LOWER TOWNSHIP
POLICE
NJ

DETECTIVE SERGEANT
ROBERT D. MARTIN

CAPTAIN
ERNEST J. NASPRETTO

POLICE
DEPARTMENT
CITY OF NEW YORK

THICK BLUE LINE

PROLOGUE

Officer Douglass heard the call of a suspicious person. He knew that the officer who handled that area was on dinner break. Douglass advised the dispatch center he would respond to the complaint, as he was nearby.

He rounded the corner and observed a short, chunky male with a plaid flannel jacket running from the headlights and search light of the patrol car. Douglass saw him run into a yard and thought he could cut him off by rounding the corner to the rear of the property and being there when he exited. Douglass knew that a wire fence enclosed the rear of the yard and figured the fleeing suspicious person might have some problems getting through it. Douglass hit the brakes. The patrol car lurched to a stop on the wrong side of the road. Douglass began to exit his vehicle and saw that the fleeing suspect was having problems getting through the fence. The officer grabbed the suspect's jacket, as the little guy was squirming out of it. Douglass tried to get a better grip but the suspect managed to break free.

He jumped up and started running across the street, through a vacant lot, toward a wooded area leaving his jacket behind. Douglass managed to catch up with him and grabbed him by the shoulder, still moving forward, the suspect turned and faced Douglass as their momentum carried them toward the wooded area. Douglass didn't want this guy to get away and knew he wanted to catch him before he got into the woods and possible cover. Douglass knew he had him as his hand tightened on the suspects shoulder as the suspect swung around to face him.

The rookie stopped his patrol car at the residence that the initial call had been initiated. He knew Douglass was doing him a favor responding to the call. He had heard the call over the radio as he was finishing his dinner break and was aware that Douglass was handling the complaint of a suspicious person. The second officer now on the scene exited the vehicle to observe the property owner at his open door yelling that another officer had chased the guy through the yard. Shots rang out, the rookie jumped behind a tree for cover not knowing from where the shots were coming.

Moments passed and Officer Douglass somehow made it back to the patrol car and gave out a call for help. There he lay mortally wounded on the ground next to his patrol car requesting assistance. The suspect was fleeing through the woods, trying to wrap his shirt around his bleeding hand, all the time running as fast as he could. The rookie, confused by what happened, remained frozen behind the protection of the tree.

0

CHAPTER ONE

It was 11:45am, a warm day for the eighteenth of February 1994. The Pocono Mountains of Pennsylvania were covered with the most snow in 15 years. The ski slopes were covered with high school and college students enjoying Presidents Week at the Poconos. The skiing conditions were excellent.

The THIRSTY CAMEL, a rustic bar and restaurant found close to Camelback Ski Area, would have been crowded if it had been 5pm. The young ski freaks would have begun their partying mode. However, at this time of the day, it was usually quiet and the time was used by employees to prepare for the 'apres ski' fun seekers.

Bob Martin and Jack Trombetta entered the empty bar and parked themselves at a location that would afford them a good view of the entrance. The procedure was a ritual. Cops always wanted to see who was coming and going. Martin and Trombetta were confronted with a young, petite, and blonde barmaid.

"Hi, Can I help you, gentlemen?"

"You sure can. I'll have vodka and cranberry and he'll have vodka and pineapple," said Martin. "Make that Smirnoff Vodka. I want to do a friend a favor," added Martin. Martin wanted to use a product, his liquor salesman friend, Bob DeNinno, distributed. The little blonde was quick to prepare and serve the drinks. She then quietly returned to her bar cleaning chores. "Man, she is really talkative, must have had a bad night," stated Martin.

"Don't be so loud, she probably heard you," replied Trombetta.

"She should be, more friendly if she wants to make a living at this trade." Martin recalled that being friendly and talkative as a bartender always put big tips in his pocket.

Martin had been a bartender before he had become a cop. He often thought about his four-year career as a bartender. Actually it was helpful when it came to dealing with people as a Police Officer.

Martin held his drink in the air. "Well, here's to the last day of a great ski vacation."

"Yeah, if our wives don't spend the remaining money at the Mall," replied Trombetta.

"You know we could have probably saved money if we had taken them skiing," said Martin.

1

"They will, no doubt, spend some major dollars," replied
Trombetta.

Both men reflected on the women who were most important to
them.

Bob Martin and his wife, JoAnne, had been married for 16
years and were most comfortable when they were together.
They owned two timeshares and were always traveling
somewhere. It was easy for them to travel. Bob and JoAnne
had two children. Tara, age 23, who was now living in the
Martins' household and Bert, short for Robert, age 20, who
was living in Iowa. Bob's grandfather was known to everyone
as Bert. Bob always thought highly of him so he decided
that the legacy would live on.

JoAnne was great with her step children and had always
treated them as her own. Bob and Jo loved to travel and
enjoy themselves. When they decided to travel, they got a
babysitter for the adopted greyhound, Samantha, who was also
a member of the family and they were on their way. This ski
trip was being spent at a two-bedroom condo at Shawnee in
the Pocono Mountains. Bob and JoAnne had arrived on the
13th of February and intended to leave on the 19th.

Jack and Lynn, his wife, arrived on the 16th of February and
wished they had arrived sooner. However, they still had
school age kids to contend with. Joe, age 18, Gina, age 16,
and Jack, age 14, made up the remaining family members.
Jack and Lynn hated to leave them with in-laws because these
kids would often rewrite the family rules to take advantage
of their grandparents. Jack's in-laws, the Durante family,
were the built-in baby sitters. They lived right next door
too the Trombettas. Jack would often relate that maybe
having children wasn't really his forte. Jack and Lynn had
been married 19 years and were waiting for the time that the
children would be on their own.

The Martins and Trombettas often traveled together. It
seemed that they were always taking yearly trips to skiing
resorts. Bob and Jo had been skiing for ten years and for
the last four years Jack and Lynn made the trips when they
were close to home. Jack never wanted to stray too far from
the kids. Actually, Jack didn't like skiing but Lynn
enjoyed it and was getting very good at getting down the
slopes gracefully. Jack on the other hand was more adept at
sliding onto the bar stool.

They were close friends and enjoyed each other's company.
Bob and JoAnne often talked about the fact that they seemed
to become close friends with members of good Italian
families. Both Bob and JoAnne had close Italian friends
when they were growing up and each of them spent a lot of

2

time enjoying the Italian culture, not to mention the food. The other close friends of the Martins were Bob and Lorraine DeNinno. If the Martins weren't traveling with the Trombettas, they were off to some island paradise soaking up the sun with the DeNinnos. The Trombettas were the traveling companions for winter sports and the DeNinnos went to the warm weather climates. Martin especially liked to visit liquor distilleries when traveling with the DeNinnos. Bob DeNinno always got VIP treatment, free drinks and complimentary bottles of the finished product. Bob and JoAnne often talked about the fact that they were fortunate to travel with close friends and not get on each other's nerves.

Bob and Jo always hoped to get the DeNinnos and the Trombettas to a resort where they all could enjoy each other's company. Bob had no idea that he would soon be adding more Italian friends to his list of "goombas" . . .

Robert D. Martin, Jr. and Giacomo J. Trombetta had been friends since becoming police officers with the Lower Township Police Department, Cape May County, New Jersey in 1974. Martin, age 26, and Trombetta, age 20, after five months of patrol duties attended the New Jersey State Police Academy at Sea Girt, New Jersey. Martin was one of the three oldest trainees and Trombetta one of the three youngest in the class. They could write a book about their ten weeks of academy life. Martin had started one a few times but just couldn't get into spending the time required to complete such an endeavor. They began the academy in October 1974 and graduated during the second week of January 1975. A graduation party to end all was given by the sixty-two member class. Bob and Jack didn't attend. Neither of them drank alcohol so why waste the time attending. Jack was a born again Christian. He would talk about being born again to anyone that would listen and often to those who wouldn't. He felt his Christianity would not allow alcohol so he didn't touch the stuff. Bob had decided drinking seemed to be at the root of a lot of personal problems. Martin did not drink alcohol for eight years. Trombetta utilized the two-hour drive to and from Sea Girt on Mondays and Fridays to spread the gospel. Martin listened out of courtesy, at first, but began to take interest. Eight months after graduation Bob Martin became born again and always credited Jack for explaining the steps of salvation.

Upon graduating the academy, Jack was assigned to a patrol squad and Martin was assigned to the Cape May County Narcotic Strike Force in an undercover capacity. Martin had hoped for this assignment but didn't think he would get the nod. He thought a veteran officer would have been assigned. Well, he was happy with the assignment but not the training.

3

One week after graduation he was back at the academy
attending an advanced narcotic's class for undercover
operatives. This place had been a hell hole for ten weeks
and there he was again. Martin found out really quickly
that the atmosphere was much different. The instructors
treated you like a human being as opposed farming animals,
which had been the case at the basic class that had lasted
for the longest ten weeks of his life . . .

Martin always remembered the fact that Trombetta had been
the only Lower Township Officer to congratulate him on his
assignment to the Strike Force. The majority of officers,
old and new thought the job should have gone to a seasoned
officer. Martin had a very productive stint working
undercover and always thought he should write a book about
the many interesting experiences. He just couldn't make
himself spend the time. Upon leaving the Strike Force,
Martin was assigned to the Detective Division at the Lower
Township Police Department. It seemed a natural job
progression. Now, he really had some officers upset.
However, he remembered Jack Trombetta congratulating him and
wishing him well. Martin was quick to adapt and succeed as
a detective. He was able to utilize contacts he had made as
a bartender to provide him with an impressive investigative
and arrest record. He found out quickly that personal
friends and acquaintances were most helpful in providing
information that made him look like a hero. Martin often
thought that he would someday write a book about some of
these people. However, he just never got around to it. He
learned very quickly that even when arresting someone to
remember that they could well supply the information that
would lead to the next case. Bob Martin really enjoyed
obtaining confessions from perpetrators and turning them
into informants.

Jack Trombetta had wasted no time either. He pursued his
patrol duties like a man on a mission. The streets weren't
safe for drunk drivers when Trombetta was on duty.
Trombetta also made a real effort to get to know the
juveniles in his patrol area. Jack knew that these kids
committed most of the crimes in his area but that they were
also a wealth of information.

Trombetta would often talk to perpetrators about salvation
and before they knew it they were spilling their guts about
the crime they committed. Jack was good at reading people
and being aware of their physical actions and reactions.
This ability made it easy for him to become a good
interviewer and interrogator.

Jack cared about people and he also cared about what they
thought of him. So, many times, he would spend time in
conversations with people that would lead them to believe

4

they were long lost friends. He really wasn't happy when people didn't like him.

Subsequently, Martin and Trombetta would prove to be an impressive and productive investigative team. However, they would also prove to be a supervisor's nightmare. They worked best when left to their own devices. They enjoyed giving ulcers to their boss. They had a way of manipulating supervisors especially when they teamed up on them.

Martin and Trombetta gazed into their fourth drink. "Hey, Jack, you want something to eat?"

"No, not, right now. I don't want to ruin a good buzz. Let's drink some more, go get the wives, and come back for a late lunch."

"Sounds good to me," replied Martin. "Hey Jack, do you remember when we didn't drink?"

"No, I don't remember. Was it long ago?"

Yeah too long ago Martin thought. Martin always wanted to write a book about it. He just never got around to it.

There they sat, each a Detective Sergeant and beginning their twenty first years at the Lower Township Police Department. Martin had been a detective for more than eighteen years, Trombetta for thirteen. Martin had more time as a detective than any active department member. Trombetta was a close second. Trombetta, however, was the Senior Detective Sergeant. They had taken a civil service exam for sergeant and each received the same score. Trombetta had been hired two weeks before Martin so seniority took precedent. Both men often chided each other about who was the real boss. It didn't really matter. They were usually on the same wave length. Each respected the other's abilities and was aware of each other's strong and weak points. They worked together well and used each others ability as required.

"Hey, Jack, remember when we were partners, worked cases and didn't drink?"

"Yeah, I remember. People used to say we were no fun. What do you think could have happened, Trombetta laughed?"

Martin raised his glass, "I don't know, twenty years of dealing with scumbags, I guess."

"We should have gone skiing," Martin said, sounding disgusted.

Trombetta chuckled and replied, "Sure, we would have paid thirty dollars a lift ticket, made two runs down the slope and be seated at the bar really enjoying ourselves. Stop complaining and order another drink."

"Jack, I wonder how the kids are doing?"

"I don't know, I haven't called my in-laws yet," Jack replied.

"I'm not talking about your kids. I mean our kids."

The kids were six detectives that were assigned to Martin and Trombetta. Jack and Bob were affectionately referred to as mom and dad by their six charges. Jack was the loving mother with affection, understanding and requests for action. Bob was the voiceful father with discipline and direct orders. Together they obtained results from the "kids."

Jack would always say, "Ask your father?"

Bob would say, "Did your mother tell you to ask me?"

The kids knew, however, that no matter what they did Mom and Dad would stand behind them to the bitter end. Mom and Dad just wanted the truth and then they would deal with the problem.

Bob and Jack each remembered supervisors who wouldn't back up their men when it was needed. When the kids were bad, Mom would lovingly reprimand and forget. Dad would etch the violation in his mind and not expect to see the same mistake again.

Jack swallowed the vodka and pineapple and stated, "We can retire in July of 1997 if everything goes right. It will be sooner than that, if we use all our time on the books."

"Tell me about it. I'll be in Montana or Colorado putting people on a ski lift. Maybe I'll even tell them to have a nice day. It depends on how I feel," laughed Martin.

"You go to the cold weather. I'm going to Florida and get a job with a D.A. as an investigator," Jack said.

"You gotta be kidding. You'll have a boss who expects you to work and do real police things," said Martin.

"Bob, how many drinks have we had?"

Martin counted the swizzle sticks. He replied, "Seven for each of us."

"Do you think we would blow a .10 on the Breathalyzer?" asked Trombetta.

"If we don't pick up the women we will be in more trouble than a DWI arrest," Bob answered and then laughed at Jack, "We can't drive we'll be breaking the law."

"You steer and I'll work the pedals. They can bust us both," stated Jack.

The detective sergeants, only slightly inebriated, drove to the mall, down the street about a half mile. They realized they could have left the car with the girls and walked to the bar. They parked and waited for their wives. Ten minutes passed and the girls appeared as they left the Mall. They approached with smiles on their faces. Only one thing was worse than the wife going shopping. Two wives going shopping together had to be worse. Their arms were loaded with bags and they had large smiles across their faces.

Both men looked at their wives and thought about how fortunate they were to be married to such attractive women. Both worked out regularly and didn't appear to be their age. Lynn Trombetta was thirty-eight and JoAnne Martin was forty-one.

Jack Trombetta smiled as he told Bob, "If they ask, tell them we had three drinks and we want to take them back for a late lunch."

Bob looked at his watch and stated, "It's three forty-five, we better say an early dinner."

"Yeah, that will sell," replied Jack.

The ride back to the bar resulted in conversation about what had been purchased. The girls were overjoyed with their purchases. But, then again, they always were. They could go shopping for toilet paper and consider they were happy shoppers.

Back to the bar they went and quickly ordered dinner. Both men ordered more drinks with dinner and eventually two rounds of after dinner drinks. Each man was now definitely feeling a buzz . . . a big buzz . . .

Dinner conversation started with what was purchased at the mall and ended with each man stating they would never marry again given the circumstances. Was it because no truer love could be found or the amount of money spent at the mall? It was 6:45pm when they all returned to the condo to relax and engage in a night of movie watching.

Once they settled in, the conversation centered around retirement and future vacations together. The Martins and Trombettas enjoyed having fun together and the conversations they had, most often, were sometimes quite interesting but always quite funny. It wasn't long before Lynn and Bob would begin to fall to sleep and Jack and JoAnne would be conversing with each other. Bob and Lynn had reverted to childhood. When the street lights came on, they fell asleep. Jack and JoAnne conversed about the fact that their spouses were always falling asleep. The decision was being made about what show would be viewed on television. The conversation then turned to what time they would be leaving the following morning to return home.

Bob gazed to where Jack was seated. "Hey, Jack, I guess nothing happened in Lower Township that was of major consequence."

Jack quickly responded, "No, if so, they would have called us."
Martin replied, "Did you give them the number here?"
Trombetta quickly answered, "Nope, did you?"

"They would call our home and the kids could tell them," Martin replied.

Trombetta laughed and stated, "If they had called, they would not have received much of a response. We have been shitfaced since Wednesday."

Martin smiled and responded, "You bring out the worst in me, Jackie."

"We're on vacation, so let's enjoy," joked Trombetta.

Bob and Lynn were just dozing off when the phone rang. The time was 8:40pm. Jack answered figuring it was one of his kids, natural kids. It was Gina, his daughter. She called to advise the vacationers that a neighbor had contacted her and advised that a Lower Township police officer had been shot. The shooting had reportedly occurred about an hour before.

Jack immediately hung up and called dispatch at LTPD. In an almost silent conversation Jack learned that Officer David C. Douglass had been shot while answering a suspicious person call. It was learned that he was in critical condition and being transported by rescue. The dispatch further indicated that a perpetrator was identified and being sought. Jack advised that they were en route and would arrive in about three hours. Jack hung up the phone and a silence hung over the foursome. Jack said, "They are going to need us. We better get moving. Let me say a prayer."

The prayer was said. Everything was packed so quickly it was hard to believe. Women just couldn't pack things that quickly. Everyone was diligently removing things from drawers and closets and packing suit cases. It had taken both girls days to pack everything for the trip to the Poconos. It only took minutes to pack everything for the return trip.

Bob checked the refrigerator and removed the left overs that had accumulated. They were all running around making sure nothing was left behind. Jack in his normal mode was basically watching everyone else pack while he made a feeble attempt to appear busy. He had a way of getting others to do his work.

Jack was pressed into service to carry the items out to the vehicles. The packing was completed in record time and both cars left the snow covered parking lots at exactly 9:00P.M. Bob and Jack would drive and did not look forward to the three hour ride home and the thought of what confronted them upon arrival.

The Buzz was gone . . .   THE VACATION WAS OVER . . .

CHAPTER TWO

The two vehicles followed the winding mountain road. A
solemn silence took over the Martins' vehicle. It was if Bob
and JoAnne Martin could not force themselves to talk. Bob
was thinking about the fact a fellow officer had been shot
and was quietly praying that Officer Dave Douglass would
survive and that life would go on for all as normal as
possible.

JoAnne was grieving for Debbie Douglass, Dave's wife. JoAnne
and Debbie had been childhood friends, attending the same
schools, playing as children on the streets of Cape May,
N.J. and growing up together. JoAnne had been a bridesmaid
in Debbie's first wedding. The marriage didn't work out.
But, JoAnne remembered how Debbie managed to raise her
daughter, Tina. When Debbie met Dave, he quickly became the
father figure for Tina and the husband that Debbie deserved.
JoAnne remembered Debbie having two children with Dave.
David junior and Courtney made up the rest of the Douglass
family.

JoAnne was thinking about the Martin Hall of Fame. She
smiled to herself as she thought about her friend Debbie and
family. The Hall of Fame comprised collages of pictures on
the walls of the Martin home. The pictures included
friends, relatives, sights and scenes that were instant
memos of Bob and JoAnne's life together.

JoAnne remembered the yearly pictures of the Douglass
children that Debbie dutifully provided each time
photographs were taken. JoAnne prayed for her friend and
family.

The Martins' vehicle entered Interstate Eighty and without
checking the rear view mirror Bob knew that Jack would be
close behind. Jack and Lynn usually were not able to spend
the time on vacation that the Martins were. The Trombettas
had three kids to worry about and the Martins didn't. This,
was no doubt, the reason for Jack and Lynn to travel in a
separate car. Over the years this arrangement worked well
and became a normal course of the vacation. Bob and JoAnne
always arrived at the vacation site first. Bob would call
Jack with the exact directions and Jack and Lynn would show
up a few days later. The trip home would consist of Jack
and Lynn following the Martins home.

Many times over the years Bob would lead the way to and from
vacation locations until Jack found himself in familiar
territory at which time he could find his way to his
destination. Bob went over the directions in his mind. He
would take Interstate Eighty out of Pennsylvania through New

Jersey to Interstate Two Eighty to the Garden State Parkway. Bob knew that once on the GSP Jack's driving technique would change abruptly. Jack wouldn't think about the rules of the road or the traffic laws of the State of New Jersey. He would be a man on a mission. The mission at that point would be to get home as quickly as possible. The thought of an accident, breaking the law or violating the rules of the road would be the furthest things from Jack's mind.

Bob thought about how Jack always relied on others to do things for him. It was as if Jack couldn't bother himself with doing things on his own if he could get someone else to do them.

Throughout their careers together, Jacks reliance on Bob was evident from fact gathering and report writing to interviews and interrogations. Everyone would always kid Jack about what he would do if Martin stopped doing for him. Bob Martin never wondered. He knew that Jack could do whatever had to be done. Martin also knew that Jack wouldn't do it for long. Jack would just groom someone else to do the everyday stuff that always seemed like a drag.

Jack Trombetta knew he didn't need someone to do his work. He also knew that it was easier for him if someone did so.

Bob always knew that when the shit hit the fan he wanted Jack involved. It didn't matter if the situation called for mental or physical ability. Jack could be quick with his hands and he was also quick with his mind.

Bob thought about what must be going on in Lower Township. He knew that the kids, of the Detective Division, were very busy. Bob experienced a sense of guilt over not being there to direct, support and take part in the investigation. Martin hoped that nothing had been overlooked and that everything was going as smoothly as possible.

Bob knew that the Swat Team had probably been activated and that would mean two fewer detectives for investigative duties. Det. Bill Hienkel was a Swat Team member as was Jack Trombetta. Martin thought that as soon as they got back to the police department Jack would probably be heading the Swat Operations.

Martin remembered the three years he had spent on the Swat Team. He recalled that the training and equipment left a lot to be desired. However, many things had changed and the LTPD Swat Team had become well trained and well equipped since then.

It then struck Martin morbidly that the training and

11

equipment of the Swat Team were in a big part due to the
likes of Dave Douglass. The team would be lacking a key
player on this mission.

"JoAnne, are you awake?"

"Yes, what is wrong?"

"Nothing, I was just thinking how helpless I feel in this
car."

JoAnne moved close to Bob and embraced his arm. "Hon., try
to keep your mind on your driving and get us home so you
can be of some help," she urged.

JoAnne hated it when Bob drove faster that 65 mph. She had
gazed at the speedometer often as it maintained a constant
70 mph. JoAnne knew that this wasn't the time to lecture
Bob about breaking the speed limit.

"Don't worry I'll get you home safe and sound, just don't
tell me to stop for gas. We have more than enough to get us
home," Bob replied. JoAnne took personal offense at the
gas tank going below half full. She always felt that meant
half empty.
Bob looked at the mileage marker and observed they were
just approaching the entrance to the GSP.

Martin directed JoAnne to try and contact the police
department on the cellular phone. JoAnne did so with
negative results. Those phones never worked when you
needed them.

Bob continued to pray for Dave and his family. "Lord,
you're will, be done and if I am to take part in anyway,
please guide me and give me the strength to do so."

Jack was following Bob and figured that as soon as he got
on familiar ground, the GSP, he would speed up and get to
the P.D. Jack was thinking about all the snow that was on
the back roads and how he would have to be extra careful,
especially knowing he was driving with a buzz. He knew he
didn't need an accident at this point. Why had he had so
much to drink? He remembered when neither he nor Bob drank
at all. They each knew that the booze was not for them.
Yet they didn't seem to care. A drink at dinner had turned
into before dinner drinks, at dinner drinks and after
dinner drinks. Jack knew that sooner or later they would
each take control and stop the drinking. He just didn't
know when.

Jack tried to watch the roadway and keep his mind on his

driving. It normally would be a three-hour drive to get home. He wanted it to be much quicker. What was going on at the P.D.? Who was handling the investigation? Did they make an arrest? Most important, how was Dave? These questions kept filling his mind and he began to feel frustrated at not being in the middle of things.

Trombetta couldn't believe that this was happening. Why was it that every time he and Lynn went on vacation something catastrophic took place? Jack's grandfather had died. Jack's sister's father-in-law passed away. The last vacation resulted in a return home to the death of Lynn's grandmother. Jack would often kid Bob about the fact that every time the Trombettas went away. They returned to a funeral. Jack thought about his stay at the FBI National Academy and while there he was advised that a fellow policeman and friend had fallen from a roof and died.

When would these terrible incidents stop? It had gotten to the point that the Trombettas didn't want to go on vacation for fear of something happening. Jack knew better. He didn't believe in bad luck or bad omens. His Christian beliefs taught him that God had control over everything. Nothing was left to chance.

"Lord, please watch over Dave. You're will, be done." Jack began to pray as he drove.

Jack was worried about having had too much to drink and tried to be extra cautious. He and Bob had at least fifteen drinks. He knew that he probably would have had more if they had stayed at the condo relaxing. That was different. He would not be expected to do anything but go to bed. Now, he knew that he would be expected to assist with a major investigation. He had to sober up.

Jack looked over at Lynn. She seemed to be in a trance. She wasn't saying anything just staring at the roadway. Jack was thinking about what an empty useless feeling he had. He shouldn't be in his car in Pennsylvania. He should be in Jersey and maybe he would have been at the shooting and have been able to change the course of events. He knew his mind was wandering and he would have to stay focused and not feel sorry for himself. Here he was worrying about why he wasn't in Jersey. He should be worrying about Dave and his family.

Jack began to think about the Swat Team and the fact that Dave was a big part of that team. Jack was the team leader and had tried to instill a close relationship among all the members. They had to be close. They could be responsible for each others' lives. Jack was thinking how he always busted Dave's chops about being overweight. Dave would

lose weight to get in shape and then the appetite would
take control and that waist line would expand. Jack knew
Dave had a never-ending battle of the bulge. Jack wanted
all his guys to be in the best condition. It was
important. You never knew when the team would be
activated. These guys depended on each other under all
conditions.

Jack thought about how he had made each man promise to
maintain an elitist secrecy about all that they did as a
team. When they would go away for maneuvers, they would do
some goofy things. They would work hard and party hard.
Whatever they did as a team stayed with the team. Jack had
given them each a silver dollar as a token of friendship
and camaraderie. They had to stick together under all
conditions to be effective.

"God, please don't let Dave die. I'm not ready for that."
Jack thought how selfish that sounded. Here he was
thinking about himself. He had to stay focused.

Why hadn't he talked to Dave about salvation and the Lord?
He hadn't even been a good example of Christianity when in
Dave's company. Sure Jack had provided positive examples
but he had also been with Dave and the Swat Team when they
were partying.

Jack could recall times when he could have testified to
Dave about the Lord Jesus Christ. Jack couldn't do it.
Jack knew he wasn't living the Christian life as he should.
Selling a product to someone was difficult when you didn't
make use of the product yourself.

Lord, please, help me to help myself, Jack thought as he
kept his eyes on the roadway.

Jack knew he had to get his own life in order. Christians
used the word, backsliding, when describing someone who was
not living the life of a born again believer. Jack was
definitely a backslider at this point in his life.

Jack was startled from his thoughts when the car phone
rang. He picked it up and it was his son, Jackie, who
advised him that Dave was in critical condition. Jackie
had heard a news release on local television and relayed
the information.

Jack began thinking once again how he gave Dave a hard time
about being fat. It was almost as if Jack was trying to
justify his thoughts when all of a sudden he began thinking
of the good things he had aided Dave in achieving. Jack
felt good about helping Dave to become a training

instructor at the P.D. and pushing for him to be placed on the Tactical Patrol Unit. These were positions that officers with less than five years service just didn't get. Jack began to feel a little bit relaxed thinking about the positive things he had helped Dave to attain.

Lord, please, let Dave live. There is so much I have to say to him. Please, give me the chance. Jack's mind returned to the stretch of highway before him.

Lynn knew that Jack was not in a talkative mood and he was probably thinking about all the things he hadn't said to Dave, but wished he had.

Lynn knew that Jack was very close to the members of the Swat Team and that he always spoke highly of each member. She would get upset when Jack would go away with the team on training missions. A few times these missions lasted for a week. She was not happy being without Jack during those times.

She didn't even like the fact that Jack was on the team, let alone a team leader. Why didn't he let younger guys do these things? Why did he have to be so bent on being involved in such things? Sometimes Jack was like her oldest child.

Lynn looked at the GSP roadway before her and thought that once at home Jack would not be home until he had to sleep. She thought about the many times he would work on a case until it was completed without getting much sleep. Why do cops do such things?

Lynn thought how Jack had passed the Martin vehicle and was wondering what Bob and JoAnne were talking about. She then realized that they were probably staring at the highway also. She knew that Jack had probably thought about the fact that vacations seemed to be bad news for her and Jack.

Lynn noticed that Jack was driving fast but knew she shouldn't mention it. She thought that he had seemed to sober up as soon as they left the parking lot of the condos.

Lynn began to think about the fact that Jackie had called indicating Dave was in critical condition. At least Dave was not dead. She was glad Jackie had called. Sometimes the kids did act like normal, responsible human beings.

Lynn prayed that Dave would survive and that Dave's family would have the strength to handle the terrible incident. She gazed at Jack and he seemed to be deep in thought. Normally when he had this look she would engage him in

conversation and provide her feelings on the topic. She
knew that this was not one of those times. She sat staring
at the roadway before her.

The silence in the vehicle was morbid and disheartening.
Both the Trombettas and the Martins drove homeward
experiencing the same almost sickening silence.

CHAPTER THREE

The GSP seemed to go on forever. Bob looked at the next
mileage marker. It indicated 90. Bob knew that he had
about an hour and one half to go. He hoped Dave Douglass
would survive the attempt on his life.

The miles slowly crept by even at 75 mph. Bob hoped that
JoAnne would not look over at the speedometer. She really
hadn't had much to say about how fast they were traveling.
JoAnne had noticed the speed indicator reach 80 mph at
times. She knew, however, that bringing it to Bob's
attention would be fruitless. She had noticed Jack speed
by when both cars reached mileage marker one hundred. She
thought that at least Bob wasn't driving as fast as Jack.

Bob had not noticed Jack go by for he was thinking about
things to come. He just wasn't sure of what they might be.
The miles continued to slip by and JoAnne couldn't help
think about how drunk Bob and Jack had been prior to the
bad news. She couldn't believe the sobering effect each
man experienced. JoAnne just worried about each man's
driving and prayed they would get home safely.

JoAnne thought about the many times Bob would be called
into work on various details and that he had always
returned home safely. He would come home with the normal
cuts and bruises but rarely with major injuries. She
remembered the time she had received a call from Jack while
she was at work. Jack advised her that Bob had been in a
traffic accident while involved in a vehicle pursuit.

Bob, then a detective, had been riding in the front
passenger seat of a police vehicle along with Detective
Rich Hooyman, who was driving, and Lieutenant John Maher,
who was sitting in the back seat. The officers were on
their way to the garage to pick up two vehicles when they
heard a call indicating a neighboring police agency, Middle
Township, was in pursuit of a red sports car containing
three black males. The vehicle was stolen and the
perpetrators were eluding police.

Rich Hooyman had just stopped at a local bank so Bob could
make a deposit. When Bob walked out of the bank, he heard
the excited voice of an officer in pursuit. "District 12,
I am in pursuit of a red Trans Am entering your Township on
Fulling Mill Road. District 12 do you read me? Twelve do
you read me?"

Dispatch responded, "10-4, keep me advised of your
location."

"District 12, to all cars, be advised Middle Township is in

pursuit of a red Trans Am, more info will follow."

Martin looked at Rich and stated, "If that driver doesn't know Fulling Mill Road he won't make it through the first curve." The three officers were well aware that during their careers many accidents resulting in fatalities occurred on that dangerous stretch of sharp curves and straightaways.

"He'll probably go to Bayshore Road and head out of our town if he knows the area," stated Lt. Maher.

Det. Rich Hooyman asked, "Well what do you guys want me to do?"

At the same moment Martin and Maher said, "Go get him."

Hooyman warned, "Buckle your seat belts, you know how I drive."

Rich drove the vehicle northbound toward the location of the last radio transmission. The officers heard the radio calls of the pursuit cars taking part in the chase. The adrenalin was high and the chance for problems increased with each moment that passed by. All the officers knew that pursuits were accidents waiting to happen. Hopefully no officers would be involved.

The Middle Twsp. Police officer in pursuit keyed his radio and said, "District 12, be advised he is south bound on Bayshore Road and at a high rate of speed."

"District 12, he just went past me at the WaWa store," indicated a Lower Twsp Officer. Hooyman knew that the WaWa was a block away from the Middle Twsp. Officers transmission. This guy was moving and he was heading into the center of town.

The officers began to converse about what they should do. They each knew the daily contingent of school buses would be stopping along the pursuit route any minute discharging their riders who were eager to get home from a long day at school.

They decided to position themselves in front of the Lower Twsp. Police Dept. It was located on Bayshore Rd. in Villas. They knew the school buses would be approaching from the south at any time and the stolen vehicle with pursuit vehicles following were southbound on the same roadway, a two lane roadway that widened with shoulders in front of the Police Department. The stolen vehicle was fast approaching from the north and the school buses from the south.

Rich looked nervously in the direction of the stolen vehicle. "Well, what do you think, Bob?"

"We can't let them get by. They will kill somebody," Martin stated.

Lt. Maher advised, "You guys do know that we can't set up a road block. They aren't legal. Didn't you see the last Attorney General directive?" The three men laughed simultaneously.

"His ass oughta be here now," added Hooyman.

Martin said, "Rich, pull out into the roadway and face south bound. He will come up right behind us. He won't have a lot of time to react after he exits the curve near Anco Aluminum. He will be able to stop but there won't be much time to try and maneuver around us or try to avoid stopping unless he hits us."

"Oh, great! So we sit here knowing he is going to hit us and being I'm driving I get the heat for any accident," said Hooyman.

"No, not at all, Rich," laughed Martin, "The Lieutenant is here. This whole thing is his fault."

All laughed in nervous anticipation of what was to come.

Hooyman slowly entered the roadway and placed the 1984 unmarked Dodge Diplomat onto the southbound shoulder waiting to hear or see the approaching speeding vehicle. Martin grabbed the radio mic and stated,"D-1 to the cars. Let us know when he approaches Anco." Martin looked at Hooyman and Rich knew he was to place the Dodge in the south bound lane when the stolen vehicle approached.

Lt. Maher directed, "When the car is in site, I'll let you know. Just keep looking forward and worry about driving this car. Bob, keep an eye on the roadway for buses and pedestrians."

"Car Charlie two to Delta one," sounded over the radio.

Martin responded to Charlie two, "Go ahead, Captain." Bob knew the transmission was from Capt. Don Douglass, a pipe smoking ex-partner whom he had worked with closely for four years.

"The vehicle is approaching my position at the 7-11 store now. They just passed me. They are doing about eighty. They'll be on you in seconds!" The Captain was hollering the sentences in rapid succession.

Lt. John Maher began to brace himself by holding on to the rear of the front seat and the back rest of the rear seat. Maher peered out the rear window of the police vehicle waiting to see the red sports car enter into sight. He figured the driver would have about fifty yards in which to react to the police car in his path. Maher also knew that a vehicle going eighty miles an hour would not be able to stop completely in such a short distance.

Detective Hooyman knew that he would no doubt have to do some serious driving. He thought to himself, "I better do this right or these guys will never let me live it down. At that point Rich knew he would begin to accelerate slowly when Maher told him the vehicle was in sight. Hooyman figured that the impact speed would be diminished if he could gain speed at the point of impact.

Martin nervously glanced to his left at the Police Department entrance and observed that the civilian staff standing in front of the building. There, also stood Chief Bob Denny. They looked like spectators at a sporting event, cheering for their favorite team.

As Martin turned his head to glance at the approach area Lt. Maher shouted, "There they are!" In seconds Hooyman accelerated and the braking of the sports car could be heard and the smoke and smell of rubber engulfed the red car.

It all happened so quickly that Martin was unable to brace himself for the impact. The rear of the police vehicle raised off the ground violently as the wedge type front end of the sports car launched itself under the bumper. The driver of the red car had begun to attempt a stop but at the last possible moment accelerated in an attempt to push the Dodge forward and out of his way.

Hooyman had floored the gas pedal in an attempt to speed away from the point of possible impact, trying to lesson the initial force of metal on metal. Hooyman felt the impact in his lower back. The Old Dodge had begun to accelerate but seemed to stop. It was at this time that Hooyman realized the rear wheels were no longer on the ground. The red car was lodged underneath the rear end and the wheels could find no traction.

Martin felt the snap in his neck. He was forced forward against the shoulder harness of the seat belts. At this point the driver of the red car slammed on the brakes and the impact and the sudden stop caused the Dodge to leap forward off the hood of the sports car.

The driver of the sports car attempted to maneuver around

the old silver Dodge in his path. Hooyman began to gain
control of the Dodge as its rear wheels found traction.
Simultaneously, Hooyman and Martin observed that the rear
view mirror had been knocked off in the impact. Martin
screamed,"Rich, I'll tell you were to go." Martin began to
turn to his left as the red car did the same. Martin
indicated the move to Hooyman and he did the same. The red
car then braked and veered to the right in an attempt to
pass on the shoulder. Martin began to turn to his right
and observed the approaching school buses in the northbound
lane. "Rich, the buses!" Martin screamed. "Go right, Go
right." Hooyman turned the wheel violently to the right.
"Rich, force him into the curb, keep to the right."

Hooyman fought the steering wheel and continuously rammed
into the side of the red sports car next to him. Martin was
looking out of his side window and everything was going in
slow motion. He could see the faces of the black males in
the vehicle next to him. He noticed the gold tooth of the
driver as he grimaced each time the Dodge rammed the Trans
Am. The fiberglass of the Trans Am was no match for the
metal of the four door Dodge.

Martin noticed that the red car seemed to be disintegrating
before his eyes. The front fender and the driver door
peeled off. The rear view mirror flew off as did the door
handle. The window seemed to pop out undamaged as it flew
over the top of the red car. The driver of the sports car
seemed determined to get out of the path of the constant
ramming motion of the Dodge. Hooyman continued to force
the Trans Am into the shoulder but observed a vehicle
exiting a cross street directly in the path of both cars.

Hooyman hoped the senior citizen driver would see what was
happening and throw his car in reverse. No such luck. The
old guy sat there mesmerized at the wheel of his 1982
Chevette, the perfect senior citizen mobile, good on gas,
easy to maneuver with a 'I BRAKE FOR TURTLES' bumper
sticker displayed on the rear bumper.

Martin and Maher were screaming "Force him over...Force him
over!"

Hooyman hollered, "There's a car in front, in front...."

Martin and Maher saw the face of the old man, a look of
fear and disbelief. The old man was in the direct path of
four tons of metal, fiberglass and various flying car
parts. So there he sat in a dead stare.

Hooyman turned the Dodge to the left in an attempt to avoid
the inevitable. The red sports car did the same with the
room that was now provided. The senior citizen sat frozen

at the wheel. Hooyman avoided striking the old Chevette, but the Trans Am braked and slid into the Chevette coming to an abrupt stop. Smoke and the smell of burning rubber was everywhere. The faces of the kids on the school buses were plastered to the windows. They couldn't believe what they were seeing. This was really neat...

Before the smoke cleared the officers quickly exited the police vehicle. Their adrenalin was pumping and it was their intention to do bodily harm, if need be. Lt. Maher began to pursue the front seat passenger, who had left the Trans Am and was running towards a wooded area. Det. Hooyman gave chase to the rear seat passenger, who had followed his partner in crime.

Detective Martin, who was closest to the driver of the battered stolen vehicle, reached through the missing window grabbed the black youth by the neck and yelled, "You move, you bleed." Martin really liked that phrase. Martin had his gun stuck in the kids face.

Martin, however, was not aware that Capt. Douglass had arrived at the scene and with his weapon drawn was on the passenger side of the Trans Am. "Hands on your head, slide across the seat and step out toward me, do it slow!" yelled the captain. The black male with a pleading look on his face along with tears of fear in a low voice begged, "Don't shoot, don't shoot, you tell me move I bleed, he tell me move slow outta da car. I ain't movin, please help me."

Martin and Captain Douglass dragged him out and would laugh later about his reactions. The black youth was handcuffed and placed in a marked unit to be transported to the P.D. Capt. Douglass and Detective Martin then began to search the wooded area for the remaining perpetrators. Douglass noticed that Martin seemed to be pale and was rubbing his neck.

"Hey, Bob, are you alright?"

"I don't know. I'm having trouble moving my head from side to side," replied Martin. "I feel like I'm going to puke on your windshield."

"You might have a concussion," said Douglass.
Douglass immediately called rescue and Martin was out of the manhunt and on his way to the hospital.

Martin was in the ambulance on his way to the hospital as he heard the reports that both Hooyman and Maher had caught up with their suspects and placed them under arrest.

JoAnne stared into the passing GSP asphalt and remembered

that Lt. Maher was the only officer not to receive
injuries. Detective Rich Hooyman was out of work for two
weeks with a back injury. Bob had been out of work for
three weeks with back injuries and a hearing loss that
resulted in the addition of two hearing aides, hearing
aides that were always being left in pockets that would be
frantically searched by her husband prior to them going
through the wash. The cost of $2000.00 per washing was more
than could be afforded. Both Bob and Rich received
workmen's compensation for their injuries but it was never
worth being injured.

JoAnne remembered Bob coming home from a subsequent
Juvenile Court hearing concerning the incident and
indicated that the three youths were given probation. This
had been only the seventh vehicle they had stolen and they
were deemed salvageable by the judge.

One year later the driver of the Trans Am was being pursued
once again in a stolen Trans Am and after crashing ran from
the vehicle into a salt marsh area at the Jersey Shore and
was found two weeks later floating face down. He would not
be stealing anymore Trans Am's. Sometimes justice
prevailed.

JoAnne' mind stopped wandering and she was back to reality
thinking how quiet Bob was being during the ride home. She
could tell that he was anguishing over the injury to his
friend and fellow officer. The silence was broken when Bob
picked up the cellular phone and dialed the Lower Township
Police Department. Bob was speaking to someone and
suddenly blurted, "He what? He died? I'm at mile marker
fifty eight, I'll be there in about one hour. Does
Trombetta know yet? OK."

JoAnne knew what had happened and grabbed Bob's arm as he
began to sob. She couldn't understand the unintelligible
words coming from his mouth. Martin was devastated by the
news. He couldn't believe it. He was sure someone would
call back and say it was a bad joke. No one called.

Jack was on the car phone talking to a dispatcher not
knowing that Bob was doing the same thing. Both were now
advised of Dave's death. A sharp pain went through Jack.
The feeling was indescribable. Jack couldn't believe the
bad news. How could this be happening? This was
unbelievable. Jack tried to choke back sobs and tears.
Lynn grabbed his leg and could see the pain Jack was in. He
tried to speak with the captain in an attempt to sort
things out. The captain advised Jack that he would be
needed for some Swat missions and that he should get to the
P.D. as soon as possible.
Jack began to think how the Lord was in control no matter

how bad things looked. Please God, give this scumbag perp to me, he thought to himself.

Jack looked down at his speed indicator and saw that he was doing one hundred miles per hour. He had to get back as quickly as possible. He wanted to be there for any Swat mission that took place. He wanted to be there when the guy was arrested, preferably killed.

How can Dave be dead? This can't be happening. Why did we go on vacation? We should have stayed home. What if, what if, what if........

The miles were flying by as the speed stayed at one hundred. Jack's eyes were on the road ahead but his mind was elsewhere. He thought he saw blinking red lights behind him and figured it was a rescue vehicle or ambulance on a run to Burdette Tomlin Hospital. Jack then realized he was only minutes from the P.D. Jack ignored the lights until Lynn mentioned that the car looked like a State Police vehicle.

Jack quickly realized it was a Troop car and pulled over quickly and exited his car. Jack didn't realize it but he was running back to the Troop car with his jacket flying open exposing his 9mm service weapon stuck in the front of his pants. Jack looked like a crazed maniac with a gun.

Lynn had been telling Jack to slow down but he wasn't listening. She kept telling him that the lights behind them belonged to a police car but he kept stating that it was a rescue vehicle. When Jack finally decided he was being stopped, he had screeched to a stop and hopped out of the car like he was out of control. The way Jack looked, the cops may have thought he was some kind of a nut.

The two troopers in the vehicle were surprised that the vehicle that had been clocked at 98 miles per hour had pulled over and stopped so abruptly. The driver of the Troop car was busy trying to stop his vehicle and was paying attention to pulling over safely and not being in the line of oncoming traffic. The other Trooper was exiting the vehicle in an attempt to get in position to affect a more than routine traffic stop. This nut was doing almost 100 mph. He had to be drunk or wrecked on some kind of drug.

Almost immediately Jack was on top of the Trooper driving the police car. The driver had just looked up and realized that this guy was running at him and it looked like he was carrying something in the waist of his pants. "He's got a gun!" the driver hollered as the other trooper began to draw his weapon. The driver now had his weapon out and was trying to exit his vehicle. Jack yelled, "I'm a cop, I'm a cop." Jack's hands went up in the air as he screamed he had identification in his pocket. "I know I was flying. I'm going to Lower Twsp. P.D. We had an officer killed and I'm a Detective Sergeant," yelled Trombetta. The driver of the Troop car now realized he recognized Trombetta as he slowly reached for his ID. The trooper reassured his partner that Jack was on the job and they both holstered their weapons. Jack was fumbling through his pocket when the Trooper said, "Hey, Sarge, we're sorry to hear about your guy. Takeoff, we hope you get the fuck that shot him."

Jack ran back to his car and headed to the P.D. The rookie trooper looked at his training officer and said, "We could have shot him and have had to live with that for the rest of our lives. Shit man, he's a cop." The seasoned trooper looked at the tail lights of the Trombetta vehicle as it screeched away and said, "I hope he don't kill himself before he gets there."

Jack didn't even think how crazy he must have looked to the troopers that had stopped him. The only thing on his mind was getting home and getting involved with this case. Neither Jack nor Lynn had given any thought to the fact that Jack had almost been shot by troopers who may have perceived him to be a mad man with a gun tucked in his pants.

Jack began to think about all the police cars he had seen on the parkway and the fact that they hadn't stopped him. Maybe they had seen the P.B.A. police shield in his rear window. The shield was often very helpful. It was especially helpful when you were speeding. Most police officers would honor the fact that you were a fellow officer and extend you the courtesy of a verbal warning if you were exceeding the speed limit by more than what was considered safe. There were fringe benefits to being in the law enforcement profession. Lawyers extended professional courtesy to other lawyers, doctors did the same to other doctors but when cops did it the public got pissed. Screw'em, he thought to himself...

Jack sped away from were he had been stopped which was about four miles from the P.D.

CHAPTER FOUR

Jack pulled into the rear of the police department. Lynn knew she would probably not see him again anytime soon. She kissed Jack and told him to be careful. Lynn pulled away and was awe struck by all the cops and equipment at the Lower Township Police Department.

As Jack exited his vehicle he saw Det. Bill Hienkel standing near the swat van. Jack could see that he appeared relieved at seeing him. He also noticed Patrolman Lou Russo standing next to Hienkel. Jack thought how Lou looked like a robot going through motions, but not having to think about what the next motion would be. He had a look of shock on his face and didn't seem to notice that Jack had arrived. Jack made a mental note that he didn't want to subject Russo to any decision making duties during the SWAT actions that would probably take place. Jack wasn't to sure that Russo would be able to handle any major decisions.

Jack acknowledged both men and walked into the conference room of the Township Hall. He went looking for his brother-in-law, John Maher, who was the captain. Jack entered the room and observed total chaos. Everyone was talking and it didn't appear anyone was listening. Jack decided real quickly to get to the point. "John, you said on the phone that there were four or five places you wanted the swat team to hit. Where are they?"

The captain began to advise Jack about the four locations that were possible hiding places for the perp. He indicated the locations on a priority basis and Jack realized quickly that the Captain Maher's last choice was Jack's first.

Jack decided than rather argue his feelings at this point he would meet with the swat team and find out some more background on the incident. He exited the building and on his way into the police department advised Hienkel to get the available team members to meet in the captain's office. Jack couldn't believe the amount of personnel and equipment that was all around the building. The faces on everyone were the same. Everyone acknowledged Jack with glances. No one seemed to say anything, just stares, acknowledging the pain with which they were all dealing.

Jack entered the Police department and was met with more of his department brothers. It seemed everyone was lost for words. Jack saw Det. Donohue and told him he would be in a meeting with the swat team and that Martin would be arriving shortly.

Jack saw the chief sitting at his desk and they each stared

at one another and words weren't forthcoming. Jack eventually advised he was having a meeting with the swat team to plan some warrant entries.

Jack entered the captain's office and slowly the members of the swat team arrived. Jack was thinking that this investigation would be over quickly. As soon as they killed this perp the investigation would be complete. He figured that he would prepare the team for what was ahead of them. If he could figure out a way to eliminate the perpetrator they wouldn't have to worry about sitting around in a court room prior to appearing before a judge. A lot of money could be saved by just doing away with the guilty party. This should turn out to be a quick arrest and investigation.

Jack began to formulate in his mind exactly what he and his team were going to do. He had been trained for this type of work and felt positive about his abilities and those of his team. This would probably turn out to be very cut and dry.

Little did Jack know that this case would the most mentally and physically frustrating investigation he would ever encounter.

CHAPTER FIVE

Bob was thinking that as fast as Jack was going he was
probably at the Police department and getting filled in on
what had happened. He hoped that Jack and Lynne had made it
back safely. It was 11:50pm when Bob pulled into the
driveway and immediately noticed that his daughter, Tara,
was not at home. Her car was not in the driveway. Tara was
soon to be twenty four and at that age she was still young
enough to believe that midnight was the beginning of party
time.

Bob opened the door and went immediately to the alarm panel
and deactivated it by entering the code. Martin recalled
that about six years prior a couple of burglaries took
place in the neighborhood. He would rather be safe than
sorry so he installed the alarm.

Bob thought about how the house he had built went from
eight hundred square feet to over twenty five hundred feet
in the sixteen years he had lived there with JoAnne. Bob
walked to the bedroom to get a holster for his duty weapon
and began to think the house was too big for three people
and a dog. He then remembered that the dog had to be picked
up at the kennel.

He had a daughter going on twenty four who could have taken
care of the dog but instead he had opted for the kennel.
Bob remembered that his daughter had trouble taking care of
herself let alone a 75 lb. greyhound. Oh, sometimes he was
too hard on his daughter. She really was a good kid who was
working her way through nursing school, when she could get
out of the party mode. There he was mentally giving her a
hard time again. She was a young person who loved to have a
good time. She would go to school during the day, work from
4pm to 12pm and then party until three in the morning and
return home for some sleep. Then she would start the
entire cycle once again.

How could he be thinking about such trivial bullshit when a
friend and fellow officer had been murdered? Maybe this
was the mind's way of taking the pressure off, he thought.
Bob removed his shirt, put on some deodorant and pulled a
sweatshirt with the Lower Township Police emblem on the
left breast over his head. He removed the metal
rechargeable flashlight from its charger, grabbed his
holstered weapon and started towards the door.

He realized JoAnne was out of the bathroom and must have
gone out to the car to await him. He thought about how she
always had to go to the bathroom anytime he was in a hurry.
That girl must have kidney problems he thought as he

laughed to himself thinking about all the stories he could tell about her trips to the bathrooms of the world.

Someday he would write a book about JoAnne and her kidneys. However, he really didn't think it would sell. People do spend their money in ridiculous ways, he thought. JoAnne would buy items at retail so she could have things to sell at her yard sale at a reduced rate. Didn't she realize she was losing money? Bob was forever telling JoAnne that these yard sales didn't make money. She didn't listen. Life with JoAnne was interesting to say the least.

JoAnne started the car and waited for Bob to leave the house for the trip to the police department. Bob exited the house and JoAnne saw the ritual take place as he hurried down the steps. He placed the metal flashlight under his arm and slipped his holstered 9mm Smith and Wesson into his waste band. JoAnne thought about how many times she observed this ritual take place during her years with Bob.

Bob was thinking to himself that Jack was probably at the station and no doubt meeting with the swat team in preparation for action. He entered the family car and JoAnne pulled out of the circular driveway in front of the Martin home. She thought about how much she hated maneuvering around the trees that lined the driveway. If only Bob would cut some of them down. This wasn't the time to bring up the subject.

JoAnne noticed that the Trombetta car wasn't in the driveway. The Trombettas lived about 100 yards from the Martins. Not only were the two families close friends, they were close neighbors.

JoAnne thought about how the tree lined street had been so desolate when Bob had first told her he was going to build a house there. She never dreamed that years later there would be so many police officers living on the street that it would be referred to as "Pig Alley." JoAnne hated those two words. She was proud of her husband's profession and despised the connotation.

Most often she was more upset by someone calling Bob a pig than he ever would be. How he would react always depended on the situation, but he never seemed to let it bother him. Cops seem to be able to take a lot of things in stride. That was part of the job.

The five minute trip to the police headquarters went quickly. JoAnne pulled into the entrance of the Police department and was mesmerized by the vast array of uniformed and non-uniformed police officers in front of the building. There had to be close to 100 men and a few women there.

Bob knew that these officers were standing by and would be ready to provide assistance as needed. They represented every department in Cape May County. Some were sleeping in their cars. Most of them were on their own time and not being paid for the work that they would be undertaking. Little did they know that the work they would take part in would lead them to a County dump and the dirty duty of searching 50 tons of trash? No one knew what was to come. If they did, it wouldn't have changed their minds. A fellow officer was dead and no matter what it took the job would be done. That's how cops are.

JoAnne followed the curving driveway to the rear of the Police Department and was overwhelmed by the amount of marked and unmarked police vehicles in the rear parking lot. She had seen activity in the past but nothing of this magnitude. She could not imagine how all this equipment and personnel could be managed.

Directly in front of her was the swat truck. JoAnne saw Detective Bill Hienkel in the dark sinister clothing of the swat team. Bill was placing weapons into the vehicle. She thought of how glad she was that Bob was no longer in that squad. She remembered the many times he was called out in the middle of the night for raids and arrests. On one occasion she made the mistake of listening to the police scanner to keep on top of the action.

She had pleaded with Bob to get a scanner so she could listen in on some of the calls. He had always advised her it wasn't something she should be listening to. She badgered him until he finally purchased a programmable bearcat Scanner. It was so neat. Now she could listen to what was going on within a thirty mile radius. JoAnne thought how it was like being on top of a breaking story. One night Bob had been called out on a swat mission and as he left she turned on the scanner. She eventually heard that the team was affecting the arrest of an armed individual who was barricaded in his home and threatening to kill his selve. She thought about how tense all the voices on the radio sounded. She began to pray that everyone would be safe.

She listened for about an hour and a half until she heard an officer transmit in an excited voice, "Where's Martin? Where's Martin?" The transmission was followed by a loud sound that JoAnne thought was a gun shot. She froze staring at the scanner and began to sob uncontrollably. She begged the scanner to tell her everything was O.K.

30

Moments later she heard Bob's voice state, "Everybody relax, that sound was a car backfire, the guy is coming out the front door with his hands on his head." JoAnne jumped up, unplugged the scanner and placed it in a closet where it is still located. She decided she didn't have to be on top of the news any longer.

JoAnne observed that the County K9 team was standing at the rear of their vehicles and that the dogs were barking and moving about inside the four wheel drive vehicles.

It was difficult for her to find room to stop due to the many vehicles and officers that were milling about. JoAnne noticed that a few news vans were located in the rear of the parking lot. She thought of how Bob always mistrusted the media people. He often referred to being "burnt" by them on one occasion and not giving them a second chance. Many times he said he would write a book about the incident. He just never got around to starting.

JoAnne found room to stop. Bob leaned over, kissed her and said, "Listen, Jo, it is going to be awhile before I get home. Probably, late tomorrow or early Sunday morning. I'll try to stop home to shower and change, but, don't expect me anytime soon."

JoAnne kissed him again and said, "I'll be praying for you. Be careful, I love you."

JoAnne watched him approach the entrance and she slowly drove away. She prayed all the way home.

CHAPTER SIX

Martin exited the car and walked towards the rear entrance
to the headquarters. He approached the police personnel
entrance and keyed in the entry code. He thought how
ridiculous the security was at the department. Even the
Coca Cola deliverer had the code for the easy access back
door. One time Martin had completed a special report to
the now retired Chief of Police about the security
problems. It was one of those things that got filed and
forgotten.

Martin entered the station house and made the turn in the
hallway to the Detective Division. The division offices
were right next to the offices of Capt. John Maher and
Chief Don Douglass.

Detective Edward Donohue, Donohue with an o, was standing
in the hallway and saw Martin coming. "Yo," Donohue said.
Donohue was forever providing this two letter greeting. He
spoke without moving his lips and it drove Martin crazy.
Martin had hearing aides but people who didn't move their
lips always sounded as though they were mumbling. He always
had trouble hearing what Donohue had to say. Oftentimes
Martin would acknowledge as if he heard what Donohue said
even when he had no idea what Donohue was talking about.

Donohue had been a detective for approximately one year and
was still getting his feet wet in the world of the
Detective Division. Martin looked at him and thought this
will be the biggest case this guy will ever work on. It
was a shame it had to be the death of a fellow officer.
Martin recalled that initially Donohue had problems during
interviews and interrogations. He was such a nice quiet
guy that suspects would take over the conversation and it
seemed like Ed thought it would be rude to interrupt.
Donohue, however, had been making excellent progress and
was a stickler for details.

Martin could see that his detective seemed to be in a
trance. Sensing this he decided to cut to the quick.

"Ed, we have our work cut out for us. Are you alright?"

"Yeah, I guess," answered Donohue.

"Don't guess, Ed. Fill me in on what happened and where
everyone is and what their assignments are at this time."

Donohue responded slowly and tried to be precise. He knew
no matter what he offered that Martin would still have more

questions for him. Donohue did the best, he could,
considering the circumstances and the chaos going on. He
updated Martin on the last four hours.

Martin stared at Donohue in an attempt to read his mumbling
lips. I wish this guy would speak up, he thought to
himself.

"Ed, where is Trombetta?" asked Martin.

"He is in the captain's office with the swat team. He just
walked in a couple of minutes ago and the chief told him to
get ready for some action. I think they are going to hit a
couple houses."

"Ed, don't tell me what you think, tell me what you know,"
directed Martin. Donohue loved to tell the whole story and
Martin didn't need it at this point. He was trying to
ascertain where his people were and what they were doing.
He didn't have time for anything more than the short
version. Martin thought to himself how he had upset a lot
of people over the years by cutting them off so they would
get to the point. Tough shit, he thought.

He hated to wait for the real story when he was in a hurry
to get things done. Martin was forever asking questions
and then ask the person responding, "Is this going to be a
long story?" Hell, even Joe Friday from Dragnet always
said, "The facts, nothing but the facts." It always
astounded Martin that people would use so many words to say
so little.

Martin thought about how Detective Bill Hienkel loved to
tell stories and that these stories would make great
material for a book. One day Martin would have to sit down
and start writing.

Detective Donohue advised Martin that Detective Chris
Winter was at the scene of the shooting. Detective Tom
Keywood was interviewing witness along with Detective Jim
Moy. Detective Mike Brogan was at the scene of a related
arson and Detective Bill Hienkel at the swat team meeting.
Donohue further indicated that he had just completed an
interview and was headed to another.

Martin asked Donohue, "Is Hooyman handling the
investigation?"

"No, replied Donohue, the Captain is."

Martin was not happy with the response. "Where's Hooyman?"

"The Captain sent him to the scene to coordinate manpower

with the County Crime Unit."
Martin thought to himself, why is it that the captain would take the most experienced investigator he had and have him direct human traffic? He could not believe what he had heard. There must be a good reason.

Martin had worked with Hooyman over the years and saw him become a methodical and by the numbers investigator. He was the kind of guy who would be great with evidence collection and control but not the greatest with regard to interviewing techniques. Martin remembered when he was teamed with Hooyman when Rich had first become a detective. Martin thought about how he did not trust him at first. Martin always maintained that a person had to prove his loyalty and trustworthiness first and then he would take the time to get to know the guy and his abilities.

Trombetta and Martin maintained that a detective should take care of his own when necessary and they should learn real quickly that most of the patrolmen they thought were friends would soon become just passing acquaintances.

When you became a detective and were able to maintain a friendship with someone you were close to as a patrolman, that friend was well worth keeping. The others became guys you worked with.

Martin thought about how Hooyman, as a patrolman, was one of those guys you worked with. He was a conscientious street cop but didn't maintain any type of friendship with the guys working as detectives.

Martin and Trombetta had just returned from a year and a half long undercover operation. They had been involved in an investigation that led to the arrests and convictions of numerous Gambino, crime family members. The FBI would call it the 'Pizza Connection'. Who would have ever thought that mafioso were working the streets of Cape May County, New Jersey. Both detectives had cultivated an informant that comes along once in a lifetime and together the three became an interesting team. The careers of the two detectives could have stopped at that point and they would have enough stories to tell for the rest of their living days.

The Gambino investigation provided an interesting investigative endeavor for the team of Martin and Trombetta. It resulted in the confiscation of over two hundred and fifty thousand dollars, the arrest of Gambino family members in three states and the country of Italy. Two members of the Gambino crime family were still fugitives and four were still in prison in the United States. One million dollars worth of heroin and cocaine had been seized during the execution of search warrants and the culmination of drug buys. Yes, it certainly was the substance of which good books were made.

So, here they came, the conquering undercover heros, returning to their department to be confronted with a new detective. Detective Richard Hooyman had been assigned temporarily to the Detective Division when it was determined that Martin and Trombetta would be working with a county, state and federal Task Force. Hooyman remembered that Martin had worked undercover about ten years prior and that Trombetta was undercover for the first time.

Hooyman had called Martin on one occasion and asked if he could use his desk during Martin's stay at the strike force. Martin said yes, but just half of the bottom drawer. Martin figured that he might as well bust the new guy's chops a little. Hooyman figured he was the new kid on the block so half was better than none.

Hooyman remembered being told that when Martin and Trombetta returned he would be partnered with Martin. The story was that then Chief Bob Denny thought it was time to separate these two roving, rogue detectives before they found cases in another country.

Hooyman remembered the first night with Martin as a partner. He had been given a talk about being trusted and looking out for his partner's best interests. Weeks went by and Hooyman began to see how detectives really operated. His preconceived notions of the prima donnas of the police department were short lived. He found out quickly they worked hard, long and furious when there was work to be done. Down time, however, would lead to conversations that often times resulted in lifestyle changes for Hooyman.

As Martin was trying to figure out why Capt. Maher would have sent Hooyman to act as a liaison with the County Crime unit, he thought about a conversation he and Hooyman had during some down time while driving through the Township of Lower.

"Hey, Bob, now that we have been working together for a month, how do you think I'm doing?" asked Hooyman. Martin thought to his self this guy must be crazy. He has to know I'm going to tell it like it is.

"Well, Rich, you talk so much that you're getting on my nerves." Martin was relating to the fact that every time the conversation was at a lull Rich would try to keep it going, usually with trivial small talk that just took up time. To Martin's surprise Hooyman stopped the small talk almost immediately.

One month later Hooyman again made the mistake of asking
how he was doing. Martin responded,"Your cigarette smoking
is killing me."

Hooyman responded, "Well, I haven't been talking as much
and I guess I'm more nervous so I smoke more."

"You are killing me with second hand smoke and I am not
ready to die at this time," advised Martin.

Two weeks later Detective Rich Hooyman went to a hypnotist
and stopped smoking. Rich was the kind of guy that liked
to please. Martin also found out as time and numerous
cases went by that he could also be trusted and would back
you up when it was required. The partnership continued.
Hooyman was not a good interrogator but his by the numbers
approach made him a good interviewer. He became a
meticulous fact finder and a stickler for details. His
ability to handle evidence was put to good use on a regular
basis. However, he started talking again. Martin decided
he would put up with the small talk.

CHAPTER SEVEN

Martin, after getting a quick briefing from Donohue, went
to the chief's office. There, he found the mayor and three
Lower Township Council members. The chief was seated behind
his desk. He had a worried look on his face that was quite
evident.

Chief Don W. Douglass, at this time, had been chief for
less than two years and was confronted with the loss of a
police officer. He had enough to do just attempting to
make everyday decisions and changes within the department
that had been under the direction of the same former police
chief for over thirty years.

Don Douglass had been one of Martin's detective sergeants
when Martin had returned from the County Narcotic Strike
Force in 1977. Martin was assigned to DSG. Don Douglass
and they soon became an interesting investigative team.
Don's brother, Robert Douglass, was the other detective
sergeant and was the boss of the division. The Douglass
brothers were always arguing and Martin loved to instigate
the arguments.

Martin had long hair that was over the shoulders and a
Fu-Manchu mustache. His hair coupled with his less than
conservative clothing made him look like a scum bag. Martin
was six foot tall and weighed one hundred sixty pounds
soaking wet. Don Douglass was a short, slightly overweight
patrol sergeant who was now in charge of what appeared to
be a burnt out hippie left over from the late sixties.

Martin recalled their first duty tour together and thought
about how the then Chief Denny had advised them he wanted
an increase in drug arrests and an increase in arrests for
burglary and theft. Don Douglass looked to his new partner
and thought to himself that it probably wouldn't be a
difficult task. Martin looked like a drug user, thief and
burglar all rolled into one. If worse came to worse he
could probably arrest Martin.

They walked out of the chief's office and Douglass asked,
"Hey, Martin, do you want to go back in uniform?"

"Not if I have a choice," answered Martin.

"In that case you better show me how you are going to make
us look good. After all you look more like a scum bag than
a cop."

"I guess you think the old man was serious?"

"Yeah, about as serious as a heart attack," laughed Douglass. Martin looked at Douglass in his hush puppy style clothing and said, "Well, if you're going to look like that, you stay in the car and I'll call you when I need you". They both laughed and hopped into an unmarked and went to what was referred to as the West End Jetty. It was that area of the beach where a canal separated the bay from the ocean. It was a local hang out for those who liked to party.

They had no sooner pulled into the parking area when they promptly made three arrests for possession of pot and found fifteen grams of hash on a sweet unsuspecting female drug dealer, who Martin had been following off and on for about three months while working undercover with the Strike Force. Martin thought she had been in too many of the wrong places at the wrong time. He was right. She quickly became a working informant for the two detectives. She along with many others provided them with an endless list of arrests and good information.

She had made the remark to Don Douglass that he dressed like a school teacher and looked like a cop. "See, what did I tell you," said Martin? "If you don't want to stay in the car or behind some bushes, you are going to have to change your look."

The next day Douglass arrived for the four to twelve shift with an afro and looking like SUPERFLY. Martin thought that the purple platform high heeled shoes were a bit much. He didn't have the heart to tell Don. However, he sure got a good laugh at the site before his eyes.

At one point in their partnership Don Douglass started carrying a leather purse which held his gun strapped over his shoulder. Martin found it difficult to equate the then crazy gung-ho detective sergeant with the solemn faced chief that sat before him.

Martin reflected on the somber look that was covering the chief's face. He glanced at the three council members. Each exhibited the same expression. The female council member sobbed quietly. The detective sergeant looked at the chief and said, "I'm here. Where do you want me?"

The chief didn't hesitate. "You are the case officer on this one. Trombetta is in charge of the swat team. Jim McGowan is the case officer for the County Prosecutor's Office. You will be working with him. I know I don't have to tell you I don't want the County running the show."

Martin thought about McGowan and earlier had decided that

he was probably the most experienced investigator at the Prosecutor's Office. McGowan had retired from Philadelphia Police department and went to work for the Prosecutor in Cape May County.
Martin knew he was competent and thorough.

The chief then began to relay general information about the shooting to Martin. The council members sat quietly as the information was provided. There was nothing new. The same information had been related by Det. Donohue. The chief did, however, make one statement that stuck with Martin.

"Bob, half a dozen witnesses are stating that the perpetrator was a white male, wearing a flannel shirt and blue jeans. He was also wearing a wool cap, dark in color and looked like he walked with a limp or a shuffle in his step." The chief then hesitated for a moment. "There's one thing that bothers me. We have one young female witness who states that she observed the described suspect in the area but that he was Oriental and not white."

"So you have approximately six witnesses saying the perp is a white male and one indicating the perp is Oriental," asked Martin?

"That's about the size of it," Chief Douglass answered.

"Also, I'm sure you know that the place that houses all the Oriental workers for the Chinese restaurant, nearby, was torched around the time of Dave's murder," added Douglass.

Martin knew he had asked the chief to repeat himself. Martin, however, wanted to hear the statement one more time. He knew he would have to remember not to forget the possibility of an Oriental suspect. He gave the possibility a quick thought and decided there were not many Orientals living in Lower Twsp. nor were there any Oriental informants. Martin also knew that those Orientals living in the Township were not knocking on the doors of the Police Department to provide information about anything. They basically kept to themselves and handled their own problems. He hoped the perpetrator was not an Oriental.

Martin thought that the case would be more easily solved if the perpetrator was a local scum bag. The local shit heads always made the same mistakes. They would leave something at the scene or they would eventually tell someone what they had done. That someone would drop the dime to one of the investigating officers during the investigation. There wasn't much honor among thieves contrary to popular belief. Martin glanced around the chief's office making eye contact with each face as a courtesy before departing the office.

"I'm going to meet with McGowan and see what's what,"
Martin said."
"McGowan is in your office," the chief advised.

"Listen, Chief, I will keep you posted as often as I can.
If you don't see me for a while, it's not because I'm
ignoring you."

"Hey, Martin, we gotta get this guy."

"We will," replied Martin as he exited the office.

Martin knew they would arrest the perpetrator. He just
wasn't sure how long it would take to do so.

CHAPTER EIGHT

Detective Sergeant Robert Martin entered his office. He
normally shared its one hundred square feet with Trombetta,
Hooyman and the vast array of radio and computer equipment
that Hooyman kept on hand. There wasn't much room for
fifty guys in a building that totaled four thousand square
feet.

Lt. Jim McGowan was seated at Trombetta's desk which was
right next to Martin's. Both desks were covered with a lot
of paper. There were three or four other individuals
standing in the small office. Martin didn't pay any
attention to them and if asked later couldn't say who was
present.

McGowan turned from the desk. "Hi, Bob, I guess it's you
and me on this one."

"That's what they tell me," replied Martin.

"I heard you were coming back from the Poconos with
Trombetta."

"Yeah, vacation is over."

"Let me fill you in on what has happened so far," stated
McGowan.

McGowan spent the next thirty minutes reviewing what had
taken place thus far in the investigation. Martin had heard
the story for about the fourth time and now was getting a
good understanding as to what had happened. McGowan then
went into what was presently taking place. When he was
finished, Martin had an idea where everyone was located and
what they were doing.

McGowan then stated that Capt. Maher was presently in the
conference room of the Township Hall along with police
administrators from other jurisdictions. McGowan also
related that an assistant prosecutor was also at the
meeting. Martin was trying to figure out why an AP would
be at such a meeting when McGowan supplied the answer.

"The AP is discussing the use of the Swat Team," stated
McGowan.

"Why is he involved with that?" asked Martin. "He should
not be involved with tactical stuff".

McGowan answered, "You can bet the AP will be around for

every decision that has to be made, tactical or otherwise."

Martin knew that the new assistant prosecutor and was supposed to be the criminal attorney savior of the Prosecutors office. Martin had not met him yet.

"Jim, how can you work with these lawyers?" asked Martin.

"Hey, it's easy. Don't argue with them and make them think all the ideas are their's. That way they don't bug ya," instructed McGowan. Contrary to what many civilians think, cops normally do not like most prosecutors, although theoretically they are supposed to be on the same side.

Martin thought about how the last prosecutor had problems with his staff winning cases in court. The local defense attorneys had been winning the majority of cases that had gone to court and the record of the Prosecutors Office was less than admirable. Why was the Assistant Prosecutor or A.P. as they were known, sitting in a meeting where cops were discussing "police work" as opposed to legal bullshit. Maybe the AP was the type of guy who was really interested, maybe even a police groupie or cop buff. Martin chuckled at the thought. One way or the other something was up.

Martin could not believe that the AP would be taking part in tactical decision making. He told McGowan he was going over to the conference room and wouldn't be long.

Martin exited the building and once again noticed the numerous police personnel standing around awaiting an assignment. He entered the rear door of the Municipal Office Building and saw that the hallway was filled to capacity as was the court room. Uniformed and plainclothes police were everywhere. Some were talking, most with looks of total disbelief on their faces. Martin nodded to a few faces he was familiar with and proceeded to the conference room of the building.

Under normal conditions the conference room would hold fifteen people comfortably. Conditions, however, were not normal. The room was overflowing with people. Many police administrators representing most Police Departments from the Cape May county area were present. Martin recognized all the faces except for one. Seated at the conference table to the right of Capt. Maher was a short balding guy with glasses. Martin tried to place the face but it didn't register. It was interesting to note that four local police chiefs were among the administrative officers in the room.

Martin directed his gaze to Capt. Maher. Martin had assisted with the background investigation of John Maher about fifteen years prior. John Maher was the

bother-in-law of Jack Trombetta. Most of what Martin knew
about Maher had come from Jack. John was a wiz with facts
and figures and when faced with a problem was not afraid to
ask for help. Maher was the type of cop who would make a
good attorney.

Martin also knew that Capt. John Maher had two
shortcomings. He was a chronic procrastinator and he had
zero experience as a criminal investigator. Maher had
risen quickly through the ranks by excelling in the
productive art of civil service test taking.
Capt. John Maher would back his people one hundred and ten
percent even when things got tough.

Martin laughed to himself as he thought about the captain's
ability to talk non-stop about anything, anywhere and any
place. John Maher also had a bad habit that drove most
people crazy. He did his best talking when he was eating.
Whether on the phone or in person he was always shoving
something in his mouth when he was talking.

John Maher was a good guy to have on your side in any
circumstance if you could just keep him quiet and keep food
from entering his mouth. He was excellent at thinking
while speaking and rarely put his foot in his mouth.   In
fact, he was most frequently putting pretzels in his mouth
when talking.

Martin looked past Capt. Maher seated at the head of the
table and noticed that Lt. Don Lombardo was talking on the
phone. Don was advising the communications operator to
relay orders to patrol officers. Martin had also assisted
with the background investigation of Don Lombardo back in
1977.

Lombardo had been assigned to the Detective Division for
eighteen months and had been a productive patrolman prior.
Just tell Don what you wanted done and he took care of it.
He was always reliable and could get things done. Don
wasn't a good interrogator so for most of his detective
time he handled check cases. You just had to point him in
the direction of a bad check case and he would handle it.
Don, however, was always repeating himself. Martin and
Trombetta would often joke about the constant repetition.
They were ushers at Don's wedding. Martin was Godfather to
Don's youngest boy.

Lombardo was a cop's cop with one problem. He would allow
things to get on his nerves to the point of chewing off all
his fingernails until they disappeared. Martin always
figured here was a guy ripe for ulcers and stomach
problems. He really let things get to him and usually
worried about lawsuits emerging from something in which his

43

people might get involved. Sometimes Martin thought that
Don Lombardo actually liked to worry about things.
The room was full of the noise of many conversations. Most
were conversations centered on the disbelief of the
occurrence. Martin was attempting to catch the captain's
eye when the unknown bald guy asked, "How do you plan on
using the swat team on these search warrants?" Maher
ignored the question and acknowledged Martin's presence.
The noise was to the point where it was impossible to hear
and or understand what was being said. Maher knew Martin
couldn't hear well, even with hearing aides, so he started
to speak much louder.

"Bob, you just get here?" asked Maher.

"Yeah, captain, about forty five minutes ago. I have been
getting filled in on some of the info," replied Martin.

"So you know what's going on?"

"In general, captain, I met with the chief and McGowan..."

Maher cut Martin off before he could finish the sentence
and stated, "No, not about the shooting. I'm referring to
the houses we want to hit with the swat team. We have info
that this perp stole a gun locally and used it on Dave."

Martin recalled Det. Donohue providing information about
the possible suspect and the attempt to locate him.
Donohue had indicated that a local scum bag fit the
description of the perpetrator and was being looked at very
closely. The detective had indicated that an individual
known to Martin as a drug user had his residence
burglarized on Wednesday, February sixteenth. During the
burglary a shotgun and a 357 magnum revolver were taken.
The victim indicated that our possible perp was the guy
that had probably burglarized his residence.
Martin began thinking about Donohue's information and soon
realized that everything pointing to the possible
perpetrator was very circumstantial. Martin had been
involved with this individual on many occasions and knew
that he had a very extensive record. Martin also knew that
this guy made a concerted effort at committing crimes
against people he was related to, knew well, or worked for.
He rarely victimized people he didn't know. Martin
couldn't recall this guy pulling off jobs at random. If he
had killed Ptlm. Douglass it would have to be related to
someone or someplace he was attached to whether by blood,
friendship or someone he did odd jobs for. This guy had a
multitude of shortcomings but Martin didn't believe he was
a cop killer. Martin also knew that anything was possible.

Martin began to respond to the captain's statement when the

bald guy asked, "Did anyone find out if the victim of the
burglary had any bullet casings that had been fired from
the 357 that was stolen?"

Martin gazed at the subject and asked, "Are you talking to
me?"

Captain Maher must have realized that Martin did not know
the identity of the bald guy. "Bob, have you met the
assistant prosecutor?"

"No, I haven't, but I guess I'm going to.

Maher started to introduce the AP but the AP started a
conversation with one of the Chiefs of Police sitting at
the table. The AP appeared busy looking at notes and did
not extend his hand, neither did Martin. Martin remembered
that a new AP had been hired recently to head the criminal
section of the prosecutor's office. The story was that he
was suppose to be the savior of a legal team that had been
having problems winning cases against local defense
attorneys. The AP's reputation, or at least the talk of
his reputation, indicated that he possessed some impressive
legal abilities. Martin knew from past experience that
time would tell, especially with a case as high profile as
this one.

Martin directed his conversation to Capt. Maher. "Captain,
I'll have to pull the case file on the stolen 357 magnum
that he is referring to and get back to you. Right now, I
don't see the importance of that information," Martin
added.

The AP looked up from his notes and stated, "We need this
type of information to add credence to our search warrant
affidavits."

"I understand that, but are we going to have time to
compare shell casings with a spent projectile we don't even
have in our possession? The autopsy on Dave probably won't
be completed until the afternoon. It will then take two
hours to bring it back here. I think that at this point we
are wasting manpower chasing after spent casings that may
or may not have anything to do with our shooting. I'm going
out to see if we can get some more info." It was very
apparent Martin was not intimidated by the AP. Martin heard
something come out of the AP's mouth but didn't pay
attention to it. He went looking for Jack Trombetta.

Martin entered the Police department and went directly to
the captain's Office where Trombetta was conducting a
meeting with the swat team. Upon entering Martin saw the
team members with their heads bowed being led in prayer by

45

Trombetta. Jack looked up and acknowledged Bob. "What's
up," asked Jack.
Martin related the story about the AP and Trombetta
laughed.

"He probably has no idea what he's talkin' about. Why
don't these ass holes stay out of stuff they know nothin'
about," stated Trombetta.

"Listen, Jack, when you guys start hitting places be
careful and don't do something stupid," instructed Martin.
Trombetta had a crazed look and stated, "If he resists,
he's dead. We just prayed about it."

"Jack, what I mean is that I don't think this guy is the
perp."

"You're kidding," Trombetta was obviously astonished.

"No, I just have a feeling, so try to do it by the
numbers," advised Martin.

Martin turned to leave the room and observed confused looks
on the faces of the other swat team members.

"Guys be careful and do what you got to do," stated Martin
as he closed the door behind him. He prayed that they would
be careful and not do anything stupid.

The door to the chief's office was open. Martin noticed
that the chief seemed to be trying to catch his attention.
"Chief, "I'm not sure this guy we have zeroed in on is
going to turn out to be our shooter," stated Martin. The
chief stared at Martin and said, "It was your guy, Winter,
who came up with this suspect. Have you seen him yet?"

"No, he is still at the scene," stated Martin.

Martin knew he had to hook up with Detective Chris Winter
and see what he knew. Winter was a detective for about
three years and his biggest shortcoming was his inability
to admit he was wrong. He was a hard worker who was
conscientious and would one day be an outstanding
investigator.

Martin saw Donohue in the hall and asked more questions
about the burglary and theft concerning the 357 handgun and
advised him to get some more information from the case
file. Martin started to his office and saw Detective Jim
Moy enter the hallway. "Jim, what are you up to?"

"Sarge, I just took a witness home," replied Moy. Martin
was thinking about the fact that Moy had joined the

Detective Division just a month ago. What a way to get
baptized into investigative work. "Do you have something
for me to do?" asked Moy.

"I want you to fill me in on what you have done since the
beginning of this mess."

Moy began to appear visibly nervous and before he could say
anything a communications operator was on the intercom
advising that Det. Brogan was looking for Sgt. Martin.
Martin went to his office, grabbed the phone and was
advised by Brogan that the perpetrator's sister had been
stopped in a car and should she be brought to the station.
Martin advised him to do so. He hung up the phone and
turned to Moy and said, "You and I are going to interview
the perp's sister and find out where he is hiding."

"All the rooms are being used," said Moy.

"We'll use the lieutenant's office," stated Martin.

They started down the hall and both men entered the office
and found five cops sitting around two desks. The
conversation centered, around the hope that the perpetrator
would be found and he would resist. Martin advised the men
that he needed the office for an interview. The men didn't
seem to be reacting as quickly as Martin had expected.
"Hit the trail! We need this room," Martin snapped. The men
immediately left the office.

Martin directed Moy to sit at the large desk and to record
pertinent information while he talked to the girl who
Brogan was bringing to the Police department. Martin
advised Moy that they were going to be real nice to her and
see if they could get information about her brother.

Moments later a short, blonde female in her mid twenties
was led into the room by Detective Brogan. It appeared that
she hadn't slept in some time and her clothing was a bit
disheveled. Martin was familiar with her and she
recognized him immediately.

CHAPTER NINE

"Hi, Mary, do you remember me? I'm Det.Sgt. Martin and this
is Det. Moy. We would like to ask you some questions about
your brother and some of his friends. I sure would
appreciate it if you would help us out. Why don't you have
a seat and I'll get you something to drink, if you like,"
opened Martin. She nodded her head that she remembered
Martin and asked for coffee. Moy went to get it.

Det. Moy returned with the coffee and observed that the
female was seated in a straight back chair in front of one
of the two desks in the room. Martin was in a straight
back chair seated directly in front of the girl. Martin was
leaning toward the subject with his hands clasped together
as though he was praying. Moy remembered Martin had wanted
him seated behind the large desk. He quickly sat down.

"Mary, it's important that you listen real closely to me. I
know you are going to tell me all you know about your
brother and his friends. I'm sure you know how important
this case is due to the fact a police officer was killed. I
have been involved with the members of your family before
and all of them have been truthful with me." Martin knew
that the family was always less than truthful but he was
attempting to get this girl to cooperate and he would say
or do whatever was necessary to get positive results.

Martin really wanted to say, that her entire family were
low life scum bags and she was no better. He knew,
however, that such a statement would not get cooperation.
Martin was thinking how he hated to placate low lifes in an
attempt to secure information and cooperation.

Det. Moy was watching Martin and listening. Martin
motioned to Moy as if he was scribbling on paper and Moy
knew he should start taking notes.

Martin interviewed the young lady for about a half hour
before she began to provide worthwhile information. She
indicated that her brother could not have possibly been
involved in the shooting because he had been at her home
during the time period in question. Martin continually
asked her to repeat and reiterate almost every statement
she made. Moy was beginning to think the note taking job
was a real drag. Martin never liked to take notes when
interviewing mainly because he felt it turned off people
from being candid. Talking to someone and taking notes was
distracting to the person being interviewed. It would
often make them feel like the entire conversation was too
official. When people felt that way they tended to freeze

up and not be talkative.
The conversation between Martin and the girl went on for
about a half an hour when Jim Moy sensed that the interview
was coming to a close. He was relieved that the note
taking session was over. Martin leaned toward the subject,
placed his hand on her arm in a reassuring gesture and told
her to relax and that he would get her some more coffee and
then she could go over her story with Det. Moy. Martin
stood up quickly and asked Moy to step outside. He excused
himself.

"Jim, what I want you to do is pay attention to your notes,
go back in and have her go through the whole thing again.
Pay close attention to every statement and indicate any
discrepancies in your notes. When you are finished let me
know and I'll review everything and we will both go at her
again. Hopefully, we will get everything she knows. I'm
sure she knows about the burglary of the guns and maybe she
can tell us who has them. She hasn't told us much that is
truthful. Everything she gives we have to drag out of her.
I want her to be more helpful. So we are going to keep
working on her. She will loosen up."

Martin opened the door and directed Moy to get another cup
of coffee for the subject. Martin placed his hand on the
girl's shoulder and stated, "I know you are tired but I
know you are also aware of how important this is. We sure
don't want your brother or his friends to be accused of
something they didn't do. Everything you tell us is very
important and I know you don't want your brother to be
hurt."

Moy entered the room with the second cup of coffee. Martin
stated, "Det. Moy is going to go over a few things with you
and when I come back I'll do my best to get you out of
here". Almost as an afterthought Martin added, "I'm sure
you will tell Det. Moy the truth. Everything you have said
has been most helpful and we really do appreciate your
help".

Martin entered the hallway and was met by Det. Donohue who
advised that he had made contact with the burglary victim
who would look for some shell casings from the 357 magnum.
Martin was thinking about the interview of the girl and was
sure he could obtain consent to search her residence for
her brother and the proceeds of the burglary in question.

Martin walked to the Municipal Building and entered the
conference room. He advised Captain Maher that he would
have a consent to search the home belonging to the perp's
sister in an hour. Maher told him to contact members of the
Middle Township Police Department who were located at the
residence making sure no one left or entered the residence.

Martin knew the captain would be glad about the consent to search. He knew that it would be hours before a search warrant affidavit would be reviewed, redone, reviewed and eventually signed by a judge. Prosecuting attorneys always wanted the affidavit airtight. It seemed that they wanted to be sure the case was won long before the first report was even written. Most cops always look at assistant prosecutors as Monday morning quarterbacks who found it easy to throw for the touchdown after making sure that all defenders had been eliminated. It sure would be nice if police work could be done that way. The hell with split second decisions. Let's just tell the victim of an aggravated assault that even though it was her boyfriend that broke her nose and jaw she is going to have to identify him in a lineup.

"Hey, are you sure the sister is going to give you consent," asked the AP? "Make sure she makes a knowing and intelligent waiver or we could have some problems at a suppression hearing."

"Yeah," grunted Martin as he continued his way out of the building. Martin was thinking to himself that he got along better with defense attorneys than with prosecutors who were supposed to be on his side.

Martin realized he didn't advise the A.P. about the shell casings. No big deal. He would tell him later. Let him worry about it some more.

Bob returned to the Police department and went directly to his office.

CHAPTER TEN

Jim McGowan was taking care of phone calls and trying to
get a handle on all the assignments that were being
assigned. He knew from past experience that you could not
allow even the smallest thing to get by you in an
investigation like this.

Jim was thinking how after retiring from an interesting and
productive career in the Philadelphia Police Department he
had decided to make permanent residency in Cape May County,
a place he and the family had vacationed over the years.
He still had kids to get through college so he figured he
might as well get a job doing what he knew best, police
work. He got a job as an investigator with the Cape May
County Prosecutor and figured he could cruise along with
minor cases and a paycheck that would help the college
bound family members. Little did he know that the caseload
would be as heavy and in this case, the shooting of a
police officer, so crucial.

"Jim, I am going to go back and get consent to search the
location on our alleged perp from his sister," said Martin.
"I think she should be ready to give it all up now."

"Do you think she'll give him up?" asked McGowan.

"Yeah, she will. She's afraid we are going to pop him. So
she will do her sisterly duty and save him from injury,
pain, suffering and Trombetta," stated Martin. McGowan sat
back in the chair and added, "You know, Bob, I'm not sure
this guy is involved. It just doesn't feel right."

"Jim, I feel the same way. We have to eliminate this
suspect real quick, before everyone decides they have their
man. Let me finish up on this girl, get our so called perp
in here and eliminate him or arrest him. If he isn't
involved we still can take him down on the burglary,"
stated Martin. McGowan picked up his notes and stated, "We
have received all kinds of phone calls from people who know
this guy saying he did the shooting. But, I think they are
listening to the police scanner and adding fuel to the
fire. You know how these shit heads are."

"I agree," said Martin. "O.K., I'm going to start on the
sister again and see what I come up with."

McGowan stated, "I'm going to have the witnesses re-
interviewed and see if something was missed."

Martin entered the office where Det. Moy had been
interviewing the alleged perp's sister and immediately saw

Moy give a positive nod. Martin knew the girl had become more cooperative and would now probably provide some worthwhile information.

Det. Moy indicated that the girl wasn't sure where her brother was hiding and she had heard he was scared because the police thought he had killed a cop. She also advised that her brother and his friend had burglarized a house and had taken a handgun and a shotgun. She thought they had sold it to a guy from Delmont, a small town in the northern part of Cape May County.

She also provided the names of the individuals involved and did her best to indicate their present whereabouts. She repeatedly indicated that she didn't want her brother hurt for something he did not do. Martin couldn't help but laugh at her statement, "My brother might steal things and use and deal drugs but he would never shoot a cop".

Martin had Moy obtain consent to search form. It was filled out and signed by the girl. She authorized the police to enter her residence and search for stolen property and her brother. She maintained neither would be found at her residence.

They quickly left the Police department as Martin coordinated a meeting with the guys from Middle that were sitting on the girl's residence. Martin, Moy and the young lady met with Middle Township officers. The officers at the scene were members of the Middle Swat Team. Martin requested that they enter the residence just in case. The girl provided a description of the interior.

The officers entered and quickly reported that the house was clear, except for the dog shit that was all over the floors. It was ascertained that the young lady had a puppy that was suppose to stay on the front enclosed porch. However, it had gotten into the house and left its calling cards. Martin was glad Middle went in first. He was impressed by the quick, clean entry they had made. Now they would quickly and cleanly have to clean their shoes of the multitude of soft items left behind by the pup. The young lady was far from a good housekeeper. The house was only clean of stolen items. Cleanliness was not an attribute of this young lady. How could people live this way? Martin had asked himself that question many times during his career.

How could people ever get to the point when they lived in conditions that were so deplorable? Both Martin and Moy had experienced these conditions many times and weren't surprised by anything anymore. Searching places like this was a drag. However, someone had to do it. They made a concerted effort not to step in any of the soft items on the floor.

The residence was searched thoroughly and nothing was found.

Martin and Moy then returned with the girl to the Police department during the ride both investigators talked to the young lady in an attempt to have her do some leg work and find her brother. The detectives knew that they would need her cooperation to locate her brother quickly. During the conversation Martin began to think that perhaps other family members could be contacted to expedite the locating of the possible perp. The problem, however, would be whether or not they could be trusted.

Something had to be done and the possible perp had to be located and interviewed. If he wasn't the shooter a lot of investigative time and effort had been expended to eliminate someone who possibly should not have even been a suspect.

The detectives escorted the young lady into the police department and directed her to the lieutenant's office. Martin knew he had to get information from her that would indicate the location, of her brother. He was entering the office when he heard Detective Donohue say, "Bob, the swat team is going to hit a place on Woodlawn Avenue. It's right where that girl came from." Donohue was referring to the female Martin was interviewing. "She was in a car with a male and another female and the house on Woodlawn is where they were headed".

Martin asked if they needed a warrant. Donohue indicated they called on the phone and requested entry. Martin knew that Jack was cutting corners to save time. Martin wondered if Trombetta received a knowing and intelligent waiver. He laughed to himself thinking that the AP may not be happy with Trombetta's actions.

Martin went into the office and confronted the young lady about the location of her brother. He also informed her that the swat team was presently hitting her friend's house on Woodlawn Avenue. The young girl was visibly upset by the statement. "Is that where your brother is located?" Martin asked.

"No, he isn't there, but Linda who lives there knows where my brother is hiding." The statement just flowed from the girl's mouth. Martin went out the door and hollered for Donohue. Donohue stuck his head out into the hallway and acknowledged Martin's request to have Trombetta bring Linda to the station.

It was at this time that Martin was asked by a dispatcher what was going to happen with the guy in the holding cell. Martin was confused because he was not aware of anyone in the cell. It was ascertained that when Det. Brogan had brought the alleged perp's sister to the station he also brought the male passenger in the vehicle with him.

Martin went back in to confront the young girl. She immediately identified the subject as a friend of her brother's. She looked down at the floor and appeared to be thinking and blurted out, "He's the guy that stole the guns with my brother." Martin was excited by the remark but didn't want to exhibit his feelings to the girl.

"Where are those guns now?" asked Martin.

"I know they sold them the day after they took them. I think my boyfriend, Ken, knows who bought them."

"Does anyone else know about the guns?"

"Friends of my brother's who live on Frances Avenue probably know something," she added.

Martin was aware of the residence on Frances and knew that it would be worthwhile to check that location for the alleged perp. The information was relayed to Trombetta and the swat team would eventually search the location and once again consent would be obtained. Martin again laughed to himself knowing the AP would not be happy. Don't forget the knowing and intelligent waiver, Martin thought to himself. He knew Trombetta would handle the search and all the bases would be covered.

The young lady provided some more information and then indicated she was thirsty. Moy obtained more coffee for her. Martin, standing next to her, placed his hand on her shoulder and asked, "Mary, where was the last place your brother was staying?" The girl looked worried as she slowly lowered her head and answered, "We took him to my grandmother's at about 7:30 P.M." Martin patted her shoulder reassuringly as Moy returned with the coffee.

Martin told Moy to obtain a formal statement from the girl with regard to all the information obtained from her. He then left the office to find out what was going on with the swat team.

Martin glanced at his watch. The time was five thirty in the morning. The time was flying by and it was hard for Martin to put all that had happened into perspective. People were running in and out of the Police department.

Food and beverages were being delivered continuously.
Local grocery and convenience stores were sending trays of
cold cuts. The donut shops were providing a continuous
supply of sweets. Coffee was being made by the gallon.
Finding a place to sit down and have a quick sandwich was
next to impossible. It didn't matter. Martin and Trombetta
couldn't bring themmselves to eat anything at this point in
time.

CHAPTER ELEVEN

Martin entered his office and saw McGowan jotting down
notes while talking on the phone. McGowan finished his
call and turned to Martin. "Bob, these witnesses are still
sticking with the perp appearing to be a white male. Now we
have two people who are saying they saw two perps in the
area, both fitting the same description. They also
indicated that a small white car was seen in the area and
that the perps may have used it to leave the scene. Maybe
re-interviewing these witnesses wasn't a good idea. They
seem to be changing their stories," lamented McGowan.

Martin seemed disgusted and stated, "You know how people
are, Jim. They start listening to the police monitor and
listening to other people and before you know it we have a
bunch of parrots saying the same thing. The guys doing the
re-interviewing are not asking for clarification. They are
asking for the whole story and they start to lead these
people into making statements that aren't the facts."

Martin continued, "Jim, I don't have to tell you how
witnesses are. They will tell you what you want to hear if
you lead them. I think the guys on the street are set on
this white male perp scenario and they aren't leaving any
openings for new information."

"Well, we have to get this alleged perp in here and see
what he has to say," advised McGowan.

"Well, that's what I came down to tell you. The sister is
talking and she gave us a lot of info. She gave us some
more info on the weapons and her brother and I'm sure her
brother is hiding at his grandmothers. He is hiding because
he has heard the cops are looking for him and he figures if
they think he shot a cop they are going to kill him,"
Martin advised.

"Bob, how the hell would he be hearing this stuff? Just
from friends?" asked McGowan.

"Sure, Jim, every time one of our guys asks someone about
him that someone starts talking and before you know it, the
perp is hearing the story."

McGowan then replied,"Yeah, not to mention his whole
fuckin' family has police radios and know everything that
is happening. Bob, either make this guy or eliminate him,
the sooner the better."

"That's what we are going to do, Jim. The only problem we

will have is the fact that we don't have an abundance of suspects. We have to start looking for our second possibility, the Oriental," stated Martin. "It's going to be difficult to make everyone believe that the scum bag we've been looking for didn't have anything to do with the shooting."

"These guys really think he is the bad guy in this case," McGowan said.

"Well, we can pop him up for the burglary and the theft of the weapons. Plus, we'll be saving the shit head from getting shot by a pissed off cop," Martin laughed then continued. "Jim, I have to get a couple people in here for statements and we will have enough to charge him on the weapons and then I will get either his sister or his old girlfriend to call and make sure he is at the grandmother's house and we will bring him in."

McGowan grinned, "Don't let Trombetta and his boys kill this guy."

"That might be more difficult than identifying the real perp," Martin added, as he laughed and walked out of the office.

Martin met with Moy, Brogan and Donohue and indicated to them what was needed as far as formal statements to tie up the burglary and stolen weapons case. Moy had just completed obtaining the statement from the perp's sister and advised that she was sure her brother was at his grandmother's.

Donohue looked at Martin and asked, "You don't think this guy killed Dave, do you?"

"No, I don't think he is our guy," stated Martin.

"If he didn't do it, who did?" asked Donohue.

"Ed, if I knew that we wouldn't have wasted all this time. Listen, Ed, we will get this guy quick if he is a local. It won't be so quick if he's not," Martin said somberly. "We have a lot of work to do and people to re-interview. We have to eliminate this scum bag and move on the best we can."

Martin could tell by the expressions on the faces of the detectives that they didn't think he was correct in eliminating this guy. He wasn't in the mood to converse about his reasons nor did he think he had the time to waste. He once again advised the detectives what was required and they each walked down the hallway.

"Hey, Sarge, what should we do with all the info from these phone calls," asked Moy as he was walking down the hall.

"I want the info on intelligence forms and then I want them on my desk. I'll review, prioritize them and assign them to you guys to follow up," Martin answered. He knew that oftentimes the detectives would get information that they thought sounded good and would spend time looking into something that may have already been checked out. These guys would think that they had a hot lead that would make them a hero. Most often the lead would go nowhere. However, Martin knew that this stuff had to be followed up. He knew that these guys were going to be real busy without having to waste valuable investigative time on wild goose chases.

Martin walked down the hall knowing the guys would be pissed that he thought they couldn't prioritize. He wanted to review each call that came into the Police department about the shooting. Martin approached the back door to the Police department and Capt. Maher entered the door. "Bob, what's up? Anything new?"

"Yeah, Captain, we will have the scum bag real soon. We will have charges on the burglary and weapons. Then we have to find our murderer," added Martin.

"You really don't think this guy shot Dave?" asked Maher.

"I am starting to get feasible alibis for this guy's time from different individuals. Time will tell. As soon as we pick him up and talk to him, then we will know what's what."

The Captain stared at Martin and stated, "Bob, I want you to interview the guy when he gets here. Don't assign it to anybody else." Martin definitely wanted to speak to this guy. If his idea about this perp not being the shooter was wrong, he wanted some time alone with the scum bag that shot Dave.

Martin turned from the Captain and started to walk away. He remembered that he wanted to tell the Captain about all the calls coming into the station with info on the shooting. "Hey, Cap, the guys are getting a lot of telephone calls on possible info on the shooting."

"You can bet that the radio operators are also taking phone calls," stated the Captain.

"Well, what I want to do is have all the calls placed on

intelligence forms and sent to me for review and subsequent action when need be," stated Martin.
"No problem. I'll put out a directive right now that indicates all that type information goes to you on the proper form," advised Maher.

"Thanks, Captain. That way nothing should fall through the cracks and I'll be able to sift out the bull crap," stated Martin as he entered the office where the alleged perp's sister was waiting for him.

"Mary, I just want to thank you for being so cooperative. I know you want to get home to your kids and get to bed. I am going to ask you to sit tight for a few more minutes. I am going to get a car to take you home. It is going to take a little time though because everyone is so busy. You understand that, don't you?" Martin knew that he couldn't let this young lady leave. She would be on the phone in seconds to her brother.

"I know." She paused and then said, "I hope you get the guy that shot your cop."

"We will."

Martin thought it was odd he was saying he would when at this point he wasn't sure where he was going to find a perp. He made a mental note to look into the story about the witness who saw an oriental male in the area of the shooting.

CHAPTER TWELVE

Martin went to the Detective Office and asked Donohue for
the intelligence forms on the phone call tips that had been
coming into the Police department. Donohue advised that
some were on scratch paper and had to be placed on the
proper form. Martin began to review the information.

Many of the tips provided information about the alleged
perp the police were already attempting to locate. It was
evident that many of these callers provided nothing more
than the type of thing you would hear over the police
scanner. Many times the cops on the street and more often
the dispatchers had too much to say on the radio. People
would listen to these transmissions and often pay more
attention than the police personnel to whom the messages
were intended. Martin thought to himself how he and
Trombetta had a real problem with personnel who had
diarrhea of the mouth.

Guys loved to tell their girlfriends and family members
information that should be kept in house. They didn't
realize the many problems that had been initiated over the
years due to cops' big mouths. Many guys would say things
in an attempt to make themselves look good in the eyes of
the listener. Usually those guys would have their
statements come back to bite them in the ass when they
least expected.

Martin recalled the time a now retired detective sergeant,
Bob Douglass, made a statement about an area of the
Township that was a parking and make-out spot for would be
lovers. A guy drugged out on PCP picked up a five foot two
by four and had decided he was going to rid the beach of
the lovers that dwelled in the secluded area. The whacko
came upon a guy and girl who were naked and smashed the guy
in the back of the head. The unsuspecting young lady on
the bottom pushed her now limp partner onto the beach where
he was quickly whacked again by Mr. Congeniality. The
victim died from the first blow but sustained about five
more hits before the perp realized there was a young lady
rolling around on the beach naked and screaming her lungs
out. The other lovers in the area figured they were
hearing the screams of a young lady at the pinnacle of
ecstasy.

The maniac grabbed the young lady's foot and began dragging
her to the water's edge. It was his intent to kill her.
She managed to escape and ran down the beach screaming for
help. The perp was eventually grabbed by an officer who
was probably in the area watching the love making activity

as opposed to doing real police work. His report, however, would eventually indicate that he was on routine patrol of the area when he heard screams and saw the perp running after a naked girl.

When Detective Sergeant Douglass arrived and subsequently took over the investigation he made it known that he felt there would eventually be a homicide at the location. It had just been a matter of time. The area was ripe for problems. Eventually the Detective Sergeant returned to the Police department and began talking to the many reporters about the incident and the fact that he always knew there would be trouble on that beach. The area he was referring to was known as Diamond Beach or the Gold Coast. It was a developer's dream. Many local and out of state investors were dumping money into the area buying as much vacant property as they could get their hands on. It was envisioned that this area would be a mecca for timeshare condos and condo homes.

The day after the murder the newspapers, radio, television and the subsequent issue of Philadelphia magazine indicated in big headlines "GOLD COAST OF CAPE MAY COUNTY-A MECCA FOR LUST, LOVE AND MURDER" according to Detective Sergeant ROBERT DOUGLASS of the LOWER TWSP Police department

Well the shit hit the fan and two weeks later DSG. Robert Douglass was back in uniform working the streets. From that time on his story telling was more subdued.

Martin had learned much from Bob Douglass. He was an excellent interviewer and interrogator and a wiz with fingerprint comparison. He never seemed to get frustrated when a case was going nowhere and he always had informants to contact when things got slow. Martin laughed to himself as he thought about the DSG's biggest short comming, he was unable to stay awake. He was always falling asleep at the most inappropriate times. Martin recalled not wanting to be a passenger in any vehicle that was being driven by the DSG. His sleeping during interviews and interrogations provided some of the funniest situations Martin had experienced while a member of LTPD.

On one occasion DSG Douglass was interviewing a male burglary suspect. He was leaning back in his rocking swivel chair with his feet on the desk and was appearing to be paying more attention to the task of cleaning his nails than to the suspect he was interviewing. In the middle of the interview he fell fast asleep. The suspect looked at Martin as though he could do something about the sleeping detective sergeant. The suspect asked, "What's the story with this guy? Is he ignorant or something?"

61

Martin answered, "No, he is bored to death with your bull shit and so am I. So just sit there and be quiet." He looked at his watch and timed the silence. Eleven minutes later the DSG opened his eyes resumed cleaning his nails and stated, "So are you ready to tell the truth and stop the bull shit?" He said those words not appearing to know that he had been asleep for about a total of fifteen minutes. The perp responded, "Yeah, I'll tell you the truth. Are you ready to listen?" Douglass stared at him and said, "Sure, that's what I get paid to do." The guy eventually went for fifteen residential burglaries and was on his way to county jail.

Martin remembered after the paper work they went for coffee. "Hey, sarge, you fell to sleep right in the middle of that interview."

"I didn't fall asleep. I was collecting my thoughts," replied the DSG. "You have to stay on top of these guys if you want results." Detective Sergeant Bob Douglass always had an answer.

Douglass had retired but his antics and abilities were missed. Stories about him were always being told and always amused all that heard them.

Martin always tried not to say everything he thought nor believe everything he heard. He had a problem with regard to refraining from saying what he thought but he never believed everything he heard. Especially if it was coming from a cop who heard it from a cop who heard it from......who heard it from....and so on. Cops were like old ladies when it came to gossip.

CHAPTER THIRTEEN

Martin could tell from the tips he was reviewing that too
much had been said already. People would repeat what they
heard and investigators were wasting time on leads that
were worthless or had already been looked into and were
proven to be dead ends.

Martin went into his office and began to relate some of the
so called tips to McGowan. McGowan listened to a few and
stated, "You realize that most of this is bull shit and a
waste of time."

"You're telling me." replied Martin.

"Don't let the AP see any of those or we'll be on wild
goose chases forever", added McGowan.

"Yeah, I have them all being directed to me. I'll sort them
out prioritize them and assign them to the guys if they
warrant any follow-up."

McGowan advised Martin that he had observed the detectives
bringing some witnesses into the detective office and the
captain's office. Martin assumed that these were the
individuals that would provide more information on the
alleged perp.
McGowan and Martin began to update a chronology of events
that McGowan had begun when he was handed the case.
McGowan was from the old school and had all his information
and facts in order and would often pause to elicit Martin's
ideas or input with regard to what had transpired.

McGowan started to read the information received from a
young female who had witnessed what she believed to be a
short oriental male wearing a plaid flannel shirt, possibly
blue in color with what appeared to be blue jeans. He was
wearing a ski type hat and was startled by her as she drove
into an intersection that the subject was crossing.
McGowan indicated that the time was right but five other
witnesses said they observed a white male wearing the same
clothing. McGowan also mentioned that the young girl
advised she wasn't sure if she could really describe the
face of the suspect. She could only state that he was
surprised to see her vehicle, enter the intersection, and
that she had almost struck him. She further advised that
his eyes bulged out when he realized her car was about to
strike him. He was visibly shook up and seemed to be in a
real hurry. She was positive, however, that he was

oriental.

The two investigators discussed the stories of the
witnesses looking for discrepancies and attempting to
ascertain if perhaps any of the witnesses had time to
converse with each other about what they had seen prior to
being questioned by police. Oftentimes witnesses could be
led by the statements of others; therefore, rendering
information that was decided upon by mutual agreement
rather than what was actually seen.

McGowan and Martin also began to discuss the reliability of
the witnesses and categorized them with regard to how
credible they appeared. Eventually they decided to list
the witnesses from most reliable to least reliable based on
what they indicated and compared to what the investigators
knew to be fact. This list, hopefully, would provide the
investigators with positive indicators that would lead them
to a more valid description of the perpetrator and a better
understanding of what took place at the incident.

McGowan indicated that in the very beginning of the
investigation the description of the white male suspect was
all that was available. Initial responding officers at the
scene along with detectives had come up with the name of
the individual that the Swat Team was presently trying to
find.

The initial investigators at the scene were taking what
they had and attempting to match it with a local scumbag
they could agree upon. This type of analysis was done by
good cops and often resulted in positive results. However,
when more information is turning up in the investigative
process, reevaluation is necessary. McGowan and Martin
agreed that it was time for a major reevaluation of all the
facts and information that had been received.

The investigators decided that the first witnesses to be
re-interviewed would be those whose stories revealed even
the smallest differences in observations, descriptions and
opinions. Too many times cops would obtain opinions from
witnesses and inter mingle those opinions with fact.

Martin and McGowan knew that at the time of the incident
the cops at the scene were working under extreme pressure
and were attempting to assist an injured victim, secure the
scene, obtain information from witnesses and arrest the
perp. This was the way it was always done. They were
taught this procedure at the police academy.

No one, however, had ever taught them how to handle the

fact that the injured victim was a mortally wounded friend and fellow officer. You are never prepared to see your friend and brother officer lying on the ground in a pool of blood. Those officers were working under extreme conditions. Both investigators knew it was easier at this point in the investigation to sit back and review everything with a critical eye. The investigators at the scene weren't afforded such a luxury. They had to make split second decisions and react to the immediacy of the situation and do the best they could with what they had at the time. Both investigators also knew that the cops who had made those initial decisions would not be happy with Monday morning quarter backing by someone who had not been there. Cops also didn't like it when they were proven wrong, especially on a major case.

Many of the young cops on the force took constructive criticism in a negative fashion. If you didn't agree with their explanation of events you were the enemy. Patrol officers always seemed to have problems with detectives. They viewed detectives as the prima donnas who forgot where they had come from. Detectives would look at most patrol officers as the guys who didn't go the extra step to solve a crime. Patrol would just take reports of incidents and turn it over to detectives for solving. Detectives figured that most patrolmen filled in the blanks on report forms and didn't really try to solve any crimes.

Detectives hated to see "TOT" at the end of a patrolman's report. TOT meant "Turned Over To." The "TOT" was always followed by the word "detective." Patrolman may not like detectives but they sure liked to turn over the investigation to them. If patrolmen would just complete the basic investigative procedures detectives would be happy. If detectives were put back in uniform patrolman would be happy. That's how it is in police departments throughout the USA.

Martin and McGowan continued to review the witness information and decided that as soon as the alleged perp was definitely ruled out they would zero in on the oriental connection. They had nothing else to go on at the time. Each investigator wished that he were wrong. It would have been a cut and dry if the alleged perp was the shooter. They almost hoped they were wrong about the alleged perp. They knew they weren't wrong.

Neither investigator could envision where this investigation would lead them after they ruled out the white male suspect. Little did they know it would be a six week investigation that would lead them to the streets of New York, city. It would be six of the most frustrating weeks either investigator had ever faced.

Martin and McGowan continued to review, evaluate and prioritize. Every so often one of the detectives would enter the office with a question about the interviews they were conducting.

Martin wanted them to finish the interviews and have the alleged perp picked up and brought to the Police department. The, detectives were obtaining information with regard to the burglary and theft of the weapons by the alleged perp and his friend. They were attempting to ascertain where the guns were located, where the perp was at the time of Dave's shooting and if the perp was at his grandmother's residence. Last but not least Martin wanted one of these people to place a call to the perp to verify his location. He then figured that once the Swat Team was in place at the location a call would be placed to the perp by police directing him to simply come out with hands up.

It had been ascertained from the alleged perp's sister that there were probably at least five adults in the grandmother's residence along with at least four children. Police had been at the location many times in the past and were quite aware of the layout of the structure. Police referred to the house as a "pit". Cops were used to entering the homes of scum bags and they usually found them to be real pits.

Many times over the years Martin and Trombetta had been in some real interesting homes. Martin recalled serving a search warrant on a house of a, would be, biker gang. Surveillance had revealed six guys and two girls were living in the home that had two bedrooms and about seven hundred fifty square foot of space. It had been ascertained that they were dealing a large quantity of speed, methamphetamine, to the local shit heads. When the team of detectives and uniforms hit the house it was quite interesting to say the least.

Police entered the residence quickly as they would on any such raid. The idea was to take everyone by surprise and not provide them with any time to react. The entry teams entered the front and rear of the residence. The team members knew exactly which rooms they were assigned to enter and secure. Trombetta was at the back door with an entry team and two search teams. Martin was at the front door with the same amount of help. Simultaneously the front and rear entry teams hit the doors.

Martin had quietly checked the front door and found out it was unlocked. He knew he didn't have to worry about smashing the door. Trombetta had never checked the back

door and really didn't care to. He wanted to kick the door
in, it was more his style. So what if you later found out
the door was unlocked. The shit heads would have to repair
or in most cases replace the door. What the hell, they had
broken the law and probably making more money selling drugs
than the cops protecting the public. The cost of a door
was nothing to them.

Trombetta also knew that kicking an unlocked door would
make a good story to tell after the raid was over and
everyone was sitting around bull shitting about what a
great job they did. That's how some cops reduce stress.

The teams quickly entered and went to the areas they were
supposed to secure and search. Martin's team took the
front bedroom. The hollow core bedroom door was locked but
the lock wasn't much and a kick at the locking mechanism
opened the door quickly. Martin and his two team members
found a well endowed female without clothing and two naked
would be bikers all taking part in some type of sexual
encounter. To the untrained eye, it appeared as though the
moving, squirming mass of numerous tattoos were attempting
to interact with each other in what appeared to be a
non-religious ceremony of some type.

Martin stated, "Excuse me, folks, as soon as we can get you
untangled we will serve you with this search warrant." The
three looked at the officers and the only response was from
an overweight, tattooed male who stated, "Ya gotta do what
ya gotta do." The subjects dressed and were led to the
living room and advised to sit on the floor. They provided
no problems to the officers.

Trombetta and his two man team entered the rear door to a
bedroom that was unlocked. Immediately Trombetta observed
a male and female enjoying their sexual activity.
Trombetta yelled,"Freeze, Police." The nude female looked
up and replied, "We ain't done yet, cut us a break."
Trombetta was surprised by the statement and stated, "Make
it quick, we have work to do." Trombetta then added, "Not
quick enough, put your clothes on and go with these
officers." The guy and girl removed themselves from their
precarious position, dressed slowly and took their places
on the living room floor.

The remaining search teams rounded up the strays and all
were sitting on the floor in the living room. The officers
all knew their search assignments and began their
respective tasks. They were now able to pay more attention
to the surroundings and observed that the place was a
housekeeping disaster.

The floors were strewn, with trash, dirty clothing and the

remains of at least six beer parties that had no doubt been real interesting get togethers. It was the day after Christmas and the results of opening gifts were also lying all over the floor of the residence. Various types of food stuffs were all over the place and there wasn't a clean dish in the house. Three puppies, Christmas gifts, had left many small gifts throughout the humble abode. The place would not be featured in Good Housekeeping.

The officers had been searching the residence for about three hours when one of the scum bags stated, "Hey, Officer, can I have my ointment." The cop asked, "What ointment?"

"We all have some type of rash and a couple of us have the crabs," stated the dirt ball. One of the females added, "This place is full of all kinds of creepy crawlies."

Eventually an ounce of meth was found in the kitchen closet along with drug paraphernalia and six hundred dollars in cash. The owner of the house stated that the drugs were his and he also admitted to distributing the drugs to anyone with the correct purchase price.

The officers left the residence with one under arrest and as they returned to the Police department they began to itch and scratch. The officers were now carriers of numerous types of little crawling creatures. Two gallons of some type of disinfectant was provided. Many of the officers stripped and began to pour the stuff all over their selves. Martin decided that to do so would be worthless for he would have to wear the same clothes until he got home. He went home that night to his back door, stripped himself of all clothing and poured the disinfectant all over himself from head to toe.

Martin's wife was laughing at him as he jumped around in the cold outdoors while pouring the cold liquid on his body. Martin immediately showered and rubbed on an ointment that had been provided by a local pharmacist.

The clothing was put in the trash can and Martin monitored himself for little crawlies for a week. The incident provided a lot of laughs and story telling for quite some time.

CHAPTER FOURTEEN

The silence that had taken over the office as Martin and
McGowan were formulating strategies was interrupted by
Detective Donohue. "Hey, Sarge, this girl Linda wants to
talk to you before she says anything. She's in the
captain's office waiting for you."

Martin was trying to remember who the girl might be and as
soon as he saw her face he recognized her as a falsely
accused writer of bad checks. Martin recalled that he was
able to prove her innocence even after she had been
identified by bank tellers. A look alike had been the perp
and this girl was getting a bad deal.

Martin also recalled taking a statement from her when she
had been assaulted by her boyfriend. It then came to
Martin's mind that she was the ex-girlfriend of the alleged
cop killer. She even had a couple of kids with him.

Martin entered the office, extended his hand and greeted,
"Hi Linda, how are you?" She shook his hand and replied,
"I have been doing real well since I got rid of him,"
referring to the guy everyone was now trying to locate.

"Oh, I didn't know you split up," said Martin. She
continued to look at Martin.

"Yeah, I took your advice after the last time he beat me up
and threw him out. I'm getting my life together. I stopped
doing drugs and I'm staying clean. Once in a while I smoke
a little pot to keep my head straight." Martin thought, why
did they always say they were off drugs but still smoked
pot? He laughed to himself.

"You got promoted since I was here last time," stated
Linda.
"You deserve it, you are always are fair with everyone,"
she added. Martin thought to himself if fairness was
criteria for promotion someone should tell civil service.

"Well thanks, Linda. What can I do for you?" Martin
wanted to get the show on the road and figured enough small
talk had taken place.

"You always treat me like a person instead of a scum bag
and now I want to do something for you. Do you remember
when everyone thought I had written all those checks and
you didn't believe I did?" she asked. Before Martin could
answer she stated, "You even met with my mom and step dad
and told them that it wasn't me who was writing the checks.
I know where he is and I'll help you get him. I'll do

whatever you want."

"Linda, I appreciate that and I can sure use your help,"
stated Martin.

"I haven't lived with him for quite a while, but he
contacts me all the time with his problems. I know he broke
into a place the other day with his buddy and they got some
guns, sold them and bought some dope. He would never kill a
cop. He does some crazy stuff but I know he wouldn't do
that," she said. "I talked to him about fifteen minutes ago
and he said he hoped the police wouldn't shoot him. He
heard the police were looking for him. A few of his friends
heard it on the police scanner and they called him. He is
hiding at his grandmother's house and is afraid to go
outside." She was very candid with Martin and he thought
she was being truthful.

"Linda, did he say anything about the cop that was shot?"
asked Martin.
"He said that he didn't shoot the cop and that he didn't
even have a gun. He said that he was at his sister's
drinking beer when people started calling him about the cop
being shot. He hadn't been out when the cop was shot. He
was watching T.V. Listen, Sergeant Martin, I don't really
care much about him but I'm sure he is getting a bad deal
on this one."

"Well, Linda, what we have to do is get him in here safe
and sound and I'll talk to him. I'll make sure no one
hurts him. He is going to have to give himself up and then
I can help him out," added Martin. "Linda, would you make
another call to him for me? I just want to make sure he is
still at his grandmom's."

"I'll do whatever you want," stated Linda.

Subsequently the call was made and it was ascertained that
the alleged perp was still hiding at his grandmother's
residence.
Contact was made with the Swat Team and Trombetta was
advised he could set his men up and that a call would be
made to the residence. The suspect would be advised to exit
the front door with his hands on his head and wait on the
porch for further instructions from Trombetta.

The Swat Team, down to just four members, obtained help
from The Wildwood Crest Swat Team. The Crest Team set up
an outside perimeter and the Lower Team would affect the
arrest and subsequent search of the residence. The Lower
Township Swat Team was a six member team. Dave Douglass
had been an integral part of that team and his absence was

felt. One other Swat Team member had been on vacation
which left the team with minimal manpower. The team had
already searched three residences and one vehicle.

Martin was thinking to himself that the frustration of
searches that provided negative results was no doubt taking
its toll on the team members. He prayed that they wouldn't
do anything stupid.

The team took up positions of cover as they awaited the
call to be made to the suspect. Martin had advised
Detective Donohue to place the call to the suspect and to
explain what was required. Martin also advised Donohue to
request that the owner of the property allow police to
search the residence after the suspect was arrested. The
suspect was advised that he was being arrested for a
burglary and theft.

Donohue advised the perp to pay strict attention to any
directions he was given when he exited the house. Donohue
placed his hand over the phone, looked at Martin and said,
"I hope this asshole moves and they blow his fuckin' head
off."

Martin glanced at Donohue and stated, "What ever they do,
better be done by the numbers. Ed, this guy didn't shoot
Dave. He committed a burglary and he's a scum bag, but they
shouldn't kill him for those reasons."

Trombetta looked to the locations where he had positioned
the team members. Jack was ready to kill this guy and he
knew the other team members would do the same. Trombetta
was thinking about what Martin had said about the suspect.
Martin didn't think he was the shooter. Jack hadn't had
time to talk to Bob to really understand why he didn't
think the suspect had killed Dave. Jack knew the team
members would take the guy out if he did anything other
than what he was directed. Jack just wanted everything to
go smoothly and he didn't want any of his people hurt.

Each of the team members knew what their jobs entailed and
they were each ready to do whatever had to be done. Jack
worried about Russo but had to use him because he was short
manpower. Jack hoped that Russo could do what had to be
done. Jack observed that the front door of the residence
had opened and that the suspect was coming out of the door
onto the porch with his hands on his head. When the perp
got to the porch he froze awaiting Jack's instructions.

Jack could see his face and fear was what Trombetta
observed. This guy was scared to death. Jack thought to
himself that the guy looks more like he doesn't believe
this is happening. Jack could see that this guy thought he

was being arrested for a burglary and didn't expect all of the people and the Swat Team at his front door. Why would all this activity, people and equipment be there to arrest him just for a little burglary?

Jack was trying to stay focused on his job but began to think to himself that this guy doesn't have the look of someone that knows he has been had and being placed under arrest for killing a cop. Jack thought that Russo better not get trigger happy. Jack looked quickly at Russo and he still appeared to be dazed over all that had taken place. Trombetta directed the suspect to slowly walk down the steps, toward the front yard. Trombetta and Hienkel would provide security and cover.

Patrolman Russo would have a laser scope honed in on the suspect's head and Patrolman Paynter would cuff the suspect.
Trombetta and Hienkel were holding ballistic shields that were able to stop most bullets. Jack kept thinking to himself he should have made someone else the shooter. It was now too late. The suspect slowly walked towards the front of the yard. He reached the center of the yard when Trombetta yelled at him to stop. Trombetta then directed him to assume a prone position and he and Hienkel placed themselves and their shields between the suspect and the front of the residence. Trombetta noticed the red dot of the laser scope dancing across the face and head of the suspect. Russo had the scope and his weapon trained on the suspect's head. The eerie sight made Trombetta think how easy it would be to kill this guy if need be. Russo could feel his insides tightening in anticipation of the suspect making a move. His finger tightened on the trigger as the red dot of the laser scope fell between the eyes of the scum bag on the ground in front of him. Come on, do something hinky, I want you to move, do something you piece of shit. These thoughts raced through Russo's mind. Trombetta gave the order to cuff the suspect and Patrolman Paynter did so. Paynter now had his hands on this low life shit head and was hoping he would do something that would give him reason to break his arm or better yet do something to make Russo kill the fuck.

When Russo was sure Paynter was in control of the suspect he allowed his finger to vacate the trigger and rested it on the trigger guard. It was no longer necessary to watch the red dot of the laser scope direct a path to the possible demise of this low life piece of shit. He lowered the weapon and assisted Paynter. The suspect was whisked away into an awaiting patrol car. The Swat Team after being advised a consent to search had been given by the owner of the property entered the residence looking for any items they believed to be evidentiary in value. Nothing was found and they eventually left the scene and returned to the police department

Trombetta was sitting in the Swat Van, a remodeled ambulance, thinking to him self that this guy sure didn't act like a cop killer. Maybe this wasn't the right guy. Trombetta figured that Martin would probably be interviewing the suspect and hoped they would then know if they had the right guy as soon as possible. The Swat Team returned to the Police department Trombetta decided he would wait around to see what Martin could get out of the suspect. Jack continued to think that the suspect was shook up but it didn't appear to be over shooting a cop.

Something about the look on the suspect's face told Jack that the investigation was just starting...

CHAPTER FIFTEEN

The suspect was transported to the station and was placed
in the holding cell after again being searched. His shoes,
belt and personal items were taken from him and placed in a
property locker in the cell area. The dispatcher advised
Martin that the suspect was in the cell. Martin and
McGowan were sitting in Martin's office waiting for the
piece of shit.
McGowan looked at Martin and asked, "You dealt with this
guy before, right?"

"Yeah," replied Martin. "He won't be a problem. He is
usually pretty closed mouth and when he knows he is had he
clams up and asks for an attorney."

McGowan thought for a moment and said, "Well, I think you
should talk to him by yourself and see what happens."

Martin nodded, "I'll get him out of lock up and get
started." Martin requested a patrol officer to bring the
prisoner to the office. McGowan left the office and wished
Martin good luck.

When the suspect entered the office Martin observed he
didn't seem too upset about his predicament. Martin stood
up from his chair extended his hand and began,"How ya been,
Willie?"

"Alright til' this mess," replied the suspect.

"Have a seat," directed Martin, pointing to a straight back
chair. Martin wanted to put the suspect at ease and started
with some small talk about the suspect's family members.
Martin thought to himself that this guy seemed pretty calm.
"Listen, man, I didn't kill no cop. That's what this is all
about. Right? Ya' know, I'm pissed about the guys with
the black suits coming to my grandmother's," stated the
suspect, referring to the Swat Team members. "I might have
stolen some shit, but I'm no cop shooter. Them guys
might've killed me and I didn't even do anything. This
whole deal is bull shit. I ain't no cop killer."

"Well, Willie, that's what I want to show. If you didn't do
anything you shouldn't have to burn for it." Martin
immediately noticed that Willie was getting emotional. This
was very odd for this loser. In the past encounters with
this guy he only got emotional when he wasn't involved in

something.

Tears started to form in the suspect's eyes. Martin could
see he was trying to hold back the tears but he was having
a hard time doing so. "Mr. Martin, it's like I said. I
might steal and do drugs, but I'm not a cop killer. I just
wouldn't do something like that. O.K., O.K. I broke into a
house with the guy you got in the cell and we stole some
guns and sold them in Delmont but that's it." The suspect
began to compose himself. "I'm telling you the truth, Mr.
Martin. I didn't shoot nobody."

"Listen, Willie, you know the routine. I'm going to give
you your rights." Martin knew he had to give this guy his
rights, and also that the guy had already heard his rights
when he was arrested by the swat team. Martin also knew
that he would probably ask for a lawyer.

The suspect looked at Martin and said, "Hey, I know my
rights, I'm not gonna' intimidate myself." Martin was sure
the shit head meant, incriminate, but why correct him.
Intimidate was probably the biggest word the guy knew
except for methamphetamine.

Martin was trying to read him his rights when he stated, "I
got nothing to say except I didn't shoot no cop. I stole
some shit but I ain't no cop killer." The suspect then
added,"I got nothing else to say without a lawyer." Martin
finished the Miranda warning and the suspect signed the
rights form. Martin called for a patrolman to return the
suspect to the holding cell. The suspect accompanied by
the officer turned and stated, "I hope you get the guy".

McGowan came back into the office and looked at Martin.
"What da ya think?"

"Jim, he didn't do it", answered Martin. "He is too calm
and doesn't appear to be worrying about anything. This guy
would be looking for a deal if he did anything. My money
says we need to find a new suspect. It's like I said in the
beginning this guy only rips off or hurts people he is
related to or knows as a friend or someone he has done odd
jobs for. He doesn't hurt people he doesn't know. He
didn't have anything to do with Dave's death."

"Shit," mumbled McGowan.

Martin stood up and went next door to the Chief's office.
The Chief was sitting with the mayor and a council member.
"Chief, Willie isn't our guy. He didn't shoot Dave,"
advised Martin.

"You sure?" asked the Chief.

"Yeah, we'll verify his alibi and follow up on the guns he stole, but I'm sure." Martin looked at the Chief and added, "Now, it's time to look for the Oriental guy." The Chief stared at Martin and stated, "I had that feelin', keep at it." Martin turned and exited the office.

Martin left the Chief's office and exited the police department on his way to the conference room to advise the Captain. Captain Maher was on his way back from the conference room and met Martin between the two buildings. "Captain, that suspect is not the guy were looking for," advised Martin.

"You're kiddin'," stated Maher. "You sound like you're positive."

"I just finished interviewing him and he's not the guy who shot Dave," reiterated Martin.

"What da ya think?" asked Maher.
"I think we gotta find another suspect, and I gotta feelin' it ain't gonna be easy," mumbled Martin.

"Bob, I have all the faith in the world in your abilities. I know you will find this guy. Hopefully, it will be quick," added Captain Maher.

"Thanks", replied Martin, reluctantly.

Trombetta saw Martin and knew immediately from the look on his face that they didn't have Dave's killer.

Both men started into the Police department and Maher stated, "Oh, the prosecutor is next door with the AP and the County Chief of Detectives. They want to see you and McGowan about what's going on."

"Hey, Captain, Jim and I are busy. We don't have time for a bull shit session about where we are going with this case," replied Martin in a sarcastic tone. "I'm sure they will come looking for us when we don't show up." Maher laughed. He knew Martin wasn't going to make a meeting with the powers to be, a priority. Both men started down the hall to their offices.

Martin entered the office and McGowan was on the phone. McGowan hung up and stated, "I was talking to the guys at the crime scene. They are finding a lot of items that might help us out on a suspect. They will get back to us as soon as they get it logged."

"I hope they find something to help us out. We have one

young girl saying she thinks she saw a surprised looking oriental that she probably couldn't identify," said Martin disgustedly.

"Oh, Jim, your boss is here from the County and he wants to meet with you and me next door." Martin could see by the look on McGowan's face that he was not happy with the news. "He is going to want to know where we are going with this case. I don't have time to see him. We gotta figure out where we are going with this case," stated McGowan.

"I'm too busy to sit around bull shitting. Let's wait till they come lookin' for us," stated Martin. "Why do these attorneys want to have so many meetings?" asked McGowan as Martin left the office.

Martin observed Moy walking down the hall. "Jim, what are you up to?" asked Martin.

"I am going to take two witnesses home. We are done with them," answered Moy.

"Jim, don't you take them home. Get a patrolman to transport. I need you here," stated Martin.

"O.K.,Sarge, I'll set it up."

"Jim, when you are done with that, ascertain whether or not they searched the interior of the car that Willie's sister was driving," directed Martin.

"I'll ask Brogan," stated Moy.

"Yeah, that's right, he was there when they grabbed her," added Martin.

Brogan, was in the detectives office and heard the conversation. "Hey, Sarge, I was there. We searched everything but the trunk."

"Why didn't you do the trunk?" asked Martin.

"Well, she wasn't the owner of the car. She was only driving it," stated the detective.

"Mike, she was in control of it. She can give consent," stated Martin.

"Sarge, the owner of the car, Willie's friend, was in the car, too," stated Brogan.

"Didn't you ask him for a consent?" asked Martin.

"No, I figured we would confiscate it and take it to
impound and then get a warrant," stated Brogan.

"Mike, we could have had it searched by now and not had to
worry about a warrant," said Martin in a disgusted tone.

"I'll get consent from the owner now. He is still in our
lock-up," added Brogan.

"Mike, they just served him with warrants on the burglary
and gun theft he did with Willie," advised Martin.   "He
invoked his rights and isn't talking anymore. Mike, don't
worry about it. I'll figure something out," advised Martin.

"Mike, get all your notes in order and try to start getting
some reports on paper," added Martin.

"Yeah, that's what I'm doing," advised Brogan as he
returned to the detective's office. Martin saw Moy coming
down the hall, "Jim, did you get rides for those people?"

"Yeah, patrol is taking them home," stated Moy.

"If you get some free time, start doing some reports,"
instructed Martin.

"O.K., I'll get started right now," advised Moy. Martin
knew that the last thing these guys wanted to hear was to
start doing reports. Martin knew from experience that all
these guys would be putting the report writing off until
the last minute. This was a big case and they all wanted
to be involved in every aspect. Guys tend to forget about
the reports until they have so many to do they become
overwhelmed and start making mistakes. Martin didn't even
have a suspect. He sure couldn't afford any mistakes.

Martin also knew he would have to start watching the time
these guys were putting into the investigation. All of the
detectives would want to stay on around the clock until
someone was arrested. These guys get upset when they are
told to go home when a case like this is being
investigated. They all have good intentions, but they
don't realize the consequences of their actions.

Martin knew that at anytime another incident could take
place and he would have no fresh investigators to handle
the investigation. He also knew he needed guys to handle
any other daily incidents that might require that a
detective be assigned. He knew these guys would be pissed
when he started to monitor their hours, but it had to be

done.

Martin knew that Trombetta would say that they should all hang around, because you never knew who you would need in a situation such as this. Jack didn't want them to think he was the bad guy sending them home. He knew they would take it personal wondering why they had been sent home and another detective was allowed to remain on duty.

Martin knew that he would be the bad guy in this decision. He laughed to himself. He always was the Dad with the kids and Jack was the Mom. Martin knew he would have to tell Trombetta not to give in and let the kids work till they dropped. Many people thought Jack was always the hard drivin' kick ass detective. Jack was more compassionate and thoughtful than most people knew. Martin made a mental note to mention it to Jack.

The thought of the un-searched car was back in Martin's mind. He wanted to solve that problem as quickly as possible. Martin believed that the County Prosecutor and Chief of Detectives would look at it as a loose end. They wouldn't accept the fact that Willie and his cronies were not involved in Dave's shooting. Martin wanted to get the investigation off of those individuals and on to a new track. The only track available was the one that pointed to an Oriental suspect.

A lot of time had been wasted, Martin thought to himself. Granted the time was spent following the lead available. Martin couldn't help but think that other possibilities should have been looked into at the very beginning of the investigation. Hopefully that lost time wouldn't affect the outcome.

Martin looked into the detective's office and told Brogan to track down the location of the vehicle. Martin knew it was either at a gas station or at the Township yard. Brogan advised he wasn't sure where it was towed but that he would locate it.

Martin walked past the dispatch center and heard a dispatcher advising someone on the phone that one hundred sandwiches were needed to feed some of the personnel. The logistics of an investigation of this magnitude were overwhelming. No one would question overtime, investigative expenses or any monies that were spent in an attempt to catch a cop killer.

The local politicians were already making statements about the fact that they supported the endeavors of the Police Department as they went about the business of finding the

suspect who committed this heinous act. The politicians
had even mentioned a reward of some type. Martin knew they
would jump on the bandwagon and make all kinds of promises.
He also knew that somewhere along the line they would jump
off and forget the entire episode. The cops would not nor
could not forget. The incident and the investigation would
be with them for the rest of their lives.

Martin walked down the hall and observed the faces on the
guys. Their expressions still registered disbelief at what
had taken place. Some of the Lower guys seemed to be in a
daze. Someone needed to give them a kick in the ass and
get them moving. They all wanted to take part in the
investigation and would do anything they were told.
However, for some reason there wasn't much self motivation.
Martin knew the reason was quite evident. The death of a
friend and fellow officer was like losing a family member.
Cops spent more time with fellow officers than they did
with their wives and children. The family of officers was
many times stronger than an officer's blood relatives.

Martin looked at his watch. The time was eight in the
morning. He had to think a minute to recall what day it
was. It was Saturday, February nineteenth. Martin thought
to himself that he should find some time to run home, take
a shower and put on some clean clothes. He had to remember
to make time. He was walking past the Dispatch Office when
he observed three trays of cold cuts and trimmings. A line
had already formed and guys were chowin' down. It didn't
matter that they weren't eating the breakfast of champions.
Time was not relevant nor was the type of food to be eaten.

Martin made the turn into the dispatch room. He looked
over the vast array of fattening items. He thought that
perhaps he should refrain from the many cholesterol laden
food stuffs. His gaze took in the salads and he couldn't
resist. He was hungry. Martin made a ham sandwich, grabbed
some coleslaw and potato salad and thought to himself that
the fact he had dropped about twenty five pounds and had
kept it off for over a year was a good reason not to be
eating the garbage he was already shoveling in his mouth as
he walked down the hall.
Cases like this always changed eating habits. Guys who
wouldn't be caught dead filling themselves with fat laden
goodies always seemed to forget their healthy eating habits
when food was spread out before them. Martin walked to his
office advising everyone that the food had arrived. The
serving line at the buffet became long, in short order.

Martin sat down at his desk and as he was eating,
remembered, that someone had told him that the missing
vehicle was taken to the Township garage. He got on the
phone and advised dispatch to let the detectives know they

no longer had to search for the missing impounded vehicle. The thought of losing an impounded vehicle was a bit embarrassing. Detective Brogan, however, would often times, misplace things. He was highly motivated and self starting and at fifty years of age that in itself made Martin think he shouldn't bad mouth the guy for losing something as trivial as a scum bag's car. Brogan oftentimes did a lot of things without really thinking them out and more often than not would make mistakes that would come back to bite him on the ass.

Don't pick on Brogan, Martin thought to himself, he meant well and now the vehicle had been located. Martin wondered how was it that all of a sudden he remembered the location of the vehicle. He assumed someone must have told him and initially it hadn't registered. Martin hoped that this was the only thing that hadn't registered. Maybe he needed some sleep. He had now been awake for over twenty six hours.

Trombetta walked in the office with a sandwich in his hand and sat down. He had a tired and worried look on his face.

"Bob, do we have anything that is pointing at a good suspect? I can't believe we spent all night tracking down the wrong guy," Trombetta shook his head as he spoke. Bob could tell Jack was in one of his "We blew it" moods.

"We went with what we had. We played it out and did what we had to do," answered Martin.

"Yeah, but you said all along that you didn't think we had the right guy. It was like everybody had blinders on and we went after the guy because there was nothing else to do." The frustration in Jack's voice became even more apparent.

"Jack, don't worry about it, we just have to move on and follow our next lead. I have a good feeling about this. We are going to get this guy, whoever and where ever he is."

Jack looked at the ceiling. "I wish I felt so sure."

"Listen, finish your sandwich and we'll take a ride. I have a car we have to search," said Martin. Trombetta looked confused. "Jack, it's a long story and a waste of time but the prosecutor wants it done. We aren't going to find anything and it should have been done when they grabbed the perp's sister, but Brogan....." Before Bob could finish Jack laughed and said, "Say no more. It's another Brogan story." Both men laughed as Jack devoured his sandwich.

They advised the officer that was keeping a log of all activities as to their intentions and got into an unmarked

car and went to the Township garage. Upon arrival, they
realized they didn't have a key for the door. They noticed
a Township employee who was working with recyclables
staring at them. Martin recognized him. "Hey, Tim, do you
have a key for the garage?"

"There might be one in the shed," he said as he entered the
small structure. He exited quickly and provided Martin
with a ring of about fifteen keys. Martin and Trombetta
moved quickly to the garage door and with the second key
entered the large structure that was utilized to repair
Township vehicles.

In the first bay they found the early eighties model
vehicle that they would search for any type of contraband.
Both investigators knew that the prosecutor was hoping that
a weapon would be found hidden in the car and that it would
match up with the bullet that killed Dave Douglass. They
both knew they were pissing in the wind, but if it wasn't
done they would never hear the end of it. Maybe everyone
would finally start looking for a new suspect.

"Hey, Bob, do we have a search warrant for this wreck?"
asked Trombetta.

"You don't want to know," replied Martin. Both men
completed their search of the vehicle and secured it and
then locked the garage. They entered the unmarked and Jack
asked, "Do you want to ride down to the scene?"

"No, I can't. I have a meeting with the county guys at
9am." Martin looked at his watch and it read 8:50am. They
returned to the Police Building. Jack dropped Martin off
and went to the scene of the shooting by himself.

Trombetta was on his way to the scene when he was advised
by radio that the Captain wanted him to respond to the
scene to replace the patrol sergeant who was in charge of
protecting and securing the scene.

On the way to the crime scene it was hard for Jack not to
feel guilt about being unavailable when the incident had
taken place. Jack was sure he may have been able to
provide his knowledge and expertise and perhaps more would
have been accomplished initially. The questions Jack
wanted to answer were racing through his mind as he drove.
How did it happen? Why did it happen? Why didn't the
responding officers catch the perp? Didn't three officers
respond in seconds? How could three officers be there so
quickly and not apprehend the perp? Did they react to the
shooting aggressively or were they taken by surprise and
find it difficult to respond? Was a perimeter set up
immediately? If there was, how did the perp escape? Were

there more people involved? Was a vehicle used? How did
they direct the investigation to the wrong perp? Was it
the only info they had at the time? Jack couldn't clear
his head of all the questions.

CHAPTER SIXTEEN

Trombetta pulled up to a uniformed officer who directed him
were to park. Jack immediately went to the shooting scene.
There was still quite a bit of blood in the area. Jack
found he was not able to look at the blood. He began to
have thoughts of Dave. Trombetta had to look away to
compose himself. Why Dave, Lord, Why Dave??????

Jack knew he had to get busy or he would be a basket case.
He observed that a field search was taking place. He had to
get involved and get his mind on something else. If he
kept busy he could keep a correct perspective and a more
directed mind set.

Trombetta directed the patrol officers at the scene to
continue their protection of the crime scene and looked
around for the evidence technicians. He could see that
they were providing instructions to the field search
personnel. Jack saw Captain Maher park his car and walk
towards him.

"Jack, what's going on?"

"We are starting a search for evidence that may be related
to the incident. It appears that the perpetrator went in
that direction." Jack pointed to a hedgerow about fifty
yards away. The captain looked and observed that a long
line of officers, the majority of them were from Wildwood
Police department, had begun their shoulder to shoulder
search of the area.

Jack walked around asking the officers how long they had
been at the scene and the majority indicated that they had
been there all night. Jack immediately grabbed the
captain's attention and requested relief for those
officers. Within ten minutes Jack observed new faces being
briefed and taking over the many posts that were necessary
during such an investigation. Jack remembered what Bob
Martin had said about one investigator at the Police
Building maintaining a log of all activities that were
being coordinated from that location.

Jack saw Officer Flitcroft arrive at the scene and asked
the captain, "John, is there a problem with using Flitcroft
to maintain a log of events for me."

"No, no problem, he is all yours." The captain walked away
to speak to Detective Winter. Jack told Flitcroft exactly
what he wanted and he watched as the officer obtained a
yellow legal pad and began his task. Trombetta then met

with Eugene Taylor. Gene was the evidence technician for the County Prosecutor's office.

Gene Taylor was a local Cape May County boy who was raised in Wildwood Crest, NJ. His family had roots in the small vacation borough. His father and grandfather had been cops in the Crest and his dad, known as "Scoop" Taylor, was a well known personality in Cape May County. Scoop had been a police officer in the Crest and when Memorial Day rolled around each year he would take over the duties of coordinating the Beach Patrol during the tourist season.

Scoop had three daughters and Gene was his only son. Gene's Mom had her hands full with the kids and Scoop's constant quest to get ahead. Scoop Taylor was a cop, captain of the Beach Patrol, and a businessman, entrepreneur. Gene's father at any given time owned a restaurant, a bar, a motel, and a sporting goods store. He was friendly with a few names in professional sports and oftentimes was in various partnerships with them. Scoop Taylor was a very personable, gregarious guy that knew everyone.

Gene worked for his dad in some of his successful endeavors and eventually began going out on his own. Gene took a few jobs from working on pleasure boats to delivering beer. While attending Lycoming College in Williamsport, Pa. he worked his summers at the Barefoot Bar at Diamond Beach in Lower Township. Gene always wanted to get involved in Law Enforcement and graduated college with a degree in accounting. Gene figured he would become an FBI Agent.

Gene was recruited out of college and went to work as an accountant with Conoco/Dupont and after nine months he knew that it wasn't for him. Things were slow with applying to the Feds so he decided on a police career in Arlington, Virginia. He progressed quickly and after extensive training in evidence collection and preservation he passed the examination for promotion to agent. He worked with the investigators that handled crime scene evidentiary procedures.

Gene Taylor spent five and a half years with Arlington and at one point knew he and his family would be moving back to New Jersey.

Gene being a cop was privileged to ongoing case investigative information. He was shocked when he heard that a neighbor living behind him had been tortured and murdered in her home. Her husband was a photographer for National Geographic and was on assignment out of the country. She had been abroad with him and had returned home to complete the sale of their Arlington home. Little did she know that a convicted felon and serial murderer, Timothy Spencer, would end her life in a brutal, hideous manner during Thanksgiving, 1988.

Gene decided rapidly that he was not going to have his family subjected to the crime that was taking place so close to home. Arlington was changing and Gene didn't want to be a part of what was going on.

Gene returned to his old stomping grounds and quickly went to work at Taylor's Market, a family run business. He was quick to decide that he missed police work and took the Civil Service Examination for a position at the Wildwood Crest Police department. He was going to be following the steps of his grandfather and Dad.

Gene also knew that the process would be a slow one so he also applied to the Cape May County Prosecutor's Office for a position in the Investigation Section. The Prosecutor's Office showed an interest so he took the position.

The Prosecutor's Office had decided to initiate a Crime Scene Unit for evidence collection and preservation. The team would handle major case evidence procedures throughout Cape May County. Gene was the right person for the job.

He quickly decided that the job was right for him. The pay left a lot to be desired but that he could live with it, figuring it would increase proportionately as his experience grew.

Gene was sitting at home on Friday the eighteenth of February when the phone rang and he was told that an officer had been shot in the face in Lower Township and that he was to respond to that location. Gene quickly called LTPD and spoke with a dispatcher who seemed to be a wreck. Gene knew it was going to be difficult getting information about the incident from people who were so involved and upset. He did manage to get a location of the incident and ascertained that the officer was on his way to medical care and that the prognosis was not good. Gene immediately headed to the scene.

Gene drove up to the area and was stopped by a Fire Police Traffic Officer. Gene noticed Fire Apparatus and Fireman all over the area. Gene knew he was about three blocks from where he was told to respond. Initially he had a problem talking the Traffic Officer into letting him get to the scene. Eventually he was able to persuade the guy into believing he was an investigator with the County Prosecutor's Office.

Gene got closer to the scene and parked his vehicle. He

observed over one hundred policemen in shock. Sure they
were trying to do their jobs, but the trauma they were
experiencing was evident from the way they looked and
acted.

Gene couldn't believe the amount of administrative officers
at the scene. They seemed to be from every department in
Cape May County. He also couldn't believe that they all
seemed to be standing in what he considered the crime
scene. You're not supposed to stand in the crime scene!

Gene looked around for the familiar faces of Jack Trombetta
or Bob Martin. He knew these guys should be in charge of
what was going on. He quickly ascertained that they had
been on vacation and were now on their way home. Gene saw
Chief Don Douglass and immediately spoke to him with regard
to getting the scene as secure as possible considering the
overall circumstances.

Things quickly came to order and Gene coordinated and
implemented evidence preservation and collection. Gene was
quick to see that there was blood in the area where the
officer went down and he also observed blood on the other
side of the street. Gene noticed that the on-scene command
post was set up too close to the actual scene of the
shooting. He was quick to suggest relocating the command
post.

Gene methodically went about making his initial
observations and deciding on his mode of investigative
procedures. He continually made written and mental notes
of his activities and ideas as they came to mind. Gene was
hearing that the local cops were looking for a known scum
bag. He had been told they were hot on his trail and would
pick him up quickly.

Gene, with this information, was surprised when he came
across a jacket near where the officer had been found.
Gene had checked the contents of the pockets and was seeing
things that made him think the perpetrator might be
Oriental. He found a business card and key chain that
advertised Chinese businesses. He had heard that a house
only a few blocks away that had been burglarized and set on
fire housed Oriental restaurant workers. The jacket seemed
to have been pulled off of the perpetrator by a barbed wire
fence that he apparently tried to hop over or crawl under.
Gene just figured that the coat must have been worn by the
perpetrator and leaving it behind had not been the
intention of the guy that shot the officer.

Gene was seeing items of evidentiary value that would
excite any evidence technician. The coat contained the
Chinese business card, keys and other papers. There were

suitcases that were left at the scene and contained what
appeared to be personal clothing items belonging to the
Oriental restaurant workers. There was blood in more than
one location. Gene observed that the officer's weapon had
been retrieved at the scene. He was quick to ascertain
that it was fired once and the ejected casing had "stove
piped". Cop talk for the gun jammed. Somehow the weapon
had been discharged but something had stopped it from
ejecting the casing and re-chambering the next bullet.
Gene could see that a lot of work had to be done and a lot
of theories discussed.

Gene Taylor could also see that a heavy frost was starting
to form. It was, after all, February. He knew that what he
couldn't get quickly would have to wait until the frost
burned off in the morning. He went about his job
methodically. This was going to be a very important case
and he did not want anything to go wrong.

Throughout the night with the help of lighting and many
officers he was able to locate and mark most of the
evidence. He did not want anyone to obliterate anything
that may lead to the killer of the officer. He made every
attempt to find every piece of evidence related to the
incident.

When morning finally rolled around it took a while for the
frost to burn off. Once it did Gene was able to direct his
people as they continued to locate and mark evidence.
Markers were put in place, sketches were drawn and
photographs were taken. Eventually all the items had to be
preserved and packaged. The job was a long and tedious
endeavor. Gene did not want anything to go wrong and he
made sure it didn't. He wanted everything done by the
numbers. He made every effort to leave no stone unturned.
Gene was also quick to pick up what other investigators had
to offer. He knew from past experience that good ideas and
information oftentimes came from others. Gene was not the
type of guy that wouldn't listen. Prior to final sketching
and collection Gene decided to conduct a final search of
the scene to make sure everything had been located.

Gene saw Trombetta had arrived at the scene. They greeted
each other and started to relay information as to what had
been happening. Each investigator had been at different
locations and involved in different aspects of the
investigation. Each was hearing many things relating to the
case for the first time.

Jack didn't know much about Taylor but he had heard he was
a very thorough technician. Jack knew that a case like
this one would make or break Taylor's future with regard to
his reputation. Trombetta hoped that all would go well.

His first observations of the scene indicated that everything with regard to evidence had been very methodical.

Jack was meeting with Taylor when the Chief of the County Detectives approached both investigators. Jack thought that the chief seemed listless and tired. Jack knew the Chief of County Detectives for twenty years.

"Chief, Gene and I are forming a search party for evidence. We are going to place them shoulder to shoulder and search the entire area. First, we are going to search what we feel is the path the perp took when he was fleeing," Trombetta advised.

Taylor began to explain his preliminary findings to his chief and Trombetta listened intently. This was the first time Jack had really heard the information about the shooting first hand. He was hanging on every word and paying close attention. A few times he interrupted to clarify information.

Gene was saying that the amount of evidence collected was noteworthy. He indicated that fibers, blood, clothing and even hairs of the perpetrator had been collected. Gene was extremely happy about a sneaker print he located and casted. Gene told Jack if he ever saw the sole of the sneaker that made that print he would recognize it immediately. It was forever embedded in his mind. Gene went on and on about his findings. He indicated that DNA would play a major part in the evidence portion of the investigation.

Jack noticed that when Gene began to tell what the evidence revealed about the actual weapon discharge, the Chief, began to sob and had to control the tears. Jack knew that if he didn't walk away he too would be crying uncontrollably.

The Chief had only recently been appointed to the County Chief position. He knew this was a very important case. This would be the first cop shot and killed since he took control of County Investigations. The Chief knew, too well, the importance of bringing this suspect to justice. Gene Taylor quickly realized that everyone was so emotional about what had happened. It wasn't easy to remove your feelings from the task at hand. He knew, however, that they must do so.

The search area was divided into grids and the search team began an exhaustive search of the area. Each time an officer found a noteworthy item a technician was notified and the area was protected for further examination. The

search team members would place small yellow cones and
marked flags to denote the item. When the area search was
completed the cones that were placed seemed to form a path
that apparently the perpetrator took as he was fleeing.

Taylor knew that they would have to conduct similar search
patterns throughout the area until all items were located,
reviewed, bagged and tagged as evidence. Items as small,
as a drop of blood, were found along the path of the
fleeing perpetrator. Officer Douglass' portable radio was
also located. Gene knew that many items were being found
and he was very happy. It would take evidence to seal the
fate of the bastard that killed a cop. Gene was aware that
the witnesses did not appear to be able to provide much
information on the description of the perpetrator.

The search continued and Jack saw County Investigator Marie
Hayes arrive at the scene. Jack had known Marie for quite
a few years and considered her a thorough investigator.
Marie usually handled sex crimes but everyone became
involved in crimes of this magnitude. Jack knew Marie
could be a real gung-ho women's rights sort of person when
it came to sex crimes. He also knew she was methodical
when she investigated something.

Jack immediately found the County Chief and requested,
Marie coordinate a house to house check for witnesses.
Jack knew that this had been done early on in the
investigation. He also knew that oftentimes people failed
to mention important information until they had time to
think about what they had actually witnessed. He also knew
that many times so called witnesses when given more time to
think about an incident would formulate fantasy type
information. He had to take the good with the bad and then
sort it all out.

Investigator Hayes immediately went to work. She was
provided a team of officers and she went about the task of
coordinating and implementing the canvas of the
neighborhood.

Trombetta noticed Captain Maher, speaking with the Chief.
He then observed them leave the crime scene area. The time
was 12 noon and Trombetta knew it was about time for him to
get something to eat. It wasn't that he was hungry but he
knew he better get something in his stomach if he was going
to keep working. Jack had now been awake for twenty nine
hours and he was sure he would not be going home anytime
soon.

Moments later Trombetta was relieved by a Patrol Sergeant.
The log of activities was being maintained as was a list of
all personnel who were being utilized. The search was

being conducted and was in the capable hands of Gene
Taylor. Jack was impressed by Gene's abilities and
thoroughness.

Jack was leaving the scene when he observed six or seven
detectives from other jurisdictions arriving. He knew that
they would be utilized in one way or another. Trombetta
gazed around as he was leaving and observed more police
than he could count. Many of them were on their own time.
He even saw officers who had retired from various local
police departments. When a brother officer was killed
manpower was not a problem. Trombetta knew that these guys
would do whatever was necessary to track down this piece of
shit cop killer.

CHAPTER SEVENTEEN

Martin was sitting in his office speaking to McGowan. It
was decided Jim McGowan was going to visit the scene in an
attempt to get a bird's eye view of what took place and to
possibly turn up some new leads. Martin was going to clear
up all the information about the wild goose chase in
relation to the first suspect. He knew the County
Prosecutor was going to want to make sure the eliminated
suspect was totally out of the picture. Martin began to
attack the task by preparing a list of interviews. Some,
would be in person, others could be handled by telephone.
The majority of the individuals to be spoken to were local.
There were a few that were about a half hour away. Martin
wanted his people to remain local and formulated a list of
tasks. He then wrote a list for out of town contacts that
would be conducted by investigators from other departments.

Martin completed the list and was approached by Sgt.
Hooyman. "Hey, Bob, do you want to visit the scene?"
Martin looked at his watch it read one fifteen in the
afternoon. "OK, I'm ready when you are," replied Martin.
They were leaving the office as Martin was instructing the
detectives on their next investigative tasks. Both
Sergeants entered the vehicle and Hooyman took the wheel.

"What do you think?" asked Hooyman.

"Well, Rich, I wish I could tell you who the perp was. If
we don't get something real fast this could be a long drawn
out investigation." Martin paused between thoughts and the
silence seemed to go on forever. Bob eventually broke the
silence. "I'm hoping we are going to get to the scene and
someone is going to say they have a witness who will name
the perp. I guess that's too good to be true."

Rich stared at the highway and effortlessly continued to
the scene. "You know, we spent a lot of time following a
worthless lead," stated Hooyman. "I think a mistake was
made last night when I was placed in charge of all the
human traffic in and out of the crime scene. I think I
could have better been utilized coordinating investigative
efforts until you and Jack got here.

"There were a lot of mistakes made early on with regard to
case coordination," Hooyman continued. "Your detectives did
what they thought was best but you could see that they had
no real direction. They quickly put all their eggs in one
basket and didn't keep their eyes open for other
information. They were just going to run the first lead
down until it panned out or proved fruitless." Hooyman's

words echoed Martin's thoughts.

Hooyman made the statements and then after short time added, "I sound like a Monday morning quarterback."

Martin felt the same frustrations and stated,"Rich, they went with what they had and gave it their best shot. They didn't have anything else to go on. The main problem they had was the fact that once their minds were set on the so called perp, they put all their efforts in one place. They should have allowed other angles for investigation. It isn't their fault. One thing is for sure, we have exhausted any possibility that the initial suspect and his cronies have any connection." Martin was watching the road go by thinking about what he had said.

He was quickly jolted into reality when Hooyman pulled the vehicle near the crime scene area. Martin could not believe the amount of emergency vehicles, marked, unmarked and personal. Bob couldn't estimate the amount of police personnel. The officer in charge of traffic directed them to a parking area. They exited their car and immediately met with a patrolman who logged their arrival onto the scene. Martin was glad to see that things seemed to be handled in a thorough and professional manner.

Martin said he liked what he was seeing. "Bob, believe me, this is much more under control than last night. It was nuts last night," Hooyman said.

"Rich, you have to realize that you guys had a cop shot and caring for him was the most important function you could possibly have." Martin could only envision the chaos that must have taken place. He knew, however, that maintaining some type of investigative order and control was done to the best of the abilities of the officers who had been present.

Hooyman walked Martin through the area. They met up with Jim McGowan at the scene and all three investigators slowly made their way in an attempt to recreate as much of the incident as possible.

Hooyman directed his attention to the evidence gathering that was still taking place. He was quick to observe that it appeared that no stone had gone unturned. Hooyman watched as members of the evidence search team found what they thought may be evidence. Hooyman followed the path of blood drops and various pieces of marked evidence and could quickly see the perpetrator's path of flight. It was also evident that Officer Dave Douglass had no doubt caught the perpetrator, and that he was then shot by the perpetrator and returned fire.

How had his gun jammed? Why did this happen? Why Dave?
Who did this horrible act? These questions were going
through the minds of every officer who had any knowledge of
the incident.

Hooyman, Martin and McGowan received a complete briefing
with regard to evidence from Gene Taylor. His expertise
and insight was evident in his presentation and explanation
of all the information he provided. Martin and McGowan now
had a more complete and detailed understanding of all the
events that surrounded the murder of Officer Dave Douglass.
It was now up to them to find the guy that did the
shooting.

The three investigators entered their vehicles and returned
to the Police department. Martin, looked at his watch and
mentioned to Hooyman that the time was 4:10 p.m. Hooyman
indicated he was hungry and mentioned that the food at the
Police department was probably gone by now. Martin didn't
respond but figured if it was more would be forthcoming.
The ride to the department was silent. Both men were
thinking about all they had observed. Martin was thinking
that every officer had a theory as to what had taken place.
He was tired of hearing theory. Martin was hoping to have
obtained enough facts at the scene and from speaking with
Gene Taylor that he could put together a solid case. They
arrived at the Police department quickly.

CHAPTER EIGHTEEN

Martin noticed that a tray of hoagies and various types of
salads was set out on a counter top in the dispatch office.
Hooyman and Martin made their way through the line and
grabbed enough to fill their paper plates. There were
about fifteen guys in line. Martin immediately met with
McGowan and sitting with him was Jack Trombetta. Each man
was chowin' down on the food before them. Martin sat at a
desk in the small office and began to eat.

"Hey, Bob, were did you get the soda?" asked Trombetta.

"It was in Dispatch in boxes on the floor," Martin
answered.

"Go get me one," said Trombetta. Martin quickly
answered,"Get your own." Martin laughed at the thought.

Trombetta was forever having someone get food, drink and a
multitude of other things for him. Trombetta's wife, Lynn,
was a saint. That girl was always providing Jack with
something. Even Jack's sisters were always kidding him
about how he never did for himself when he could find
someone to do for him. Martin remembered times when Jack
was first hired and he wouldn't even go into stores to buy
a soda. He would always find someone to run his errand.
Many times it would take him an hour to talk someone into
getting him a sandwich and a soda. Finally just to shut
him up someone would run his errand.

Trombetta hollered down the hall to no one in particular.
"Hey, someone get me a soda." Moments later, one of the
rookies walked in with a can of Coke. Trombetta was now
ready to eat. He devoured his food in moments and started
to light up a cigarette. "Yo, Jack, at least wait till
we're done eating," suggested Martin.

"Trombetta, I didn't know you smoked," said Jim McGowan.

"Well, I didn't for years and then I started again."

Martin looked at McGowan and said, "Yeah, Jim, he didn't
smoke, didn't drink and didn't cheat on his wife. The only
thing that he doesn't now do is cheat on his wife," added
Martin.

"Yeah, well, I can stop anytime I want to," answered
Trombetta as he walked from the room to smoke his

cigarette. Martin laughed, "Jim, he doesn't buy
cigarettes, he bums them. Maybe when it starts costing him
money he will stop."

"You one of those guys, Trombetta," asked McGowan.

"No, I buy my own once in a while. Don't listen to Martin,"
stated Trombetta. "He drinks too much."

McGowan looked at Martin. "I thought you and Trombetta were
bible toters. I didn't know you drank."

"Well, I didn't for about eight years, until Trombetta got
me drinking again," Martin said as he laughed.

Bob and Jack knew that backsliding in the Christian faith
had been taking place in their lives and each man was
embarrassed at his lifestyle as of late. Recently, they had
started going to local bars on Friday afternoon after work
just to unwind. At least that's what they told themselves
and anyone who would listen. They had started hitting a
few local establishments around the first week of
Christmas. Jack had been going on weekends since May and
had picked up the bad habit at the FBI National Academy.
Jack liked to call his drinking escapades "Networking." It
was one of those FBI words that actually meant "shit
faced." Usually, Trombetta would put the word out during
the week that the "boys" were going drinking on Friday.
Before long the young guys would all join in and they would
meet at a local bar and take it from there.

Martin didn't really like all the young guys showing up.
They always wanted to talk police work. Martin's days of
talking police work were over. He would rather talk about
retirement. Jack on the other hand would talk to the young
guys. He did so mainly because if he was nice to them they
would buy the drinks. Jack didn't like to spend money at a
bar unless it was absolutely necessary.

The sandwiches were eaten and Trombetta reentered the room
after roaming the hall smoking his cigarette. The three
men were sitting at the desks when Trombetta said, "Well,
where is this investigation going now." Martin replied
quickly, "We have to find a new suspect and the only place
we have to go is the Oriental angle."

"We have to start on the residents of the house and the
workers at the restaurant and bar. We have to get a list of
all employees," Jim McGowan said.

"I told Moy and Keywood to make a list of all the employees
and to take Polaroids of each one. I also told him to find
out which ones can speak English and also to find out what

dialect they speak," Martin advised.

"You mean some of them don't speak English?" asked
Trombetta. "This is going to be real interesting."

The investigators talked about all that had taken place up
to this point. It was almost like therapy as they related
their thoughts and ideas.

It bothered Martin that Jack seemed so negative about the
chances of grabbing the perp. They all knew that if they
didn't find him quick, chances were they may never locate
him, especially if he wasn't a local scum bag. Both Martin
and McGowan had given up on the idea of the suspect being a
local. They knew that the investigation was now going to
be directed towards an Oriental suspect. Little did they
know that they would be conducting their investigations in
the largest and most populated city in America.

The telephone rang and McGowan answered. A short
conversation took place and after hanging up McGowan
advised that the call was from the pathologist. "They
retrieved a 38 cal. slug from Dave's body." Everyone was
hesitant to reply when Trombetta finally said, "Well, now
the liberal press won't say, perhaps he shot himself in a
scuffle with the perp." LTPD officers carried 9mm Smith and
Wesson's and a 38 cal. slug certainly couldn't be fired
from a 9mm weapon. Even a public defender knew that. The
men found it difficult to talk about the autopsy and
McGowan sensed this and offered no further information. He
knew that if they wanted to hear it they would ask. It was
evident that Martin and Trombetta were very uneasy with the
conversation and probably would never ask.

The men talked for about an hour reviewing the information
over and over. Martin hated to rehash the same stories
again and again. He knew, however, that some cops did
their best investigating by rehashing the incident over and
over in an attempt to catch something that may have been
missed.

Trombetta looked at his watch and realized the time was now
six thirty in the evening. McGowan indicated he had some
phone calls to make. Trombetta stated that he was going to
touch base with his wife. Martin decided that this would
be a good time to run home, take a shower and put on some
fresh clothes.

Martin hopped into the unmarked vehicle and made the five
mile trip in quick time. He didn't pay any attention to
the cars parked in his driveway. If he had he would have
noticed his daughter's car was not there.

Martin entered the door and was quickly greeted by his wife
and dog but not in that order. JoAnne heard the car pull
into the driveway and hurried to the door to greet her
husband. The dog was already standing in front of the door
with her tail wagging. JoAnne had to wrestle with the dog
to jockey for position at the doorway. She opened the door
as Bob exited the unmarked police car.

Trombetta also decided to run home and see the family.
Jack wished that he hadn't as he walked in the door. It
seemed like every family member was in his dining room and
kitchen. They all wanted to know what was going on with
the investigation. He wasn't in the mood to talk. He was
polite and indicated that things were moving along.

He didn't want to say that he wasn't sure whether or not
they would catch Dave's killer. Everyone asked how Dave's
wife was doing and they also asked about Dave's kids. Jack
made a mental note to mention to Bob that they had to pay
Debbie and her family a visit. Jack knew that neither he
nor Bob were looking forward to the meeting.

CHAPTER NINETEEN

JoAnne could see that Bob appeared tired and looked exhausted. She was glad to see him come home but figured he was making only a pit stop to change clothes. She hugged him as he walked through the door. Bob almost tripped over the Greyhound while trying to pet her and hug and kiss his wife in the same movement. "You really look tired, Hon," JoAnne said.

"I am tired," laughed Bob. He looked at his watch. "I've been awake for about thirty six hours."

"Did you get the guy yet?"

"Not yet."

"I just came home from Debbie's. I wanted to feed the dog and then I'm going back. There are so many people there and the majority of them are sitting around crying and really not helping matters any. Debbie and I were talking about old times and how things were when we were kids. It seemed to take her mind off the tragedy for a while. People keep stopping by to show their support and offer their help. They all mean well but the house is in chaos." JoAnne thought that what she was saying might sound like she was being too critical. She knew, however, that everyone was concerned and wanted to offer their help and support.

JoAnne realized that she was following Bob around the house as he went from room to room removing his clothes and eventually entering the bathroom to take a shower. JoAnne entered the bathroom and sat down on the toilet and continued to talk as Bob showered. The dog was laying on the floor and JoAnne was petting her as the conversation continued.

"When I was at Debbie's I heard that you guys were going to be arresting the guy that did the shooting," said JoAnne.

"What you heard isn't so," said Bob.

JoAnne knew that Bob wouldn't offer any information about the incident other than to say that the suspect was under arrest or that they were still looking for him. JoAnne always hated that about being a policeman's wife. She never seemed to know anything before it came out in the newspapers.

Bob always made it an effort not to tell her much of anything. He always figured that if he didn't say anything, he would never have to worry about JoAnne saying something she shouldn't to someone who need not know. JoAnne wasn't getting anywhere with the conversation about Dave's shooting so she decided to change the subject.

"Tara hasn't been home yet. She didn't come home last night nor has she called."

"Remember when I said she figured we wouldn't be home until tonight. I told you she would stay at her friend's. I just love having a daughter who doesn't seem to give much thought about advising us as to her location," said Bob disgustedly.

"Don't say that. Maybe there's a good excuse," said JoAnne.

"Earth to JoAnne, get a life, will ya? This is the nineties. Kids don't think about how something looks or how we might feel about it," stated Bob.

"Well, you shouldn't say that," added JoAnne. Bob dried himself and declared, "I hope she walks in right now. I am in the mood to have a short talk about her life."

JoAnne hoped Tara wouldn't return home at that time. "If she comes home when I'm not here, make sure you let her know how we feel," stated Bob. "I'm about ready to do something I will probably regret.

JoAnne knew that Bob was just mad about the fact he had advised her a few times with regard to coming home late and he was tired of saying it. It wouldn't be long before he let loose on Tara.

Martin wasn't happy with his daughter's choice, of some, of her friends and was most upset with the fact that he had spoken to his daughter on other occasions about her relationship with her friends. She seemed to gravitate toward some losers now and then. Why couldn't she find some nice people? The worst part about the situation was she was an attractive, intelligent kid who was working hard at obtaining her nursing degree and would probably make something of her life if she played her cards right. Bob knew that he didn't have time to worry about it at this point. He only wished that his kids had learned from all the mistakes he had made. Lord knew that he had told them about many of the low points of his life. Martin had hoped

that hearing those stories would have registered something
in their minds. Society had really become a liberal place
to raise children.

Martin despised how liberal everything and everyone was
becoming. It made him sick to his stomach and when it
involved friends and family it made him sick in his
heart.......Maybe he needed a drink. Perhaps on the
conservative side he should take some time out to say a
prayer. He went to the bedroom to find some fresh clothes.
He never got around to saying the prayer. Nor did he have a
drink.

Bob quickly dressed and advised JoAnne that he was headed
back to work and he was not sure what time he would be
returning home. He had no idea when he would be getting
some sleep.

JoAnne indicated that she would be going back to Debbie's
and that if he needed to contact her he could do so at the
Douglass home. Bob hugged and kissed the dog or was it
JoAnne, as he was walking out the door. He chuckled to
himself as he left. He wasn't sure what he and JoAnne had
talked about as he was getting cleaned up. JoAnne waved as
he drove away. She knew her husband had his mind on police
work and everything else was going to be taking a back
seat.

JoAnne Martin was familiar with the scenario. She had been
a cop's wife for sixteen years and had dated Bob for two
years prior to marriage. She hoped Bob would not do
anything that he would regret. She knew all too well that
he was always telling people what he thought of them when
perhaps a little tact and reserve would accomplish the same
goal. However, she always liked the fact that he told it
like it was.

Jack was unable to talk to Lynn due to all the activity at
his home. He could tell that she was concerned with, his
well being. She knew that this case was different than
most and that Jack would be having some problems coping
with what had happened. She wanted to talk to him but it
was a little impossible when more than a dozen people were
hanging around.

Jack made some small talk and provided some general
information about what had taken place. He knew that he
may as well get back to the department. Jack said his
good-byes and hopped in the car for the trip back to the
police department.

Jack drove to the station with thoughts about Dave going
through his mind. He had so many questions about the

incident. He hoped that one day he would have all the
answers. He drove and prayed, asking for God's help.

Jack thought about how Bob seemed so sure they would make
an arrest. He felt guilty that he didn't feel the same
way. How, would they ever find a Chinese perpetrator if he
wasn't one of the local restaurant workers. Jack thought
about the language problem and felt helpless. He didn't
like the feelings he was experiencing. He wanted to be in
control of all situations. This case was going to be
difficult. He kept thinking that they had to solve it fast
or the passing time would work in the scum bag cop killer's
favor. Jack continued to pray as he drove into the parking
lot and entered the police department.

CHAPTER TWENTY

Bob returned to the police department. The time was seven fifteen in the evening. He walked in and observed another group of guys standing in line for food and beverages. He was immediately met by McGowan who advised him that the County K-9 unit was once again being contacted to explain the trail they had followed from the scene of the shooting. Jim indicated that it had to be clarified as to whether or not the trail that had been picked up by the dogs went back to the Chinese restaurant.

Martin thought if that was so perhaps this case could be closed quickly. He knew, however, that such a scenario was too good to be true. Martin never really did think much of tracking dogs and hoped that their findings wouldn't put the investigation on the wrong track.

Martin was walking down the hall when he saw FBI Special Agent Jack Reemer. Bob recalled Trombetta saying that Reemer had been at the scene early in the morning and that he had offered his services along with those services that could be supplied by the FBI.

Trombetta and Martin had worked with Reemer on some major cases in the past. The Gambino investigation was one of those cases. Reemer was the man to have on your side when you needed the help of the FBI. No one, at this point, knew how much this investigation would need help from federal, state, county and local agencies throughout the United States. Neither did anyone realize that eventually Interpol resources would be utilized. The investigators were in for a very long haul but weren't aware of all that would be involved in solving the murder of Officer David C. Douglass of Lower Township Police Department.

Martin was thinking to himself that whenever an investigation reached the point that many agencies were involved bureaucratic bull shit always seemed to get in the way. You always had to worry about not stepping on someone's toes or upsetting some desk sitter who really knew nothing about the day to day shit the investigators were going through. Martin knew this would be one of those cases.

Reemer approached Martin, extended his hand and said, "Bob, I'm sorry about the loss of your officer. I'm here to help. Whatever you need, just ask." Martin knew Jack meant what he said and replied, "Thanks, Jack, I'm sure we will be taking you up on your offer. What do you know up to this point?"

"Well, I was at the scene and just finished meeting with Jim McGowan. He said you had gone home to take a shower." Martin didn't want to cut Jack off but he sure didn't want to tell the story another time. Martin then stated,"Jack, if you talked to McGowan you know everything I know." Bob didn't mean to sound quick in his response but he knew he did. Martin thought he should provide more information as a courtesy and just to be pleasant. Bob hated the social mores of conversation.

"You know that we will probably be directing our efforts to the fact that our suspect is an Oriental," advised Martin.

"Jim was saying that you ruled out the local you grabbed and that you were going to have your hands full with the Orientals that lived in the house and worked at the restaurant," mentioned Reemer.

Both men were walking to Martin's office as they talked and met with McGowan and Trombetta who were conversing about what steps should be taken next.

Jack saw Bob and asked, "You have eaten at the Chinese Resturant, haven't you, Bob?"

"Yeah, a few times," advised Martin.

"Do you know any of the people that work there?" asked Jack.

"Not really, however, I can tell you the majority of them do not speak English", answered Martin.

"Oh, great, this is going to be real interesting," added Trombetta.

McGowan had a look of frustration on his face. "This case is getting more difficult by the hour." The investigators all shared the same thought. Little did they know, they would be using interpreters from four agencies before the case was solved. Martin had mentioned earlier that there were many dialects in the Chinese language and now repeated the same thought. Reemer indicated that he was aware of that fact and further, that he may be able to provide the first help on behalf of the FBI.

Once again the detectives reviewed all the facets of the case and were trying to formulate a work list of investigative activities that was structured and productive.

Martin and McGowan had already begun the wheel turning on obtaining a list of workers at the restaurant. They knew they would need interpreters to interview the workers. Both men wanted those interpreters to be cops. They would have not only translation skills but the ability to read the movements, voice inflections and all the things cops looked for when they were interviewing people.

Martin heard Jack Reemer speaking to Trombetta with regard to support groups. He had already initiated contact between these groups and Debbie Douglass. Reemer advised that she would be getting a lot of help financially, emotionally and spiritually. She was going to need all the help she could obtain. Martin knew that this was not going to be easy, on her. Martin was already dreading seeing her for the first time. He knew that it would not be easy.

Martin put his mind back to the investigation and asked Jim McGowan, "Do you know of any Chinese Philadelphia cops?" McGowan had retired from there and should know if Philly could provide this kind of help. "I know they have an Asian Gang investigative team but I don't think they have that many guys assigned. I'll make some calls," McGowan added. Reemer heard the conversation and interjected, "I'm sure we could provide someone if they are available." Reemer was aware of an Asian Investigative Team that was based in Newark and a Task Force for Asian Gang investigation in New York. Reemer added, "I can make some calls and maybe come up with some people."

Trombetta perked up and said, "Yeah, this is what I like to see, progress in an investigation. Let's kick some ass." Everyone looked at him and grinned. Trombetta loved to be a cheer leader. He wished he really had something to cheer about. Calls were made and messages left. It was now a matter of waiting for a response from the respective agencies.

Jack Reemer indicated that he had to leave and that he would advise the others with regard to the FBI's response to the request for a Chinese speaking agent. McGowan started to review witness information as did Martin. Trombetta decided to take a walk through the halls to speak to some of the officers from other departments that were assisting with everything from investigative work to picking up sandwiches at local food stores. Jack found out that all the businesses were being generous and many had even sent food items to the Douglass home for those people who were helping Debbie in her time of need. Why did it take a tragedy to get people to help one another?

CHAPTER TWENTY ONE

McGowan made a phone call and advised Martin that a complete list of all the evidence at the scene was en route to LTPD as where pictures of all the items. Martin knew that upon the arrival of these items there would be a lot of information that would require follow up investigation. Martin and McGowan had heard preliminary reports on the evidence and had formulated some ideas and theories. Now they would be able to ascertain exactly what investigative leads would be derived from the evidence.

Martin began reviewing some of the reports that the investigators were providing. He picked up one, from Detective Chris Winter, which indicated that he had obtained a list of employees at the restaurant who had been at work at the time of the incident. It also indicated who had not been at work that evening. Martin made a note of the information and continued to review the report and noticed that it indicated the Chinese residence had been burglarized on two other occasions in January. Household items, personal items, a small amount of cash and a female's bicycle had been stolen during the burglaries.

Martin remembered these incidents and recalled assigning detectives to investigate them when they had occurred. He jotted the information down. Martin also wanted to remember, Winter had utilized good investigative skills and intuitiveness in seeking out the information. Winter had heard that one witness had reported seeing an Oriental near the incident prior to the shooting and had remembered that Orientals had been utilizing the burglarized residence for dormitory type housing while working at the local Chinese Resturant. Martin wanted to mention, to Winter, he was doing a good job. Bob knew he would probably never get around to it. Martin laughed to himself that Trombetta would commend guys for everything and that he always seemed to forget. That was probably another reason why the kids of the Detective Division called Jack "mom" and Bob "dad."

Martin then reviewed information obtained by Detective Jim Moy that detailed the interview of the witness who observed the Oriental subject. This was the witness Winter had mentioned in his report. Martin reviewed the information closely and ascertained that the young female witness was a bit frightened and surprised when she observed the Oriental male dart in front of her moving car. The witness had to slam on her brakes to avoid running over the subject. Her description was hindered by her fright upon seeing the subject. Martin knew she would have to be interviewed again as he jotted down the information.

Martin looked at his watch and the time was 9 p.m. He knew that the informational road block near the scene would have been completed and he was wondering if they had obtained any worthwhile information. This type of investigative tool was used often by police in an attempt to ascertain if anyone traveling the roadway during the hours of the incident may have seen or heard anything that would be helpful with regard to the investigation. Martin hoped something positive had been uncovered.

Subsequently it was ascertained from a bus driver, who drove the route past the Chinese residence, that he had a passenger that was Oriental on his bus the evening, of the incident. The driver further indicated that he had dropped off that subject near the residence. Martin made a note that this subject would have to be interviewed formally. Martin then related some of these facts to McGowan who listened intently. McGowan indicated that he would have some of his investigative staff contact the local transportation companies in the area. McGowan figured he would have them contact cab companies and New Jersey Transit. Before long, there would be cops riding all public transportation that would service the area. Martin and McGowan didn't realize that from this action they would eventually obtain a complete description and a composite drawing of the man who shot and killed Officer Dave Douglass.

McGowan had left the room to speak with a county investigator and when he returned he was carrying Polaroid photos of all the evidence that had been found at the scene. He also had quite an extensive list of all the items obtained by Gene Taylor. Martin was impressed with the results of Gene's work. He really was a thorough investigator. Martin was glad Taylor was running the show as far as the evidence aspect of this case. It was quite evident to Martin and McGowan that this case would eventually be solved with the items that Gene Taylor had recovered. Taylor had no idea that his work at the scene would eventually lead these investigators to the killer of Dave Douglass.

A list was prepared with regard to what had to be accomplished in regard to the evidence items. Martin and McGowan slowly reviewed each item and conversed about its importance and what investigative follow up was required. The investigators decided that they would complete the list and early the following morning assign investigators to handle each task. Neither Martin nor McGowan had been paying much attention to the time and had no idea what time it was. Martin looked at McGowan as Trombetta entered the office. Jack immediately grabbed the pictures and started to review them.

Chief Don Douglass entered the office and he too began to look at the photos. The chief then said,"I want you guys to get home and get some sleep. I notice you have been sending other guys home for rest, Martin. Now it's your turn. You too, Trombetta. Get out of here and come back in the morning."

Martin and Trombetta looked at each other and Trombetta started to speak when the chief ordered, "No bull shit, hit the road. I'll see you in the morning." Each of the men knew it was futile to argue so they started to stand when McGowan stated, "We all need some rest. We have a lot to do tomorrow." Martin made sure that all LTPD's detectives were off the schedule and had gone home for some rest. They all knew that they couldn't accomplish much at this time. They all agreed to return first thing in the morning and get things rolling once again. Martin noticed there was still plenty of food in the dispatch center. It seemed to multiply rather than deplete.

Martin entered the unmarked vehicle and started the five mile trip home. He observed that Jack was just in front of him on the way home. Martin looked at his watch. The time was one thirty five in the morning. Martin knew that his wife would probably be wide awake and waiting for him. He realized that it had been twenty eight hours since he had left the Poconos with the bad news. The time had gone so quickly since he had returned to Lower Township. His time had been consumed with the investigation. It had seemed that the rest of his life was on hold. He was in the unmarked police vehicle on his way home to get some much needed rest. He thought about the many times in the past when he would be involved in an investigation and work non-stop until the case was close. Such an occurrence was not unusual to most cops, especially investigators. He knew, however, that this case was not going to be solved quickly. Martin thought about the fact that a perpetrator was not identified and that a lot of time had been wasted looking into the wrong suspect.

Martin tried to justify in his mind the time utilized to placate his sense of having wasted the time. Sure, he knew that it was the best lead at the time, but, he couldn't help but think that all the eggs should not have been placed in one basket.

The five mile trip home went quickly. Martin pulled into the driveway and saw that the lights were on inside the house. He turned off the car and saw the front door open and his wife standing there waiting for him to enter.

JoAnne had been accustomed to Bob returning late following an investigation and hoped he had good news. She had been speaking with other officers' wives and had been listening to the news.

She hadn't heard much but thought perhaps they may have gotten a break in the case and would be close to solving it. That belief, however, was washed away when she saw Bob's face as he entered the house. JoAnne hugged him and asked, "Are you, alright? You look exhausted, are you hungry? Do you want something to eat?" Bob laughed to himself and smiled as he replied, "Which question do you want me to answer first?"

"I haven't seen you in over twenty four hours and I'm concerned," JoAnne lamented.

"Okay, I am tired, I'm not hungry and I don't want anything to eat," Bob said with a grin.

Bob decided the first thing he wanted after hugging his wife was to get a shower. The family pet, Sam, was under his feet as he made his way to the bathroom. That dog would not stop until Bob made a fuss and at least rubbed her back.

The shower felt good and almost seemed like a luxury. Bob was drying off as JoAnne entered the bathroom and began to relate what had been going on at the Douglass household. She had been visiting Debbie since Bob had returned home earlier in the day for a change of clothes. She was explaining to Bob all that had taken place and was mentioning how many people had stopped to visit with Debbie Douglass. JoAnne mentioned that Debbie was really taking things very hard and needed sleep. JoAnne had been there from 11 am Saturday morning until 10pm Saturday evening. JoAnne had only left for the short time when Bob had seen her at home in the early evening. JoAnne found it difficult to relate the names of everyone who had stopped by to express their concerns. Everyone was very concerned and all were attempting to help in any way they could.

JoAnne was thinking about the faces of the police officers that had visited and how they all appeared to have the same look of disbelief on their faces. This entire occurrence was hard to believe for everyone involved.

JoAnne watched Bob as he began to brush his teeth and said, "You better get to bed before you pass out."

"I'm going to as soon as I'm done," stated Bob. He finished in the bathroom and made his way to the bedroom. "I didn't see Tara's car out front."

"I didn't want to bother you with her whereabouts, but she hasn't come home yet," stated JoAnne reluctantly.

Bob responded quickly, "She will be home tonight because she figures we will be returning from the Poconos. She stayed at her friends last night, figuring we would still be in the mountains. I don't have time to worry about her lifestyle, but I want you to talk to her as soon as she walks in the door."

JoAnne knew that the worst thing that could happen was for their daughter to walk in before Bob got to sleep because he was in no mood to hear her side of any story. Bob got into bed. JoAnne kissed him and left the room. She was hoping he would get some sleep and at least be somewhat rested before he went back to work. JoAnne waited up until 2:30 am to speak with Tara but she had not returned home. She slowly got into bed so as not to wake Bob. She really didn't have to be so careful. He was rolling around and not appearing as though he was getting much sleep. JoAnne heard Tara decode the house alarm and looked at the clock, it read 3am. JoAnne was not going to speak to Tara at this time of night. She figured morning would come soon enough.

Jack had driven home feeling almost useless. How was it possible they didn't have the right guy under arrest? They had a thief locked up, not Dave's killer. Jack felt totally disgusted. He knew that his lack of patience was not going to work to his benefit in this investigation. Jack knew that Bob had been assigned as case officer but he also felt as responsible for this investigation.

Jack pulled into his driveway and knew everyone was asleep. He immediately got into bed and found out quickly that he was having a hard time dozing off. Jack just lay in bed waiting for morning. He wasn't sure whether he had slept or not. He awoke early to find Lynn in the kitchen.

"Hon, you got home late. Did you get any sleep?" asked Lynn.
"No, none," Jack replied.

"Well, what's going on with the case?"

"Not much," stated Jack.

"Did you get the guy?" asked Lynn.

"No, not yet."

Lynn got the idea that Jack wasn't interested in talking about the case. She decided to be the dutiful wife and help him find his way out of the house and on his way to work. Lynn knew that when Jack was this way there wasn't much she could do.

Joe, Jack's oldest son, walked into the kitchen and began asking the same questions Lynn had asked. Jack cut him off and said, "Joe, we didn't catch the guy yet."

"Dad, do you think you will?" asked Joe.

"Sure, we'll catch him." Jack said it but he didn't really believe it.

Jack figured Bob was already at work. Maybe he had made some coffee. Jack was right. Martin didn't have a good night's sleep either.

Bob had rolled over and looked at the clock. It was 5:00 am and he knew he would not be able to sleep any longer. He went to the bathroom, showered, shaved and dressed. He bent over to kiss JoAnne and she awoke, "You're going in already? You should get some more sleep." She knew she was wasting her time as Bob said, "I'm on my way, see ya later. I'll try to call you when I can. Love ya."

"Hon, happy birthday," JoAnne said meekly, knowing it was anything but "happy."

"Thanks. I totally forgot it was my birthday," said Bob as he left the room. "Listen, Jo, don't plan on anything. I'm really not in the mood to celebrate. In fact, I'm not going to celebrate this birthday until I arrest this guy." JoAnne just sighed. She thought about the gifts she had purchased and the fact that they would now be sitting around wrapped until Dave's murderer was arrested. She felt guilty with the thought. She was worrying about gifts lying around and Dave had been shot and killed. She knew Bob meant what he said. There would be no birthday celebration until this investigation was completed. Those gifts would stay wrapped for a while.
Bob was quickly out the door, started the car and was driving to the police building. He looked, at his watch, it read 5:35 am. It was Sunday, February 20th and he had been born 46 years before. Boy time really flies when you're having fun, he thought to himself as he entered the LTPD headquarters. The parking lot at the Police Department was relatively empty compared to the previous day. Martin knew that as the morning rolled on the parking lot and the building would swell with manpower and

equipment.

Jack had left his own home a little after Bob and before
going to the Police department he wanted to drive past the
crime scene. Jack did so and afterwards wished that he
hadn't. He couldn't help but think what Dave must have
gone through. Jack quickly headed to the department for the
coffee fix he needed.

CHAPTER TWENTY TWO

Bob went immediately to his office and began to read the intelligence information that had found its way into his mailbox while he was gone. The forms were filled out by police personnel and would include any information pertaining to criminal activity within the Township. The information may be first hand knowledge, conclusions of criminal activity reported to them or information obtained from the public. The forms numbered twelve and Bob began to review the information.
The first sheet indicated that the suspect ruled out the night before was really Dave's killer. It was provided by a woman who was walking through a food store and happened to overhear a statement made by a tall dark complected, dark haired man. The man had made the statement in a low voice but the woman had heard it distinctly and reported it to police. It also indicated that if a reward was available that she would like to be provided same.

Bob laughed to himself as he started to read the next report and subsequently all of them. Each and every report referred to the perpetrator as being the suspect that police had already eliminated. Bob was thinking that this was going to be a long investigation. Martin made a note to contact some of the local informants to see if they had any information whatsoever. He knew that he was wasting his time but knew it had to be done. Martin was sure that the suspect was going to be a short, Oriental male. What a great description. It would fit practically every Oriental male known to Martin.

Martin decided that as soon as Detective Bill Hienkel arrived at the station he would have him review all the radio transmissions pertaining to the incident and prepare a formal report. Hienkel was very good at operating the Dictaphone equipment and also had a good ear for deciphering all the radio traffic and phone calls that would have been recorded during the incident. Martin continued to list assignments for the day and made a note to check with Detectives Moy and Keywood to make sure they obtained a complete list of Orientals working for the Chinese Resturant. Martin also noted that he wanted the restaurant's work schedule for the past two months. He knew that it would be needed to track the whereabouts of the workers.

Bob heard someone approaching his office and turned to greet Trombetta as he entered. Trombetta immediately grabbed his cup and poured some of the coffee Martin had made. He then sat down and started to tell Martin that he thought the prosecutor's office was spending too much time

on investigating leads that were really useless. Martin
agreed with most of Trombetta's statements. They usually
did agree on most things and when they didn't, they were
usually able to put their heads together and come to a
workable compromise and solution for whatever problems
confronted them.

"Bob, last night when we left I heard an investigator from
the county say that they were going to be following up on
information about the suspect we eliminated. That's bull
shit and a waste of time," stated Trombetta.

"I know," advised Bob.

"Listen, we can't let them go off on these tangents. It
will waste a lot of valuable time. We have to do
something," added Trombetta. Jack looked perplexed and
then made one of his most often used comments. "I'll just
tell those ass holes that I'll kick any of their asses if
they try to screw with this investigation."

Martin laughed, "Jack, listen, let's not worry about what
they are doing. McGowan is good and he understands where
we are coming from. That's the important thing. Let the
rest of the county guys go on their merry way and we will
go ours. Whenever they request one of our guys to assist
them on what we think is a ridiculous venture we'll make
sure we have our guys assigned to something else.
Eventually they will just go on by themselves and we can
direct our guys to do what we think is necessary. If we
think they are on the right track we can send someone with
them. The bottom line is that no one is going to take this
investigation away from us and no one is going to direct it
but us. If we do everything tactfully there won't be any
complaints. If they bust our balls about something then
we'll do what we got to do."

Jack knew that Martin had thought out everything he had
said and knew that apparently Bob had been getting the same
vibes. Jack grinned for the first time in two days and
said, "Bobby, I love it when a plan comes together."

"Hey, Jackie, only my wife calls me Bobby and when she does
she kisses me."

"Well, Martin, don't hold your breath. We're close but not
that close." Jack left to get more coffee.

Moments later Jack returned with a cup of coffee contained
in a plastic FBI mug. The mug had not been washed in over
thirty days. Trombetta had, however, wiped it with a paper
towel on one or two occasions. "What are you doing?" asked
Trombetta.

"I'm making a list of assignments for the day," answered Martin.

"Well, find something for me to do. I don't want to sit around here all day. I'm glad you're the case officer and not me."
"How about if you coordinate search teams to check the trash receptacles at the mall around the Chinese Resturant, re-canvass the neighborhood and to drain the pond near the mall," suggested Martin.

"I won't have to do a report, will I?" joked Trombetta.
"I'm going to need a lot of help. I'll start contacting other departments to provide manpower, assign team leaders and I'll supervise. That is probably going to take most of the day."

"When you're done, come see me and I'll find something else to keep you busy, Jackie," said Martin, as a smile spread from ear to ear.

"I'm sorry I asked," said Trombetta as he drank from his germ infested FBI plastic mug.

"Hey, Jack, couldn't the Feds afford to give you a ceramic mug. After all, you gave them eleven of the best weeks of your life at the National Academy."

Bob was referring to the FBI training center for, law enforcement, personnel from around the world. Jack had recently completed the school and for years had tried to talk Martin into applying. When Bob and Jack had worked with the Feds on the Gambino Investigation Bob was offered the chance to attend the school but graciously turned it down. Martin felt that when he retired from police work the last thing he would want to do would be more police work. The contacts made at the FBI National Academy were most useful in Law Enforcement endeavors but Bob didn't think such training and contacts would aide in his desire to retire as a ski bum. Hence, Martin couldn't be talked into applying. He had no idea that he would soon see how important and useful Jack's National Academy contacts would be.

Martin and Trombetta conversed about the names of local cops from surrounding jurisdictions. Jack indicated even the retired guys would respond. They came up with a list of names of seasoned investigators and good cops. Jones and Schaffer of Ocean City, Feeney from Sea Isle City, Saduk, Kirwin and Tomkinson from Middle Township, Fedderoff, Sheehan and Boyd from Cape May City, Quinn and Merkel from Wildwood City, Stevenson and Kill North Wildwood City, Miglio, McGaha and Stocker from Wildwood Crest, the list continued to grow before Martin and Trombetta realized that those individuals and many more would show up without being requested.

Jack started making phone calls and Bob continued to pour over paperwork and assignments. 8am came quickly and uniformed and plain clothes personnel started to arrive at the station. By 9am the contingency of manpower and equipment along with every TV News Team in the Tri-State area was at Lower Township Police Headquarters. The press had been very cooperative and seemed genuinely concerned with the situation. They even provided help when requested and even when not requested.

The donuts arrived by the box and coffee was plentiful. Bob noticed Detective Hienkel walking down the hall with two donuts in his hand along with a can of cola. Bob thought to himself how Buzz Hienkel was always careful with his caloric intake. "Hey, Buzz, get healthy will ya," chided Martin?

"Hey, Sarge, I'll shit this out in a minute," advised Buzz.

Martin laughed to himself and thought Buzz always did spend a lot of time in the john after a good meal. "Buzz, your going to kill yourself with that crap you put in your body," added Martin.

"Yeah, I know," replied Buzz.

Martin had completed a list of work assignments that would keep his kids busy for the rest of the day and beyond. Jim McGowan entered as Bob was leaning back in his chair. Trombetta was doing the same as he just completed a phone call to the North Wildwood Police Department and requested manpower.

"You guys look like your comfortable," said McGowan.

"Hey, we've been here since before the rooster crowed," answered Trombetta.

"Yeah, Jack, Martin probably was and you were rolling over for your second sleep," laughed Jim.

"How come I always get the bad rap?" asked Jack.

"We all know that Martin does all the work and you take all the credit," said McGowan.

"Don't pick on Jackie. He has been 'networking', lining up people for search teams," said Martin.

116

McGowan laughed," I bet he has. He figures that the more
people he lines up the less he will have to do." All three
men laughed. Bob thought the laughing did not seem whole
hearted and hearty as was the norm with most conversations
among police. Dave's murder didn't leave much room for
guys to enjoy funny remarks.

McGowan quickly began to share his ideas with regard to
investigative endeavors. He also mentioned that the
prosecutor's office was still pushing follow up
investigative work with regard to the local suspect who had
been eliminated by the Lower Township investigators.
Martin looked at Jack who knew that Bob would have
something to say on the matter.
"Jim, for your info, beware that as far as we are concerned
we are finished with that bull shit. If you want to send
your people on a wild goose chase knock your socks off,"
Martin said sternly.

"Bob, my hands are tied, I don't have a choice," stated
McGowan.

"I know that, Jim. I'm just saying we do have a choice and
we choose not to have anyone available for assignment for
what we think is bull shit busy work," advised Martin.

"Hey, I understand you have to do what you have to do."
Jim knew that Martin and Trombetta would not be happy with
the information, but he also knew that they were aware he
had to abide by the directives of his boss. McGowan was
glad that these guys had minds of their own. He also knew
that the investigative manpower could be used for better
things.

The silence of each man reflecting on the prior
conversation was shattered by the piercing sound of the
intercom. A dispatcher advised that police from various
agencies were in the building looking for Trombetta, who
quickly left the room to direct the men to the Township
Building conference rooms.
Jack was going to need a lot of room to brief the officers
and coordinate the activities. He didn't realize that the
various searches, neighborhood interviews and investigative
activities would keep his contingent of officers busy for
close to twenty-four hours of non-stop work. Martin and
McGowan began to discuss each other's list of investigative
activities for the day. Martin then gave his investigators
their assignments.

Martin had to qualify the fact with each detective that the
local suspect was eliminated from the suspect list and that
they should no longer give any thought to his involvement.

117

Detective Ed Donohue was the most reluctant to accept, the directive. Donohue would oftentimes attempt to rekindle interest into the local suspect. Other investigators' interest into the eliminated suspect would lead Martin to many verbal altercations. Martin believed there was proof positive that the perpetrator was not a local scum bag. He did not wish to waste anymore time or investigative efforts nor did he want to engage in conversations about the issue with everyone who believed otherwise. It was a closed issue. He just wished others felt the same way.

Initially Martin would explain all his reasons and investigative findings to anyone that asked. Eventually he would become visibly upset each time it was brought up. Martin wanted to catch the bad guy. He did not want to spend time talking about something that he considered finished and complete. Martin knew that many people would consider him uninterested in their ideas. Eventually he didn't mind telling them that he was no longer interested in their thoughts on the matter. What the hell. He wasn't in this business to make friends. He was trying to catch a cop killer. Martin never did care who liked or disliked him. Sometime that attitude worked to his benefit other times it didn't. He didn't care.

The assignments were made and the two investigators reviewed a chart that McGowan had prepared at home. The chart was a list of events with regard to the entire incident. It provided a chronological order off all investigative steps of the last two days. The chart made it easy to view everything from another perspective. Each man indicated their ideas and concerns. They also determined what further actions must be taken. It was easy for them to see what things had to be done over. Sometimes investigators fail to do or ask the obvious. You could get away with that type of investigation on cases that weren't so high profile and important. A murder case was not the time to take short cuts.

Martin and McGowan began to reflect on some of the statements that had been obtained from the various witnesses. Some of the witnesses actually saw things that were important to the case. Some, however, saw things that had no evidentiary value and in some regards were detrimental and time consuming as far as the overall case was concerned.

Martin recalled a husband and wife who had observed smoke coming from the home the Chinese lived in at around 7:30 p.m. the evening of the shooting. They also indicated they observed two white males driving a small vehicle exit the rear of the residence. Both McGowan and Martin knew the information from these individuals had to be considered and verified. Thus far, in the investigation, the information had not been accepted as fact. Neither McGowan nor Martin thought the people were providing exactly what they had witnessed. It was almost like the witnesses were fabricating information to assist the police in the investigation. Martin made a mental note that this information had to receive more attention as soon as a detective was free.

Martin went to the clerk's office where three clerks were working diligently at their typewriters. He asked to see the completed statements and was quickly provided six completed statements. Martin took them to his office and he and McGowan began to slowly read and digest each statement.

The phone continuously rang and was answered by one or the other of the investigators. The interruptions were non-stop. Investigators would interrupt to turn in their assignment sheets and to advise Martin and McGowan of their findings. It was up to Bob and Jim to decide what information was useful and act on it.

Detective "Buzz" Hienkel walked in and began a long dissertation on information he had followed up on that indicated the local scum bag was the shooter. Martin felt his temperature rising. He had advised his men not to spend any more time on that suspect. Martin tuned out the story coming from Buzz and tried to tell himself not to freak out. Finally Martin snapped, "Buzz, get to the point. What are you saying?"

"Well, people on the street are still saying that we had the shooter and let him go," replied Buzz.

Martin glared at Buzz and advised, "Buzz, we are the cops. We have information the people, on the street, are not aware of and we know for a fact that what they are saying is bull shit. I can't make it any clearer. Don't waste anymore time. Do something constructive and don't waste your time and mine." Martin was upset that his senior investigator was still beating a dead horse. Hienkel decided at that point he would spend no more time on the subject. Martin made a mental note to try and smooth Hienkel's feathers the next time he saw him.

Trombetta entered the Township court room and quickly decided that maybe he should have volunteered for a different job. Jack was sure there were over one hundred police officers in the room. He knew he had a lot of details to assign them. He also knew that this type of work could be a logistical nightmare.

Jack looked around the room and quickly observed that

everyone was looking to him for direction. Well, he
thought to himself, I have to handle this one. He knew he
couldn't "sluff" this job on someone else. "Guys, I want to
thank you all for showing up here today. We have a lot to
do, so I guess I'll get started. I am going to need a group
of guys to search through about fifty tons of trash."

Jack was astonished when almost every hand, in the room,
went up into the air. These guys were volunteering for the
worst possible duty. Jack decided quickly that he would
need about thirty guys for the trash duty at the County
Dump, twenty for checking dumpsters near the resturant,
twenty five guys for neighborhood canvassing and the
remainder for a search detail for the weapon that may have
been discarded.

Jack began to split the group into teams and appointed team
leaders to handle the various duties. He then advised all
the men and women to break up into their teams and
instructed them as to their exact duties. Jack didn't
realize that it had started to rain and all of these people
would be walking around in the rain all day long. These
men and women diligently carried out their work assignments
throughout the day and never complained. Every person
involved hoped that he or she would be the one to provide
the least little bit information that would lead
investigators to the killer of Patrolman Dave Douglass.

Jack was almost reluctant to ask for volunteers for the
dump duty but he knew it had to be done. Some of the
dumpsters at the restaurant had been picked up and
transported to the county facility. It was in a large pile
that had already been sectioned off and was awaiting the
search team. These cops would search all day and turn up
nothing that would be useful. They would eventually
retrieve over one hundred items that would have no bearing
on the case. They knew, however, that every item may be
important. These cops would spend ten hours searching
through fifty tons of trash.

They used rakes, shovels, picks and their hands in an
attempt to play a part in catching a killer. A cop killer.
The officers searching the dumpsters would spend six hours
and would not turn up any worthwhile evidence. The
canvassing team spent five hours interviewing and
re-interviewing people in the neighborhood with negative
results. The team searching for a weapon searched for five
hours and never found a weapon. The same team assisted the
Townbank Volunteer Fire Company and for almost fifteen
hours pumped water from a small lake in an attempt to lower
the water level so a search team could walk through the mud
in search of a weapon.

The members of the Townbank Volunteer Fire Company were
more than helpful. They were totally committed to doing
all they possibly could. Patrolman Dave Douglass was also
a member of their company. The lake was practically
emptied, however, no weapon was found. Jack was depressed
that all of his endeavors for the day did not provide a
shred of evidence.

Martin and McGowan had been busy throughout the day.
Investigators came and went. Martin had contacted the New
Jersey State Police and requested a composite artist. One
of the witnesses that observed the Oriental suspect
indicated she would be able to provide some details.
Martin and McGowan didn't believe she would be able to
provide a good description of the suspect. Due to the fact
she was quite startled when she observed him the
investigators didn't think her composite would be helpful.

Martin requested composite artist Sergeant Lou Trowbridge.
Martin had used Trowbridge in the past and knew he was not
only an excellent composite artist but he also had an
uncanny ability to read his witness. When Trowbridge was
finished with the witness he could tell you whether or not
the likeness you were looking at was a true representation
of your suspect. The State Police advised Martin that they
would provide the artist on the following day.

Martin had been reviewing the statements from witnesses and
knew that he could use Trowbridge and obtain two or three
composites of possible suspects. The witnesses differed in
their descriptions so perhaps Trowbridge would be able to
come up with a likeness of the one guy they should be
looking for. Moments later Martin received a phone call
from Lou Trowbridge. He advised that his office had
contacted him and that he wanted to confirm the appointment
and get some background. First, however, he extended his
condolences.

Martin talked with Trowbridge for a short time and hung up
the phone. He was hoping that the state police composite
artist could break the case for Lower Township Police
department

121

CHAPTER TWENTY THREE

Martin had just finished the phone call when his phone rang. A dispatcher advised him there was a Randle Elliot to see him. Martin couldn't think who this guy might be and reluctantly left his desk to meet him. Martin opened the door and Mr. Elliot said, "Hi, I'm Randy Elliot, I own the property, were the shooting took place."

Martin immediately remembered Mr. Elliot. Over the years since Martin had been a cop at Lower Township Mr. Elliot had lived at the same location. Mr. Elliot then stated, "I was raking my yard this morning and I found this key. It was found near the same location that your guys found all the stolen property the other day." Martin looked at the key. It was contained in a plastic sandwich bag. Elliot indicated that he had picked it up and was wearing gloves when he did so. "I don't know whether it is important but I figured I better bring it in." Martin looked at the key and observed that on one side in small letters the inscription China Town HDW 58 E. B. Way 0843525. On the opposite side was the inscription Made in USA, Star, 6 ARZ.

Martin figured that the key had probably fallen out of one of the stolen cases or packages that had been taken from the Chinese residence and left on the Elliot property. He thanked Mr. Elliot as he showed him out of the Police department. Martin walked to his office and thought that he had just wasted about fifteen minutes of his time. He was sure he could have completed more important tasks. He could not have been more wrong. In his hand, he had held the key to the investigation.

Martin entered his office and advised McGowan of what had transpired. McGowan indicated that after it was bagged and tagged he would make sure the key was placed with the rest of the evidence at the County. McGowan also had more important things on his mind. He was preparing more assignments for the county investigators who were contacting the various public transportation companies throughout the area. McGowan decided that he would have the investigators ride the various buses and taxi cabs that service the area in an attempt to obtain information from passengers and drivers. He knew it would be a long shot but it had to be done.

Martin was just about to pick up the phone when Detectives Moy and Keywood entered his office. "Hey, Sarge, we interviewed the restaurant owner and he gave us a list of his present workers. We took pictures of them and ascertained that three out of about thirteen speak English.

There is one of the three who speaks English that you can really understand," Moy reported.

"Sarge, we tried to ask them some questions but we couldn't get anywhere," stated Keywood. Moy looked at Martin and added, "We asked him if he had any problems with employees past or present. He said he never had trouble with anyone nor did he ever fire anyone since he opened the business. He says he uses some employment agencies in New York City for workers. He also said that his house that is used by the workers has been burglarized about three or four times. He also states he has no reason to believe that the burglaries are related to any of his people."

"Did you tell him his ass was out?" stated Martin.

"No, Sarge, I figured you would tell him when you saw him," said Moy as he chuckled.

"Jim, somebody at that restaurant knows what happened and we have to find out who it is," stated Martin. Keywood looked puzzled, "You really think so, Sarge?" McGowan answered before Martin opened his mouth, "No doubt about it."

Martin thought this was the second time the restaurant owner had been asked about possible suspects and he still indicated he never fired anyone or had problems with an employee. Martin made a mental note to contact a friend who had once been a cop and ask him about the owner and his business. Martin knew this ex-cop had done some work for him and that he spent some time eating at the restaurant. Moy was telling McGowan about the alarm system that had been installed in the residence owned by the restaurant owner when Martin caught on to the conversation. McGowan stated to Martin, "We have to find out who the alarm installer ...." Moy cut him off, "I have the name and I found out it was never activated. The alarm was functional but had not been hooked up to central receiving. It would only make noise at the house and would not alert the Police department or an alarm company until it was certified."

"Keywood checked our records and found out they never had it certified for use," added Moy. Martin looked at McGowan, "Hey, Jim, wasn't the alarm unit found in the rear yard of the Chinese residence?"

"Yeah, it had been ripped off the wall and thrown out in the back yard," replied McGowan. Martin picked up the phone and called the alarm company that had installed the unit. He requested a description of the unit and some paperwork that would explain how it functioned.

Martin looked at Moy, "Jim, did you ask about Caucasian employees."

"Yeah, Sarge, the restaurant owner is preparing a list of past and present employees. You guessed it. He has never had problems with any of them either. This guy must be the most easy going bar and restaurant owner I ever met," laughed Moy.

Martin advised the two detectives to work on some reports. He would have more assignments for them as soon as they got caught up. They left and headed straight for the sandwiches that had just been delivered. The local businesses continued to donate food for the officers that were still working around the clock.

Detective Hienkel entered the office. "I am done with the tape on the incident. Do you want the notes?"

"No, Buzz, give it to the clerks and get it typed up into report form," instructed Martin. "Hey, Buzz, anything interesting?"

"Well, it really sounds like the rookie lost it," replied Hienkel. Martin knew he was referring to the cop who showed up at the scene after Dave Douglass.

"Don't go spreading that around, that's all we need," said Martin.

"Hey, Bob he really screwed up."

"Buzz, keep it under your hat for now," added Martin. "Brogan messed up too. He told everyone at the shooting scene that the arson at the Chinese house wasn't connected to the shooting. He said it as soon as he got to the fire scene." Buzz could see Martin was getting upset when he asked, "Did anyone wonder how he could make such a snap judgement?"

Buzz thought for a moment and stated, "The Captain told him right away that he better do some investigating before he decides."

"Good."

Martin was glad someone was keeping an eye on things as they were occurring. He knew that under such conditions guys often started talking before they got their brain working. He hoped that nothing had been screwed up in the early stages of the investigation that would make it difficult or impossible to catch the shooter.

"Sarge, there was another problem too," said Buzz.

"What else happened?" The disgust was apparent in Martin's voice.

"It took them twelve minutes to decide to call out the swat team."

"Hey, Buzz, I'm sure it was nothing personal. They probably found more important things to do," joked, Martin. Hienkel knew he was getting nowhere with his problems. He started out of the room as Martin added, "Buzz get something to eat and then I'll have something for you to do." McGowan looked at Martin and stated, "I wonder if he will have anything positive to say about this investigation."

"He's alright," said Martin, "Sometimes his story telling takes precedent over his ability to realize he sounds like no one can do the job as well as him. I put up with his stories, because when the shit hits the fan I like him around."

Martin thought how all the detectives had there own idiosyncrasies and how each one had to be treated differently. Oftentimes egos, attitudes and the ability to get along with each other worked against the members of the Detective Division. Somehow everything still managed to get done and guys were able to work together and party now and then. Martin and Trombetta each knew that they couldn't force all the guys to be friends. They could, however, dictate that they work together and get the job done.
Martin and McGowan continued to review the events of the investigation and provided assignments to the investigators. They knew all too well that as long as they had work that had to be completed the investigation would be making progress. They also knew that when they ran out of work to do the case would begin to get cold and solving the shooting would be more difficult.

Throughout the day they made phone calls to numerous Federal, State, County and local agencies. A few investigators from other agencies began to contact them with regard to Asian gangs pressuring Chinese Restaurant owners for cash. These gang members would extort money through bribery and kidnapping and would terrorize the Chinese businessmen into paying large sums of money to be left alone. Martin and McGowan certainly didn't need that kind of activity to enter into their investigation. Each man knew that this was going to be a case that would be solved on evidence and possibly some good breaks.

The two investigators began to review the names of the Orientals that had to be questioned. McGowan decided to contact Jack Reemer in an attempt to get an interpreter involved. McGowan had contacted Philadelphia Police department and had been advised that they only had one Chinese speaking officer and he was presently involved with an Asian gang case. Philly had provided the name of a New York contact who may be able to assist. McGowan, however, had remembered his boss saying to contact the Feds. He figured he better follow orders and do so.

Reemer advised McGowan that a translator would be available on February twenty third or twenty fourth. Martin was disheartened that they would have to wait and was hoping to get something going as soon as possible.

Trombetta entered the room and saw the look on Martin's face that always indicated a problem. "Hey, you pissed or something."

"No, I'm just thinking about the fact we need some translators here as soon as we can get them," said Martin.

"Did you try the Feds?" asked Trombetta.

"Yeah, we have to wait three or four days."

"That's bull shit," said Trombetta as he raised his voice. "We got a freakin' murder of a cop and they can't get us someone who can speak Chinese."

McGowan could see that Jack was entering his aggressive mode. "Jack, these translators aren't easy to come by. Just relax. We'll have someone hear as soon as possible." McGowan got up to go to the bathroom and Martin and Trombetta continued the conversation.

"Jim indicated that his people want him to use the Feds for a translator," stated Martin.

"What's it matter who we use as long as he speaks the language?" asked Trombetta.

"I agree, Jack, but if we start making waves we are going to be on the shit list again," laughed Martin.

"That's no big deal. You're used to it.," Jack answered.

"Yeah, the county hates my guts and little do they know it's you who puts me up to it. I have broad shoulders, any suggestions?"

"I know a guy in China I can call," said Trombetta. "He will tell me who I can contact."

"China, are you kiddin'? Well, do it. Don't let me stand in the way of progress," said Martin.

"The county is going to be mad at you when they find out this was your idea, Bobby."

McGowan entered the office and Trombetta left to use another phone. Martin decided it was time for a sandwich. He walked down the hall and observed that some of the guys from the various details were returning to the Police department. They were all wet from the rain and smelled like trash. They had been taking turns searching through the tons of trash and returning in shifts to eat at the Police department.

Martin couldn't help but think about all the guys working on their own time in an attempt to bring Dave's killer to justice. He even saw a couple guys who had retired during the last few years. These guys were from other departments. The brotherhood was strong. Stronger than most people could imagine. Many of the officers helping in the investigation didn't even know who Dave was or anything about him. They did know that he was a cop and brother. That's all that mattered.

Martin saw Trombetta in the hallway and Jack indicated that he had made the statement about calling China just to keep McGowan on his toes. He also advised Bob that he really wasn't sure how he would speak to the guy in China. Jack really couldn't recall how well the guy spoke English. This guy was among those Jack had met while at the FBI National Academy in Quantico, Virginia. Jack oftentimes had memory problems, Bob thought to himself.

CHAPTER TWENTY FOUR

Martin and Trombetta found an empty room. Doing so was a
major accomplishment in such a small building and under the
conditions. The Captain had left his office and the
detectives who had been there had gone for sandwiches.

Jack shut the door so they would not be interrupted.
Trombetta spoke first. "Where do we go from here? It
doesn't look good. We don't even have a suspect. I have a
bad feeling about this one. We have to make something
happen. The county is still running around tying up loose
ends on the perp we ruled out. They aren't going to be much
help."

Martin knew that Jack was frustrated. "Jack, listen, we
are going to get this thing done. We hit some road blocks,
but, we are working around them. I'm telling you we are
going to get this guy. We have a ton of evidence that has
to be processed. Who knows we might get some prints or do
something with DNA. Taylor got some blood, hair and
clothing. Believe me, I have a good feeling about this
case."

Trombetta started to relax a little and said, "Taylor did a
good job at the scene. He found a lot of stuff. There was
even a lottery ticket in the jacket the perp was wearing.
Maybe we can do something with it. What about that key that
Elliot brought in?"

"You never know," said Martin. He didn't want to tell Jack
that he figured the key was more of a long shot than the
lottery ticket. He continued, "We just have to keep
pushing. We will just keep following leads and check out
all the evidence. Once we start the interviews of all the
workers at the restaurant we will probably come up with
more leads. It's just a drag we can't really communicate
with them."

Neither Martin nor Trombetta realized just how frustrating
communication would prove to be when it came to
interviewing the Oriental witnesses and suspects. The two
investigators were dealing with a culture they knew nothing
about. Jack's closest contact with Chinese people was on a

vacation with the Martins. He was talked into eating Lobster Cantonese and liked it. He also obtained a taste for Tsing Tao beer on that vacation.

Trombetta also mentioned that Gene Taylor had found a piece of newspaper, apparently from a Chinese publication that had a telephone number written on it. It had been found in the pocket of the jacket that had been torn off the perp. The investigators knew they had a lot of evidence to follow up on.

Trombetta wished he hadn't been on vacation when Dave was murdered. Maybe he and Bob could have made a difference. He knew it was wishful thinking. There was a knock at the door. Martin opened it and Captain Maher walked into his office.

"So, Bob, what's going on?" asked John Maher. Jack could see by the look on Bob's face that he did not want to relate the progress of the investigation. Jack jumped in and started to update the Captain on what had transpired. Martin was thankful he didn't have to tell the whole story again and slipped out of the room as Jack went on with his update.

Martin walked down the hall. Trombetta usually knew when Martin wasn't in the mood for conversation. Jack knew that this was one of those times. Bob knew that the brass absolutely needed to know what was going on. He just hated to be the one who always had to relay the information. Martin hated long conversations that usually resulted in little or no progress.

Martin went to the bathroom, locked the door and threw some water on his face. He dried his face and said a prayer. "Lord, please watch over Jack and me in this one. Give the shooter to us and we will take care of the rest." Martin knew that his request was less than Christian. Martin had to question his intentions and less than Christian lifestyle during the past six or eight months. Would the Lord even pay attention to his prayers and requests? He had a lot of nerve approaching God with his requests considering his recent backsliding. Martin knew he had to get his life in order, for some reason it wasn't happening.

Martin returned to his office with a platter of food in his hand. It was now six thirty in the evening. The time had flown by and Martin and McGowan were still handing out assignments. Martin was going crazy reviewing all the Crime Stopper information that was coming across his desk. Coupled with the intelligence reports from the troops the paper was piling up. Martin had requested all of the information be funneled through him. He knew that this way he would be on top of every piece of information that came into the Police department

Everyone knew that all information had to be on paper and that Martin was the recipient. Martin counted the forms and then began to sort out the fifty one pieces of information. He made three files. The first group included the information that required immediate follow-up. The second group was to be followed up at a later date. Last and least was that information that Martin considered useless. Martin was always preaching prioritization to the detectives that worked for him. He hoped that his method of prioritizing would once again provide good results.

Sgt. Bob Martin hated to see the detectives working on leads that were useless and a waste of time. He would have them work on what he considered important and when they had some slow time he would assign the less important information for follow-up.

Trombetta entered the office and sat down to talk to Martin and McGowan. Jack saw that Bob was reviewing the leads and asked if there was anything good. Martin looked up, "Fraid not, Jackie. Just a bunch of busy work for the kids. We haven't really received any information that seems to be worthwhile. We have to start talking to the workers at the restaurant and then we'll get something to go on. When we get the translator here we can kick ass and get this show on the road." Martin reflected on what he had said and was starting to believe that the workers were the key to the entire case. He hoped that the owners would have provided information about past employees that would prove fruitful. He was upset that they hadn't. He figured that they would have had someone that would have a grudge against them. Jack listened to Martin and sternly commented, "We have to get this translator here now. Why are we waiting?"

McGowan looked up, "Jack, we are way ahead of you. The Feds will be providing someone as quickly as possible. Chinese speaking cops aren't a dime a dozen."

"Why don't we use one of the employees that speak English? He can be our translator," Trombetta suggested.

"Jack, how will we know that what he is translating is the truth?" asked Martin.

"Man, I'm just frustrated. We have to get something happening. I feel like we're not accomplishing anything."

"I know what you mean but we have to be careful when it comes to interviewing these people," advised Martin.

Trombetta looked discouraged and added, "Yeah, I know. I'm just pissed over this whole mess."

McGowan knew that these guys were venting and figured he would let them talk. He knew that eventually they would realize that without the translator their hands were tied. He didn't know, however, that they had other plans for obtaining a translator.

Martin also knew that there was plenty of work that still had to be done with regard to witness statements, evidence review and composite drawings. He couldn't help think that when they did interview the Chinese workers that one of them would identify the shooter. It was just a matter of time. He didn't want to wait but knew that the wait would be worthwhile.

Detective Sergeant Rich Hooyman entered the room and advised that the various search teams had been providing trash bags full of items that could possibly be considered evidence. "Bob, you're not going to believe what these guys have been bringing back," said Hooyman. "Come on outside I'll show you."

Martin and Trombetta followed Hooyman to the rear of the Police department and observed a pick up truck load of items that the search teams had seized. The items ranged from clothing to bank deposit bags. Martin didn't see a gun. The three men looked at the truck load of items and knew that there probably wasn't a piece of worthwhile evidence in the pile. They also knew, however, that someone had to go through the so-called evidence and make a decision as to its importance or lack there of.

Hooyman was looking at the other two Detective Sergeants and knew that they were not going to have the time to check this stuff piece by piece. He quickly took control of the situation. "Listen, I'll check out each thing and categorize it into yeah, maybe and no way. When I'm done with it I'll get you to review what I've done. That way we will all have had a chance to find something that might be worthwhile." Martin and Trombetta were overjoyed at Hooyman's offer and Martin said, "Knock your socks off, Rich. I appreciate it."

"I know you guys have better things to do. This way we can get it over with and still have more that one person deciding on whether or not we have something worthwhile or we have a bunch of trash." Hooyman thought about his last statement. He sure didn't want to be digging through all this shit. However, someone had to do it. Rich also thought about the search team from the dumpsters that had not returned with all their findings.

Rich decided he would enlist some help from some of the volunteers and start unloading the truck. He would secure everything in the outdoor bike pen and start first thing in the morning sorting through the remaining items. Hooyman knew there was no room inside the Police department and further that some of this stuff smelled like a fish factory on a hot summer night. The bike pen was used for all the lost and stolen bicycles that showed up at the police department. It was lockable and secure. Hooyman enlisted the help of four cops and started his task.

Trombetta went into the clerk's office and grabbed some of the reports that had been completed along with some of the completed formal statements. He wanted to review what had been ascertained and hoped that perhaps he could find some important things that may have been overlooked. Martin continued his work with the intelligence sheets and McGowan was attempting to bring the prosecutor up to date on what was going on.

Martin decided that he should review the time that the detectives had spent at work and quickly ascertained that he better send some of them home. Trombetta walked in and observed Martin preparing a list as to who would be scheduled for work the following day. "Bob, why don't you just bring them all back in the morning?" Jack asked.

"Jack, I have to have someone to handle the regular shifts. We are still accountable to cover what ever else might happen."

"You know how these guys are. They all want to be here. They aren't going to be able to sleep anyway. They're going to think you are sending them home because your mad about something."

"Jack, we can't keep them all on. Sooner or later they have to sleep. Not to mention the fact that if something happens we have to have fresh investigators to handle the problem." Martin knew Jack was right about the guys wanting to stay on. The kids would probably be mad at Dad for sending them to bed, but they would get over it.

Jack knew Martin was right about the need for fresh investigators, but he wouldn't be the one to send the guys home. "You're right, but you tell them."

"Yes, mom." Martin quickly exited the office and sent the day shift guys home. It was eight in the evening and he told them to return to work the following morning. The three day duty guys each complained that they still had work to complete. Martin advised them to finish it

tomorrow and repeated his order for them to call it quits.
He knew they were upset. He also knew that one day they
would realize he was doing the right thing by sending them
home. He then made a mental note to send the night shift
detectives home at the normal time. Martin figured that by
eleven p.m. there would be no need for them to stay on
duty. Martin also knew that if something did come up he
might have to keep them on and possibly call the day shift
guys in early. Something told him that they would all get
some rest that evening. They may not be mentally ready for
sleep. They would, however, be physically ready for sleep.

Martin walked down the hall and could hear the guys
complaining about being sent home. He let them bitch to
one another and in about ten minutes hollered down the
hall. "Good night guys. Go home!" The kids reluctantly
went home to bed.

It was midnight before Martin and Trombetta left the Police
department. The Police department was now manned only by
the normal 12 to 8 shift patrol squad. That squad would
spend their evening getting tags from the vehicles at the
Chinese restaurant and keeping an eye on any Orientals that
traveled through the township that evening.

Martin drove home and found his wife was still awake. He
knew that she would ask him if there was any good news. He
also knew that he would have no news to provide. Trombetta
pulled into his driveway. He knew Lynn would be sound
asleep and would probably not even know what time he had
come home. He was right. Neither Jack nor Bob would get
much sleep. They would continually think about what should
be done next.

CHAPTER TWENTY FIVE

Bob was back in the office at six in the morning on
February twenty first. He reviewed the crime stopper
sheets and intelligence forms from the midnight shift. Jack
rolled into the office at seven and immediately began
talking about his ideas with regard to the investigation.
Bob advised that those ideas had already been explored and
investigated. Bob knew that Jack had been thinking about
the case all night. Trombetta continued to mention
investigative angles that either Bob or McGowan had already
discussed and implemented.

Jack then mentioned that there was some information that
had to be followed up with regard to the bus drivers. It
was good to bounce things off of each other. Trombetta was
always able to come up with ideas when it seemed there were
none to consider.

Jack's frustration was high and Martin felt the same way.
The investigators continually tried to think of things that
may have been overlooked or forgotten. Little did they
know that they would continue to rack their brain over the
intricacies of this case until an arrest took place.
The investigators had a couple cups of coffee and played
devil's advocate with themselves. Were they forgetting
anything? They certainly agreed that the translator was
the most important thing that had to be done. Jim McGowan
entered the room and grabbed his first cup of coffee. He
immediately began talking about some information pertaining
to the evidence that had been found at the scene by Gene
Taylor. McGowan was excited by the findings and indicated
that some of the items would require follow-up with regard
to origin and importance.

McGowan advised that he also had some of his investigators
following up on a bus ticket that had been found in the
pocket of the jacket that had been torn off the perp when
he fled the scene. He advised that they also recovered a
Peking Restaurant business card from the pocket and on the
reverse side printed in English was "DEAR BUSDRIVER I SPEAK
NO ENGLISH PLEASE DROP ME OFF AT TOWNBANK ROAD BEHIND
JAMESWAY NEAR TRAFFIC LIGHT AT NORTH CAPE MAY."

Martin and Trombetta were excited with the news and
immediately started asking questions of McGowan as to what
steps should be taken next. McGowan let each man talk and
then advised that he had already implemented their
suggestions. He also advised that he had a few
investigative ideas of his own that were being looked into.

McGowan needed two Lower Township detectives to follow-up
on some bus drivers who lived locally. Martin had already
directed Patrolman Dave Adams to obtain a listing of the
New Jersey Transit drivers who lived in the Township and
made a mental note to find out what he had uncovered.
Martin also prepared an assignment sheet for Detective
Donohue to interview the drivers, once located.

The two phones in the office started to ring and every call
seemed to be from investigators from other departments that
had information with regard to Asian gangs utilizing
extortion methods to obtain cash from Chinese restaurant
owners.

Martin did not believe that extortion rackets were part of
the scenario with regard to Dave's shooting. However, he
knew he had to review such scenarios. He knew from
experience that everything had to be considered when you
had little or nothing to go on. He did believe now more
than ever that the entire incident was related to the
restaurant workers. Someone in that place knew something.
It was a matter of time before they would get some *key*
information. Martin was thinking about that,
to himself, when he thought about the word "key."

He recalled that two keys were found at the scene. Martin
mentioned the keys to McGowan who advised that it appeared
one of the keys was for the Chinese residence that was
burglarized. Maybe the perpetrator had a key to the place
and committed the burglaries at the location with a key and
then covered it up by breaking a window or a door. There
were many possibilities. He didn't realize at that time the
key would turn out to be the "KEY" to solving the murder of
Patrolman Dave Douglass.

Detective Chris Winter entered the office. "Sarge, I just
got off the phone with Philly Police department. They
checked all area hospitals and no one reported any injuries
that may have been gunshot wounds." Martin had advised
Winter to contact all area hospitals to ascertain if they
had any recent patients exhibiting wounds that may have
been the result of a gunshot.

"Chris, contact Jersey, Philly, Delaware and New York City
hospitals," instructed Martin.

"I checked all but Delaware and New York," replied Winter.

"Then you didn't check'em all," added Martin.

"What I meant was," Winter started to provide an excuse and

135

Martin cut him off. "Just do what I asked. You don't have to explain."

"O.K., but I was going to do those other places," Winters mumbled as he left the office. Jack laughed, "Boy, Chris never does anything wrong and always has an answer."

Martin chuckled, "That's why I was giving him a hard time."

"If he learns to admit mistakes and except the fact he isn't always right he'll turn out to be a good investigator," Jack said.

"Yeah, Mom, I know," added Martin.

McGowan was busy reviewing paperwork and was continuously interrupted by phone calls. Martin was experiencing the same on the other telephone in the office. Trombetta decided to walk the halls and see what was going on amongst the men.

CHAPTER TWENTY SIX

The minutes drifted into hours and it seemed to Martin and McGowan that the telephone became a physical appendage. They had spoken to agency after agency about Asian gangs and their activities. Everyone, they spoke too, had an idea as to their perpetrator. Both investigators were polite but they knew that they didn't really agree with the scenarios they were hearing. They continued to make notes of their conversations but really thought they were wasting their time.

McGowan said, "I just got a call from Rybicki. He told me there is a guy in county jail that should be interviewed. He says he may know something. How about I run up there? I need to get out of this place for awhile. I understand that Chris Winter knows this guy. Do you mind if he goes with me?"

Martin quickly responded, "No problem, he's not busy right now." Martin hollered for Detective Winter and advised him of the interview. Martin also asked Winter about the night of the incident and the fact that Winter had initially directed the investigation towards the local scum bag they had eventually eliminated. Chris Winter provided his reasons and Martin was quick to see that Winter had made the right decision with the facts that he had on hand. The only mistake was it should have been mentioned that the scum bag was only a possibility and not definitely the killer of Dave Douglass. Winter also explained that he had been assigned to the crime scene from the beginning of the investigation and hadn't been able to monitor what was going on with regard to the search for the local scum bag.

Martin could see that the men on the street had turned the information Winter had provided only as a possibility into a verified murder suspect. Martin thought to himself he was real glad nobody shot, Willie, the local scum bag. In minutes McGowan and Winter were out the door and on the way to County Jail.

Martin was thinking about things to do and remembered that the husband and wife witness team had to be re-interviewed with regard to their observations at the Chinese home. He looked through the assignment sheets and then forwarded it to an investigator.

Martin was continually answering the phone and receiving alleged leads. Each lead had to be checked out and Martin

thought about all the time that would be wasted looking
into blind alleys. Martin continually prioritized the
information, attempting to weed out the crap. He knew his
detectives were making contacts with everyone who had to be
re-interviewed or interviewed for the first time.

Trombetta indicated that he was going to go to the Cape May
City Police Department and speak to Detective Sergeant Nick
Fetteroff who might have some worthwhile information.
Detective Moy entered the office as Jack was leaving.

"Hey, Sarge, I set up two formal interviews for tomorrow
morning. I tried to get them in today but they can't get
away from work," Moy reported.

"No problem, Jim. Listen, I have a job for you and Brogan
at the Kentucky Fried Chicken near the Chinese Resturant. I
want you to check with employees there and ascertain if
they had any Oriental enter the business between 7:30 and 8
p.m. on the night of the shooting. Then check with the
employees at the Chinese Resturant and get the one who
speaks English to ask if any of them had been at the
chicken place." Martin finished his directive and Moy left
the building.

Captain Maher entered the office and asked Martin how
things were going. After some small talk Maher asked if
there was anything he could do to assist. "Well, Captain,
I am going to send Keywood down to re-interview the people
who called in the suspicious person the night of the
shooting." The Captain knew that Martin was referring to
the husband and wife who had requested a police response
that resulted in Dave's shooting.
Martin continued, "If you could, I would appreciate
yourself and another person go with Keywood and do a walk
through of the entire scenario. Pay close attention to
elapsed time and exactly what the witnesses are stating.
Hopefully they will remember something they may have
missed. Plus we will have a more accurate account of
exactly what took place." The Captain quickly said, "I'll
take Lombardo with me. Where is Keywood?"
"I'll have him meet you there in fifteen minutes," replied
Martin. The time was twelve noon.

Martin sat thinking about the Chinese workers at the
restaurant and decided to call Detective Moy on the radio
and instruct him to bring the English speaking workers back
to the Police department one by one. No sooner had Martin
done so and the phone was ringing once again. He knew it
would be more information with regard to the incident.
Martin got off the phone and decided to advise the
dispatchers that it would now be up to them to spend more
time screening the phone calls and to fill out intelligence

138

forms with the necessary information.

The calls were taking up too much of his time. He also
advised the dispatchers to put through those calls that
they deemed needed immediate attention. He made a mental
note to check with the dispatchers on the hour to review
the information.

Trombetta walked into the office and advised that his trip
to Cape May Police department was fruitless. Martin filled
him in on what was going on and once again they began to
review what investigative work had been completed. Jack
again expressed his frustration with the lack of
translators and his feelings of uselessness. Martin knew
that other things had to be investigated so he wasn't as
upset that they still didn't have translators. Martin did,
however, know that it wouldn't be long before the entire
case rested on talking to the Chinese restaurant workers.
Martin hoped that by that time the translators would be
available.

Jack knew Bob was busy and probably hadn't been checking on
the interviews the kids were conducting. Jack decided to
check. "Hey, Bob, I'm going to check on the kids and make
sure they are asking all the right questions. I am noticing
that they are spending too much time going over things that
they should have been gotten on the first interview." Jack
knew he was being critical, but this was a case that
required that everyone be doing their best investigative
work. Jack started out of the office, "I'll start spending
more time with the kids so you don't have to worry about
them screwing up, Dad." Martin laughed and said, "Thanks,
Mom."

"If I criticize them I'll blame it on you, Dad," said
Trombetta as he walked from the room.

McGowan and Winter returned to the office. McGowan
indicated that their interview didn't provide any
information with regard to the shooting. They were going to
grab a sandwich and Martin followed them to what now had
become a buffet of lunch meats and salads.

Once again Martin couldn't help but think about, the
business owners, providing the food items. The citizens
and business owners in the township were really helping to
make things easier on the many investigators that were
working many long hours to bring a cop killer to justice.
Martin knew that he would never forget the support provided
by those individuals and organizations.

Detective Donohue saw Martin, "Sarge, the dispatchers just
advised me that a couple of weeks ago there was a fight in

the bar, attached to the Chinese Resturant." Martin was
aware that the restaurant owner had opened a bar attached
to the place.

Martin and Trombetta along with Rich Hooyman had spent a
few Friday evenings there since the Christmas holidays.
"There was a fight there between some Orientals and some
Hawaiians," advised Donohue.

"Ed, if you're not busy, take care of it," said Martin.

"I'm on my way."

Martin thought to himself that maybe this was the lead they
were looking for. Martin didn't allow himself to get too
excited.

CHAPTER TWENTY SEVEN

Martin grabbed a platter of food and returned to his office
when he was notified that the state police artist had
arrived. Martin knew Sergeant Lou Trowbridge from past
cases and was glad he was assigned. Martin went to the
back door of the Police department and welcomed Trowbridge.
Martin asked if he was hungry and directed him to the food.
The men then went to Martin's office where everyone had
congregated to eat.

The officers filled the room and there wasn't much room to
stand let alone sit and enjoy a sandwich. Some of the guys
that had finished eating made room for the new arrivals.
Martin and McGowan began to fill the artist in on the
incident. They explained that they would need him to
prepare at least three composites during the next week.
Sergeant Trowbridge indicated that he would make himself
available. He also advised that his boss had told him that
the case was a priority and that he was to drop everything
else and make himself available to do what had to be done
to catch this cop killer. The information about the
shooting was provided and the food was eaten.

Dispatch advised that they had the young female witness who
had observed the Oriental subject dart in front of her
vehicle in the waiting room. Trowbridge explained that he
would need a quiet room to interview her. Martin
immediately took him to the conference room in the township
building next door. He waited until the state police
sergeant had his equipment set up and brought the witness
into the room. Martin made the appropriate introductions
and left the room.

Martin knew, as he walked away, that Lou would obtain a
good composite likeness from the witness. Martin also knew
that if the witness was not the best subject that the
composite would be worthless. Lou would be able to tell how
good a witness he was interviewing.

Martin returned to his office and McGowan lamented, "I
don't think she is going to give a good one." Martin,
felt the same way. Trombetta heard the conversation and
asked, "Why are you guys so critical of this witness?"

"Read her statement," Bob said as he handed the typewritten
pages to Jack. After reading it, Jack asked, "You think she
was too scared to be able to provide a good description?"

"You got it, Jack," answered McGowan.

"Isn't this the witness that Moy said saw everything and could ID the shooter," asked Trombetta?

"Yes it is. He also had a witness who saw the little white car with the shooter and another guy in the driver's seat," said Martin.

"Moy has a problem when it comes to interviewing. He automatically believes what they tell him before he spends time looking into the information they have provided," added Trombetta.

"He becomes too personal with the subject he is interviewing and decides to place credibility instead of taking the information for what it is worth and working with it," said Martin.

Trombetta laughed and added, "Well you take care of it, Dad, I don't want another kid mad at me."

Martin thought for a minute and said, "He'll come around. He is new at this thing we call detective work." They all laughed and each began to think about the composite that Trowbridge was working on.

The three officers were already feeling negative about the composite but they didn't tell anyone else. Why make everyone unhappy? They all knew that the composite would be only as good as the witness observations would allow. They knew that this witness may have been too shook up to be able to provide a good description of the suspect's facial features. They were interrupted by Chief Don Douglass.

"Bob, I want to have a departmental meeting this afternoon. Trombetta came up with the idea and I think it's a good one. I have the dispatchers calling all off duty personnel. It is scheduled for five P.M. I want to make everyone aware of what's going on in the investigation. I know there will be information you can't provide, but I want them updated on where we are. I don't want rumors floating around about what is going on with this case."

The chief paused for a moment then stated, "Bob, I want you to give a short synopsis of where we are and where we want to go."

"Sounds good, chief, will do," replied Martin. The chief left the room and Trombetta said, "I like that idea. The guys will appreciate it. This way they will all feel that they are taking a part in this investigation."

McGowan said, "You guys do what you have to do. I'll hold down the fort."

Martin gazed at his watch. It was two forty five in the
afternoon. Martin was wondering how the detail was going
with the captain, lieutenant and Detective Keywood. At
almost the same moment Trombetta indicated he was going to
go down to the scene and see how the guys were doing.
Martin laughed to himself at how many times he and
Trombetta seemed to read each other's minds. Trombetta was
leaving as a dispatcher entered and handed Martin about a
dozen intelligence forms. Martin quickly reviewed and
prioritized them and assigned the follow-up to various
detectives. He would keep the day shift detectives on until
eight in the evening and then send them home for some rest.
He had brought the four to twelve guys in two hours early
and would send them home at the end of their normal tour of
duty.

The public was still providing information that was old and
stale. Martin hoped that something would come in that
would blow the case wide open. He knew they needed a
break. He also knew that because they had heard nothing
yet from any informants about a shooter that this case was
probably going to be a long haul. He was sure that a local
resident had not shot Patrolman Dave Douglass. It was hard
for him to believe that the shooter probably arrived in
Lower Township by bus and probably left the same way. He
hoped a bus driver would be found and would provide helpful
information.

Detective Ed Donohue entered the office and advised that he
had interviewed the individuals that had been in a fight at
the resturant. He advised that they were American Indians,
not Hawaiians, and he felt the incident was not related to
the shooting. Martin saw another lead go down the tubes.

Detective Brogan arrived at the Police department and
advised that his interview of the people at Kentucy Fried
Chicken was fruitless. The leads were drifting away.
When was something going to turn up that they could react
too immediately and obtain positive results? Martin would
be asking that question for quite some time. More time
than he desired.

Martin began to review the names of the witnesses that had
to be interviewed and those that would require formal
statements. He reviewed the notes of initial contacts with
so-called witnesses. He didn't see much that would direct
cops to the perp. Many of the witnesses had information
about Caucasians being at the residence around the time of
the shooting. Martin was sure that these individuals would
turn out to be volunteer firemen. Martin hollered into the
detective's office. "Heah, anyone in the office?"

"Yo, what's up?" Donohue responded. I need to know what volunteer fireman arrived at the fire scene in their own vehicles and also get a picture of them." Martin wanted to get the ball rolling, even if it was rolling the wrong way. "Once you get them, take them to the witnesses that saw white guys and see if they can ID the photos."

Donohue immediately contacted the Fire Department and started the ball rolling. Detective Winter started to contact the witnesses to set up an ID session. Martin looked over the names of other witnesses and saw that McGowan made a note that one of the bus drivers may be able to identify a suspect that had been dropped off near the Chinese residence.

Martin heard some voices in the hall. Captain Maher, Keywood and Lombardo had returned. They immediately entered the small office and offered the witnesses' account.

Mr. and Mrs. Hillman had been standing in front of their residence having a cigarette at about seven thirty in the evening on February eighteenth. Their residence is one block away from the house that was occupied by the Chinese. They noticed that a man wearing a dark flannel shirt or jacket was walking along the hedgerow on the west side of their property. He was bending down and seemed to be placing some type of object on a pile of items that were already sitting on the ground near the hedgerow. The male began to walk eastwardly away from the items across their yard and headed to the main street, which was Townbank Road. Mr. Hillman indicated that he thought the man was acting in a suspicious manner and decided to follow him. Hillman entered his car and drove east on Townbank Road. As he entered the intersection slowly he observed the suspicious individual crouched over and shuffling his feet as he walked. Hillman watched him approach the side of the residence that housed the Chinese workers of the resturant. Hillman drove towards that residence and turned his vehicle onto the opposite side of the street. He placed his car in such a position that he was able to view the residence. Moments later he observed the same subject exit the rear west side of the house. Hillman was now able to see that the subject was wearing dark pants and had a ski cap pulled down over his ears. The subject appeared to be about five foot six inches tall weighing approximately one hundred sixty five pounds.

Hillman continued to watch the subject and noticed that he began pushing an item that appeared to be on wheels. He thought that it may have been some type of duffle bag with small wheels. The subject continued to push the item down the street towards the Hillman home and placed the item

near the others that had been secreted in the hedgerow.
The subject then returned to the Chinese residence a block
away. Hillman immediately returned to his home and called
the Police Department. The Police log indicated the call
was at seven thirty seven P.M.

Hillman then looked out his front door and observed the man
now wearing a dark colored ski type parka. The subject was
no longer wearing the jacket or flannel shirt. Hillman was
sure, however, that it was the same individual with a
different coat. When the man walked under the street light
he could see that the jacket was open and underneath, was,
what appeared to be a dark and light colored plaid flannel
shirt. Hillman walked to his front step and watched the
subject walking towards the hedgerow. The sound of a
vehicle motor could be heard approaching and a police car
turned into the intersection off of Townbank Road.
Mr. Hillman saw the subject change his direction with the
arrival of the police car. The man walked in a northerly
direction and began to run past the front door of the
Hillman home. Hillman indicated that the subject was about
twenty feet away and was running through his yard
approaching a low barbed wire fence that bordered the north
side of the residence. The strands of barb wire were low
to the ground. As the man ran towards the wire, he tripped
over it making his jacket cling to the barb wire. The
police officer stopped his vehicle and began to exit. The
subject was on his feet and running before the officer got
out of his car. The man crossed the street and was heading
in an easterly direction across an open field. On the
opposite end of the field was the rear of the Chinese
residence.

Hillman advised that the officer was chasing the subject
and was gaining on him and yelled, "Freeze, you mother
fucker." The officer reached out to grab the subject as he
went out of Hillman's view. Immediately thereafter Hillman
heard what sounded like two gun shots. A crack or pop
sound followed by a loud pow. Mr. Hillman then advised
that he saw the officer returning to his vehicle but could
not provide any further information other than observing
two or three other cars arrive. One of those cars had
arrived right behind the vehicle of the officer who gave
chase. The other one or two a short time after the officer
had returned to his car.

Hillman indicated that the officer who exited the first
vehicle was a "short guy with a mustache." Martin knew
Hillman was referring to the rookie. Hillman advised that
he could tell that the officer heard the shot ring out.
The officer crouched down behind a tree when he heard the
shots and seemed to linger there for a while as if he was
figuring out what he should do next.

145

Neither Mr. nor Mrs. Hillman were able to provide a facial description of the subject because he always seemed to be looking down at the ground.

Martin listened intently to the information as did all who were present. Martin believed now more than ever that the subject was an Oriental. The description provided by the young girl who witnessed a similar subject was almost identical. The clothing and ski mask were the same. Martin knew, however, that the girl would not provide a good facial description but hoped he was wrong.

At least these three witnesses had observed the same subject and were able to describe his movements for approximately ten minutes. If only, the young girl, had not been startled when she observed the subject's face. If only....If only....

Martin, McGowan and Trombetta looked at each other as if to say "All we need is someone who can describe the asshole's face."

Martin ended the silence and advised Keywood to start a formal report on his findings. Martin knew that the information was almost exact in content with the information supplied by Hillman the evening of the shooting.

Martin, Trombetta and McGowan remained in the office as the others left the room. The three investigators tried to determine if there were any discrepancies from initially supplied information. There were no differences. They knew they had a real good witness on their hands, the type who was very exact in his rendition of events. If this case went to trial they knew Mr. Hillman would be a key player.

Trombetta left the office and McGowan and Martin began to review intelligence forms and Crime Stopper information. Donohue returned to the office and advised that he had obtained photos of the firemen who had been at the fire scene. He stated that only two had arrived in their own vehicles. Each of them had been wearing dark colored, plaid flannel shirts. They had also been driving small light colored cars. Donohue advised that Winter had made contact with the three witnesses. Martin knew he was referring to those witnesses that had observed the two Caucasians at the scene of the fire.

McGowan wanted to eliminate the Caucasian theory as much as Martin. They knew they were on the right track. At least they hoped they were on the right track.

Both men returned to their paper work as Donohue left the office. The telephone started to ring and McGowan picked it up. The look on McGowan's face indicated that it was nothing more than more stale information that had already been eliminated.

CHAPTER TWENTY EIGHT

Trombetta entered the office. "Bob, we have to get to the meeting." Martin couldn't believe it was five P.M. already. Both investigators left the Police department and made their way to the Township Court Room next door. When they entered they found every member of the department was seated with apprehensive and passive looks on their faces. Fifty policemen and four off duty dispatchers were seated in the court room facility.

Captain Maher immediately took control of the meeting. He expressed his concern about all of the men and how they were holding up under the present conditions. He thanked everyone for their untiring work and involvement. He then relinquished the floor to Chief Douglass who directed the meeting toward the investigation. The Chief advised that Martin would provide a lengthy and factual update with regard to everything that had transpired.

Chief Don Douglass spoke for about ten minutes and turned the meeting over to Martin. Martin could sense that everyone in the room felt helpless with regard to solving the murder. They all had looks on their faces begging for some positive insightful information from him. Martin had prepared a complete synopsis of the case and started by bringing them up to date on the incident, evidence and suspects. He also went into information obtained from witnesses.

Martin was thinking to himself that perhaps he was being too winded and was saying too much. However, when he would try to shorten the format someone would ask for a clarification or have a question. He knew he would have to provide the long version of every aspect of the entire investigation. He knew he had to leave out certain points and investigative endeavors. Every man and woman at the meeting could be trusted. However, Martin knew from experience that all too often, well meaning cops, mention something to a family member that would find its way to the public.

Martin couldn't allow that to happen, especially relating to information that was kept secret. All investigations generated information that was known only to chosen investigators. This was done to maintain evidentiary information that was only known by the perpetrator and subsequently ascertained, by the investigators. Often this type of information would tie an individual to a particular crime. It also prevented crackpots from "confessing" to a heinous crime. Some crazy people would confess to anything.

Martin began to relate exactly what Dave Douglass had been
confronted with when he responded to the suspicious person
complaint. Martin could feel himself becoming emotional.
He managed to hold back the tears but didn't know if he
could manage through the rest of the meeting.

Martin continued with the information and began to provide
information from the autopsy. Bob thought that perhaps
this wasn't a good idea and changed the presentation in
mid-stream. He then continued on providing information
with regard to witness accounts of the events that led to
Dave's shooting. Martin finished his overview and asked if
there were any questions. Immediately hands went up.
Questions would soon take up close to forty five minutes of
the meeting. The majority of the questions were about the
local scum bag that had been eliminated. The consensus
amongst the troops was that the decision to eliminate him
as a suspect was too hasty. Martin let them go on about
their beliefs and ideas for about fifteen minutes. It was
evident that Martin was not interested in what they had to
say about the subject. He did, however, let them go on
until there was a lull. Martin then took control of the
meeting once again and glared at the audience of police
personnel. "Guys, listen up, I can't put this any other
way. We will not spend anymore time even talking about the
possibility that our shit head from town shot Dave. He did
not do it and we are not wasting anymore time trying to tie
him into something he had no part in. Are there anymore
questions about what I have talked about up to now?" It was
apparent that Martin was not going to entertain anymore
questions about the eliminated shit head.

Trombetta knew that Bob was pissed so he chimed in, "Listen
guys what we need is, any, info you may have or may hear in
the future. Just keep filling out the intelligence sheets
and getting them to Martin. He makes sure that each one is
looked into and either verified or eliminated. We need any
stuff you can give us." Martin knew Jack was trying to
placate the guys and bring the intensity level down a few
notches.

Martin calmed down and said, "I want to thank everyone for
all the information that has been provided thus far. Some
of it has been most helpful and we will continue to follow
up on everything you guys provide. Believe me when I say we
are doing everything we can to catch this guy. We are using
every agency we can to obtain assistance. Sooner or later
we will get this guy."

Martin felt himself getting emotional and he tried to
control himself. "I want you guys to know we need your
help on this. You have to keep beating the bushes and
provide us with everything you hear. We especially want to

hear about any info with regard to Orientals in the
community. I'm talking about any that you have had contact
with that was negative in one way or another. Think about
your past contacts and let us know if anything peculiar
comes to mind. You guys can help with this case and we need
all the help we can get. I know there are a lot of you guys
that are looking to move up in the ranks. I can't speak for
the other sergeants or the brass. I can speak for myself
and I'm telling you that I don't have far to go for
retirement. I won't retire until the guy that killed Dave
is in jail."

Martin felt the tears starting to flow and he began to sob.
The guys had never seen hard ass Martin shed a tear over
anything. Martin tried to continue to speak but the tears
would not allow understandable words to come from his
mouth. Chief Douglass saw that Martin was going to have to
get himself together and interjected, "Guys, I feel the
same way Bob does and I retire sooner than him. So if
anyone wants my job you better get out there and catch this
piece of shit."

Trombetta began to provide information from all the details
he had coordinated. The men listened intently and Martin
soon provided some insight on where the investigation was
headed. Martin decided to close the meeting.

"Guys, don't be upset if it seems like we aren't telling
you everything we are doing. With an investigation of this
magnitude we can't find time to be telling you everything.
We are interested in what you have to say. We will try to
update you when we can. We have uncovered information that
we believe will take this investigation to New York City."
Martin was thinking about the lottery ticket, the key from
Chinatown Hardware and the fact that other evidentiary
information was pointing to the City of New York. He did
not want to begin to fill the officers in on this
information. Martin continued, "When it does, I won't be
around to provide you with much of anything. I'm sure I'll
be spending a lot of time in the Big Apple. So don't think
we are ignoring you. That's not the case. I can only ask
that you continue to supply any information you become
aware of and try to be patient. Believe me when I tell you
we are going to get this piece of shit."

The Chief knew Martin was finished and he asked Trombetta
to say a prayer. Trombetta was caught off guard and didn't
feel real good about providing a prayer. He knew that his
life as of late had not been the most Christian like. He
was embarrassed to think that he felt hesitant about
praying. He was quiet for a few seconds as everyone bowed
their heads.

"Heavenly Father, please give us the strength to do your will, guide us through this investigation and lead us to the person that killed Dave." Jack hesitated for a moment as he began to get emotional. He fought back the tears and continued. "Lord, please be with Dave's family and provide them with their needs. Lord, we rely on your guidance and direction. Continue to be with us as we work to close this case and bring Dave's killer to justice. Provide us with success in spite of ourselves. We ask these things in the name of the Lord Jesus Christ, Amen."

Everyone in the room provided the Amen and the men slowly left the courtroom. Jack's guilt intensified as he fantasized about blowing away the fuck who murdered Dave Douglass. Was it worth burning in hell to murder a murderer?

CHAPTER TWENTY NINE

Martin looked at his watch. They had been at the meeting
for two hours. It was now seven P.M. He was anxious to get
back to the office and see if anything positive had taken
place. He walked to the Police department with Trombetta
and they conversed about the meeting. They entered the
building and observed a line of guys getting something to
eat. They both went to their office and met with McGowan.
He indicated that the artist had completed the composite
and was getting something to eat.

New Jersey State Police Sergeant Lou Trowbridge entered the
office with a sandwich in his hand. He acknowledged Martin
and Trombetta and started to explain the composite that he
had drawn. McGowan had already shown the drawing to the
two investigators. Martin told Lou to finish his sandwich.
Lou ate quickly then began to explain his interview and
drawing session with the witness. "Well, guys, let me put
it this way. We have good news and we have bad news. She
definitely saw your man. Her description of the clothing,
his height and his physical demeanor is right on the money.
She is a little shaky on weight. The suspect may be pudgy
but not fat. The bad news is that her rendition of his
facial description is not good."

Martin interrupted,"Lou, are you saying that the guy we are
looking for is not going to look like this composite?"

Without hesitation Lou answered, "That's right. She was too
shook up to be able to give a good indication of this guy's
facial features. She was frightened and shook up by this
guy running in front of her and was too scared to really
remember his face."

The investigators knew she would not be able to provide a
positive facial description. Their belief had now been
substantiated by someone who dealt with witnesses
regularly.
Trowbridge was a specialist and they knew he was good.
They knew they still needed to put a face on their Oriental
suspect. Somewhere, someplace there was someone who had
seen this guy. They had to find that someone. It seemed
that once again they had come to another dead end.

Trowbridge said he had to leave and that he would return if
needed. The men exchanged thanks and hoped that they would
be meeting again, very soon.
Many loose ends were being tied together, by the
investigators. Witnesses were being eliminated as were
possible suspects. The list was endless. Martin, Trombetta
and McGowan continued to meet with investigators and review

their findings.   Trombetta would always provide Martin with
updates of his contacts. He knew that Martin had to be
aware of all that was going on.   It was the only way to
avoid repetition.

Detective Winter entered the office and advised that three
witnesses were shown the pictures of the two Caucasian
fireman.   One of the witnesses indicated that they were the
individuals seen at the fire scene. Two of the witnesses
indicated they were not sure but that it was possible that
the two volunteer firemen were the individuals seen near
the Chinese residence the night of the shooting and fire.

Martin looked at McGowan. "Jim, as far as I'm concerned
there are no white guys involved with this incident. All
our efforts are pointed in one direction."

"I'm still going to have to placate my bosses, however, I
agree with you. We're going all out on the Chinese
connection," McGowan said.

"Jim, have we gotten any phone records from the Chinese
house or restaurant?" Martin asked.

"My people are preparing paperwork to obtain records on all
the phones at the business and residence," answered
McGowan.
"Jim, that's going to take some time. I'm going to have my
guys ask the owner and subscribers if they will provide us
with any telephone bills they might have laying around."

Martin wanted to get things moving and didn't want to wait
for all the bureaucratic bull shit that it would take to
get a court order.   McGowan knew where Martin was headed.

"Do what you have to do. Just don't tell my people I know
what you're doing." McGowan knew Martin's idea would
expedite things and he didn't believe it would cause any
problems.   McGowan also knew that the prosecutors and
attorneys would sit around for hours talking about what
Martin had done and would eventually realize it was not a
problem.   Jim thought to himself, "That's why lawyers get
all the big bucks."

Martin wanted to see the records from the restaurant, bar
and residence as soon as possible.   He figured simply
asking for the bills, was the quickest way. Jack entered
the room and Bob provided an update. It was midnight and
the three investigators decided to go home and try to get
some sleep.
They went home but sleep had not been coming easy.

CHAPTER THIRTY

Martin arrived at the Police department just before six AM. He was thinking and rethinking his investigative plans for the day. Trombetta rolled in about an hour later and was followed two hours later by Jim McGowan.

McGowan said that he had been at a meeting with the prosecutor's office. Jim relayed what his office was attempting to do with the found lottery ticket. Martin and Trombetta paid close attention.

The investigators hoped that somehow the ticket could be tracked down. They were putting a lot of faith in the New York Lotto system. McGowan advised that they should be able to tell where the ticket was purchased and provide a date and purchase time. That little slip of paper could prove to be a very valuable piece of evidence. Maybe it belonged to the perp and he played it regularly. If so, it may lead them to the perp. McGowan indicated that the AP believed that the Lotto Commission would be able to provide a history of where and when the numbers were played, in effect, a history of the numbers in question.

Rich Hooyman entered the office and advised that he, a patrol sergeant and the administrative lieutenant would be coordinating Dave's funeral. It was going to be held on Thursday, February 24th. Hooyman indicated that they were expecting about five thousand mourners. A notice had been teletyped to all police departments in the United States. Many agencies had already responded. Martin and Trombetta were not looking forward to the ceremony. Jack did not want to speak at the services. Martin was thinking that Trombetta would be asked and that he would comply. Jack felt that he was presently not suited to speak at such a ceremony. He kept thinking how he had not been living the good Christian life and was embarrassed to face the Lord in prayer. Hopefully someone else would speak.

The investigators spent the next two days following leads. The intelligence forms were continually prioritized as were the Crime Stopper information forms. Martin assigned investigators to more interviews than they had ever expected. Everyone was working to his capacity. Tempers became short and nerves frazzled.

Martin and Trombetta thought and rethought every topic that had anything to do with the case. McGowan had to put up with their outbursts and try to keep them in tow. He was glad these two guys didn't work for him. Jim knew they were competent, hard working investigators but it drove him crazy that he could never figure out what they might do next. Guys like this had to be allowed to go their own way. Once they got hold of the ball they would score or somehow cancel the game.

The investigators and patrol officers wrote and rewrote their reports. Many times Martin after reviewing the reports would direct that they be rewritten. Many of the officers thought he was being too critical. Martin didn't care what they thought. He and McGowan knew that they wanted this case to be as perfect as they could make it. These, pain in the ass, forms may one day be subject to all kinds of scrutiny by defense attorneys at trial.

Martin kept looking for the rookies report. He knew that the Rookie had followed Dave Douglass to the scene. The incident was actually the Rookie's assignment and Dave had arrived first. The Rookie was the second officer to arrive. Martin wanted to make sure that the report was adequate. Martin figured The Rookie may have a problem documenting what had taken place. Time would prove Martin correct.

Martin and Trombetta were frustrated that they could not speak to the Chinese. Both the investigators felt that they had to be able to utilize their interview and interrogation techniques. Strict translation would not be enough. They had a good way of relating to the subjects and utilized good acting abilities while interrogating scum bags. They really felt out of place not being able to use what they considered their strong points.

Jack Reemer of the FBI was constantly spending time at LTPD aiding in the investigation or attempting to obtain an agent to be used as a translator. Reemer knew that he was not able to obtain a translator until the day of the funeral but he didn't want to tell Martin and Trombetta. These guys would go ballistic. Reemer advised McGowan and indicated that he would do his best to do something sooner, but he was sure the translator would not be available until February 24th.

Jack and Bob had talked about Jack making a call to his friend in China. Jack had indicated that the he knew another guy from the FBI National Academy who could probably help out with translators. Jack said he was the lieutenant in New York City who solved the Son of Sam case. Jack laughed when he mentioned the infamous case and thought about Lieutenant Ernest Naspretto of the NYPD. Jack remembered that this guy had a line of bull shit a mile long and that he also loved to take over beer drinking establishments with his ability to sing, old, Italian songs. Jack thought it was also funny that "Good Ole Ernie" also performed a repertoire of Country Western all time favorites. There weren't too many cops, especially New

155

York City cops, who could sing "O Sole Mio" and then go right into "Your Cheatin' Heart." Lt. Naspretto had absolutely nothing to do with the Son of Sam case.

Bob thought it was premature to call the guy in New York and suggested they wait and see what transpired with the FBI translator. Jim McGowan was listening to the conversation and interjected that he hoped Martin and Trombetta would at least find out how the other translator worked out before they involved anyone else.

Jim knew that his boss had advised the FBI that the investigation would wait until their translators were available. Jim also knew that Martin and Trombetta would only wait so long. He didn't blame these guys for wanting to get the show on the road. McGowan had been around long enough to know you shouldn't make people mad if you wanted something from them. Martin and Trombetta didn't seem to care. They would go elsewhere for help.

Capt. Jim Rybicki of the Prosecutor's Office had told McGowan that he had contacted the NYPD and left a message with the Major Case Squad. McGowan hoped that help would be provided before Martin and Trombetta began their quest to the Big Apple.

The information had been forwarded to the NYPD by fax and was sitting in the mail box of the Major Case Squad. Rybicki had forwarded a copy of the composite completed by Lou Trowbridge. McGowan had told him it would not match the killer but Rybicki felt that he should forward it to New York just in case.

Martin and Trombetta were under the impression that the composite would not be released to anyone. They were sure it would not be a good likeness of the shooter or for that matter anyone who may be involved with the incident. A poor composite could come back to bite them on the ass at a trial.

CHAPTER THIRTY ONE

It was Wednesday morning, February 23rd. New York City was just getting out from under a major snow storm. There was a faxed wanted poster on Detective Sergeant Joseph Piraino's desk, located in the Major Case Squad office on the eleventh floor at One Police Plaza. There was a generic looking drawing of a male oriental wanted for questioning in connection with the homicide of a Lower Township, New Jersey police officer. Lt. Joe Pollini received the fax on Tuesday and had put it on the desk knowing full well that Piraino would immediately start making inquiries. He was right.

Piraino called the number on the poster which went to the Cape May County Prosecutor's office and spoke with Captain Jim Rybicki.

"Hi, my name is Joe Piraino. I'm a Detective Sergeant from the New York Police Department's Major Case Squad. I just saw the wanted poster for the Lower Township homicide," Joe stated.

"Thank God you called. I may need your help," Rybicki said.

"Jim, anything you need, you got. We're your partners in New York City." The words sounded like they were coming from God.

"It appears that Asians were involved and I know you have a big Asian population. I can use some detectives that speak fluent Chinese. If anything does come back to New York City, can you help us?" Rybicki knew he was about to get an affirmative answer.

"We'll open up a case and I'll assign a detective. Detective Ruben Santiago and myself will be available to you twenty-four hours a day." Piraino proceeded to give Rybicki his office, beeper and home phone numbers. Rybicki didn't offer any more information and Piraino didn't ask for any.

Immediately following the conversation Piraino had Detective Santiago run a computer check on all arrested Asians who fit the description on the wanted poster, male, Asian, stocky build, 40's. The computer spit out over a hundred names, not all necessarily fitting the description but definitely all Asian. Piraino faxed the sheet down to Capt. Rybicki.

That night on his way home to Staten Island, Joe Piraino
stopped at various precincts throughout Brooklyn that had
sizable Asian populations and dropped off the printed
wanted posters.

He spoke to many cops and asked that they spread the word,
to debrief any Oriental prisoner or informant to ascertain
if anybody heard anything about who might have killed a cop
in New Jersey.

Detective Sergeant Joe Piraino was no stranger when it came
to helping other police agencies. He had always prided
himself in helping any cop anywhere anytime. One time it
almost got him killed.

On December 5, 1991, Piraino while assigned as the
Detective Squad Commander at the 68th Precinct in Bay
Ridge, Brooklyn, received a call from Grand Rapids,
Michigan. A detective was requesting assistance in
locating a man who had kidnapped, raped, left for dead
naked on a road a 26 year old woman. The Grand Rapids
Police Department had developed information that the
individual's mother was living in Bay Ridge. Joe was
literally in the middle of combating the Colombo organized
crime family's civil war. Every day another mobster was
showing up dead in Joe's precinct. He was getting a lot of
heat from downtown. On a personal level Joe was facing the
greatest tragedy of his life. His mother, Mary, was dying
of cancer.

Within twenty-four hours of the phone call Piraino and two
detectives forced their way into the Bay Ridge apartment.
There was a long hallway. At the end of the hallway was a
bedroom where the man wanted for the brutal rape was in a
phone conversation with a minister back in Grand Rapids.
As the cops entered the room the individual didn't feel
religious anymore and pulled a nine millimeter pistol from
the small of his back. Before the rapist could become a
murderer Joe was on top of him. He and the detectives
disarmed him, Joe picked up the phone and advised the
minister that his parishioner had an appointment with
destiny. Joe's mother died five days later.

Piraino loved cops and loved being a cop. He fell in love
with a police officer's shield long before he ever wore
one. His older sister, Angela, would take him to the
neighborhood library on Caton Avenue and Flatbush Avenue in
Brooklyn. There would always be a cop walking the beat by
the library. Joe was nine years old. The first thing he
would notice on the cop was not his gun or his uniform or
his nightstick or his hat. It was the cop's shield pinned
to his chest. He would just stare at it.

One day the cop asked, "What are you doing here by yourself?" Joe told him that his sister was inside the library and he was just waiting for her. The cop said, "You should also be in there reading." Joe told him that he wanted to be a cop. The cop told him then he had better do well in school, a thought routinely echoed by Joe's mother. The cop and Joe became buddies.

Joe's father, Joe, Sr., was a locksmith in a state mental facility. Occasionally, he would take his son to work. At a very young age Joe observed some nasty sights in the various mental hospitals. He felt sorry for severely retarded people, including some children, who seemed to be caged up. Years later, while attending Brooklyn Prep High School, he would help the Jesuit priests after school in teaching disadvantaged kids, many with mental problems.

In 1972 there was an anti-establishment mentality among America's youth. Brooklyn Prep was holding a "career night" for its seniors. There were over one hundred graduating seniors. Joe was literally the only one to go the classroom with the FBI agent. Joe had made it known to everyone that he wanted to be a cop. Other students gave him the nickname "Popeye" after the main detective character in the French Connection movie.

The 71st Precinct covered Joe's neighborhood. As a junior and senior he would hang around the station house. Eventually some of the detectives became friendly with him and let him hang around the office. It got to the point where this kid, Joe, became a trusted figure in the detective squad. The lieutenant would let him do some clerical work and even answer the phones. Joe loved to answer, "Seven-one detective squad." Little did Joe know that seventeen years later he'd be in charge of detectives at that very same precinct. Although Joe's parents thought it was weird for their son to like to hang around cops, they certainly weren't adverse to it.

In September 1972, Joe enrolled in John Jay College for Criminal Justice. He attended classes at night and got a job as an administrative aide with the FBI. New York City was facing a major fiscal crisis and there wasn't a police test in sight. In fact, in 1973 over three thousand New York City cops would be laid off.

In 1974 Piraino went to work for a notorious special state prosecutor named Maurice Nadjari. His title at this point was investigative clerk. Close but no cigar. In 1975 armed with three years administrative experience with the FBI and the Special Prosecutors Office and an associate's degree from John Jay, Piraino got a job as a "rackets investigator" for the Manhattan District Attorney's Office.

Although he wasn't a New York City cop, Investigator
Piraino had full police powers and carried a gun and badge.
Joe continued to attend John Jay at night to obtain his
bachelor's degree.
Investigator Piraino worked in the District Attorney's
office for five years and initiated over one hundred
arrests. Many of the investigators were actually laid off
New York City cops. By the late seventies New York City
was back on its feet and rehired the laid off cops. In
addition, a police test was given in June of 1979. On his
twenty-seventh birthday, January 26, 1981, Joe realized his
boyhood dream and was appointed to the New York City Police
Department. Five months later upon graduating the Police
Academy he just stared at his own NYPD shield, the same way
he had stared at the one worn by the cop walking the beat
by the library eighteen years earlier.

Officer Piraino was destined to spend very little time in a
police uniform. As a rookie assigned to the 73rd Precinct
in Brooklyn, Joe was asked to assist the family of a police
officer who had been shot and paralyzed from the waist
down. The cop was an academy classmate named Donald Rios.
Joe and Donald had become close during training. Piraino
was temporarily assigned to the Rios family through the
Employee Relations Division. He spent literally every day
with Donald Rios and his family for five months. Donald
would often get very depressed and speak about suicide. It
was a very draining experience for Joe. Although he would
never fully recover Officer Rios eventually regained use of
his legs. The sight of his friend Donald being crippled
due to a criminal's bullet left a lasting impression on
Joe. He disliked criminals, but he really hated cop
shooters.

A Brooklyn assistant district attorney who had transferred
over from the Manhattan DA's office contacted rookie cop
Joe Piraino at the 73rd. Joe had just been assigned there
after the Rios assignment. He was eager to learn patrol.
Although he had hung around and worked with cops for over
ten years he really knew very little about patrol work.
Joe's entire background was investigative in nature. It was
to remain that way. The assistant DA had worked with Joe in
the Manhattan DA's office. She knew he was sharp and could
do undercover work. She needed a cop to cultivate an
informant named "Cream Soda" and infiltrate a criminal
establishment connected to the Colombo and Lucchese
organized crime families. It was supposed to be a ninety
day assignment. Eighteen months later Joe was wondering if
he'd ever see a uniform again.

The place was called Vinny's, located in Red Hook,
Brooklyn. It was a haven for wannabe wiseguys, the lowest
of the low. Police Officer Joe Piraino was now a wise ass

punk livery driver named Joey Vitale. He drove around in a
white Cadillac and carried absolutely nothing that would
identify him as a member of the NYPD. For eighteen months
"Joey" played numbers, made bets, took bets, bought guns,
got involved with prostitution, loan sharking, fenced
stolen goods, sold untaxed cigarettes and did all the
things he basically despised. He also took a bad beating
which resulted in a broken nose and a week's hospital stay.
It got to the point where he felt he was losing his
identity.

The only cop he kept in touch with and could talk to was
Donald Rios. It got so bad at one point Joe put on his
uniform in his home and looked into the mirror just to
remind himself whom he was. The case broke in its
eighteenth month and thirty ass holes went to prison. Joe
remained at the Brooklyn DA's office and worked on various
other undercover assignments. On June 1, 1985, Joe Piraino
was promoted to detective and assigned to the 7th Detective
Squad in Lower Manhattan. He was very happy.

Detective Piraino's talents would become apparent to
Detective Sergeant Joe Pollini of the Major Case Squad.
Pollini had observed Piraino's handling of some homicides
and particularly a highly publicized hostage situation
which occurred in September of 1986. A despondent, drunk
and drugged up twenty-seven year old man was holding a 007
folding knife with a six inch blade to his four year old
daughter's throat at a Human Resources Administration
building on E. 3rd Street in the Ninth Precinct. Although
it wasn't his precinct Joe responded anyway when he heard
the call on the radio. The media was all over the place.
Joe entered the location and observed that this maniac had
already cut the little girl by her ear but she seemed okay.

Joe kept the despondent father engaged in conversation and
wrote out a "letter of amnesty" that the psycho could sign
in order not to be prosecuted. The guy fell for it and
when he put the knife down to sign the document Joe jumped
him. Case closed. No one injured. In July of the following
year Piraino was assigned to Major Case working for
Sergeant Pollini.

On September 29, 1989 Detective Piraino was promoted to
sergeant. He was assigned as patrol supervisor in Coney
Island's 60th Precinct. He had absolutely no idea what he
was doing on patrol. Less than two months later he was back
in the Detective Bureau where he belonged. He worked in
various Brooklyn Detective Squads, the 62, 66, 71, 70 and
68 which covered a wide variety of neighborhoods. In
December 1993 now Detective Sergeant Piraino was back
working in the Major Case Squad for now Lieutenant Joe
Pollini. Little did Joe Piraino realize that he was soon

to be involved in one of the most interesting cases of his career. He also didn't realize that he soon would become very close to two gung ho cops from Lower Township, New Jersey.

CHAPTER THIRTY TWO

Martin and Trombetta sat at their desks and reflected on
what McGowan was saying but they figured the more people
working on the case the easier it would be to obtain help
when it was needed. McGowan knew that these guys would get
their own translators if they felt things weren't moving
fast enough. The investigators followed up on endless dead
ends.

Everyone who was involved became frustrated with the
constant investigations that seemed to lead nowhere.
Members of other departments who were trying to be helpful
continually supplied information that lead to nowhere. The
frustration level continued to increase daily.

The county investigators were still following up on the
first suspect. McGowan was embarrassed but knew that
Martin and Trombetta understood his predicament. Martin
and Trombetta had to answer to Chief Don Douglass. They
knew it was more important for him to be happy with them
and their actions as opposed to the Chief of County
Detectives and the Prosecutor. The investigators provided
Chief Douglass with updates as often as possible. Martin
advised him that the investigation was going to probably be
headed out of town and possibly out of state.

Don Douglass just said, "Do what you have to do. Just stay
out of trouble." Douglass knew that these guys would get
the job done. He knew better than to question them with
regard to their techniques. He knew that no matter what
happened they would generate some interesting stories.

Martin began conducting meetings with the investigators to
allow them to provide their insights and provide
information about their findings. A few of the meetings
included investigators from the county. The meetings
included updates on everyone's investigative activities.

The Patrol Division continued to stop endless scum bags in
an attempt to obtain information. On one occasion Detective
Brogan stopped a van load of Orientals and had them
transported to the Police department. It was ascertained
that they were Vietnamese and they operated a fishing boat
locally. No one realized that months later those Vietnamese
would be indicted for smuggling illegal aliens into the
United States. Brogan's intuitiveness eventually led the
FBI and INS into a major case.
The investigators continually obtained license plate
numbers and descriptions of all vehicles that frequented
the Chinese Resturant, bar and house. The public
continually called with information regarding Orientals

that seemed suspicious. The investigators tried to handle the Oriental subjects in such a way that they didn't seem harassed. It wasn't easy.

The Chinese restaurants and fast food locations throughout Cape May County were checked out, including a listing of all workers. Martin knew that it might be necessary to interview those individuals if leads did not direct investigators to the perpetrator.

The Transit Authority and Cab Companies were as helpful as possible and interviews were being conducted of passengers and drivers. The travel logs had to be reviewed to insure that everyone was interviewed. Martin directed a patrolman who had contacts with the county airport to fly over the area of the shooting and obtain photographs and a video representation of the entire scene.

It was decided to have Agent Reemer speak with the owners of the restaurant. It was believed that perhaps the owner would understand the importance of any information he could offer if he was talking to an FBI Agent. During the interview the owners would indicate for the fourth time that they had never fired anyone or had a problem employee that quit.

Reemer also advised the owners to provide loss statements with regard to the other larceny and thefts that had occurred at the house utilized by their Chinese employees. This was the third request that had been made. It was important to ascertain what had been stolen from the residence in the past and compare it with what had been found near the Hillman residence the night of the shooting.

Martin and McGowan met with the owner, of the alarm company, Keith Eaves. His company had serviced the residence that housed the Chinese. Martin remembered Keith from when he was a teenager and worked for his father who founded the company. It was necessary to determine if the company had done lock work at the location as well as obtain information about the alarm system.

The Chinese workers had been displaced from their residence due to the fire damage and were now being housed in numerous locations throughout the township. Investigators were assigned to track them down and obtain current addresses. Everyone was busy with follow-ups and initial lead investigations. The coordination of the effort was time consuming and frustrating. Martin, Trombetta and McGowan seemed to be the most frustrated. No doubt due to the fact that they were aware of each and every activity that took place.

164

The frustration was eating at them. Trombetta's smoking habit was beginning to take its toll on everyone. Martin knew that to get Jack to stop smoking he was going to have to make an arrest. It would be worth any amount of work. Trombetta was smoking like a chimney. Every lead they pursued didn't seem to gain them any ground. The ground they were looking for would be the ground on which the perpetrator was standing.

CHAPTER THIRTY THREE

Jack entered the office and sat down with a look of defeat on his face. "What's up Jack?" asked Martin.

"The Captain just told me I have to speak at Dave's funeral. "I'm not ready for that. I'm not ready for it but I know I should do it."

"Well, then if I were you I would start thinking about what I was going to say," said Martin. "Most of your contact with Dave was because of you both being on the Swat Team. You should draw on those experiences."

"That's what I plan on doing. I thought you would have a better idea. You have to help me out here," said Jack.

"Sorry, Jackie, it's all yours. I don't think I could get through it," said Martin.

"Well, if I lose it during the funeral you are going to have to take over," added Trombetta.

"You better get working on it."

"I tried to tell John that I wasn't the one to be giving this eulogy. I tried to pawn it off on you. John wouldn't let me slide out of it. He started on me about duty, honor and the fact that someone had to do justice to Dave. I would feel guilty if I didn't speak. Sometimes it makes me mad that he knows how to push my buttons," added Jack.

"I guess that's what makes a captain a captain," said Martin.

"Oh, you're a big help. Thanks for, all, your input partner," said Trombetta sarcastically. "I knew I would be doing this so I have been thinking a lot about what to say. I just wish my life lately had been a better example." Trombetta sat quietly reflecting on what he had said.

"Jack, it's five o'clock. Why don't you go home and start getting something on paper? We aren't going to be doing anything earth shattering here." Martin knew that the assignments had been listed and everyone was busy. He didn't think that by everyone hanging around it would solve the case any quicker.

Bob continued, "We have a lot to do tomorrow as far as the funeral is concerned. Jim is going to be handling the investigation from here and using all of his people. Reemer will be here with the translator and they will be busy

166

trying to figure out what these Chinese really know. The
State Police are going to handle all activity in the
Township from midnight tonight through midnight tomorrow.
That way all of our guys will be at the funeral."

Martin knew that Jack should spend some time formulating
what he would say. Jack reluctantly went home. "Let me
know if anything happens," Jack said as he exited the
office. Everyone knew they were to be in uniform for the
funeral and it was evident that police officers from
everywhere would be attending. Calls had been coming in
all day verifying that many departments from around the
United States would be represented.

The next day would be a very sad day for everyone involved.
Martin couldn't help but think that under most conditions
when a cop is killed the perp is under arrest by the time
the funeral takes place. He was upset that Dave could rest
in peace until the perp was dead or in jail for the rest of
his worthless life.

Martin and McGowan began tying up lose ends. Martin began
to prepare a list of assignments for the day of the
funeral. Martin worked on questions to be asked by the
translator when he interviewed the Chinese workers. He
along with Reemer, McGowan and Trombetta each provided
questions they felt needed answers. Both investigators made
sure that the day of the funeral would still be a day of
work for cops that weren't members of the Lower Township
Police Department. McGowan knew that the Lower guys would
not be of much help once the funeral was underway. McGowan
made a mental note to enable those who would be working a
chance to extend their condolences.

Martin was making some phone calls when Captain Maher
entered the office. "Bob, don't you have to get a uniform
ready?"

"Yeah, Captain, I do."

"Why don't you get out of here and spend a little time at
home tonight," added John Maher.

"As soon as I finish up here, Captain."

Martin finished the phone calls and reviewed assignments
with McGowan. It was seven thirty in the evening when he
left the Police department. The short drive home seemed to
take forever. Bob was thinking that an arrest had not yet
been made. It was embarrassing to him that the perp had
not been arrested. It was difficult for Martin to go home
from work each night not having made an arrest. This
murder case would be the most important of his career. He

had to make an arrest. He knew that he would. He just
didn't know when.

Martin gazed at Trombetta's house as he drove past. He
could see the light on in Jack's library through the window
and observed Jack bent over the desk with his chin resting
on his hands. Martin felt sorry for Jack and silently
prayed that Jack would be able to collect his thoughts and
provide a eulogy that would do justice to Dave's memory.
Martin knew that Jack would come through. He always did.

Jack was looking at the tablet before him and reviewed all
that he had written. He kept thinking that he wanted to be
one of the mourners not one of those speaking at the
funeral. It seemed that he was always placed in this role.
Why couldn't he mourn like everyone else? Jack began to
feel guilty about feeling as though he was burdened by what
laid before him.

Dave gave his life and here Jack was feeling sorry for
himself. Each time he would review the points he hoped to
make, he would begin to loose control and cry. He hoped
that he wouldn't break down at the funeral. He knew,
however, that he would. He thought as he cried that the
Lord was allowing him to mourn as he prepared the eulogy.
He had never looked at it that way before. This process
really was his time to think about Dave and mourn the loss.
The Lord was allowing him this personal time to think about
Dave and to get himself together. Jack prayed out loud to
his maker. "Heavenly Father, thank you for allowing me
this opportunity to rejoice in the fact that you are in
control of all things. Watch over and guide me so that I
can honor you and do justice to the memory of Dave. Please,
Lord, I know that you have afforded me this honor and that
I don't deserve it. My own life has not been as Christian
like as I know it should. Please forgive me for questioning
your divine wisdom and providence. Lord, please forgive me
for all my transgressions and continue to guide me. I ask
all these things in the name of your son, The Lord Jesus
Christ."

Jack began to put all his notes into a fluid presentation.
He thought how he hadn't heard his kids arguing with Lynn
or each other. The household was almost too quiet. The
entire family had each been thinking about what Jack was
doing and were silently praying that he would complete his
task. Jack wasn't aware that his in-laws Roz and George
Durante were in the kitchen speaking with Lynn. She also
was concerned that Jack had to provide the eulogy. It
seemed that he was always being pressed into service at
funerals for friends or family. But, this time was very
different. She hoped and prayed that he would get through
the funeral.

Her father looked at her and said, "Hey, Lynn, don't worry,
Jack will do good. I'm telling ya he will be alright. Yeah,
he'll do good. Yeah, don't worry." Lynn thought to
herself, why does my Dad always repeat himself. Lynn's
mother looked at George and said, "You're right, George,
you're right." George responded, "I know, Roz, I know."

Martin pulled into his driveway and JoAnne was at the door.
She knew he wouldn't be too talkative so she tried not to
bother him. "Are you hungry, hon?"

"No, I've been eating sandwiches all day. I'm going to
weigh a ton before this case is over. I have to get a
uniform ready for tomorrow. The last thing I want to do is
attend a funeral."

Martin knew his statement sounded cold. He didn't mean it
to sound that way. He didn't want to attend anyone's
funeral. It meant that someone's death was final. He now
had to face that fact. He knew that the Douglass family
would be facing the same cold hard fact.

Bob hoped that everyone would be able to get through the
day. He knew it wouldn't be easy for anyone. He also knew
it would be especially difficult for the family of
Patrolman David C. Douglass.

Joanne tried to make small talk and once in a while
actually got Bob to speak. It was quite evident that he
wasn't going to talk about the investigation. She made
repeated attempts to provide him with information about her
day and what was going on with the Douglass family. JoAnne
had been speaking to Debbie and her family and was trying
to get Bob to take part in a conversation to get his mind
off of his work. She knew she was wasting her time.
She began to tell Bob about the conversation she had with
Tara and she could see that he was not interested. She
then decided that she would help get his uniform ready for
the funeral.

"Hon, where are your medals?"

"What are you talking about?" asked Bob from the kitchen.

JoAnne was in the bedroom. "The medals, that go, on your
uniform shirt?"

"I don't want them on the shirt," stated Bob. "I have never
worn them, why start now?" Bob couldn't give two shits
about those freakin' medals.

"You should wear them. They were awarded to you and they

169

should be on your shirt."

"Hey, Jo, everyone will be wearing the same uniforms and we should all look alike. I don't need some medals on my chest to make me stand out from the rest. I just want to go unnoticed and get it over with."

"You should be proud to wear them," said JoAnne in a low voice. Bob didn't respond to her statement but eventually said, "Don't worry about the uniform. I'll take care of it after I get a soda. Hey, do we have any booze?"

"No, we don't," advised JoAnne. There was a bottle of rum in the closet but she didn't think Bob needed it.

Bob slowly prepared his uniform and thought about JoAnne mentioning the medals. Martin thought to himself that if the guys all wore their medals they would look like something out of a cop movie. Martin always liked that the New Jersey State Police had some of the most highly decorated officers and they all wore the same uniform without medals. The hell with egos.

Bob finally slept through the night. His body was finally catching up on some sleep.

He awoke at six in the morning, showered and for the first time in days was able to read the local newspaper. There was a story about the pending funeral and mention of the fact that police were still looking for the killer. JoAnne entered the living room and saw that her husband was reading the paper. "You haven't read the paper since Dave was shot. I kept them for you. They are all in the closet." She could see that Bob was beginning to cry. He threw the paper to the floor and sobbed uncontrollably. JoAnne sat next to him and hugged him. She didn't know what to say and she started crying. They both sat encircled by each other's arms crying like small children.

"I can't read anymore of the paper," said Bob. "I have to be present when they put Dave in a grave and I haven't even caught the bastard that killed him. I want this sucker in my hands so I can do Dave justice."

"You will catch him. You said yourself you would get him. I know you will," said JoAnne.

"You don't understand. The longer it takes the harder it becomes. I have to get this guy soon or I'll be looking for him for a long time. The job of catching him becomes harder as every day goes by. These newspaper people don't know shit and they make it sound like we aren't doing anything. I don't want to read anymore papers until I catch the bastard. I'll get him, Dave, I swear I will." Bob began to cry again. JoAnne knew that there was nothing she could say to help her husband. She continued to hold him until he got up to get a handkerchief. JoAnne picked up the paper from the floor and placed it in the closet with the collection she started the morning after the shooting.

Bob was standing in the bedroom wiping the tears away when all of a sudden he fell to the floor and started doing push ups. He didn't know why. It was as if he had lost control of his body and whoever was controlling it decided he needed exercise. Martin was counting each repetition out loud. When he reached forty he pushed out ten more and fell to the floor. The tears flowed once again as he mumbled, "I'll get him, Dave, I swear I'll get him." Bob was exhausted and emotionally drained. He laid there for a while and decided he needed another shower. JoAnne heard him showering and made up her mind she was not going to ask him why.

JoAnne looked at his uniform and realized that he didn't wear it very often, funerals and special occasions only. She was proud of her husband in or out of uniform and she was also proud of what he did for a living.

Bob exited the bathroom and quickly put his uniform on and prepared to leave the house. JoAnne knew he was early. He didn't have to be at muster until 9 o'clock. She also knew that he would want to get into work and review what may have taken place during the night. His mind was on the case and would be until the killer was caught.

Bob hugged and kissed his wife and told her he would see her at the funeral. She knew that he would find her even in all the confusion that would be taking place.

CHAPTER THIRTY FOUR

Martin arrived at the Police department at 7:30 and
immediately realized that the New Jersey State Police were
handling all calls in the Township of Lower. He entered
the rear entrance and observed State Troopers processing
individuals they had arrested for warrant violations and
minor offenses. The local scum bags were not able to bull
shit the troopers with promises of information or talk of
other violators. Local cops were always willing to cut a
break to the regulars if it would lead to something
worthwhile. Troopers knew that they could make some
arrests and get some stats under their belts. They weren't
beholding to any scum bags in this town. Chances were that
they would never be working in the township again. Martin
went to his office and as he did four or five Troopers
extended their condolences. Martin exchanged some small
talk and eventually sat down behind his desk and began to
review the paperwork from the day before.

This quiet time afforded him the chance to get things done.
He felt funny in uniform. He was glad everything still
fit. He didn't wear it very often. When he did he at
least wanted to look presentable. He pulled a shoe shining
kit from his desk drawer and slowly put a shine on the
black uniform shoes.

He was thinking of all the work that went into the funeral.
He remembered that Sergeant Rich Hooyman along with others
had been coordinating the funeral procedures. Many officers
had been assigned numerous tasks. They really had their
job cut out for them. The coordination of such an event
could be mind boggling.

There were thousands of cops and firemen expected to
attend. They had received confirmations from as far west
as New Mexico. Every state on the east coast was
represented. Police Officers always managed to show up at
these miserable occasions. He hoped that the Douglass
family would be able to handle the events of the day. He
knew it would be very difficult. Representatives of Lower
Township Police Department and the New Jersey State Police
had been working for the last four days trying to
coordinate all that had to take place. The entire funeral
was a large production. No one realized how much work went
into such an event everything from the funeral arrangements
to the parking of perhaps thousands of vehicles. Those in

attendance had to be fed and in some cases housed.

The fact that Dave Douglass had been a fireman also provided some problems with regard to coordination of the funeral. Both agencies wanted to provide a funeral befitting their fellow member. Each department wanted to take control of the funeral.

Martin started to hear people entering the Police department and for the first time looked at his watch. The time was 8 o'clock and he remembered that they were to report to the St. John of God Church at 8:45.

Martin heard an unfamiliar voice on the intercom, "Is anyone waiting for a Rocco DeNote?"

"Yeah, let him in," hollered Martin. He couldn't believe this dispatcher didn't know that Rock was a retired officer. The guy had been shot in the head in the line of duty. Now some shit brained dispatcher didn't want to let him in the building. Martin hurried to the door and opened it. Rocco was standing there and saw Martin glaring through the dispatch window at the dispatcher. Martin quickly realized that the person working the window was a relief dispatcher and she probably was not familiar with active officers let alone one who had retired.

"Rock, I'm sorry they kept you out here."

"Don't worry about it. I'm not," laughed Rocco. Martin and DeNote hugged and Rocco whispered, "Sorry to hear about Dave."
"Thanks, Rock." Both men had tears running down their cheeks. They patted each other as Lt. Don Lombardo began to hug both of them. Now all three men were sobbing. Rocco pulled away and fumbled through his pockets looking for a handkerchief. Each man then did the same and they began to get control of themselves. Small talk ensued. Rocco then asked, "What are we doing about funeral procedure for retired personnel?"

"That's easy. You go with us," said Martin. "I have an old badge you can put a black band on and hook it to your trench coat."

"Hey, Bob, if you don't mind I'll wear my old badge," said Rocco. Martin forgot that retirees maintained their old badge when they retired. Rocco pulled badge number thirteen from his wallet and Martin put a black band on it and hooked it to his trench coat. Martin remembered that the badge numbered thirteen had once been assigned to him. Everyone use to kid him about how unlucky it would be. Badges use to be handed to new guys when they were hired

and as they progressed in seniority they would receive a
lower number badge. That practice had ceased a few years
back. Now when a new guy was hired he kept his badge until
he was promoted to a higher rank. Martin thought about the
unlucky number thirteen.

Rocco on the other hand looked at badge number thirteen as
a red badge of courage. Rightfully so, he lived through a
point blank shotgun wound to his temple, with badge number
thirteen pinned to his chest. Rocco had been a cop's cop.
One who could be counted on, in every situation. He cared
about people and would do his best to take care of the
public. He went out of his way to treat the public as
human beings. Some cops found that impossible to do. Rocco
loved to have a couple beers with friends and converse
about whatever came to mind. Rocco was a thinker and was
one of those people whose eyes always told you his mind was
about ten feet ahead of what was coming out of his mouth.
Lombardo said that he would get Rocco to the funeral.
Martin took part in some small talk and then had to get to
the staging area.

Martin went looking for Chris Winter. He had told Chris
that he would travel to the funeral with him. Winter had
found two patrol officers who needed transportation and he
was talking to them. Martin talked to a couple of the state
troopers and a couple of guys from the county who were
standing in the hallway. Martin was thinking about Jack
Trombetta who was no doubt sitting in the church reviewing
in his mind what he intended to say about Dave Douglass.
The two investigators had been working together so long
that it seemed odd when they weren't together. They each
were able to function without the other but for some reason
they were almost like siamese twins when it came to getting
the job done. Things seemed to happen when they were
together feeding off of each others thoughts, ideas and
actions.

Martin then met with Jim McGowan who intended to man the
phones for a while and then go to the funeral. McGowan
indicated that Jack Reemer would be doing the same and that
they would arrange for someone to be working the case
during the entire time the Lower Township guys were away
from the police station.

McGowan had an idea that most likely the investigation
would slow up a little on this day but it could not come to
a halt.
McGowan knew Martin was uncomfortable because he was
leaving the center of investigative activity. McGowan also
knew that Martin and Trombetta would return to the Police
department as soon as they could.

Martin heard Chris Winter calling for him and advising that they were leaving for the church. They, along with two patrolmen, quietly entered the marked unit. They turned from Bayshore Road onto Townbank Road and immediately saw hundreds of vehicles parked on the roadway. Uniformed officers from other jurisdictions were handling the parking. The New Jersey State Police were answering all calls for service in the township. Cops from many departments from throughout the county would assist in answering calls during the entire day.

Police Officers were always willing to go the extra distance for each other. They all knew that the funeral could have just as easily been for one of them.

Martin observed that the officer directing them to the staging area was a member of the Delaware River Bay Authority Police. One lane had been left open and three lanes had been utilized to park police vehicles. Winter slowly drove past the vehicles and Martin looked to his left and stared at the place were Dave had been shot. The house that had been burned by the perpetrator was still ringed by the yellow police tape surrounding it. Martin thought to himself that it was almost sickening that the funeral was taking place so close to the location where Dave had been shot.

They were directed to the Church and quickly parked in the designated area. They had to walk past many vehicles and it suddenly struck them just how many different uniforms were walking around the area. Martin thought there must be two thousand guys here. He knew that more would be showing up. There was still about two hours to go before a procession of uniforms would enter the church to pay their last respects.

Cop after cop approached the Lower Township officers to extend their condolences. The morbidity of the meetings became monotonous. The Lower guys understood it but felt very uncomfortable with the exchanges. Martin noticed the many news vans at the church. He was uncomfortable with their presence. He also knew that they too had a job to do. Helicopters were flying overhead. Martin didn't look up to see the logos that may be painted on them. This was going to be a very long day. A day he knew he would never forget.

Martin saw his wife and some police wives she had caught a ride with to the church. The women had decided to travel together. They all knew that their husbands were going to be very busy during this damp chilly morning. Each, were hoping their husbands would be able to handle the events of what would be a long day. JoAnne really thought that a day away from the investigation would benefit her husband.

Bob Martin, on the other hand, would rather be finding Dave's killer. You didn't bury a cop without the killer being dead or in jail. Bob was hurt that the killer was not in jail....or even better, dead...

Bob told JoAnne and the girls where they had to sit in the church. They each were trying to find their husbands for some small talk and encouraging words. The thousands of uniformed officers were spending time trying to locate others they may have met in the past. These officers oftentimes had spent time in a Police Academy or an in service training facility. Perhaps they met at a union event or had been involved in an investigation that brought them together. Meeting old friends and colleagues always happened at the funerals of fallen officers. It made somber occasions somewhat tolerable. Martin was walking around in a daze. Cop after cop extended condolences and wished him well with the investigation.

Martin came across his mentor, retired Detective Sergeant Bob Douglass. They shook hands and Martin said, "Hey, Putt, how ya doing?"

"I'm alright, how about you?" asked Bob Douglass.

"Well, I'm hanging in there. This is a case I wish I didn't have to investigate," added Martin. "Yeah, I had to investigate a lot of crimes but never a cop killing."

"Any good leads?" questioned Douglass. Martin was embarrassed to tell the truth.

"Bob, we have followed every ridiculous piece of information along with the good stuff and we are no closer to locking up someone than we were on the first day," stated Martin dejectedly. "I need a big break."

"What did I always tell you?"

Martin immediately answered, "If a local pulled the job, you'll hear about it real fast. If not, you better look elsewhere. Believe me, Putt, I'm sure it isn't a local and there is a good possibility this scum bag is in New York City. I'm sure I'll be headed there in due time. I hope it is soon enough so that this sucker doesn't disappear." Douglass could see Martin was not happy with the investigation. He also knew he didn't want to sound like he was telling his protege to get his ass to New York.

"You'll get this guy, I'm sure. Just keep at it." Bob Douglass had all the faith in the world in Martin's abilities and cop sense. He knew that if the case could be solved, Martin would do it. He also knew that if Trombetta was working the case and if Martin could prevent him from killing someone, the case would have two bull dogs nipping, at the heels of, the perpetrator.

"Listen, Bobby, if there is anything I can do ask? I have access to private investigators and some national investigative agencies, maybe they might be some help," added Douglass. He had been a private investigator since his retirement and he was willing to provide whatever assistance he could.

Martin observed other retired Lower Township officers approaching and they all began exchanging greetings. He knew that everyone was going to ask him about the investigation. Television and news coverage teams were all over the place. A large assembly room at the church complex had been set up for coffee and donuts for the thousands of police officers.

It was evident that the news people were looking at the department patches on the sleeves of the police uniforms. They would spot a Lower Township patch and immediately begin to ask questions about the case or about Dave Douglass. Martin was talking to an officer from another jurisdiction when a camera was pointing at him and a newsperson introduced her self. "I was at the news conference and I recall that you are the case officer in the Douglass murder. Would you be willing to talk to me on camera and answer a few questions?" Martin did not like talking to news people and looked around hoping to find Trombetta. Jack liked being in the limelight and Martin would much rather Jack talk to this young lady.

"You look much different in uniform," she said, "I knew it was you when I saw the name tag."

Martin seemed uncomfortable. "Listen, I'm not one to talk to the media. No hard feelings, but I'm really not interested." Martin hoped she would just go away.

"Sergeant Martin, I know you can't answer any questions about the case. I was just hoping to get some information about your feelings with regard to the turnout here today. It is really a great display of togetherness among police officers."

Martin relented and said, "O.K., go ahead."
The camera light went on and the reporter stated, "I am speaking with Detective Sergeant Bob Martin of the Lower Township Police Department. Sergeant, could you explain the feelings you are experiencing today?" Martin looked at the

reporter and answered, "As you can see, there are thousands of police officers here today to honor a fallen brother. They have come from many states to offer their condolences and to pay their respects. It is a shame that when this many officers get together it is usually because of the tragic death of one of their own. We have come together to honor Dave Douglass and I am glad to see that so many officers have attended."

"Sergeant, do you have any idea how many officers are here today?"

"No, I don't, however, I would estimate the number will be in the thousands."

"Do you have some thoughts with regard to Dave?"

"Yes, I can tell you he always was there when you needed him and he would always go the extra step. He was very involved in the community and spent a lot of time involved in community based programs. He will be missed but he will never be forgotten." Martin finished the sentence and found himself on the verge of tears.

"Sergeant Martin, you are the case officer on this case. Is there anything you can say with regard to the investigation?" Martin was upset she asked the question but knew she couldn't help herself. "I can only say we have committed all available resources toward the apprehension and subsequent conviction of the individual or individuals that were involved in the murder of Patrolman Dave Douglass." The reporter knew that Martin was finished talking and as if on cue she said, "Thank you for speaking to me." Martin turned and walked away as the camera lights went off.

Martin walked out of the large building that was full of uniforms lined up for coffee and donuts. He exited and outside the door could see the vast amount of uniformed officers beginning to form ranks. The New Jersey State Police had a contingent of close to a hundred officers lined up. Martin thought how professional they appeared. Those guys always looked like they belonged in uniform. They took pride in their appearance. Martin looked around and observed a long line of civilians waiting to enter the church. This was a very fitting ceremony for Patrolman David C. Douglass.

Martin saw Rich Hooyman hurrying around speaking to various brass from the New Jersey State Police. Martin approached him and noticed he was speaking to Lt. Hay. Martin knew Hay was the funeral ceremony coordinator for the state police. They exchanged greetings and Martin asked, "Excuse me, Rich, could you tell me if they have a camera set up inside to record the ceremony? I think it would be a fitting remembrance for the family."

"I'm way ahead of you, Bob. He is already set up inside and he will also be doing some taping outside. He will be the only camera inside. We decided not to have any news cameras on the inside of the church."

"Just checking, Rich, I should have known you would have taken care of it."

Trombetta was inside the church with the officers that were handling the Honor Guard and pallbearer duties. He was sitting in a small room reviewing what he would say during the ceremony. Jack did not want to make any mistakes and he wanted to honor Dave in such away that others would be able to know and understand the man as he did.

Jack prayed that he would be able to honor the memory of Dave and that the Lord would allow him to get through the ceremony without interrupting himself with a flood of tears. Jack knew he would get emotional and that if he did it was the will of God. He continued to review his notes. The church pews were filling with dignitaries, friends, family, acquaintances and even people who never met Dave Douglass. They were all there to take part in this final tribute to a fallen Police Officer.

Martin observed a staff writer for the Atlantic City Press taking notes. He knew Meg Tornetta as a hard working journalist who handled news reporting for the southern part of Cape May County. She was busy taking notes and speaking to individuals to obtain insights into this momentous gathering of thousands of people. She wrote, "One by one, they came Thursday. Some to say goodbye to a friend, some to say goodbye to a brother. All to say goodbye to a man who gave his life for his community."

Martin was glancing at the sky. He was glad that the rain had stopped. It was a bit chilly but the sun was trying to peek through the clouds. Martin hadn't realized it but people had been waiting in line for more than ninety minutes to file through the church paying their final respects to the fallen officer. The church was filled to capacity and people were standing in the rear isles in an attempt to gain a spot to observe the proceedings.

People had been filing into the church since 9 AM. The viewing wasn't supposed to start until 10. The large amount of people necessitated a change in plans. The entire area around the church was a sea of blue uniforms interspersed with civilians by the thousands. By day's end over five thousand people paid their respects.

The Lower Township Police Department had filed into the Church at 1 p.m. They slowly marched to their seats and sat down on command. Every eye in the church was upon them. They all appeared to have faces of disbelief and humbleness was evident. People in uniform usually didn't appear to be humble. They usually had a look of confidence, almost a look of bravado. These people were hurting and their faces and demeanor showed the pain. They were sitting in front of the coffin and they tried not to look at it. None of the officers wanted to show their emotions. They were police officers. They were supposed to handle death situations in a professional and distinguished manner. None of them seemed to fidget in their seats. They continued to look forward and past the coffin that held their brother officer and friend.

The civilians in the church continued to watch the officers as if they were going to do something that the civilians would be expected to respond to. After all, police officers were expected to provide help to the public. The public seemed to be hoping to do something that would be constructively helpful. Everyone sat quietly.

The interior of the church was ringed with flower arrangements numbering close to one hundred. The flowers were arranged as police badges and fire emblems. There was an eerie silence as the Lower Township officers took their seats. The only sounds to be heard were the sobs and crying of the many mourners.

The Rev. Dozia Wilson began to talk about growing up with Dave Douglass. They had been boyhood friends while growing up in Cape May Point. The small town at the south end of New Jersey was the type of town where everyone knew each other. Dave had been brought up in the southern part, of Cape May County, and seemed to know everyone. He had been a security guard in the small town and during that time obtained a job at the Cape May County Correction Center. He knew he wanted to be a cop and while waiting to apply for testing for a local police department he took the job as a county corrections officer. He was well liked by his superiors. They liked the fact that he was always interested in bettering himself.

Dave would apply for any training that came along. Before long he had completed many different types of training classes. He continually strived to make his law enforcement resume as impressive as possible. Eventually he became a sheriff officer in Cape May County and while there served in many capacities. He quickly became a jack of all trades, a weapons instructor, dog handler and a training officer at the County Corrections Center. In his heart he always wanted to be a Lower Township police officer. His dream came true in 1989.

Trombetta recalled doing the background investigation on Douglass. Jack was impressed by all the training Dave had undergone while working for the county. Everyone Jack talked to indicated that Dave was committed to law enforcement and would be a conscientious cop. Dave was involved in all types of community activities. He always took part in programs for kids. He and his wife, Debbie, had operated the Cape May City Roller Rink for many years.

Dave maintained an avid interest in the midget football league to which his son belonged. He was a member of the Townbank Volunteer Fire Department and served as its president. Dave was always busy with some community activity. The day after Dave's murder a fire commission election had taken place and Dave's name was on the ballot. He was elected to the position.

Dave had been a member of the Lower Township Police Department for four years and prior had been a County Sheriff for thirteen years. Everyone in the church listened intently as the speakers talked about the life of Dave Douglass. Jack Trombetta sat quietly reflecting on what he would say. He was prepared, but wasn't sure if he could hold, back, his emotions.

Jack quietly prayed that the Lord would allow him to do justice to the memory of Dave Douglass. It was Jack's turn to speak and he walked slowly to the podium. Jack cleared his throat and began.

"There is no greater love than this - that one lay down his life for his friends. The community was your Dad's friend," Trombetta directed his words to Dave's three children who sat teary eyed and gazing. Their eyes focused on nothing in particular.

Trombetta stepped away from the microphone as tears began to stream down his cheek. He removed a white handkerchief from his pocket and tried to wipe the tears away. The tears continued to flow.

"Dave lived every minute of the day and he was always there when you needed him. He enjoyed life to the fullest and always made himself available to help anyone that needed assistance. Dave's favorite line was 'life is good and we're livin large.'"

Jack referred to the words of the Swat Team logo that Dave had helped design. "Honor, loyalty and courage, those words

were what Dave was all about. On that night, what was Dave
doing? Dave was being Dave. He was responding to a call
that had been dispatched to another officer. Dave was
responding because Dave was being Dave. Where was he? He
was there. He was always there when he was needed. That's
your Dad," Jack said to the children of Dave Douglass.

Jack went on to provide an analogy into the man, Dave
Douglass. He did so by comparing Dave's life to the three
word motto of the Swat Team. Jack made sure that everyone
walked away knowing that Dave was honorable, loyal and
courageous. Jack had set out to make people aware of
Dave's qualities as a police officer, a man and a father.
Jack did the job in a personal and poignant way.

Jack was handling his emotions as best he could. He
continued, "Whenever there was a problem and your Dad was
on duty he was there." Jack began to cry as did everyone
who knew Dave Douglass. Jack wanted Dave's children to
understand their Dad, the police officer. Jack's ability
to talk to kids was showing itself in a positive and
explanatory way.

Jack continued to provide insights into Dave Douglass.
When he finished, a procession of police and firemen
started to file past the casket in a quiet quick step
movement. Thousands of officers filed past in a reverent
manner. The procession, lasted almost forty five minutes.
As the thousands of uniformed personnel filed by the
members of the Lower Township Police Department looked
straight ahead.

Seated in the middle of the first row of Lower Township
officers sat Martin with tears streaming down his face. He
was sitting mourning the death of a friend and fellow
officer and he couldn't clear his mind of the fact that
even though Dave would be buried he couldn't be at rest
until the killer was found. Martin mourned for Dave but in
a sense felt sorry that he had not made an arrest in the
most important case of his career. Martin felt embarrassed
that there he sat feeling sorry for himself. This day was
to honor Dave and his memory not to be sitting around
feeling sorry for yourself, because a case hadn't been
solved.

Martin could not help but think about everything Jack had
said. Bob knew that Jack probably didn't think he had done
a good job putting his thoughts to words. Bob on the other
hand felt that his partner had come through once again.
Martin thought about telling Jack what a great job he had
done. Martin also knew that he probably wouldn't say a
word about it. At this stage in their partnership he and
Jack could just look at each other and thoughts and ideas

were conveyed. Telling each other what a good job they did was not important to these two men. They knew what each other was thinking. That fact alone made them a good team.

The Lower Township guys all sat solemnly staring forward. It was now time for them to pay their final respects to Dave. The rose to attention and slowly filed past the coffin containing the body of Patrolman David C. Douglass. They then slowly approached Debbie Douglass and offered their condolences and respects. Martin looked at Dave's lifeless body and in a low voice said, "Dave, it isn't over until we lock this scum bag up. We promise you it will happen." Bob was talking for himself and his partner, Jack Trombetta.

Martin then approached Debbie and as she sat he bent over and hugged her. They both were crying and Martin whispered in her ear, "I'm gonna get this guy and when I do you will be the first to know." The tears were flowing down Debbie's cheeks as she said, "Please, get him."

Debbie eventually stood and walked to the casket and pulled a blanket up to her husband's chest and kissed him for the last time. The entire church was silent as the casket was closed. The cover of the casket was supposed to be lowered slowly and quietly. Inadvertently, the casket cover crashed down with a loud noise. Everyone was stunned. Those with tears in their eyes cried out with the finality of the loud sound of the casket closing. Martin was startled by the sound and thought to himself it was Dave's way of bringing attention to the fact that it wasn't over until an arrest was made.

Slowly but surely the entire church emptied as the police personnel lined up outside for the mile long processional march to the Cold Springs cemetery. The members of the Lower Township Police Department stood four abreast, saluting as thousands of other police and fire personnel lined up for the funeral procession. Douglass' casket was carried out by members of his department. The American flag draped over it blew in the stiff crisp breeze.

The color guards and bagpipe bands lined up and the funeral march began. Lower Township led the march. A Lower Township police car, Dave's patrol vehicle, was first in line followed by the fire truck he was assigned to as a volunteer fireman. They were followed by five motorcycles. Next in line was the hearse which was surrounded by members of LTPD.

The uniforms seemed to line up in an endless sea of blue behind the hearse. Many civilians who had attended also fell in line behind the thousands of uniforms. The bagpipe band drummers played a steady, heavy cadence throughout the route to the cemetery.

Eventually the procession snaked its way to the grave site. The Lower Township police formed a line on two sides from the hearse to the grave site. The bagpipe band slowly began to play "Amazing Grace." Tears could be seen flowing down the cheeks of the seasoned and rookie cops and firemen.

Eventually the final words were spoken and the bugler played taps. Debbie was sobbing and her children sat crying. The reality of the finality of the circumstance had hit everyone. Dave was gone, never to be forgotten.

The flag was folded by Lower Township police and handed to the chief. Chief Don Douglass, his face pale and his steps almost in slow motion, presented the flag to Debbie Douglass.

The crowd slowly began to disperse as Debbie approached her husband's coffin and placed a red flower on it. Everyone said goodbye to a father, son, brother, police officer, fireman and a friend.

The large crowd slowly disappeared from the grave site in an almost eerie act of magic. A short time before thousands stood at the cemetery. Now the site was empty except for the cemetery personnel who would bury the coffin.

Two locations had been set up to provide food and drink for the thousands of people who had attended the funeral. Virtually every ounce of food and beverage had been donated as had the two halls that were utilized. Some of the officers in attendance found themselves drinking large quantities of alcohol in an attempt to forget what they had just been part of.

Martin and Trombetta went to the first reception site at the church. They found it difficult to do anything other than think about solving the case. They each walked around in an almost dazed like stupor talking to fellow officers and friends and not really paying attention to what was said by anyone.

Eventually Bob and Jack returned to the station house to check with the investigators and ascertain if anything new had come to light. Everything was status quo. They almost wished someone had solved the case in their absence. Jack Reemer and Gary Chan had been re-interviewing the workers from the restaurant to no avail.

Gary did indicate that one of the workers from the restaurant, Roy Choo, was being very cooperative and helpful. Choo was helping with translations of those dialects that Chan was not so fluent.

Bob and Jack sat down and in a short time their wives showed up at the station. Most of the Lower Township detectives had returned to the station after leaving the reception and their wives had followed them. They split up into small groups and found their way into the vacant offices. They all were talking about the funeral and the proceedings. There was food and drink in the dispatch office so the officers and their wives began to eat. Martin thought to himself that this investigation had sure put a hurting on his eating habits. He laughed at the thought. He should be worried about the case not his waist line.

It was decided that they should all attend the second reception site at the Townbank Fire Hall. They had put this off until last because they knew it would be a difficult time. This reception would be much more personal. Everyone would be local cops, fireman and family. The feelings would be intense.

Everyone knew it would be difficult to maintain and control their emotions. Bob and Jack managed to stay for about two hours and when they left they both stopped at the station one last time before going home. They quickly determined that nothing earth shattering had taken place. They left for their homes and for the first time they spent an extended period of time talking to their wives about what was going through their minds about Dave and the investigation. Neither of the investigators was coping very well with the fact that Dave had been buried but his killer had not been arrested. Bob and Jack prayed themselves to sleep.

CHAPTER THIRTY FIVE

Martin arrived at work at six in the morning on February 25th. The funeral was over and the entire service was like an unfinished book. It was difficult for Martin to put Dave to rest. Dave couldn't rest until the arrest was made. Bob had stopped at the Police department after the funeral was over the night before. He had spoken with McGowan, Reemer and Gary Chan. They had indicated that after speaking to six of the Chinese workers they had no real positive information that would lead them to the killer. Gary Chan, the FBI translator, had advised that he was having a problem with communication. Some of the subjects being interviewed spoke different dialects. Gary suggested bringing in another translator who might be able to assist.

The Feds were going to work on getting another agent to aide with the dialect problem. Martin remembered he had advised the Feds that a problem would probably arise due to the many dialects spoken. That was why he had obtained the dialects spoken by each worker. He had directed Detective Moy to obtain that information from the owner of the restaurant. Moy had done so and Martin had advised Jack Reemer. Reemer, however, didn't want to tell Bob he could only get one translator, assigned to the case. Reemer figured that at least they would have someone that could talk to some of the workers and they would figure out what to do next.

Martin sat at his desk and began to review the intelligence and crime stopper sheets. This was becoming a ritual. He was sick and tired of worthless information. It seemed that no one could provide information that would lead to the shooter. The frustration was becoming too much to handle. Martin realized that his frustration with the case was making him more and more miserable with every passing day. He hoped that he wouldn't alienate someone because of something he might do or say. This case was providing more headaches and heartaches than any case he had been involved with in his career.

Working undercover had provided challenges. Those challenges, however, could be confronted head on and you could deal with the issue. This case only provided dead ends. Dead ends aren't easy to deal with, especially when it concerns the murder of a friend and fellow officer.

Trombetta walked into the office and immediately began talking about how frustrated he felt. What a team, Martin thought to himself. Each discussed what had transpired during the interviews of the Chinese workers. Bob filled

Jack in on what he had learned from Reemer, McGowan and Chan.

McGowan arrived at the office and once again the investigators began conversing about the fruitless interviews. FBI Special Agents Gary Chan and Jack Reemer showed up right behind Jim McGowan and all the investigators were conversing about the interviews from the day before.

Gary Chan had spent the night at the Atlas Motel in Cape May City. The Satt, family, who owned and operated the motel were always cooperative and helpful to the local police departments. They always managed to find room for investigators no matter how booked up they were. They also would provide reasonable rates and on some occasions would not even charge for the rooms.

Chan began to explain to the investigators the background of many Chinese, living, illegally in the United States. Many of them paid $30,000 to come to the states and then worked to pay off the debt. Chinese gang members often ran the illegal immigration schemes and treated the aliens as if they owned them. In all reality they did. The immigrants would be placed on ships from mainland China and would live in conditions of squalor while on the boats. Once in the United States they would serve at the whim of the gang members who arranged their delivery into the U.S. They would work long and hard hours to repay their debt. Then they would hope to disappear into the population of the United States.

The vast majority of the illegal Chinese aliens were hard working people who were looking for a better life. Many would pay off their debt to the gangs and after much hard work start small businesses that would lead them to independence. The gangs, however, would often reappear in the lives of the aliens and utilize extortion and kidnaping to extract even more money from their prey.

Bob and Jack listened intently to Gary Chan's synopsis and both were very interested. They each felt that perhaps a Chinese gang had somehow been involved in Dave's shooting. At least it was something they could sink their teeth into to find Dave's killer, maybe.

The investigators reviewed and discussed the statements of the Chinese workers who had been interviewed the day before. They then formulated questions for those workers that would be questioned throughout the day. Jim McGowan had a county investigator assigned to take photographs and fingerprints of each subject they interviewed. They all knew that some of these people would be illegal's. They

187

assumed that the INS would be interested in those
individuals that did not legally belong in the U.S. of A.
Little did they know that their assumption would turn out
very wrong.

One, of the most, interesting items of potentially
important information that had been obtained the previous
day centered on two workers. It was ascertained that since
Dave's shooting two male Chinese workers had gone to New
York City and had not yet returned. They were due to arrive
for work as the investigators were meeting. Martin figured
that this was probably what they were looking for. He and
Trombetta asked Chan what the other workers had said about
the two men.

Chan advised that the two were from an area of mainland
China that provided most of the Chinese young males that
became gang members when they arrived in the United States.
The men were from the Province of Fujian. Chan described
the province as a fishing area that produced individuals
who seemed to gravitate toward illegal activities. Martin
and Trombetta compared what they were hearing to the
fishermen that lived and worked in Cape May County. There
were those who worked hard and were good citizens and then
there were those fishermen who only wanted to take part in
their next shipment of illegal drugs. The many docks in
Cape May County afforded drug smugglers a relatively safe
haven for their activity. No matter how many times
investigations would result in arrests of those individuals
there would be someone to take their place.

The Chinese gang members were much more organized and
deadly. Martin and Trombetta listened to every word Chan
had to say. They knew they were getting close to Dave's
killer. They knew the two men would not return to work and
that they would be hiding from authorities. Bob called the
owner of the Chinese Resturant and asked if the two workers
had returned. The owner, said that they were late and that
they probably would not arrive until around 7pm. He was
sure they had missed the morning bus from New York to
Atlantic City, but they'd show up on a later bus. Martin
and Trombetta figured he was wrong. He advised that as
soon as the two men arrived he would bring them to the
Police Department. None, of the investigators expected the
delivery of the two "gang members."

Martin assigned two detectives to transport the workers who
were scheduled for interviews. McGowan, Reemer and Chan
conducted the interviews and utilized the conference room
in the building next to the Police department A short time
later Martin and Trombetta were alone with each other and
their thoughts. They finally had something to investigate
that seemed like a good lead. They couldn't wait for the

two workers to return from New York City.

Throughout the day people were interviewed and leads were checked out. Both Martin and Trombetta knew that they had to keep their investigators busy. They didn't want them to have too much time to think about the fact that the case didn't seem to be gaining any ground.

Martin was going through the assignment sheets from the Twenty-third of February. He hadn't done so since the funeral and saw that Detective Ed Donohue had spoken to a bus driver that had recalled transporting an Oriental male sometime in the past month. The subject had been dropped off at the Townbank Road location and picked up at the same location.

The driver indicated that on one occasion the subject put a bicycle on the bus and on another occasion he had to assist the subject load luggage onto the bus. According to Donohue's report the bus driver would be able to provide the exact dates and times once he reviewed his log book. Martin called Donohue into the office to clarify the information.

Donohue relayed that the driver was a good witness and was pretty sure that on January 28th and on two times prior he had picked up the same subject at the Townbank Road location. The driver thought the passenger pickup was about seven thirty P.M. on each of the occasions. The description of the individual matched the description provided by Mr. and Mrs. Hillman. Martin could feel a weight being lifted from his shoulders. He could envision the two workers returning from New York City and one of them fitting the description as provided by the driver and the Hillmans.

Trombetta suggested, "How about the two guys don't come back from New York? If they are involved they would be crazy to return."

"Let's not think about that, Jack," said Martin. Martin didn't think they would return either. Why would they return if they were involved?

Trombetta reminded Martin that similar information had been received from another bus driver. This driver had recalled dropping off an Oriental on Townbank Road on the evening of the incident. Initially, he didn't think much of the passenger. Upon being advised by police investigators that the subject would have been picked up in Atlantic City he began to think otherwise.

The bus driver remembered that the passenger had a card that indicated he could not speak English. The driver also

remembered that the subject wanted to go to Townbank Road.
Martin couldn't figure out why he hadn't seen a formal
statement from the bus driver. McGowan walked into the
office for some paperwork and Martin asked him about the
bus driver.
McGowan advised that a county investigator had arranged to
meet with the driver at one in the afternoon. Martin
suggested that Lou Trowbridge, the composite artist, be
notified. McGowan indicated that the bus driver was sure he
could provide a good description of the subject's face.

Martin had obtained Lou's home number and caught him at his
home before he left for work. Trowbridge indicated that he
would be available at about three in the afternoon. Martin
figured that once the statement was completed Lou could
interview the driver to obtain a composite. Martin now had
two bus drivers who were providing some positive
information about a possible suspect.

Martin was looking through a file that contained telephone
bills for the Townbank residence. McGowan advised that he
had reviewed them and was in the process of obtaining
subscriber information on some of the numbers. There were
many calls to New York and a couple to Georgia. There were
also many calls to overseas destinations.

McGowan mentioned that a slip of paper found in the jacket
left behind by the perpetrator had a New York telephone
number, written on it. They were in the process of
obtaining subscriber information on that number. McGowan
also stated that the number found in the pocket did not
match any of those found on the telephone bill. Martin and
Trombetta began to talk about the importance of going to
New York City. They both figured the two subjects would
not return from New York and they would be on their way to
the Big Apple.

McGowan left the office to return to the interviews of the
Chinese workers that was going on in the conference room.
Jim entered the room and returned to his seat at the
conference table. He along with Reemer and Chan had
interviewed seven of the workers who could not speak
English. They had ascertained a lot of information about
the history of the workers and the restaurant. They had
not, however, received much information about a suspect.

McGowan was hoping that someone would indicate that the two
guys who were still in New York were bad individuals.
Everyone indicated they were hard workers and never got
into any trouble. McGowan did not want to believe them.
One thing drove him crazy about interviewing the Chinese
subjects. It seemed that you had to ask them pointed
questions with regard to every topic you wanted to hit

upon. If you asked them a question you could not expect an overview of their thoughts or ideas about the topic. You had to make sure you were asking exactly what you wanted answered. They seemed to qualify every answer they gave when confronted with a discrepancy. Getting information was time consuming and repetitive.

McGowan knew that these interviews were going to take forever. He also realized that these people would have to be re-interviewed as time went on. Jim was frustrated with their cryptic answers and the fact that Gary Chan had problems with some of the dialects. Jim McGowan knew that they were going to have to find other translators.

Chan seemed content with his findings and believed these workers had no idea who shot Dave Douglass. Gary Chan also hoped that the two workers would not return from New York City.

The people he was talking to were hard working immigrants who just wanted to make money to send home to family in China and various parts of the United States. Gary Chan wanted to find something positive he could tell Martin and Trombetta. He knew they were counting on him and he wanted to come through for them. The interviews went on into the early evening when the investigators finally broke for dinner.

Martin and Trombetta had reviewed every piece of paper that related to the case. They had been hoping all day that the translator would have some positive information. They were all sitting in the office eating sandwiches and talking about the interviews. It wasn't long before Martin and Trombetta were once again frustrated with the direction this case was taking.

They were thinking that nothing else could go wrong when the phone rang and it was the owner of the Chinese Resturant. Martin picked up the phone and Trombetta saw by the look on Martin's face that something was wrong. Martin hung up the phone and said, "Our two guys have returned from New York. They either are not involved or two of the most stupid criminals ever." Gary Chan could see the looks on everybody's faces that they had put all their hopes in the two workers.
Chan spoke, "Listen, guys, maybe they aren't the shooters but let's hope they know something." Reemer added, "Hey, you never know." McGowan looked up and stated, "One way or another we have to talk to them."

Martin asked Gary, "Aren't these guys Fujian or whatever you call it?"

"Yes, they are," stated Gary. Martin knew that Gary didn't speak Fuch and Gary knew what Martin was thinking.

"Bob, I found out from one of the other workers that one of them speaks my dialect also, so I will be able to speak with him." Gary was hoping he could establish a rapport with the one subject and utilize him to speak to the other. Gary had some knowledge of the Fuch dialect but he didn't want to stake his career on it.

They finished eating as the restaurant owner arrived at the Police Department with the two would be suspects trailing behind him. Martin met him at the front entrance door and instructed him to introduce the two subjects. The tall thin subject was Stevie Yuk and the second small stocky subject was Sieh Wong. Martin advised him to tell them that they were going to be interviewed and that they would be at the Police Department for some time. He did so and told them to follow Martin. Martin advised him that he did not have to wait and that the subjects would be returned to the restaurant when the interviews were completed.

Martin observed that each subject seemed to be grinning. They almost seemed to be enjoying the attention they were receiving. The restaurant owner said one last phrase to the subjects and after they responded he advised Martin what had been said. "I tell them they must speak truth and help you," he stated. "They say they will," he added. Martin looked at his watch. The time was 7:20 p.m. Gary Chan took both subjects into the chief's office and began his interview.

Martin, Trombetta, McGowan and Reemer sat in the detective office finishing their food and talking about the fact that the subjects probably weren't involved because they had returned. The frustration level was extremely high. Martin and Trombetta wanted to blow up on someone just to relieve some of the tension. However, neither of them realized that they seemed ready to do so. One hour had gone by when Chan entered the detective office and advised the investigators that he was finished with Sieh Wong and that he could be taken back to the restaurant.

"What did you get from him?" asked Trombetta.
"Nothing."

"That's freakin' great," said Martin in disgust.

"I am sure he doesn't know anything," said Chan. "Stevie knows some things and I want to spend some time with him alone."

"Well, get a patrol car to transport this guy back to the

restaurant," said Trombetta. Martin hollered to dispatch
and the subject was returned to work. Everyone had a look
of despair on their faces. They couldn't get used to set
backs. Set backs seemed to be the forte of this
investigation. Would they ever get a break in this case?
Every time they got their hopes up they were confronted
with another negative finding.
Trombetta couldn't help but think the investigation was
going nowhere. Nothing seemed to be going right. When
would a real break occur? One of these workers had to know
something. Maybe Stevie Yuk knew something. Hopefully
Gary Chan would be able to get Yuk to talk.

Gary Chan was interviewing Yuk and decided that he would
appeal to his sense of family. Chan advised Yuk that he
was going to bring in the murdered officer's relative.
Chan went to the detective office and advised Martin that
he wanted him to act as if he was a relative to Dave
Douglass. Martin agreed and they both entered the room.

Immediately, Chan began to speak and Yuk had a look of real
concern on his face. Martin could see that the subject
really seemed concerned with the hardship that the family
of Dave Douglass was going through. Yuk spoke and Chan
subsequently translated. "I told him that you were a close
relative of Dave's. He was sorry for your loss and he would
do everything he can to help you find the killer. Just sit
there and look sad. When I start to raise my voice look
like you want to kill somebody." Martin listened to Gary
and Yuk converse in Chinese for what seemed like hours.
When Chan raised his voice Martin knew it was time to go
into his act. It wasn't difficult at all for Martin to
look like he wanted to kill someone. He wanted to do just
that. Martin moved around in his chair to get Yuk's
attention and then stared at him with a look that made Yuk
wish he wasn't in the room.

The conversation between Chan and Yuk continued and
eventually Chan looked at Martin. "Bob, I told him you
were crazy over losing a family member and that you
wouldn't rest until the killer was brought to justice. I
also told him you were nuts and that sometimes you couldn't
be controlled. He said that he is on your side and will
help by doing anything we ask. So I want you to look at
him, smile and slowly nod your head up and down." Martin
did so and the subject had a small smile part his lips.

Chan also advised Martin that Yuk had provided information
about a subject named Yi Liang Liu and that the information
would be very helpful in identifying and locating him.
Chan also stated that the restaurant owner's wife and he
could provide a good description of Liu. Chan was
optimistic about the subject, Liu. Martin was hoping maybe

they had a lead that would take them somewhere. Martin
immediately thought of Lou Trowbridge preparing a composite
as soon as possible.

Chan indicated that he was sure Yuk was not involved in any
way but that he would be most helpful. Chan stood up and
indicated that the interview was over. He told Yuk that he
would be contacted to take part in a composite as soon as
possible. Yuk shook the hands of both investigators and was
returned to the restaurant. The time was 11:45 p.m.

Martin and Chan explained to Trombetta and McGowan what had
taken place with Yuk and began to formulate their next
move. They all decided that whatever would be done could
not be started until the morning. Gary Chan indicated that
he would not be available the following day due to other
commitments that couldn't be broken.

They were all excited about the possibility that Yi Liang
Liu may be a possible suspect and wanted to find him as
quickly as possible.

It was decided to use Roy Choo, a cooperative restaurant
employee, as an interpreter for the interviews that would
be conducted the following morning. Roy had been helpful
throughout the investigation and could speak all the
dialects. Roy Choo also seemed to have a genuine concern
for helping the investigators. The investigators had
decided to clarify some points of interest with the
restaurant workers and they knew they wouldn't need a
police translator to assist. They all put on their coats
and began to exit the station house. It began to snow as
they entered their cars.

Martin hoped the snow would stop and would not accumulate.
The last thing they needed was a major snow accumulation to
slow things up. Martin knew it would be a drag driving to
New York in the snow.

Trombetta was driving home oblivious to the heavy falling
snow. He couldn't help but think about getting to New York.
 He and Martin both knew that was where this case would be
solved. Jack thought about how he was going to influence
Martin to start pushing a trip to New York. Then he
remembered Martin had mentioned going to New York, but
when?

Reemer drove home slowly as he thought about the fact that
his FBI cohorts in New York seemed to be dragging their
feet. He wanted to tell Martin and Trombetta that things
were going full force but they weren't. He knew that he
wouldn't be able to placate those guys much longer.

McGowan was thinking about how he would tell the prosecutor
that Martin and Trombetta were going to New York no matter
what anyone said. Why did he have to be in the middle of
this mess? He knew everyone was depressed and frustrated
and wanted this case to come to a close.

Gary Chan had a long trip home and somehow knew that this
snow storm was going to give him headaches. The winter had
already produced more snow in North Jersey and New York
than they had in years. He sure hated driving in this
stuff.

They all reflected on what they thought should be done
next.
At least there were still things to do. The investigation
had not dead ended yet.

CHAPTER THIRTY SIX

The following week of investigative endeavors went by quickly. Saturday and Sunday had been utilized to re-interview the restaurant workers. All past and present employees that had been revealed by the restaurant owner and his wife had now been interviewed. However, the owner's still maintained that they had never fired anyone nor had anyone quit. The investigators knew that they were not providing the truth.

The workers had provided names of subjects who had left the restaurant. The only problem was the names were always nicknames and could not be identified or traced. The investigators had a page of descriptions and nicknames of individuals they could not locate. An all out effort was made to secure telephone records and review them for calls that may lead to the killer.

The legal system had placed road block after roadblock in front of the investigators as far as telephone records were concerned. They all began to call in favors that had been owed them at the telephone companies. They knew the court orders would be days in coming so they improvised. Before long they had phone records for two telephones at the restaurant and one telephone at the Chinese residence that had been burglarized and burnt.

They went to the task of obtaining subscriber information with regard to the numerous telephone numbers they had accumulated. Before long they had pages of numbers and subscribers that had to be contacted. However, they had to know exactly what to say. They may be talking to someone that knew the perpetrator and they did not want to alert him as to their intentions.

Martin and Trombetta were especially fixed on getting the restaurant owners to cooperate. They advised their detectives to put some pressure on the restaurant and bar owner that might bring about their cooperation. The Immigration and Naturalization Service was contacted in hopes that it would apply some pressure. The investigators really didn't care about illegals but hoped that pressure from such an agency would make the owners decide to cooperate.

The investigators also decided to contact the Labor Board and the IRS in an attempt to pressure the owner into providing all the information they had. It was evident that the owners weren't trying to protect an individual. They were attempting to protect their business.

What was it going to take to get them to cooperate with the investigation? Why would they hold back such important information? Both Martin and Trombetta felt that the owners were withholding information that would lead them to Dave's killer.

Martin contacted a friend and ex-cop turned Private Investigator, Dave Iannucci. Dave knew the owners of the Chinese restaurant. He had indicated that the owners had recently fired a cook for being too slow and a waiter because of a theft problem. Martin and Trombetta decided to have Gary Chan and Jack Reemer interview the restaurant owners to show that even the F.B.I. was involved in this case. The result of the interview revealed a list of three nicknames that the owners now remembered. Two of the individuals, a cook and a waiter, were already known to the investigators. They did not, however, reveal the name of the waiter that had supposedly stolen from them until they were confronted with the information. They advised they had forgotten about Vincent, a waiter they had fired because they thought he was taking money. Now the investigators had four nicknames of possible suspects, Chong, Chu, Liu and Vincent. Now all they had to do was find out who these people were. Liu still seemed to be the best of the four.

The investigators were doing everything they could to locate Liu. Every agency possible was being utilized. The State Department of Labor proved to be very helpful. A list, of all the employees, reported by the owners, for the last two years had been obtained and it was quite evident that he was not good at keeping records.

It was ascertained that restaurant workers came and went regularly and that New York Employment agencies were utilized to provide employees. The workers would be hired through the agency and provided a bus ticket to the restaurant. They would be given a place to sleep and would work fourteen hour days for fourteen days and then, be given, two days off. Most often they would travel to New York City by bus and spend their off days with family or friends in familiar surroundings. They received anywhere from $600.00 to $1500.00 per month depending on their abilities and expertise. The average pay at the restaurant was about $800.00 per month. The owner could keep overhead costs low when he was paying his employees such low wages for such long hours.

The investigators often conversed about what investigative endeavors had to be initiated. They would go over the same ground again and again. They had to be positive they left nothing out. There was no room or time for mistakes.

197

On Monday the 28th of February the investigators attended a
meeting at the Cape May County Prosecutors Office. The
County big wigs were in attendance as were representatives
of the F.B.I. and Lower Township Police Department. Martin
and Trombetta were interested in hearing what Gene Taylor
had to say relating to evidence. They were hoping he would
be able to provide some insights to the technical
laboratory testing that would be required.

Trombetta and Martin were admitted to the Prosecutors
Office and directed to a small conference room. Seated
around a large table were the Prosecutor, the Assistant
Prosecutor, Chief of County Detectives, Gene Taylor, Lt.
Jim McGowan, and Jack Reemer. Martin and Trombetta sat
down as the meeting began. The time was exactly 9am.
Coffee and donuts were available and Trombetta quickly
grabbed his share of each.

The Prosecutor turned the meeting over to his First
Assistant who immediately began to explain how he had
initiated an investigation into the lottery ticket that had
been found in the jacket left at the scene by the shooter.
The AP indicated that he felt that the perpetrator could be
located through this ticket. The investigators at the
meeting thought it was possible but not very probable.

It was known that the Oriental culture is very
superstitious with regard to numbers. It is also no secret
that many Asians engage in gambling. Many people play the
same lottery numbers over and over and it was hoped that
perhaps the perpetrator did the same. The killer of Dave
Douglass had a New York Lottery ticket in his coat pocket
with the numbers 01-03-07-08-18-38 and 02-05-14-16-17-32.
Captain Jim Rybicki of the Prosecutors Office entered the
room and advised that he had made contact with a
representative of the New York Lottery Commission and it
had been ascertained where the ticket was purchased.

Rybicki also stated that the Commission would provide a
listing, or history, of Lottery play with regard to the
numbers during the last few weeks. It was also mentioned
that perhaps other State Lottery Commissions should be
contacted in an attempt to secure a history of play in
regard to the numbers. The perpetrator may have worked in
other restaurants along the east coast. There was a remote
possibility that the perpetrator could be located through
his use of the Lottery.

Reemer then began to discuss what the F.B.I. was doing in
regard to the case. He advised that Taylor would be taking
all the evidence to the F.B.I. lab for testing and
analysis. He also provided a quick review of what

information had been obtained during the interviews of the Chinese restaurant workers. It appeared that he was finishing his presentation so Martin directed a question to him.

"Jack, what's the story with what we asked the Feds in New York to look into?" Martin was referring to telephone subscriber information, interviews of Asian employment agency personnel, checking the store where the Lottery ticket had been purchased and checking into the origin of the key found at the scene. The Feds had also stated they would try the key at some of the addresses that came up on the subscriber list. Martin knew that none of the tasks had been completed. If they had the Feds would have advised. It was time for Reemer to pay for the sins of his New York partners.

"The New York Office hasn't got back to us at this point." Jack Reemer knew that his statement would not be accepted without a reply. He was getting embarrassed.

"I think at this point we should be sending some people to New York," said Martin. "We can't wait for them to get free time to spend on our investigation. We should hook up with some New York cops and get this show on the road." Martin knew that he was bringing up an unpopular issue. The county wanted to give the Feds ample time to conduct their investigation. Martin and Trombetta were tired of waiting for results.

"Ya know, Bob is right," stated Trombetta. "We are wasting time. Dave's shooter will be back in 'friggin' China by the time the Feds in New York get around to doing something."

Trombetta thought for a few seconds and added, "We should also be thinking about initiating a task force if this investigation looks like it will go on for a long period of time. We have to be planning for the future and everyone has to be doing their share as quickly as possible. If they can't then they shouldn't be involved." Jack was going to make them commit to a mode of action.

McGowan agreed with Martin and Trombetta but he knew that the prosecutor wanted to provide the Feds with ample time to complete their tasks. McGowan interrupted, "Jack, Bob and I have been talking about getting NYPD involved in this investigation. It is their city and they know what goes on in it. We have made some preliminary contacts and they indicate that they are more than willing to do whatever they can."

"This is a major investigation and we have to conduct it by the numbers. The AP is handling this case as far as legal counsel and we feel that the Feds should be involved in every aspect possible. There is a lot of evidence involved and they will get it all. I don't want to alienate them by circumventing the New York Office," the prosecutor sternly stated.

Jack Reemer could see that Martin and Trombetta weren't happy with the prosecutor's statements. He also knew that neither of the investigators really cared what he had to say. Once they made their minds up to do something they would do it. He was right.

Reemer tried to calm them down. "There is an Asian Task Force comprised of NYPD and FBI guys. I have been advised that NYPD is aware of the incident and that they are talking to informants. The task force provides information back and forth so I'm sure my guys in the New York office will be notified of whatever NYPD finds out."

Martin and Trombetta looked at each other and their gazes indicated that they were going to talk things over and do something positive. The Chief then indicated that if the investigation became long term that he would coordinate a task force to maintain the investigation over a long period of time. Trombetta and Martin were glad to hear that but hoped that it wouldn't be necessary. They just wanted to find the perpetrator and make an arrest. The longer the investigation became the more difficult the case would become.

Everyone seated at the table wanted the same results. The ideas they had with regard to achieving those results weren't always the same.

Gene Taylor then began to review each piece of evidence that had been found. Martin and Trombetta were impressed with the findings. They knew quickly that even if a confession was not obtained from the scum bag shooter that they could still get a conviction. Gene Taylor and his evidence technicians had done a remarkable job. Gene indicated that he was attempting to identify each piece of stolen property that had been recovered. He advised that it was a slow tedious process because of the language barrier. Gene provided insight into the technical aspect of the evidence with regard to DNA and numerous blood samples that had been recovered at the scene. Gene indicated that he was sure that he had found two different blood samples. He was sure one was Dave's and had to assume the other belonged to the shooter. Gene had found human hair, fibers, clothing, and shoe prints. The evidence list seemed endless. They just had to catch this guy and Gene Taylor could make the case. Both Martin and Trombetta finally felt some relief. They knew they had a lot to do

but at least they had a competent evidence technician who
could provide invaluable assistance.

Martin looked at McGowan and he too had a look that
indicated he felt some relief. McGowan had already heard
most of the information supplied by Taylor but somehow it
seemed like he was hearing it for the first time. In the
past he had been getting the information piece meal.
Hearing it all at once provided a new perspective. McGowan
was reviewing in his mind all that had to be done with
regard to follow up on the evidence that had been found.
Many of the items had already been verified, investigated,
retained for inclusion in the case or ruled out as far as
importance. McGowan thought mainly about the key found in
the yard by Mr. Elliot, the telephone number written on a
piece of a weekly issue Chinese newspaper, and the lottery
ticket.

McGowan had a feeling that these were key pieces of
evidence that had to be tracked down to their origin. He
knew that Gene Taylor would handle all the technical
aspects of the evidence testing and comparisons. He also
knew that he and Martin as case officers would have to do
their share of investigative work to clear up any problems
that might arise with regard to investigating the origins
of the evidence.

McGowan thought about the name Vincent. He remembered it
had been provided by the workers at the restaurant after
repeated efforts to get them to give information. McGowan
recalled that he and Martin had decided they did not
believe the subject had any involvement. McGowan just
decided to log the name in the back of his mind in case
other leads became exhausted. McGowan tried to pay
attention to Taylor as he continued to provide the
evidentiary material.

Taylor confidently and expertly reviewed each piece of
evidence. There was no doubt there was no better man for
this part of the investigation. Martin and Trombetta
continued to listen intently as did all in attendance.
Gene finished his presentation with an overview of what
tests would be conducted by the FBI lab. Taylor stated
that all of the items to be tested would be taken to the
lab after the meeting and that he personally would
transport and deliver them.

The meeting ended with the prosecutor stating that all was
going smoothly with the investigation and that major
advances were being made. Martin and Trombetta didn't feel
that way. They just wanted to get to New York City and
start beating the streets. They knew they would be able to
make better progress than the Feds.

McGowan spent the day clearing up paper work and writing reports. Reemer returned to his office with the hope of lighting a fire under the New York office. Martin and Trombetta returned to LTPD and coordinated various follow-up investigative assignments for the detectives.

Throughout, the rest of the week investigators obtained background information on Liu. It was verified that he had family in Atlanta, Georgia and further that he had indicated he was going to move there after he quit the Chinese Resturant. He quit on January 17 and had in his possession a Chinese Resturant business card that had the directions written on the back in English. Detectives now had one of the restaurant employees who advised that he had written the information on the business card and personally gave it to Liu when he had started employment in the middle of September. It was also ascertained that Liu spoke Mandarin and Fujin.

Trombetta could see that Bob was totally focused on locating Liu. He knew when to leave Martin alone and not bother him. Jack figured that as soon as he observed Bob slow up on his activity he would ask him more about Liu.

Martin was working with McGowan in an attempt to find out as much as possible about Yi Liang Liu. During the week they would engage the services of Jack Reemer and his contacts. They eventually ascertained that Liu had obtained a N.J. Motor Vehicle personal I.D. car and had provided an address on Delsea Drive, Millville N.J. A check of that location revealed that it was a Chinese restaurant.

They decided to use Reemers' contacts with INS. None of the investigators realized that they were wasting their time. They would eventually find out that the INS had a lot of records they might provide but as far as authority on the street the INS would prove useless.

McGowan indicated that Capt. Rybicki had made contact with New York Police department and that they could send a Chinese speaking detective. McGowan provided the telephone number to Martin and he immediately began dialing the number. Martin found himself speaking to a Detective from the Missing Persons Squad of NYPD. Martin had hoped for someone from a Homicide or Robbery Unit but he was willing to take whatever he could get. Martin provided directions to the investigator and advised him that all his expenses would be taken care of by Lower Township. The NYPD Detective advised that he would be arriving on Friday, March 4, in the early afternoon. Martin completed the call and contacted the Atlas motel in Cape May to set up a room for the investigator.

Martin was apprizing Jack of NYPD's pending assistance when the phone rang. It was Sergeant Bob Merriman. Merriman was a friend of Trombetta's who lived in Georgia. Jack had asked him to do some investigative leg work with regard to a phone number that had been traced to Georgia. They put him on the speaker phone. Martin and Trombetta listened while Merriman stated that he had tracked down the telephone number and had already ascertained that an individual by the name of Liu lived at the location and worked at a food business in the area. He also indicated that from what his people observed there was no one fitting the description of Liu as provided by Trombetta during an earlier conversation. Merriman stated that he would put a surveillance team on the business and residence for the night and advise his findings as soon as possible. Martin and Trombetta thanked Merriman and Jack hung up the phone.

Trombetta looked at his watch and stated, "I talked to Bob Merriman at about ten this morning. It is five in the evening now and this guy has already told us more in less than eight hours than the Feds in New York have been able to provide in two weeks."

McGowan walked in and they filled him in. He immediately suggested setting up a call from Stevie Yuk to the Liu residence in Georgia to find out if Yi Liang Liu was at the location. Reemer advised that Gary Chan would be arriving and could translate the conversation.

Martin was advised that there was a call for him. He picked up the phone and answered, "Detective Sergeant Martin, can I help you."

He immediately heard a familiar voice state, "Heah, Beuybindle, sorry to hear about your guy." Martin knew immediately he was speaking to his old partner Jack Harron. They often referred to each other as 'Beuybindle'.

It was their way of joking with each other about how, bureaucratic, police work and the resulting police paperwork had become during their partnership together. Jack Harron had been the type of guy whose company you would want if stranded on an island. He was McGyver before McGyver was on television. He could make anything you needed out of anything you had on hand. He was another guy who always took Martin home for lunch and dinner before Martin was married. Jack and his wife Pat were two more people that should have claimed Martin on their income tax.

"Heah, Beuybindle, thanks for calling. How's, Florida and what are you doing with your life," said Martin?

"I didn't call to talk about me. I wanted to tell you to keep pluggin'. You'll get this shit head. Just hang in there," stated Harron.

"Heah, Jack, I appreciate the call. I'm going to get the scumbag. I just don't know how long it's going to take."

"Are you the lead on the case? Is the County givin ya' any shit? Don't let em' run your show." Jack Harron was on a roll and Bob thought he hadn't changed a bit since he left police work.

"Yo, Jack, you know me I'll do what I have to do and I got Trombetta to help."

"Oh, shit, you are in good company. You know, Trombetta, he'll do anything for God, country, family and friends," said Harron as he laughed.

Martin knew Harron was right. Trombetta always had said the same thing and lived by that credo.

"Well, Beuybindle, get busy. I just wanted you to know I was pullin' for ya', and don't take any shit from the County.
Don't do anything stupid and loose your pension over it," added Jack Harron.

"Thanks, Beuybindle, take care," said Martin as he hung up the phone. He was glad to hear from his old friend and partner.

The investigators went about tying up loose ends throughout the rest of the evening. Chan eventually arrived at about nine at night and Yuk was picked up at his employment to take part in a consensual intercept of his conversation to the Liu residence in Georgia.

Martin began setting up the equipment as he and Chan went over the questions they wanted Yuk to ask once he was talking to someone at the Georgia residence. Yuk arrived and Chan began conversing with him and explaining what the investigators wanted him to do. He immediately agreed, signed the consensual intercept forms, as required by the prosecutors office, and the telephone call was made.

Martin listened intently as Yuk conversed with a subject who was the brother of Liu. Gary Chan paid close attention to what was being said and was trying to keep Martin filled in on the conversation. It was quickly determined that Liu was not in Georgia and was believed to be in New York or

New Jersey.

Gary Chan reviewed the conversation with Yuk and
subsequently Martin prepared the tape for the next
conversation to the New York number. Yuk made the call and
found out Liu was no longer staying at the number but was
possibly working in North Jersey at a Chinese restaurant.
The problem was that no one was sure. Yuk was told to
indicate that he may be able to find Liu a job and that if
anyone at the New York location was to see Liu they should
have him call Yuk.

It was also indicated the Liu still had personal belongings
at the New York location and that they were sure he would
be returning. They advised Yuk they would pass on his
message.
Upon completion of the call the tape was rewound and marked
as evidence and provided to Chan. Gary indicated that he
wanted to have it reviewed because the Fujin dialect had
been used throughout the conversation and that he wanted a
second opinion on exactly what was said.

Martin advised Chan to explain to Yuk that it was very
important for him to contact the police as soon as he heard
from Liu no matter what the time or place. Martin gave Yuk
a business card and included a private number. Yuk was
told to have Roy Choo assist him whenever he called the
investigators.
Yuk was returned to his place of employment. Martin and
Chan advised McGowan, Trombetta and Reemer of the findings
and all the investigators called it quits for the night.

Martin made the trip home reflecting on what had been done.
He prayed out loud that Liu would contact Yuk and that
investigators could get their hands on him. Martin thought
to himself how deserted the roads were on the ride to his
home. Martin couldn't remember the last time he arrived
home at a decent hour. When was the last time he had
dinner with his wife, the last extended conversation with
JoAnne or Tara? Martin was thinking to himself that he was
not even sure about the last time he and JoAnne had made
love. He laughed to himself. He must really be busy. Sex
hadn't been on his mind. He made a mental note to ask
JoAnne about the last time. He usually didn't forget
something that important. Apparently he had more important
things on his mind.

Martin passed Trombetta's home and saw Jack was home and
that the house was dark. Jack must have hopped right into
bed. Martin made a mental note to ask how Jack's sex life
was coming along. Bob started to think maybe he was
abnormal. He parked the car and entered the house. JoAnne

was still awake and in the mood to talk. It seemed as
though they had not had many informative conversations
since Dave was killed. She knew that he should talk about
what he was feeling. She also knew that Bob never told her
much about any case he was working on. He always
maintained that what she didn't know couldn't hurt her.
JoAnne, however, loved to be in the know.

"Hi, hon, how ya doing?" said JoAnne.

"I'm okay. Why are you still awake?" questioned Bob.

"I wanted to see you and see how things were going."

"Well, we are making headway but haven't arrested anyone
yet," replied Bob. JoAnne knew that Bob had just finished
the conversation on that topic and that she would hear no
more.

"How is Jack holding up?"

"Well other than wanting to kill every Chinese man we see
and burn every Chinese restaurant in the county he is doing
fine."

JoAnne hugged Bob. He was on his way to the bathroom as she
was telling him to take a shower. He wasted no time in the
shower and as he was getting out to dry off JoAnne entered
the bathroom and he was quick to see that she was naked.

They embraced and in due time they found their way to the
bedroom. The only thing on their minds was each other.
The love that they felt for each other was overwhelming as
was the physical attraction. They made love, eventually
falling asleep in each other's arms.

Bob was wide awake at five in the morning and JoAnne was
awakened by his movement. Bob turned to her and said,
"Thanks for last night, I needed that."

"You're welcome, Hon Bun."

"We hadn't made love for two days and I figured I would do
my wifely duty." JoAnne laughed as she said the words. Bob
didn't remember the lovemaking that had happened two nights
ago. It must have been enjoyable. It always was. Boy he
did have a lot on his mind. He was even forgetting whether
or not he had taken part in a sex act.

It was March 3rd, 6:15 in the morning when Martin drove to
work thinking that the investigation into Dave's shooting
was going nowhere. When were they going to get a break?
Something had to happen. The FBI was supposed to be trying

the key in the doors of all the known locations in New York
City. They were supposed to have checked the hardware
store where the key had been made. They were also supposed
to have put the word on the street for information. Jack
Reemer had pulled out all the stops to get assistance from
the Feds in New York City. Martin was upset that nothing
positive seemed to be happening.

Trombetta was lying in bed unable to sleep and decided he
might as well get ready and go to work. The thought kept
going through his head that it appeared the Feds in New
York were useless. He decided to mention to Bob that they
had to do something to get the Feds on board. What was
holding them up? It seemed that every time he or Martin
mentioned something to Reemer about the Feds in New York
there was a discomfort in Reemer's voice.

Martin arrived at the Police department at about 6:25 am.
He entered the building and thought how desolate the
parking lot seemed to be. It was nothing like the week
before. The only police vehicles and equipment at the
Police department belonged to Lower Township. The mass of
officers that had been at the Police department the week
before was gone. Martin thought to himself how it almost
seemed like he was on his own. He knew, however, that he
could get all the help he needed if he asked. Martin was
languishing in his frustration. He unlocked the door to
the office and noticed that there were no Crime Stopper
bulletins or intelligence forms in his mail box. The
information from the patrol guys and from the public had
ceased. Martin sat down at his desk, leaned back and
stared at the ceiling.

He was hoping that Yuk would get a call from Liu. This
case needed a break. Martin knew that they were going to
have to keep digging and that sooner or later a lead would
direct them to Dave's killer. He was thinking about New
York and the fact that they were still waiting to hear what
the Feds had uncovered.

Trombetta entered and caught Martin in a trance like stare.
"Hey, are you alright? You look disgusted."

Martin looked at Jack and said, "These stinking Feds are
getting on my nerves."

Trombetta immediately replied, "I was thinking the same
thing. As a matter of fact I was going to mention to you
that we should give up on those guys in New York and do
what we have to do."

"Well, I agree this is bull shit. I say we go to New York
and do what we have to do. I have been trying to let the

county and the Feds work the New York connection. McGowan
said that the County had turned over New York to the Feds.
It made sense at the time, but, not any longer." Martin
was on a roll. Trombetta loved it when Martin was like
this. It usually meant he was going to tell somebody off
and it usually worked out where Jack didn't look like the
bad guy.

Trombetta liked it better when everyone liked him. Jack
cared about the perception. Martin cared about getting the
job done no matter what others might think. Trombetta could
be the same way but he had to get mad first.

"Is McGowan coming here today?" asked Jack.

"Yeah, about ten or eleven," said Bob.

"How about Reemer?"

"I think he said he would be here this afternoon."

"Well, when they get here we will tell them what we intend
to do," stated Trombetta.

"We'll meet with the Captain and the Chief when they get
in," said Martin. "We better run this by them."
"They won't care," said Trombetta.

"Yeah, you're right. I just thought it would be nice," said
Martin as he smiled.

Both men began to review reports and paper work pertaining
to the case. Martin was looking at the composites that had
been drawn by Trowbridge. He knew that two of them were
going to be real close likenesses of the suspects. The
other had not even been released to the media or even other
officers. Both McGowan and Martin had made it real clear
that to release that composite would be a mistake. They
both knew it would not resemble the individual they were
looking for.

Neither of them knew that Capt. Rybicki had already sent
the composite to New York and that Sergeant Joe Piraino was
passing it around. Trombetta observed Martin looking at the
composites and thought to himself how Martin seemed to be
spending a lot of time gazing at the two ever since they
had been completed. "You really think they are good
likenesses, don't you?"

"Yeah, I sure do. We are going to find out that both of
these guys are involved," said Martin.

"It sure looks that way," said Jack. "It sure seems odd,

though, that the old chubby guy did the shooting."

"The young guy set up the burglaries and the old guy pulled
them off. None of the workers can identify the composite of
the old guy. They all agree, though, that the young guy is
Yi Liang Liu," said Martin.

"Hey, Bob, did Stevie Yuk get back to you about contacting
Liu?"

"Yeah, he went to New York after work on Saturday night. He
came back yesterday in the afternoon. That guy, Roy Choo,
the one that speaks English, brought him to the station and
acted as translator. Stevie said that he left a message
with Liu's roommates to tell Liu to contact him down here
at work as soon as possible. I told Stevie to tell him he
needed another job and that perhaps he could find him one."

"I think this guy, Stevie, is trying to be helpful. So is
Choo," Martin commented.

Jack was quiet for a few moments and then said, "I wish the
owner was more co-operative. He is too busy trying to cover
up his illegal workers. He just wants to stay out of this
mess so it doesn't affect his business. From what I
understand his business has gone down the tubes since the
shooting. I hope it's true. He deserves to go broke."
Martin readily agreed.

"Well, we had Yuk make phone calls and had him go to New
York and leave messages for Liu. Hopefully, we will hear
from him," added Martin.

Jack looked confused. "When did you have him call New
York?"

"Last night, before we left he called New York and
Georgia."

"That's right, I forgot. I must be going goofy," Jack said
and smiled. Martin was thinking that Jack had gone goofy
long before this case.

Martin heard the Chief and Captain next door and mentioned
to Trombetta that they should speak to them about traveling
to New York. "Yeah, before we do that I want to call
Merriman in Georgia," Trombetta said. Martin remembered
that he was the guy Jack had called to check on one of
Liu's relatives near Atlanta, Georgia. Merriman was one of
Jack's contacts from the FBI National Academy. Jack looked
at his watch and saw that the time was 8 am. He figured
Merriman would be in the office.

Bob knew that Jack had Sergeant Bob Merriman of Chatham County Police department checking on Liu's relative and on the location where he worked and lived. Jack had faxed a composite of Liu to him when it was determined that Liu may be in Georgia looking for employment. Both investigators knew that there was a possibility that they may even be traveling to Georgia if Liu was found there.

As an afterthought Jack asked, "Hey, didn't I already get a call from Merriman about the composite?"

"Yeah, you did, but we faxed him the other one after your call," said Martin.

"Man, I'm starting to lose it," replied Trombetta.

These men had so much on their minds that they were having trouble remembering what they had completed and what still had to be accomplished. They each knew that such action was not a good sign. Damn, they wanted to get this case over with and make an arrest.

Stevie Yuk, however, had originally thought that Liu had been in Georgia but may have returned to New York City. The calls indicated that Liu had probably not been in Georgia but the possibility still had to be checked out. It was fortunate that Jack had the contact in Georgia to follow up on the Liu connection in that state. It saved a lot of time.

Both Martin and Trombetta couldn't believe how these aliens traveled around the United States in search of jobs. The majority, of them, couldn't speak English. It amazed both investigators that these people found it easy to travel from state to state and secure employment. The majority of them were hardworking people who just wanted to get ahead.

Jack made the call to Georgia and had to leave a message. His friend was not at work yet. Jack laughed and said, "I'm at work. Everyone should be at work."

Bob and Jack entered the Chief's office and sat down. The Chief knew that these guys seemed unhappy and figured he would hear the entire story. They each went on for about fifteen minutes before Don Douglass spoke. "Listen, I told you guys to do what you had to do and go where you have to go. Don't worry about what it is going to cost. Just don't get arrested in some other jurisdiction for doing something stupid."

"Don't worry about that, Chief," said Trombetta.

"Hey, Trombetta, don't tell me that if both of you guys get

pissed off at somebody you might not do something goofy.
Martin handcuffs people to trees and leaves them," said
Douglass with a grin. Martin knew what he was referring to
and didn't say a word.

Martin and the then Detective Sergeant Don Douglass had on
one occasion chased a juvenile burglar into the woods.
This kid had been giving them grief pulling burglaries for
about four months into the summer. Martin and Douglass
happened onto a burglary in progress and this kid came
running down the street. They chased him down in the
woods. Both officers realized that they didn't have enough
to charge the kid for burglary. Martin figured that the
only justice available was whatever he and Douglass could
render. So at just about dusk Martin had the kid put his
arms around a tree and he handcuffed him. The officers
waited until it got good and dark and then returned to
release their prey. The kid never pulled another burglary
and never appeared before a judge. The officers had done
their part to rehabilitate a chronic offender.

Martin later told the kids parents what had transpired.
They believed that the incident was instrumental in having
their son get his life in order. The worst part about the
incident was the fact that the kid was allergic to poison
ivy. No one noticed that it was growing at the bottom of
the tree. The kid made the mistake of sitting down at the
base of the tree. He was wearing loose fitting shorts.
His manhood was rendered useless for awhile due to his
allergic reaction. Sometimes justice prevailed. Martin
always said he would write a book about the incident. For
some reason he never got around to it.

Both the Captain and the Chief wanted the investigators to
take this investigation on the road. The administrators
felt it would be necessary to do so to shake things up a
bit. They also knew that they had two very frustrated
investigators on their hands. Perhaps if they were to go
to the big city they could take some of their frustration
out on someone who probably deserved it.

The Chief told Martin to take what ever money would be
needed from the investigative funds that were available.
He also supplied them with a credit card to be used for
lodging. "If you guys run out, of money, let me know,"
stated Chief Douglass. "I'll get it from the treasurer. I
had a lot of promises from Council Members and I'll
probably have to take them up on those promises."

"Just try to stay out of trouble and call home now and
then," added Captain Maher. He knew that New York City was
a far cry from Lower Township. He also knew that these
guys would not be intimidated by the 'Big Apple'.

Both men walked from the room as Jim McGowan was walking toward the office they had been sharing. "Pack your bags, Jim, we're going to New York," said Trombetta.

"Why?" asked McGowan.

"We're going to catch a bad guy," chuckled Martin.

"Yeah, Jim, somebody has to go. The Feds aren't doing anything up there. Even Reemer is embarrassed," stated Trombetta.

"I just came from a meeting with the prosecutor and he maintains we should just sit back and wait for the Feds to do their job," stated McGowan.

Jack then said as his face got red, "Screw that shit head. We had it with him. Jim, it has been over two weeks since we asked the Feds to check on the key. We aren't waiting for other agencies anymore. This is getting ridiculous. Martin and I are going to get something happening no matter what it takes. If we piss off some people in the process, so be it."

McGowan knew he was wasting his time and that Jack was right. The prosecutor's office had advised the Feds that they would await their response before they made any other moves in New York City. McGowan hated to be in the middle of this, especially when he knew that once these guys got their minds set on something they were committed.

"Hey, Jack, today is the day you call your buddy in New York. Let's get this show on the road," said Martin.

"Sounds good to me, Bob Bo," replied Jack.

McGowan wanted to slow them down a little. "Well, let's go over some stuff and see what we need done in New York." Jim was hoping that they would listen and understand that perhaps the Feds were more suited to get things done. He knew he had to do it in such a way that these guys wouldn't be offended. Jim knew that if he pissed them off they would get goofy.

McGowan felt like he was trying to calm down two irate teammates who were upset with the coach's directions and had a better idea on how to win the game. Jim, however, also thought that the Feds had dropped the ball and hoped somebody would get them back in the game.

One of the patrolmen walked by and mentioned that lunch had been delivered. McGowan knew that this was an opportune

time to change the subject. The three were making
sandwiches when Reemer entered the dispatch office and
started putting together a platter. Trombetta kidded
Reemer about his arrival time and then asked if the Feds
would ever spring for lunch. Reemer laughed and said, "The
check's in the mail." Bob and Jack had heard that one from
the Feds the entire time the Gambino investigation was
underway.

Martin and Trombetta could never figure out how the Feds
got things done. They always had so much bureaucratic bull
crap to go through. Martin always got a kick out of all the
forms that the Feds had to fill out. They had to put
everything on paper. They had so many forms that you
needed an index to figure out when each form was needed.
Jack always told Martin he should write a book about the
Gambino Case. Jack figured Bob would be able to supply a
pretty funny rendition of the case. Jack got a lot of
laughs listening to Bob relay the conversations he had
monitored while sitting on the wire.

Bob had been cooped up in a room with three other guys
monitoring telephone conversations of members of the
Gambino family. There was also a translator on the wires
twenty four hours a day. Martin told some pretty funny
stories about what he had heard on the telephone. He would
always say that the most interesting information he
obtained was the many recipes for Italian food that the
female members of the Gambino family had provided each
other over the phone. Jack was right. Bob should write a
book about that investigation.

The men loaded up their plates and returned to the office.
Martin asked Reemer, "Hey, Jack, have you heard anything
from your people in New York?" Trombetta hoped he would
say yes. He knew Martin would embarrass him if he didn't.

"I have a call into the office and I'm waiting for a call
back," answered Reemer. Trombetta figured Martin would
accept that statement for the time being. He was right.

McGowan changed the subject by mentioning, "Bob, have you
heard from Stevie Yuk this morning?"

"Not yet. It's still early."

"I hope something comes out of that," Reemer commented. "I
spoke with Gary Chan last night. He said he met with Stevie
in New York over the weekend and that he gave him some
money in hopes it would influence his assistance."

Trombetta laughed, "How many forms did Gary have to fill

out?"
Reemer also laughed and answered, "Jack, sometimes we fill out the forms after the fact."

"Hey, Bob, did you hear that? Sometimes the Feds bend the rules."

"We have a form for that," Reemer added.

McGowan and Reemer began to review the information obtained from all the interviews they had conducted. Martin and Trombetta listened and questioned various aspects of the interviews. It was indicated that Stevie Yuk was becoming most helpful and had provided some key information in regard to Liu. It had been revealed that the business card that had been found at the scene had been in Liu's possession. He did not speak English and he utilized the card to provide bus drivers with information as to his destination when using the transit system.

Yuk also felt that Liu was an honest man and a hard worker who was trying to make money to pay off the debt he incurred when he came to the United States. Yuk did not believe that Liu was involved in any way with criminal acts or wrong doing of any type. The investigators hoped Yuk was wrong.

The investigators sat around discussing whether or not they had utilized Yuk in the most productive way. They all agreed that having him make the calls last evening had been a good idea and hoped it would lead to something positive. Trombetta decided it was time to call Merriman again down in Georgia.

Trombetta was dialing the phone when Reemer stated, "I can have my people in Georgia start watching the location. Did we get a location on the telephone number yet? I can start the paperwork for a court order to the Telephone Company." Reemer was trying to be helpful but Martin knew Trombetta's phone call had already accomplished more results in Georgia than the Feds could accomplish in such a short period of time. Neither Reemer nor McGowan knew that Trombetta and Martin had already started the wheels turning in Georgia. Trombetta had done so when the possibility was only being discussed. He and Martin both knew they had done the right thing. They also knew, however, that other investigators thought they should have waited.

Martin watched Trombetta place the phone on hold and get up to go to another room. Jack was leaving the room and glanced at Martin as if to say, "I'll take care of Georgia right now. Don't get the Feds involved down there." Martin caught the glance and never answered Reemer.

Martin changed the subject. "Hey, Jack, did your buddy at INS ever come up with a photo of Liu?"

"I'll call him now," said Reemer.

Martin left the room to find Trombetta who was motioning for him to enter the detectives' office and sit down. Martin listened to Trombetta talking to his friend in Georgia.

Jack interrupted Merriman, "Bob, I told him about the phone call last night. He still says he will continue to watch the place and see if he can find anything we may be able to use."

"Jack, give him the phone number of Liu's relative and see if he can find the place. Then maybe they can set up surveillance and look for our boy." Martin could feel himself getting excited over the possibility that Trombetta's Georgia contact was a hustler that could get things done.

"Bob, I did that the last time we talked." Martin thought to himself and then said, "You're right, I forgot." They had made so many calls and spoken to so many people that they were both forgetting what they had done. They each knew that their forgetting things, was dangerous. They both had a lot on their minds.

Jack extended his thanks to Merriman and hung up the phone. "Bob, he will do what has to be done. He will get back to us real quickly. I know him and when he says he will do something, he does." Martin trusted Jack's judgement as if it was his own. Now they just had to wait.

Bob then advised Jack to give the guy in New York a call. Martin knew that the investigation was going to New York City. Jack called Ernie Naspretto. Jack figured that this guy could get him some help in the Big Apple. Jack listened while the phone rang and an answering machine clicked on. Jack left a message.

Jack had advised Bob that Ernie was a normal good guy. Bob and Jack each used the word "normal" to indicate that someone was like themselves in most respects. If Jack said the guy was normal that's all Martin had to hear.

Martin and Trombetta had worked together long enough to accept without question each other's like or dislike of most people as the gospel. Both men had the ability to decide who was worth knowing and who wasn't. Jack, however, was not as vocal when it came to letting them know they

weren't worth knowing. Martin on the other hand took up
Jack's slack. Oftentimes, Jack was embarrassed by Bob's
vocalizations of distrust and dislike for someone. Bob
didn't mind telling them to their face. Jack had to be
angry to do so. Bob seemed to do it as a pastime.

Martin's wife was always telling him not to be so blunt.
Bob told her he inherited this trait from his father.
JoAnne would tell Bob he was being like his father. Bob
took it as a compliment. JoAnne didn't mean it as a
compliment.

Martin liked the fact that his Dad said what he thought and
meant it. Martin's father was more outspoken than him and
much, more blunt. Martin would always joke with JoAnne
saying that when he grew up he wanted to be just like his
Dad. JoAnne lived with it, reluctantly. She was the nice
one in the family.

They left the room to talk with McGowan and Reemer. Reemer
was pretty excited and advised INS had found a picture of
Liu and that he had directed Gary Chan to pick it up and
get it to Lower Township. Reemer indicated that from the
description it appeared that the composite information
provided by Yuk and the wife of the owner was very
accurate. Martin and Trombetta were starting to think
things were coming together. They both knew, however, that
this case was loaded with obstacles.

McGowan had been on the phone. He hung up and stated,
"Bob, Roy Choo says he has some information for us. Can you
get one of your guys to pick him up?" Martin hollered
across the hall and barked out the directive.

Trombetta looked at Martin and predicted half heartedly,
"This is going to be the break we need." Martin just
smiled. He didn't think so but didn't want to break
Trombetta's heart. They all conversed about what Choo would
have to say. Martin didn't think it would be anything
worthwhile. However, he held out hope that perhaps he was
wrong. In a short time Choo was brought to the Police
department

Choo entered the office. Martin and McGowan started to
interview him and it was immediately ascertained that a new
suspect was being thrown into the works. Choo indicated
that he had remembered an individual named Vincent who had
worked for the restaurant for a short time. It had been
believed that he had stolen money and had been let go for
that reason. Choo felt that perhaps Vincent had a bone to
pick with the restaurant owners.

The investigators remembered that Vincent's name had come

up earlier in the investigation. Choo was most helpful and provided everything he knew about Vincent. When asked why it took him so long to remember Vincent he replied, "I just tink' of him cause' he call me today." Martin's and McGowan's ears perked up. "What did he say? Why did he call?" Both investigators were in the more interested listening mode.

"He call me to say he hear about problems at restaurant and want to know what going on here. I tell him what happen then tink' I should call you."

Martin and McGowan now had another Chinese suspect to find. Choo advised that he was in Mt. Vernon, New York. "Hey, Jim, where the hell is Mt. Vernon, New York?" asked Martin.

"I'll be damned if I know," stated McGowan.

Choo was returned to the restaurant while Martin, McGowan, Trombetta and Reemer kicked around the new suspect scenario.
Martin and McGowan had placed the information on the back burner once before. They still felt they had made the correct decision by putting off looking for Vincent. It had to be looked into but that it would go on the back burner once again for the time being. They made the right decision.
It was the second time Martin and McGowan had heard the name Vincent and had decided that they didn't think he had any involvement. From what Choo had provided this guy spoke English very well and would not have known enough about the present workers to be cognizant about their belongings and room assignments. Whoever did the jobs had, inside, information. Vincent had been gone too long for any of his knowledge to be current. Martin and McGowan would be correct in their decision to not waste time on Vincent.

McGowan and Reemer decided to return to their offices to catch up on paperwork. Martin and Trombetta sat looking at one another as if they didn't see each other. They both stared into each other's faces without really seeing anything.

Martin broke the silence, "You know, Jack, this case is taking too long. The longer we go without an arrest the more frustrated I get."

"I know, what you mean, I hope we get this guy. I am having bad feelings about this whole thing. We have to get this guy."

Trombetta was pretty down and now Martin wished he had not

217

initiated the conversation. "We will get him. It is just
taking more time than I figured. I know we will get Dave's
killer. I just don't know when," Martin lamented.

"I wish I was as positive as you. I just don't think we
will get this guy. It really has me worried. Why should the
Lord give this guy to us? I am embarrassed to ask for
God's help." Trombetta was not happy with how his life had
been going lately and he knew that the Lord was not happy
with it either.

Martin reflected on the fact that when Trombetta's
Christian life was lacking so was his own. Each of them
knew they had to get back on the right track.

A lot had happened since Dave's shooting but they still
hadn't arrested the perp. They were both mindful of the
fact that others were waiting for them to solve this case.
They could not go through life with this case in the open
file. They would not be able to retire without someone
paying for Dave's death.

McGowan and Reemer were in the hallway conversing about
were the case was going and decided they had some things to
get done. McGowan had to return to his office to complete
some reports. Reemer wanted to go to his office to do the
same. Martin and Trombetta decided to go get something to
eat. They began to do so when the dispatcher advised them
that a Detective from NYPD was in the lobby.

CHAPTER THIRTY SEVEN

The excitement was evident on their faces as they went to
greet the detective. They both knew that things would
start rolling now. They had a real cop who could speak the
language. Some small talk took place as the men greeted
each other and they immediately went to work.

It was immediately decided to re-interview those restaurant
workers who seemed to have the most information during past
interviews. Martin, Trombetta and the New York detective
began the interviews after the NYPD guy had been brought up
to date on the investigation. Detective Chris Winter played
taxi, transporting the workers to and from the restaurant
one at a time.

Three hours went by as did four interviews. Martin and
Trombetta felt that they had gotten nowhere. They decided
to speak to the restaurant owner's wife, once again. The
NYPD guy was given some background on her and was advised
that the investigators thought she was a bit of an airhead.
She seemed to be unable to grasp the importance of the
entire incident.

It was later ascertained that her demeanor and actions were
not a show. She was just one flighty female who had a
problem putting her thoughts together. Maybe it was the
language barrier. Martin and Trombetta just knew they
hated to have to listen to her or watch the stupid faces
she made while being interviewed.

It was evident that the New York guy was also having a
problem with her. He began to become very frustrated and
at one point told her that there was a good possibility
that the entire incident had been initiated by Chinese gang
members who preyed on wealthy Chinese restaurant owners.
He told her that she should keep an eye on her children for
fear that gang members may kidnap them. He was hoping to
strike a chord that would lead her to being more
cooperative. He advised her not to be reluctant to provide
an employee list and that she had better do so immediately
or she would feel the wrath of the NYPD. She left the room
crying.

Jack got Bob alone and said, "Why in the hell did he scare
the shit out of her? He should have spent more time before
he gave up on her." Bob Answered, "Good question, I hope
this guy knows what he's doing."

Martin and Trombetta left the office as he was calling NYPD to advise he was staying for the night. Martin looked at his watch. It was 7PM. Martin advised Detective Chris Winter to take him to dinner and also to get him set up in the motel for the night. Martin advised the detective that he and Trombetta would pick him up in the morning and have breakfast before getting started.

Winter and the detective left for dinner at the Rio Station Restaurant.

Trombetta looked at Martin as they left the Police department Bob could tell by the look on his face that he wasn't happy. Trombetta stated,"I expected more."

Martin replied, "These people just don't want to provide information."

Trombetta gazed past Martin and said, "No, I meant, I expected more from the New York detective. I don't know what his experience is but I don't think he was much of an interviewer or interrogator."

"I agree with you," replied Martin.

"He said he was assigned to missing persons," stated Trombetta. "Maybe they do things differently. We need some Chinese cops who can bust balls and get the job done."

"You guys still here?" asked Chief Don Douglass. The Chief had walked into the Police department to find out how they had done with the interviews. Both Detective Sergeants vented their frustrations along with providing what had taken place. The Chief could tell they were not happy with the day's work. "Why are you guys sitting here? Go home and get some time with your families."

"We have too much to do," stated Martin.
"I go home and I'll sit around like a zombie," stated Trombetta.

The Chief looked at them, "If you don't want to go home, go someplace and unwind. I don't care where you go just get out of here."

Both Detective Sergeants knew they might as well hit the road. This would be the earliest they had returned home since Dave had been killed. They each felt kind of guilty about leaving work. They agreed to meet in the morning and pick up the New York guy.

They went home sat on the couch and stared at the television. The members of their families tried to strike up conversations to no avail. Eventually they went to bed and rolled around formulating what they would do next. Their respective family members knew they were hurting and frustrated and tried their best to do all they could to help with the pain and frustration.

Martin was lying in bed thinking about the interviews of the restaurant workers. Why were these people so reluctant to provide information? Getting information from them was worse than pulling teeth. It had been ascertained that the Chinese residence had been burglarized a total of five times. The victims had failed to report the burglaries to police. The owner eventually did after the third burglary incident.

Martin recalled that over and over again the workers were asked about disgruntled employees. The owners were also asked to provide information on past employees. The owners were also reluctant to provide anything. Eventually the restaurant owner indicated that he remembered that a worker, named Liu, had quit either the fifteenth or sixteenth of January. He had wanted a higher salary and was denied. The owner indicated that this subject appeared "slow and sneaky".
It had been determined that the rooms he had stayed in had never been burglarized when the residence was hit. This information was pointing the investigation to Liu.

Martin being unable to sleep continued to think about Liu. Liu had been interviewed by the INS and was photographed and fingerprinted after the contact. It had taken INS almost a week and a half to verify the information and provide the photograph and prints. The information had been provided to Martin and Trombetta just prior to the detective showing up from New York City.

Information had also been received that Liu had a New Jersey identification card provided by New Jersey Motor Vehicle Department. The address on the card came back to a Chinese Restaurant in Millville. The investigators decided to go to that restaurant and do some digging.

Trombetta had been rolling around in bed unable to sleep and thinking about going to the restaurant in Millville the next day. He was fantasizing in his mind that they would enter the restaurant and that Liu was running out the back door in an attempt to elude police. Trombetta thought about how he would beat the shit out of Liu when he caught him. This guy did not deserve to live. Not after what he had done.

Trombetta wanted to give this suspect the justice he so rightfully deserved. Jack thought about how Liu was the key

to this investigation. Once Liu was caught the case would
be unlocked and come to a close.........Trombetta
dozed.....

Martin was thinking about the fact that Gary Chan and
Stevie Yuk would be meeting in New York City the following
morning and that they were going to attempt to locate Liu.
The FEDS, had even authorized a $100.00 payment to Yuk to
compensate him for using his day off to assist
investigators. Martin thought about the cash payment by
the FEDS. Getting money from them wasn't easy. Reemer
must have been owed a favor somewhere along the line.
Maybe Chan and Reemer chipped in the cash. Everyone wanted
to find LIU.

The telephone rang and after JoAnne picked it up she handed
it to Bob. "Bob, this is Chris. Did I wake you up?"

"No, I'm laying here thinking about the case. What's up?"

Chris Winter paused for a moment and said, "This New York
guy is an ass hole. All he did was complain through
dinner. The sucker orders the best steak in the house and
complains. All he talks about is how good the food is at
the restaurant owned by him and his wife. I just dropped
him off at the Atlas. I hope he gets indigestion and dies.
He's an ungrateful fuck."

"Chris did you say anything to him?" asked Martin.

"No, I figured I would call you and let you know what was
going on."

"Alright no problem, I am having breakfast with him in the
morning. If he has something to say I'll be on him like
stink on shit." The two took part in some more small talk
then hung up. JoAnne didn't even ask what Chris had talked
about. Bob and JoAnne rolled over to get some sleep.

Both Martin and Trombetta felt that they had just fallen
asleep when they awoke and were on their way to the
station.
They arrived together. The roads had been a mess during
the last two weeks. The weather had been terrible, ever
since Dave's funeral. It had been snowing and cold.

Driving had been a real drag, especially for the guys
traveling from north Jersey. Gary Chan had been caught in
a couple of snow storms and had to stay in Cape May County
on a few occasions. Northern New Jersey and New York City
were having one of the worst winters in a long time. South
Jersey was usually spared the ravages of snow. The
southern coast of New Jersey was just not conducive to lots

222

of snow fall.

The Detective Sergeants entered the Police department and Martin reviewed the incidents that had taken place over night. Even though they were deep in the middle of an investigation they were still responsible to make sure other cases were being handled. The telephone rang. Trombetta answered and Chris Winter was immediately telling Trombetta he thought that the New York detective had taken advantage of the hospitality last evening. Winter advised that the investigator from New York had himself one expensive dinner, not to mention that during his feast he bad mouthed the restaurant but continued to chow down.

Trombetta was telling Martin the juicy details as Winter was relating the incident. Jack hung up the phone and mentioned to Martin that they were expected to meet the NYPD guy at 8:30 am. He also expected to meet the two Detective Sergeants for breakfast at the Atlas in Cape May City. Martin indicated that Chris had called him last night and he was aware of what had gone down with the ungrateful detective. Martin and Trombetta were deciding on the schedule for the day while driving to the motel restaurant to meet the detective.

When they arrived they had the girl at the desk ring the detective and they waited for him to get off the elevator. The three investigators entered the restaurant and were promptly seated and handed breakfast menus.

The NYPD guy immediately began telling the two detective sergeants about the restaurant he and his wife owned. He also began telling stories about his investigative abilities and the many important cases he had investigated. Both Martin and Trombetta continued to look at the menu. Jack ordered a bagel and coffee. Martin had wheat toast and coffee. NYPD ordered pancakes with strawberries and whipped cream along with eggs on the side. The two south Jersey cops thought this guy was a little much.

He began bad mouthing the food and how it was served. He was mentioning how terrible the waitress was and that he would never employ such an individual. Trombetta could tell by the look on Martin's face that he was about ready to advise the Detective that he was a guest and should just smile and be grateful.

Trombetta knew, however, that Martin would not be very tactful. Trombetta immediately began talking about the work schedule for the day in an attempt to change the subject. Jack did not want to be embarrassed by Martin when he went off, even though the guy deserved it. Martin had a way of not being very tactful. Jack mentioned that they had a few more restaurant workers to interview and also that they wanted to go to as many of the area's Chinese restaurants as possible.

Jack had already made plans to go to the Millville restaurant were Liu's name had come up. Trombetta had set up a meeting with McGowan and an INS investigator for that evening in Millville. They were going to check out a restaurant and a house where many of the Chinese workers lived. Trombetta wanted the New York guy to go along to act as the interpreter. Jack didn't know that Martin had already decided not to go to Millville. Martin knew that Chris Winter would also be going with them and that Jack Reemer may also travel along. They would have more than enough bodies to effect any action.

Martin had a family get together to attend with JoAnne's family and she would not be too happy if he didn't make it. Throughout the investigation thus far he had been ignoring his wife. He knew he had to make some amends. Sure, she was understanding, but she was still a woman. Bob knew that enough guys were going to Millville. He had a feeling that Millville was going to be a bust anyway.

Breakfast was completed and the waitress brought the bill. Martin immediately acted as though he was handing the bill to the New York detective and stated, "We got dinner last night. It's your turn." Jack knew Martin was going to let loose on the guy. Jack immediately grabbed the bill from Bob and said, "He's kidding." Jack smiled and handed the bill back to Martin. As they left the table, Bob said, "That waitress did a great job. I left her ten bucks."

Jack hoped NYPD didn't respond. Martin was ready to let go with a tirade even a Chinese Detective assigned to Missing Persons would understand. The guy didn't say anything and entered the elevator to pick up his overnight bag from the room and Martin checked him out at the desk. Martin advised the clerk to extend his thanks and gratitude to the Satt family for once again coming through for Lower Township Police. The Satts always found room for guests of Lower Township and always provided top quality accommodations and good food at a discount. Most often they could rent their rooms for more money but they always were willing to help the Police Department and did so regularly.

Martin was trying to figure out the NYPD detective. Maybe he had a rough week at work or maybe his wife didn't want him to leave home for an investigation in south Jersey. Sometimes guys didn't function right for a multitude of reasons. Martin was deciding to write it off. The guy had been nice enough to show up and at least make an effort to help.

224

The detective followed Martin and Trombetta to the Police department and the three immediately got to work. They slowly and methodically interviewed the remaining Chinese restaurant workers. They completed the assignment by one in the afternoon. Martin had previously advised Chris Winter to arrive at work at one to take the detective to all the area Chinese restaurants to interview workers in an attempt to obtain some leads. Winter arrived and they left the Police Department. Trombetta and Martin reviewed what the workers had said and compared it to what had been provided earlier.

The stories were still the same. They had uncovered nothing new. Both cops were frustrated and were just looking for things to vent their frustrations upon. They wanted this case to come to an end. They wanted the Feds in New York to do something. They wanted real cops to assist with the interviews and interrogations of these people whose language they did not understand. They wanted the County to agree that they should be in New York, not Cape May County, looking for leads. Martin wanted the guys in the department to stop asking questions about the investigation. He had answered the same questions over and over again. He had reassured the same guys over and over again.

Each cop had his idea of what should be done. Little did they know that all, the things, had been completed. These guys were only trying to be helpful. Martin knew that talking to them about their thoughts or ideas was a waste of time. He did not, however, want to make them think he was not interested in their investigative thoughts. Some of the theories were far from realistic. How do you tactfully tell a guy his idea sucks? Martin couldn't be bothered with trying to make the guy feel good about his ridiculous idea. Trombetta usually did that for Martin. Trombetta could tell when Martin was about ready to let loose and he would always intervene to keep people happy.

The times when Jack felt the same as Bob often turned out to be real interesting. When both of them went off on some loser it wasn't fun to be present. They tried not to do that too often.

Trombetta mentioned that tonight in Millville they would find what they were looking for. Martin didn't feel that way. He felt Millville would be a waste of time. He didn't want to bust Jack's bubble. Martin didn't tell Jack that he thought Millville would be a wild goose chase. Trombetta knew, however, that Bob didn't think much of the Millville connection just by the way he seemed to stay out of any conversations regarding it.

Martin and Trombetta continued to review reports and try to think about anything that they may have missed or perhaps failed to follow up on. Winter walked into the Police department. The time was 4:45 p.m. Winter immediately advised Martin and Trombetta that they had been to every Chinese restaurant in the area and spoken to every worker with negative results. Trombetta suggested they go get something to eat prior to going to Millville. Martin wished them the best with their trip and returned home to get ready for dinner with his wife's family.

Martin knew that all the relatives would want him to talk about the investigation. He also knew that he would have to be polite but that he wouldn't tell them much. He knew that short of telling them that he hadn't caught the perpetrator there wasn't much to say.

Martin sat through the get together like a zombie. He was thinking about the guys in Millville. He was hoping they would turn up something. He knew, however, that they weren't going to find anything. It was a feeling and it proved to be true.

Trombetta, and the guys got something to eat and met, the other investigators, at a prearranged location and decided on how they would handle the investigation. Jack wanted this to go right and he was going to make sure it did.

Jack, Chris and the New York detective had met McGowan, Reemer and an INS agent whose name Jack couldn't remember in a parking lot. Jack indicated how he wanted to enter the restaurant and what he wanted done. Jack could tell the INS guy seemed unhappy with Jack's plan. The guy started to indicate that he didn't have the authority to bust into the restaurant and start checking the papers of immigrants. He advised that he had to initiate a telephone call to advise the owner that he intended to visit the establishment and check the papers of his employees. Jack couldn't believe what he was hearing. Jack looked at the guy and said, "What kind of bureaucratic crap is that? You'll never find illegals that way." Chris, chimed in, sarcastically, "I bet you don't make many arrest on guys without papers." McGowan knew the conversation was going nowhere and stated, "Listen, Jack, Chris and I will go to the rear door of the restaurant."

McGowan looked at Reemer and stated, "You guys go to the front and strike up a conversation with the owner." Trombetta had indicated the same scenario in the beginning of the conversation so he was happy with the plan.

Before any more conversation could take place Jack, Chris

and McGowan started to the rear of the restaurant located on Delsea Drive in Millville. The restaurant was located in a small mall type setting and the men didn't think they would have any problems.

The three investigators entered the rear kitchen door just as Reemer and the INS agent were talking to the owner at the front entrance to the kitchen. One of the cooks started to run to the back door and Chris Winter quickly grabbed him and said, "What's up man? Going on a break?" Trombetta and McGowan saw that Chris had the guy under control and they kept an eye on the others in the kitchen. The owner was upset with what was going on but he didn't want to be too vocal because he was aware that he was employing a few illegals.

Chris showed the workers the composites and, of course, no one recognized either individual. The restaurant owner supplied the address of a home he owned which housed his workers. He advised that some of his employees who were off for the evening would be at the residence.

After the investigators were finished with everyone at the restaurant they went to the other location. As they arrived it was pretty evident that the workers had received a call. They were scurrying about the residence and yard and leaving the premises as quickly as possible. They were all rounded up. Jack couldn't help but laugh to himself as Chris Winter who was as tall as Michael Jordan was running after them and grabbing the little Chinese guys who were scurrying about. Jack thought it reminded him of a Praying Mantis closing in on a mosquito for the kill.

Chris had grabbed one guy who was running out the door and asked, "Excuse me, but, do you have any monosodium glutamate I can borrow?" Chris had a way with words. Chris later indicated that the residents were like a bunch of ants escaping from an earthquake that was devouring their ant farm. Jack would later tell Bob that he should ask Chris about all that had taken place at the house. Jack knew that it would be good stuff for a book.

Jack was especially critical of the INS Agent. Jack couldn't believe that the agency was so powerless and almost worthless.

CHAPTER THIRTY EIGHT

The weekend had gone by quickly. It was March 7th and
Dave's killer still hadn't been arrested and the
investigation was progressing but not the way Martin and
Trombetta had hoped. Martin was sitting at his desk when
the phone rang. It was Jack just checking to see if Martin
had arrived at the station. Jack indicated that he would
be at the office shortly. He just wanted to ascertain if
anything had happened Sunday that was worth knowing. Jack
had managed to stay home on Sunday for the first time since
Dave was shot. He even managed to get himself to church
along with the rest of his family.

Bob had promised JoAnne that he too would stay home on
Sunday. He went into the office for four hours then
returned home. She was happy that even though he didn't
stay home he at least only spent a half day.

Bob advised Jack that the only noteworthy happening was the
fact that Gary Chan hooked up with Yuk in New York City and
they were once again trying to locate Liu. Gary had told
Bob that he and Yuk had been all over Chinatown in an
effort to locate Liu. Chan advised that if Liu didn't get
the messages left all over the city on this visit he
probably was a long distance from New York's Chinatown.

Jack advised Bob he was getting a shower and would be at
the office shortly. Bob looked at his watch and saw that
it read 7:20 am. Martin decided to check the printout for
the weekend. He tried to keep updated on other happenings
in the township. He and Jack were still responsible for
other crime through out the Township. The kids had been
doing a good job following up on those cases that fell
within their realm of responsibility. He and Jack were
fortunate that they didn't have to tightly supervise the
kids who made up the detective bureau. Bob made a few
notes about some burglaries he noticed that had taken place
in the north end of the township.

He thought about the fact that Chan had stated that Yuk
would be returning from New York on the afternoon bus.
Martin hoped that Liu would get the messages Yuk had been
leaving with everyone who had any relationship with the
hard to find Asian.

Jack showed up and began filling Bob in on the Millville
investigation and how worthless the INS investigator had
been. Jack spent an hour explaining to Bob the
shortcomings of the investigative branches of the Federal

Government.

McGowan called and indicated that he would not be at Lower during the day because he had a few reports he had to catch up on. Jack laughed and indicated that they were probably reports of the Millville investigation which had produced nothing.

Jack was happy with the fact that he was managing to stay away from report writing on this case. Jack made an exerted effort to be with someone who could do the reports. Jack was fully capable of completing a good report. It was just less strenuous on his mind if someone else would provide the case facts and mention Jack's name now and then.

Bob and Jack were soon meeting with the Chief and the Captain and filling them in on what had taken place over the weekend. The conversation once again began to center around the fact that the investigation was pointing north to New York. Captain Maher questioned as to whether or not both Bob and Jack should be going to the big city together. The Captain was feeling them out on the importance of both traveling to New York. Both Bob and Jack quickly came up with many reasons why they should go together.

The Captain then felt that it would be important that due to the fact that he was in ultimate control of the detectives and the investigation that perhaps in the absence of Martin and Trombetta he should become totally familiar of every aspect of the investigation. Martin thought to himself that the Captain was chewing off a bit more than he could chew but went to his office and came back with the working file pertaining to the Douglass case. By this time the file was contained within a legal case carton and was quite large. It was divided into many various categories. Martin began to explain the set up to the Captain. The Captain asked if perhaps there was an easy way to review the vast amount of paperwork. The file contained everything from notes to case reports.

Martin quickly went to a section entitled case synopsis. He removed it from the carton and handed it to the Captain. The Captain quickly observed that the document was fifteen pages long and referred to various other reports and documents contained in the carton. The Captain advised that he would review it in order to be on top of the case. There was always the possibility that if something happened to Martin someone in the department would have to take over the investigation. The Captain knew that Jack was knowledgeable about the case but that knowledge would be generalized while Bob would have all the facts in his head and Jack would use him for a ready reference. That was the way these two guys always worked. The Captain wanted to be secure in the fact that someone else in the department had as much in-depth knowledge about the investigation other than Martin. He made up his mind that he would be that person.

Captain Maher left the office with the synopsis. He entered his office and shut the door. Martin and Trombetta were talking to the Chief when they were advised that some detectives from a municipality in Atlantic County were looking for them.

Martin and Trombetta met the two detectives and it was ascertained that they had a home intrusion in their area and that it had been pulled off by Asians. They had a file of about five jobs that had taken place in Ocean and Atlantic counties. Martin and Trombetta listened to their idea that the killer of Dave Douglass was probably part of the Asian Gang that was pulling the jobs in South Jersey. Martin had looked into that possibility in the beginning of the investigation and he and McGowan had decided early on that their case was not the typical home intrusion that was being undertaken by the Asian gangs.

Martin still provided them with a lot of the case facts but knew he was wasting time. After about two hours the two detectives decided that they would return to their municipality and still felt that perhaps the Lower Township Case was like their case. Martin knew that they felt Lower Police department was working the wrong angle on their case.

After the two had left Jack said, "You were pretty nice to those guys."

"Well, they thought they were doing us a favor. They thought they could help us out with this case."

"I know, but, you knew right from the beginning that they didn't have anything we could use. I figured you were going to embarrass me and tell them they were stupid or something," added Trombetta.

"I figured they came all the way down here to give us this information that I should at least listen to them," said Martin.

"I could tell that a couple of times you were getting ready to tell them they were full of shit," said Jack. "You had that look on your face. You know the one that says, I hear you but what you're saying is a bunch of shit."

"Don't tell me you felt any different than I."

"I didn't," said Trombetta. "I was just waiting for you to freak out on them. It didn't appear they were hearing your objections. I figured sooner or later you would let them have both barrels." Jack looked at Martin smiled and added, "I think you're getting soft in your old age."

"You would have crapped your pants if I had told them they were idiots and threw them out," said Martin. "Like I said, they were nice enough to come, I was nice enough to hear them out."

Jack smiled and said, "Yeah, you're getting soft, Bobby."

The Captain walked in and handed the case synopsis to Martin. "Do you realize how difficult it would be for someone to grasp all the information in that paperwork?" asked Captain Maher.

"This is a pretty confusing case," said Trombetta. "That's why I have Bob remember everything and I just pick his brain. I want to keep my head fresh for any new information," added Trombetta with a grin.

"There is no use in me trying to obtain enough knowledge about this case to answer all questions," said Maher. "You guys have a lot of information to keep in your minds. When you leave town, just leave a number where I can reach you. If I need something, I'll call you for the info," said the Captain as he smiled.

The Chief entered the room and looked at his investigators and stated, "You guys need a break. Get out of here and relax for awhile. Get the cobwebs out of your heads."

Maher looked at the Chief and said, "You want cobwebs? You ought to read the synopsis." The Chief laughed and stated, "That's why I have these guys."

Jack and Bob decided they would visit a local club for a few drinks. They left the station and picked up Martin's personal car and were on their way. Neither of them were too keen on taking a department car and parking it at a drinking establishment, let alone be drinking and operating a department vehicle. They had enough problems with the investigation.

They drove to the club and parked. Bob hit the buzzer at the entrance and both men entered the Villas Fishing Club, a private club that had been in existence for almost seventy years. It catered to the local members who liked a cheap drink and a good meal. A couple of guys in the department were members and could take guests to enjoy inexpensive drinks and food.

Detective Winter's brother, Gus, was a full time bartender at the club and had told Bob and Jack they could be his guests whenever they felt the urge. Gus was behind the bar as they entered. They looked around and found a seat at the end of the bar. A large picture window behind them provided a good view of the Delaware Bay. The bay is a large body of water and on a clear day you can see the state of Delaware on the opposite side. The wind was turning all the waves into whitecaps. It would not be a good day to be floating around in the Delaware Bay.

Jack and Bob each had been fishing in the bay and had learned to respect its ability to change from a calm lake into a torrent of wind and waves. Neither of them spent much time with a fishing pole in their hands. You didn't have to be a fisherman to be a member of the fishing club. You just needed a sponsor with pull to become a member.

"Hey, guys, how ya doing?" asked Gus. "Sorry to hear about Dave. Have you got the guy who did it?"

"We're working on it," answered Martin.

Both investigators felt uneasy sitting in a bar when they felt they should be looking for the killer. They knew, however, that they needed a break and that there would always be down time in the investigation. That was the worst thing about cases like this. Sometimes there was nothing to do but let time pass. They had left the "kids" assignments that had to be completed. They did feel, however, that someone might see them and wonder why they weren't spending all their time catching the killer.

Both men ordered a drink and as they sat patrons and members of the club approached them with their condolences. They were touched that so many people seemed to care. They hadn't spoken to many people on the street since the incident. Sure they had talked to witnesses and scum bags but they really hadn't talked to John Q. Public. It was evident that the public cared and was interested in what was going on with regard to the investigation. Both men couldn't supply much information but the people seemed to realize that they could not expect the officers to provide them with an update on the investigation.

Many of the card carrying members of the Villas Fishing Club were retired cops and firemen from Philadelphia, PA and Camden, NJ. They knew how these guys felt about losing an officer. They extended their regrets and then went on about their business. They knew that these guys wanted to have some down time without being bothered. Eventually both men began to talk to each other about what had been going on in the investigation.

"Hey, Jack, what ever happened with the guy you called in New York?" asked Bob.

"No one was home, so I left a message," answered Jack.

CHAPTER THIRTY NINE

It was about two o'clock in the afternoon. It was a rare
moment in the Naspretto household. Ernie was home, but his
wife, Grace, and fifteen month old daughter, Angelina, were
out somewhere. It was rare that Ernie found himself alone
in their modest Glendale, Queens home. He, almost, savored
the moment. Of course, he loved his family, but an
occasional moment at home all by his self was nice. The
red light was flashing on the answering machine.

"Hi, Ern, it's me, Jack Trombetta. Remember me from the FBI
Academy?"

Ernie immediately broke into a smile. Do I remember Jack
Trombetta? That's like asking do I remember the pain and
constant itch of hemorrhoids, thought Ernie. How could he
forget him? Actually, Ernie was quite fond of Jack. They
met at the FBI National Academy two summers earlier. NA
Session #170, June 21, 1992 to September 4, 1992. It was
eleven weeks neither one would forget. 249 cops from all
over the world attended this session. Everyone knew and
remembered Jack. He was known for his unending quest to
have a good time. Jack spent most of that summer either
intoxicated, attempting to get intoxicated or hungover.

Ernie and Jack hit it off right away. Maybe it was the
"Italian Thing". The first time they met was in an
extremely boring forensics class. There were about thirty
cops in the room. It was the first day of class and the
instructor had everyone say a little something about
themselves. Where you were from, the type of jurisdiction,
what your assignment was, etc. All Ernie had to say was
Lieutenant, New York City Police Department, patrol platoon
commander. One of the benefits of coming from New York
City was that a description of the jurisdiction was not
required. Jack on the other hand was from a small
jurisdiction.

"Jack Trombetta. I'm a detective sergeant in Lower
Township, New Jersey. We have thirty thousand, population,
in the winter and about one hundred fifty thousand,
population, on a hot summer weekend. It's basically a
summer resort area. We handle a lot of white trash."
Everyone in the room was a little uneasy with Jack's less
than professional description of the community he served.
After all, this was the FBI National Academy, the Harvard
of Law Enforcement. Only one half of one percent of all
law enforcement officers in the nation got a chance to
attend this very prestigious school and this fuckin' cop

was calling people "white trash". These officers were supposed to be above these kinds of statements. Ernie liked Jack right away.

Although they could both be bad boys, Ernie hid it much better. He came across as the guy who would actually do his homework and reading assignments and write his own term papers. He jogged everyday, made his bed, said his prayers and sometimes used big words. If he drank it was in moderation. However, some perceived him as the type that if he got into a fight, especially if he was winning, he'd think nothing of stepping on some mutt's throat and pissing in his mouth. The perception wasn't far off base.

In daylight hours Jack always looked ill. He had that "I gotta throw up my guts" face. He never made his bed, never did his homework and basically had no idea what the hell he was doing at the FBI National Academy. Yet, he came across as a fierce competitor, a leader, an extremely loyal friend and an excellent street cop who couldn't give a shit about rules and procedures. He was one of the five finalists to be selected for "class representative", who makes a valedictory speech on graduation day. Oh, yes, Ernie certainly remembered Jack.

They hadn't spoken in over a year. Jack always said he'd come to New York, but he never made the trip. Ernie called Jack the last couple of times. Like all those high school friends you swore you'd keep in touch with they basically lost touch. Anyway, Ernie was very happy to hear Jack's voice and wondered what prompted the call. He couldn't wait to call Jack back until he heard the next line.

"They killed one of my cops. One of the guys I worked with." Ernie felt the smile immediately leave his face. Oh, shit! The next lines got even worse. "We think it's a Chinese guy from New York. I could use your help. Can you call me back? Thanks, Ern..." Ernie sat on the edge of his bed and thought how the fuck can I help this guy?

Ernie Naspretto was promoted to captain two weeks after graduating the FBI National Academy. He was now Captain Ernest J. Naspretto, Executive Officer, of the 60th Precinct in Coney Island, Brooklyn. As an Executive Officer, Ernie was second in command, working for a senior captain, a twenty two year veteran named Dale Riedel. Ernie had only eleven years on the job when he made captain. At 34 years old he was probably one of the youngest captains ever in the Department. Well, that was a year and a half and thirty five pounds ago. Everyone who knew him was more impressed with Ernie's career than Ernie was.

The New York City Police Department had over 30,000

uniformed members. There were approximately 22,000 police
officers, 3500 detectives, 3500 sergeants, 1100 lieutenants
and about 400 captains and above, which include deputy
inspectors, inspectors, deputy and assistant chiefs, and
bureau chiefs.

The Lower Township Police Department had 47 members total,
including only one captain. Ernie knew Jack had very
little perspective of the enormity of New York City and its
police department. Jack undoubtedly had some illusory
understanding of Ernie's power as a captain in the almighty
NYPD. Ernie was just one of the hundreds of captains.
Even worse, he was a patrol captain who didn't even have
his own precinct. There are 75 precincts in the city,
therefore only 75 captains could have their own patrol
command. Ernie, like many other captains, was just a
"brand X", an "executive officer" who assisted the
commanding officer

The promotional process in the NYPD up to captain was
determined by very difficult and competitive civil service
exams. Ernie excelled in test taking. He scored somewhere
in the middle of the sergeants' list and closer to the top
on the lieutenants' and captains' lists. Promotions above
captain were discretionary usually based on politics,
dedication, and proven abilities. However, for one's
abilities and dedication to be recognized and result in
promotion, a candidate had to engage in an incredible
amount of politicking. Ernie couldn't do that. He had
seen some captains sell their souls, sell out their cops,
and suck up to politicians and big bosses in a quest to
move up the ranks. The thought nauseated him.

Ernie knew he was a "captain for life" within three months
of his last promotion. He was assigned to a detail in
Crown Heights, Brooklyn, where hundreds of Hasidic Jews
were protesting outside the 71st Precinct station house
because one of their members was arrested for beating up a
black vagrant, who the Hasidics claim was a burglar. Ernie
was given strict orders that nobody, except cops, was to
enter the front door. One of the local councilmen walked
out of the front door, signaled to one of the Hasidics to
come in and attempted to reenter. Ernie knew exactly who
the councilman was but pretended he never heard of him.

"Do you know who I am? Who are you?" the councilman
demanded.
"I'm in a police captain's uniform. It's obvious who I am.
Who the hell are you?" Ernie shot back. He had absolutely
no tolerance for supposed "leaders" who expected you to
know who they were. The cops were not used to seeing the
councilman being spoken to like this. They loved it. The
councilman ran to a chief, the borough commander of

Brooklyn South, and wanted to file a complaint. Another
captain walked over to Ernie and explained the realities of
political life in Brooklyn South and who that raving
councilman was. Ernie waited for the senior captain to
finish, then said, "Fuck that little twerp."

Over the next two months there were at least two other
incidents with the councilman. Each time Ernie did the
direct opposite of what the councilman demanded. It got to
the point where Ernie was being reprimanded by an inspector
who relied on this councilman for promotions. After the
inspector's dissertation on what being a captain was all
about and how Ernie had to "grow into the rank", Ernie
said, "I'd like to piss on that little ass hole's corpse."
The inspector transferred Ernie to the 60th Precinct in
Coney Island, the farthest possible precinct from the
councilman's district. Everyone, including Ernie, was very
happy with the move. But, it was very apparent that
Ernie's meteoric rise through the ranks would end at
captain. That was fine with him. No problem. He was
content and actually liked the idea of people thinking he
was a bit of a psycho. The reputation he had as a rookie
cop stayed with him and even magnified as he moved up the
ranks. But, how was he going to help Jack Trombetta find a
cop killer?

Ernie never worked in the very elite Detective Bureau, but
he had many friends who were detectives. He truly envied
and respected detectives. He may have outranked them, but,
he always wanted to be one of them. Ernie's entire career
was in uniformed patrol. Although he knew and socialized
with many detectives he was not truly cognizant of the
bureau's mores. You would have to work in the Detective
Bureau to be acutely aware of the differences between
patrol and investigation. Ernie most certainly had a
patrol mentality which limited his perspective of the
department as a whole.

The patrol mentality at his level was rather basic: Every
command for itself. Although his outlook may have been a
little crude, it did reflect the realities of precinct
command. Each precinct was divided up into sectors. Patrol
units and foot posts patrolled the area. If it didn't
happen in your precinct, you weren't concerned. It was
that simple. i.e. a large event, i.e. a parade,
demonstration, a concert, etc., required personnel from
other precincts, written requests through channels were
submitted to the borough headquarters. One captain would
never just call another captain and ask to borrow ten cops.
No such animal. All requests had to be approved and
sanctioned from "downtown". Emergency mobilizations at
large scale riots were the exception. Everything else
required "paper", pain in the ass, fuckin' paper.

So how could Ernie help Jack find a Jersey cop killer who happened to be a Chinese who probably looked just like every other Chinese guy and was now hiding somewhere in the biggest city in the world? The first thing he had to do was return Jack's call. In less than ten seconds he went from he couldn't wait to talk to Jack to he wished Jack never called.

Ernie knew Jack would describe the killer as a young Chinese gang member. As a lieutenant, Ernie had worked in the 109th precinct in Flushing, Queens for three years. Flushing had a huge Chinese and Korean population. Virtually every business on Main Street or Union Street was owned by Asians. All the signs were in Korean or Chinese. Ernie used to joke about having war flashbacks and reliving the horrors of combat every time he saw those signs. He was never in the military, but the rookie cops didn't know that. The area had many problems with Asian gangs with names like Born to Kill, Korean Power, known as "KP", and White Tigers. All, these little mutts looked alike to Ernie. The typical profile was male, between 16 and 21, very thin, spiked hair and the sudden inability to speak or understand English when arrested. Legitimate identification papers simply never existed for these little bastards. Ernie hated them. But, then again, Ernie hated all criminals.

The Asian gangs were notorious for extorting money from Korean and Chinese business owners. Robberies, kidnapping and criminal mischief were trademarks of these gangs. They often engaged in "turf battles" in the Fifth Precinct which covered New York's world famous Chinatown. A major obstacle in arresting and prosecuting these gang members was a reluctance by the victims to cooperate with the police. It was hard enough to identify and arrest these pieces of shit when serious crimes occurred in New York. How the hell could Ernie and Jack find one of these creeps that did something in New Jersey? Ernie felt like tits on a bull.

Ernie called the number Jack left on the machine. In the most professional voice he could come up with he asked for Sergeant Trombetta. As soon as Jack came on the line Ernie said, "Jack, you terd, what's going on?" Jack broke into a grin and started to laugh. Ernie's voice conjured up some happy memories from the National Academy. For a split second they forgot why the call was being returned. Then Jack explained that one of his cops was shot and killed on a burglary call. The shooter was apparently Chinese and that evidence from the crime scene may link the killer to New York.

"Jack, it's bad enough that this happened, but to try to nail one of these gook fucks is almost impossible. These fuckin' gang members all look alike and could hide in sidewalk cracks. They're like fuckin' roaches. Not to mention that it is almost impossible to get cooperation from the Chinese community." Ernie was slightly embarrassed by his own pessimism.

"We don't think the guy is a gang member," Jack countered.

Ernie couldn't figure how something like this could happen with a Chinese "perp" not being a gang member. However, once Jack gave the description Ernie felt a little better.

"He's a heavy set guy about fifty years old."

"Now, that's very different. You're telling me a fifty year old chink killed a cop? That's gotta be the first time that's ever happened in this country," Ernie said, his voice filled with apparent amazement. This mutt did not fit the profile of the typical Asian criminal. Thank God, Ernie thought.

"Well, what do you got? What do you need?" Ernie asked, his voice sounding slightly more confident.

"This happened two weeks ago. We think the guy may have worked in a Chinese restaurant down here."

"Why do you think the guy's from here?" Ernie asked.

"We found a New York lottery ticket and a key with 'Chinatown' stamped on it at the scene."

"What do the people from the restaurant say?"

"They're being totally uncooperative. They say they don't know anything." Ernie was not surprised to hear that. Jack continued, "We can't really do a good interrogation on these guys because we're having problems with the language."

"Have you tried the FBI for help or translators?"

"Ernie, the Feds are freakin' useless. The local guys are trying but the New York area is no help at all. They sent down a guy who is fluent in Chinese but he is no interrogator. He doesn't even speak the right dialect for some of these people. We told the New York Feds about the key and gave them some addresses where the key might fit. It's been two weeks, they haven't done shit. I don't want to work with these guys. I want a cop!!!"

The frustration was apparent in Jack's voice. He asked
Ernie if the New York City Police Department had any type
of unit that dealt with Chinese criminals. Ernie
immediately thought of the Intelligence Division but wasn't
sure.

"Let me make some calls and I'll get back to you. But, I
tell ya, Jack, this is going to be a tough one. If the
mutt was black, Spanish, Italian, Irish, anything else
would be easier than Chinese. I'll call ya back." Ernie
hung up feeling sorry for Jack. He could imagine the
frustration, pressure and feeling of helplessness that Jack
was experiencing. Suddenly, Ernie was feeling the
pressure. He thought, I'm just a patrol cop. How the hell
am I going to help catch a Chinese cop killer?

He looked up the number in the NYPD phone directory and
called the Intelligence Division. A female sergeant
answered. She sounded very pleasant. Ernie tried to
explain the situation in New Jersey and inquired as to
whether there was an "Asian Squad" or something like that
in the Intelligence Division. The sergeant said that there
was a unit that dealt with gang intelligence but that was a
different unit within the Intelligence Division. Ernie had
called the unit that handles the Mayor's security. Rudolph
Giuliani was the new mayor of New York City after winning a
hotly contested very close election over the incumbent
David Dinkens. Ernie adored Giuliani and despised Dinkins.
"Do me a favor, please?" Ernie asked the sergeant. "Tell
Rudy I love him. I mean I really love him. I want him to
adopt me." The sergeant laughed. Most captains didn't
talk that way.

Ernie was about to call the other unit when he thought
better of it. The "intelligence gang" unit didn't sound
like an enforcement unit. He didn't need intelligence
information, he needed sharp street cops. Ernie's old
precinct came to mind. I'll call Don, he thought to
himself.

Ernie had a very good friend, a sergeant that worked in the
109th Precinct Robbery Unit named Don Costello, who seemed
to know everything and everyone in the Department. They
had been friends for eight years. They met when they were
rookie sergeants assigned to the 103rd Precinct in Jamaica,
Queens. Don was transferred to the 109 and Ernie arrived
there about three years later. Only Ernie was a lieutenant
now, Don was still a sergeant. Ernie routinely reminded
Don of the rank differences.

Don Costello is six foot four and weighs about 290. His
suits usually don't fit well and he speaks very slowly.
Ernie used to say if you asked Don the time it took him ten

minutes to give you an answer. Costello would pause when he
spoke, almost moan like he was constipated. Ernie said to
him once, "One of these days you're gonna take a really big
shit. Then you'll speak like the rest of us." He was one
of the sharpest cops Ernie ever met.

Costello could get confessions from all types of criminals.
He would plop himself in a chair and sit next to the
individual who was arrested. Although he was very big, his
demeanor was very non-threatening. He'd talk about
basketball, the Yankees, cars, clothes, just about anything
other than crime. Most criminals would look at him and
think they'd get over, no problem, because this guy is
stupid. Shortly thereafter, many would be signing
confession statements.

Two punks from Queens had committed a string of robberies
at doctors' offices throughout Flushing and Bayside.
They'd walk in, produce handguns and rob the doctors, the
nurses and the patients in the waiting room. They would
take money, jewelry and whatever else they could grab.
Eventually they were caught. A veteran detective was
trying to interrogate them in the interview room, at the
109 detective squad. He was getting nowhere. They were
cocky and told him to fuck off. Sgt. Costello looked at
their background sheets and noticed that one had attended
Catholic grammar and high school. Costello walked in and
took a seat next to the "perp with the attitude".

"I see you went to Catholic school. Man, Catholic school
was tough, those nuns! But, listen, I know you've got some
sense of decency. It's a credit to your parents that they
cared enough to send you to Catholic school. I know you
must feel a little sorry that you let them down. You know
we got a lot on you. You're gonna go to jail. You stole a
Christhead from a woman at one of those doctors' offices.
The thing has almost no value to anyone else. It might be
worth twenty five bucks, if that. But, to her it was
priceless. Her only son died of leukemia last month. He
was 24. Just before he died he gave it to her. She had
given it to him when he was seven years old. He wore it
everyday until he died. Can you please tell me where you
pawned the jewelry you stole so hopefully we can give her a
little bit of her son back?" Costello pled with the saddest
of eyes.

The punk's eyes started to swell with tears. The veteran
detective had a big lump in his throat. This was a real
tear jerker. The punk gave it up. He gave a statement and
signed a confession. The detective said to Costello later
that day, "That's a heavy story. I didn't know that."
Costello answered, "Neither did I. I just made it up as I
went along." They recovered 90% of the jewelry in that

241

case.

Ernie called Costello. "Don, this is Captain Naspretto.
You're still a sergeant, right?"

"Yeah, yeah, yeah. You're still short and ugly, right?"
Costello shot back.

"Listen, terd, I need help with something. It's heavy."

Ernie went on to explain what happened in Lower Township,
New Jersey. "I know you deal with these Asian fucks all
the time over there. These guys need help interviewing the
workers in the Chinese restaurant where the shooter may
have worked. They tried the FBI, it was a waste of time.
The Feds sent some fuckin' Yale type who speaks Chinese.
The chinks talked circles around him. He isn't much of an
interrogator. They need some cops who can deal with these
people on their own level. Basically, they need someone to
go down there, kick their fuckin' asses, and find out the
deal." Without hesitation Costello said, "Tommy Chin and
Keith Ng."

Ernie remembered Detective Tommy Chin. Ernie had been a
patrol lieutenant in the 109 and Tommy was in that
precinct's detective squad. They rarely dealt with one
another, but the few times they did, Ernie was impressed.
He remembered Tommy as a very respectful, pleasant, sincere
individual. But, he never saw him interrogate anyone.
Could he verbally knock the shit out of someone? Ernie
didn't know Keith Ng. Chin and Ng were both assigned to
the Queens Robbery Squad. They were affectionately
referred to as the "Ninja Squad."

"Oh, yeah, I remember Tommy. Nice guy. But, Don, I really
don't need a nice guy here. I need a scum bag."
"Keith Ng is a maniac. Tommy keeps him in line, but
they're a great team. They work off of each other,"
answered Costello.

"Great. Let these guys know I'm gonna call them."

Ernie hung up. He felt slightly better than he did when he
first heard Jack's message. But, he knew it was going to
be a long shot.

CHAPTER FORTY

Thomas Chin was born in the Bronx in 1953. His parents,
Guy Nen and Yee Wan, immigrated to the United States in the
1940's. In an effort to assimilate into the American
culture and expedite his attaining U.S. citizenship Guy Nen
Chin joined the army during World War II. His wife and
their five children remained in China until after the war.
Upon their reuniting the Chins settled in the Bronx and
opened a Chinese laundry. Three more children, including
Tommy and his twin sister, Rose, would be born in America.

Tommy grew up with few Chinese friends. Most of his
friends were black or Hispanic. While in grammar school
Tommy and his American born siblings were forced to attend
a weekend Cantonese class in Chinatown. He hated it.
Tommy's parents stressed education, especially with their
American born children. Cantonese is one of the major
dialects of Chinese. Tommy's family spoke a little used
sub-dialect of Cantonese called Toisan. Although the Chins
wanted their children to assimilate into the American
culture, they also wanted their American born children to
revere their great Chinese heritage. Tommy never did
become fluent in Cantonese.

Tommy always wanted to become a cop. His family dismissed
it as a childhood fantasy. As far as Guy Nen and Yee Wan
were concerned Tommy wasn't going to be anything until he
graduated college. Hopefully, by then, Tommy would forget
this cop thing. Upon graduating Hunter College in 1977
with majors in Sociology and History and a minor in
Psychology Tommy became a teacher. He taught third and
fourth grade in Chinatown. Teaching wasn't for Tommy.

In June 1979 Tommy took the police test and was called for
the job in 1980. Out of respect for his parents who
strongly voiced their disapproval he turned down the job.
At twenty-seven years of age Tommy was too young to be a
cop, so his parents felt. Tommy worked many jobs. He was,
an administrator, in the New York Hospital registrar's
office and a postal worker. At one point he also held a
job with UPS. None of these jobs gave Tommy a sense of
fulfillment. Finally, in 1984 he became a cop. This time
his parents did not voice any objection because they now
believed Tommy at thirty years of age could make his own
decisions.

On July 14, 1984 Thomas Chin was appointed to the New York

City Police Department as a probationary officer. However, he would never do conventional patrol work or wear a uniform. In 1984 there was a major problem evolving with Chinese gangs and the violence associated with them, especially in Chinatown.

The Police Department's Organized Crime Control Bureau, which handles narcotics trafficking, extortion, gambling and just about anything else involving gang related activity, needed a "UC", an undercover officer to basically work the streets and infiltrate these gangs. At the time there were few Chinese cops. But, this UC had to be more than just Chinese. He had to be streetwise, a little older, and have no typical cop mannerisms, including speech. Being thirty, single and raised in the South Bronx, Tommy was made to order.

Rookie cop Tommy Chin was given fake identification, an automatic pistol which resembled what street thugs carried, not what NYPD cops carried in 1984, and a beautiful Corvette to drive around in. He was a wise ass punk. He grew up with enough of them of all races that playing that part came easy.

For four years Tommy was deep undercover. He bought drugs, gambled, and developed information on loan sharking and prostitution activities. He was not just a Chinese hoodlum. He was a street hustler. His investigations covered the widest of gamuts, a united nations of criminals. Tommy hooked up with Italians, Irish, Blacks, Hispanics, and of course, Asians. Many went to prison. Before he ever got a chance to wear his blue uniform, Police Officer Thomas Chin was promoted to detective.

In 1988 Detective Chin was transferred to the 109th Precinct Detective Squad in Flushing, Queens, an area which had a huge Asian population and the accompanying problems. His perspective changed dramatically. He was now conducting investigations, no longer starring in them.

The Asian crime wave rapidly spread throughout Queens. Tommy's abilities and experience were required on a borough level. Eventually Detective Chin was transferred to the Queens Robbery Squad, which also had its offices in the 109th Precinct station house but handled cases which crossed, many Queens precincts. His knowledge of major Chinese dialects was limited, but his demeanor and his ability to break down barriers with Chinese victims and criminals was a major asset. He demonstrated genuine empathy for Chinese victims who normally don't trust police and a "don't yank my chain" attitude with gang members. But, even with gang members he rarely lost his cool. At 5'8", 165 lbs., his style was more subtle and tricky than intimidating.

Sgt. Costello told Tommy to expect a call from Captain
Naspretto. He also informed him of the incident down in
Lower Township, New Jersey. Tommy could not believe what
Costello had just relayed. A Chinese guy killed a cop
during a burglary. No way. Bad as these mutts could be
they never shot at cops. There had to be some mistake.
Without knowing the facts Tommy reasonably assumed he would
be needed to interview Chinese residents and workers in
that area. He also knew that his partner, Detective Keith
Ng, would be needed.

Keith Ng was born in Canton, China in 1960. In 1976 his
parents uprooted the family and headed for the better life
in the United States. His older sister, Yeeso, had
immigrated to America in the mid-sixties. The family
settled in New York's lower east side. Keith's parents,
Fuk Miu and Shui Yuk, were factory workers. Life wasn't
great, but it was better than living in Canton.

Keith graduated high school in 1980 and signed up with the
Marines. For two years he learned the art of
interrogation. Although it was peacetime all branches of
the services needed individuals skilled at interrogating
and debriefing prisoners of war. Part of Keith's training
included psychology courses.

In 1984 Keith Ng returned to civilian life. He enrolled,
at New York Technical College. He happened to notice a
recruitment poster for the New York City Police Department
in one of the hallways at school. Keith took the exam just
for the hell of it. In 1986 he found himself learning how
to be a cop in the Police Academy.

Police Officer Keith Ng was sent to Chinatown's Fifth
Precinct. It seemed like the most natural place for him to
be assigned. Keith truly felt a sense of accomplishment in
that he viewed himself as "a bridge between the Police
Department and the Chinese people". He was fully aware
that most Chinese people considered police officers
corrupt. One Chinese proverb proclaimed, "Good metal was
never made into a nail." Cops were the nails. They were a
wasted resource. Keith did not believe that and did
whatever he could to change the thinking of Chinatown's
residents.

Although there were approximately two hundred Asian police
officers in the NYPD, Keith was the only one raised in
Communist China. He was fluent in the major Chinese
dialects, Mandarin, Cantonese and Fuchianese. In 1989 his
skills were required by the Queens Homicide Squad. There
had been numerous Asian gang related murders in the 110th

Precinct, which covered Elmhurst, Corona, and Jackson Heights. Initially, Keith was used only as a translator, however, detectives started noticing the pitch in Keith's voice changing. His actions became more demonstrative as the interviews proceeded. His translations were turning into interrogations. His Marine training was showing through.

One specific case which catapulted Police Officer Ng from a translator on loan from the Fifth Precinct to an invaluable interrogator occurred in 1990 in Coney Island, Brooklyn. Five members of a Chinese gang called Tong On were walking on Surf Avenue. Apparently an unsuspecting Korean man had bumped into one of the five. An argument ensued and the Korean was shot dead. The five gangmembers ran to a nearby subway station where they were cornered by the Transit Police. Of course, they pulled the "I don't speak English routine". Keith was called to translate. At first, he asked the questions as posed by the detectives, then he went in his own direction. Before the end of the night Keith had obtained incriminating statements from the non-shooters and a confession from the shooter.

On February 28, 1991 Keith Ng was promoted to detective. He was now well beyond "a translator on loan." In April 1992 he was transferred to the Queens Robbery Squad.

Tommy and Keith became partners more because of design than choice. It seemed only natural for the bosses to hook up these detectives to address the needs of the growing Asian population, which included victims and criminals. Although they respected each other's abilities and background, their styles clashed at times. Tommy was Chinese, American born Chinese, and his knowledge of the language and the various dialects was limited. He needed Keith's linguistic abilities. However, Tommy felt his style sometimes got lost in Keith's translations.

Tommy rarely raised his voice while Keith would turn almost maniacal. Keith needed Tommy's polish. The combination, although sometimes strained, worked and their reputation as a team spread throughout the detective bureau. Other members of the Queens Robbery Squad referred to them by their affectionate title, the "Ninja Squad".

Tommy explained the bare facts of the Lower Township case to Keith. Like Tommy, Keith could not believe an Asian criminal shot a cop. Yes, they were bad motherfuckers, but shoot a cop? Keith was perplexed.

The call from Captain Naspretto came the following afternoon. Tommy remembered him as a lieutenant assigned to the 109th Precinct as an Integrity Control Officer then

246

patrol platoon commander. He did not know him well, but he knew all the cops liked him, which was rare for an ICO who was supposed to be the captain's hit man on disobedient cops.

"Tommy, how ya doing? It's Ernie Naspretto, remember me?"

"Sure, Lieu, I mean captain. How are you?" Tommy answered.

Whenever Ernie called another member of the department and identified himself as "Ernie" he certainly did not expect to be referred to by his rank. But, he also knew that Tommy Chin was too polite and professional to call him by his first name so he let it slide.

"I guess Don spoke to you about the cop that was killed in Lower Township. These guys need help, Tommy. Can you and this guy Ng help out?" Ernie felt a little funny asking these guys to go down to Lower Township, a three hour drive, and play detective on their own time. Tommy didn't hesitate for a moment.

"Yeah, we'll do whatever we can."

Ernie was glad to hear the reply. Ernie explained the case in a little more detail. He knew, Tommy, like himself, would assume that the shooter was a typical young Chinese mutt gang member. Upon hearing the description of a middle aged heavy set Chinese man Tommy was even more perplexed.

Tommy explained that he and Keith were currently entrenched in a heavy robbery kidnapping trial involving, of course, Asian thugs. However, hopefully, they wouldn't be needed for the entire trial and they'd go down to Lower Township as soon as they could.

Ernie called Jack's office after the conversation with Tommy Chin. He felt much better about this call than his first return call to Jack. Detective Sergeant Bob Martin answered the phone.

Ernie did not know Bob Martin so he identified himself as Captain Naspretto from New York. Bob responded, "Is this Ernie?" It was apparent Jack had told Bob all about Ernie.

"I'm Jack's partner. Man, we've heard a lot about you. We really appreciate your help in this mess."

Again Ernie started to feel some pressure but this time at least he had some resources for the Lower Township Police Department to utilize. Bob and Ernie conversed for a couple of minutes. The conversation ranged from goofing on

Jack to what a waste the Feds in New York had been. Ernie liked Bob right away, which was unusual because Ernie liked very few people right away and he hadn't even met Bob yet. Jack took the line.

Ernie explained that two Chinese detectives, one with a serious attitude, were willing to come down to re-interview the previously uncooperative Chinese restaurant workers. Jack was ecstatic. He was going to have cops, real cops, interview and interrogate these people who couldn't give a shit that Dave Douglass was shot dead by one of them. There would be no language excuse and these were New York City cops! Thank you, Ernie.

Jack's excitement actually made Ernie get a little excited. Ernie explained that Detectives Chin and Ng were involved in a trial and would try to come down sometime next week. Jack said he'd make sure they were comfortable in a good hotel and well fed. Everything would be paid for by Lower Township. He also said that he and Bob would be coming up to New York to try to do the things the Feds simply couldn't be bothered with, mainly finding out were that key fit. Ernie felt himself getting pessimistic again. How in God's name were these guys going to find the one door lock which would open with the key found at the murder site in Lower Township in a city of millions upon millions of door locks. Ernie didn't want to tell them that he thought they were fighting a losing battle.

Jack was talking in almost immediate terms. He and Bob would probably come up before Tommy and Keith would go down. Jack wanted to know about hotel arrangements.

"What are you, stupid? You ain't staying at any hotels. You'll stay at my house," Ernie said as though there were absolutely no other considerations.

"No, Ern, I don't want to put you out. Besides I'll be with Bob. We'll just stay at a hotel."

"You and Bob will stay with me and I don't want to hear any more shit. You stay with me or don't even bother coming up here," Ernie was not just being polite, he was very serious and Jack knew it.

Jack reluctantly agreed and there was no more discussion on it. Ernie thought to himself that it took a cop killing to get this fuck to visit me. What a piece of shit. He couldn't wait to see Jack and lay a guilt trip on him. Jack said he would know in a day or two when he and Bob would be coming up.

Ernie and Jack got off the phone and Ernie thought about

the fact that he would soon be seeing Jack and would undoubtedly have to take Jack's jokes about being overweight. Ernie made a mental note to contact Don Costello and thank him for his help.

Jack finished relating the story to Bob and they each had about three drinks and departed the Villas Fishing Club. They each knew that they had an early day the next morning. They went home, had dinner and thought about the next step.

CHAPTER FORTY ONE

Tuesday, March 8th started out as a slow day. Everyone was
catching up on reports and reviewing old assignment sheets
to make sure they were placing the correct information into
their reports. The morning was dragging on slowly.
McGowan, Reemer, Trombetta and Martin had planned to meet
at Lower Police department at eleven in the morning. It
was about twelve thirty when Reemer showed up. Bob and
Jack had completed a lot of busy work and McGowan had just
arrived from completing reports at the Prosecutors Office.

They were conversing about traveling to New York. Martin
was complaining about the fact that the New York Feds
hadn't done much with regard to leg work on the case. Jack
began voicing his opinion and McGowan seemed uncomfortable
with the conversation. Reemer then handed Martin copies of
four reports from FBI Agents who had been working the case
in New York City. Martin read the four pages very quickly.
Trombetta was extremely surprised that Martin was turning
the pages so quickly. Jack figured that after all this
time the reports would no doubt be extensive and intensive.
Bob had a look of total disgust on his face and handed them
to Jack and walked out of the office.

Jack read the first page: ON 3-1-94 NAMED BELOW ENTERED
THE CHINATOWN HARDWARE STORE LOCATED AT EITHER 57 OR 59
EAST BROADWAY, NEW YORK, NEW YORK. A RACK OF BLANK KEYS
WAS OBSERVED, AND SEVERAL BLANK KEYS CHECKED. ALL KEYS
OBSERVED BORE THE INSCRIPTION "CHINATOWN HDW 084-3525.

Jack quickly read the report and in disgust quickly looked
at the next three pages. Each page was just as short and
basically indicated the same worthless information. Jack
threw the papers on the desk and walked out of the room.
He found Martin in the men's room throwing cold water on
his face. Jack looked at Bob and said, "Do you believe
that shit? We waited all this time to find out that the
friggin' Feds in New York were as worthless as tits on a
bull. I have friggin' had it with them. I can't believe
those ass holes. What kind of cops are they?" Jack
quickly answered his own question. "They aren't cops.
They're assholes!"

"Jack, I have had it with the damned Feds. I don't care
what the Pros says or anybody else for that matter. From
here on in if we want it done we will do it ourselves. I'm
gonna tell Reemer he can tell the Feds to kiss my ass."

"Yo, Bob, it isn't his fault. The Feds from down here have

been great. It isn't their fault." Jack knew he wanted to
calm Martin down before he said something to Jack Reemer
that he didn't deserve to hear.

"You're right, Jack, I'm just pissed that we wasted all
this time for nothing, absolutely nothing."

Jack thought for a minute and was telling Bob just to
ignore the reports and let it pass as one of the detectives
entered the men's room and advised that their was a call
for Martin.

They both returned to the office and observed McGowan
reviewing the reports. He also had a disgusted look on his
face. Jack Reemer was sitting at a desk looking over some
paperwork. Reemer looked over at McGowan and asked a
question about a phone number he was checking on.

Martin walked over to the phone and picked it up.
"Detective Sergeant Martin, can I help you? Hi, Roy, how
are you? Say that again." The investigators all looked at
Martin and observed a business like look on his face. Jack
had worked with Martin long enough to know when he was
hearing something important. Jack motioned to Reemer and
McGowan to remain quiet.

Roy Choo was on the other end of the telephone and advised
that Steve Yuk had just received a phone call at the
restaurant. Roy took the call and ascertained that it was
Yi Liang Liu asking for Steve. Roy advised Martin that he
told Liu that Steve was busy and that he would take a
message for him.
"Roy, did you get a phone number as to where Liu can be
reached?" asked Martin. Every face in the room had heard
Martin's question and they were all staring at him in
anticipation of the answer. "Yes, Sergeant Martin." Roy
provided the number to Martin and he wrote it on a yellow
legal pad. Immediately it was picked up by McGowan and was
handed to Jack Reemer. "Well, it's in North Jersey,"
stated Reemer. "Yeah, we have to run a check on it," said
McGowan. Trombetta watched Martin on the phone to see if
he could see a look on Bob's face that would indicate that
it was good information. Martin finished the conversation
with Roy Choo by saying thanks and requesting he call back
with any further information. Trombetta knew Martin had
something.

Jack Reemer quickly picked up the telephone and was calling
his office to obtain a location on the phone number.
McGowan was on the other phone speaking with an Assistant
Prosecutor in an attempt to obtain a court order for
getting the subscriber information with regard to the
number. Martin had a look on his face that indicated to

Trombetta that he had other plans with regard to the number on the yellow legal pad.

Trombetta followed Martin into the hallway where Martin stopped. He indicated to Trombetta by his actions that he wanted to listen to what McGowan and Reemer were saying to the people they were talking to on the telephone. After a short time Martin and Trombetta went into the next office.

"Jack, this is a phone number to a Chinese restaurant where Liu is working. They are going to spend a lot of time trying to legally figure out where this number is located. I'm not waiting for that." Martin picked up the phone and began dialing the number. Jack watched as Martin made the call. He knew Martin was going to play dumb on the phone to obtain as much information as possible from whomever he was talking to.

Martin listened to the phone ring a few times before it was picked up. "Golden Crane Restaurant, can I help you?" Martin knew he was listening to a Chinese male and quickly stated, "Hi, I'm calling to find out what time you close tonight." The person on the other end responded, "Ten P.M."

Martin quickly stated," I'm coming from out of town. Could you tell me the easiest way to get to your restaurant?"

"We are located near 206 right off of interstate 80 in Succasunna."

"What is the exact address?" Martin asked in the most polite voice he could come up with.
"Number 15 Route ten," was the quick response.

"Do you specialize in hot and spicy?" asked Martin with a smile on his face.

"Yes, we do, sir."
"Thank you," said Martin as he hung up the phone.

Jack had been listening to Martin and watching him write everything down. Jack quickly asked, "Where the hell is Succasunna?"

"Let's get the map out of my desk," said Martin.

Both men entered the office and observed that McGowan and Reemer were still on the phones. They were still talking about subscriber information. Martin opened a drawer to his desk and took out a road atlas.

Martin opened it to the index and found the town of

Succasunna, NJ. He didn't realize it at first but he and
Jack had passed the town every time they traveled to the
Pocono Mountains in Pennsylvania. They had driven right by
the night Dave Douglass was murdered.

"Let's go to Succasunna and pay Liu a visit," Jack said.

"We have to get a translator to go with us or it will be a
wasted trip," Martin advised.

"Shit, you're right," replied Trombetta. McGowan had heard
the two talking and excused himself from his phone call
knowing something was up. Martin motioned to Reemer to
hang up the phone. Reemer did so and stated, "The
subscriber search is in the works. We'll have it tomorrow
morning."

"Good, the AP was talking about an affidavit for a court
order," said McGowan.

"Well, I'll have the info but we still need the order to
back it up," Reemer said.

"Hey, guys, my man Martin called the joint and ordered
Lobster Cantonese. We are on our way to pick it up."
Trombetta laughed at his own joke.

Martin added the address and location of the town. Reemer
looked at Martin and said, "You just called the place?"

"Yeah, why not," asked Martin.

"I don't know," answered Reemer with a smile on his face.
Trombetta quickly added, "Jack, see if you can hook up with
Gary Chan and have him meet us in North Jersey at this
restaurant."

Reemer thought for a second. "He had some kind of a meeting
in Newark today. I'll reach out for him." Martin knew that
was Fed talk for "I'll try to find him."

McGowan chimed in. "I guess I should call the Pros and tell
him to forget about the court order."

"Guess so," said Jack in a sarcastic tone. "I love it when
a plan comes together, Bobby." Martin laughed.

Reemer was on the phone trying to locate Chan. He was
advised that Chan would contact him as soon as possible.
McGowan stated, "Well, until we get a translator we can't
go anywhere. I am going to return to the office and do
some paper work." Reemer indicated that he was going to do
the same. Martin looked at his watch and it was three

thirty in the afternoon.

"If you come up with Gary Chan, give me a call," said
Martin to McGowan and Reemer.

Martin got on the phone and called information to ascertain
which police agency covered Succasunna. He quickly
obtained the number of the Roxbury Township Police
Department. Martin dialed the number and spoke with a
Lieutenant Gary Sweeney. Martin filled him in on the case
background and Sweeney replied that his department had sent
two men to Dave's funeral. He would be more than willing to
help in any way possible. Martin requested that Sweeney do
some background on the restaurant and its employees.
Martin advised that he would be visiting Roxbury Township
as soon as he could locate a translator. Sweeney provided
a few numbers were he could be reached and the conversation
was complete.

Martin was hanging up the phone as Trombetta asked if they
could expect help from Roxbury. Martin indicated that
Lieutenant Sweeney sounded like he would provide whatever
they needed. Sweeney even indicated that he would set up
reservations at a local Holiday Inn. Martin was sure this
guy would be helpful.

Reemer and McGowan had left before the phone call to Lt.
Sweeney. Martin looked at Jack Trombetta and said, "Let's
celebrate. We'll be going to Succasunna tomorrow."

"Where to?"

"Let's go to Rio Station."

The two investigators left the station and within minutes
were sitting at the bar throwing back their favorite
alcoholic beverages. "Why don't we have a couple drinks,
call our wives and invite them over for dinner?" Martin
suggested.

"Lynn will be taking a nap," said Trombetta. "She won't
want to come here."

"Well in that case, we'll have a couple drinks and head
home. We will probably be traveling to North Jersey in the
early morning."

They sat and drank a few drinks and were talking small talk
when Martin's beeper went off. Martin looked at the number
and saw Jim McGowan's number. Martin looked at his watch.
It was four forty five. He and Jack had been at the Rio
for almost an hour and a half.

Martin went to the phone booth and called McGowan. "Jim, what's up?

"Bob, I got a call from Reemer. He says that Gary Chan can meet us in Succasunna at about eight to eight thirty. Why don't you meet me at the Ocean City parking area off of the parkway as soon as you can and we'll go from that location."

"Listen, Jack and I have to pick up some stuff. I assume we're staying over night." McGowan answered yes.

"Both you guys going?"

"Absolutely."

Martin pulled another quarter from his pocket and called Captain Maher and filled him in on what was taking place. John Maher's only reply was "Do what ya gotta do." Martin returned to the bar and told Trombetta to finish, his last drink. Both men left the bar and hopped into their vehicle. They conversed about what they should pack and how they were going to beat the shit out of Liu if the opportunity presented itself.

Martin dropped Jack off at his home and as he drove into his own driveway JoAnne was right behind him. She followed Bob into the house as he explained that he had to pack quickly, pick up Trombetta and meet McGowan. JoAnne knew not to ask any questions and she helped Bob pack. Bob changed clothes, grabbed the suitcase, kissed JoAnne and was out the door as she said, "I'll be praying for you guys, be careful."

Martin pulled into Jack's driveway as he came running out the door with a brown paper bag in his hand. "Yo, Jack, what the hell is that? Your lunch?"

"It's my clothes. Lynn couldn't find a suitcase for me."

"You look like a bag person."

Martin quickly made it to the parkway and they were on their way to meet McGowan. They pulled into the parking area at about six p.m. McGowan quickly berated them for taking so long. They didn't have the heart to tell him they had been busy getting shit faced when they got his call. They didn't have to tell him. He could smell the booze.

"Listen, you alcoholics," said Jim, "We are going to my house to pick up my stuff then we have to pick up Reemer."

"Sounds good to me, Jimmy," said Jack as he smiled. Martin

was in the front passenger seat and Jack was in the rear. Martin knew that once at McGowan's home Trombetta would sneak into the front seat before they pulled away. Jack hated to be in the back seat of a car. McGowan packed quickly and they were on their way to pick up Reemer. Reemer exited his home with his suitcase and entered the rear of the vehicle with Martin and they were on the road. Everyone kidded Trombetta about his brown bag suitcase. Jack could not be embarrassed. He didn't care about trivial things like what his luggage looked like.

Martin quickly utilized McGowan's car phone to contact Lt. Sweeney at Roxbury Township and advised they were on their way. Sweeny indicated that he would expect them at about 8:30 p.m.

Jack Reemer started a conversation about the fact that his daughter was stopped by a State Trooper. Reemer was asking Jack and Bob if they had any PBA courtesy cards that he could give his daughter. Most often if you were able to provide such a card when stopped you may just receive a warning for a vehicle violation.

Reemer's mentioning of the subject started a conversation about each man's kids and the problems the kids caused. In general, all the guys had good kids but they could easily find funny negative stories to share with each other.

Trombetta started to light a cigarette. McGowan advised Trombetta that smoking wasn't allowed in the County vehicle. Trombetta persisted and eventually started smoking with his window rolled down and directed the smoke out the window.

Trombetta turned on the radio and started skimming through the stations to find something familiar. Everyone kidded him about his choice of music. Trombetta would attempt to explain the inner hidden meaning to each song he found on the radio.
He would only listen to each song for a short time and change the station. Martin was used to his constant station surfing. Reemer and McGowan appeared to be getting a headache from the ever changing musical format.

The worst part of the music situation was listening to Trombetta try to sound like the musical artist on the radio at any given time. Trombetta's voice sounded like a food processor with a rod knock.

The Led Zeppelin release of Ramble On blared from the radio. Trombetta made his most concerted effort to sound like Robert Plant. He sounded more like Bea Arthur following a tonsillectomy.

256

Everyone made fun of Trombetta's singing ability. Jack
didn't care. He still smoked, sang and changed the station
repeatedly. Martin had worked with Jack long enough to
know that he would continue to do what he could get away
with. After quite a few songs, cigarettes and channel
changing the County vehicle pulled up to the Roxbury
Township Police parking lot. There was quite a bit of snow
plowed into large piles all over the area.

They entered the building and Martin spoke to a dispatcher
who seemed to be expecting them. Lt. Sweeney was summoned
to the dispatch center and quickly introduced himself to
everyone. He led them to a squad room where they could
talk.

Sweeney had spent some time obtaining background on the
owners and workers at the restaurant. He indicated that
the owner maintained a residence that housed approximately
seven workers. He also advised that the owners had been
the victim of a home intrusion in the past. Everyone's
wheels were turning trying to implicate Liu with regard to
the home intrusion. The Jersey boys were feeling more
positive about Liu with each word they heard. Sweeney and
the members of the Roxbury Township Detective Unit had done
a good job of obtaining and providing information about the
restaurant personnel.

The men were waiting for Gary Chan to arrive, before they
would attempt to pick up Liu. They were conversing about
how they would enter the restaurant and get Liu to return
with them to the Police Department to be interviewed and
hopefully interrogated. McGowan and Reemer were afraid they
would spook Liu and possibly lose him.
"You guys go in the front. Martin and I will go in the
back. Roxbury guys can secure the perimeter. That chink
won't disappear," Trombetta said confidently.

Trombetta knew that Liu worked in the kitchen and if he was
going to flee he would exit the rear of the building. Jack
wanted to make sure that he and Martin were waiting at that
door. Jack was hoping the guy would run. He wanted this
thing to get physical. He and Martin both had a lot of
anger they would be more than willing to share with Liu.

Lt. Sweeney was listening to the investigators and was
about to add his agreement with Trombetta's idea when the
phone rang. The dispatcher indicated that FBI Agent Chan
was at the front desk.

Chan was directed to the squad room and after greetings
were out of the way he was filled in on all the
information. Martin looked at his watch as the

conversation between Chan and Reemer was centered upon how the entry to the restaurant should take place.

Martin had already decided he liked Trombetta's mode of entry. Reemer stated to Chan, "How bout we go in the front door, sit down and order a late dinner?" Martin looked at Trombetta. Trombetta knew by the look on Bob's face that he was about ready to go to the restaurant and pick up Liu without any help from anyone. Chan replied,"I'll go in first and get a table. You can follow and make like you are meeting me for dinner. Then somehow I'll make my way to the kitchen. I'll say I got lost looking for the bathroom. I'll be able to verify if Liu is in the kitchen. Jim can be out front, Bob and Jack out back. The uniform guys can be located around the outside perimeter of the building. I'll ask the owner if we can speak to Liu and then we'll go to the kitchen. That way we have total control of the situation."

Martin interrupted as Reemer began to reply. "Listen, you guys go in the front, walk to the counter." Martin was pointing at Reemer and Chan. "Jim will stay in front of the building at the door. Jack and I will go to the rear of the building with the Lieutenant and we can go inside the kitchen and do what we have to do. This whole thing is starting to sound like a soap opera that was canceled." Lt. Sweeney knew Martin and Trombetta were getting a little upset with the entry scenarios that were being suggested.

Sweeney offered, "You guys are running the show but I can go in the back door with Bob and Jack and if there is any problem as to why we entered I'll tell them I am following up on a health complaint."

Martin immediately stated, "Let's do it. Can you get a guy who likes to run, just in case?" Sweeney advised he had just the right guy waiting in the hall. Sweeney opened the door and introduced a guy built like a tree trunk who ran the hundred in under ten seconds. Martin and Trombetta now knew they wouldn't be chasing anyone. This guy could catch a gazelle and once he had his hands around its neck he was fully capable of ripping off its head. Bob and Jack began to really hope Liu decided to run.

McGowan by this time had grown tired of listening to the entry scenarios and sided with Trombetta and Martin. McGowan, Chan and Reemer went in one vehicle, Sweeney, Martin and Trombetta in another. The tree trunk took his patrol car.

The restaurant was only a few blocks from the police department. The men quickly took up their positions. Martin took a position near the rear door that opened into

the kitchen. Martin peered inside and saw Liu. Martin
immediately motioned to Trombetta that Liu was in the
kitchen. Trombetta was behind a fence and could see four
people in the kitchen but he could not tell if Liu was one
of the four. Sweeney and the Tree Trunk were patiently
waiting for the Lower Township guys to make a move. Martin
was waiting for Chan and Reemer to enter the kitchen from
the dining room door. It seemed to Martin that a long
period of time had passed and that the Feds hadn't entered
the kitchen. He hoped they hadn't sat down to dinner and
were waiting for their Pu Pu platter.

Martin gazed at Trombetta who was motioning to Martin that
someone was about to exit the rear door. Martin quickly
observed that it wasn't Liu. Martin decided to let the guy
walk out. The short Chinese man walked to a vehicle and
began to drive out of the rear parking lot. Martin and
Trombetta knew that he had observed the uniformed guys at
the rear of the building. As quickly as the vehicle had
departed it returned. The driver had driven around the
building and returned to the rear of the restaurant. He
exited the car and Martin and Trombetta simultaneously
followed him into the kitchen. They knew they had to make
their move. Sweeney and the Tree Trunk followed right
behind them.

Martin went to the front of the kitchen and approached Liu.
The composite of Liu was perfect. There was no question in
Martin's mind. Trombetta watched Martin and saw that one of
the cooks was picking up a carving knife. Quickly the Tree
Trunk grabbed his arm and removed the knife. Martin had
stated, "Yi Liang Liu," as he approached the man they had
been looking for. He was short and thin and smiled a
nervous smile. Martin extended his hand as if to shake the
hand of Liu. Liu extended his, Martin was holding on to
Liu's hand as if he was shaking hands and with his left
hand he grabbed Liu's right arm. Martin decided he
wouldn't let go until everything was under control.

Reemer and Chan upon hearing the commotion in the rear of
the restaurant came through the doors from the dining area.
The owner of the restaurant hollered, "What you want? Why
you here?"

Sweeney in a monotone voice declared, "I'm Lt. Sweeney and
I'm investigating a health violation. Are you serving
dirty won tons in this joint?"
The Chinese restaurant owner didn't know what to say.
Martin and Trombetta chuckled. Sweeney added, "Keep calm,
we'll be outta here in a minute." Sweeney with a grin on
his face, pointed at a tray of Won Tons and said, "Is this
all the Won Tons?" No one answered. Sweeney let it ride

with a smile on his face.

Trombetta walked around the kitchen glaring at the employees. He was hoping that one of them would give him eye contact so he could rip his face off. Jack was in one of those moods.

Gary Chan was conversing with Liu as Martin still held on to his arm. Chan stated, "Bob, he says he will come with us to the police department for an interview." Martin let go of Liu as he was guided to the patrol car by Tree Trunk. They assured the owner they would return Liu if possible. No one thought Liu would be going back to the restaurant.

It was quickly decided that McGowan, Reemer and Chan would interview the suspect. Martin and Trombetta would be outside the room and would listen and subsequently interrupt with questions or information if they desired.

Upon arrival at the Police department, Liu was quickly taken into the squad room. Martin and Trombetta followed him into the room and just stared at him. Liu smiled nervously. They were both looking at him like they were going to kill him. His nervous smile turned into a look that said. "Those guys don't like me."

McGowan, Chan and Reemer began the long arduous task of interview and interrogation. Martin and Trombetta stood outside the door listening to every word. Trombetta had to repeat much what he was hearing because of Martin's hearing problem. The time passed slowly. Martin looked at his watch and said, "Jack, they have been at it for over two hours and this shit head isn't going for anything. It's time for somebody to bust his balls."

"I'm surprised that McGowan hasn't let loose on him," Jack replied. At that exact moment McGowan's voice could be heard bellowing in the hallway, "Listen, all you keep saying is that you don't know nothing. I want you to explain what happened to the business card you had in your possession and tell me why your belongings were never stolen while you lived at the house near the Chinese Resturant." Gary Chan quickly translated the questions into Chinese and everyone waited for Liu's reply.

Liu spoke and Chan translated, "I gave the card to a new employee after I didn't need it any longer and I don't know why my things weren't stolen from the house." Martin and Trombetta knew McGowan wouldn't be happy with the answer.

They were right. McGowan went off on another tirade and Liu could be heard sobbing. He began to cry and speak at the same time. Chan advised that he was saying he had no knowledge of the murder nor the burglaries and thefts at the residence. McGowan screamed, "You're lying, you shit head. You're gonna find yourself face to face with the guys in the hallway. They just want to kick your ass. One of them is the brother of the cop that was killed." Chan translated and Liu began to cry uncontrollably. McGowan kept up the tirade and Chan continued to translate for Liu. Martin and Trombetta were listening as Liu could be heard speaking while he was crying. Chan stated, "He wants to talk to the brother of the murdered cop."

Reemer looked at McGowan and each had a look on their faces that indicated they felt the guy was ready to talk. They had been questioning him for three and a half hours and had finally got him to let loose. Reemer quickly exited the office and motioned to Martin to come in.

Martin entered with Trombetta behind him. Trombetta immediately began staring at Liu. Liu started to cry once again. McGowan stated, "I think he is ready to talk. Have you heard everything?" Martin and Trombetta nodded in the affirmative. Liu began talking and Chan started to translate. Everyone had a look of relief on their faces. Chan, however, was pessimistic.

Chan began to shake his head in the negative as he listened to Liu. Everyone looked at Chan as he stated, "He says that he is very sorry for the loss to your family and that he knows it is a matter of honor. He says that he wants to help you find the killer of your brother and that if he knew anything he would help." Everyone's face showed the dissatisfaction with Liu's reply. Trombetta screamed, "Tell that Chink motha I'm gonna kill him!" Liu didn't need a translation. He was looking at Trombetta as Jack walked toward him. Liu lowered his head and began crying uncontrollably once again.

Martin looked at Jack and said, "This is going nowhere. We gotta get this guy to tell us something."

McGowan said, "Listen, let's start all over. We will try again and if he won't go we'll see if we can get him to take a polygraph. The only problem will be doing it with a translator." Martin remembered being told by Expert Polygraph Examiner, Dick Arther, that using a translator was always difficult because of not being able to understand voice inflections and the like. McGowan also knew that it was a long shot but they weren't getting anywhere.

Martin and Trombetta turned to leave the room and Liu spoke to Chan. Chan translated, "Bob, he is saying that he hopes

he remembers something to help you honor your family."
Jack looked at his watch as they sat down in a small office
near the squad room. The time was 12:25 in the morning.
Jack lamented, "They aren't getting anywhere."

"We are wasting our time. He is either a real hard ass or
he really doesn't know anything. I don't want to think we
spent all our time finding this guy and he had nothing to
do with Dave's murder," Bob moaned.

"He's involved, I'm telling you he's involved," said Jack.

"I think so too," said Martin. "We just have to get him to
admit it."

"He isn't going to tell them anything else tonight. We
should let him go home set up a surveillance and then once
he is sitting back thinking he beat us, pick him up in the
morning and hit him again. Maybe his guard will be down."

Martin thought for a few seconds and said, "I like that
idea. I'm going in and tell McGowan." Martin exited the
office and listened at the door of the squad room. When he
knew nothing of major consequence was happening he entered
and Reemer approached him. Martin advised Reemer of
Trombetta's idea. Reemer liked the idea and said, "We are
going to try one more time and if it doesn't work we'll try
again tomorrow."

Martin left the room and advised Trombetta. Both men knew
that Liu wasn't going to talk, at least not at this time.
They hoped that perhaps he would be so psychologically
devastated when he was brought in again that he would then
tell the truth.
Martin looked at Trombetta. "We are wasting our time hear
now. We might as well get Lt. Sweeney to take us to the
Holiday Inn."

Lt. Sweeney entered the office and told the Jersey guys
that he could give them a marked unit that they could use
until the following morning. Jack quickly said, "We don't
want to tie up one of your patrol units. Just get us a
ride. That's all we need." Sweeney drove them to the
hotel.

They entered the Holiday Inn and noticed that the bar and
restaurant was still open. Each man was starved and
thirsty. Sweeney was talking to the female desk clerk and
then spoke to a waitress who was passing by. Sweeney
informed Martin, "All you have to do is give this lady a
credit card and tell her how many rooms you want. I
already checked you guys in."

Martin pulled the Township credit card from his wallet and the clerk took an impression of it for subsequent billing.

Sweeney advised that he would tell the other investigators that Martin and Trombetta were at the Holiday Inn. Martin said, "Tell them we're at the bar." Sweeney smiled a mischievous smile.

Martin and Trombetta took their belongings up to their room and quickly came down to the bar. The bartender and waitress were talking. The bar was empty. Martin grabbed a basket of pretzels that was on the bar and he and Trombetta started munching immediately. The waitress and bartender kept talking, almost ignoring the two cops.

Martin was getting impatient and said to Trombetta, "What is their problem?"

"Don't say anything, will ya." Trombetta didn't want to be embarrassed by any remark Bob might make. Martin looked at his watch and it was 12:45 AM.

The bartender walked over and asked them what they wanted to drink. Both men ordered draft and Martin asked, "Is it too late to get something to eat?"

"We close at one."

Martin and Trombetta knew that they were planning on drinking for more than fifteen minutes.

The waitress walked by and Martin asked, "Could you tell me if there are any bars that stay open after one?"

"I'll be right back," was her reply.

"Hey, Jack, are you getting the feeling that no one wants to talk to us?"

"Yeah, it's like they are avoiding us."

Both guys poured down the beers and ordered two more. The waitress returned and advised that there was a bar about three miles away that stayed open until three AM. She then inquired, "But you guys have to stay in this building, Right?"

"What do you mean?" asked Martin.

"Lt. Sweeney told us that you guys were a couple of criminals that had to stay here under house arrest and that if you left we had to contact him at the police department."

Martin and Trombetta looked at each other and grinned. Nice guy! Lt Gary Sweeney had pulled a good one on them. No wonder no one wanted to talk to them. Martin immediately removed his Police ID from his pocket as did Trombetta. The waitress looked at the badges and ID cards and laughed.

"That Gary is a real nut. We should have known he was pulling a joke on you guys." Everyone had a good laugh and the bartender set up two beers on the bar for each of the guys.

Trombetta then asked if there were any taxi cabs in the area. The waitress advised that when she finished her duties she would take the guys to the bar nearby. She told them it was the least she could do. The guys agreed.

They quickly finished their drinks as the waitress finished her work. They entered her car and were on their way to the open bar that was nearby. It had started snowing again and the guys were thinking that they had seen enough of the snow.

The waitress was making small talk about her being an unwed mother and had a little girl that she had to pick up at the babysitter's. She also said that if she could have talked the babysitter into watching her daughter overnight she would have partied with the guys. Both guys pretended to be disappointed.

They passed a go-go bar that advertised "Nudes All Night." The waitress said, "I can tell by the rings on your fingers that you don't want me to leave you out there." Martin thought how funny the statement sounded. Jack rarely wore a wedding ring. For some reason he had it on his finger for this trip. Moments later she pulled into the parking lot of a respectable looking establishment that advertised "Music Til Closing." Both guys thought it was a far cry from "Nudes All Night", but the music would not get them into any trouble. The waitress offered to come back in a couple of hours to pick them up and return them to the Holiday Inn. They graciously declined.

Trombetta felt cheap about the girl driving them to the bar and in his most gallant manner said as he fumbled through his wallet, "Here is a PBA Courtesy card. If you ever get stopped hand the officer the card and maybe he'll extend you the courtesy of not writing you a ticket." She thanked him, said goodbye to both men and drove away warning, "Don't get into any trouble." Both men knew better.

They entered the bar and saw about eight people at the bar
and four or five tables that were being utilized by about
fifteen people. They sat down at the bar and each ordered
a beer and Martin quickly ordered onion rings and
mozzarella cheese sticks. Martin had seen the menu on the
chalk board on the wall behind the barmaid.

Both guys looked around and observed a nice bar restaurant
and what appeared to be clean cut patrons. A guy who
looked like Soupy Sales was playing a guitar and singing
Led Zeppelin's song "BABE I'M GONNA LEAVE YOU." Martin
thought to himself that every song he heard lately was from
Zeppelin.

Martin took a sip from his beer and then went to the
telephone to call Roxbury Police department and let the
guys know where they should stop when finished with Liu.
Martin knew that Reemer, Chan and McGowan would also need a
few drinks to unwind.

Martin and Trombetta ate the goodies and washed them down
with a few more beers. Martin changed to Grand Mariner on
the rocks and Trombetta started drinking Vodka and
pineapple juice. It was two fifteen before they knew it
when the door opened and the rest of the entourage entered.

Martin and Trombetta made eye contact with the
investigators as they entered. They could tell by the
looks on their faces that they had not accomplished
anything. No confession or useful information had been
obtained. Jack and Bob felt so down they didn't even say
hello to the other guys. The guys took up seats at the bar
and ordered some drinks. After about fifteen minutes of
silence McGowan lamented, "We didn't get shit from the
guy." It was evident that Jack and Bob didn't want to talk
about Liu.

"We sent him home to bed and we're going to pick him up at
9am. I don't think he has anything to do with Dave's
murder," Chan said.

"I'm still not sure," McGowan added.

"I need another drink," said Reemer.

Trombetta said, "Bob, buy these guys a drink. It's the
least you can do." Martin ordered drinks for everyone.
More onion rings were ordered and all the guys were pouring
down the drinks as if they were on a mission to get drunk.
McGowan started to harass Martin and Trombetta about
leaving during the interview of Liu. Trombetta was
attempting to justify their absence and finally said, "We

either had to leave or break in the room and kick the shit outta that chink. No offense, Gary."

Martin added, "Jim, how would you explain that one to the prosecutor in the morning?"

McGowan chuckled and ordered another round of drinks. Eventually everyone had paid for a round of drinks but Trombetta. McGowan busted his chops until Trombetta broke out twenty bucks from his wallet. The money had been secreted away in the tiny recesses of a long forgotten hiding place in the wallet.

Jack reluctantly threw it on the bar as the barmaid stated, "Sorry, fellows, the last drink was last call." Trombetta quickly picked up the twenty and returned it to its hiding place. He hoped he never had to take it out again. Jack hated to buy drinks when someone else could.

McGowan looked at his watch. It was three AM. Everyone threw a tip on the bar. Jack said, "Hey, Bob, get the tip." They all laughed and exited the bar. They entered McGowan's car and returned to the Holiday Inn. McGowan, Reemer and Chan had stopped and obtained their room keys before going to the bar. They all walked up the stairs to the rooms. The rooms were all situated on the same floor and in close proximity.

Chan entered one room, Reemer another and McGowan entered his room. Martin and Trombetta entered the same room as McGowan stated, "You guys even sleep together!" Chan laughed as Reemer asked, "Hey, Jack, do you scrub Bob's back or does he do your's?"

"Hey, we are saving the taxpayers money while you guys are ripping them off. Are you too good to sleep in the same room?" Jack countered.

"You two give new meaning to the phrase 'Closeness Counts'," Chan said.

Trombetta said in a feminine tone, "Don't bother us, we are going to bed."

Trombetta quickly turned on the television and found the Honeymooners. Both men removed their clothes and hopped into their separate beds. Trombetta laughed at Ralph Kramden and said,"Hey, Bobby, that's us. The Honeymooners."

"Go to sleep and stay out of my bed," Bob said firmly.

Both guys had a restless night. Martin woke up early,

which was his normal routine. He reached for his watch on
the night table. It was 5:35 AM. He got out of bed and
took a shower. He tried to be as quiet as possible. He
didn't want to wake up the other half of the Honeymooners.

After dressing he went down to the lobby and found the pay
phone. It was 6:15 and he knew JoAnne would be awake
getting ready for work. She answered the phone and it was
good hearing her voice.

"Good morning."

"Hi, hon bun, did you get the guy that killed Dave?" asked
JoAnne.

"Nope, this may be another dead end," said Bob. JoAnne
knew that she should change the topic of conversation.

"Did you sleep good last night?" she asked.

"Well, not really. We went to a local bar restaurant and
stayed til closing. Then I had to listen to the
Honeymooners with Jack. It's a long story. I think I got
about two or three hours sleep."

"Well, I won't tell you not to stay out late drinking."

"Good, don't tell me that." They both laughed. JoAnne
decided to change the subject once again. "Our son called
from Iowa last night." JoAnne was referring to Bert. "He
asked if he could move out here and stay with us for awhile
to get his life together."

Bob listened for a moment and asked, "What is so wrong in
his life at this point?"

"He feels that he needs a change to get some structure in
his life and begin a career in law enforcement. He figures
you're the best person for that and I agreed with him."

"Well, I know we both want what is best for him so give it
some thought and when I get home remind me and we'll talk
some more and make a decision."

JoAnne knew that Tara was not going to be happy with having
her little brother to deal with once again. She had been
living with Bob and JoAnne for more than a year while she
pursued her nursing education. She also had moved to
Jersey from Iowa in pursuit of a career. Having both adult
children in the house would probably prove interesting,
especially with one bathroom. JoAnne thought about the
practical things. Usually, Bob failed to think about taking
a number to use the bathroom.

They exchanged goodbyes and Bob grabbed two cups of coffee from the table that was set up in the lobby. He also grabbed two muffins and started up the stairs to the room. Normally he didn't eat anything in the morning. This stuff was free, so why not? McGowan was just coming down the hallway and after seeing Martin asked, "Where's the coffee?" Martin provided the directions and McGowan went to the lobby.

The time was 6:45 AM. Bob knew Trombetta would still be sleeping. Martin quietly unlocked the door and entered the room. "Bobby, do I smell coffee?"

"Yes, Jackie, you do and yes, I got one for you. I knew you wouldn't have Lynn around to serve you and I wanted you to feel at home."

Jack laughed. "See, we are like the Honeymooners. Give me a kiss."

Martin had absolutely no intention of making Jack feel that much at home. They both laughed. Jack took the coffee and muffin into the bathroom. Martin sat down finished the goodies and watched the morning news.

It had been decided that the guys would meet in the lobby at 8 AM and meet Lt. Sweeney at a local restaurant for breakfast. They checked out of the motel and were on their way. They walked into the restaurant and Sweeney was sitting at the counter talking to the waitress. He quickly acknowledged them and moved to a table and began rearranging the tables to make room for six of them.

They conversed about what they intended to do. They concluded that they would immediately scare the crap out of Liu and hoped he would break. Chan maintained that he didn't think Liu was involved in any way. The other guys figured Chan was wrong. Liu had to have some involvement. None of them wanted to face the fact that they may have run into another dead end. This investigation was an ongoing lesson in frustration. They were all getting tired of getting nowhere fast.

Sweeney sent a patrol car to pick up Liu and hoped that the sight of the marked unit and an intimidating cop would scare him. In a short time Liu was back into the now familiar surroundings of Roxbury Township Police department Liu looked scared. He had the look the guys had hoped for. Martin and Trombetta along with Chan started the interview. Not much time had passed when they were both looking at each other realizing that they were not getting anywhere.

Both Trombetta and Martin kept telling Chan to not only repeat what they were saying but to do it with the same tone and demeanor. Chan had been doing so during the entire interview. Martin and Trombetta were too frustrated to notice. Chan had used every scare tactic and conversational mode he could think of. Martin and Trombetta could not believe this guy was not involved. They were quickly getting emotional and Chan began to think that they were no longer acting. How could he tell these maniacs that Liu was not involved? Chan knew that no matter what he told them that he would not change their minds.

Chan said that Liu would take a polygraph test to clear his self in the minds of the investigators. Martin and Trombetta figured he was just stalling for time. Trombetta started screaming, "If I find out you're lying, I'm gonna make you wish you never met me. Do you understand me, man? I'll fuckin' kill you. Do you know what I'm saying?"

Martin then spoke in a low but firm tone. "Gary, tell him that when we find out exactly what his involvement is we are going to pay him a visit."

Martin was nose to nose with Liu and Trombetta's chest was making contact with Liu's shoulder. Liu began to cry uncontrollably. He started to mumble and cry at the same time. Trombetta screamed, "Don't cry, you punk."

Chan stated, "He is saying you are scaring him and he didn't do anything wrong. He has been saying the same thing since last night." McGowan then came into the room and said, "Let's just set up a polygraph and get this guy tested. It's the only way we will know for sure."

Both Martin and Trombetta felt that doing so was admitting defeat. They knew, however, that they had no alternative. Reemer walked into the room and once again began to question Liu about the business card that he had admitted to having in his possession, the same business card that had been found at the scene of the murder. Reemer wanted to clarify that Liu had either lost the card or misplaced it.

Liu finally indicated that he had given it to a new employee maybe sometime in December or January. Liu just couldn't remember which employee. At this point both McGowan and Reemer were getting frustrated with Liu's answers. Every time he provided an answer it was as if he was concealing something. Chan still maintained that Liu was innocent of any involvement and was so scared that he couldn't think straight. Everyone else thought that Liu was pulling a snow job.

It was noon before the guys decided that they would give up on Liu until they could have some New York cops interrogate him. McGowan and Martin figured they would set up a polygraph and then take it from there. Liu indicated that he was moving back to New York City. He was returning to his apartment over top of the Japanese restaurant on 14th Street. The Golden Crane was changing ownership and the new owners were hiring all new employees. Liu would be looking for a new job in the Big Apple.

Liu was returned to his workplace and the guys went out to lunch. They ended up at the same restaurant they had been at in the morning. Sweeney had bought breakfast. McGowan picked up the lunch bill. Of course Jack had to coerce him into it.

The conversation during lunch centered on Liu, of course. The guys were talking about the fact that they did not observe any fresh wounds on him. They had all observed that Liu was not even bearing any scratches. They had kept in their mind the fact that Dave Douglass had no doubt wounded the suspect when he was fleeing. Gene Taylor had found two distinct blood types. The FBI Lab had come to that conclusion upon receiving the evidence for processing.

The guys then began to thank Sweeney for everything he had done. Sweeney indicated that if the guys from South Jersey needed anything at all they just had to call. They all exchanged business cards and they were on their way back home. Sweeney hung around the restaurant as they left. The waitress came up to him and was filling his coffee cup when he stated, "Those guys from Lower Township are going to find the killer. It's just a matter of time." The waitress really didn't understand what he was saying. She knew not to ask. It really didn't seem like Sweeney was talking to her.

The ride back to South Jersey was long, boring, uneventful and frustrating. It seemed like Trombetta smoked a pack of Marlboro Lights. No one had much to say.

CHAPTER FORTY TWO

March 10th was a day of paperwork for Martin and another day of frustration for Trombetta. Jack walked the halls of LTPD venting his feelings upon whoever wished to listen. While Martin was doing reports Jack had filled the administration in on all the information with regards to Liu.

Jack continually stated that they still weren't done with Liu and that eventually a couple of New York detectives would probably break him. Jack knew Bob felt the same way. Jack figured that it would be a good day to fill in the on duty guys about what was going on with the investigation. He walked into the office and saw Martin reviewing notes. "Hey, Bob, what do you think about me giving Patrol a little briefing on what has been happening?"

"Sounds good to me. I'm glad you want to do it. I'm not in the mood."

Jack looked at Bob and commented, "It's not looking good, is it?"

Martin replied, "Jack, I know we are going to get this guy. I just don't know when." Jack wished he could be as optimistic.

Martin spent the rest of the day completing reports and spending time on the phone. At one point the phone rang and it was Dick Arther. Dick had trained and certified Martin as an Expert Polygraphist. Dick immediately began telling Martin that he had received a call from an investigator at Cape May County. Martin was listening intently but was a bit confused with the conversation.

Arther advised that he had recommended Martin as the Polygraphist the County should use in conjunction with a translator for a case involving a Chinese suspect. Martin now realized that Arther was talking about the Douglass case. Martin advised Dick Arther about his involvement with the case. Dick apologized and stated he was not aware that it was Martin's case. Arther then indicated that he would recommend another Polygraphist. He didn't want the Polygraphist to have personal interest in the case. Martin was flattered that Dick Arther had recommended him for the job. It was a good feeling knowing that his teacher thought highly of his abilities.

Arther extended his condolences with regard to the loss of a fellow officer and provided Martin with the name of another polygraphist and a translator he had utilized in the past. Dick also questioned Martin about the interview of Liu. After he heard the entire scenario he stated. "Well, Bob, from what you told me I believe that if neither you nor McGowan could break this guy even with a translator, you probably are wasting your time with a polygraph. You're going to find out he isn't involved." Martin did not like what he heard. Dick Arther had to be wrong. Time would tell.

The time went by quickly. When four o'clock rolled around Martin and Trombetta were sitting at home feeling as if they had accomplished nothing. They both spent an evening of watching television but not paying attention to anything that was on it.

JoAnne and Lynn had talked to each other on the telephone while their husbands sat around comatose. Both wives expressed their concerns about their husbands well being. They were starting to worry about the fact that the case wasn't solved yet. They knew, however, that they shouldn't mention the concerns to their husbands. It was their job to be attentive, understanding and supportive. Both wives were good at those things.

Neither Bob nor Jack had noticed that their wives had been taking part in a lot of phone conversations lately, most often with other family members who were wondering what was going on with the investigation. Lynn and JoAnne knew that the best thing they could do was to keep their husbands insulated from these phone calls. Sometimes the guys really had no idea what their wives went through.

JoAnne on one hand loved to talk on the telephone and would talk forever, as long as she wasn't busy. She had been busy trying to insulate Bob from what he considered garbage calls. Lynn on the other hand hated to talk on the telephone but she did, so Jack wouldn't be bothered.

Neither, Jack or Bob had given much thought that the girls were also stressed out over this investigation. The guys were too busy worrying about solving the case. They hadn't been giving much thought to family matters.

The next day at work Martin and Trombetta spent much of the morning meeting with the Chief and Captain. The talk was about financing the investigation when it led the investigators out of town. They also talked about the idea of reward money for information. Neither the Chief, nor Captain, we're worried about finances. They felt pretty sure that township government had committed itself early on in the investigation. They were ready to hold the members of council to their word.

The Chief indicated that a Republican council person stated she could get close to fifty thousand dollars donated for a reward. The Chief advised that once the Democrats heard they too would get some donations for a reward.

Both the Chief and Captain were easy to work for and they would only be critical if either Martin or Trombetta let their emotions take over and cause them to do something stupid like kill the perpetrator without just cause. Sometimes actions like that might get administrators upset. When noon rolled around the Chief told Martin and Trombetta to take some time off, spend some time with the family and return fresh on Monday.

Bob and Jack decided on lunch at the Villas Fishing club. They made sure the shift was covered for the rest of the day and took a couple of the "kids" with them to the Fishing Club. They decided that everyone needed a break. It was Friday and everyone needed to unwind. Bob and Jack knew that they weren't setting good examples by taking the kids to get shit faced. However, neither man seemed to care. The investigation was bogged down once again and both Martin and Trombetta felt that maybe a few drinks would get the problems off their minds. The guys sat down to eat and drink and before they knew it they were all calling home to say they wouldn't be showing up for dinner.

The conversation was purposely kept from centering on the investigation. Jack was doing his best to make the guys aware that he and Bob really wanted to think about nothing. Nothing, other than the next drink.

CHAPTER FORTY THREE

In New York Captain Ernie Naspretto had just returned home
from a day tour and it entered his mind that he wanted to
thank Don Costello for his help. He had tried to catch Don
a few times and on each occasion Don was busy. Ernie
wanted to thank him for the Chin/Ng connection and let him
know the guys from Lower Township would be coming up
sometime the following week. Ernie praised Tommy and Keith
for being so willing to help out on their own time. Then
true to form Don nonchalantly suggested Lower Township make
a formal request through the Police Commissioner's office.
Ernie's patrol mentality and detective bureau ignorance
were shining through.

"What do you mean? How do they do that? This job would
send detectives to another state on company time to help
solve a crime that happened in that state? Are you
serious?" Ernie kept shooting out the questions.

"Have them call the PC's office. Tell them what happened
and that these Chinese detectives are needed for
translation and interrogation," Don instructed. Ernie
wondered if there was anything that Don didn't know about
this job. It was about 5:30 in the afternoon. By six
everyone at headquarters would be gone for the weekend.
Ernie wanted to give Jack this information right away and
hopefully get that request in so it would be official by
Monday. Ernie figured Jack would have gone home by this
time.

Ernie didn't know that the Lower Township Chief of Police,
Don Douglass, had told his two Detective Sergeants to go
have a drink on him and wind down a little. He knew these
two investigators were working their collective butts off
and needed a break.

Ernie called Jack's home and his son, Jackie, answered.
His parents weren't home. Ernie asked him to beep his dad
and have him call back right away. Within ten minutes Jack
called Ernie back.

"Where are you?" Ernie asked.

"At the fishing club," replied Jack.

"Are you drunk, yet?" Ernie's voice was half serious, half bustin' chops. Jack laughed and said no. Ernie continued, "Listen to me, this is very important. I just found out that you can make things go more smoothly if you officially request assistance through the Police Commissioner's office. This way, those detectives can go down there on department time and not have to worry about scheduling." Ernie instructed Jack to have the highest ranking member of his department call immediately to get things rolling. Jack wrote down the number for the fax and the office, thanked Ernie and hung up. Jack returned to the bar where Bob was seated and ran all the information past Bob. Bob, called Chief Don Douglass at home and provided him with the information.

The Chief returned to the Police Department and prepared the necessary requests and had them faxed and also made a call to the PC's office in New York. He spoke with an officer who advised he was waiting on the information and would get it to the Commissioner immediately.

The Chief then beeped Martin and advised him everything had been completed. Don Douglass then entered his police vehicle for the ride home. He couldn't help but think about how extensive this investigation had become. He knew Martin and Trombetta would be spending a lot of time in the Big Apple. He wasn't sure whether he should worry about them or the fine citizens of New York City. He laughed to himself as he drove home.

Martin and Trombetta sat at the Villas Fishing Club and even after promising them selves they wouldn't talk about the case did so anyway. They wondered where the investigation would lead next. They conversed for a short time while the young guys were trying to get up a game of shuffleboard or darts. They knew they would finally be going to New York City. It sure had been a long wait. Many times either Martin or Trombetta said they had to get to New York. Each time they had done so something came up that put the halt to their trip.

Jack indicated that he wanted to call Ernie once again and advise everything was taken care of and that the PC's office had by this time received the necessary paperwork. Jack knew that Ernie was doing as much as he could to get things happening. Bob agreed that Jack should at least make Ernie aware that things were finally going in the right direction.

Jack walked from the bar and Bob yelled, "Hey, Jack, tell Ernie I love him." Jack responded quickly, "That's okay, but no playing Honeymooners with another lover, Bobby."

The senior citizens at the bar were beginning to wonder
about these two detective sergeants. Bob looked at his
drink and noticed both he and Jack had three drinks each
lined up. They better stop talking and start drinking so
they could get caught up. Bob knew that wasn't a good
idea, but what the heck. They were unwinding.

CHAPTER FORTY FOUR

Meanwhile, in the Naspretto home Ernie was thinking that
now the NYPD Major Case Squad, which fell under the parent
command of the Special Investigation Division, would be
assigned this case. Although Ernie did not know much about
the detective bureau, he did know that the Major Case Squad
was big time. He was very impressed with his own
department for being so willing to help. Ernie also felt
like a ten ton boulder had been lifted from his shoulders.
His good friend Jack Trombetta called for help and he was
able to provide it. Thank God for Don Costello!

Great, the resources would be provided. But would they be
able to nail the shooter? Was he back in China or anywhere
else in the world? How long would the NYPD provide
assistance? Would they reach a dead end and just give up?
Ernie knew Jack would never give up, but he also knew the
realities of life in the big city. If they were going to
nail this bastard it better be soon. Ernie knew it wouldn't
be long before Jack and Bob would be paying him a visit.

Ernie couldn't help but think about the pressure the Jersey
guys were under. He knew that they wanted to solve this
case and that the longer it took the harder it would be to
do. He knew that he would help these guys in any way
possible. No matter what it might take. He would be
rekindling a friendship with Jack and would probably find a
new friend in Bob. He nor Bob and Jack had any idea that
this working relationship and friendship would eventually
bring them all very close together. They had no idea what
God had preordained. They would soon find out.

Ernie was very happy that at least his department was going
through the right motions. If the effort would result in
anything was another issue. Jack and his partner, Bob
Martin, would be coming up and staying at Ernie's house.
There wasn't a doubt in Ernie's mind that his wife, Grace,
would be the perfect hostess.

Ernie and Grace were married for three years. They met on
March 20, 1985 at a fund raising benefit, what the cops
call "a racket", being held for a cop who had been indicted
for shooting a crazed woman who was threatening other cops
with a knife. All charges were eventually dropped against
the cop. There were literally thousands of cops in the
main ballroom of the LaGuardia Sheraton in Jackson Heights.
Grace was an executive secretary for the hotel's manager.
She attended the racket because she always had a soft spot

in her heart for cops and she certainly wasn't adverse to meeting a nice guy. Her father, Thomas Brauchle, had been a cop for the Port Authority. Shortly after retirement he died of a heart attack while trying to break up a fight at a school bizarre. He was 46. Grace was 4.

Grace grew up in a two room apartment in Astoria, Queens. Her mother, Angelina, who everyone called Ange, taught her daughter, the ways of "the good Italian wife". Ernie, however, was not sure of the exact role of the good Italian husband and their love affair was off and on for four years.

Ernie and Grace got back together for the last time in December of 1988. Grace had seen a newspaper article in the Daily News written about Ernie. He was an outspoken sergeant assigned to the 103rd Precinct in Jamaica, Queens. The article highlighted how Ernie would go out of his way to embarrass incompetent district attorneys and lenient judges by apprizing his friends in the media how messed up the system was. Ernie was one of the few cops who realized that he, too, had first amendment rights and if the bosses didn't like it, fuckem'.

Apparently, Ernie as a sergeant was the same as Ernie as a police officer. In fact, he was probably worse, Grace thought. She wrote him a letter. He called as soon as he received it and they were married in Las Vegas on January 10, 1991.

Ernie couldn't deal with a big Italian wedding. He despised all the politics and the planning involved. Too many of his friends had great weddings and lousy marriages. He vowed never to have a big, stupid, gaudy wedding and hopefully have a good marriage. Although she preferred a more traditional wedding, Grace knew Ernie would be unrelenting so she agreed to go to Vegas. Six months later they had a very small church ceremony in Astoria. Grace's, brother, Denis, told Ernie at the second wedding, "You're the only dope I know who married the same woman twice. At least I had the decency to marry a different woman my second time."

Grace was an excellent homemaker, cook, and all around partner for Ernie. Her infinite pleasantness overshadowed his tendency to be less friendly. Although he was polite he was not quick to warm up to new people. Whenever Grace wanted him to meet her friends or coworkers Ernie would say something like, "If I've gone this far in my life without knowing them, I can probably go a lot longer without knowing them." Grace on the other hand treated Ernie's friends like gold. She sent them birthday and Christmas cards and bought their children little gifts. Ernie would tell his friends, "You better hope I die first, cause if she goes, so do the cards and gifts." She invited many couples over for dinners. She always made Ernie look good. Ernie's friends would always wonder what she saw in him. Ernie often wondered the same thing.

The telephone rang in the Naspretto home and Ernie answered to hear Jack on the other end advising that everything was in the works. They only conversed for a short time before Jack advised that he had more important things to do. Ernie knew he meant getting his butt back to the bar stool.

Ernie began thinking about Jack and Bob and the fact they would be visiting. Jack and his friend, Bob, would be house guests of Ernie and Grace, who was now four months pregnant. Angelina was fifteen months old. Although Grace would do whatever she could to make things comfortable for Jack and Bob, Ernie still felt a little funny about seeing Jack after a year and a half.

Ernie left the FBI National Academy at about 185 lbs. which fit his 5'8" frame just perfect. He was running five miles a day, watching his diet and was in very good shape. That lasted for about three months after the academy.

After Angelina was born the running stopped, the watching of the fat intake stopped and the weight gain started. Ernie was now 220 lbs. He knew Jack would have a field day with him as soon as they laid eyes on one another. He wasn't looking forward to that.

Jack actually got in worse shape while at the FBI National Academy. His partying resulted in a fifteen pound weight gain. He only ran when he absolutely had to and he hated going to the gym, usually because of the hangovers. However, Ernie knew Jack had gotten back into shape right after graduation from the academy. The last time they had spoken was the week Angelina was born. Jack said he had lost the weight he had gained while at the academy and was going to the gym everyday. Unfortunately, Jack in good shape was the real Jack, while Ernie being thirty pounds overweight was the norm. He had fought the "Battle of the Bulge" his entire life and lost on a regular basis.

CHAPTER FORTY FIVE

Back at the Fishing Club Martin looked at his watch. The time was 7:45 p.m. Martin, Trombetta and four of the kids from the Detective Division where still drinking and had all contacted their wives and advised them they would be getting home late. Jack looked at Bob and said, "Do you realize we have been here since noon." Martin responded, "Yeah, I needed this, Jackie."

They had been drinking for eight hours. Neither of them could tell how many drinks they had consumed. They each had been unwinding and really not talking about the case.

Jacks conversation with Ernie had been the only time they conversed about the case. Their kids, however, wanted to talk about the incident and constantly dwelled on it. Bob had mentioned repeatedly that he didn't want to talk about the case. He had made up his mind that he and Jack were going to get drunk and forget that they felt like they had accomplished absolutely nothing with regard to solving the case. Sure, they knew that a lot of leads had been followed and information had been received and looked into. It was work that had to be done. They, however, wanted an arrest.

Bob and Jack were sitting at the bar and Tom Keywood, one of the "kids", approached Bob. Jack knew that Tom was going to ask about the case. Jack also knew that Bob had already told Tom on about three occasions in the last three hours that he didn't want to talk about the incident. Tom Keywood was so drunk he certainly couldn't remember what Bob had said. Jack turned and said, "So, Tommy, where are we going after we close this place?"

Tom responded, "You guys are the bosses, you tell me." Before Jack could reply Tom was in Bob's face. Jack could tell Bob was going to say something sarcastic. Before Tom could say anything Bob advised, "Tom, you have to break the habits you have." Tom was taken back by the statement and asked, "What da ya mean, Sarge?"

"Tommy, whenever you have something to say you get right in my face and then you have to touch or grab me. Believe me, I'll give you my undivided attention without your closeness."

Tom replied, "People are always telling me I'm in their space."

"They're right, Tom, believe me," said Martin.

Jack could tell that Tom was hurt by the statement but he was too drunk to realize it. Jack also knew that Martin didn't mean anything derogatory. He was offering constructive criticism. Jack, on a few occasions, wanted to tell Tom to get out of his face. Tom didn't let the statement bother him and asked,"Sarge, you're going to catch this guy, aren't ya?"

Jack knew Martin didn't want to talk about the case and figured he would cut off the conversation before Bob blew up. Bob was getting in the Dad mode so Jack became Mom. Jack changed the subject by saying, "So, Tommy, where are you taking me after we leave here?"

Tom then began talking about other locations they could visit to continue what was looking like an all night party. Jack then told Tom to talk to the other kids and work out the logistics of whose cars would be used and who would be designated drivers.

Jack looked at Bob and said, "You owe me, I kept him from buggin' you about the case."

"I just wanted to go to a quiet place, sit, eat, relax and get shitfaced. Why does everyone want to bust my chops?" Bob wondered.

"Well, they don't mean anything," said Jack.

"Jack, how many times have I said, I don't want to talk about police work. Let's talk about something important like who is buying the next drink." Jack didn't want to talk about cop shop stuff either, but, he knew the kids couldn't help themselves. Jack figured he would screen everyone that wanted to talk to Martin. He didn't want Bob chastising the kids.

Everyone continued to drink and they all were taking part in a lively game of shuffle board. Jack was being his normally competitive self and Bob liked the game because no one was talking cop stuff. Martin walked over to the bar and grabbed his drink. Detective Ed Donohue was sitting at the bar drinking a beer. Martin reached over to grab his drink and noticed that Ed seemed to be bummed out over something. "What's the matter, Ed, your beer warm?"

"No, Bob, I'm sitting here thinking how Dave is dead and we all are partying," said Donohue.

"Hey, Ed, snap out of it, we all feel the same way."

Martin took his drink and walked away. Jack saw Martin approaching with a pissed off look on his face. "What's the problem? Somebody talking shit? We'll kick their ass," Jack said. "I've been drinking rum. It makes me nuts. It makes me want to kick ass."

"No problem," advised Martin. "I think it's time we headed home."

Jack looked rejected and said, "We are all going to a place in Wildwood and keep this party going." Martin looked at Jack and said, "Jackie, if you go to Wildwood tonight you'll probably end up in trouble. You're right, rum makes you wacky."

"Come on, man. Don't let me down. Let's go to Wildwood with some of the kids," pleaded Jack.

"Let the kids head out and we'll stay here and relax over a few more drinks. I don't think it's a good idea to go to Wildwood. I got a bad feeling about going over there."

Jack figured he would make one more try to change Martin's mind. "Listen, if you don't go the kids are going to think you're mad at them."

"I'm not mad at them. There just getting on my nerves with police talk. I'm going home." Jack knew as Bob waved goodbye that there was no changing his mind.
Martin got into his car and headed home. Jack went back to the shuffle board game and told the kids that Dad was tired and was going home. He also said that Mom was ready for Wildwood. Everyone left the Fishing Club.

Martin was driving home and had a bad feeling that Jack was going to get jammed up in Wildwood. He pulled into the driveway of his home, shut off the car and looked at his watch. The time was 10 p.m. Bob walked in the door and JoAnne was sitting on the couch. Bob walked over and kissed her. "Did you drive home?" JoAnne asked.

"No, the invisible chauffeur drove me home," answered Bob.

"You are in no condition to drive."

"You're right," said Bob. "I'm also in no condition to listen to a bunch of crap either." Bob knew JoAnne wasn't nagging. She rarely ever did. He knew she was just concerned. "Listen, I think I'm going to Wildwood to find Jack. I have a bad feeling he is going to get jammed up tonight." JoAnne looked at Bob and said, "He's a big boy, he can take care of himself." After she said it she knew it was the wrong thing to say.

"Hey, JoAnne, you don't understand all that we have been going through. Tonight we were unwinding. We needed this. We have to get all the stuff off our minds. I'm worried about Jack getting jammed up."

JoAnne could see that Bob was getting emotional but she didn't want him to drive anywhere in his condition. "JoAnne, you know he's my best friend. Shit, he's like a brother. I can't sit here thinking he is going to have problems and not be there when the shit hits the fan."

"Listen to yourself, you're cursing."

Bob laughed and said, "You haven't heard me curse. All I said was shit. That's not gonna keep me out of heaven."

"Yeah, but, if you go to Wildwood in your condition you may do something you'll really be sorry for and then think about your plans for heaven."

At that point, Bob's, emotions coupled with the alcohol took control. "I'm worried about Jack. I'm worried about when we are going to catching Dave's killer."

Bob was rambling, he could tell he was ready to break down. He was not sure if it was precipitated by his feelings for his partner or the pent up feelings about Dave's death.

"You just don't know JoAnne. You don't understand. I insulate you from all the crap that goes on and then you don't support me when I need it." JoAnne knew that Bob must really be drunk. She knew that he often insulated her from a lot of things he was involved with. She also knew that he was sure that she supported him.

JoAnne walked into the kitchen and grabbed a glass of water for her husband. When she returned Bob was lying on the sofa and was in his snoring mode. She sat down and placed his head on her lap and ran her fingers through his hair. She prayed quietly for her husband, for Jack and for all those involved in the investigation into the murder of Patrolman Dave Douglass.

Jack was already at Seasons in Wildwood. He and Keywood had been the only two that kept the party going. They met Bill Mastriana at the bar. Bill was a new, young cop on the force and had known Jack from working out at a gym prior to Bill being hired at the Lower Township Police Department. Mastriana was known as "Bill Ding," because he was as big as a building. Bill was a weight lifter who enjoyed staying in shape.

Bill had been at Seasons for about two hours by the time
Jack and Keywood arrived. He had taken his girlfriend Kim
to the nightspot so they could have a few drinks and enjoy
the music. Bill was just getting a comfortable buzz when
the other guys showed up. He was quick to notice that both
guys were feeling no pain.

Bill was thinking that Jack had an odd look on his face.
If he had known Jack better he would had known the face
meant trouble. Jack had been drinking rum and it tended to
make him a little nuts. For some reason Bill decided to
keep an eye on him.

They got drinks at the bar and Bill led the guys back to a
table where Kim was seated. The five of them were talking
and enjoying the music. Bill looked at Jack and could see
that he was annoyed by the look on his face. Bill
questioned, "Yo, Jack, what's up?"

"That guy over there is breakin' bad with his staring over
here," said Trombetta in a disgusted voice. "Look at him
he's harassing that girl at the bar." Bill looked over as
the guy who was over six foot tall and weighed about 230
pounds grabbed the girl by the arm. The girl pulled away
and said something and turned in an attempt to ignore the
guy.

Bill immediately recognized the guy. A few months earlier
Bill Ding had a few words with the guy and two friends
stopped what may have been a good fight. Bill didn't
realize it, but Jack was observing the situation. He may
have been drunk but he was sizing up the guy and also
noticed that the wise guy had a friend standing next to him
who was also acting obnoxious. Jack was planning in his
mind exactly what he would do if the occasion presented
itself.

Bill noticed that the guy was now staring at Jack and
pointing in Jack's direction. This guy, apparently,
noticed Trombetta looking his way and the guy now said
something to his friend. They both looked at Jack and
grinned. Jack saw their faces and said to Bill, "As soon
as they go to the men's room I'm going in and kick some
ass. They're starin' at me like I'm some piece of shit."
Bill knew Jack was serious and decided he better not let
the detective sergeant get himself in any trouble.

The girl who was standing next to the guys seemed to have a
look on her face that said, "Please get lost!" The big guy
kept pawing at her and started to grab her waist. She
moved from him and started to slap the guy as he grabbed
her hand in mid air. Jack was out of his chair, like a

shot, from a cannon. In one move Jack lunged forward. His right hand pushed the smaller guy out of the way and left him reeling backwards. Jack thrust his left hand toward the big guy's throat as he turned to see what happened to his buddy. Jack caught the guy totally off balance and knocked the wind out of him. Jack was holding on to the guy's throat with the fingers and thumb of his left hand.

Bill had reacted a little slower than Jack and as he noticed Jack choking the guy he could see Jack was pulling back his right arm. Bill had been in enough fights to know that this guys head would wobble like a 'Joe Palooka' doll when Jack connected. Bill knew Jack would really hurt this shit head. Yeah, the guy deserved it but it wouldn't be worth Jack losing his job. Bill pushed at the smaller guy who was trying to get at Jack. For the second time, that shit head landed on the floor.

Bill caught Jack's arm just as the roundhouse got underway. Bill Ding used his bulk to pull Jack away and got him to let go of the guys throat as the second shit head fell to his knees. No one noticed that during the melee the girl who was being manhandled had run to a bouncer and pointed out the two ass holes that were grabbing and harassing her. The bouncer knew Jack and had figured that Jack and his buddy were handling the problem. As the ass holes were thrown out of the bar the big guy was saying he couldn't breathe.

Everything quickly calmed down. Jack decided it was time to start drinking water. Keywood, who had been in the bathroom for the entire episode, felt like he missed the best part of the evening.

Martin who had been sound asleep on the couch at home suddenly awakened in a cold sweat and startled JoAnne. He had been asleep on her lap and she had dozed off. JoAnne asked Bob what had made him so startled. He couldn't answer her question. They both got up and went to bed.

Keywood and Jack hung around the bar until closing. Jack after consuming about two gallons of water left for home and bed. Keywood did the same. Bill Ding, had kept Jack out of a lot of trouble.

CHAPTER FORTY SIX

It was Monday March 14th. Bob and Jack had planned on
traveling to New York City to meet with the New York Major
Case Squad. They had arrived at the Lower Township Police
Headquarters at seven o'clock in the morning. They figured
it was going to be a week of in-depth investigation.

They were sitting around talking about what they intended
to do once in New York. Neither had noticed that the
message light was blinking on their telephone. The light
finally caught Jack's eye and he played the recorded
message. It was from Jim McGowan and he advised that there
was a meeting at 9am at the Prosecutor's Office. The
Chief, of County Detectives, wanted Trombetta to attend.
McGowan also stated that Martin was to meet him at the 8am
to leave for New York. Jack immediately proclaimed,"Those
suckers don't want us going to New York together. They are
trying to keep us from working together on this. I don't
want to go to some ridiculous, worthless meeting. That's
all these ass holes want to do. Keep having meetings that
don't accomplish anything." Trombetta was getting loud.
It was easy to see that he was not very happy.

"You're probably right," said Martin. "What do we do?" The
Chief walked in and heard them talking. He advised that he
wanted a Lower Township representative at the meeting. He
further advised if Martin was going to New York then
Trombetta better be at the meeting. He knew Jack wasn't
happy but he wanted someone at the meeting to get things
moving to New York.

Jack eventually attended the meeting that was totally
worthless. Jack indicated to the Chief upon his return
that it was nothing more than rehash of what had taken
place thus far. Jack was not happy about the fact that he
was unable to go to New York.

McGowan and Martin made the three hour trip to New York
City. The Lower Township cops needed to interview the
members of the Kan Fat Quey family. The phone number
listed to that family was written on the piece of the
Chinese newspaper that had been found in the killer's
jacket. The look up on the number came back to Quey in New
York City.

Detective Ruben Santiago of NYPD was aware that the Jersey
guys were going to need some assistance locating and
speaking to the members of the Chinese family. Detective

Sergeant Joe Piraino had coordinated the pending arrival of the Jersey guys and directed Santiago and Detective Tom Nerney to make them selves available. Santiago knew he needed one of the guys who spoke Chinese to accompany him. Tom Nerney suggested Detective Simon Kok from the Missing Persons Squad. Over the years Tom had come to know Simon Kok as a genuine, dedicated professional who had absolutely no use for criminals, especially Chinese criminals. Unlike the passion and emotion of a Keith Ng, Detective Kok was low key and performed like a reliable, well oiled machine that always produced.

Simon Kok was no stranger to violence, neither professionally or personally. He had lost an older brother to gang violence years earlier. Although he rarely spoke about his early years as a cop, Simon had worked in a deep undercover capacity for almost seven years. The nature of that assignment remains confidential to this day, but it did require him to live two distinct lives.

Born in Chinatown and raised in Brooklyn, Simon was basically brought up by his father, Chun, who owned a restaurant on Church Avenue in Brooklyn. His mother, Wo-que, had died from cancer. Chun Kok would never approve of his son being a cop. Only after Chun retired and moved back to Hong Kong did Simon take the police test. Appointed to the NYPD in January 1982, Police Officer Kok never wore a uniform. Before even entering the Police Academy he had been pulled into the Intelligence Division. He could not tell anyone that he was a police officer; although his brother, sister and soon to be wife knew. They had no idea what he was doing for the department but knew not to ask. Simon had no gun, no shield, no police identification and no back-up. He was one of whatever it was that he was infiltrating.

It would be almost seven years before Simon Kok actually held his own police shield. By that time, the shield was gold. Detective Kok entered the police academy as a seven year veteran. Upon graduation he was assigned to the Missing Persons Squad.

McGowan and Martin had made the trip to New York to meet with the Major Case Squad detectives. They conversed the entire trip about where the investigation was going. McGowan and Martin wanted to interview some people in the Big Apple and Martin couldn't wait to try the key in some doors. When they arrived in New York they realized that they were lost. McGowan figured the easiest way to get to Police Plaza was to call the Major Case office and get some new directions. McGowan had written down the directions as they had been provided to him but for some reason they were driving in circles around Battery Park.

McGowan used the car phone and spoke with Detective
Sergeant Joe Piraino. He told the Jersey guys to sit tight
and that he would pick them up, and they could follow him
back to One Police Plaza. In a matter of minutes he showed
up, introduced himself and they were on their way.

Piraino led them to a parking area under the Brooklyn
Bridge and they made the short walk to the police
headquarters. Martin and McGowan couldn't help but notice
the bag people living in cardboard shanties under the
bridge. Piraino walked by them like they didn't exist.
They entered the building and immediately had to display
their identification. The Jersey guys had to register and
get passes to enter. Joe Piraino walked them through the
process. Martin couldn't help but notice the brick facade
on the interior of One Police Plaza.
On the wall was a memorial to fallen officers. It was a
most reverent and impressive sight. Even with all the noisy
activity it seemed to require a quietness.

They got through the security and entered an elevator and
went to the eleventh floor, the home of the Major Case
Squad. Piraino directed them to a cubicle in the office
area that was his office. The main office or bullpen as
detectives called it was pretty large with desks
accommodating about twenty-five to thirty guys. Around the
perimeter were offices and cubicles that provided office
space for secretaries, supervisors, storage and
administrators. Martin thought to himself that it was a
pretty good set up. Supervisors and administrators could
easily keep an eye on all the detective activity within the
confines of the large room. Joe Piraino immediately became
a gracious host. He offered all the normal things
maintained in a working detective section, coffee, coffee
and more coffee....

Martin and McGowan sat down in Joe's office and from where
Martin was seated he could look out the door. He noticed a
short, trim guy probably in his late forties to early
fifties. The guy looked like a well fit retired Marine and
was keeping very busy on the phone. Martin always liked to
use the phone to expedite investigations. He hated when he
had to tell guys working for him that they should be
spending more time on the phone and less time riding around
in circles. Lots of detectives thought that if they
weren't in the office the supervisors would assume they
were out running down leads. Martin liked to run down
leads on the phone as well as coordinate future
investigative actions.

He liked to see a guy busy on the telephone. Martin
unconsciously turned up the hearing aid in his right ear so

he would be able to pick up what the investigator was talking about on the phone. Martin could hear that the investigator was referring to himself as Tom and was talking to various people about a cop killing that occurred in South Jersey. This guy was working on Martin's case. Martin was impressed.

Martin and McGowan were told by Joe Piraino that he had been authorized to provide as much help as possible and that they were welcome to set up office within the Major Case Squad room. Joe indicated that he would provide detectives to accompany them and assist with anything that was needed.

Joe was a very soft spoken guy and Martin was thinking to himself that this guy is too quiet and reserved to be a cop.
Joe Piraino should be a priest. He seemed like the kind of guy that liked to hear his soft spoken voice solve the problems of the world. Martin didn't usually get along with this kind of guy.

The three investigators were talking about the composite of the shooter and deciding as to how it should be disseminated to the public. Piraino indicated that he had an investigator that could get it plastered all over national television if necessary.

Joe asked about offering a reward for information. He indicated that he could have bulletins printed in the police print shop and have them all over New York in a short amount of time. Martin was thinking to himself that this place really had the resources. McGowan was thinking that the prosecutor had told him not to do anything without clearing it through the, prosecutors office in Cape May County. McGowan was trying to think of a nice way to inform Martin that they should wait on the advertising for information scheme that was being offered by Piraino. Martin kind of changed the topic of conversation when he advised Piraino that he and McGowan wanted to run down some leads and talk to some people located at various addresses in New York City.

McGowan pulled out a list and explained that telephone numbers had been located at the crime scene scribbled on paper and that they had obtained addresses for other telephone numbers that had come up during the investigation. Martin indicated that they had a few telephone numbers that they still didn't have addresses for. Piraino advised that he would be able to obtain addresses through the police computer for any numbers that weren't known.

Piraino then called for Detective Ruben Santiago to meet
McGowan and Martin. Martin thought that this guy looked
like Jimmy Smits, the famous actor. The only difference
was Ruben had a mustache. The introduction went quickly
when Piraino asked Tom Nerney to enter the office. Martin
figured that would be the marine looking guy on the
telephone. Nerney put the phone down for a minute and
quickly walked into the room. Martin observed that this
guy didn't seem to waste time doing anything. He talked
fast, walked fast and took part in introductions fast.
Before anyone realized it Nerney was back at his desk on
the phone. Martin realized that as Nerney sat down at his
desk he had answered about seven or eight questions that
had been asked of him by Piraino, McGowan, Santiago and
himself. Martin liked this guy and was glad he was involved
in the investigation. Santiago left the office to run some
phone numbers to ascertain address locations and also to
verify what the Jersey guys already had with them.

Piraino asked if anyone was hungry and advised that there
were plenty of good places to eat around the area, within
walking distance. Martin and McGowan were more interested
in interviewing some of the people on their list.

Piraino once again brought up the fact that a reward would
probably get results in New York City. Martin immediately
picked up the phone and called Chief Don Douglass in Lower
Township.

"Heah, Chief, its Martin. I'm at Major Case in New York and
they are advising it is a good idea to start some type of
reward advertisement for information." There was a silence
for a few seconds and Chief Don Douglass stated, "Well I
have been approached by two members of council who are
telling me that they are sure they can get a hundred
thousand dollars donated to be used as a reward."

"A hundred thousand! You got to be kidding," stated Martin.
Joe Piraino heard the amount and looked at Martin.

"Bob, tell him you only need thirty thousand. That's a
magic number to the illegals from China. That is the
amount they have to pay to get into the United States. It's
a good figure to get them talking." The Chief put Martin
on hold, while he made a call to the Mayor. McGowan was
thinking that the prosecutor was not going to be happy with
this announcement. Martin had already made up his mind
that if he got the go ahead from the Chief he was going to
have Joe Piraino contact the print department and have them
at least run a sample copy. They could hold off
distributing them until the prosecutor was happy.

"Bob, I just got off the phone with the mayor. He said go

with the thirty thousand for now and if we need more it
will be in reserve. He said that the republicans and the
democrats are fighting over who is going to give the most
for the reward."

Martin hesitated and said, "These politicians have made
offers in the past and then didn't stick by them. I hope
they don't burn us." The chief responded, "Yeah, they will
be burning themselves if they don't come through." Martin
agreed and then advised the chief that they were getting
ready to start checking at some of the locations in New
York City. The chief was aware that they would be
interviewing possible witnesses and maybe get lucky and
find the door that would be opened by the key found at the
scene.

"Hey, Martin, don't get in any trouble up there."

"Yo, Don, you know me better than that."

"That's why I said what I said," advised Chief Don Douglass
as he laughed and hung up the phone.

Joe Piraino then stated, "Bob, you called your chief by his
first name."

"Joe, my department is not as large as yours and he was my
partner when he was a detective sergeant. As a matter of
fact, his wife fed me for about a year or so."

Piraino was a bit confused by Bob's statements. "I guess
it's good to come from a smaller department, that way at
least you know everybody. I'm use to calling the Chief,
'Chief'. Not to mention his wife never made me a dinner let
alone feed me for a year." Piraino laughed at his
statement as did Martin. McGowan was still thinking about
the fact that the Prosecutor was going to be upset about
the reward and especially the fact that Martin already had
asked Joe to start the printing press.

Joe then advised that he was going to call Missing Persons
to get Simon Kok to accompany them to some Chinatown
locations. Simon was fluent in Chinese and would be worth
his weight in gold when it came to interviewing and
translating. Moments later Simon entered the office and
the introductions took place once again. Martin observed
that Simon was a soft spoken well dressed investigator that
appeared self assured. Martin thought that Santiago and
Kok seemed to be operating on the same wave length. Martin
thought that if they were going to partner a Jersey guy
with a New York investigator he would like to be with Tom
Nerney. He looked like a guy who had been around and
would probably know enough people to get anything done and

get it done quickly. Santiago and Kok were younger and probably less experienced. Martin had made up his mind he would travel with Tom Nerney. He just had to figure out how he could make it happen.

Moments later while Piraino was working out the logistics of the investigative endeavors for the day Martin had his chance. Joe mentioned that he would be going on the interviews with three of his men. Martin quickly stated, "I'll go with the busy guy on the telephone." Piraino replied, "No problem."
Santiago, Kok and Nerney were running down addresses, phone numbers and checking with the printing department of the NYPD. Piraino was still listening to the case facts as supplied by Martin and McGowan. Nerney entered the room and advised that he was just talking with representatives of "America's Most Wanted" and he was pretty sure they could get the story on television if they couldn't locate the shooter in New York. Nerney then introduced a guy who walked into the office who was a representative of the photographic and printing department of NYPD. This guy provided many insights into getting the information out to the public. He left with a copy of the composite of the shooter and advised that he would come up with a flyer to be distributed throughout New York. Nerney then mentioned he would have it on local and national television as soon as he got the go-ahead.

Martin was once again impressed by the way Tom Nerney handled himself. A prototype of the stereotypical television hard nosed detective, Tom Nerney's reputation throughout NYPD Detective Bureau preceded him wherever he went. Never married, he devoted his life to putting bad guys in jail and he was very good at it.

Martin had worked with a few guys from NYPD in the past but never anyone from Major Case Squad. Martin still hadn't met Ernie Naspretto and that meeting would only come about because Trombetta had met Naspretto at the FBI National Academy. Martin really only knew Ernie's name and nothing else since they hadn't met yet. He had no idea that Naspretto and Tom Nerney were good friends.

Ernie Naspretto first met Tom in 1990. Nerney had called Naspretto when he was a Lieutenant at the 109th Precinct. Tom was investigating the homicide of an off-duty police officer who had been shot and killed outside his home after intercepting a car thief. The incident occurred in 1987 in the confines of the 109th, before Ernie was assigned there. Tom explained that he had been referred to him by the 109th's former commanding officer. "I was told that you're the guy to talk to if things have to get done," Tom said. Not one to run from compliments, Ernie was flattered.

Nerney needed uniformed officers to close off the street where the officer had lived. He had arranged for the highly acclaimed show "America's Most Wanted" to film a re-enactment of the murder in hopes that more leads would develop. Nerney requested "a detail of one and ten", meaning one sergeant and ten cops. The day of filming Ernie supplied himself, two sergeants and twenty-five cops. Needless to say with that contingent of blue uniforms there were no problems taping the episode.

Ernie spent over twelve hours with Tom that day and was quite impressed. Tom Nerney looked like a TV detective. He dressed impeccably and was immaculately groomed, his full head of closely cropped graying hair and mustache perfectly in place. He spoke in a deliberate, yet flowing professional manner. He rarely cursed and showed respect to the uniformed officers and supervisors who were present. Although it was very apparent that this detective was a confident true professional who knew he was excellent at what he did, there was nothing pretentious about him. His 5'9" medium build frame was not imposing, but his piercing blue eyes and perfectly chiseled face sent a message: Don't even think of fuckin' with me. Those same eyes softened when he smiled and showed genuine empathy for crime victims and their families. Ernie thought to himself, "I'll never be like this guy, good thing I studied and made boss."

Tom was thrilled with Ernie's cooperation. He was very happy with the uniformed presence during the filming. It made life a lot easier that day. He also knew this young lieutenant was very serious when he asked if there was anything else he could do. Tom took him up on his offer a couple of weeks later. He needed a bar owner and his dirtbag patrons to be abused and harassed. Evidently, the killer had contacts at the bar which was a neighborhood eyesore and located within blocks of the shooting scene. Ernie hand picked ten of the meanest, ugliest, nastiest, biggest and sharpest cops assigned to the 4 x 12 shift.

Lt. Naspretto's instructions were basic: Cross little children and old ladies across the street, smile and say "Good evening" to the legitimate area residents, tip your hats to the ladies and terrorize the white trash mutts that frequent the bar. Stand right by the front door of the bar and fuck them wear they breathe. Let them know that you can't wait to use your new toy that tests for drunk drivers.

This went on for about two months. The cops and the community loved it. The mutts stopped frequenting the place and the bar's owner was forced to legitimize the

business. Unfortunately, the drive didn't result in the
information Nerney needed, but it sent a message. He
certainly appreciated the effort and Tom and Ernie
developed a good relationship. Yes, Ernie definitely knew
Detective Tom Nerney. He also knew that the killer of
Officer Dave Douglass would pay dearly because Bob Martin
picked "the busy guy on the telephone." Ernie recalled
telling Grace, "This guy Bob really knows his shit.
They're gonna catch this mutt."

The son of a phone company employee Tom Nerney was born in
1939 and grew up like thousands of other kids in middle
class Queens during the 40's and 50's. His brother, James,
was very well behaved and became a Franciscan brother. Tom
certainly wasn't a criminal, but he was also far from being
a saint. He enlisted into the Marines in 1959 without
consulting his parents. Tom knew his family, especially
his father, James, Sr., would approve and be very proud. A
tear rolled down James' cheek when Tom told him. That tear
was a definite sign of approval. Tom was a marine for five
years, assigned to various bases in South Carolina,
Tennessee and Hawaii. He attended aviation courses and
also learned Japanese and French. In 1964 he was back home
working for Pan Am trying to find lost cargo. He took the
police test.

Nerney was appointed to the police department on March 28,
1966. Upon graduation from the academy he was assigned to
the famous and infamous Tactical Patrol Force, known as
TPF. At the time TPF was used to quell riots and basically
step on marauders like bugs. They were very effective.
Even the regular precinct cops were afraid of them. Tom
made over three hundred arrests in his first four years. A
very important arson arrest in 1970 opened the door to the
elite detective bureau.

In 1970 narcotic conditions were handled by the detective
bureau. A couple of years later the Organized Crime
Control Bureau was formed to address narcotics and
prostitution. Nerney was a narcotics investigator assigned
to Brooklyn. His normally perfectly pressed military
looking uniform was replaced by dirtbag looking flannel
shirts, leather jackets, blue jeans, and anything else that
made him look like a street mutt. His clean shaved face
and marine looking haircut gave way to an ugly beard and
long anti-establishment style hair. His police cruiser was
traded for a Harley-Davidson hog.

Nerney was placed in a team with six veteran investigators.
Each was mandated to make at least four arrests per month.
The team worked as a unit and the arrests were given to
each investigator based on seniority. Usually by the third
week of the month the six senior guys did what they had to

do and really didn't worry about whether Tom "got on the sheet" or not. Any arrests made during the last week of the month would go to the new kid, Nerney.

Tom knew the guys didn't give a shit about his numbers by the end of the month so he had to get innovative. He started making undercover buys with his own money. That practice would never be allowed today. Although unorthodox, his self initiated undercover operations easily insured his arrest quota for the month. In 1972 he was promoted to detective.

Normally, promotion days are big events in the NYPD. Promotees wear their best dress uniforms. Hair is cut and shoes are shined. Friends and families jam the auditorium at One Police Plaza and cheer when the names of the new detectives, sergeants, lieutenants, etc. are called and the promotees walk across the stage, salute the Police Commissioner and accept their new shields. Then the parties begin. Tom Nerney with long hair and beard, leather jacket and chains rode his Harley-Davidson up to headquarters, parked on the sidewalk, took an elevator to a clerical office which housed the "shield desk", dropped off his silver shield, picked up his gold detective shield, got back on his motorcycle and took off. The combination of his undercover assignment and having to live with the fact that his brother had died the year before in a car accident would not allow Tom to partake in normal festivities.

On his tenth anniversary on the job, March 28, 1976, Detective Nerney was assigned to the 76th Precinct Detective Squad in Brooklyn. The area was a mixed bag of hard working lower and middle class whites, mostly Italian, and Blacks and Hispanics living in housing projects. Although Tom was sharp on the street and made hundreds of arrests, this experience did not provide the interviewing, interrogation, and case management skills required of a precinct detective. The beard and long hair were gone, out came the perfectly tailored suits.

"Can you type, kid?" were the first words spoken to Tom by a thirty year veteran detective named Bill Keenan, known as "Lefty." Lefty made Tom his project. He would teach Tom how to interview a crime victim and witnesses, interrogate a suspect, and make an interrogation seem like an interview and visa versa. He taught Tom the mores of different ethnic or racial groups. Tom learned when entering an Italian household you had to eat something and drink some wine, especially if it was homemade. There was no negotiation, you just ate and drank.

Lefty taught Tom how to deal with victims, especially the families of homicide victims. You had to show empathy and

sympathy. You had to gain trust so no matter how the
investigation turned out the victims would know you gave it
your all. That, in itself, would help the victim cope. He
taught him crime scenes, how to identify and preserve
evidence. Tom worshiped Lefty.

In 1980, Lefty was forced to retire because of the 63 year
old age limit. He died from a heart attack sixteen days
later. Lefty's death devastated Tom. He knew, that Lefty,
more likely died from a broken heart because he could not
do what he loved best, being a good investigator and
getting the job done. Working the squad without Lefty
produced a big void in Tom's life. Over the preceding six
years Tom had assisted some FBI agents in bank robbery
investigations which had occurred in the 76th Precinct.
They were impressed. In 1982 Nerney was assigned to the
FBI/NYPD Joint Bank Robbery Task Force. In 1986, he was
transferred to the Major Case Squad. One of the main
responsibilities of the Major Case Squad is to investigate
police officer homicides.

In July 1987, a round faced, pleasant, young detective
named Joe Piraino was assigned to the Major Case Squad.
Joe had only six years on the job but had an impressive
background.

Eleven years had passed since Bill "Lefty" Keenan had first
asked Tom, "Can you type, kid?" Now, Tom had assumed the
role of Lefty and Joe was the eager student. They had
something in common from day one. They both liked to put
bad guys in jail.

When Bob Martin had made the request to work with Tom
Nerney he saw a look of approval on Piraino's face. Bob
knew nothing of the relationship the two men shared. He
could, however, see the look of respect and admiration on
Joe Piraino's face. Joe looked out into the direction of
Nerney and stated, "Harvey, you'll be teamed up with Bob."
Harvey, just nodded. Bob thought this guy Tom Nerney must
be nicknamed Harvey. Whatever the case, Bob knew that
these guys must have some history.

They certainly did have a history. Tom Nerney saw Joe
Piraino as a genuine dedicated professional who wanted to
learn, although it was apparent he already knew a lot, more
than Tom did when he met Lefty. Joe was aware of Tom's
reputation and was in awe of him. There was never any
"down time" for Detective Nerney. He was always busy. If
he wasn't on the street beating the bushes he was on the
phone lining up bushes to beat. Joe thought of Tom as an
independent loner who did not need a partner. However, it
was apparent that to "qualify" as Tom's partner you had to
be his friend. For reasons known only to them, they

296

referred to each other as "Harvey."

Joe noticed that Tom's desk was always cluttered. Placed neatly to the front of all the on line booking sheets, detective informational reports and all other kinds of papers were the Marine Corp flag, pictures of wanted felons, including a cop killer, and a picture of Lefty, who Joe initially thought was Tom's father. There was a major rule for all assigned to the Major Case Squad: Do not use Tom Nerney's desk for anything.

The case that cemented their partnership was a cop homicide. On October 18, 1988 two New York City cops were killed in upper Manhattan in separate incidents. Officer Christopher Hoban was killed in an undercover drug buy that went bad in Harlem. A couple of hours later in Washington Heights, Officer Michael Busczek was shot at point blank range as he attempted to stop a suspicious man who "may" have had a gun. Detectives Nerney and Piraino were called at their homes and assigned to the Busczek shooting. Piraino responded to the scene of the shooting, 161st Street and Broadway. Nerney went to Columbia Presbyterian Hospital to interview the slain officer's partner, Joe Barbato.

There is an unwritten commandment in the New York City Police Department: Cops who fire their weapons don't make any statements for an absolute minimum of two days after the incident. If the shooting is particularly sensitive the cop won't talk to anyone until after the grand jury proceeding. When Tom Nerney showed up at the hospital in his tie and jacket he was stopped by the PBA delegate. There was no way Busczek's partner was going to talk to Nerney. Tom tried to convince the delegate that he was one of the good guys and would keep the conversation totally confidential. The delegate acting like a bouncer at a bar just shook his head. A board member from the PBA showed up and recognized Tom. Within minutes Detective Tom Nerney was interviewing Officer Barbato.

"I'm the best friend you have right now. I want to catch the person responsible for killing your partner. It's that simple," Tom told the trembling cop. Meanwhile, Piraino was canvassing for witnesses around the area of the crime scene. Information developed by Tom and Joe provided the incident scenario.

Officers Mike Busczek and Joe Barbato were exiting an apartment building were they had just handled an assignment. Busczek noticed a couple of men who seemed suspicious. Busczek had an incredible ability to pick out people who were carrying guns. He had affected hundreds of gun arrests. The two men sensed they were about to be

stopped by the cops and started to run. Busczek and
Barbato were right behind them.

Busczek grabbed one of the men from behind and had him in a
bear hug. The other male backtracked and put a bullet in
Busczek's heart. Barbato emptied his weapon at the fleeing
cop killers but missed. At the crime scene was a jacket.
Apparently it belonged to the individuals that had been
grabbed by Busczek. Evidently, the dying officer pulled it
off his back. Inside the jacket was a set of keys.
Detectives Nerney and Piraino were going to do anything and
everything possible to find out what doors those keys
opened in the biggest city in the world.

One of the keys was rather unusual. It was a miwa key that
was placed in a lock horizontally instead of the normally
vertical way keys work. The key actually resembled a metal
computer card. This type of key could not be duplicated
unless the locksmith had the person's name on file with the
coded combination. Tom and Joe obtained a list of all
authorized miwa locksmiths. They literally went through
thousands of files at dozens of locksmiths throughout New
York City in hopes of finding the file card with the same
code combination as the key found in the jacket. They got
lucky in Jamaica, Queens.

There was a locksmith located on the corner of 165th Street
and Jamaica Avenue. The locksmith was about to close for
the day when Tom and Joe showed up. He looked at the key
and instantly said, "I made that." He pulled the file card
and sure enough the code matched. The person named on the
card was Pablo Almonte who resided five blocks away from
the locksmith.

The detectives went to the location and found the miwa key
opened a security gate. Another key on the ring fit one of
the apartment doors. They had found the residence of the
bastard that Officer Busczek had grabbed. Subsequent
investigation revealed that Almonte had fled to the
Dominican Republic. His sidekick and the murderer of
Officer Busczek was Daniel Mirambeaux, who had also fled to
the Dominican Republic.

Mirambeaux was captured and about to be extradited when he
supposedly committed suicide by jumping off a balcony. No
one cared if the story was true as long as the fuck was
really dead and he certainly was. Spanish speaking
detectives from the Major Case Squad went to the Dominican
Republic and fingerprinted the corpse. It was Mirambeaux,
case closed.

Although these cases were horrific, Tom and Joe were
excellent at capturing cop killers. A year later, Joe was

promoted to Sergeant. Four years later he was back as Tom's boss, but the reality was he was back as Tom's partner. It suited both of them just fine. The two "Harveys" were back together and the first major mission for their renewed partnership was to catch the killer of Officer David C. Douglass of the Lower Township Police Department.

Martin didn't know the history behind the two "Harveys," but he knew that he liked what he saw in Tom Nerney. Martin still had to figure out Joe Piraino. He seemed too soft-spoken and accommodating to be very effective with dirtbags or uncooperative individuals.

Martin liked the way everything was going. Santiago and Kok returned with the verifications on telephone numbers and addresses. Piraino reviewed the locations and said they could be checked immediately and that he, Nerney, McGowan and Martin would travel in one car and that Kok and Santiago would travel in another. It was also decided that all the investigators would go to the locations and conduct any interviews with all the investigators present. They had to make stops on First Avenue, East Broadway, West 28th Street, 17th Street and then back to East Broadway. Martin recalled that the last time he was in New York he attended a Christmas Show with the family. Prior to that the last visit to New York was when he was about twelve years old. His Aunt took him on a tour of all the interesting New York City sights. The cases he had worked with NYPD officers in the past had taken place in Jersey.
He sure didn't like the city and wished he was back in South Jersey. Everything was just too fast and busy. Martin couldn't feel comfortable in New York City.

CHAPTER FORTY SEVEN

They had entered the two vehicles in the parking garage
under One Police Plaza. They exited through the security
exit and entered the traffic of the big city. They snaked
through the afternoon traffic and made their way to the
first stop.

They pulled up to 40 First Avenue, the residence of the Kan
Fat Quey family. Martin could see the building was a high
rise structure. Piraino indicated that it contained small
units that were sold as condominiums and that they probably
were all one and two bedroom units.

They approached the door and found it was locked. There
were two old woman sitting in the lobby who looked at the
six investigators all wearing suits and trench coats. One
of the white haired ladies slowly got up from her chair and
it seemed to take her forever to get to the door. Martin
laughed and said, "I'm glad we don't need a quick entry.
This lady is moving about as fast as my daughter when she
knows there is work to do around the house." Joe Piraino
showed her his badge and requested she open the door. She
complied and after opening the door stated, "Hi, boys,
looking for some fun." She smiled, glanced at her friend
and said, "Hey, Marge, these fellows are all cops and their
lookin' for a good time." They both laughed. Joe Piraino
was very gallant and pleasant as he said, "Sorry ladies,
we'll have to take a rain check on the fun. We are on the
job." Madge looked at her friend. "See, Mary, we finally,
have some free time and these good lookin' boys are busy."
Both of the ladies were in their early eighties and still
had a good sense of humor.

The cops got on the elevator and went to the eighth floor.
When they exited the elevator they looked around for
apartment 8-H and when they found the door Simon Kok
motioned for everyone to be quiet and he listened at the
door for a moment. Martin noticed how the four guys from
New York all had their hands on their weapons that were
concealed. At first Martin thought they were overreacting.
He then thought to himself that this was the big city.
Cops were killed here regularly over trivial bullshit.
Nothing was trivial when it came to being prepared. Martin
let his hand rest on the Smith and Wesson 9 mm auto tucked
in his waist band. He knew that McGowan probably left his
weapon in the glove compartment.

Kok listened for about thirty seconds and whispered that he
believed he heard three or four voices and that they were
talking about the school day and what was for dinner. The
conversation was in Chinese and Kok was translating.

Kok knocked at the door. A female voice answered in
English. Kok responded in Chinese and the door immediately
opened and a small oriental woman was looking at Kok's
police ID. She immediately smiled and in Chinese invited
all the cops into her small apartment. Kok translated that
she wanted everyone to take a seat and make them selves
comfortable. Martin observed that there were two young
males and a young female also in the apartment. It was
evident that dinner was being prepared. Martin could smell
what he thought was pork boiling in a pot on the stove.

The investigators except for Kok and Santiago made their
way to the living and dining room area. They were
nonchalantly checking the rooms for other people. Martin
was impressed by the way they did so without upsetting the
people who lived in the residence.

Kok told the investigators that Mrs. Chui-Sheung Quey said
that she lived at the residence with two sons, ages 18 and
14, a daughter age 17 and her husband age 51. She further
stated that her husband often worked at Chinese restaurants
in New Jersey. The officers were beginning to think they
may be on to something.
McGowan was thinking about the piece of newspaper that was
found in the jacket left behind at the scene by the
perpetrator. It was a small piece of paper that had been
torn from a Chinese newspaper that was published in
Chinatown in New York City. The piece of paper had a phone
number written on it. The phone number came back to the
residence of Kan Fat Quey.

Mr. Quey was a chef who was presently working at a
restaurant in Trenton, NJ. Mrs. Quey indicated that her
husband was working his last day at the restaurant and that
he would start a new job the next day. She further advised
that she did not know the name of the new restaurant or the
location. She thought that it was in North Jersey,
somewhere.

Martin asked Kok to ascertain if Mrs. Quey had a recent
photograph of Mr. Quey. She left the room after Kok had
asked her. She went to get a family album. Her oldest son
came in the door carrying a bunch of books with a book bag
slung over his shoulder. He immediately started asking
questions of his sister and brother. They were all
speaking in Chinese. The cops felt uncomfortable since

301

that Simon Kok had followed Mrs. Quey when she left the room. Kok either heard or sensed someone else had entered the residence. He returned to the living room with Mrs. Quey and immediately started talking to the oldest son.

Kok indicated that Ringo Quey, the oldest son, was the man of the house in his father's absence. He was just looking out for his family.

Ringo asked quite a few questions in English. Joe Piraino spoke to him and calmed him down. He was visibly upset that his father may be a suspect in a crime. The officers all stared at Ringo to the point that he was becoming nervous. The guys all realized that Ringo Quey was a spitting image of the composite that had been drawn by Lou Trowbridge of the New Jersey State Police. His age was much too young but he looked exactly like the composite. The cops figured that Ringo probably looked like his father. They were waiting patiently for Mrs. Quey to provide a recent photograph of her husband.

It seemed like they waited more than an hour for Mrs. Quey to locate a picture. When she did it turned out to be an old picture. When the guys saw it they realized Kan Fat Quey couldn't be the guy that shot Dave Douglass. Mr. Quey was bald. The perpetrator had a full head of hair. The guys knew they had another false alarm and probably a dead end.

They knew they had to interview Kan Fat Quey but they now did not believe he was the shooter. It also was evident that he never worked at the restaurant in Lower Township. Now the best thing that could happen was that Quey had given his phone number to the guy that shot Dave. They were very anxious to speak to Mr. Kan Fat Quey.

Mrs. Quey repeatedly asked the officers if they were hungry or thirsty. The entire family was most hospitable and tried to be helpful. Once Ringo felt his father was not in any real trouble he too tried to be as helpful as possible. The guys eventually left and were assured that Mrs. Quey would contact Simon Kok when she heard from her husband. At that point Kok would set up an interview with Quey.

The detectives then began many of the business and resident locations that had come up in the investigation. The many phone numbers they had looked into provided them with the addresses that had to be checked. Martin and McGowan got a real tour of Chinatown. They had stopped at hardware stores, restaurants, lottery locations and residents throughout Chinatown. They did a lot of leg work that provided only negative results.

During the time Martin was with Nerney he learned a lot about the workings of the Major Case Squad. Tom Nerney was a seasoned detective who knew all the ropes. He was also a very sincere individual. Martin could tell that Nerney was taking a personal interest in the case.

It was getting dark and they wanted to stop at one more location to see if Liu had returned to his 17th Street address in New York City. They figured that they could keep him on his toes. The Jersey guys had kept his identification papers after interviewing him in North Jersey. They figured they would then have a good reason to revisit with the guy they still thought was involved in the shooting of Dave Douglass.

The cars pulled up to the location. It was a three level structure. There was a Japanese restaurant on the street level floor. It appeared to be an upscale type establish from the outside. The neon lights in the window were impressive and one of the signs advertised fresh sushi.

The group of investigators split up. Everyone went into the restaurant except Martin and Nerney. They were standing outside the restaurant on the sidewalk. Nerney indicated that they should wait outside. He explained that it was a courtesy. He didn't feel there was much use in having everyone enter the restaurant and upset the patrons. It was evident that Nerney was listening to what was going on in the restaurant through the opened door. He was also keeping a close eye on what was going on as was Martin.

Simon Kok went immediately to a bartender and asked for the owner. McGowan figured Kok also spoke Japanese. Moments later Kok said, "Hey, another Japanese restaurant owned and operated by Chinese." Everyone laughed at the statement. Almost immediately the owner exited the kitchen and approached Kok. McGowan watched and listened as Kok began to converse with the short Chinese man. Joe Piraino and Ruben Santiago kept an eye on all the workers who were scurrying around. Ruben was in the kitchen and Joe in the dining area with Kok and McGowan.

Simon was translating and indicated that the guy was upset that the cops were at his establishment and that he knew nothing about a guy named Liu and had no idea why his phone number would turn up in a police investigation.

Martin and Nerney still outside heard the raised voice of the owner and Nerney made the move to enter. Martin followed behind. Both men entered and the owner became more belligerent. Martin was waiting for Kok to start screaming at the guy. Kok looked at Piraino who seemed as

calm as ever. Simon indicated that the guy was not being
helpful and wanted everyone to leave his establishment.

Martin was waiting for someone to read this guy the riot
act. They were investigating a murder of a cop and this
guy was worried about his sushi. This guy was ranting and
raving in Chinese. Martin noticed that Joe Piraino was
walking toward Kok and the restaurant owner. Joe had been
speaking to one of the waiters. Joe interrupted Kok.
After some small talk Joe walked away from Kok placed his
arm around the shoulder of the restaurant owner and in his
most quiet and reserved voice said, "I am Detective
Sergeant Joe Piraino. I am with the Major Case Squad of
NYPD. I am told you have indicated you don't speak English
and all of your people are legal immigrants but they have
no papers. It is not my intent to give you a hard time.
It is my intent to make sure you cooperate with a murder
investigation." Joe looked directly into the owners eyes
and asked, "Do you understand me?" The owner looked at Joe
and shook his head in the negative. Joe immediately
squeezed down on his shoulder and in a harsh voice that
almost scared Martin said, "Well, maybe you'll understand
this you shit head. You will cooperate completely with my
people or I'll have every health inspector in the City of
New York checking your fuckin' sushi. Now let me see some
identification and start speaking English before you wish
you never met me." As Joe finished the sentence his voice
trailed off and Martin could see by the look in Joe's eyes
he meant what he said.

The little guy immediately reached into his pocket pulled
out his wallet and removed a New York drivers license. He
then in perfect English said, "These fine officers wish to
check our identification papers. I want all my employees
to comply." Joe let go of his grip on the guy's shoulder
and smiled and said, "Thank you, my good man." Martin now
knew that he liked this smooth talking, soft spoken
reserved New York Police Detective Sergeant. Joe Piraino
could also be a nut when the chips were down. Martin no
longer had qualms about Joe Piraino.

Tom Nerney could see the look on Martin's face and said,
"That's Harvey for ya." They both laughed.

They eventually checked all the IDs and then went up the
stairs to the Liu apartment. No one answered the door. A
resident in another apartment opened the door and advised
the detectives that about six or eight Chinese guys lived
there but they were all probably at work.

The detectives then returned to One Police Plaza. It was
decided that Joe Piraino would get the Jersey guys over the
Verrazano bridge. Everyone left with the Jersey guys being

assured that Kok would contact them when Mrs. Quey called back.

Martin and McGowan were traveling behind Piraino. They traveled through the traffic in the city. Piraino expertly got them around every delay. When they reached the toll plaza Joe made sure the Jersey guys didn't pay. He then pulled over and walked up to the car.

Martin rolled down the passenger side window. Joe looked in and said, "My guys will call ya' as soon as they know sometin'. Drive careful and listen guys. We have a partnership that is going to catch a cop killer. Keep that in mind on your way home. I'll be talkin' to ya'."

Joe hurried away, entered his unmarked police vehicle and drove off. Martin knew the guy was serious. Martin really liked this guy Joe Piraino.

Martin and McGowan made the three hour trip home and decided that they would be doing paperwork the next day. They agreed to call each other with any new news or events.

CHAPTER FORTY EIGHT

The morning of March 15th found Martin at his desk
reviewing reports. Trombetta walked in and saw Martin
reviewing a pile of Uniform Investigation Reports, known as
UIR's. Trombetta looked at Martin and said, "Listen, you
won't find one from the Rookie in there." Martin knew that
the Rookie was the first officer at the scene after Dave
had been killed. He also was the officer who had received
the initial call about the prowler. Jack added, "Remember,
I told him not to do his report until he talked with you.
He didn't tell me he was going to the mountains on
vacation. So to make a long story short we're still
waiting for his report."

Martin thought for a minute and said, "I'll talk to him."
Martin obtained his phone number for and called him.
The Rookie apologized for not getting in touch with Martin.
He then indicated that he was a little confused about what
should be in the report. He started to ramble on about the
night of the incident. His thoughts and statements were
disjointed and didn't make a lot of sense. It sounded like
he was trying to justify what appeared to be a slow
response.

Martin was thinking that this guy should get some
counseling. He seemed to go between doing heroic deeds and
then possibly making a mistake. Martin said, "Listen, man,
I am going to write a short and sweet report for you. If
it gives the basic facts about your response, that is all
we need. Once it is done, review it and if it indicates
what happened sign it. Remember, that we have reports from
everyone at the scene and from all the guys that responded
with you. We want to make sure there are no
discrepancies."

Jack was listening to the conversation and after Martin
hung up said, "Boy, he is thick. Doesn't he realize he
made some mistakes and you are trying to help him out. He
better do some thinking about everything that took place.
I think you're right. That boy needs some help. "
Martin thought for a minute and asked, "Didn't he meet with
the counselors when they were here?" Trombetta responded,
"No remember, that's when he went on vacation to the
mountains." Martin dropped the subject.

Both guys continued to review every report in an attempt to
ascertain if any changes had to be made. The task of
reviewing and coordinating the paperwork was a job that
neither of them enjoyed. They both knew, however, that
Martin would do it. It was a working agreement between
them. Martin always seemed to do that stuff and Trombetta
agreed to let him do it. It was agreed that Jack would fill
in the other detectives and give them some work assignments
that still had to be completed. Jack would also remind
them to get up to date on any reports that had to be done.
Bob and Jack also filled in each other on what had taken
place the day before. Before the day ended they met with
the Chief and Captain and brought them up to date.

Jack was glad to hear that Bob had good feelings about the
guys in New York Police department's Major Case Squad. Jack
made it clear that no one at the County would stop him from
making any more trips to North Jersey or New York City.
Bob knew Jack was serious. These guys always seemed to get
more done when they were working together. It was almost
like the Good Lord wanted them to be "Siamese Partners."
That's the way it had been since their Police Academy days.

They finished up for the day and went home. They both had
decided to get in some exercise. Jack went to Muscle
World. It was a gym that Jack had been going to for about
ten years. His wife worked there. Bob got on the tread
mill at home. Each guy worked up a good sweat. It was the
first real physical workout the guys had taken part in
since Dave's murder.
March 16 found both guys in the office deciding what they
would do next. They made a work list of things to be done
and after reviewing it revised it throughout the day. They
both were making phone calls to all the agencies that had
been assisting them. It was imperative that they obtain
reports of everyone's involvement in the case. They spent
most of the day getting everything together.

Throughout the day patrolmen would visit both men and
Trombetta would fill them in on what was happening with the
investigation. Jack usually did so because he knew Bob
would be doing paper work. He also did it because he knew
that Bob could be a little caustic when someone was having
trouble understanding the intricacies of such a detailed
investigation. Martin took it for granted that the guys
should have some knowledge of police work. What the hell
they were cops. Jack on the other hand was more like a Mom
and would explain things to the guys when they weren't sure
about something. Jack knew Bob could do the same thing if
he wanted to. He always seemed to be busy, however.

Jack was sure glad Martin did all the paper work and phone
contacts. That alone enabled Jack to shoot the shit with

the guys. He knew that if Martin got overwhelmed he would ask for help. Jack would be there to do what had to be done. Martin knew that most of the guys in the department always kidded Jack about not doing paper work or the everyday stuff of investigations. Martin also knew that Jack could and would do it when necessary and that it would be done right.

Martin looked at his watch and the phone rang. The time was 3:30 p.m. Simon Kok was on the phone and indicated that he had just talked to Quey and ascertained that he was working in Budd Lake, New Jersey at the Lucky Garden Restaurant. Simon indicated that he and Ruben Santiago would be willing to travel to that location in the early evening to interview Quey. Martin placed Kok on hold and immediately called McGowan. Jim indicated he would be ready as soon as he packed some clothing. Kok was advised and a meeting was set up for 7:30 p.m. Kok provided the directions.

Martin and Trombetta advised the Chief and Captain and were on their way home to pack once again for a trip to North Jersey. They looked at a map and ascertained they were heading back to the same area they had visited a few days before, when they interviewed Liu. They made up their minds they would stay in the same Holiday Inn. They knew they would be pulling another late night.

They had returned to their homes and packed. Bob packed, Jack on the other hand had told Lynn about the brown paper bag incident and she now had a suitcase that was pre-packed and waiting for him. Lynn knew that if she packed it Jack would have everything he needed. Lynn also placed a personal item in the suitcase that Jack wasn't aware of. Jack and Bob each called their wives at their place of employment and once again were on their way north after meeting McGowan.

These guys were starting to log some miles on the trips that took them to North Jersey and New York. Most often their conversations were about the case and what investigative steps they taking. Oftentimes the conversation also centered upon Trombetta's smoking habit. Martin and McGowan couldn't stand being the receivers of the second hand smoke. Jack didn't care. He figured they were cry babies. Jack would continually say that as soon as they caught Dave's killer he would stop smoking.

They had no sooner entered the Garden State Parkway and Jack had lit up and was changing the channels on the radio. McGowan asked Jack why he never let a song finish before he changed the channel. Jack said he got bored with the tune. McGowan and Martin had decided that they would count the

cigarettes Jack smoked and how many times he changed the
radio station. They always got tired counting.

They made it to Budd Lake, New Jersey and waited at the
prearranged location for the arrival of Kok and Santiago.
Martin and McGowan filled Jack in with regard to the two
guys from New York.

Earlier in the day Martin had contacted Lt. Sweeney of the
Roxbury Township Police Department. He had advised Martin
that his Detective Frank Schomp would be able to supply
Martin with the names of a couple detectives who handled
Budd Lake. Martin remembered speaking to Frank Schomp the
night they interviewed Liu. Schomp filled them in on the
workings of the police departments he was acquainted with.
Martin spoke with Schomp and he was told that Detectives
Joe Kluska and Jim Dunn were members of the Mt. Olive
Township Police Department. That department covered the
Budd Lake area. Schomp assured Martin he would contact the
two detectives and set it up so the guys from New York
could use their offices to interview Quey. Martin obtained
directions from Schomp and the meeting was set up.

It was about 7:45 p.m. when Kok and Santiago arrived.
Trombetta was introduced and the guys immediately decided
that the New York detectives would pick up Quey and then
follow the Jersey guys to the Mt. Olive Police Department.

The directions led the guys to a small shopping center.
The detectives from Mt. Olive Township had a store front
office in the shopping center. It was away from the main
headquarters of the Police department. Everyone became
acquainted and the Mt. Olive guys provided a full run of
the facility. Trombetta filled them in on what had taken
place with the investigation thus far. Martin, McGowan,
Santiago and Kok went to work on Quey.

Quey was the right age for the perpetrator but he sure
didn't fit the composite. He seemed to be forgetful about
the places he had worked within the last few years. He was
not good about providing a lot of detail when answering
questions. Martin figured it was the same problem they had
been having with all the Chinese they had spoken to. You
had to be real direct and explain your questions or these
people would not expound. They never seemed to provide
information unless they were asked pointed and direct
questions. When they did answer you had better make sure
you worked the question until it was dead. Otherwise you
may not get the complete answer.

The interview of Quey was very frustrating. He had a
terrible time recalling names, faces and facts. It seemed
more like he was trying to hide something as opposed to

309

forgetting. Everyone was getting frustrated with the
questioning. To make matters worse, Trombetta, Martin and
McGowan were fresh from obtaining no information from Liu.
They were now confronted with another possible suspect or
witness who didn't appear to be very helpful.

Quey was questioned for two hours and it was quite evident
they had gotten nowhere. Once again McGowan asked Kok to
ascertain if Quey could possibly remember any of the names
of people he had spoken to while at an employment office.
This question had been asked of Quey in a variety of ways.
The guys had a hunch that perhaps Quey had met Dave's
killer while hunting for a job. Perhaps they had exchanged
names or numbers. These people were always networking when
it came to getting jobs.

Quey had now been asked to recall names and numbers for
about the fifth time during his interview. All of a sudden
he removed a small telephone and address notebook from his
back pocket. McGowan asked Kok why it took so long for
Quey to provide the book. Kok responded that he had never
specifically asked Quey if he kept a record of such
information. He had only mentioned it this time out of
frustration. Immediately McGowan started reviewing the
address book as Martin and Trombetta asked questions of
Quey. They were becoming old hats at using a translator.

Kok had a very calm and subdued demeanor. Santiago took
notes as Kok did his job. Martin and Trombetta by their
voices and actions indicated to Kok that it was time to put
some heat on Quey. Almost on cue Kok began to become a bit
irate. He indicated to Quey that he was not being helpful
and that it appeared he was withholding information. They
began to badger Quey and McGowan started asking about the
entries in the telephone address book. It was decided to
ask Quey about each entry. There were a total of seventy
one entries. It was going to be a long night. The Mt.
Olive guys sent out for pizza and the guys from New York
and New Jersey ate while they interviewed. Even Quey, the
Chinese chef, had some pizza.

It was ten thirty in the evening before the guys figured
they were getting nowhere with Quey. Either he didn't know
specific information or he could not recall. The
frustration level was extremely high. The guys from Mt.
Olive figured the interview would get physical. Martin and
Trombetta knew that they couldn't afford such action. Not
to mention they knew better. It appeared McGowan was the
most frustrated. He repeatedly referred to the address
book and Quey could not or would not remember. McGowan
couldn't figure out how someone could put down a phone
number and a name then not remember the person or why they
listed the information. McGowan started to think the guy

310

was mentally slow.

They were getting nowhere fast and they needed a break. It
was decided that they better start being nicer to Quey and
indicate to him that he should contact them if he
remembered anything. They spent another forty five minutes
just being nice to the guy in an attempt to get him to
cooperate in the future.

Quey repeatedly advised that if he could recall something
he would contact Simon Kok. Quey was very interested in
getting back to his job. He had only been employed for one
day and the cops had taken him out of work early. He was
worried that he may not have a job. Quey indicated that
the restaurant owners are quick to fire you when you get
old. When you are young you can work faster and you can
work longer hours without becoming fatigued. When you get
older you aren't as fast and the restaurant owners won't
keep you on the job. Quey said that he was being laid off
more and more all the time. He still had three children he
wanted to get through college before he could stop working.
Quey knew he would have to work the rest of his life to
enable his children to make something of them selves.

The guys were telling Quey about how friendly and
cooperative his family had been. Quey was glad to hear
that they had honored him by helping the investigators.
Quey asked the investigators if they liked they could come
to the restaurant sometime and he would provide them a
special meal. Everyone graciously accepted but no one
expected to return to Budd Lake, New Jersey again.

The time was 11:50 p.m. when they dropped off Quey after
thanking the guys from Mt. Olive Police department for
their help and hospitality.

Simon and Ruben said that they had to return to New York.
They both had day tours in the morning. Martin, Trombetta
and McGowan pulled into the Holiday Inn they had stayed at
earlier in the month. They were too tired to stop for a
couple drinks.

They woke up in the morning to four inches of snow and
couldn't wait to get back to South Jersey. The ride home
was a smoke filled, radio station changing trip that only
Jack Trombetta could arrange.

Martin and Trombetta went directly home. They decided to
spend the night at home with family. Sleep came quick but
morning came faster. Martin and Trombetta were back to
work again.

During the remainder of the week Martin and Trombetta had

made day trips to New York City doing what they felt had to be done. They didn't want to tell the Prosecutors Office and they couldn't tell Ernie Naspretto or he would have wondered why they weren't staying with him. They had decided that they would travel back and forth.

Bob and Jack had returned to the many apartment complexes and Chinese restaurants to try the key in as many doors as possible. They did so continuously without any luck. They had advised their "kids" to call them if anyone from the prosecutor's office was looking for them. They figured they would say something to stall for time and then return home if need be. They were both very good at talking their way out of sticky predicaments.

Whenever they were in their office they continued to review the reports from all the agencies that were coming across their desks. Sergeant Rich Hooyman was covering for them. He would run interference whenever anyone was looking for them.

During the week they had also attended a meeting at the local FBI office in Linwood, NJ. Reemer had requested their appearance. Those in attendance kicked around everything that had to be done and the Feds provided some insights into the evidence that had been shipped to Quantico. Martin and Trombetta attended the meeting but would have much rather been pounding the streets of New York City.

When they went to the city they tried the key in every door lock that might have accepted it. They also placed it in a few locks that they knew wouldn't open. They were desperate. They wanted to find Dave's killer.

They had been tracking down telephone numbers and address locations. They kept plugging away but it never seemed that they got any real breaks. The long trips back and forth gave them a lot of time to talk about theories and ideas. They each had a lot of both. They just didn't have any answers. It was answers that they needed. When would they get a break in the case?

Many times during the trips they were able to converse about God's part in the investigation. They each knew that the Lord Almighty played a major part in their lives and the lives of everyone involved. They knew that they had not been living a real Christian lifestyle. Many times they would pray that things would work out. They knew God had control. It was just hard turning everything over to the Lord Jesus Christ.

There they were thinking about God on one hand, wanting to kill Dave's shooter on the other and further wanting to have a few drinks before they returned home. Would God watch over and help them in spite of themselves? They prayed that he would be with them throughout the course of the investigation. They were sure God wouldn't let them down. Sometimes they were so sure they would drink to it.

Throughout the remainder of the week Martin and Trombetta continued to review all reports. Trombetta made an effort to speak with the members of patrol to provide them with updates. Martin continued to provide work assignments for the kids. He figured if he kept them busy they would spend their time productively. All the detectives didn't have to be reminded to keep busy. Bob, however, wanted to keep them on track. They still had a tendency to let poor information lead them to take part in unproductive investigative endeavors.

Martin spent Friday, March 18th, going through all the intelligence information that he had placed on the back burner in the initial stages of the investigation. He now figured the kids could look into the information. He knew that it would no doubt be unproductive, but, it was now a good time to get the work completed. He knew that somewhere in the investigation the Prosecutors Office would be asking about some of the old information. Martin wanted to be a few steps in front of the prosecutor's annoying inquiries.

The day ended with everyone having an impromptu meeting at the Fishing Club. Either they hadn't realized it or no one wanted to mention but it had been one month since Dave had been killed. McGowan, Reemer and Chief Douglass met the kids along with Martin and Trombetta.

They kicked around a lot of ideas and threw back a lot of drinks and eventually got something to eat. Martin was home by five P.M. and figured he better take the little woman to dinner. He knew he could put down some more food and his wife would be happy that he spent some time with her.

McGowan, Reemer and the Chief left the club about the same time as Martin. Trombetta and the kids decided to call it a night.

Jack and Bob were back in the office early Saturday morning. They decided on a game plan for the next week and made it to church on Sunday morning.

On Monday, morning, March 21st, Martin and Trombetta received reports from the County and the Feds. They spent the morning reviewing the reports and ascertaining if follow-up was required with regard to what was contained in the reports. During the afternoon they had been receiving many calls from the press with regard to the one month anniversary of Dave's death. Both Bob and Jack were embarrassed that they hadn't made an arrest and already more than a month had gone by.

They made the decision to go to New York City the following day. McGowan was going to be out of town and they figured that they would better serve the investigation if they were in New York City. They wanted to leave on Monday but figured they better get the kids squared away on assignments and have them handle some follow-up investigative work.

Bob and Jack had planned on leaving Tuesday in the morning but once again the County Prosecutor had set up a meeting for all the investigators to review the case. Local, County and Federal people were in attendance and once again Martin and Trombetta had to hear about how everyone was doing everything to catch Dave's killer. However, they still hadn't made an arrest.

Bob contacted Joe Piraino at Major Case and advised him that they would be meeting with him on the following morning. Joe indicated that he would provide them with whatever manpower and equipment that was required. They would be taking part in some surveillance and investigative background work and were looking forward to getting things moving with Major Case once again.

Bob and Jack eventually left for the Big Apple at about six in the evening. Once again the trip was a clone of every other trip Jack and Bob had taken. Bob, was the driver, Jack smoked and changed channels on the radio. Once in a while they would run ideas passed each other and a lot of the time they would think about Dave Douglass and his family. They knew that everyone was waiting for them to make an arrest. Maybe this trip to New York City would provide some real concrete information that would lead them to Dave's killer.

CHAPTER FORTY NINE

It was Tuesday night, March 22nd. Ernie had attended a
Columbia Association meeting in Elmhurst, Queens, and was
on his way home. The NYPD's Columbia Association is a
fraternal organization of Italian-American police officers.
It claims over six thousand members. Ernie had been a
board member for four years but had to step down after he
had made captain and Angelina was born. The captain's work
schedule, especially a rookie captain's schedule, simply
wouldn't allow for too many extra curricular activities.
He also did not want to take any time from Angelina. But,
he still attended the monthly general meetings.

It was about ten o'clock and Ernie saw the unmarked Chevy
with the little antennae sticking out of the rear corner
panel and New Jersey plates parked in his driveway. He
felt an anxiety about meeting Bob Martin for the first time
and seeing Jack after a year and a half. He also didn't
want to hear Jack's comments about his obesity. Ernie
walked in the front door and saw Jack standing in the
living room. They embraced. Jack looked great, damn it.
He was trim, vibrant, and looked like a twenty-two year old
kid. He must have cleaned up his act since the FBI
National Academy. He looked healthy. He looked ten times
better than he did when they graduated from the academy.
Ernie could see the look of disapproval in Jack's eyes.
Ernie was fat and looked fifty three. "What happened to
you? Look at that belly," Jack stated. "Fuck you, Jack.
I'm a captain now. I don't have to be in good shape. I
order guys like you to do my work," Ernie answered. "It
took a cop getting killed for you to come visit me." Bob
just stood there smiling nervously.

Jack introduced Bob to Ernie. Bob looked a little older
than Jack but didn't have an ounce of fat on him. Don't
these guys eat, Ernie thought to hisself. Bob also had the
look of an unrelenting determined veteran investigator who
meant business. He was the kind of guy that always stood
watching and taking in everything that was going on around
him. He looked like the kind of guy that should be a secret
service Agent protecting the President. Ernie noticed Bob
was wearing two hearing aides which made him instantly
respect his new found friend. Ernie knew he also needed a
hearing aide but refused to get one. It drove Grace crazy.
It was getting to the point where she had to actually face

Ernie for him to hear her. Whenever he spoke on the phone,
the whole house had to be quiet. One of his wise ass
friends had been sending him hearing aide brochures
anonymously for the past three years. That was probably
the same "friend" who was sending hair replacement
advertisements.

So there they stood in the Naspretto's living room, two
slim good looking detective sergeants with full heads of
hair who were in their forties but looked much younger and
an overweight, balding, hard of hearing, middle aged
looking thirty five year old captain. Ernie needed a
drink. They said goodbye to Grace and Ernie took them to
Kate Cassidy's on Woodhaven Blvd., about ten minutes from
his home.

Ernie had been frequenting Kate Cassidy's Pub for twelve
years. The owners are retired cops who love to cater to
the cop crowd. They had seen Ernie go from rookie cop in
1982 to captain in 1992. Jack, Bob and Ernie walked in and
a lot of cops who had attended the Columbia meeting were
there. When Ernie told Brian the bartender why Bob and
Jack were up from New Jersey the drinks were on the house.

Bob and Jack could not believe how concerned all the New
York cops seemed to be. Neither of them would remember any
of the names of the guys. They would, however, remember
how concerned they were with the fact that Lower Township
had lost an officer. These guys treated Bob and Jack like
they were old friends. The Jersey boys had probably met
fifteen or twenty New York cops and they hadn't talked to
one they didn't like. The bartender kept the drinks
flowing. Bob was talking to him about when he had been on
a squad that served outstanding warrants on felons. He was
an interesting guy to talk to. They all had a mutual
interest. They were cops and they all hated cop killers.
Jack was talking to a sergeant who pointed out three New
York cops who had been shot at while on the job. The
Jersey boys began to be glad they didn't work in the big
apple. Bob would say it but Jack's ego wouldn't allow him
to agree. They both knew they were in the big city and
that they had a big job ahead of them. They had not eaten
all day and even though it was late they each ordered a
burger and fries. They ate, drank and talked. Everyone
that entered was introduced to them and everyone wished
them good luck.

They also received many offers of help from everyone they
talked to. Bob and Jack were getting some real good
feelings about New York cops. There really was a
brotherhood of cops and it was alive and well in New York
City. Bob and Jack were unwinding and enjoyed the feeling.
Ernie was figuring he was the most sober and that the

morning would be arriving all too soon. Ernie looked at
his watch and it was almost one in the morning. The
morning had already arrived. Ernie said "drink up" and
they were on there way to Ernie's house for some sleep.

Grace had prepared the beds for her house guests. Jack
would sleep in the sofa bed in the living room. Bob would
have his own room upstairs. At about three in the morning
Angelina woke up and started crying. It was literally the
first time she had woke up in the middle of the night in
over six months. Ernie couldn't believe it. Her wails
filled the whole house for almost two hours. Earlier in
the night at Kate Cassidy's Ernie had bragged on how
Angelina always slept right through the night.

Angelina's crying didn't wake up Jack because he wasn't
sleeping to begin with. Bob claimed he didn't hear
anything that morning. Everyone was awake and sitting at
the breakfast table by eight o'clock, everyone except
Ernie. He plopped down around nine. Jack and Bob hardly
ate a thing. Ernie ate and ate. Jack made a couple of
comments and Bob was still being nice. Instead of saying
"Fuck you" to Jack, Ernie saved energy and just gave Jack
the finger. Ernie's mom always told him not to speak when
his mouth was full.

They were going to meet Jim Rybicki and Gene Taylor at the
Major Case Squad in Manhattan sometime between ten and
eleven that morning. Later in the day the four New Jersey
cops would meet with Chin and Ng at the 109th precinct in
Queens. Ernie would be their driver. There was no way he
was going to allow these guys to drive themselves anywhere.
Attempting to catch a cop killer was not the time to learn
the streets, highways and horrendous traffic patterns of
New York City. Ernie was scheduled for a ten to six tour.
He called a lieutenant at the 60th Precinct and told him
he'd be at headquarters all day and would check in
throughout the tour. Lieutenants never questioned
captains.

Jack, Bob and Ernie sat around the table. Jack was playing
with Angelina who was sitting in a high chair. Bob was
talking about Detective Sergeant Joe Piraino and Detective
Ruben Santiago and how helpful and cooperative they had
been. Ernie was just finding out that Bob had already been
to Major Case and had already worked with some of the guys
from Police Plaza. Ernie had recognized Ruben's name.
They both were assigned to the 23rd Precinct in East Harlem
twelve years earlier. Ernie remembered Ruben as an
excellent street cop. In fact, only recently Ruben's face
had been all over the newspapers and television after he
helped solve the kidnaping of a millionaire. Ruben
actually found the victim, who was in bad shape but alive.

317

The investigation generated great publicity for the department. Ernie didn't know Joe Piraino.

Bob started filling Ernie in on some of the specifics of the case, including the lack of assistance from the FBI in New York. Jack got that psycho look in his eyes when Bob mentioned how uncooperative some potential witnesses had been. It was the same look he had during the softball games at the FBI Academy. Jack started pacing in the living room. "If they cut off my head the rest of my body will go after this ass hole!" Ernie looked at Jack and thought of Arnold Schwartzenegger in the movie "Terminator". Jack then apologized for cursing in front of Grace and Angelina. Ernie said, "Don't fuckin' worry about it."

Bob continued to fill Ernie in on most of the case. Ernie looked at Jack and asked, "Did you know all of this stuff? You look like you are hearing some of this for the first time." Jack laughed and said, "Bob keeps all this stuff in his head. Rather than me trying to remember it I just ask him. You can tell you never worked with a partner. Man, Ernie, don't you know nothin' about police work?"

Ernie thought for a moment and said, "I know enough to get myself a partner like Bob and have him do all the work. What do you do, Jack, take all the glory when the case is solved?" Jack laughed and said, "Tell him Bob. I can work when I want to, can't I?"

Ernie smiled and said, "I carried you through the FBI Academy and Bob has no doubt carried you through your career. I hope you're good for something, Jack."

Bob began talking about the fact that he had already been to Major Case on two occasions with regard to the case. He indicated that Jack had stayed in Lower Township and was supervising the detectives working on the case. Ernie inquired, "What did Bob do? Call you every fifteen minutes and tell you what to do?"

Bob mentioned that he had been working with Detective Nerney while at Major Case. Ernie asked excitedly, "Did you say 'Tom Nerney?'" Grace looked at Ernie and they each had a look on their faces as if they had just won the lottery. Grace had heard Ernie speak of Detective Tom Nerney a couple of times over the years. "Is he involved with this investigation?" asked Ernie very deliberately. Bob said yes. "My friend you could not have mentioned a better name in this entire department," Ernie said with a very broad smile.

At that point Ernie felt a confidence that had eluded him

since Jack's initial phone call. The combination of Jack's psychotic resolve, the vibes Ernie felt from Bob Martin, and now the addition of a guy Ernie believed to be the absolute best detective in the New York City Police Department meant Officer Douglass' killer would most likely be caught.

The guys finished breakfast, got dressed and said goodbye to Grace and Angelina.

CHAPTER FIFTY

Wednesday, March 23rd had been planned. First Jack, Bob and Ernie would meet with Joe Piraino and Ruben Santiago at the Major Case Squad at One Police Plaza. Captain Rybicki and Investigator Gene Taylor from the Cape May County Prosecutors Office would also meet them there at eleven in the morning. Parking was always a nightmare at police headquarters but not for captains.

Ernie was driving the Lower Township unmarked Chevy. He pulled right up to the cop assigned to the security gate at headquarters and showed his shield, the cop saluted and up went the gate. Ernie often said this was the absolute best part about being a captain. Bob and Jack never experienced parking problems before.

In the lobby Jack and Bob had to sign in, present ID and obtain security passes. Bob had been there before and seemed to know the routine. Jack followed along. Ernie hadn't been at headquarters in a long time. In fact, he very rarely ever went to headquarters, but he was impressed with the apparently new security measures. They took the elevator to the eleventh floor. Piraino and Santiago were waiting for them. Detective Ruben Santiago and Ernie recognized each other immediately. A decade earlier they had been rookie cops assigned to Spanish Harlem's 23rd Precinct. Ruben looked exactly the same, thin build, good looking, perfectly groomed. Ernie looked like he had over twenty years on the job and was heavier that Ruben remembered him.

"You're doing great, Ruben. Saw you all over TV and the papers last month with that kidnaping caper," Ernie said.

"You're not doing bad yourself, captain," Ruben smiled.

Ernie couldn't believe Ruben called him "captain." Bob Martin had already called Major Case and advised that they would be arriving with Capt. Ernie Naspretto. Joe Piraino was standing nearby trying to figure out who the "captain" was. Ruben introduced them. Joe was very polite but it was apparent to Ernie that he was trying to understand what a patrol captain was doing at the Major Case Squad with detectives assigned to a cop homicide.

"I'm only here as a soldier. Anything I can do to help

320

out, let me know. I told my command I'd be here for the day," Ernie explained. Joe smiled a polite smile but still couldn't understand why this patrol captain from Coney Island was there. Detective Greg White then walked in. "Hey, Ernie, how's it going? You involved with this?"

Detective White and Ernie worked in a rookie training unit together in 1982. Greg was the only black in the unit and was affectionately referred to as "Greg White, the black guy." Gregg had been a very active cop and worked for years in Brooklyn's 75th Precinct Detective Squad. He had handled more homicides in a year than most cops see in their entire career. They shook hands and complimented each other's success since their rookie days.

Gregg was built like a fullback and looked like a movie star. Referring, to both, Ruben and Gregg, Ernie said, "I was never sharp enough to be a detective so I studied instead." Joe just stood there wondering if this captain was going to be a pain in the ass. Then Ernie said something that loosened Joe up.

"There is no better investigative unit in this department. If this mutt can be caught, these guys will help you get him," Ernie told Jack and Bob. There was sincerity in his voice and everyone in the room appreciated it. "Where's Tom Nerney?" Ernie then asked.

"He's at court today," Joe answered wondering if Ernie knew everyone in the office except him. Jim Rybicki and Gene Taylor then walked into the office. Bob Martin introduced them to everyone. Bob could see Ernie staring at Gene Taylor. Gene was tall and built like a linebacker. He had a Marine flat top with a mustache that didn't move when he talked. He seemed to glare at whom he was talking to.

Ernie looked at Gene and whispered to Jack, "That guy looks like he's fun at parties." Everyone shook hands and it was time to get to work. Deputy Inspector Charles Alifano walked in and immediately said hello to Bob Martin. Ernie didn't know Bob had already met him. Bob introduced him to all the Cape May County guys.

Bob had met Deputy Inspector Alifano the second time he had been to Major Case and was impressed with how concerned he had been about catching this cop killer. Alifano had told Bob that he had personally spoken to Chief of Detectives Joseph Borrelli and he would provide all the help necessary to catch this cop killer. Borrelli had indicated that Lower Township could use New York's equipment, vehicles and men. Borrelli stated that he had about 33,000 cops at NYPD and that Bob Martin would have them at his disposal. Borrelli only requested that Martin not use them all at once. Martin liked Alifano and Borrelli immediately.

Alifano was the commanding officer of the Special Investigation Division, which was the overhead command of the Major Case Squad. A thirty-three year veteran of the NYPD he had a reputation for being a fair, honest, very competent supervisor. Alifano was known for being a family man who never displayed any animosity or anger. He was always low keyed. Tom Nerney called him the Perry Como of the police department. Coincidently, the inspector's son worked for Ernie at the 60th Precinct.

Sgt. Chuck Alifano headed the precinct street narcotics enforcement unit. Ernie made sure he mentioned that and what an asset Chuck was to the precinct. Whether it was true or not and it was, Ernie made sure Inspector Alifano knew he was Chuck's boss. The inspector appreciated the comments and Piraino again wondered if this captain knew everyone in the police department except him.

Lieutenant Joe Pollini entered the room and greeted Bob Martin. Bob introduced him to everyone and as the conversation continued Pollini asked Martin, "Who's the guy with the mustache?" Martin could see that Pollini was looking at Ernie as if he was a bad carnival act or an annoying politician trying to get votes. Pollini asked in a low voice, "Is that guy with you?" Bob could tell there was a lot more to the question. The meaning to Pollini's rather simple question was, "Who the fuck is this clown?" With a slight mischievous smile Bob just answered, "No, man, he's with you. That's Ernie Naspretto, he's a captain in Coney Island."

"What the hell is he doing here?" Pollini looked at Martin waiting for an answer.

Upon hearing that the guy with the big mouth who acted like a game show host was a NYPD captain, Pollini thought, "Wonderful, fuckin' wonderful. A detective wannabe. Just what this case needs."

Martin thought to himself that Ernie seemed to know everyone except the bosses in control. Piraino and Pollini were the working bosses of this unit. If you screwed with them you wouldn't get anything accomplished.

Martin decided to tell Pollini that Ernie was a close friend of Jack Trombetta and that he had provided lodging and a ride to Police Plaza. Martin also added that Ernie was willing to provide any help that he could and that he wasn't flashing his rank around Major Case. Pollini seemed to be at ease and then he asked Martin to accompany him to the office of Captain George Duke, the commanding officer of the Major Case Squad.

Ernie noticed Pollini talking to Bob. Although they had
never met, Ernie remembered him from a cop homicide which
had occurred when they both were sergeants. On February
26, 1988, a rookie cop named Eddie Byrne was literally
assassinated as he sat in a marked radio car guarding the
home of a witness who was going to testify against a major
drug dealer in Jamaica, Queens. The murder drew national
attention, including an inquiry from President George Bush,
who referred to the incident on national television.

Ernie was a patrol sergeant at the time in the 103rd
precinct where the rookie had been assigned for only a
couple of weeks. Pollini was one of the lead supervising
investigators. Byrne's killers were in custody within five
days of the murder. Ernie vividly recalled how Pollini
came across as, a know nonsense, focused, take charge type
of guy. Ernie was happy to see that Pollini was involved
with this case. Pollini, however, was less than thrilled
that a detective buff captain was sticking his nose where
it didn't belong.

Ernie walked over to Martin and Pollini. "How ya' doing?
I remember you from the Eddie Byrne case," Ernie said as he
extended his hand to Joe Pollini.

"Yeah, that was some case," Pollini had a polite smile as
he shook Ernie's hand. Bob could tell Pollini was really
saying, "Yeah, well, I don't remember you, ya flamin' ass
hole."

Martin followed Pollini to the commanding officer's office.
A big guy stood up from behind the desk. It was Captain
George Duke. Martin thought this guy looked like a retired
Marine Colonel who had seen action around the world. Duke
shook Martin's hand and said he had heard Martin was
heading the investigation and that he would help in anyway
he could. Duke advised that his people would supply
whatever was needed and that if Martin had any problems he
should bring them to the attention of Lt. Joe Pollini.

Pollini then advised Duke that the heavy guy with the
mustache was a Captain Ernie Naspretto from Coney Island
and that he was a personal friend of Martin's. Duke stated
that Alifano had already advised him. Pollini further
advised that Naspretto was willing to help if he could.
Duke said it would be no problem. The three men then all
returned to the main office were everyone was still
congregating.

Deputy Inspector Alifano then said something that was music
to Ernie's ears. "This is an absolute priority. We'll do

whatever has to be done."

Being from patrol Ernie certainly wasn't used to, hearing deputy, inspectors speaking like that. Everything on patrol required ten million forms and okays from a chain of command that seemed endless.

Alifano saying "Do whatever has to be done" was a signal to Piraino which translated to "Don't worry about overtime. Use whomever and whatever you need and catch this son of a bitch." Alifano then added that the Chief of Detectives was interested in this case.

The Chief being "interested" meant Alifano's directive was sent with the chief's blessings and that Sgt. Piraino's unit better catch this cop killer, the sooner the better. Ernie knew the Chief of Detectives very well but decided not to mention it, at least not now anyway. Ernie's discretion probably saved Piraino from terminal annoyance.

Chief of Detectives Joseph R. Borrelli was among the most notable law enforcement figures in New York, if not the country. A highly revered thirty five year veteran he was referred to as "Joe the boss" by those working under him, which was basically everyone in the elite detective bureau. Undoubtedly his biggest claim to fame and the case which catapulted him to cop superstardom was the notorious "Son of Sam" investigation in 1976-77. A captain at the time, Borrelli spearheaded the investigation of the psychopathic serial killer who terrorized a city which was supposed to be used to terror. The investigation, arrest and closing of that case made Borrelli a household name in New York City.

Ernie had read three books on the Son of Sam case and could convince any civilian or young cop or cop from another jurisdiction that he had actually worked on the case. In the summer of 1992 he had half the FBI National Academy believing he and Joe Borrelli solved Son of Sam. The reality was Ernie was an eighteen year old college student when Son of Sam was lurking around Queens.

Over the years Ernie got to know Borrelli pretty well. A combination of luck, coincidence and destiny made their paths cross more than a couple of times. Borrelli was the inspector in command of the Fourth Division in 1981 when Ernie graduated the police academy. At that time the rookies were placed in an "NSU", Neighborhood Stabilization Unit, which covered all the precincts in a given division. Each division usually had three to five precincts. The fourth division had four which included the 19th, 20th, 23rd and Central Park Precinct. The NSU's reported directly to the inspector. The first day Inspector

Borrelli met the rookies he referred to himself as "God." Ernie never forgot that and used the same line often as a sergeant, lieutenant and captain.

Rookie cops stayed in this unit for about six months then were transferred to precincts. When the rookies in this particular NSU were about to be transferred to various precincts they held a big party at a local restaurant and invited Inspector Borrelli out of respect. No one expected him to show up. Not only did he show up, he came early and stayed late. He even brought his wife, Fran. Borrelli made a comment about the music tapes being played. "Why don't you people put on some Jimmy Roselli?" the inspector asked realizing most of these "kids" probably never heard of the great Italian singer.

Ernie set a world land speed record as he ran to his orange 1971 Dodge Dart, opened the glove compartment and ran back to the restaurant with his Jimmy Roselli tapes. Within seconds the whole restaurant was hearing Roselli's powerful voice belting out "Mala Femmena." Borrelli was impressed that this kid, Ernie, knew and actually liked Italian music. Then the inspector really tested this kid.

"Yeah, this is great, but I really like to hear Roselli sing saloon songs," Borrelli waited for a reaction. Ernie pulled out his eight track carrying case and asked, "Which volume, one, two or three?" Ernie literally had every album Roselli ever recorded. Borrelli couldn't believe it. Later that night Ernie proclaimed to the other rookies, "It's good to be Italian. You know what I mean?"

Throughout the years Ernie kept in touch with Chief Borrelli, usually through Columbia Association functions. Once Ernie became a board member of the fraternal association he went out of his way to cultivate contacts with big bosses. He didn't do it to suck up to them, and even if he did it never worked. Ernie worked in patrol since the first day out of the academy. He did it to ensure that these bosses wouldn't forget the vowel at the end of their names. Big bosses being proud of their Italian heritage could only strengthen the power and influence of the Columbia Association. It was no secret that Borrelli was very proud of the vowel at the end of his name.

Ernie liked Borrelli and it seemed like their paths would cross on and off the job. Borrelli was well known by cops all over the East Coast and for that matter throughout the United States.

Joe the boss didn't work his way up to the most prestigious job in the department by being a nice guy. Even Ernie had

one negative dealing, with him. On November 4, 1983, Ernie
had a serious accident while driving a police car in a
typical rookie haphazard fashion. A call of a man with a
gun at the corner of 110th Street and Park Ave in the
confines of the 23rd precinct had come over the radio.
Ernie was driving car #1330 and wanted to be the first car
at the scene. In his haste he went right through a red
light and was struck by a car driven by an elderly man.
Fortunately, the man was uninjured, but Ernie and his
partner sustained concussions and a lot of bumps and
bruises. Car #1330 was D.O.A. Borrelli told the precinct
captain to ground Ernie for life, which meant he would
never ride in a radio car for as long as Borrelli was the
division commander. Two months later, Ernie was
transferred to Queens, where he was allowed to drive a car,
as long as Borrelli stayed in Manhattan.

Every once in a while Ernie would get up the nerve to ask
Chief Borrelli for a transfer to the detective bureau. The
Chief usually responded with something like, "The only
bureau you'll ever see is the equipment bureau." The
reality was Chief Borrelli actually attempted to get Ernie
into the bureau as a lieutenant, but there was a hold by
the Police Commissioner on all transfers from patrol. By
the time things loosened up Ernie was about to be promoted
to captain. Although it didn't work out, Ernie was
extremely flattered that the Chief had made the attempt.

Although he was considered a gentleman by all who worked
under him, everyone knew that you did as the Chief said.
Chief of Detectives Joe Borrelli wanted this Chinese guy
caught. He better be caught. End of discussion.

Piraino began to explain the plan for the evening.
Surveillance would take place at the business locations
were the lottery tickets had been purchased in the past.
Those locations consisted of a candy store on East
Fourteenth Street, a liquor store on Avenue B. and a
grocery store on Grand Street. The plan involved about
fifteen men, each assigned a specific task. They would
start the surveillance at five in the evening and continue
it until eight p.m. Everyone was hoping that the mutt
would decide to purchase another lottery ticket at one of
the locations he had utilized before.

TARU, Tactical Assistance Resource Unit, would have a
surveillance van set up right in front of the candy store
with the lotto machine on East 14th Street. Detectives
inside the van would film anyone and everyone buying
lottery tickets. There would also be a man inside the
lottery store posing as an employee and there would be
surveillance teams outside the location. These teams would
follow and or pick up anyone that fit the description of

326

the perpetrator.

The non-descript van was equipped with surveillance cameras able to pick up a pimple on a mosquitos ass from a hundred yards away. Ernie felt like a tourist as Piraino explained TARU's ability. Ernie was beginning to like this detective stuff. The Cape May crew had worked with similar equipment throughout their respective careers. They didn't seem to be impressed. Ernie took an interest in the way Martin was requesting that teams be set up at.all of the locations that had been targeted as Lottery Ticket purchase sights. Martin explained that if the mutt had bought tickets at the locations in the past, around the same time, then they should be set up on all of them. Ernie liked the way that this guy said what he thought even to the members of the largest police department this side of Moscow's army.

Jack Trombetta, after hearing Martin, also indicated he felt the same way. Piraino then advised that they would set up at all locations and use the video camera equipped van at the 14th Street location. Everyone agreed and seemed to have a good feeling about the busy location.

It was decided that everyone would meet back at Major Case Squad's office at four in the afternoon. It was eleven in the morning. It had been arranged that Martin and Trombetta would be taken to the 109th Precinct by Ernie. Bob and Jack were to meet the "Ninja Squad", Tommy Chin and Keith Ng.

Rybicki and Taylor went along and it was decided that all would make the trip in one car with Ernie driving. Piraino and Santiago advised that they had about four or five hours work that they had to take care of on a kidnaping case. Ernie was impressed with how these guys just kept working case after case and prioritizing their time.

Ernie and the Jersey guys decided to take Rybicki's car. They had to walk down under the Brooklyn Bridge where it was parked. They approached it and observed that it was wearing a parking ticket. Ernie was embarrassed and before he could grab the ticket Martin was stuffing it in his pocket. "Bob, give that to me, I'll take care of it." Bob figured Ernie would probably pay it rather than try to get it dismissed. "Don't worry about it, Ernie, I have influence. I'll get it taken care of when we come back," said Bob. Jim Rybicki, a guy who did everything by the numbers stated, "No, really, I'll pay it." Martin laughed and stated, "Jim if my influence doesn't work they will have a warrant out for your arrest."

Rybicki didn't laugh. "That's what I'm afraid of." Taylor didn't seem to notice the ticket or worry about how or if

it would be taken care of. Everyone piled into the new
Chevy Caprice and Ernie took the wheel. They took the
Brooklyn Bridge to the Brooklyn-Queens Expressway and, of
course, hit traffic. Ernie pulled a couple of maneuvers
and got them to the 109 by 12:30. During the ride Jim
Rybicki kept on saying how appreciative he was for all the
assistance the NYPD was rendering. Ernie downplayed it.
If they only knew that he was more surprised and
appreciative than they were. Ernie was actually very proud
of his department for doing what was being done. It was
truly a learning experience for him, not to mention he was
getting to play detective. He would have paid these guys
for the opportunity.

During the drive, every time Ernie went past a landmark he
would mention a story. They passed Shea Stadium and Ernie
talked about the time he was working crowd control and a
mugger beat and robbed an old lady who went to all the Mets
games. Ernie explained how he chased the guy down and after
running six blocks he tackled the mutt and beat the shit
out of the guy when he pulled a knife on him. The collar
brought Ernie the prestigious "Mayor's Award for Valor."
Ernie thought Rybicki seemed impressed. Ernie noticed that
Bob wasn't showing any reaction. Ernie thought to himself
that Jack probably told Bob that Ernie was a bullshitter
and made up heroic stories. Gene Taylor never cracked a
smile nor said a word. The story was, in fact, bullshit
and there is no such thing as the "Mayor's Award."

The 109th Precinct is located on Union Street in Flushing,
Queens. Since the early eighties the Chinese, Japanese,
and Koreans had moved into the business district in droves,
replacing many of the old fashioned Mom and Pop shops that
once flourished in the area. The late seventies had
economically been devastating to Flushing. The Asians
brought it back to life. Union Street ran parallel to Main
Street, which was the heart of the business district.
Virtually every restaurant, store and office building had
Oriental characters written on the facades. The Jersey
crew couldn't believe they were in America.

"Can you imagine a Korean or Vietnam veteran having too
much to drink being dumped in the middle of this area?
Wanna talk about flashbacks. Forget about it," Ernie
commented. Everybody laughed, except Gene, not even a
smile. This guy always had a marine look on his face.
Someone should poke him to see if he sleeps with his eyes
open, thought Ernie.

They parked across the street from the station house. At
least five cops recognized Ernie as soon as he walked
through the front door. Two years earlier he had been a
lieutenant breaking balls and having some fun in this same

precinct. He spoke briefly with a couple of the guys then brought the Jersey cops up to the Central Robbery Squad on the second floor. Big Don Costello was waiting for them.

Tommy Chin and Keith Ng were on their way back from court. They would arrive any minute. Ernie introduced Don to the Jersey crew. On the trip out Ernie explained how Don was responsible for setting them up with Tommy and Keith. Bob was explaining some of the details to Don when Ernie received a message to call his command.

The administrative lieutenant, a twenty-eight year veteran named Jeff Shore, informed Ernie that the Chief of the patrol borough wanted him to attend a meeting being held at four that afternoon between opposing factions of the Jewish community in Seagate. Ernie went ballistic. Seagate was a co-op community which was in the middle of a civil war between the Hasidic Jews and every other faction of the Jewish religion. It was apparent these groups, although Jewish, despised each other and, as usual, the cops were caught in the middle.

"Jeff, I'm with the Major Case Squad today. We're trying to catch a fuckin' cop killer. I ain't got time for this political bullshit. Call, Jimmy Morrisroe, let him know what's going on. Maybe he could get me out of this shit," Ernie directed. Deputy Inspector Morrisroe was the division commander who never overreacted to anything, very unlike some of the bosses over him. He knew Jimmy would squash everything once Jeff explained the Jersey situation. He also knew that Jeff was excellent at getting rid of anything or anyone that Ernie deemed annoying, which were many things and many people. It was one o'clock.

"I'll call you back in an hour. See what you can do. Thanks, Jeff." Ernie was obviously mad as he hung up the phone. Jack asked if he had to leave. Ernie said he would know in an hour. Tommy and Keith walked into the crowded squad room. The Jersey guys looked at them like they were celebrities. The "Ninja Squad" was what the Jersey crew had been waiting for. They needed good street smart detectives who could speak Chinese and cops who could use their proven interview and interrogation abilities to catch this Chinese cop killer. Everyone was all handshakes and smiles. Then they got into the details of the case.

Bob Martin did all the talking. Everything about the case he revealed from memory. He explained the actual homicide, the evidence at the scene, the business card, the writing on the back of it, the lottery ticket, the key and the very uncooperative Chinese restaurant workers and their boss. He also got into the assistance, or lack of, from the FBI and how Detective Gong's interviews didn't go as well as

expected perhaps because his forte was as an NYPD Missing
Persons investigator. Martin couldn't make himself believe
that perhaps the restaurant workers had nothing to provide.

Bob asked Tommy and Keith if Ray Gong the detective from
Missing Persons had supplied the copy of the case file they
had given him for delivery to Chin and Ng. When they
answered no Bob and Jack looked at each other with
obviously pissed off expressions. Bob had hoped these guys
would have already had a working knowledge of the case from
reading the case file they had given to Gong. Bob
continued with what was required down in Lower Township.

Bob was very professional in his presentation to Detectives
Chin and Ng. He had everyone's undivided attention. Jack
just stood there looking like a handsome well dressed
psychopathic killer. Except for Jack, everyone in the room
looked like corporate executives listening to a proposal
from a CEO on expanding or merging or investing 6.2 million
dollars. Tommy and Keith looked like the businessmen from
overseas that Bob was trying to lure into the firm.

Bob had completed the facts of the case as they were known.
Bob could tell he was providing all the necessary
information because there were no interruptions requesting
clarification. Bob could also see that these guys from
NYPD didn't interrupt just to hear themselves talk. These
guys were investigators not wanna-bees with a million
questions because they didn't listen or just wanted to make
people think they were evaluating what they had heard.
Martin never had time for wanna-bees. That's why he always
seemed to have trouble with investigators who had never
been cops and found themselves working for a prosecutor's
office, most often because they knew some politician who
got them a job.

Bob noticed that Tommy Chin and Keith Ng were doing more
than listening. The looks on their faces told Bob that
they were dissecting and evaluating all the facts Bob layed
out before them. Their faces indicated more than just
interest out of courtesy. These looks showed a desire to
know every aspect of the case to mentally formulate their
plan of investigative attack. They knew they would be
interviewing people who were withholding important facts.
Bob noticed how Jack was observing the "Ninja Squad" guys.
He knew Jack well enough to realize that he was observing
the same indicators in the faces of these guys.

Detective Ng was very interested in the killer's
description, especially as it related to age. A middle
aged chubby Chinese man shooting a police officer just
didn't make sense. A young punk gang member possibly might

shoot a cop, but even that was unlikely. Both Ng and Chin
had seen the aftermath of Asian violence, but neither had
ever heard of these mutts even pointing a gun at a cop.
How could a fifty year old Chinese man do something like
this when teenage punks wouldn't even think of it?
Everyone waited for Bob to finish. When he did there
weren't a lot of questions. Bob had covered the incident
from top to bottom. Tommy Chin clarified a few points and
Keith then spoke for the first time. Ernie, Jack, Gene and
Jim just looked at each other uncomfortably as Keith spoke.
Don smirked. Ernie whispered to Don, "What the hell is he
saying? I can't understand a fuckin' word." Don just
smiled. Jack looked at Ernie but said nothing. However,
his eyes asked, "Can you understand this guy?" Ernie's
eyes answered back, "No way." For reasons known only to
God, Bob understood everything Keith was saying.

Bob was even conversing with him. Even Tommy Chin was
impressed that someone other than he knew what Keith was
saying. Tommy was use to translating Keith's statements so
everyone could understand. Tommy almost looked relieved
that someone else understood Keith.

Keith not only was Chinese, his English sounded like it was
Chinese. He spoke very quickly and ran his words and
sentences together. His rendition of the English language
made it sound like it was a foreign language.

Keith was making comments to Martin about what had been
indicated about the Chinese restaurant workers. Keith was
explaining that they just wanted to keep their jobs and get
their pay. He advised that basically they were hard
working people who didn't want any problems.

Keith said, "Me, Tommy tawk dese peoper, we get storry fwom
dem. Dese mudda fuckas betta tell twuth." Bob stated, "It
will be good to get the truth from them." Everyone figured
that Bob must have been happy with whatever Keith had said
because he had a smile on his face. If Bob was happy, all
the Jersey guys were happy.

Keith asked about extortion or kidnaping taking place among
the Chinese community in Lower Township. It was obvious to
Bob Martin that Keith Ng felt this incident had to somehow
be connected to Asian gangs. Jack, Ernie, Gene, Jim and
Don just sat there with their mouths open trying to figure
out what Bob and Keith were talking about. Tommy Chin just
gazed at Bob and nodded occasionally as Keith spoke.

The only words that Jack, Gene, Jim, Ernie and Don
understood coming from Keith's mouth were "Mudda Fucca."
It wasn't hard to get the meaning of those two words. Jack
had given up trying to understand what Keith was saying so

331

instead he counted the number of times "Mudda Fucca" was used in a sixty second period. Later, that day, Jack told Bob that Keith had used the infamous expression an average of 72 times a minute.
Bob understood everything between the 'Mudda Fuccas'. Keith explained that the relatively minor things that had been stolen in the series of burglaries before the Douglass homicide can be attributed to poor people with criminal dispositions from the Fu Chin province of China. Personal items, underwear, toothpaste and other clothing would be more important than a stereo or TV. Keith also mentioned that an older out of work Chinese man would steal those types of items to provide for the care of his family if indeed he was out of work and was having problems securing a job.

Bob was asked if the Feds had provided any help with interviewing the restaurant workers and owner. Keith didn't wait for Bob's answer and stated, "Da FBI, dem mudda fuccas, deh all some computa operata, never solve mudda fucca cwime." Keith also had some choice words for Chinese restaurant owners. "Chinese restwant owna, mudda fuccas, dey tweet da peoper rike shit, speciawrry der own..."

Bob then explained that there were thirteen Chinese restaurant workers, eleven of whom spoke no English, who had to be re-interviewed. In fact, it was beyond the interview stage. Bob needed Chinese interrogators. Keith interjected, "You need good Chinese interrogata, a mudda fucca, to punch perp in da face."

It was almost two o'clock. The meeting went well. The Jersey crew got great vibes from Tommy and Keith even though they really didn't understand what the hell Keith had said. It must have been a cop thing.

Ernie called back to Lt. Shore to see what the story was at Seagate. "I spoke to Morrisroe. He said don't worry about it. I'll take care of it." Jeff's words made Ernie relax, however, he made a decision at that point. Any work Ernie would do on this case from that day on would be while off duty. In this way Ernie wouldn't have to worry about any "captain bullshit" while he was with Jack and Bob. Ernie was a captain assigned to the 60th Precinct in Patrol Borough Brooklyn South, not the Detective Bureau. If something requiring a captain's presence occurred in his precinct the borough commander, a two star chief, would not want to hear that Captain Naspretto was in Manhattan or Queens living out a detective fantasy. The chief would be pissed and he would be right.

As a captain, Ernie could usually make his own hours. He would work around this case. It would mean long days and

more time than usual away from his family, but it would be
less stressful. Ernie also knew that Grace would be very
supportive. She could be the wicked witch of Glendale when
Ernie wanted to go out with the boys, but for something
like this, Grace, pregnant and all, was the greatest
partner in the world. She would have preferred to be on
the street following leads. That way she could try to keep
Ernie out of trouble.

Bob had set up future contact with Tommy and Keith and
everyone said their goodbyes. They headed back to
headquarters. Ernie took a different route. He took them
over the Triboro Bridge and down Second Avenue in Spanish
Harlem through the 23rd Precinct where Ernie had worked ten
years earlier with Ruben Santiago. He showed them a couple
of locations and told some "War Stories", some of which he
made up. Perhaps he had made up all of them. He wasn't so
sure anymore.

"Yeah, I blew some mutt away right in front of that subway
station. Made my first bank robbery collar on 96th Street.
Delivered twins on Lexington Avenue. Did it with some
Puerto Rican chick right in the radio car behind
Metropolitan Hospital." Jim and Gene didn't know what to
think about Ernie. Bob thought he was full of shit but
wasn't sure. Ernie knew Jack knew he was full of shit but
loved playing head games with the other guys. But, it
wouldn't be long before everyone in the car knew Ernie was
so full of shit it was coming out of his ears and getting
on everybody.

They got back to headquarters around three o'clock, ate
lunch, and were back at the Major Case Squad by three
thirty. Joe Piraino introduced everyone to Captain George
Duke, the commanding officer of the Major Case Squad. Duke
acknowledged Bob as if they were old friends. Ernie was
thinking to himself that Bob seemed to know everyone and
was comfortable around them also. Bob made himself at home
parking himself at a desk, using phones and conversing with
the detectives in the room.

Duke was a seasoned veteran of the Detective Bureau. As a
Lieutenant he had commanded some of the busiest detective
squads in the most dangerous precincts in Brooklyn, the
75th and 77th. Anyone that walked into Captain Duke's
office knew that although he resided on Long Island, his
first love was Brooklyn, where he was born and raised.
There were large aerial photos of Coney Island and pictures
and pennants of the Brooklyn Dodgers all over the walls.

George Duke was into cops and robbers. He loved hard
working detectives and had no tolerance for laziness. He
wouldn't ask anyone to do something he hadn't already taken

part in. Many times he still got involved in the day to day investigations that came to the attention of Major Case.

Duke had another love, golf. He, also, had one major hatred. It was for the FBI. Considered a tough but very fair boss, Duke demanded loyalty, not to himself, but to the law enforcement mission. Anyone who violated that trust could not work for George Duke. A week earlier Sgt. Piraino was briefing him on the Lower Township homicide. Duke simply nodded and waited for Joe to finish then said, "Just do it."
He made sure that Joe Piraino would have whatever was required to conduct this investigation. There would be absolutely no restrictions.

Joe introduced Ernie as Captain Naspretto. Suddenly, Ernie got a little embarrassed as George smiled and shook hands. Ernie knew George had to be thinking what the hell he was doing there. There were captains and then there were captains. Ernie had thirteen years on the job. George had over thirty. Ernie was from patrol. George was on patrol before Ernie was in grammar school. The investigators on this case reported to George not Ernie.

Ernie had no idea that Bob Martin had already advised Duke about Ernie and the fact that he was along for the ride and wanted to do whatever he could to help regardless of his rank.
Ernie just wanted to help his friend, Jack, his new found friend, Bob, and most of all he wanted to get the mutt that killed a brother police officer.

"If you don't mind I'd like to just hang around and help out. I'm just a soldier in this. I won't get in the way," Ernie heard himself almost pleading. Ernie thought, to himself, please don't send me home, Captain Duke. Duke just smiled figuring what the hell. Why turn away anyone who wanted to help? A resource was a resource.

Bob was busy with Joe Piraino coordinating all the surveillance set ups. Jim Rybicki was doing the same. Gene Taylor and Jack Trombetta were sitting with scowls on their faces. Jack's look seemed contrived. Gene's was no doubt his usual look. Ernie thought to himself Gene looked a little demented. But then again sometime that's a good look for a cop to exude.

The vehicle and position assignments that had been worked out were then provided to all who were taking part. The entire entourage then exited One Police Plaza and drove to their assignments. By five o'clock the white TARU van was parked directly outside Brothers Candy and Grocery at 542

East 14th Street. The van was truly "nondescript."
Anything and everything, everyone and anyone fit in on East
14th Street. On the north side of the busy two way street
was Stuyvesant Town, a complex of numerous eleven and
twelve story buildings which housed everything from blue
collar locals who resided there for decades to the 80's
arrival of yuppie business types to long time residents who
had become wealthy and would never think of leaving.

On the south side were housing projects consisting of ten
story buildings housing mostly minority residences. Many
of whom were on welfare or some type of public assistance.
Some had low paying laborer type jobs. Whatever the case,
a bunch of guys wearing ties and jackets sitting in Chevys
and Dodges scattered over a two block radius certainly
wouldn't make anyone suspicious. Even those who might have
noticed them wouldn't care one way or another. A naked man
could be walking down the street and probably not seem too
much out of place to the residents of the area. Everybody
just did his or her own thing on East 14th Street.

The two TARU detectives were filming everybody entering and
exiting the candy store, particularly those individuals at
the "lotto" counter. The patrons truly represented what is
the melting pot of East 14th Street, a well dressed thirty
year old black woman followed by a twenty year old white
kid wearing a New York Ranger shirt followed by an Asian
woman carrying some groceries followed by some Hispanic
teenagers.

Joe, Jack, Ernie and Bob were parked on a corner diagonal
from the candy store. Ruben, Jim and Gene were parked
about ten car lengths from the TARU van. Detective Simon
Kok was positioned in the store. He had previously
identified himself to the store owners and told them to
immediately signal him if anyone played the lottery numbers
01-03-07-08-18-38 and 02-05-14-16-17-32. The investigation
had already revealed these numbers had been on the person
of Dave's killer. The owners who appeared to be Arab just
nodded and asked no questions. Kok didn't offer them any
other information.

The plan was rather simple. Kok would notify the outside
units if the numbers were played and give a description of
the player. The outside units would follow the player to
his or her residence, keep detectives observing the
location to monitor anyone entering or leaving the
apartment then obtain a search warrant. Hopefully, the
player would be a middle aged stocky Chinese man.

By six o'clock Joe Piraino had loosened up with Ernie.
After listening to some of the sick conversations Ernie was
having with Jack he realized that Ernie was there truly to

help not to hinder or play boss. If anything, Ernie didn't act or sound, like a captain at all. Jack and Ernie were sharing fantasies, everything from sex to blowing this "chink bastard" away. Bob was in the rear of the unmarked vehicle directly behind Jack on the passenger side. Ernie was seated behind Joe who was driving. In less than two hours Joe felt like he knew these guys for years. Joe and Bob had already passed that plateau. They seemed to gel from the first time Bob had met Joe a week before. Now Joe seemed comfortable with everyone. Ernie noticed that even though Bob and Joe would take part in the small talk they always seemed to know everything that was going on in front of them. They were forever saying to each other, "Hey, Joe, did you see that guy in the ski cap?" "Bob, check out this guy with the grocery bag." Martin and Piraino really seemed to be paying attention to everything that was going on. Jack and Ernie on the other hand were deciding how many shots they would put into this cop killer if he ran.

Bob and Joe decided to leave the car and walk around the neighborhood to get a feel for the lay of the land if they had to chase someone on foot. Joe, of course, had been in this area before and was familiar with the location. Bob, on the other hand, wanted to see what was what. When Bob and Joe left, Ernie and Jack reminisced about the FBI National Academy. There were a couple of hot looking women cops who attended the 170th session.

"Hey, Jack, did you jerk off as much as I did?" Ernie asked in the most serious voice he could conjure up. Jack laughed and asked, "Why do you have to be so gross?" Jack, however did not answer the question. Ernie waited a couple of seconds and said, "Well?"

"Naw, I was too drunk most of the time," Jack finally answered. Then Jack brought up Ernie's weight again. Ernie was just about to say fuck you when Joe got back into the car appearing excited and asked if they knew where Bob was. At that moment Bob appeared from the court yard of the Stuyvesant Housing Complex. Both men were now in the car.

Joe stated, "There's a heavy set Chinese guy about forty-five years old behind the counter of that fish store." There was apparent excitement in Joe's voice. The fish store was located on the corner, literally within yards of the candy store. It would make sense. The mutt worked in the fish store and would play the lottery numbers right next door. Could it be that easy? Jack's eyes started to bulge. Joe immediately radioed the detectives in the TARU van and advised them to start taping the fish store. He mentioned that the guy was wearing a black buttoned down shirt and he further described the subject.

336

Bob who was now staring in the direction of the fish store now changed his look from what had been a watchful gaze into a look of anticipation. Bob exited the vehicle, crossed the busy street and blended in with the human traffic that hurried along the sidewalk. Bob seemed to return in minutes.

"He sure fits our description," Bob proclaimed. "Anything is possible. Let's keep an eye on him. He isn't going anywhere until the place closes." Joe advised all units to stand by and maintain surveillance. They would keep a watchful eye on this man who might be Dave's killer. It was decided that when the guy left the store that he would be followed no matter where he went. China if need be.

Joe, Bob and Jack began to talk about warrant procedures, jurisdictional considerations, and other detective stuff that Ernie had never had to worry about in his thirteen years on patrol. Bob stated, "If this is the guy this will be an easy end to what has been a bastard of a case." Jack gazed and added, "Yeah, too easy."
Ernie asked, "Do you mind if I take a look at the guy?"
Jack said, "Be our guest, Ernie, bring me back something to eat."

Ernie walked across the street past the store and looked at the subject. Yes, he certainly fit the description, but there was something about him that wasn't right. For the first time since he graduated the FBI National Academy eighteen months earlier, Ernie was about to utilize something he had learned in a criminal profiling course. Although the course was very interesting a patrol captain had very little use for criminal profiling. Basically the course taught how a crime scene can help profile a person responsible, especially in homicides. A crime scene could possibly advise if the parties knew each other, if the act was well planned, if it was spontaneous, if the individual was mature, immature, a scorned lover, etc. It is not an exact science like forensics, but it can be remarkably accurate.

Ernie saw the killer of Patrolman David Douglass as a loser. He was apparently a fired employee. He was disgruntled and was pulling off spiteful burglaries, stealing everything from clothes to toothpaste. He actually wore a jacket that he had stolen from one of the previous burglaries. He was also stupid in that he kept returning to the scene of his crimes, although now he would stay away. So basically Ernie saw David Douglass' killer as a fat, stupid waste product. The guy in that fish store was no loser. He looked like he was running the place. Fuck it, Ernie decided to go in and buy something to eat. Ernie saw that they sold fried chicken wings. He figured

Jack would appreciate the treat.

Ernie walked in and waited by the front counter. The subject noticed him before the young Chinese girl by the cash register saw him. The subject barked something at her in Chinese and she jumped like her job depended on Ernie being served promptly. The girl asked if she could help Ernie. Just then a well dressed black woman entered the store. Ernie stepped back and indicated he would wait while the woman was taken care of. The subject broke into a big smile and spoke perfect English to the woman. Ernie knew right away that this guy wasn't Dave's killer. His English was very good. The killer couldn't speak English.

Ernie noticed two young Hispanic teenagers also working in the store. The subject hollered orders to one of them in Spanish. The subject fit the description of the killer but that is were the likenesses stopped. Ernie ordered some fried chicken wings, paid for his purchase and as he walked past the TARU van he gave them the director's cut sign.

Joe, Bob and Jack were all looking at Ernie as he entered the car. "Sorry to be the carrier of bad news, guys, but that guy speaks three languages, including English. He's the boss over there. He ain't no cop killer. Want some chicken wings? They ain't bad."

When Ernie mentioned the fact that the guy spoke English, their hopes went down the drain. Joe radioed the TARU van and told them to start filming the lottery store again. He then notified all units that the subject was a negative ID. Ernie felt guilty about ascertaining that the subject wasn't the cop killer. He felt good, however, about saving the investigation some man hours being spent on trying to ID the subject in the store. Ernie felt like he had added something to this investigation. Not bad for a guy from patrol.

Joe, Bob and Jack were actually glad Ernie was around. He got to live out a fantasy that had become a routine bore to them. They hated following people, especially on foot. Ernie was jumping out of the car anytime one of the guys even remotely implied that someone appeared suspicious. Joe started to enjoy telling Ernie to "follow that guy." Joe was giving, a captain, orders and enjoying every minute. Ernie loved every minute also. He'd follow any individual for any reason just to see if they'd enter a car or nearby residence or subway. Ernie didn't have a clue as to why he was doing this but Joe told him to do it, so he did it.

While Ernie was out of the car on one of his numerous clandestine following episodes Jack said to Joe and Bob,

"Hey, Ernie's been following almost every possible look-a-like since we parked. Maybe one of us should do some walking." Bob replied, "Joe and I did our one each, it's your turn Jackie." Upon Ernie's return a stocky Chinese man walked by the car. Jack didn't make a move to follow him. Ernie left once again. Jack hollered, "Ern, wait a minute." Ernie stopped and listened. Jack said, "Get me some Marlboro lights." Ernie now realized that every time he exited the vehicle Jack had a request, food, candy, a drink and now cigarettes. Jack never dipped into his pocket when he asked for these things. Ernie went ballistic on Jack. The other guys loved it.

"Hey, but don't you ever go into your fuckin' pocket? I spent fifteen bucks on you tonight, ya cheap fuckin' terd." Ernie was yelling and talking Italian, with his hands and arms.

"Oh, sure, now I know who my real friends are. I ask for one little favor and this is the way I'm treated. Thanks, Ern, thanks a lot. Just forget it," Jack answered in the most serious voice he could come up with.

"Just one favor! Kiss my ass, I've been buying you little things all fuckin' night."

Bob was used to Jack's antics. He had been a victim of Jack's favors for years. Ernie was just learning, thought Bob. Then he heard Ernie say something he wished he didn't hear.

"Give me some fuckin' money you cheap bastard and I'll get your stupid Marlboro Lights."

Jack turned to Bob and asked, "Got any money, pal?" Bob already had it in his hand.

The stakeout ended at eight o'clock. Nobody purchased a ticket bearing the numbers in question. Everybody headed back to headquarters. There was a message from Tommy Chin. He and Keith Ng got a break from court and advised that they would go to Lower Township on Friday and may even be able to spend some time on Saturday. Jack and Bob were ecstatic that the "Ninja Squad" would finally get to Lower Township.

Everyone took part in a short debriefing and before long the decision had been made to call it a night. Jack, Bob and Ernie got back to the Naspretto residence about 10 p.m. Earlier in the day Grace had decided to spend the night at her mother's apartment in Astoria just in case Angelina had any more tantrums during the night. She left a big pot of cubed boneless chicken mixed with broccoli, stewed tomatoes and pasta. Jack and Bob said they weren't hungry.

Ernie basically said bullshit to that and set up three
settings, micro waved the chicken, cut up some Italian
bread and served. Everything was gobbled up within
minutes. It tasted great. The Jersey boys raved about it.

"What do you call this?" Jack asked.

"Chicken Angelina," Ernie lied. He just made up the name
at that moment. Grace had been cooking this dish for about
two years and basically just concocted it by mistake. She
never gave it a name. Ernie usually referred to it as
"Hey, Grace, make that chicken thing."

Not only were they impressed with the meal, but, Jack was
particularly, impressed with how domestic Ernie was acting.
He set the table, heated up the food, served his guests,
then washed the dishes. Jack commented on Ernie's very
pleasant demeanor. Ernie graciously accepted the
compliment by suggesting that Jack have intercourse with
himself.

It had been a long day. Jack, Bob and Ernie were in bed by
eleven-thirty. Bob and Ernie actually slept, Jack just
stared at the Naspretto's dark living room ceiling.

It was a new day and Bob and Jack were awake and dressed by
seven in the morning. Ernie had to go in for a day shift.
He wasn't about to play games with his schedule today. Bob
and Jack had worked it out with Tom Nerney that he would
pick them up about nine o'clock and they would travel to
Major Case together. Bob liked the fact that these guys
would shuttle them around. Bob hated having to drive in
New York City.

Tom Nerney showed up about eight-fifteen and they all had
some coffee and bagels. Tom was talking about the case and
they were formulating what they would be doing throughout
the day. Bob had indicated that he wanted to hook up with
Ruben Santiago and Simon Kok and make an effort to try the
key in a few locations. They had obtained the addresses
for a half dozen phone numbers that had been recorded
throughout the investigation. Bob figured it was time to
run down the locations. They knew better than to wait for
the Feds to do the job. Bob and Jack both knew at this
point the easiest way to get something done was to do it
yourself.

They had decided to hook up with Santiago and Kok and
meander through Chinatown checking as many locations as
possible. They were beginning to know their way around the
area. It seemed like they had been to all of the locations

repeatedly. They had. They continually back tracked
through many of the locations they had checked previously.
They hoped something new would come up. The guys from New
York had other cases to work on but somehow they always
managed to find room for Martin and Trombetta in their busy
schedules.

Martin and Trombetta spent the entire day running down
leads that were leading nowhere. It seemed that each day
produced another frustration. Every time they thought they
had something it turned out to be crap. They were tired of
all the roadblocks in the case.

Tom Nerney could see that they were hitting an awful lot of
roadblocks and he figured it was time for a little R&R.
Tom purposely cleared his schedule for the night and after
a few phone calls set it up with Ernie and Grace to meet
him and the Jersey guys at Abbraciamento's, a great Italian
restaurant on Woodhaven Blvd. in Queens.

Tom also wanted to take the guys to the 112th precinct and
introduce them to Lt. Phil Panzarella, a guy who had been
in the trenches of NYPD for a lot of years and had more
interesting cases under his belt than anyone around. Tom
figured the change would be good for everyone.

Tom wanted to foot the bill for the dinner. Bob and Jack
had done so a few times during the investigation and Tom
also felt that he should return Ernie and Grace's
hospitality. They had supplied him with a few meals and
good company and now was the time to return the favor.

The conversation at dinner centered on the fact that they
were eating in a fancy Italian restaurant that at one time
had been considered off limits to New York City cops. It
seemed that every wiseguy and mafia boss in the city made a
point to frequent the place. Martin wished he had a tape
recording of the entire dinner. The cop talk and stories
supplied by Lt. Panzarella would have been enough material
for three cop novels.

Between the Lieutenant and Tom Nerney a lot of
investigative history had gone under the bridge. Their
stories should have been part of a training program for
rookie detectives. The funny part, however, was that they
were as interested in the stories provided by Bob and Jack.
The sad part, however, was that even Grace wasn't
interested in Ernie's stories. Everyone did make an effort
to listen. They just wanted to be polite.

The food was fantastic and the party lasted until no one
else was in the restaurant. The owner supplied three
bottles of Anisette and the Jersey guys learned all about

espresso and cappuccino. Tom Nerney wouldn't even allow anyone to leave a tip. The treat was his. Jack was real happy that he once again didn't have to pull any money from his pocket. He did, however, mention that Bob had some money if it was needed. Eventually they closed the restaurant. The guys made plans for Tom Nerney to pick them up in the morning.

March 24th once again found Bob and Jack at Major Case. Bob and Tom went over all the case reports and began coordinating the reports from the New York guys. Jack made a concerted effort not to be involved because he knew that if he wasn't privy then he would not have to provide a report.

Jack and Joe Piraino talked about what was next in the investigation. Jack and Joe reviewed everything that they had taken part in with regard to the investigation. Joe mentioned to Jack that so far he had been pretty fortunate with regard to report writing. Jack laughed and said, "Yeah, Joe, I know what you mean. That report writing can be a real pain." Jack had not made out one report. He hoped his luck would hold out. Joe assumed that Jack was probably swamped with paper work.

Ernie worked a day tour and then met the guys at Major Case.
It had been planned that he would pick them up, take them home for dinner and then they would travel to Queens Robbery to meet with Chin and Ng.

Ernie, however, had already ascertained that the 'Ninja Squad' were stuck in court and probably would be free after dinner. Ernie decided that they would grab a sandwich somewhere and then he would take the Jersey guys to the Queens precinct to meet Chin and Ng.

Joe Piraino, Tom Nerney, Ernie, Bob and Jack went down the street and got a quick sandwich at the bar restaurant called the Metropolitan owned by ex-cops. The waitresses were beginning to recognize Bob and Jack. It seemed like every time they frequented the place the same girls were working.

The scenario was always the same. The place was always filled with cops and war stories were always floating around the room. Martin thought to himself that this place was probably the location for a lot of cases to be brought to a positive conclusion. He hoped the same would hold true with the Dave Douglass case.

After dinner the guys went their separate ways. Joe and Tom had other cases to follow up on and Bob, Jack and Ernie traveled to Queens and met with Chin and Ng. They made plans for the following day and eventually they returned to Ernie's home. The guys sat around, Bob and Jack had a few beers and they all talked about the case.

The topic of discussion was meeting with Liu the next day and then traveling to Lower Township with Chin and Ng. Bob and Jack couldn't wait for the restaurant workers to meet the 'Ninja Squad'. Ernie was wishing he could tag along. He knew, however, that he had to work and couldn't get out of it. Ernie knew that Chin and Ng would put on a good investigative show. Ernie would have loved to be involved. The guys were about to call it a night when the phone rang and Ernie picked it up.

"Hello. What's up? You're kiddin'. No, No I'll come in. I don't want somebody else to handle it." Ernie hung up the phone.

Ernie looked at Bob and Jack and stated, "I'm glad I didn't do any drinkin' today. I have to go to the Precinct. One of my guys just kicked the shit out of a scumbag and they are going to need my expertise to make this one right."

Jack looked at Ernie and stated, "Oh, so your guys are kickin the shit out of local citizens and you are going to cover it up."

"No, no, that's not it at all you fuckin' terd. They did it by the numbers. I just have to make sure the reports are right and that all the questions are answered. I take care of my people," added Ernie.

Ernie quickly threw on his coat and as he shut the door stated, "A good cops work is never done. I guess, you wouldn't no about that, would you Jack."

Everyone laughed and Bob and Jack decided to get some sleep.

Ernie worried all night that Angelina would keep everyone awake. She slept like a baby and so did everyone else.

CHAPTER FIFTY ONE

On March 25th, Martin and Trombetta woke up early. Grace,
was, already running around the kitchen making breakfast.
Both Bob and Jack were telling her they weren't hungry.
Ernie came down the steps looking like he hadn't slept all
night. Trombetta looked at Ernie pleasantly
commented,"Hey, Ernie you're fat and look like shit."

"Yeah, and good morning to you, too, terd. If you remember,
Jack, I didn't get home until 4 a.m. You mumbled something
as I walked past your bed, Sleeping Beauty."

"I heard you. You mentioned you got stuck at work because
one of your guys beat the shit out of some scumbag. If you
had any kind of memory you would have realized that I was
here when you got the call."

"Yeah, I had to make sure he got all the paper work in
order. Even in New York you can't beat people up just for
kicks. Hey, Grace, you making pancakes for these guys?"

"Don't worry about it, Grace, all we need is a cup of
coffee and a bagel," said Jack. Grace entered the room
carrying plates and silverware. Jack jumped up and using
his best line of crap said, "Grace, let me help you with
that. You should be careful carrying stuff around in your
condition." Martin was almost sick to his stomach. Martin
had known Jack for over twenty years and not once had he
heard Jack tell Lynn she was working too hard and he would
help her. Ernie also knew Jack was full of shit.

"Hey, Jack, why don't you say what you really mean like,
'Hey, Grace, set the table, cook the breakfast, have the
baby and in your spare time clean up the mess.'" Ernie
words echoed Bob's thoughts.

Ernie thought for a second and added, "You know, Jack, you
are so full of shit I don't know why Bob puts up with you.
How is it that no matter where you go, or what you do, you
always find someone to do everything for you. I worked my
ass off in the Academy and you skated and had somebody else
do all your work. I bet you never did one thing at
Quantico, did you? You were so lazy you even had someone
else sleep for you."

Jack looked at Bob and pleaded, "Tell him I can work when I

want to." Bob looked at Ernie, "Jack can work when he wants to. He just doesn't get the urge very often." Grace chimed in like a mother scolding her children.

"Stop picking on Jack. He was just worried about my health and welfare."
Ernie looked at Bob and said, "Now he has her believin' his bullshit."

Ernie then began to fill them in on the incident that forced him to stay at work until 3:30 in the morning. Martin was thinking to himself that this guy can really tell a story. He couldn't help but think that Ernie should write a book about some of the incidents. Ernie had a way with telling a story and making you think he was present when it took place. Most of the time he was sitting at his desk stamping overtime slips. Yeah, Ernie should write a book. Even if the facts were twisted a bit, it would still be entertaining.

Even though Bob and Jack said they weren't hungry Grace managed to keep the pancakes and sausage flowing. Jack took a sip of his orange juice and in his inimitable way said, "Grace, is this fresh squeezed? How do you find the time to do everything you do around this house? Ernie, you are a lucky man to have a wife like Grace."

Ernie looked up from his plate. "You're makin' me sick. Grace, give me the garbage can, I gotta throw up." Grace looked at Jack. "Oh, Jack, I'm not doing anything I don't do everyday for Ernie."

"Well, then all I can say is that Ernie is a very lucky man. He should be glad he has a fifties woman for a wife. These nineties women nowadays don't care about taking care of their husbands."

Jack thought for a moment and said,"I pity the guy that marries my daughter. She is one miserable little girl. She can't do anything for herself. Her room's a pig sty, she can't cook, and she is always in a bad mood. She sure don't take after me or my wife."

Ernie glared at Jack. "Oh, listen to Mr. Perfect speaking. I saw your room in Quantico. It always looked like a crime scene. You could have applied for Federal Fuckin' Funding to clean up the toxic shit. Those asshole democrats in D.C. would have floated you the funds. The only problem you would have had would have been talking Bob into doing all the paperwork. And you have the nerve to talk about your daughter? If she is anything like your wife, she is beautiful and a saint for puttin' up with your shit."

Jack looked at Bob and said, "Tell Ernie about my daughter."

"I'm not throwing any stones. I got a daughter of my own who is driving me crazy. You don't even want to hear it," Bob answered.
Ernie looked into the living room at his daughter Angelina who was watching Barney on television. "I'm sending Angelina to private school and then to a convent. She is going to be known as Sister Angelina."

"Hey, Ernie, All I know is these kids will drive ya nuts," said Jack. "Hey, Bob, pass the syrup," added Jack.

"I thought you only wanted a bagel. You're on your second stack of pancakes," said Martin.

Jack looked at Ernie and said, "Heah, Ernie, beings Grace is pregnant, what good Italian names have you come up with for the new addition?"

Before Ernie could answer Jack said, "Bob tell Ernie about what your family does to the kids in the family."

"Well, Ern, I have an Uncle Jack and Aunt Fran who I love and respect but they named their four kids Ronnie, Johnnie, Bonnie and Connie," said Bob.

"You gotta be kidding," said Ernie.

"Tell him your sisters kids names Bob," said Jack.

"My sister has four boys named, Vito, Gino, Nino and Dino. Good Italian names like yours Ern," said Martin.

Martin hesitated and then said, "My sister was hoping for girls. She was going to name them Gina, Nina, Pinta, and Santa Maria."

Everyone laughed and the three ate while Grace prepared and served breakfast and Ernie talked about the agenda for the day. Ernie asked about the transportation plans. He was looking at Jack when he asked the question but looked to Bob for the answer. Ernie had spoken with Ng and Chin the night before with Bob and Jack but didn't recall setting up chauffeurs for the guys. Ernie was happy that Chin and Ng were finally going to get to Lower Township. Bob refreshed Ernie's mind that they were taking their own car and doing the driving.

Bob and Jack would meet the Ninja Squad at Major Case at noon. It was their intent to find Liu and speak to him. Chin and Ng had to appear in court on a robbery kidnaping

in the morning but had been advised they wouldn't be needed
in the afternoon. Tommy Chin had made up his mind that he
and Keith would travel to Lower Township after they spoke
to Liu.

Chin wanted to be able to stay in Lower Township for the
weekend but a family emergency required that he be back in
New York City late Saturday the 26th of March. Jack and
Bob had been at Ernie's for four days and felt they had
accomplished as much as possible. They had been traveling
the streets of New York City trying the key in as many door
locks as they could. They had been all over Chinatown.
They had become familiar with the many apartment buildings
that housed many of the immigrant Chinese. They became
more frustrated daily at the fact that the key would not
unlock any of the doors.

During the last few days at Ernie's they had been on
countless surveillance of lottery locations hoping to spot
Dave's killer as he was purchasing a lottery ticket. On
this morning they were eating their breakfast making small
talk but thinking about what investigative avenues still
had to be traveled.

Ernie was unable to work with them after breakfast and it
was decided that Jack and Bob would take their belongings
with them because they would be heading back to Jersey by
the end of the day. They were excited about taking the
Ninja Squad back to Jersey. They couldn't wait to see the
faces of the Chinese workers in Lower Township when they
were confronted with the likes of Chin and Ng.

Ernie wished that he could travel with the guys and be
present in Jersey to witness first hand the Ninja Squad at
work. Ernie hated that he had to play captain. Ernie
wanted to be a regular cop. He wanted to investigate crime,
carry a detective shield and kick ass. Ernie thought to
himself, why do I have to have brains and be so good
looking? Why couldn't I just be a detective? Ernie
laughed to himself.

Ernie had a strong feeling that they would be returning to
New York very soon. He reminded himself to tell Grace to
buy more food. These guys ate like every meal was their
last. He thought that perhaps he could claim them on his
income tax. He wanted to ask his accountant if these guys
were investigative expenses. He should have asked Martin
and Trombetta who would have advised him to write it off as
informant's fees.

The breakfast table was cleared. The guys showered and
shaved. Ernie had to get to work and Bob and Jack were
going to follow Ernie. He was going to lead them to a

certain point near the Brooklyn Bridge and then the guys were on their own getting to Police Plaza, the home of Major Case.

They said their goodbyes to Grace and Angelina and followed Ernie out of Glendale and onto the congested roadway. Martin was driving. Trombetta did not like to drive. It was easier for him to sit, do nothing, enjoy the trip and the scenery. Martin was use to being Trombetta's chauffeur. Trombetta hated to do anything that someone could do for him.

Ernie pulled off at an exit for Coney Island. He waved Martin forward towards the Brooklyn Bridge. Martin had now made the trip a few times and was starting to know his way around the city. Even though that was the case he still hated being in the city. Somewhere along the line he had become a country boy. Trombetta on the other hand loved the hustle and bustle of New York. He really enjoyed it when someone else was driving.

Martin parked under the Brooklyn Bridge right down the block from Police Plaza. They made their way to the entrance. Both Detectives couldn't help but notice the bag people living in cardboard huts under the bridge. They had noticed the hovels the first time in New York and found it hard to believe that people lived that way and nobody made an effort to move them from such a high profile area.

They entered the building and obtained a pass for entry. The girls at the reception desk had got to know them very well. Martin couldn't get over how polite they always seemed to be no matter what idiot was giving them a hard time. They could be negative in the nicest way. Apparently, these girls had been working this desk for quite some time. If you gave them a hard time they politely made you wait forever to gain access. Martin and Trombetta made every effort to be polite.

They approached the attractive black girl behind the counter. "Good morning, fellas. Here are those handsome Jersey boys again," she stated to her co-worker. "You boys are becoming New York residents. I'll bet your wives sure miss having you around." She handed them passes and instructed them to place them on their jackets. "Be good fellas. If you can't be good, be careful."

They entered through the metal detectors and made the operator aware that they were carrying weapons. The officers at the detectors had even got to recognize the detectives and waved them forward. They quickly entered the elevator and proceeded to Major Case. They exited the elevator and immediately noticed Detective John Bucalo.

John was President of the Columbia Association and had been
introduced to them by Ernie a few days earlier. He had
already made the guys honorary members and was telling them
they were invited as his guest to the next get together.
Everyone at Police Plaza treated them as if they were
members of NYPD.

The guys couldn't get over how great every police employee
in the Big Apple seemed to want to render every assistance
possible. Bucalo quickly ushered Jack to the coffee. He
told them to relax until the guys from Major Case showed
up.

Trombetta and Martin were looking at all the pictures on
the wall behind Bucalo's desk. It was loaded with
dignitaries from around the world. John Bucalo was
standing next to Presidents, movie stars, heads of state,
not to mention Miss Americas and Miss Universe. Trombetta
looked at one photo of John with his arm around a pretty
girl who appeared to be Italian. "Hey, John, was this girl
a Miss America or something," asked Trombetta.

"No, that one is my daughter. She is my little Miss
America," stated Bucalo as he left the guys to wait for
Major Case. Trombetta looked at Martin and said, "She is a
beautiful girl. I'm glad I didn't say something I shouldn't
have."

"Yeah, that would have been great, Jack. I could see it
now. We would have every member of the Columbia Association
giving us the kiss of death." Both men laughed at the
thought.

It was only minutes before the guys from Major Case started
entering the office area. John Bucalo walked the Jersey
guys over to Major Case. He hung around for a time while
everyone was bull shitting about anything that came to
mind.

Eventually it was evident that everyone had work to do and
things got down to business. Martin was reviewing his
notes and Trombetta was talking small talk with anyone that
was interested. Bob eventually heard Jack talking about
the Gambino investigation or as the Feds referred to it
the, 'Pizza Connection'. They had taken part in when they
were undercover. It wasn't long before many war stories
were being talked about.

Jack was networking and loving every minute of it.
Whenever Jack wanted to make sure about a name or date with
regard to one of his stories he would get Bob involved in
the conversation. It was evident that Martin and Trombetta
had become quite at home in One Police Plaza, not to

mention the offices of the Major Case Squad.

Jack finished up his story telling and mentioned to Martin he wanted to check on the "kids" in Lower Township. Jack called LTPD and was conversing with Detective Chris Winter. Bob could hear Jack filling him in on what he and the other detectives should be doing on their end.

Jack set up the interviews for the Chinese restaurant workers by the Ninja Squad. He wanted everything to be ready when they arrived in Lower Township. Chris updated Jack on everything else that was going on in the Township and Jack provided some direction as to what should be done.

Bob could also hear Jack filling in the Captain and the Chief on what was going on. Bob was glad to hear Jack was on a role. Bob knew that he could get his notes in order and update his work log and activity records. Jack knew that Bob liked to keep the paper work up to date and he figured he would handle some of the things usually handled by Martin.

Jack had a smile on his face. He was thinking that Ernie should be around to witness the supervision Jack was providing to his kids. Jack was going to mention to Bob he should tell Ernie how indispensable Jack was in a pinch.

The time went quickly and before long Bob and Jack had just finished a meeting with the guys from Major Case about what angles they should pursue in regard to the investigation. They were deciding about lunch when Tommy Chin and Keith Ng entered the office. Martin looked at his watch and realized the Ninja Squad was right ontime.

CHAPTER FIFTY TWO

Jack remembered that Bob had mentioned that Tommy Chin and
Keith Ng did not seem comfortable in those surroundings of
One Police Plaza. Jack, on the other hand, had become very
comfortable in the office of the Major Case Squad. He knew
all the locations where coffee could be obtained free of
charge and it was close enough that he didn't have to con
someone to get it for him. Jack had even found enough New
York detectives who smoked and made it possible for him to
obtain cigarettes at no charge. Life was good in the big
city, Jack thought to himself as he reflected on Chin and
Ng.

Bob and Jack had been at Major case all morning and when
Chin and Ng entered Jack decided almost immediately to get
something to eat. Jack asked if Bob had enough money to
spring for lunch. Bob knew that Jack probably didn't have
a dollar in his pocket. He rarely did carry much cash. If
he had money on him he may have to spend it. Jack would
rather have someone else spring for incidentals, like food,
beverage and entertainment. Tommy and Keith each indicated
that they really weren't hungry and would rather start the
trip to Lower Township. It had been decided that Chin and
Ng would interview the Oriental restaurant workers and
owners of the resturant. Bob and Jack had been waiting for
this to happen for weeks. Jack decided he didn't have to
eat lunch.

They were happy to finally be able to say they were taking
the "Ninja Squad" to Lower Township. The Queens Robbery
Squad affectionately referred to Chin and Ng as the "Ninja
Squad."
Martin and Trombetta were soon to find out why.

The four detectives exited the Major Case Squad office and
Martin had talked the two Queens Robbery detectives into
stopping at Liu's apartment above the Japanese restaurant.
They hoped to speak to Yi Liang Liu. Martin and Trombetta
had told Liu that they would be contacting him again.
Martin thought that perhaps Chin and Ng may be able to
obtain some information that McGowan, Reemer and Chan had
not been able to extract from Liu.

The four Detectives traveled to the location in the
department vehicle driven by Chin. Martin enjoyed the
sights of New York when someone else was driving. However,

Martin found it difficult to feel comfortable in the Big
Apple. Martin did not like the city, any city. Jack on the
other hand enjoyed the quick pace of City life.

Martin was talking about the surveillance that had been
ongoing at the lottery locations and Ng mentioned that he
had noticed the TARU van on East Fourteenth in front of a
lottery location. Ng had mentioned that information to
Chin in a conversation they had previously. Tom Chin was
listening and thought to himself than Ng had mentioned if
the perpetrator frequented the store on East Fourteenth he
probably lived in the public housing apartments down the
street. Tom Chin remembered that Keith Ng had made the
statement nonchalantly and neither man gave it much
thought. Little did they realize that the murderer of Dave
Douglass would eventually be found living in that apartment
complex.

Tommy Chin maneuvered the unmarked vehicle through the
lunch crowd traffic and in quick time the detectives were
climbing the steps to Liu's last known address.

Martin had been at the residence on one other occasion and
had tried the key in the lock on the entrance door. The
residents of the apartment were not aware, however, that
this had taken place. The Jersey detectives still
considered Liu to be the best witness who might lead the
investigators to the perp. Bob and Jack figured that Liu
would eventually talk.

The building was less than an architectural prize winner.
There was a Japanese restaurant on the first floor. Martin
laughed to himself as they climbed the steps to the
apartment. The Japanese restaurant had been visited by
Martin along with other NYPD detectives at an earlier time.
Martin thought it humorous that this Japanese restaurant
was operated by Chinese cooks and waiters.

When the four detectives reached the top of the stairs they
paused on the landing to listen at the door of Liu's
apartment. They had all been very careful not to make any
noise as they climbed the steps. They figured that they
would much rather surprise Liu than be surprised by him.

Martin heard Ng mumble something to Chin. Tom turned to
Martin and indicated that Keith heard four or five
different voices behind the door. Ng slowly attempted to
turn the door knob and found out it was locked. Ng then
knocked hard on the door and hollered something in Chinese.
Both Bob and Jack were startled by the loudness and rapid
speech of Ng. Martin looked at Chin who quickly stated,
"Keith just told them in Fuchianese that we were the Police
and we wanted to speak with Yi Liang Liu". It sounded like

there was a lot of movement going on in the apartment.
Keith continued to yell in Chinese that the door be opened.
The door opened and standing in the entrance were five
Fujin Chinese immigrants.

Martin quickly advised Ng that Liu was not among the five.
Keith Ng again began to speak the language of the
immigrants and Martin Trombetta and Chin started to enter
the apartment. Martin could now see Liu peeking from the
doorway to the bathroom. Liu saw Martin's face and smiled.
It was like he was relieved to see a face he recognized.
It was quite evident that all the residents of the
apartment were scared shitless of Chin and Ng.

Tommy Chin maintained a watchful eye on the individuals and
continually scanned the room for any movement that might
prove threatening. Keith Ng was now pushing through the
subjects to get to Liu. Liu was smiling and was extending
his hand to Martin in a greeting. Trombetta was waiting to
see what was going to happen next and was deciding which
subject he was going to put out of commission if the
opportunity arose.

Martin was not accepting the extended hand of Liu and was
watching another individual who was exiting the bathroom
behind Liu. There were now seven people in an apartment
that consisted of a living room, dining room, kitchen
combination and a small bathroom. Wooden bunk beds had
been constructed around the perimeter walls and Tommy Chin
mentioned that there were ten bunk beds and that possibly
more people were in the apartment.

Keith Ng was speaking loud and fast in the language that
was understood by the subjects. Quickly they all stopped
talking and lined up against the sink in the kitchen part
of the living quarters. Martin was trying to listen to
Keith's words and every now and then heard the two words
that he always understood, "Mudda Fucca." Martin figured
that even in Chinese mother fucker sounded like mother
fucker.

After the preliminaries were over Keith instructed Liu to
exit the apartment and wait on the landing. Martin and
Trombetta looked around the room hoping to find items that
may have been stolen from the Chinese workers home in Lower
Township. They saw quite a bit of electronic stereo and
portable TV equipment, however, none of it matched the
description of the stolen items.

The other subjects in the room were told to relax and Chin
obtained their names for future reference. The detectives
then joined Liu and Keith on the landing and Tommy closed
the door to the apartment as he exited. Keith was speaking

to Liu and it appeared that Liu was being indifferent to
the conversation. Keith glanced at Tommy and spoke quickly
and quietly to him. Tommy then advised Jack and Bob that
Liu was not being cooperative and that Keith was going to
provide him with an attitude adjustment. Tommy quickly
added, "Relax, let Keith roll with it."
Almost immediately Keith had Liu by the shirt and was
looking like he was going to throw Liu down the stairs.
Liu had a look on his face that could only indicate that he
was about to shit his pants then die. Martin and Trombetta
were wondering how this would be written up in their
report. "Two Lower Township Detectives witness a Chinese
Immigrant plunge to his death." Chin knew that Ng was only
playing games in the hope that Liu would soon see the error
of his ways. Once again Martin made out a string of "Mudda
Fuccas" in Ng's conversational tone.

Ng again raised his voice and Liu began to cry. Martin
then observed that Liu was looking at him with what
appeared to be a look of pity. Keith stated to Martin, "He
said you tell him before that the Police that was killed
was your brudda."

"Yeah, that's right," stated Martin.

"Dat good. Dat way dis rittle mudda fucca tink he help you.
He wants to help you get dis guy so he can help you honor
your family, dis is good. Shake his han, pat on back or
sometin. Say, Shay Shay, a couple times, he like dat."
Martin knew that shay shay was Chinese for thank you. Keith
added,"Rook rike you mean it. Den we tell dis Mudda Fucca
we see him in couple days and get outta here."

It all happened so quickly. Keith and Tommy indicated that
Liu was reluctant to say anything with the other subjects
so close by. He didn't want them to think he was helping
the police. So Keith had told him to tell the others that
the police would be back in a few days to check his green
card and immigration paperwork.

Martin asked Ng what all the screaming was about at the top
of the stairs. "Oh yeah, the rittle Mudda Fucca piss me
off. He say you already talk to him and he tell you he
don't know noffing. He give me bunch of shit I figur I
straighten his ass out. I tell him he don't cooperate I
trow him down steps. He start to cry rike baby. I tell the
mudda fucca he get on my nerves. I tell him I kill him, dat
mudda fucca. I was fuckin piss off at dat mudda fucca. He
probably upstair shittin his mudda fucca pants righ now."
Ng grinned and Tommy Chin acted as if it was another day in
the life of the Ninja Squad. The detectives entered the car
and returned to One Police Plaza.
Trombetta and Martin were sitting in the back seat of the

NYPD detective vehicle. Chin was driving and Ng was
reliving the meeting at the top of the stairs. Jack was
trying to understand what Ng was saying. He decided that
he would never be able to figure out what he was talking
about. Jack couldn't believe that Martin was able to
understand Ng. Jack didn't realize but even Martin could
not believe he could understand Ng.

It was decided that they would return to Police Plaza to
drop the Jersey guys at their vehicle. Chin would then
lead the Jersey guys out of the city and onto the Garden
State Parkway. Once there Chin would follow them to Lower
Township, Cape May County, New Jersey.

Martin hopped into the driver seat of the unmarked Chevy
Caprice and in seconds was driving behind Chin and Ng. The
traffic was normal New York City. Cars were double parked
all over the place and traffic was at its normal stand
still. Martin didn't realize they were headed for the
Holland Tunnel. They weren't getting anywhere in the
traffic and Trombetta noticed that Ng seemed to be waving
his arms around and hollering out the window of the NYPD
detective car. Trombetta mentioned it to Martin and they
both watched as Ng became more animated in his actions.

Keith almost seemed like he was an animated cartoon. They
finally realized that he was screaming at the traffic and
pedestrians who were in the roadway. Ng and Chin had
become frustrated at the stopped vehicles and slow moving
pedestrians. Ng was screaming, "Heah, you mudda fucca's
get out of street. Heah you, mista, get on mudda fucca
sidewalk, where you berong." Trombetta noticed Ng becoming
more frustrated. Chin stated to Ng, "Keith, don't get
upset just grab the light." Ng reached under the seat and
placed a Kojak light on the roof of the vehicle.

Trombetta said, "If they start flying we will never keep up
with them."

"Turn on the siren and put the light in the window. We
either follow them or be lost in New York City. Take your
pick," Bob said.

Trombetta knew Martin wasn't kidding so he went into
emergency mode. Here they were, two Jersey cops screaming
through the streets of New York City behind the Ninja
Squad, one of whom was screaming and hollering out the
window, the other who seemed to be on a kamikaze death raid
driving onto the curb to get through the traffic. The
scene appeared to be out of a cops and robbers movie.

Trombetta laughed and wondered, "How would they be driving
if this was an emergency?" Trombetta answered his own

question. "Hey, this is an emergency. We're trying to catch a cop killer." Martin laughed and continued to take part in the Bonzai run through the city. The entire incident stopped as quicky as it had started and they were traveling through the Holland Tunnel on their way into Jersey.

They quickly entered the Garden State Parkway and in a matter of hours were pulling into the parking lot of Rio Station. Martin always took his wife to Rio Station for drinks and dinner. JoAnne told everyone that whenever it was her turn to cook they would eat at Rio.

Bob always did the cooking and told everyone that the only thing JoAnne ever made for dinner was "reservations." Bob and JoAnne could be found at Rio Station about three nights a week. They liked the atmosphere and they especially liked the food. Bob and Jack would also frequent the bar for a cold one now and then.

It was 5:15 p.m. when they entered the restaurant. They were immediately seated and the waitress who knew Bob asked if the investigators wanted a drink. Bob introduced the waitress, Sealy, to the New York guys. She was familiar with Jack. The investigators all knew they would have a long night of work so they all decided on soda. They were looking at menus and making up their minds on what they would order when Sealy returned with the soda. Sealy had been working at the Rio for seven years. She started there when the place opened. Bob and JoAnne had been regular customers during those seven years.

Bob had already explained the menu to the New Yorkers and they were interested in the crab cakes that were a house specialty. Bob assured the guys that the crab cakes were always fantastic and that the portion was more than filling. Bob hadn't noticed but the special for the evening also featured crab cakes but as always the case with the specials the portion was reduced. Sealy brought it to Bob and Tommy's attention. Keith Ng was talking to Jack and not paying attention to the information supplied by the waitress. Bob could hear Keith talking and continuously heard a string of "Mudda Fuccas' finding their way into the conversation.

Tommy Chin had a look of embarrassment on his face as he listened to Keith. Sealy paid no mind to the profanity and listened and made note as Bob ordered the crab cakes from the regular menu and Tommy ordered the same. Jack quickly stated, "Give me the same thing Bob is having, please." Sealy then asked Keith for his order. He quickly stated, "Cra cake, preez." Sealy asked, "Regular or special?"

"Cra cake," was Keith's reply.

"Yes, regular or special," asked Sealy once again.

"Yeah," answered Keith. Bob knew the conversation was going nowhere and could hear the frustration in Keith's voice. Sealy once again asked, "Regular or special?"

In his most rapid speech pattern Keith stated, "Cra cake, mudda fucca'." Tommy quickly said, "He'll have the regular menu, please."

It was apparent from the look on Keith's face that he was use to having Tommy order for him. Keith spoke so rapidly that most people could not understand his fast paced Chinese rendition of the English language. Sealy was either not embarrassed by Keith's response or perhaps she hadn't understood his reply. She asked, "Baked or fried potato?" Bob saw the look on Tommy's face and knew he wished he could answer for Keith. Keith quickly stated, "Fry, fry, mudda fucca." Sealy jotted down the information as though all she understood was that he desired fried potatoes. When she asked what type of dressing he wanted Bob could see that even Jack's face was registering the question, "Did Keith say he wanted 'mudda fucca' crab cakes and fries?" Keith wasn't paying attention to Sealy's question about the salad dressing and as she started to ask the question again, Tommy cut in. "He'll have the house dressing."

Bob figured that Tommy answered because he didn't want Keith to ask, "What kine dressin do you have, mudda fucca?" Sealy finished writing the order and smiled as she left. Bob could tell by the look on her face she didn't have a clue as to what Keith had said. Bob figured Sealy was better off not knowing.

The guys conversed through dinner as to what they intended to do with the Chinese workers Tommy and Keith would soon be interviewing. Bob and Jack provided what they considered a list of possible witnesses who were holding back information. It was decided who would be spoken to and in what order. It was also decided that they would not use the police department facilities for the interviews. Bob had indicated that all of the possible witnesses were very familiar and had become comfortable within the confines of the small and almost personal facility.

It was decided that they would bring the subjects to the confines of the new public safety building in the airport complex. The investigative section had been set up earlier as a sort of substation for the detectives during the renovation process. It was loaded with building material and stacks of old furniture that awaited cleaning and eventual use. The complex would prove a little eerie and maybe even scary to someone who had never been there before.

Bob explained that the subjects were very comfortable around he and Jack and that they had already been interviewed by Gary Chan, the Chinese speaking FBI Agent. Bob indicated that Gary had been a real gentleman during the interviews. Jack advised that he wanted the "Ninja Squad" to put these subjects on notice that they were being interviewed by real cops. Bob and Tommy laughed as they understood Keith to say, "We scare deez mudda fucca's goohd. Dey wish dey neva meet us. What I need is a Chiney Commoonist uniform. Den, I scare shit outta dem." Jack saw Bob and Tom grinning but had no idea as to what the hell Keith had just said.

The guys left the restaurant and went directly to the new Police Department which was still under construction. The kids had cleaned up a few of the rooms that could be utilized for interviews. Tom Keywood and Ed Donohue were standing by waiting for their bosses and the "Ninja Squad."

It was decided that they would start with the individuals whose stories had seemed most suspicious. The kids went to the restaurant and picked up one worker at a time. They would bring them to the building and take the subjects to a room were Chin and Ng would be waiting for them.

Bob, Jack and the kids were sitting in the room next door listening to what was going on. All the interviews started out the same way. Tommy Chin would calm the people down and obtain background information and then start to question them about any knowledge they had with regard to the incident. Chin would complete his very calm and almost pleasant interview and then Keith Ng would take over. His speech came fast and when he deemed it necessary he would raise his voice and would become animated.

Each subject was questioned intensively for as long as it took. During the first interview Gene Taylor entered the building. He found Bob, Jack and the kids sitting in the office listening to the interviews. They could not understand the language but the tone, volume and intensity of the voices provided enough insight for the investigators to ascertain if the 'Ninja Squad' were getting to their interview subjects.

"Hey, Gene, did the County send you to keep an eye on us?" asked Martin. Gene looked perplexed by the question and slowly responded, "No, not really."

Jack quickly replied, "Hey, Gene, who are you kiddin'? We know better. Their worried we are going to get carried away on these subjects and kick their asses. Don't they realize we are not going to jeopardize an important case."

Gene didn't want to piss off Martin and Trombetta so he didn't respond with the fact that he was told to sit in on the interviews just to keep an eye on things. Gene asked, "How long have they been in there?"

"They're on their second interview," said Martin.

"I thought one of you guys would be sitting in on the interviews."

"We decided to let the New York guys handle the whole thing. We don't know the language and we would only be in the way.
Anyway, I don't like the idea of a lot of people sitting in on an interview. You know as well as I that it isn't conducive to getting information from people. I think the best way is just to let those guys do their job. They know what they're doing."

Gene knew there was no use in trying to get into the interview room and take part in the interviews as he had been directed. He also knew Martin and Trombetta were right. Gene knew he sure didn't know the language and as far as providing insight into the case to the guys from New York he would be wasting his time. They had almost as much knowledge of the incident as anyone who had been involved with the investigation from the beginning.

Gene hung around and listened to about four interviews. The only thing the Jersey guys could make out was that Keith Ng seemed to become more frustrated with each subject. After the 'Ninja Squad' completed an interview they would escort the subject out of the office and turn them over to Keywood and Donohue who would transport them back to the restaurant and return with another person to be interviewed.

Chin and Ng would fill in Martin and Trombetta on what had transpired. If during the interviews the guys from New York had any questions about the facts of the case Chin would come out of the office and converse with Bob and Jack.

Jack and Bob figured the New York guys were going to find someone who had first or secondhand knowledge of the case. One of the workers had to know about the case. They were sure someone would provide information with regard to the burglaries, suspicious actions by one of their co-workers, phone calls to someone who was involved or some type of worthwhile information. Bob and Jack had even thought that perhaps the gun used in the shooting of Dave Douglass had been stolen from the residence of the Chinese workers.

Each of them found it hard to believe that someone came to the area on a bus with a gun knowing they were going to shoot a cop. They figured that one of the workers had been keeping an illegal weapon and did not want to admit having it in the first place. The perpetrator once inside the residence found the gun, figured he could sell it then was eventually confronted by Dave Douglass and out of fear or stupidity shot and killed him.

They were sure the perpetrator had to be an irate ex-employee or a close friend of one. Dave's killer had to be associated with the restaurant and the workers in some way. They hoped that Chin and Ng could answer some of the questions.

The 'Ninja Squad' had been interviewing for over three hours. They even decided to re-interview the subjects that spoke English. Jack sent the kids out for food and something to drink. The New York guys were getting tired but they wanted to do as many interviews as possible. Tommy Chin knew he had to go back to New York the next afternoon. He wanted to make sure that everyone of the Chinese restaurant workers and owners had been interviewed.

It had also been decided that the Chinese owners of a local motel should be interviewed. It had been ascertained that when the residence had been burglarized and burnt the residents had stayed at the motel. The phone records had been obtained and the records indicated that telephone calls had been made to the residence where Liu had stayed when he first came to the United States. Trombetta sent Keywood and Donohue to the motel and told them to bring back someone who had some information about the phone records.

It wasn't long before a phone call from Keywood advised the guys that the female owner would not co-operate. She gave some story about the fact that her husband was away in New York and that neither she nor her maintenance man could leave the motel. Trombetta looked at Martin and said, "Do you believe that bimbo won't cooperate with us." Martin quickly said, "Give me the phone." Bob took the phone and advised Keywood to put the female on. Jack made a face for all too see when he handed Martin the telephone. He knew it was going to be an interesting conversation. Everyone stopped eating their sandwiches. Jack Reemer who had arrived only minutes before could sense Martin was in a bad mood.

A female voice stated, "Harro." Martin knew it had to be the female Chinese motel owner. "Hello mam, this is Detective Sergeant Bob Martin from Lower Township Police." Before Martin could say another word the female stated, "Why you want crose my bizness, you can't do dat." "Ma'am, I do not want to close your business I want to speak to you and your maintenance man with regard to an investigation I am conducting." The women cut Martin off and Jack could tell by the look on Bob's face that she was getting on his nerves. "I too busy to tawk and so my helpa. I wir not tawk to you and he won't eeda."

Martin stated, "You're all wrong, Ma'am. You will talk and so will he or I'll close your place down quicker than you can say Kung Pao Chicken. Do you realize that you have a lot of local health and business codes you have failed to comply with and if you don't cooperate you won't be renting out any more of your sleazy stinkin rooms!"

The woman was upset and stated, "I have to stay heerr, I have many peoper in wooms."

"You're full of crap. It's March and there's snow on the ground. If you have two welfare rooms occupied you can consider yourself busy. Now give the phone to the detective. He will be bringing your maintenance man back here when he leaves. Goodbye, it's been a pleasure."

Keywood was on the other end of the phone and stated, "Hey, Sarge, she is pissed she is running around here screaming and hollering and neither me nor Donohue have any idea what she is saying." Donohue grabbed the phone from Keywood and stated, "Hey, Sarge, what do you want us to do? It's gettin' crazy over here."

Martin quickly answered, "Grab the worker and get his ass over here." Before Bob could say another word Donohue said, "I hope he gives us a problem because I'm gonna kick his ass and stuff it in the car. These Chinks are gettin on my friggin' nerves." Martin then stated, "We'll get the bimbo after we're done with the guy. Martin hung up the phone as he heard Donohue say, "Hey, One Hung Low, you're coming with me."

Martin explained what was going on to all the guys and Ng stated, "We work on dis Mudda Fucca when he get heerr. Awr nite rong you guys bwing me vickums of cwime. I want to tawk to perrpp. Dis Mudda Fucca get punch in Mudda Fucca face if he don't tawkkkk." Tommy Chin shook his head and returned to chewing on his turkey hoagie. Everyone had a good laugh and while eating filled Jack Reemer in on what had been going on.

Jack Reemer indicated that he was going to be tied up in court and that he couldn't get out of it. He wished he would be able to travel to New York. Agent Reemer was hoping to show everyone that he and his office weren't like the guys in the Feds that hadn't been very helpful. He didn't have to apologize. Martin and Trombetta already knew. Reemer was very diplomatic. He wouldn't say that the other guys dropped the ball. He would just indicate that apparently there had been some type of communication problem. Those Feds had a way with words, thought Trombetta and Martin.

It wasn't long before Keywood and Donohue returned with probably the shortest Chinese guy ever born. This guy looked like a smurf without the colored hair. The 'Ninja Squad' quickly took him into their room. Only about twenty minutes went by as Keywood and Donohue were starting on their third sandwich. The little guy could be heard crying and sobbing uncontrollably. The guys not only heard Keith Ng screaming but so was Tommy Chin. They figured they must really have something. Tommy was usually pretty calm and cool. He usually kept Keith in line. Finally the noise subsided and the crying turned into a low pitched whimper.

The guys continually heard a string of Chinese words interspersed with "Mudda Fuccas'. They knew Ng was into the interview. They all loved listening to this guy. When he spoke in English everyone looked to Martin to translate. No one could figure out how Martin, who even when wearing hearing aids had a problem hearing, could understand a guy that spoke so fast and killed the English language with every word. Martin couldn't figure it out either but somehow he understood Keith Ng.

When Keith spoke slowly it was easy. However, when he got excited and his rate of speech increased Martin had to pay close attention. Martin figured that for some reason the Lord was allowing him to understand Keith. Otherwise Keith would have been talking and no one would have known what the hell he was saying.

By the time they finished with the Oriental Smurf the time was eleven p.m. The little guy was scared shitless and didn't know a thing that would help the investigators. It was decided that Keith Ng along with Keywood would take the little guy back to the motel. That turned out to be a big mistake.

When they dropped the smurf off Ng had figured he would talk to the female hotel owner. It was quite evident that the Chinese business owner was not impressed with Ng's New York City Detective badge. Ng on the other hand was not too happy about the fact that a member of the Chinese culture would not cooperate with police investigators looking into the murder of a fellow officer. Ng called her "a Chinese Bitch Mudda Fucca."

When Keywood finally completed the story, Martin and Trombetta figured everyone that had been involved in the investigation that evening would be talking to internal affairs in short order. Keywood also advised the sweet lady that if she had a problem Detective Sergeant Martin would hear her complaints in the morning. Keywood indicated that Ng told her they would close her down by noon the following day if she didn't comply. Martin knew he was going to have to do some talking. Trombetta thought the entire affair was pretty funny, especially because the lady never got his name. As far as anyone was concerned he wasn't even present during the time that those terrible policeman picked on those defenseless Chinese, hardworking immigrants.

Everyone was so upset by the events of the evening and the possibility of being investigated by Internal Affairs that they sent Donohue out for two cases of beer and they celebrated off duty, of course.

By the time the beer was gone Chin and Ng would be escorted to the Atlas Motel in Cape May. They would be picked up at eight in the morning by Martin and Trombetta. Reemer went home, Donohue did the same and Keywood and Trombetta tried to talk Martin into going to a few bars in Wildwood. Martin opted to escort Chin and Ng. Trombetta and Keywood continued to party.

Martin finally got home at about 1 am. Trombetta and Keywood made it home at 4 am. Martin was the only one awake in time to pick up Chin and Ng. He took them to breakfast and then they returned to the new police building to finish up with three interviews of the remaining Chinese restaurant workers. Donohue relayed the subjects to the building and Chin and Ng went back to work. Trombetta showed up shortly as did Keywood. They looked a little under the weather but were still able to bring coffee and donuts.

The interviews of the remaining workers lasted until noon. The "Ninja Squad" had completed their task. They had in less than twelve hours interviewed fifteen people extensively. Martin, Trombetta along with the kids sat and listened as Chin and Ng provided the result of their findings. It had been ascertained that not one of the people interviewed had any knowledge of who shot Dave Douglass. The New York guys had obtained lots of information on what had been stolen in all the burglaries and also they had verified the names of the three or four workers who had been fired or left on their own.

Martin and Trombetta thought for sure these would be the interviews that provided the key to the crime. They both sat thinking as Tommy Chin stated, "It is also very important to know that the gun was definitely not in the house at the time of any of the burglaries. We're sure about that. Whoever killed your guy brought the weapon with them. I don't believe the perp brought it along to kill a cop, but he brought it for protection or he intended to use it on someone else if need be. I wouldn't be surprised to find out that the perp brought it to use on the owner. All of his workers hate his guts."

Chin also advised that the perpetrator was by no means involved with a gang. The perp had a grudge against the owners. Chin and Ng were sure that would be the scenario. Ng stated, "Da perp is mad at owna, maybe because he fired or, made him quit. One way or odda deez peoper awr vickums not perp."

The guys all sat around feeling once again that they had to start all over. Once again they hit a major roadblock and had to change direction. Both Martin and Trombetta knew that the information that had been obtained by the "Ninja Squad" would no doubt be real worthwhile. They just hoped its worthiness showed itself real soon. Chin and Ng had done their job. They had now assured the Jersey guys that none of those interviewed had any involvement with Dave's death.

Chin and Ng went to the men's room. Martin, Trombetta, Keywood and Donohue were sitting in the office conversing about the information they just had heard. Donohue had a look of total despair on his face and said, "We don't have anything, do we?" Martin responded immediately, "On the contrary, Ed. We now have more than we did before those guys came down here. We just eliminated fifteen people."

Ed clarified his despair. "No what I mean is we don't have Dave's killer."

"I know what you mean, Ed, and I can tell you we're getting closer," said Martin.

Jack changed the subject. "Can you believe what all those people must have thought while they were being interviewed by those two. Quite a few times last night I thought Ng was going to kill somebody."

Donohue chimed in, "I sure wouldn't want him interrogating me. Did you see his eyes? They look right through ya."

Keywood added, "When we were driving the people back to the restaurant they stunk so bad it was sickening. They were so nervous their anti-perspirant apparently was not working."
"That wasn't their deodorant that failed, most of them probably shit themselves," Jack said.

Keywood then added, "Hey, Ed, remember the guy that spoke English? When we were driving him back to the restaurant he asked if he had to meet with the New York detectives again. I told him he probably wouldn't be interviewed again. He gave a long sigh of relief and said, 'Dat ritter detective is a bad, bad verwy bad man.' "

The guys all laughed. Chin and Ng had done their job. Moments later the police radio came to life requesting that Martin call the dispatcher. He immediately did so and hung up the phone with a smile on his face. "Well, Keywood, you are in deep shit," said Martin with a straight face. The bimbo, at the motel called, and wants to talk to me about how rude you were last night."

"Hey, Sarge, it wasn't me, it was Ng," replied Keywood.

Donohue put in his two cents, "Come on, Tom, you were probably in her face and invading her space." Everyone was laughing except Keywood. He always took things seriously. He, no doubt, was thinking there would be an investigation into the matter.
"All I need is an Internal Affairs investigation," Keywood lamented.

Jack laughed and said, "Why are you worried? Bob and I are the Internal Affairs team. What are you worried about? We'll give you a fair shake, Tommy."

Chin and Ng had returned from the mens room and had heard the conversation. Ng stated, "Ret me tawk to dat Mudda Fucca bitch. She wish she was back in Comoonist China." Everyone laughed. Everyone also knew that they certainly couldn't allow Ng to speak to the female again.

Martin then picked up the phone and everyone listened as he smoothed talked the motel owner. As Bob talked Jack stated to everyone, "That's my man, Bob Bo. Before it's all over the bimbo will be giving us free rooms at her luxurious facility."

Everyone was laughing heartily. They all knew the place was a pit. Martin eventually hung up the phone. "Well guys, the little lady is at the heights of total cooperation. She was pissed at Keywood and Ng but now she

can see the errors of her ways. I think it has something
to do with the fact that I told her we would shut her down
and also her fear of Keith."

Keith asked, "What she say bout me, dat Mudda Fucca."
Martin quickly replied, "She said, and I quote, 'I don't
ebbewr want talk dat ritter man again, he crazy and cawr me
baadd names." Everyone was laughing, even Keith. Martin
added, "Keywood, she said you invaded her space."

"Come on, Sarge, cut me a break."

Trombetta added, "Don't worry Tommy we won't let her accuse
you of anything we don't think you would do."

"Tom, you're in deep shit, pal. Sarge, I did everything by
the numbers," Donohue teased.

"Sure, Ed, I know. We sent you for one case of beer and
you brought back two," Jack said.

The guys offered to take Chin and Ng to lunch, but they
graciously refused. Tommy had to get back to New York for
personal business. Everyone called it quits for the day
and Bob escorted Chin and Ng to the parkway. When they
arrived at the entrance both drivers pulled their vehicles
to the shoulder. Martin got out and ran up to the drivers
side window of the New York police vehicle. Martin
extended his hand and shook hands with the two members of
the 'Ninja Squad'.

"Guys, I can't thank you enough for coming down here. We
really appreciate your time and effort."

Tommy Chin stated, "Bob, we wish we could have found your
killer."

"Next time we do dis bwing me perp not vickums," Ng
suggested.

Martin smiled and said, "Jack and I will be up in the
beginning of the week to hook up with you guys. We will
pick up Liu and let you work on him." Martin knew that the
'Ninja Squad' would get a confession from Liu, if he was
involved.

Ng advised, "Don't wowwy, we get da Mudda Fucca dat shot
Dave." As they drove away Martin waved and said to no one
in particular, "Yeah, guys, we will get Da Mudda Fucca dat
shot Dave."

Everyone took Sunday off. Jack and Bob took their families
to church. They both figured that it was about time. Once

again they knew that they had not been good examples of Christianity, as of late, but they knew that the Lord was in total control of everything that went on. They had to get their lives in order. They prayed for forgiveness and help.

When Bob and JoAnne returned home the telephone was ringing.
Bob answered, "Hello, yeah, Dad, what's going on? How have you been?"

Bob's father warned, "Hey, boy, I hear you have been up in the big city a lot. Be careful up there. Those people are crazy."

Bob laughed,"Yeah, I know." Bob thought to himself the cops are crazier than the people on the street. He further explained to his father, "That's where the killer is so that's where Jack and I are spending our time."

"Well listen, I had a dream last night and in the dream you and Jack are lockin' up a short little Chinese guy. He was standing in a room holding a telephone to his ear when you and Jack surprise him. It's gonna be some time this week. You know I don't believe in this dream stuff but I thought I would tell you anyway."

"Thanks, Dad, I hope you're right."

There was a short silence and Bob's father said, "Make sure you and Jack are careful up there and stay out of trouble. Don't get hurt and if you hurt somebody make sure it's legal."

"All right, Dad, I'll call you when I get back after the arrest. See ya later," Bob hung up the phone hoping his Dad's dream would become a reality.

CHAPTER FIFTY THREE

Monday morning, March 28th, both Trombetta and Martin were sitting in the small room at LTPD that served as their office. Martin looked at his watch and the time was 7:05 am. Jack was drinking his second cup of coffee. He was sitting at his desk with his feet resting on it. He was staring at the ceiling and his gaze seemed to be directed at nothing in particular. Bob was reviewing a printout of the weekend activities in Lower Township. Bob was having a rough time trying to stay focused on the incidents as he read the facts about each of the calls the patrol cops and detectives had responded to over the weekend.

Jack wasn't the least bit interested in anything that had gone on. He was thinking about the events since last Monday and sat in despair. Dave's killer was still free, just living his life and doing his thing while Dave was in his grave.

Jack was not aware that Bob felt that a lot had been accomplished. Once again Jack was feeling negative about the investigation. He figured that they would never arrest Dave's killer. Jack was glad Bob felt differently. Bob had been positive that eventually he and Jack would look the killer in the face and be able to say, "It's done, it's over". Both men could then rest not only physically but most of all mentally.
This investigation was taking its toll. If someone had asked Lynn Trombetta or JoAnne Martin how their husbands were holding up, they would have received subdued assurances that both men were fine. However, they knew that their husbands were like over wound watches ready to let loose. The wives hoped that they would be able to control themselves and get through this investigation.

Jack was looking at the ceiling and reflecting on the events that had taken place since Monday, March 21st. He appeared to be in a trance. It was hard to believe that another week had gone by and it didn't seem like anything had been accomplished. Jack knew that Bob could list a long list of case accomplishments. Jack, however, felt that the arrest had to take place for an accomplishment to be realized. Trombetta could not bring himself to be optimistic. He reflected on how his life had been less than productive with regard to his Christianity lately. He was thinking that perhaps the Lord, Jesus Christ, was not going to provide the murderer of Dave Douglass to him. Jack knew he had to get his life together and get back on the right track. Please Lord help me to get myself through this, he thought to himself.

Martin could almost read Jack's mind. "Feeling like you're going nowhere fast, Jackie?" asked Bob.

"I thought we would have something this past weekend. We have waited so long for Chin and Ng to get here. Now it's over and they're gone. We still don't have anything," lamented Jack.

"That's not so. We now can feel positive that none of these people at the restaurant have anything to do with our shooting. We also know that the weapon used to kill Dave was not picked up by the perpetrator when he burglarized the house. He had to bring the gun with him. So therefore he brought it knowing he may need it for something. He had to know he may decide to shoot someone. I don't think he came all the way down here to kill Dave. He had something else on his mind. He was out to get the owners or the workers down here at the restaurant."

Martin paused for a minute and Jack spoke. "Do you still think Liu is involved? He probably did it or set it up. We have to get that sucker on our territory and break him. I want to see him squirm. He is involved in this mess in some way." Don't you think we are wasting our time sitting here talking about this. What are we going to do next?" Trombetta looked at Martin waiting for some words of wisdom.

"I don't know, Jackie. Let's get a drink," stated Martin. Jack had a look of concern on his face as Martin added, "I'm only kidding, Jackie. Listen, Chin and Ng cleared up at lot of loose ends and misconceptions for us. We now know everything we need is in New York."

Jack had a grin on his face and asked, "Then what are we doing in Cape May County?" Martin didn't have an answer. "Let's get back to New York City and see what we can do," said Jack.

"We can hook up with Chin and Ng and question Liu," stated Martin. "I also want to try that key in some more doors, and I want to ask Simon Kok to contact Quey and see if he remembered anything else," he added.

"We scared the shit out of him. I think he would have told us everything he knew."

"Yeah, but he struck me like someone who had to be asked everything over and over again to get the real answer," said Martin.

"Yeah, you have a point. Every answer he gave was like pulling teeth," said Trombetta. "Well, let's get on a roll and head to New York. I'll call Lynn and tell her we are leaving. She already has a bag packed for me," added Jack.

"A brown paper bag?" kidded Martin. Bob knew that Jack wasn't much for luggage. He had proven it on the other trips they had been making back and forth to the big city.

"No, wise ass, Lynn packed me a real suitcase with the things I need."

"I'm taking a couple suits and she even shined my shoes," said Jack sarcastically.

"Why don't you call Ernie and let him know we are on our way and see if he can coordinate a meeting with Chin and Ng," said Martin. "I'll call JoAnne and let her know we are off to New York."

Jack looked at his watch. The time was 7:45 am. Jack figured Ernie would be on his way to work but he knew that Grace would be up with Angelina.

The telephone was ringing at the Naspretto residence and Ernie was reluctant to pick it up. He had just gotten to sleep after a double shift of bullshit at work. He had to save some sergeant from the politicians and had to hang out after his normal shift to see this guy. Ernie spent about six hours of his own time trying to save this guy from himself. Ernie, however, knew it was time well spent. The sergeant was a guy with balls and brains and would one day turn out to be an excellent command officer. Ernie felt he was just doing what should be done. Sometimes you had to run interference and save these guys from themselves. Lord knows Ernie had some great bosses who had looked out for him. Now, Ernie had to look out for his people.

The telephone kept ringing and Ernie remembered that Grace had taken the baby to her mother's and was then going to the doctor. It wouldn't be long before Ernie had another mouth to feed. He picked up the phone. "Yeah," mumbled Ernie.

"I didn't wake you up, did I? This is Jack." Jack knew he had awakened Ernie and enjoyed it.

"Yeah, you woke me up, fuck Face. What do you want?

Shouldn't you be investigating a case. Never mind, I take that back. Bob is probably out investigating and you are harassing me at 7:45 in the fuckin' morning. What are you, lonely?" He loved to bust Trombetta's chops.

"No, Ern, I'm really sorry for waking you up." Jack was not sincere nor did he sound like he was.
"Fuck you, Jack. Now what the fuck do you want?"

"You keep cursing at me and I'm going to tell your wife not to feed you anymore. You need to loose about thirty pounds of ugly fat. Why don't you start by cutting off your head."

"I really need you this morning. What the fuck do you want?" Ernie was yelling.

"Ern, I just wanted to call and see if you could hook up a meeting with Chin and Ng. Bob and I are going to head your way in about a half hour."

Ernie got serious. "I talked to those guys last night. They have court early this morning and they are figuring they will be in court all day long. They are going to get Liu tomorrow." Jack relayed the information to Bob.

"Well tell Ernie we are coming anyway and we will be there in about three hours. We can go to Major Case and touch base with those guys," Bob said.

Trombetta agreed, knowing that the rest of this investigation would be conducted in New York City.

Ernie thought for a moment and said, "I'll get a few hours sleep and go with you. I'm off tonight and work four to twelve tomorrow. Grace had invited somebody over for dinner tonight but I forget who the hell it was. It's not important. You guys come here and I'll go with you."

Jack felt bad that Ernie was changing his family's plans for the evening. "Ernie, don't worry about it. We are going to stay at a Holiday Inn near Chinatown and...."
Ernie cut Jack off, "The fuck you are, dick head. You and Bob are staying here and I'm going with you today and that's that. I'm the Captain and you're the dick head who follows my orders."

"Yo, Ern, we feel bad taking advantage of you and Grace. We've probably ruined your sex life," added Trombetta.

"What sex life? There is a bun in the oven and the kitchen is closed until the bun is done. Anyway Grace likes you guys. She has a ton of questions for you about the case.

She is drivin' me nuts with questions. So stop bullshittin' and get your asses on the Parkway. I don't want to hear anymore crap. I'm hangin up. Good bye, terd," added Ernie for effect.

"That dago hung up on me," said Jack with reverence.

"Don't tell me," said Martin, "He is going with us and we are staying at his place."

"You got it," said Jack.

"I hate to take advantage of them all the time."
"Yeah, I know what you mean."

"But, I miss Grace's cooking," added Martin. "Listen, we'll take them someplace nice for dinner or lunch while we are there. That's the least we can do."

Jack looked at his watch and said, "Why don't you leave a message for McGowan and tell him we are going to New York."

"He had to go to Florida this week. Don't you remember?"

"Well, leave the message for him anyway. Someone at the county will review the messages and when they do they can't say we didn't tell them what we were doing."

"Hey, Jackie, I love it when you're sneaky," said Martin as he laughed.

Martin quickly called his wife as did Trombetta. They told them that they were on their way back to New York and would probably be there for a few days. Both wives hated to hear that, but they knew that their husbands had a job to do. They worried about their husbands working in the big city and feared for their safety. They were both glad that their husbands were partnered with each other. Many times over the years they had watched each other's back in many situations. They were extensions of each other.

The Chief of Police walked into the office and sat down. "What are you guys up to today," asked Chief Don Douglass.

Trombetta immediately advised that they were on their way to New York. Martin added,"We are wasting time hanging around here. There is no doubt in our minds that nothing else has to be done at this end."

Trombetta interjected,"Chief, the shooter is in New York and that's where we belong. The County don't...." Trombetta was interrupted by the Chief. "I'm not interested in the County. I want you guys to get to New York, find this guy and close this case."

Martin looked at the Chief and stated, "Chief, this time we won't be back until it's all over."

"We have a lot of stuff lined up that has to get done."
"We have some interviews and some locations we want to try the key at, so we are going to be busy," Trombetta added.

The Chief took a long drag from the pipe that was always stuck in his mouth and stated, "Just don't get, yourself, jammed up. Be careful up there. I don't need any more funerals and I don't want to have to bail you guys out of jail either."

Trombetta and Martin both laughed and Trombetta said, "Chief, you know us better than that. We would never embarrass you or the Department."

"Hey, Trombetta, you're talking to me not your wife. She probably believes some of your bullshit. I don't." Douglass added, "Do you have enough money?"

Trombetta looked at Martin and said, "Ask Bob. He won't let me touch the funds."

"I don't blame him. You would spend it all on booze and cigarettes."

"Chief, I'm cuttin' down. You would be proud of me," stated Trombetta.

"Hey, Chief, he has cut down on buying. He just borrows from the guys in New York," Martin interjected.

"When this investigation is all over we are going to have to do something nice for the guys in New York," said Chief Douglass. "They have really been helpful to you guys, not to mention paying for Trombetta's habits. So stop the bullshit and get your asses to New York. Keep me posted on what is happening."

Trombetta immediately called Buzz Hienkel into the office and advised him what was going on. Martin also advised him to make sure all the detectives' reports were up to date with regard to all investigations. Hienkel indicated he would take care of everything and then stated, "I'm not trying to be pushy, but is this case looking like it might be coming to a conclusion?"

Martin answered, "Buzz, I can say that, hopefully, this will be our last trip. We will keep you posted."

Jack added, "Hey, Buzz, you are in charge. Don't screw anything up."

Buzz got a sheepish look on his face and asked, "Hey, Sarge, don't you trust me. You and Bob taught me everything I know."
"Yeah, Buzz, but always remember we didn't teach you everything we know. That way we will always be one up on ya," warned Trombetta. Buzz chuckled, not really knowing what Jack meant. The Detective Sergeants walked down the hall and out the door to their vehicles. Buzz walked into the office and then realized what Jack meant. He laughed out loud as the Detective Sergeants went home to get their personal belongings together for what they hoped would be their last trip to the Big Apple.

Martin and Trombetta talked about how they felt they were taking advantage of Ernie and Grace Naspretto. They both realized that if the Township was footing the bill for all of their room and board they would have been making a lot of trips back and forth to the big city. They would not have had the money to be able to stay in motels during all of this investigation. Martin thought to himself that it was fortunate that Jack knew Ernie.

Both Martin and Trombetta felt indebted to the Nasprettos. They would never be able to show their gratitude. The Nasprettos didn't even act like they were being imposed upon. Martin thought about how his grandfather always referred to people like the Nasprettos as "Good People." Those two words summed it all up.

Martin and Trombetta had become friends with a lot of "Good People" while on this investigation. It seemed that everyone was willing to go out of their way to help the two of them catch a cop killer. Everyone they spoke to seemed to take an intense interest in the case.

The short trip to their homes was over in minutes. Martin dropped Trombetta off and then went to his own home. They quickly packed the necessary clothing and Martin picked up Trombetta and they were on their way. "Hey, Bob, do you really think we are going to get this guy?"

"Jack, I have said all along we would get the sucker."

"Yeah, but this time you're talking like we will be making an arrest," stated Jack.

"Hey, I'm thinking positive, O.K.," said Martin. Trombetta started to light up a cigarette. "Oh, man, not again. You're going to kill me with that second hand smoke."

"Don't get all shook up I'm opening the window." Trombetta hesitated and said, "As soon as we lock this guy up I'll stop smokin. O.K., Bobby?"

"Now you really gave me a reason to close this case."

Martin entered the Garden State Parkway for the three hour trip to Ernie's. Trombetta was smoking his first cigarette. Martin knew there would be more during the trip to New York. Trombetta made his usual attempt to find some music on the FM radio. He would run through the channels not waiting to hear what was playing and when he would fall upon a song that sounded familiar he would increase the volume and attempt to sing along with the song.

Trombetta's voice was somewhat like the sound of a cuisinart attempting to frappe ice cubes. Martin also thought Trombetta was tone death. However, he did have a way with coming across old music that was from the early seventies. Martin heard the familiar bass of a song by Led Zeppelin. He liked to call 'Good Times Bad Times' his theme song. Martin felt that it said a lot about his life during the late sixties and early seventies. Trombetta turned the radio to full volume and the bass was pulsing from the rear speakers in the unmarked police unit.

They both listened as Jimmy Page played lead guitar and Robert Plant wailed through the lyrics.....IN THE DAYS OF MY YOUTH I WAS TOLD WHAT IT MEANS TO BE A MAN. NOW I'VE REACHED THE AGE I TRY TO DO ALL THE THINGS THE BEST I CAN. GOOD TIMES BAD TIMES YOU KNOW I HAD MY SHARE........

They listened until the song ended when Martin asked, "Have you noticed we have been hearing a lot of Led Zepplin on these trips up and down the Parkway?"

"Hey, you know me. I don't know who did these records. I just know which songs I like."

"Well, then take my word for it, Jackie. Every time you turn on the radio we are hearing Zepplin."

"Hey, I remember them," said Trombetta. "There was a picture of a Zeppelin on the cover of their album."

"Good, Jackie, you really aren't a burn out. You really do remember something from your youth."

Martin was thinking that if investigations had theme music, Led Zeppelin was playing the theme music for this investigation. The song ended and Trombetta began cruising the channels looking for the next familiar sound. He managed to smoke nine cigarettes during the trip to

Ernie's. Martin didn't keep track of how many times he
changed stations on the radio. Martin did know whenever
Jack found a song he was familiar with. The volume would
blast Martin out of his day dreaming. Martin had been
thinking about the fact that on these journeys to the big
city they both seemed kind of quiet. They were forever
going over the facts of the case in their minds and at
times would ask each other questions in an attempt to clear
their brains.

Bob no longer needed directions to the Naspretto residence
but Ernie had provided them once again anyway. Ernie had
given them to Bob over the phone. Jack couldn't be
bothered with writing down the information. Why should he
even worry about it when he knew that Bob would take care
of everything. Jack knew Bob would have money, credit
cards and everything else they may need on this trip. Jack
hated to clutter his mind with such trivial things.

It didn't seem that the trip took three hours. In no time
they were at their destination. They pulled into the
Naspretto driveway in Glendale and Grace was immediately
standing at the open door. Ernie exited the house and
played parking attendant. Parking space on Ernie's street
was always at a minimum. Ernie provided "The Club" from
his own vehicle. He had Martin park the unmarked police
vehicle in his driveway. Ernie parked his car on the
street.

Ernie then advised Martin to place the trusty steering
wheel lock on the unmarked Chevy. There were hugs and
kisses all around as they entered Ernie's house.

Ernie asked Grace to get the guys something to drink and
they all sat down at the dining room table. Grace provided
some soda and immediately started to talk about the dreams
she had been having. She indicated that she knew an arrest
would be made in the very near future. She started to
explain her dreams and Ernie cut her off, "Yo, Grace, they
don't want to hear about that crap. They deal in reality,
not your dreams." Ernie continued, "She has been dreaming
about numbers and faces and everything else you can think
of. I think it has something to do with an abundance of
hormones because of this pregnancy." Bob was thinking
about his father's dreams. Oh, God, if only these dreams
would come true.

"Hey, Grace, why don't you make some lunch for these guys?"
Ernie was immediately cut off by Jack's response. "No way,
we are taking you guys out for lunch, dinner whatever you
want to call it. Bob has the money. So where do you want
to go? Make it someplace nice." Bob then chimed in, "No
excuses, Ernie, we are taking you guys out so let's get

started."

"No, we have the baby to worry about," replied Ernie.

"Bring her with you. Ernie, we are taking you and Grace and the baby and that's that," Bob ordered. They quickly decided to take two vehicles so they wouldn't have to take Grace and Angelina back to the house.

Grace would drive her car with the baby and the guys were going in the unmarked chevy with Ernie driving. It had been decided that after lunch Grace was going to visit her mother. The guys were going to do some police work.

They went to Lennie's on Cross Bay Blvd., about twenty minutes from Ernie's house. The joint had great Italian seafood dishes. Ernie indicated that the place was very well known and had catered to the stars. It was one of those places that exhibited signed pictures of all the stars that had visited and enjoyed the food.

They finished the late lunch and then they went their separate ways. Grace to her mother's house with the baby and the guys went to Major Case to meet up with the New York guys who were working 4 to 12.

There was a little time to kill. Ernie wanted to take the guys to his precinct and show them around. Ernie also wanted them to see how everyone jumped when Captain Naspretto was around. In the world of investigations Ernie was nothing, but when it came to the alleged "backbone of the job", patrol, Ernie was king in his precinct, well actually, almost king. The other Captain, Dale Riedel, was the commanding officer. Ernie was the "X.O.", meaning the executive officer, the number two guy. Still, over 250 people working out of the 60th precinct had to answer to Captain Ernie Naspretto.

Ernie was driving the Jersey unmarked car and stopped by a cemetery located within a half mile of his home. From the street he pointed out the grave site of the legendary magician Harry Houdini. The impressive looking grave is about 150 feet off the street and can be seen clearly. Jack and Bob found it interesting and the conversation went from Houdini escaping from the grave to how long it took Jesus to rise from the dead.

New York City's Hasidic community was preparing for the imminent death of 92 year old Menachem Schneerson, the Grand Rebbe. His health had been failing for over a year and doctors felt he would die within a very short time. Brooklyn's Crown Heights Hasidic community, where the Grand Rebbe had resided, would undoubtedly turn into a sea of mourners. The potential for chaos and conflict with the nearby Black community was great, especially after the riots of August 1991, which resulted from the death of a seven year old black child who was struck by a car traveling in the Rebbe's motorcade. Ernie knew that if the Rebbe died there would be no time for him to play detective with Jack and Bob. Every Captain in Brooklyn would be utilized for a minimum of twelve hours a day to handle the massive police details which would be needed for the funeral and subsequent mourning. Ernie hoped the Rebbe would live, at least until Dave Douglass' murderer was caught.

Ernie was explaining to Jack and Bob that the Rebbe was to the Hasidic community what the Pope was to the Catholics of the world. Actually, the Rebbe was considered by many Hasidics to be the Messiah. Ernie got into how a Messiah beats a Pope. It sounded like he was describing a poker hand. Then he got into how "our Messiah" rose from the dead within three days. "Let's see how fast their Messiah could rise from the dead. Anything more than three days, we win."

Jack and Bob got a kick out of Ernie's less than sympathetic view of the Hasidic leader's health. His commentary also showed a rather obvious disrespect for everyone's view of the Messiah. As Ernie pulled onto the Belt Parkway headed toward Coney Island Jack spoke of the imperfections of the Catholic religion and why he was born again. Ernie loved to break Jack's balls about being born again. "You know, I really wanted to be born again, but my mother told me to get lost!"

Jack explained to Ernie that the Catholic religion does not always teach the literal meaning of the new testament. Bob who was seated in the rear of the car said, "Jack, give Ernie an example. How about Christ's immediate family?"

Ernie felt as if these guys were setting him up. He knew they had used this conversation in the past to convert an unsuspecting heathen.

Jack stated in a most serious tone, "Did you know that Christ had brothers?"

"What the hell are you talking about?" Ernie was genuinely perplexed. Bob sat in the back seat and looked as though he knew Christ had brothers. Jack continued, "That's right. The bible refers to Jesus' brothers."

"Oh, come on, Jack. That's figurative. We're all brothers and sisters in the eyes of God, except for Irish people. Get real, uh." Ernie sounded like Archie Bunker.

"You see, Ernie, that's where the Catholic religion
misleads. Remind me to give you the bible verses that name
Christ's family. I could give you some bad news about Mary
and the names of the other family members. Wait til I have
a bible in my hand. I'll walk you right through some real
truth. Ernie you're living in sin."

Bob who had been sitting quietly in the back said, "Let me
have an Amen." Both the Jersey guys simultaneously
proclaimed, "AMEN!"

"Oh, great. You shitbirds are ganging up on me now,
"stated Ernie. "O.K., wiseass, what were his brothers
names then?" Ernie was on a roll now. "He probably had a
brother Dave, another named Freddy. Yeah, that's it,
Freddy Christ. I like it. Man, when those Christ brothers
get together forget about it! You wanna talk wine. It
just keeps on flowing."

Jack and Bob started laughing. They knew they would not
get Ernie involved in a heavy conversation about religion.
If Ernie was going to be saved the message would have to
come from someone else. Jack knew not to try and Bob would
rather jump in a pool of acid.

They pulled into the parking lot of the 60th Precinct.
Cops were coming and going and respectfully saying hello to
Captain Naspretto. Ernie was hoping Jack and Bob would
notice how important he was. An attractive female
detective walked by and said hello.

Ernie immediately advised Jack and Bob in a low voice, "She
wants me so bad she can't walk straight. She pulsates with
desire every time she sees me. I get a lot of that, you
know." Bob and Jack believed that about as much as Ernie
believed in Freddy Christ.

Ernie continued to show the guys around the precinct. They
entered the processing area and Ernie said, "This is where
we beat the prisoners. The guys always ask me to do the
beatin' because Italians are good at that." Bob thought to
himself, "This guy is actually in charge of this place?"
They walked through the Detective squad, robbery unit,
community policing and the communications area. Bob and
Jack were all smiles and handshakes but were bored to shit
and couldn't wait to get the hell out of there.

Ernie never told Jack but the next day the lead clerical
staff supervisor, a woman named Ronnie, walked into Ernie's
office and made some inquiries about one of the previous
day's visitors.

"Who was that gorgeous guy with the pitch black hair,
mustache and green eyes? My God, I melted when he walked
in," Ronnie proclaimed. She was obviously talking about
Jack. Before Ernie could answer Ronnie cut him off. "Is
he married? If so, does he cheat? Where in Jersey does he
live?" Ernie without hesitation stated, "Oh, him and the
other guy live together. They're queers." Ronnie figured
the Captain was full of shit but she gave up. Ernie vowed
never to tell Jack about the inquiry. He knew Jack's head
would swell to the size of Ernie's stomach.

They eventually finished the tour and Ernie took them by
Coney Island and showed them the sights. The guys thought
it reminded them of Wildwood, NJ. They arrived at One
Police Plaza and they immediately met Joe Piraino. They
all sat in Joe's office and began formulating a plan for
the evening.

They wanted to hook up with Quey but found out that Simon
Kok would not be available until the next day. They needed
him for translating. Ruben Santiago indicated that Quey
was supposed to be off the following day. It was decided
that they would wait.

They prepared a schedule of investigative work for the next
day and after completion decided to head over to Queens
Robbery to see if they could catch Chin and Ng.

As usual Ernie drove and told stories about every landmark
they passed. At one point as they passed a prestigious
looking office building Ernie went on about how he single
handedly stopped the rape of a young Puerto Rican girl
behind the building. Both Bob and Jack listened so they
would know when to laugh. They had heard enough Ernie
stories to know he was fabricating the whole thing. It did
sound good, however. Bob told Ernie he ought to write a
book. Jack stated that they both should get together and
write a book. Jack advised that Bob could write factual
information and Ernie could make up interesting stories
that would make him look like a supercop.

They arrived at Queens Robbery and parked across the
street. Ernie said hello to everyone in the place. They
all remembered Ernie Naspretto from his Lieutenant days in
the precinct. It was evident Ernie didn't have any enemies
in that precinct.

They ran into Don Costello and all sat down. Bob brought
Don up to date on what was happening with the
investigation. Don indicated that Chin and Ng had also
made him aware of what was happening with the case. They
already had a meeting set up with the "Ninja Squad" for the
next night. They were looking forward to interviewing Liu

and finding out what he really knew and was no doubt holding back.

Ernie looked at his watch and saw that it was 9pm. He decided they should hit the road and head home. Everyone said their goodbyes and the guys were on their way. It wasn't long before Ernie was pulling up to Kate Cassidy's bar. He figured the guys could use a drink. Oddly enough he was wrong. Jack and Bob each had a quick drink and Ernie could see that they really just wanted to get some sleep.

They no sooner walked into the house and Grace told Ernie someone from the precinct had just called. Ernie quickly grabbed the phone and called one of his lieutnants. He hung up the phone and explained he had to go into work to straighten out a problem. A prisoner had died while in custody and Ernie didn't want anything to go wrong with the follow up investigation. He wanted to be sure they were no problems or someone screaming they had tried to cover anything up. Ernie quickly left and it wasn't long before everyone was trying to get some sleep.

It had been a long day. Everyday was a long day since February 18th. Sleep was a luxury that eluded Jack Trombetta. During the best of times he was the lightest of sleepers. Since Dave Douglass' murder if Jack slept more than a couple of hours a night, it was a lot.

Grace, Angelina and Bob were sleeping. Jack was lying on the sofa bed staring his patented stare at the living room ceiling. He envied Bob Martin. How could he sleep through this? Bob had some problems sleeping for about the first two weeks of the investigation but now he seemed to get the sleep he needed. Jack's thoughts varied. He thought about Dave, Dave's family, how Dave would tend to put on weight until Jack would make fun of him then suddenly he'd lose the weight. He thought about Dave's killer. Where was this fuck? He fantasized about the arrest. Would there even be an arrest? Hopefully, this son of a bitch would resist and pull out a gun, the same gun he used to kill Dave. Bob and Jack would empty their semi-automatics. When the smoke cleared they'd be standing over one dead cop killer. Wounds opened, case closed. Jack kept dwelling on the fact that Bob had said from the beginning that they would get this guy. He seemed so sure. Jack just couldn't bring himself to think positive about this case.

Jack thought about Ernie, Joe Piraino, Tom Nerney and the other guys from Major Case. He was very grateful for their unrelenting assistance. He was gratified that the NYPD's Major Case Squad was handling this like Dave was one of their cops. He thought about Tommy Chin and Keith Ng.

Their interrogations of these formerly uncooperative
Chinese restaurant workers were incredible. But, where
would all these efforts lead?

Bob kept saying they weren't going home until they made the
arrest. What made him think this time in the Big Apple
would be any different from the rest? How could he ever
face Dave's wife and children or even the other Lower
Township cops until this piece of shit was caught. Bob had
even told Dave's wife that he would contact her when the
arrest was made. He would speak to her personally and not
to believe anything that didn't come from his mouth. Many
times during the investigation Debbie would call and ask
about something she had heard. Each time Bob would have to
tell her the real story.

Jack thought about what a large city they were working in.
He and Bob were out of their element. How could they be
expected to find a Chinese guy in this town that had
Chinese walking all over the place? In New York City
anything could happen. The killer was on his home turf and
knew all the angles. Jack kept thinking about the fact that
he and Bob weren't cut out for police work in New York
City.

How long could Captain Duke allow his squad to give this
case priority attention? At what point would Lieutenant
Pollini tell Joe Piraino to put the Lower Township case on
the back burner. God forbid, but suppose a New York City
cop was killed in the line of duty before Dave's killer was
caught?

A cop getting killed in New York was very possible 24 hours
a day, 365 days a year. Suppose this, suppose that,
suppose everything. Jack was fatigued but sleep simply
wasn't meant to be.

Jack thought about his family. Dave's death interrupted a
tough time Jack was having with his wife and children. If
and when this case was ever resolved, Jack's personal
problems would be eagerly awaiting him. He missed Lynn.
Even if he couldn't sleep he wished he could have her lying
beside him. Jack had been less than the perfect husband
over the past few months. Too many bar nights, with the
boys after work, were getting on Lynn's nerves. For
reasons he couldn't understand he felt himself being pulled
back to a time when he was less than the perfect son. He
remembered the problems he had put his parents through.
His rebellious 16 year old daughter, Gina, was driving him
crazy. His 14 year old son, Jackie, couldn't give two
shits about school and his 18 year old son, Joe, thought he
knew everything. Yet, these kids were saints compared to
their father when he was a teenager.

Jack grew up in the West Oak Lane area of northwest Philadelphia. He was the oldest of seven children. His parents, Lillian and Joseph, did all the right things to raise their children. They were model parents. Joseph was a carpenter and general contracting laborer. Lillian ran the house. She was a tough, but loving mother. No, meant, no! There would be no negotiations.

The Trombettas always tried to shield their children from the not so pleasant realities of life. They'd speak in Italian whenever they didn't want the kids to understand some negative gossip about another family member or neighbor. But those artificial rose covered windows were shattered by the realities of the tough Philadelphia streets.

The neighborhood had been basically white, Italian, German, Irish and Jewish. In the sixties blacks started moving into the area. The area residents were less than open minded about their new neighbors. The kids started forming gangs "To protect their turf". Jack belonged to a loosely knit group of thugs called "The Road." The name came from their hangout on Vernon Road.

School had become a waste of his time, resulting in Jack being left back in the eighth grade. When Jack finally did get to Bishop McDevitt High School the die had been cast. He would be in a rush to nowhere. Gang fist fights soon gave way to stabbings. Sometimes Jack was a victim, sometimes he was a perpetrator. It depended on the day and who jumped whom first.

Some neighborhood Vietnam veterans were using drugs like LSD and heroin and it seemed like everyone was smoking pot. Jack soon fell into that groove too. In 1970, Joseph Trombetta had enough of Philadelphia and moved to Wildwood, New Jersey. He mistakenly thought the move would help straighten Jack out.

Jack was enrolled in Wildwood High School. The fifth day of his junior year he was called into the principle's office. Jack's father was waiting there with the principle, Mr. Mancia. Although it was less than a week into the new school year, it was very apparent to the faculty that Jack Trombetta was trouble, big trouble.

"What do you want to do with your life?" Mr. Mancia asked, thinking Jack would be intimidated into some reasonable answer because of his father's presence.

"I wanna be a bum," Jack shouted. Almost immediately his father's right hand came crashing against the back of Jack

head. Joe Trombetta called his son a "dago." The word
hurt Joe more than it did Jack.

Jack quit school and moved into an apartment with a couple
of other losers who thought they knew everything. He
worked odd jobs, mostly construction, for a year.
Seventeen year old Jack Trombetta hated working to support
himself. Reality sucked. Jack's parents welcomed him back
home with the condition he return to Wildwood High School.
He did and met 15 year old Lynn Durante.

Jack was intrigued by Lynn. He actually behaved like a
gentleman in her presence. She was more than just good
looking. She was old fashioned. Lynn cooked, cleaned and
was a very loyal companion. There was only one problem, her
father, George. George Durante was familiar with Jack's
wiseguy wannabe reputation. He had absolutely no use for
him. But, Lynn's mother, Rosalyn, actually liked Jack and
saw something positive in Jack that only a mother could
see. Despite his reputation, Jack was always very polite
and pleasant to her. George on the other hand wanted to
bash Jack in the face with a brick!

Although Jack was back in school he never won any student
of the year awards. He walked around the school like he
owned it. He'd attend classes if he was in the mood and
had nothing better to do. His test scores usually depended
on who was sitting next to him.

Jack and Lynn dated for three years. Actually, Jack would
stop seeing her in the summer so he could play the field.
Come September they'd get back together. Miraculously, Lynn
accepted the arrangement and never dated anyone else, even
during the lapses. Finally, Jack's sisters, Denise and
Ann, talked Lynn into dumping Jack. They loved Lynn and
hated Jack for treating her like a piece of furniture.
Jack rapidly realized how much he loved Lynn and promised
to change. He did.

Just before graduating high school in 1973, Jack started
reading the Gospel and then became a born again Christian.
Jesus and Lynn saved Jack from himself. He even applied
for a summer job as a cop with the North Wildwood Police
Department. The cops couldn't believe it. They all knew
Jack. Most of them had brought him in for various things,
yet he never seemed to be charged with anything. But, he
was a wise ass punk in their eyes. Unfortunately for them,
Jack's father was friendly with the Mayor, Tony Catanoso,
who approved Jack's application.

After a couple of weeks the wary cops actually started to
like Jack. The kid had balls and made arrests for the same
things he was doing the previous summer. He worked six

days a week from 8pm to 4am. That September Jack found himself in Atlantic Community College. But, there was a problem. Jack could barely read and couldn't divide or multiply. He wound up taking remedial reading and math courses. A teacher named Don Payne, a retired police captain, from Delaware, liked Jack. He advised him to take all the civil service tests. Jack always scored well, not because of the written part, but because of the physical part. In the spring of 1974 he was contacted by the Lower Township Police Department. He never even heard of Lower Township, which was about twenty minutes away. Payne told him to take the job and attend school part time. Jack took his advice and was appointed on April 1, 1974. He married Lynn six months later.

Jack would be the perfect husband, father and Christian for the next eighteen years. In 1977 he took a leave of absence from the job to attend seminary in Philadelphia, a ninety mile trip each way, five days a week. He was attending school when his daughter was born. Although he wouldn't become a minister, he relished the experience.

In the spring of 1992, thirty-eight year old Jack Trombetta hit a premature mid-life crisis. Partying and drinking after work, softball games and good arrests and just about any other reason to celebrate were becoming the norm. That summer he was sent to the elite FBI National Academy. It was party time! Jack gained weight, lost a lot of stamina and skipped classes when he thought he could get away with it. It was Wildwood High all over again, except for the drugs. Jack even started smoking again.

Upon graduating the academy he shaped up, both physically and mentally. But, over the past few months he was slipping again. Lynn was justifiably getting upset. Jesus probably wasn't too happy with Jack either. The roller coaster ride had to end. Jack owed it to God, Lynn, Joe, Gina and Jackie. But, Dave's murder suspended everything for now.

It was 4am. Jack's thoughts were interrupted by the clicking of a door lock. He watched Ernie slowly open then close the front door. Despite his gruffness, Ernie was actually trying to be considerate and not wake Jack.

"Hi, Ern," Jack said as though it was four in the afternoon.

"Don't you ever sleep?" Ernie asked, sounding almost annoyed.

"You know I can't sleep," Jack answered.
"Well, I can. Good night, psycho." Ernie never broke

stride and went up the stairs to his bedroom. Jack went
back to staring at the ceiling.

Bob and Jack were wide awake by 7:30 am. They had showered
and shaved and were trying to remain somewhat quiet. Jack
had already been outside on the front step freezing his
butt off having his morning wake up, Marlboro Lights.

Bob was reading the Queens Chronicle, a weekly publication
with an impressive circulation of over 100,000. He was
reading Ernie's column "A Different Angle." Ernie had been
writing a weekly piece for six years just as a hobby, an
unpaid contributor. Bob was thinking that Ernie sure had a
sick sense of humor. His writings were pointed in an
irreverent sort of way. He sure didn't care what people
thought. Bob could see a lot of Ernie in hisself. It was
an old article that ripped the now ex-Mayor Dinkins,
homosexuals, and most politicians. Bob was thinking Ernie
should say what he really means. Bob laughed at the idea.
Ernie said exactly what he meant. Bob liked his style. "I
ought to sit down with this guy and write a book," thought
Martin.

Grace and Angelina came down the steps. Angelina
immediately turned on the TV and began watching Barney the
Dinosaur. This was new territory for Bob and Jack. Who
the hell was Barney? They soon found out. He was only the
most popular purple dinosaur on television. Grace laughed
when she saw both men sitting on the couch watching the
show with Angelina sitting between them.

Grace walked over to the couch and while glancing at the TV
said, "I think Angelina likes this show so much because
Barney reminds her of Ernie." Grace laughed at her joke.
Ernie was still in bed and couldn't defend himself.
Neither Bob nor Jack came to his defense. Maybe Grace was
right. Who really knew?

Grace asked what was on the agenda for the 29th of March.
Jack advised that two guys from Major case were going to
pick them up at 9 am. They would then spend the day at
Major Case then later in the evening they were going to
meet Tommy Chin and Keith Ng at the 109th Precinct. Grace
explained that Ernie was trying to get some sleep and then
they had some personal business to attend to and then he
had to work a 4 to 12 shift. She indicated that they
should come home for dinner when they could and that she
was sure Ernie would have it figured out on how they would
get to the 109th for their meeting with the "Ninja Squad."
They each had a cup of coffee and a bagel and right on time
the guys from Major Case picked them up and took them to
One Police Plaza.

CHAPTER FIFTY FOUR

The day was spent obtaining background information on the tenants at the apartment they were concentrating on. They also had the TARU van set up surveillance and they were taping everyone that went in or out of the complex. The guys in the van had the composite of the shooter with them and many times throughout their surveillance they would compare it to the people on their screen.

Bob and Jack teamed up with Ruben Santiago and Simon Kok. They spent the day tying up as many loose ends as possible and made repeated efforts to contact Liu and Quey. Bob wanted Quey interviewed to ascertain if perhaps he remembered something or arbitrarily would provide information that he had failed to do in the past.

They wanted to speak with Liu just to make sure that he remembered his appointment with the "Ninja Squad." Bob and Jack were sure that Liu was involved and may have even set up the burglaries at the Chinese workers' residence in Lower Township. Both detectives thought Liu had some involvement in the killing of Officer Dave Douglass..

The four detectives made many stops in Chinatown during the day. They were in and out of apartment complex after complex. They were seeing first hand how the Chinese immigrants lived. Oftentimes they would find themselves in a two room apartment with a bathroom. The four or more inhabitants would always seem to be soft-spoken and basically unknowledgeable of anything they were asked. Simon Kok was very good at getting them to relax and at least be somewhat helpful. Martin and Trombetta were always upset with the fact that they couldn't converse with the immigrants. The language barrier was a real drag. They found it difficult to impossible to utilize their investigative interview and interrogation skills.

The fact that they couldn't personally speak to the Chinese speaking victims, witnesses and possible perpetrators had been a major problem from the very beginning of this case.

Bob and Jack were getting a real education on how Chinese immigrants were forced to live and exist. Both the detectives were quick to see that the majority of the immigrants were first taken advantage of by the people who they had to rely on for passage to the United States. They would have to pay these people back a large sum of money. They would usually have to work in the restaurant business at very low wages and slowly pay back the large sum of money they owed. The restaurant owners would have cheap

labor and would take advantage of the immigrants to line their own pockets.
Most of the restaurant owners would not pay unemployment, social security or federal tax on the wages of the immigrants. The workers would be used and abused until they were no longer useful and then they were fired.

Bob and Jack were impressed by how hard working the majority of the immigrants appeared to be. These individuals came to a country whose language they didn't understand and almost immediately went to work at below minimum pay and would oftentimes travel across the United States on a bus in an attempt to relocate to a restaurant that would keep them working. Not only would they pay off the large sum of money owed to the scum that illegally got them into the country but they would always manage to send money to their families in China.

These people were hard working, industrious individuals, who would stop at nothing short of an all out effort to make it their new surroundings. Both Bob and Jack wanted Dave's killer dead but they were also gaining respect for these hard working people. They both, however, were not real happy with the restaurant owners who abused the immigrants.

The four detectives were walking up a flight of stairs to a fourth floor apartment and Bob was looking at the names scribbled in Chinese on the doors. Simon Kok saw Bob's interest and explained that the symbols indicated the names of the individuals that lived in the apartments. Ruben Santiago continually looked up and down the hallways as if he was expecting problems. Jack, too, seemed to be waiting for someone to jump out of a doorway and start shooting.

The four were approaching a landing as a door quickly opened and the occupant started screaming in Chinese. Martin, Trombetta and Santiago each grabbed for their guns. Kok immediately advised them to calm down. He spoke to the occupant and smiled. Everyone continued down the hallway and Kok advised that the subject was calling to a friend down the hall to ascertain as to whether or not they had pork for a dish he was preparing.

Kok also advised that a group of immigrants in apartment eight had an individual whose name was Liu living with them. He had obtained this information from the subject who was screaming down the hallway. The detectives wanted to speak to this individual to ascertain if he was related to Yi Liang Liu.

Kok knocked at the door and spoke in Chinese. The door quickly opened and three Chinese immigrants were standing

in the kitchen. One had just exited the bathroom, one was
standing near a small kitchen table and the other was
stirring a pot of what Martin observed to be pork.
Martin observed that a large quantity of Chinese vegetables
were on the kitchen counter and were apparently going to be
added to the pork. He was thinking he would like to be
invited to dinner. The place was pretty clean and tidy.
The kitchen, living room, dining room was ringed by a
bathroom and two doorways that led to bedrooms. One of the
bedroom doors was open and the other was closed.

Kok was talking to the subjects standing in the kitchen.
Santiago and Martin made their way to the bedrooms to see
if anyone was in them. Trombetta checked the bathroom.
The three detectives were nonchalant in the way they
conducted their search. It didn't appear as though they
were being pushy. It just appeared that they were
interested in the apartment. One of the subjects spoke a
little English and Martin was telling him what a nice
apartment they had. Martin also made an inquiry about the
food that was cooking and the subject tried to tell him
what was being prepared. Martin made out the word pork and
that was about the extent of the recipe ingredients that
was understandable.

It was ascertained that the subject who stayed in the
locked bedroom was working and that he would not be home
until the following day. It was also revealed that the
subject had a phone in the room and that his last name was
unknown. Simon Kok advised that it was not uncommon for
the subjects not to know the full name of those who they
lived with. Simon picked up a phone in the kitchen and
dialed a number that was listed to a Liu and had been found
on the telephone bill of the Chinese Resturant in Lower
Township. It was one of the many phone numbers that the
detectives had been tracking down. When Simon finished
dialing the detectives could hear the phone ringing in the
locked bedroom.

The papers of the subjects were checked. Two of the
subjects had no legal documents. Simon Kok indicated that
such a problem was not a big deal and that most of the
immigrants he dealt with never seemed to have legal
documentation. Martin and Trombetta were aware of the fact
that INS didn't really have any control over these people.
INS just seemed to spin their wheels when it came to
illegal immigrants. Kok and Santiago agreed. Martin was
hoping that they would all be invited to dinner but his
wish didn't come true. He had forgotten that neither he
nor Jack had dined on Chinese food since Dave was killed.
Jack loved lobster Cantonese and Bob hadn't found a Chinese
dish he didn't like. It was common knowledge that if what
was on the plate didn't eat Martin first he would devour it

in short order. He loved to eat Chinese food.

Kok advised the immigrants that he would make contact with
the subject who wasn't present sometime later in the week.
Kok indicated that he didn't think that the subjects living
at the apartment were involved in the case.

It seemed like the detectives had been in every apartment
complex in Chinatown since this investigation began.
Martin was even starting to remember streets and landmarks.
He had also picked up some of the language of the
immigrants he had been investigating. He knew, however,
that knowledge of a few Chinese words was a far cry from
being able to understand what they were saying.

The day went quickly and they had forgotten to eat lunch.
They had returned to the Major Case Squad office and it was
decided that Tom Nerney would take them back to the
Naspretto residence on his way home. The three hopped into
Nerney's car and were quickly on their way. Tom was more
than use to the traffic of the city and knew all the
shortcuts. The three men talked about the interview of Liu
that was going to take place that evening. Each had ideas
about what should be asked. They talked about Chin and Ng
conducting the interview. Both Martin and Trombetta felt
that it would be best if the "Ninja Squad" handled the
interview and interrogation. They all felt that those two
would obtain the truth from Liu. Martin and Trombetta could
view the proceedings from behind a two way mirror and would
be able to provide any case background information and
questions if necessary.

They arrived at the Naspretto house at five forty five in
the evening. Tom wanted to say hello to Grace, who was
putting dinner on the table as they walked in. The
greetings were quickly over and Tom said that he had to
make a stop at a local precinct to obtain some information
on another case he was working. Grace begged him to stay
for dinner but he indicated that the detective was waiting
on him. Tom left while Bob and Jack devoured a meatloaf
dinner along with vegetables, potatoes, salad, Italian
bread and dessert. Jack was kidding Grace about the fact
that Ernie was missing a good dinner. Grace indicated that
Ernie could afford to miss a dinner or two.

They were finishing dinner when the phone rang and it was
Ernie asking for Bob. He wanted to know how things had
gone during the day. Bob quickly filled Ernie in on the
day's happenings.

"Listen, Grace is going to take you guys out to the 109th
tonight and when you are done she will come and pick you
up," Ernie explained.

"No way, Ern. Just give me directions and we'll get there."

"I don't want to hear that," Ernie warned.

"Ern, I'm not kidding. Grace would have to pack up Angelina twice tonight and cart her out in this cold weather. Just give me directions and we will find the place." Ernie could hear Jack in the background echoing Bob's sentiments.

"Tell the terd to shut up." Ernie laughed as he said the words. Bob was starting to wonder if Ernie had forgotten Jack's name since he never called him by it.

Ernie continued, "Bob, the road you guys should travel is all torn up. It will take forever for me to give you other directions."

"Ernie, we will find the place."

Ernie cut Bob off. "Do you give everybody a hard time? O.K., you follow Grace out to the 109 and then you guys can back track and find your way home tonight. I don't want to hear anything else. Put Grace on." Bob could tell that it was no use talking to Ernie any longer. His mind was made up. Grace got off the phone and said, "Ernie said good luck with the interrogation."

Grace immediately tried to talk the guys into allowing her to be their taxi. She said she would drop the baby off at her mother's and she would stand by the precinct while the Chinese guy was interrogated. Bob and Jack talked her into just letting them follow her to the 109th Precinct and reassured her that they would be able to find their way back to the Naspretto residence. She immediately sat down and wrote a list of directions in case they weren't observant on the trip to the precinct. She didn't want two cops from Jersey and friends of Ernie getting themselves lost in the big city.

The guys helped Grace clear the table and after relaxing for a short time they were on their way to meet Chin and Ng. They were following Grace through what appeared to be a maze of stops, turns and lane changes. Jack stated, "Man, she drives like a truck driver. Don't lose her or we'll never find our way to the precinct."
Bob laughed and stated, "Grace and Ernie both drive like their lives depend on it." Jack stated, "In this city your life does depend on your driving ability, so keep your eyes on the road and don't get us killed."

"Have another cigarette, will ya," stated Bob.

They arrived at the 109th Precinct at 7:45pm. They were
supposed to meet Chin and Ng at 8pm. Grace said her
goodbyes and told the guys that if they had any trouble
getting home that they should call and she would come get
them.

Bob and Jack waved as she drove away. They had parked in
the police parking lot which was more like a driveway than
a parking lot. They figured that when they came out the
car would be gone. Bob made a mental note to mention their
parking spot to Chin as soon as he saw him.

CHAPTER FIFTY FIVE

The Jersey guys entered a rear door and quickly went up the stairs to the office of the "Ninja Squad", Queens Robbery. They were immediately greeted by a couple of detectives who had remembered them from their last visit. They were advised that Chin was on his way in to the office and that Ng was picking up Liu at his apartment.

Bob and Jack made themselves at home and swapped a few war stories with the detectives who were all sitting around eating Chinese food. The eight o-clock movie came on the television. It was the movie "Attica". It was about the prison riot that had taken place at the New York prison in the early seventies.
Bob was thinking how much he'd love to send Dave's killer there, if not to hell.

Moments later Chin arrived and was quickly followed by Ng. Ng advised that he had Liu in the interrogation room. The four investigators quickly decided on a line of questioning and Chin and Ng went to work. Bob and Jack decided to stay in the office while the "Ninja Squad got acquainted with Liu."

Bob and Jack tried to get interested in the movie on TV but repeatedly would ask each other about case facts that should be looked into with regard to Liu. Bob started to make a list to mention to Chin and Ng when they would take a break from the interrogation.

Bob looked at the clock on the wall and the time was 9:25pm. Chin entered the office and indicated that Liu was still telling the same story he had related when he was interviewed in North Jersey. Chin advised that they had found a few discrepancies but nothing that was really worthwhile. He and Ng were going to start getting a little harder with Liu. Martin provided Chin with the list of questions he and Jack had come up with. Chin quickly reviewed them and advised that he had covered most of them but he try again, follow up and try to trick him.

Chin walked out and Jack had a look of defeat on his face. Martin felt the same way and they began to talk about the fact that maybe Liu wasn't involved at all. How could that be? He had to be the one that at the least set the whole thing up. He was mad because he wasn't being paid enough and he was seeking retribution. If he didn't burglarize the residence in the past, he had to be the one that gave someone else the information about the location and the coming and going of the inhabitants of the residence. They didn't think he was the shooter but they had been sure he had been involved.

The movie was over at ten and almost immediately Ng entered the office with a look of disgust on his face. "He not tell much. Tommy wit him now. I go back and dis time I get dat rittle mudda fucca to tell trute. We prray game wit him, I go back dere in minute. If he do anyting in dis case we let you know soon." Ng turned and left the office. Jack looked at Martin as one of the robbery detectives commented, "The Ninja Squad is pissed now."

Martin and Trombetta smiled. Somehow they were reassured that they would soon know for sure whether or not Liu had any involvement in the killing of Officer Dave Douglass. If the "Ninja Squad" couldn't get it out of him, then Liu was actually innocent. The Jersey guys dreaded the thought.

It was 10:30 p.m. when Chin came into the office and advised Martin that he wanted him to go into the interrogation room and talk to Liu. Chin related that Liu felt sorry for Martin because that he had lost his brother. Martin remembered that he had told Liu during the interview in North Jersey that Dave Douglass was his brother. Martin had thought if he was searching for the "killer of his brother" it would put more pressure on the witnesses to cooperate.

Chin told Martin that Liu was concerned that Martin would feel dishonored if he didn't catch his brother's killer. Chin advised that he thought this guy really liked Martin. He was told by Chin just to do what Ng told him. Martin entered the room while Jack and Tommy watched from the other side of the mirror.

Liu started to rise from his chair and put his hand out to Martin. Martin shook his hand and sat down. Ng spoke in English to Martin and stated that Liu had practically no understanding of the English language and that he would interpret everything Liu had to say. Ng told Martin to appeal to Liu for help to catch the man that killed his brother. Ng told Martin to put on a good act.

Martin began to speak to Liu as though he could understand every word. Ng translated as Martin spoke. Martin could see the compassion on the face of Liu. He really did seem concerned. After about five minutes of non-stop pleading on Martin's part Ng told Martin to start crying. Immediately Bob started to make a last ditch appeal to Liu. Ng advised that he felt Liu was an emotional person and the outburst of tears from the brother of the murdered officer might get Liu talking. Martin turned on the tears and played his part to its fullest. It wasn't difficult to turn on the tears. He had done it before in interviews. He found it easy. He just had to think of a terrible incident in his life and the tears would flow. He could turn them off just as quickly. Martin cried as Liu's eyes started to fill with tears that began to flow slowly down his cheeks. Martin thought that Liu was about to tell the whole story. Tommy Chin thought the same thing and entered the room and led Martin from the office. Martin had done his part. Tommy knew that he and Keith could finish this guy off. They would now play on his emotions.

Chin looked at Martin. "Nice job. I was ready to confess." Chin started back into the interrogation room and said, "Give us about fifteen more minutes." Martin and Trombetta watched as the detectives began the task of their last ditch effort to get this guy to break. Liu was controlling his crying as best that he could. Jack looked at Bob and said, "It won't be long now. He is ready to go."

"Looks that way," said Martin as they both walked away from the window and back to the office.

About fifteen minutes later Chin entered the office and stated, "We are done. He doesn't know a thing about the murder of Dave Douglass." Jack and Bob looked at each other in disbelief. They had been so sure he had at least set the previous burglaries up for the perpetrator. They didn't want to believe Tommy but they knew he too had investigated enough cases to know whether a guy was involved or not.

Tommy saw the concern on their faces and said, "I want you to see this guy and observe how he is acting." Martin and Trombetta followed Tommy back to the interrogation room and gazed through the window. They observed a broken, verbally beaten man who was crying and sobbing uncontrollably in such a manner that it made Martin think of a prisoner of war who had been psychologically broken and had become a mentally lifeless piece of human flesh and bone. This was the face of a man who wished he knew something and would have gladly provided it. He crossed his arms in front of himself on the table and threw his head onto his arms and continued to cry and sob. His entire body was shaking and he mumbled words in a language that neither Martin nor Trombetta understood.

Both Jack and Bob recognized the fact that they were looking at the face of a suspect who had been through the most stressful interview/interrogation he had probably ever experienced or would ever be confronted with again. If this had been a war criminal held by a foreign government he would have the physical signs to show what he had been through. Liu had not been physically injured but he would never forget his meeting with the "Ninja Squad". Martin and Trombetta recognized that Liu would have done practically anything just to have Ng and Chin leave him alone. Liu continued to make statements in Chinese as though he was talking to anyone who was listening but no one in particular. Ng walked out of the office leaving Liu crying and ranting to himself. Ng approached Martin, Trombetta and Chin and stated, "He broken man, he know nuttin. He ready to admit to anyting just so we reave him arone. He doesn't know anyting bout Douglass murder."

Bob and Jack now knew the "Ninja Squad" was right. It was, however, hard to accept. Ng advised that he was going to get Liu to calm down and take him home. What could Martin and Trombetta do now? All they had left was the composite of an old fat guy that they couldn't locate.

Moments later Ng walked in with a very humble Liu. Ng advised that Liu wanted to talk to Martin. Liu bent at the waist and lowered his eyes as he greeted Martin with his outstretched hand. Martin shook his hand and Liu started to talk in Chinese. Ng translated. "He say dat he sorry for your ross and dat he hope you fine your brothers kirrer. If he fine out anyting he cawr me to ret you know. He say he know dat one day you catch the guy cause you good man." Martin continued to grip Liu's hand and responded, "Shay Shay". Martin could see the tears starting to form in Liu's eyes. Ng advised he was taking Liu back to his apartment. Chin indicated that he had some paper work to do on a case. Martin and Trombetta decided it was time to head back to the Naspretto residence.

When they pulled into the Naspretto driveway Ernie came out the front door. He had finished his 4 to 12 shift and was waiting up for the guys to return. "Well, did ya burn the shithead or what?" Ernie was waiting to hear the guy was in central booking and the key was about to be thrown away. Jack looked at Ernie and said, "Ernie, Tommy and Keith made us believers that this guy had nothing to do with the whole case. Matter of fact we started to like the guy."

"Holy shit, ya gotta be kiddin," responded Ernie. "Well, if you're hungry, let's go in and get somethin' to eat. I wanna hear the whole story." Both Bob and Jack weren't hungry or thirsty but they thought they owed Ernie the story about what had taken place. The guys sat around Ernie's dining room table conversing. Ernie felt proud of the Ninja Squad for what they had done and made a mental note to make people aware of just how good these guys really were. Ernie especially liked Jack's remark about Ng and Chin reducing the guy to "a pile of runny shit".

Ernie commented, "Hey, this guy will never break the law or do anything to make the cops want to talk to him. Keith and Tom have made him an upright and law abiding immigrant." Martin and Trombetta laughed. They both agreed. This guy wouldn't even jay walk on the streets of New York.

Martin advised Ernie that Ng had said that Liu was moving to North Carolina the following afternoon. Ernie laughed and figured he was moving because he didn't want to be around New York cops for the remainder of his life. Liu had told Ng he was moving to get a better job.

Bob and Jack had two beers apiece, while Ernie just ate and ate. Bob wondered to himself if Ernie ever missed a meal in his life. They went to bed at 3 AM.

Morning came quickly. Ernie had already left the house for a day tour. Bob and Jack were sitting around the dining room table telling Grace about the Liu interview. Tom Nerney was picking them up at 10 am. They both eventually called their wives and touched base with home. Martin contacted the Chief and filled him in and then talked to Chris Winter and advised him what was going on. Chris was told to make the other detectives aware of what was happening. Bob told Chris that it wouldn't be long before they would be calling with news of an arrest.

Jack sat there perplexed. "Boy, you sound real sure about that. What case are you working on?"

Martin replied, "I can feel it, Jackie. It won't be long. I gotta start feeling positive sometime."

"You're the one that has been thinking positive from the beginning. I'm the one that has the doomsday thoughts."

They both got showered and true to form Tom Nerney picked them up right on time and they were once again headed to One Police Plaza.

Upon entering the Major Case Squad office Jack immediately went to the coffee machine. The Jersey guys had really begun to make themselves at home with the guys from Major Case. Jack was borrowing cigarettes from anyone that walked past him. He really felt at home.

Bob immediately sat down with Jim Rybicki who had arrived with Gene Taylor. They were filled in on the Liu situation and felt comfortable with the fact that Liu was not involved.

They then began to discuss what was going to take place

that evening with regard to the surveillance of the lottery
locations. Major Case Squad detectives and supervisors
were taking part in conversations about the upcoming
activities for the evening.

Simon Kok and Ruben Santiago entered and Jack observed
Martin speaking to Simon. Kok and Santiago left almost
immediately. "Yo, Bob, what was that all about", asked
Trombetta?

"I asked Simon to see if he could hook up with Quey again.
He had a good rapport with him. What the hell? Quey seemed
like he wanted to help but just couldn't remember anything.
Maybe he needed some time. Hey, Jack, maybe I'm pissin' in
the wind, but who knows?" Jack thought it certainly
couldn't hurt.

Trombetta found someone with a cigarette and in a moment
was giving everyone second hand smoke to fill their lungs.

Martin hoped that this guy would live up to his promise and
stop smoking when Dave's killer was arrested. Catching
Dave's killer was one thing, getting Jack to quit smoking
was yet another. Martin looked at his watch. It was 2 p.m.

Martin was depressed over not having a suspect identified.
This case was taking to long. The shooter was probably in
main land China. Ng and Chin had been great, many
potential witnesses and or suspects were devoured but
nobody was in handcuffs. Martin had asked Kok to question
Quey about some of the names written in Quey's little black
phone book. Based on the original interview with Quey it
seemed a couple may have fit the description of the killer.

Simon Kok had received a few calls from Quey's wife during
the past few days. She wanted to advise Kok that her
husband was a good man and that he would never commit a
crime not to mention shooting a policeman. She was
obviously very worried that her husband would eventually be
accused of some terrible crime. Quey probably told her
that the cops were looking for a killer, a cop killer. Kok
would routinely explain that Quey was not a target in this
investigation but probably had met the killer on at least
one occasion.

Kok and Santiago had gone to Kok's desk to call Quey.
Simon was aware that Quey would be at home on his day off
from work in North Jersey. Kok asked about some of the
individuals whose names appeared in Quey's little black
phone book. Simon got some what's and where's answered,
thanked Quey and was about to hang up when he decided to
ask one more question.

"Do you remember anybody else you might have met at the employment agency you used to get work?" Kok asked.

"There was a guy, Chung Hop. I never put him in my book. I just put his name on piece of paper and put in my wallet." Quey answered. There was no pressure over the phone. Nobody was threatening him or scaring him. Quey was in the comfort of his own little kingdom, small as it was.

"How old is this person?"

"About 40 or 50."

"Do you have any idea where he lives?"

"Around 14th street."

Kok started to get a little excited. Quey's memory was in fifth gear. Kok asked calmly, "Where on 14th street?"

Quey's non-chalant answer was about to turn the biggest city in the world into a small town. Detective Simon Kok felt light headed as he heard Quey say, "Around First Avenue." The lottery place was right there! It was all Kok could do from screaming. He didn't want his voice to change pitch. It might have scared or intimidated Quey. Santiago could tell by the look on Simon's face that this conversation was going somewhere.

Kok asked Quey to check to see if this Chung Hop's number was still in his wallet. It was! Quey read it to Simon. Interestingly, Chung Hop's name was not pointed out as someone fitting the general description of the killer during the first interview with Quey in North Jersey. Quey had been questioned about all the names in the book but he never thought about the piece of paper in his wallet until just being asked by Kok. Kok thanked Quey and said he'd be in touch. Quey didn't give a second thought to the conversation he just had with the detective. Quey had no idea he had just fingered the guy that shot and killed Patrolman Dave Douglass.

Kok and Santiago did a Coles check on the number and came up with 612 East Fourteenth Street, Apartment 2C. They rapidly walked over to the Major Case Squad three offices away and told Tom Nerney, who just nodded. Bob Martin and Joe Piraino walked out of Joe's office and Joe asked what was going on. Upon hearing the news Joe grabbed Simon Kok and hugged him. "We got him!" Joe shouted, not caring how ridiculous he looked hugging Simon, who was looking at Ruben Santiago and rolling his eyes. Tom Nerney didn't show any emotion other than to look at Bob Martin and say,

"That's our shooter."

Jack Trombetta entered the room with a fresh cup of coffee and a new cigarette and asked, "Yo, what's up?"

Martin with a big smile replied, "Jackie, We finally have a door that is going to be opened by our key."

CHAPTER FIFTY SIX

Captain Naspretto worked the standard day tour on
Wednesday, March 30th. His tour would be over by three
o'clock and he'd be at headquarters meeting up with
Piraino, Nerney, Trombetta and Martin by four. Upon his
arrival, Ernie was told that Martin requested Detective Kok
to re-interview Quey in an attempt to obtain more
information. Kok had come up with some interesting
information. Jack had indicated Martin felt it might prove
very useful. Ernie felt himself getting excited, however,
he tried to hide it, especially since no one else seemed
overly optimistic. Ernie kept forgetting that the Jersey
guys had been through setback after setback.

Jack and Bob couldn't afford to build up their hopes. Sure
Bob made positive statements about making an arrest but
this investigation had been an emotional roller coaster.
Every time something seemed to break in the right
direction, they would hit a brick wall. That wall was
starting to look like the "Great Wall of China." It got
thicker and longer with every lead they tracked down.
Sergeant Piraino didn't show too much emotion, good or bad,
over the past couple of weeks so Ernie didn't know how to
gauge him. Ernie had missed the "hugging episode" with
Kok. Detective Nerney showed his usual unrelenting resolve
to solve the case.

A briefing was in progress. Bob was saying that he, Jack
and Ernie would be going to the housing complex on East
Fourteenth Street. Ernie wasn't aware of the reason behind
going to the housing complex and he looked at Jack in
question. Jack whispered to him that they had a possible
make on the perpetrator and that he may live at the
building. Martin's request of Kok to re-interview Quey had
provided a possible phone number of the mutt and the phone
number lead to an address in the housing complex. It was
decided that a surveillance of the residence would be
conducted concurrently with the surveillance of the lottery
location. The TARU unit was set up along with a
surveillance unit the Jersey guys had sent down from the
Prosecutor's Office. The TARU van would set up on the
Lottery location and the van from Jersey would set up on
the housing complex.

Ernie could feel the anticipation building. He was excited
but everyone else seemed to be remaining pretty calm.
Assignments were given to everyone at the meeting. Ernie
knew he would be driving Bob and Jack and was happy with
that assignment. He knew these guys were going to be in on

any major incident that went down. There was no way Ernie
was going to miss out on the opportunity to catch a cop
killer. It would be one "war story" that would actually be
true.

Everyone, except Bob, seemed to be taking their time to get
their portable radios, call signs and vehicle assignments.
Bob seemed to be in a hurry and Jack knew just to follow
along. Ernie questioned Jack as to Bob's quickness to
leave the building and get to the housing complex. Ernie
counted fifteen guys getting their assignments.

Bob was walking out of Major Case and advising that he,
Jack and Ernie were on their way. The time was 4:15 p.m.
Ernie had thought everyone didn't have to be set up until
five p.m. Jack was right behind Bob as he approached the
elevator. Ernie caught up and stated, "Why are we in such
a hurry?"

Jack looked at Ernie and spoke what was on Bob's mind as if
he was reading Bob's thoughts, "We're going to do some real
police work that Bob doesn't want the prosecutors people to
be aware of until it's all over."
"You got it, Jackie," said Bob. Jack looked at Ernie and
said,"I told you he had something on his mind." They were
on the elevator and Bob reached into his coat pocket and
pulled out a small envelope. "We are going to 612 East
Fourteenth Street, Apartment 2C, and find out if this key
fits the door lock." Martin grinned as he said the
sentence. Jack laughed and stated, "I love it when a plan
comes together, Bobby."

Ernie smiled. He didn't have the slightest idea of what
the hell these guys were up to. All he knew was that he
wanted to be there whenever they did whatever they had in
mind.

They pulled up to the New York Housing Authority complex on
14th Street. They parked on the opposite side of the
street. They were directly in front of the same building
that Detective Keith Ng had been staring at only a week
before. Ernie no sooner turned off the ignition and Bob
and Jack were getting out of the vehicle. Ernie quickly
followed.

"Hey, Ernie, are these buildings easy to get into or are
they locked to the public?" asked Bob.

"These places are always unlocked. They have locks that
have been broken for years," advised Ernie. They walked
through the court yard and stopped in the building's
vestibule. The inside door was actually locked, requiring
visitors to be buzzed in. Ernie couldn't believe it.

"I've been in a million housing projects. Of course, this is the only fuckin' project that has a working buzz in system." Just then a very attractive Hispanic woman who appeared to be around twenty walked through the outer doors. She was taking keys from her pocketbook. Ernie showed his shield and in the best Jack Webb voice he could come up with asked her to allow them in. She didn't say anything but smiled a big smile as she opened the door for them. She walked to the elevator and the cops headed for the stairway. Ernie was looking over his shoulder at the young lady's derriere then proclaimed, "That girl wanted me. The high beams were on. Did you notice? Her whole body was pulsating with desire. It was obvious. Did you see the way she was checking me out?" Again, with that 'pulsating with desire' line. Jack and Bob both looked at Ernie like he was as mentally sick as he was acting and laughed. They became very quiet as they reached the second floor. The hallway was empty.

They exited the elevator on the second floor. Bob got his bearings and Jack and Ernie followed him down the hallway. Bob approached apartment 2B and put his ear to the door. He was attempting to ascertain if he could hear anyone in the apartment. Ernie whispered, "Don't we want apartment 2C?"

"I want to see if this key at least fits this type of lock before I get to 2C," said Bob, in a low voice. Bob slowly inserted the key into the tumbler and it fit easily. He then attempted to turn it and it would not turn. Bob said, "It's the right type of key for these locks." He seemed excited. He then walked past apartment 2C to the next door and again after listening at the door inserted the key and it fit easily but would not turn. Bob figured that if the key would fit the tumbler and not rotate he would be able to compare the action of those tumblers with the tumbler on the lock at the door of apartment 2C. Bob then put his finger to his lips indicating that Jack and Ernie should remain quiet. The three cops then quietly walked the hallway and Bob motioned to Ernie to stand at one side of the door. Jack had already taken a position to Bob's right.

Jack had been at enough doors in his time to know exactly where he should be. Jack tapped Bob's shoulder to let him know where he was located. Jack stood behind Bob. Ernie and Jack each had their weapons at their side. Bob listened at the door and could hear the television playing and people speaking in Chinese. He slowly inserted the key and after pushing it in as far as possible and as quietly as possible he slowly tried to rotate it to the right. Ernie watched and could see that the key was turning. It was fuckin' turning! Ernie started to raise his gun. Ernie froze as Bob turned the key back to the lock position, removed it and showed absolutely no excitement or emotion as he and Jack rapidly walked down the hallway toward the elevator. Jack was returning his weapon to the holster inside his jacket. Ernie was dumbfounded by their actions.

Ernie whispered loudly, "Where ya' goin'? Let's take the fuckin' door." Bob looked back and gave a very authoritarian wave of the arm which meant, "Come on, let's go, ass hole!" Jack just kept walking. He knew they should clear the hallway as quickly as possible. Before Ernie had walked the twenty feet back to Bob and Jack he realized that taking the door would have destroyed whatever case they might have. He felt stupid. They took the fire exit and hurried down the steps and exited the vestibule into the courtyard. "We got'em now, Jackie," said Bob.

"I hope he is still in there and didn't leave the area to hide somewhere," said Jack.

"Jack, I can feel it. That shithead is in there," Martin made no attempt to hide his excitement.

It was a combination of relief that they actually found a lock that could be turned by the key and humor in the way Ernie wanted to just barge in like he was on television in an episode of "COPS".

Bob and Jack were smiling and Jack stated, "Hey, Ern, I thought you were going to shit your pants when we walked away from the door."

"Yeah, well, I'm a street cop who is use to kickin' doors. I don't think about all this James Bond shit. I suppose now you Jersey shits are going to tell me all about reasonable suspicion, probable cause and search warrants. Just save me the fuckin' law lecture and tell me what we do next. Anyway, I passed three civil service tests. I know the fuckin' law. I just got a little excited, okay?" Ernie was happy and embarrassed at the same time.

"Well, that's understandable since you normally don't get a chance to work on big cases like this," answered Jack, sarcastically. Bob laughed as Ernie's face turned red. Bob said, "Hey, Ern, stick with us, we'll make you a hero."

"Yeah, maybe you'll get a plaque as an award," said Jack as he laughed. "Fuck ya both," said Ernie with a grin. It was quite evident that Ernie was excited at the thought of all this detective cloak and dagger stuff.

They were back in the car and immediately Bob and Jack were talking about the entry into the building and the

subsequent turning of the key at the door of apartment 2C.
They were discussing the legality of what they had done.
Bob indicated that it was a public building and that they
had not unlocked the door or entered. He had only turned
the key until he felt the tumbler engage and then returned
the tumbler to its upright position. Jack stated that he
didn't like the fact that the entry to the building was
locked and required a key for entry. Jack stated,"Some
asshole prosecutor back home is going to tell us we needed
a warrant to enter that building."

Ernie suddenly turned into Captain Ernest Naspretto.
"Absolutely not! As a New York City police officer I am
licensed and privileged, mind you, to enter the common
access area of any housing project in this city. It
doesn't matter whether some ass hole locks it or not. I
just can't go into someone's apartment, but I have an
absolute right to patrol the hallways."

Bob and Jack were impressed with the confidence of Ernie's
statement and decided that a New York City police captain's
knowledge shouldn't be questioned by cops from another
state. Even Ernie was impressed with how knowledgeable he
sounded. Of course, Bob and Jack didn't know that Ernie
was guessing on the subject, although it was an "educated
guess."

Ernie thought he would change the subject and asked, "Okay
guys, tell me what you, two hero's, would have done if some
irate Chinese guy came out of one of those doors as you
were inserting the key."

Without hesitation Jack immediately said, "I would have
told him you were the building inspector and we where your
assistants and that we were attempting to ascertain if the
locking system within the Public Housing Complex was up to
code."

"See, Ernie, an excellent and experienced investigator,
such as my partner, Jack, is ready for any situation that
may arise", said Bob in a mocking tone.

Ernie glanced at Jack and stated as he fumbled with the
door handle, "I'm getting out of this car. It's getting
full of shit." All three guys had a good laugh.

Bob grabbed the portable radio and called Joe Piraino,"MC-1
from MC-5, be advised the key works." Piraino immediately
responded, "I read. I'm at your location in two minutes."
The three cops could hear the excitement in Piraino's
voice.

Moments later Joe Piraino pulled up next to them and to any

passerby on the street it appeared that from the way these
guys were acting they had just won the lottery.
Jim Rybicki had heard the transmission and asked to meet
with Martin. Martin started to walk toward Rybicki's
vehicle which was parked near the lottery location,
Brother's Grocery store. Jack hollered to Martin, "Hey,
Bobby, they're going to give you shit about trying the
key."

"So what," snickered Martin as he walked down the street.
Martin approached the vehicle and Rybicki unlocked the back
door. Gene Taylor was sitting in the front passenger seat
and Rybicki was behind the wheel. Martin could see that
Rybicki was on the telephone. Taylor whispered that
Rybicki was talking to the AP, the assistant prosecutor in
Cape May County. Rybicki stated,"Bob, they are looking
into the legality of entering a housing complex without a
warrant."

"Tell them, it is allowable as per the direction of Captain
Ernie Naspretto, NYPD." Martin figured that would go over
like a lead balloon. Rybicki didn't want to advise the AP
of that information and had placed his hand over the phone.
Rybicki looked at Bob and stated, "Listen, they are
expressing their concerns. The Chief, the Prosecutor and
the AP are thinking about what we should do." Martin
looked at Rybicki and stated, "Jim, we have been in and out
of the building and the key fits and turns the lock."
Taylor snickered and broke a grin. A small grin, for his
ever so constant stoic face. Rybicki handed the phone to
Martin and said, "You tell em'."

Martin put the phone to his ear and asked, "This is Martin,
who am I talking to?"

"This is the Pros. You are on speaker phone and the Chief
and the AP are here."

Martin heard the Prosecutor's voice and knew he was
referring to the assistant prosecutor and Chief of
Detectives being in the room. "What's up?" asked Martin.

The Prosecutor answered, "Bob, we are discussing the
feasibility of entering the housing complex and checking
out the possible location of the perpetrator you guys have
come up with."

"Well, pros, you're a little late," stated Martin. There
was silence for a moment. Martin continued, "It is legal
for NYPD to enter these public housing complexes, not to
mention the fact that the key fits and will unlock the
door." Rybicki looked at Taylor and whispered, "They don't
have to worry about getting information about their search

warrant affidavit anymore." Taylor didn't respond.

Martin didn't give anyone a chance to respond and stated, "We are set up on the store and the building where this shithead lives. We will be taping the entrance to the building and the store. Somebody ought to be working on the affidavit for a search warrant to the apartment, not be worrying about whether or not we have a right to be in the building. We have overcome that obstacle already."

There was no response from the other end. The Prosecutor finally stated, "Let me talk to Jim, please." Martin handed the phone back to Rybicki. Jim didn't get a chance to say a word. In moments he hung up. "Well, Bob, you pissed them off. They are still talking about how what you did may be illegal." Martin laughed and stated, "We could do it their way and not know anything or our way and now know we got something positive. There is no one more intent on getting this bastard and doing it right. What we did is legal and will be reflected the same way in my report. So screw them."

Rybicki asked, "Did you enter the apartment?"

"Jim, if I did I certainly wouldn't tell anyone. However, to answer your question, no. I turned the key until I felt the tumbler engage, then I turned it back and we left," answered Martin. "I also tried the key in other doors on the same floor. There were people in the apartment. I could hear them talking," he added.

"In the suspect's apartment?" asked Rybicki.

"Yeah, his too," said Martin, with a grin.

"Well, you got the prosecutor thinking. They instructed that you and I should be working on a search warrant for the apartment," Rybicki said.

"Geez, it's good to see they are planning ahead," laughed Martin.

"You know, Bob, you aren't making any lasting friends with the prosecutors."

"Hey, Jim, I probably won't be able to sleep tonight." Martin said it in his most sarcastic tone. Taylor snickered and Rybicki joined in the laugh.

"Jim, when is the van from Cape May getting here?" asked Martin. Almost immediately the driver of the van was on the radio asking for a surveillance location. Rybicki directed him to the building as Martin was exiting the car and walking back to suspect's building.

Rybicki opened the window, "Keep in touch, will ya?"
Martin thought to himself that Rybicki was starting to come
around and waved a gesture of compliance as he left.

Martin made his way to the vehicle down the street. He
entered the back seat to the smoke of Trombetta's ever
burning cigarette. Ernie immediately asked, "What did they
have to say?" Martin stated, "The County Pros isn't happy
with our actions." Jack immediately knew who Bob was
referring to and stated, "Screw them ass holes. They
probably wanted a warrant before we entered the building,
right?"

"You got it, Jackie," said Martin. Ernie had a look of
disgust on his face and asked, "Whose side are those ass
holes on? Did they think we would screw up an
investigation like this one? Listen, everything we did is
ethical, moral and legally correct."

"Go, Ernie," said Jack in a mocking tone. Ernie grabbed
for the telephone and declared, "I'll prove it to you right
now."

Ernie had the phone to his ear and heard, "Law Department,
Sergeant Galbo."

"Hey, Paul, what's up? I know you're not busy," Ernie
loved to make fun of anyone working at the police academy.
Sgt. Paul Galbo and Ernie were friends long before they
were cops. They met at St. John's University eighteen
years earlier. Ernie was godfather to Paul's first son,
Joseph.

"Is Ray there? I gotta ask him something. I would ask but
you're more stupid than me. Put him on."

Ray was Lieutenant Ray DuFresne who had been assigned to
the Law Department at the academy for the past fourteen
years. He was Police Officer DuFresne when he taught
Ernie's company thirteen years earlier.

Ernie explained the fact pattern and ended it with, "Am I,
licensed and privileged to be in that hallway?" Lt.
DuFresne answered with a simple, "Yes, you are." Thank God,
Ernie thought.

Joe Piraino pulled up with Tom Nerney in their unmarked.
Jack and Ernie were joking about how they would have
explained the situation to Joe if while Bob was opening the
door the perp tried to run out of the premises and was
inadvertently shot and killed. "Oh, hi, Joe. Listen while

you guys were getting set up we blew the piece of shit away. His dead body is on the floor of apartment 2C. Do you know a nice place in Little Italy? We thought we would have pasta and clams, some vino and a little anisette to celebrate the shithead's demise." Bob thought it's a good thing these two wackos don't work on the same force.

Bob couldn't help but think that the County Pros shouldn't be worried about the letter of the law at this point. They should be worried about whether or not these guys were going to bring the perpetrator back dead or alive. Jack and Ernie knew what they wanted to do.

Ernie heard Bob telling Tom Nerney that the key fit. Ernie looked at Tom and thought he had turned into a robot. His computer like mind started racing as he formulated a strategy to find out anything and everything about the apartment and its occupants. Ernie noticed the looks on the faces of the cops in the two vehicles. It was not a good time to be the killer of Patrolman David C. Douglass.

A white van pulled up in front of both cars. It seemed as though it was trying to find a good place to park. Jack immediately noticed it was the Jersey surveillance van. Jack asked to no one in particular, "What the hell is he doing?" He is supposed to be taping the project entrance. Why is he parking there? He should be directly in front of the place."
Ernie added, "He's double parked and a little conspicuous." Martin observed that the driver was an investigator from the County named Cramer. Martin exited the vehicle and approached the van. Cramer wound down the window as he recognized Martin approaching. "Cramer, you don't want to park here. Go across the street directly in front of that complex and tape everything that goes into and comes out of the building."

Cramer responded, "Captain Rybicki said to park right here."
"He hasn't been down here to see the best location. Move over there," instructed Martin, pointing in the direction of the building. "I'll clear it with your Captain."
Martin got back into the vehicle and saw Trombetta was on the portable radio.
"Jim, we moved your guy to a better location." Cramer had exited his van and was approaching the car as Jack was on the radio.

"Park over there," said Jack, in a sarcastic tone.

"Hey, Jack, don't be mean to him," laughed Martin.

"I don't believe he was going to park over here. He

couldn't see shit where he was parking," Ernie added.

"You see, Ern, these guys figured they received an order and they better comply. The Prosecutor's office gives orders and the guys are afraid to use their own minds to get things done. That's why they don't like me and Martin," added Trombetta.

Throughout the surveillance Ernie was constantly taking the binoculars, leaving the vehicle and attempting to view the apartment to see the perpetrator. At one point Ernie had thought he saw a Chinese man possibly in his late forties or early fifties reading the paper. Ernie would indiscreetly attempt to walk around the courtyard peering into peoples' windows with binoculars.

Martin and Trombetta remained in the car making comments about Ernie and his super snooper endeavors. Ernie was standing behind a row of bushes adjacent to the building and was peering through the binoculars.

Jack laughed and suggested to Martin, "If this wasn't such an important case I would call the local precinct. I'd tell them that there is a short little Italian guy with a mustache that has been peeping in the windows trying to check out woman getting dressed or showered. I would love to see some uniform guy show up and snatch his ass from behind those bushes."

Martin and Trombetta laughed at the thought. Trombetta added, "I wish he would get over this James Bond stuff and go get me something to eat." Moments later Ernie returned and went on a candy and cigarette run for Trombetta. Ernie would much rather walk around the neighborhood than sit in a car.

Eventually Jack had to exit the vehicle to go to the bathroom. He figured it was also a good time to take a walk around the housing complex. Ernie was thinking he never had heard Martin talk about his past. Everybody had a history, Ernie wondered about Martin's. "Hey, Bob, what did you do before you became a cop?" Martin hesitated for a minute and then stated, "Well I worked in a chemical factory, a chrome plating factory, I was an electricians helper, a bartender, an insurance salesman, worked in a wholesale warehouse, played drums in a band, was a mason's helper for my Dad, worked as a roofer, was a title searcher for a title company and worked at the Post Office as a full time mail carrier. In my spare time I went to college and was a male slut. I drank a lot, screwed around a lot and then stopped drinking for eight years. I ruined the lives of two nice girls and their families. I became a cop, met Trombetta. He told me about Christianity. I accepted

Christ as my savior and here I am Bob Martin, Mr.
Wonderful. Somewhere I started drinking again but because
of my beliefs and the fact I have, a wonderful women for a
wife, I managed not to return to my days of male sluthood.
I'm sure the Lord is not too happy with my actions as of
late but I will come around I'm sure."

Ernie wished he hadn't asked. That had been the fastest
and most informative life history Ernie had ever heard.
Not to mention it provided a lot of information. Ernie got
the idea that Martin wasn't going to provide any details,
not that he wanted to hear them.

Jack re-entered the car and immediately started talking
about how positive he was they were sitting on the right
place. Ernie stated, "Great, terd, why didn't you bring us
something to eat?" Jack didn't hesitate, "Bob forgot to
give me money."

The surveillance of the locations continued until 9pm. The
Jersey van returned to Cape May County and the TARU van
stayed on the building complex until it appeared that
activity had ceased for the evening. It had been decided
that the TARU van would set up on the Housing complex and
monitor the location throughout the next day. Everyone was
hoping that they would see some male fitting the
description entering or leaving the building. Martin and
Trombetta were positive he would look exactly like the
composite that had been prepared by Sgt. Trowbridge more
than a month before.

Everyone left and returned to Major Case at Police Plaza.
It was decided that the guys deserved a sandwich and a
couple beers. They decided to go to the Metropolitan. It
was a nice bar and restaurant that was in walking distance
of Police Plaza and was a favorite watering hole of the
local cops. It had become a favorite watering hole of the
Jersey guys also. It was owned by two retired NYPD guys.
It was a nice atmosphere and no one bothered you. If they
did they were somehow involved with police work so you
didn't mind.

Bob, Jack and Ernie got there first and were saving some
seats at the bar. Ernie immediately recognized a guy from
the job that had been a hard working cop who had been
involved in a major shoot out with some mutts and had taken
it pretty hard. His wife had divorced him because he
wouldn't seek help. He turned to the bottle and it was
easy to see that he was pretty shitfaced.

The off-duty, drunken cop immediately bought a round of
drinks for the three after he was introduced and advised
why the guys from Jersey were in New York. The other guys

from Major Case started coming in and before long there
were about ten guys in the bar who had earlier been sitting
on the surveillance. They were all unwinding and listening
to Ernie stories. Bob was now positive that Ernie just
made these stories up as he went along.

Martin thought to himself that this guy should work with
Joseph Wambaugh and write cop books. So what if they
weren't true? No one would know it. Ernie sure had a way
with spinning cop tales. Bob was finding it interesting
trying to figure out when Ernie was telling a true story.
It was a real challenge.

The time went quickly as all of the guys took their turn
relating what had taken place during the surveillance.
They all had something to eat and at about midnight they
were all on their way home to get some sleep. Little did
they know but the next few days were going to be very
hectic.

Bob, Jack and Ernie walked across the street to the
unmarked police car. As usual Ernie entered the driver's
side of the vehicle and took over the driving duties.
During the trip to Ernie's home the talk centered on the
events of the day. Everyone was pretty happy about the
fact that it appeared they had a good suspect. The
conversation was upbeat as was the general feelings and
demeanor of the three cops. Ernie was talking about what a
great job he had done during the surveillance. Bob and
Jack continually belittled, berated and chastised Ernie for
every little thing they could recall.

"Hey, Bob, did you see the way Ernie was hiding in the
bushes. He was acting like a rapist or pedophile or
something. Ernie, you're my hero," said Jack. Bob laughed
and before he could reply Ernie quickly shot back. "Jack,
get off my back, ya terd. So, okay, I got a little
excited. I'll admit. At least I got my fat ass out of the
car and looked around. Even Bob got out of the car. You
sat there like a prima donna waiting for someone to bring
you cigarettes, food, sweets and something to drink. Jack,
I decided you can't do anything for yourself. As a matter
of fact did you even go to the bathroom today? What's the
matter, your wife's not here to help you?"

Jack was grinning and Bob was laughing heartily. Ernie
added, "You know what, Jack? I heard Bob talk about how
you always had someone stop at the store to pick up things
for you to eat and drink. I remember how you were at the
FBI Academy. You even had guys pour your beer for ya. If
someone didn't get you stuff you would starve to death.
You're so lazy. You're a disgrace to the Italian culture.
You shouldn't be a cop. You should have been a Godfather

and had people kiss your ring and do things to please you.
Who wipes your ass?"

Bob was laughing and said to Jack, "Hey, Jackie, do your
Don Corleone impression." Quickly Jack stuffed two napkins
left over from an earlier treat into his cheeks. In his
best Don voice he said, "My son, Ernie, after you do my
bidding you can kiss my ring. Then you can kiss my ass."

Jack did a decent Marlon Brando. Everyone had a good laugh
and they continued to talk about what was going to take
place the following morning. Jack and Bob knew it would be
a long day. It had already been decided that they had to
get a photo line up prepared containing the suspect. Tom
Nerney had indicated he wanted to take part in the process
and would travel back to Jersey with the guys when they
displayed the photo line-up to some of the witnesses. They
knew a lot had to be done. First of all they had to get
some photographs of their suspect.

Tom Nerney had a sleepless night deciding on how to get
some photos of the suspect. Bob was excited at the
prospect of having a suspect. Since Liu had been
eliminated Bob was hoping for a new lead. He now had one.
It was difficult for him to get a good rest. Jack was also
rolling around on the sofa bed in the Naspretto living
room. He was excited by the prospect of a new suspect and
he could tell that Bob seemed to be pretty up on this guy.
They had to find some pictures of this guy on file
somewhere. Jack also worried about whether or not he would
be required to actually write a report about the photo
array. Suppose for some reason Bob was involved in
something else relating to the case? Would that mean that
Jack would actually have to do something? Bob and Ernie
are right, Jack thought to himself, I really am a lazy
bastard.

Ernie woke in the morning to find Jack and Bob sitting at
his dining room table talking to Grace and feeding
Angelina. "Don't you guys look like the epitome of
fatherhood?" said Ernie as he game down the steps. "I
guess Bob helped Grace cook breakfast and you watched.
Right, Jack?"

Jack smirked and said, "Why don't you go to work?"

Grace immediately responded for Ernie, "He has some things
to do this morning with me and then he works tonight."

"Yeah, I got some stuff to do and then I work a four to
twelve," Ernie advised. "Remember, Tom Nerney is coming
here to pick you up this morning. Hey, Grace, that reminds
me I told Tom to stop here early and get some breakfast."

413

Immediately Grace got up from feeding duties with Angelina and started to prepare more pancakes. Moments later there was a knock on the door and Ernie greeted Tom and showed him into the dining room.

Tom greeted everyone, made a fuss over the baby and immediately began to talk about setting up an appointment with two agents from INS in an attempt to obtain information on the suspect, Hop Chung. Tom indicated that they were to meet the agents at 9 am.

It was March 31st. The time was 7:45 am. Tom ate breakfast and the conversation was about preparing a Photo line-up containing Chung's picture. By 8:15 am. the investigators were on their way to the INS headquarters to meet with the two agents. The three were talking about how nice it was of Ernie and Grace to allow them to utilize their home as a motel and a restaurant.

Tom Nerney mentioned that he was sure Ernie would find a way to show up at Major Case sometime in the evening. Bob and Jack agreed. They knew Ernie would make sure he would be present when the shit started hitting the fan.

The guys met up with Agents Siu and Ceballos and they all fit themselves into the unmarked Chevy Caprice and made their way back to Jersey to an old Army Base where all the old INS records were kept. Neither Bob nor Jack knew where they were and didn't really care. They just hoped that they would be able to obtain a photograph of Chung.

They entered through a security gate and Tom Nerney was immediately recognized by the security guard. Tom indicated that he knew the guy from the job. The gate attendant was a retired New York cop. Tom made some small talk with the guy and was directed to a building located near the dock area. The car was parked and the Agents advised the investigators to follow them into the records storage building.

Both Agents upon entry into the building advised the lady at the desk as to everyone's identity and then explained what they were attempting to locate the INS file for Hop Chung. The clerk became very professional and matter of fact and advised that they would have to speak with security personnel to obtain clearance to review the items if they could be located. She immediately called and a guy who looked like a retired hard nosed cop exited an office and approached the men.

The guy looked at the five men and immediately recognized Tom Nerney. He walked right passed the INS Agents and

extended his hand to Tom Nerney. Once again Nerney knew
another person working at the facility. Tom introduced the
guy as a retired cop from New York whom he hadn't seen in
about five years. They were having a small reunion as the
INS Agents seemed to be getting a little upset with being
ignored.

Eventually Tom Nerney explained what the Agents were
looking for and the retired cop went into a long
dissertation on how important it was that the files could
only be reviewed and excerpts could be jotted down but
copies could not be made and taken from the building.
Martin and Trombetta seemed upset with the statement. Tom
had a sneaky smile on his face as the Agents went back to
the female clerk. Bob, looked at Tom and said, "You look
like you just swallowed the mouse, Tom."

Nerney immediately replied, "My buddy is just putting on a
show for the Agents. He will give us whatever we need. He
just has to make sure that the Agents think he is doing
everything by the numbers."

Bob and Jack watched as the Agents seemed to be spending an
awful lot of time with the clerk. Eventually she exited
the storage area and handed the Agents a manilla file. She
then stated, "Be advised you cannot copy or duplicate any
of this information and you cannot leave the building with
the file." Agent Ceballos advised that he was aware of the
rules and regulations and he also knew that he could sign
for some of the paperwork and take it with him if need be.

The guys all sat down at a table and began to review the
paperwork. Tom Nerney didn't spend a lot of time with the
file. He knew that he would be able to have a copy of the
file thanks to his buddy. Cops often make allowances for
cops they have respect for and know they can trust. What
the hell, the guys from Jersey and New York were looking
for a cop killer. Allowances would always be made under
such circumstances. The information in the paperwork
indicated that Hop Chung was naturalized in 1974 and that
he was a Chef at a Chinese Restaurant. It provided a lot
of useful information with regard to the background of the
suspected killer. As the Agent thumbed through the
paperwork an envelope was located and it was marked
"photo."

Tom Nerney immediately grabbed the envelope and removed the
photograph of Hop Chung. The picture was twenty years old
and as soon as Tom placed it on the table Bob and Jack's
eyes lit up. They looked at each other as Tom Nerney
pulled from his inside suit coat pocket the composite of
Dave's suspected killer. Bob smiled and said, "Jackie,
that sure looks like our boy."

Jack responded, "We got him. Don't we?" Tom compared the photo to the composite and said, "The major difference is the hair length, other than that this photo looks like a young version of your composite. We are going to have to come up with a more recent photo of Mr. Hop Chung."

The guys packed up and headed back to the Big Apple. Tom knew that his buddy at the INS record storage area would come through with a copy of the entire file. The INS guys had extracted enough information for the time being and they did supply a copy of the photo for identification purposes.

Tom took the Agents back to their office and, the three investigators, returned to Major Case at One Police Plaza. They were all excited about the suspect and figured they were on the right track. They just hoped that Hop Chung had aged gracefully. They hoped they could locate a recent photograph that would match the composite as well as the INS photo of twenty years ago.

When the three entered the office area of Major Case they were met by Jim Rybicki, Gene Taylor and Joe Piraino. They were talking about the events of the day when Lt. Pollini entered and asked for an update. Captain George Duke entered just as everyone began to run down the events of the morning.

A lot had been accomplished by all involved in the investigation. Rybicki and Taylor were working on affidavit information for a search warrant. Gene had provided a run down on all the evidentiary information he thought would be needed to justify his aspect of the warrant. Rybicki advised Martin that he had to sit down with him and pick his brain to obtain background information for the affidavit with regard to the history of the case.

Martin had forgotten that it was up to him to assist Jim Rybicki. Jim McGowan who would have handled that part of the workload had to fulfill obligations in Florida with his family and was not in New York during this phase of the investigation. Jack Reemer who had hoped to travel to New York for the investigation found himself in Federal Court providing testimony.

Tom Nerney provided his bosses information into the venture to the INS record storage area. As he was speaking a package arrived for him. It was from his buddy at the facility. The package contained the life and times of Hop Chung. The entire INS file was now at their disposal. Nerney also indicated that he directed other detectives to

contact Interpol for information on Hop Chung to include
credit card use and any business dealings. All public
agencies within New York were presently reviewing their
files for information on the suspect. The computer whizzes
at NYPD were busy coming up with everything possible on Hop
Chung. The wheels were turning and everything was looking
positive.

Martin and Trombetta just wanted to be perfectly sure that
they were on the right track. They felt good about this
suspect but they needed to be sure they were hot on the
trail of Dave's killer. They wanted a positive
identification.

Joe Pollini indicated that he wanted a driver's abstract of
Chung from the Department of Motor Vehicles. Tom Nerney
indicated that it was presently being done. Pollini knew,
that if the suspect had a driver's license or New York Sate
ID card they would have a record in Albany, New York.

Everyone provided an update as to their various assignments
with regard to the case. Bob and Jack hadn't realized that
Ernie had entered the rear of the office and had sat in on
the impromptu meeting. They assumed he must have assigned
himself to Major Case. They knew Ernie was not going to
miss out on this phase of the investigation.

Jack looked at his watch and realized Ernie must have left
his precinct and traveled directly to Major Case. The time
was three p.m. Someone sent out for pizza and sandwiches.
Everyone continued with their investigative endeavors and
continued to exchange ideas. Jack embarrassed Jim Rybicki
into picking up the tab for the food and beverage. What the
hell, the County of Cape May had the money. Trombetta and
one of the New York guys went to pick up the food.

Lt. Pollini exited his office. "Listen up. Who wants to
go to Albany? They have a picture of our boy but they
won't fax it. Someone has to personally pick it up."

Tom Nerney stated, "We won't be able to get it until
tomorrow morning. We need it tonight. That's a long
ride."
Before he finished the sentence Joe Pollini was on the
phone. In minutes the authorization to utilize an NYPD
helicopter had been received and it had been decided that
one of the Jersey guys should go along to maintain the
continuity of the picture as evidence in the case.

It was quickly decided that Taylor, Rybicki or Martin could
not go. They were needed in New York City. Ernie
Naspretto said, "Hey, what about Jack? He'll go." Martin
laughed and replied, "Hey, Jack isn't much on flying."

Lt. Pollini stated, "Well, he'll have to get use to it. He's our only choice."

Pollini returned to his office and advised that when Trombetta returned from the mens room and finished eating they had to get him to a helicopter pick up sight as fast as possible. Martin followed Pollini into his office and stated, "Lieutenant, you have to do me a favor."

"Yeah, you name it, Bob."
"Well, we have to bust on Trombetta about this helicopter stuff. Shake him up or something," stated Martin. Pollini laughed and stated, "Yeah, okay, I'll come up with something."

Moments later Trombetta walked into the office carrying a load of food. He had met the delivery boy getting off the elevator. Everyone immediately grabbed their share and started eating. Jack advised the delivery guy to give the bill to Rybicki. Rybicki was reviewing the bill and Jack stated, "Hey, Jim, give the guy a good tip. He deserves it." What the hell, it wasn't Jack's money.

Pollini came into the office and while grabbing a sandwich stated, "Hey, Jack, we need a volunteer for a helicopter ride to Albany. They have a photo of Chung." Jack nonchalantly answered, "Hey, that would be a nice trip for someone." Pollini responded, "That someone is you, Jack. You are the only one that isn't needed for getting Search Warrant affidavit info together."

Trombetta didn't respond and looked at Martin with eyes that said, "Me in a helicopter?" Bob advised, "No body else can be cut loose, Jack. I would take the trip if I could but Gene, Jim and I are stuck here." Jack didn't want to appear less than macho. He stated, "Hey, no problem I gotta go, I gotta go." He pulled out a cigarette and lit up. Jack wasn't keen on floating in the air.

Lt. Pollini then handed him a pager. Jack took it and with a confused look on his face said, "Why do I need a pager? I won't be near a phone." Pollini responded, "That's not a pager. It's a directional device. That way if the copter goes down we'll be able to locate you and the picture. That picture is important, Jack." Jack tried to crack a smile and took a long drag from his cigarette. Everyone in the room had a good laugh at his expense. Pollini told him to pick up some food and eat on the run. Jack did so and in minutes he was in a car traveling to the copter pick up point. Jack really wasn't keen on this whole helicopter thing.

418

Jack's fears quickly subsided when he realized that if he couldn't talk one of the copter guys into doing a report then he would have to do it. The fear of doing his first report of the case was scarier than the helicopter ride. Jack had to work this mess out.

Martin, Rybicki and Taylor completed their sandwiches and returned to preparing the affidavit for the search warrant. Joe Piraino had assigned Detective Henry Waite to assist. It had been decided that a New York Officer would be the affiant in the case. Rybicki was a whiz on the computer and continually revised and made important changes to the affidavit as Martin and Taylor provided more information. Jim Rybicki would eventually spend eight hours preparing the affidavit. He completed four drafts that were changed each time by either Martin or Taylor. Jim had placed himself in a corner of the room with the reports and everyone's notes placed out before him. Martin didn't envy Rybicki. He knew that the guy was going to be doing a lot of typing, editing and paperwork.

Jim looked like a worried stockbroker reviewing company spreadsheets in an attempt to decide into what firm he was going to sink all his assets. Everyone in the office had an assignment to carry out and the Major Case Squad offices seemed to be in constant movement.

Detective Christine Leung and two other Chinese detectives were preparing a Chinese language version of the Miranda warning. She had even requested the assistance of Robin Mui, the Production Manager of Chinatown's daily paper, The Sing Tao Daily.

Robin was a good reporter and always fair with his articles.
He printed the news as opposed to putting out an article that would sell papers. His ability to produce unslanted news articles would make him a friend too many cops.

Martin and Trombetta liked the way Detective Leung took charge of her job assignments. They both thought that if females were going to be cops they should take lessons from Leung.

Joe Piraino was keeping in constant communications with the TARU surveillance van that was at the Housing Complex. They had taped everyone entering and exiting the building since the previous night. Joe was hoping that they would have some news about a subject that fit the composite of Dave's killer. They had completed about four tapes at their assignment but didn't feel they had spotted the suspected perp.

The office was a hub of activity. Everyone was busy and
they all continually provided Martin or Piraino with
updates of their activities. Bob and Joe would then
coordinate the findings into investigative assignments.
The concept of teamwork was showing itself regularly in the
investigation. The present was no exception.

Tom Nerney was continually on the phone speaking to his
many contacts. He was preparing a background report on Hop
Chung.
He had four detectives from Major Case and Missing persons
doing a lot of leg work and they were constantly checking
in and providing information.

Ernie Naspretto was amazed at how everything seemed to gel
with regard to all that was taking place. Ernie was seeing
real detectives doing real detective work. He made every
effort to observe and pay attention to all that was taking
place around him. Ernie figured that some day he might be
able to utilize some of this detective stuff.

Ernie couldn't believe how the guys even took the setbacks
in stride. When it was ascertained that DMV had the photo
of Chung everyone was overjoyed. They then found out they
needed a court order to obtain it. Sure the guys bitched a
little but immediately an investigator was assigned to get
the order. It was done and faxed to DMV in short order.

Ernie was mesmerized by the way everyone seemed to be
taking part in constructive and worthwhile investigative
work. Each man had a job. As the detectives completed
their assignments they provided the result verbally to
Martin and or Piraino who then made sure the results were
recorded. The information was then supplied to Jim Rybicki
to be reviewed and if deemed necessary to be included in
the affidavit for the search warrant.

Ernie couldn't believe that these guys even had the names
of all the individuals that lived in the apartment that was
registered in Chung's name. The investigators were even
conducting background checks on all the family members.
Ernie's old friend Detective Greg White was providing a
virtual life story of the Chung family. Ernie could easily
see why Greg and his counterparts were assigned to the
elite Major Case squad. Ernie was thinking how proud he
was to be working with this team of investigators. These
guys were good and they knew what they were doing. It
seemed that they were always completing one investigative
assignment and being assigned another. No one complained
and everyone completed their tasks in record time. Ernie
was thinking that his involvement in this case was a once
in a lifetime occurrence.

Ernie was impressed how the Jersey guys just seemed to fit in with the members of NYPD. His old friend Jack and his new friend Bob knew what they were doing and did it well. If Rybicki and Taylor exemplified the other members of the Cape May County Prosecutors office they no doubt had an impressive investigative section. Even Interpol was providing information on Chung. It seemed that every investigator had contacts in every agency imaginable and that they utilized these contacts to 'get the goods' on Chung. Yes, indeed, Ernie was definitely proud of NYPD and his Jersey buddies. Ernie could now feel the intensity of the chase and he knew that the elation of the catch was getting closer. This was an aspect of police work that he simply wasn't used to.

Jack Trombetta was sitting in the helicopter wearing a set of headphones acting like he was comfortable. Jack was thinking a lot about what kept the birds in the air. The pilots were talking to each other. Jack was talking to God with regard to the abilities of the pilots and the worthiness of the craft.
He was happy with the fact that the pilot and co-pilot were Italian. He felt a certain kinship to the guys and figured that even if they didn't like him personally they wouldn't let anything happen to him. They had Italian mothers also and they knew the wrath that an irate Italian mom could produce if her son was hurt in any way.

The trip to Albany took about two hours. A representative of the Division of Motor Vehicles met the copter and provided Jack with the photograph. Jack quickly opened the envelope and thought he was going to be sick to his stomach. The photograph was taken in 1990 and the person depicted was sporting a shaved head. Jack could see that the features were similar but he was sure no one would pick him out in a line up. Jack immediately found a telephone and called Martin at Major Case.

"Bob, we got a problem."

"What's up, Jack?"

"This picture is worthless. The one we got from INS is much better, even though Chung had long hair. In this one his head is completely shaved. I say we should go with the one from INS. Martin immediately advised Tom Nerney and without hesitation he contacted the photo section of NYPD and got the ball rolling for a photo line-up based on the INS photograph of Chung. Nerney also knew that the hair depicted in the older photograph did not match the composite but the facial features were on the money.

Initially everyone was disheartened with the news but

slowly they returned to getting passed another set back and moving forward with the case. Bob and Jack were use to the set backs. Jack unhappily hopped into the helicopter for the return trip. Bob went back to working on the Search Warrant with Rybicki.

Bob, Jim and Gene continually revised the affidavit each time new information came in. All the investigators were either on the phone, at a computer or on the street running down leads and doing leg work that they hoped would lead them to Dave's killer.

Tom Nerney seemed to have made the telephone a permanent part of his head. He continually requested and obtained information and channeled it to Martin and Piraino. Nerney gazed at a picture of Dave Douglass that was on his desk. Tom had requested the photo the second time Martin had visited Major Case. Tom knew with Dave's picture staring at him he would always be focused on the job at hand. CATCH A COP KILLER.

Jack was thinking about the fact that the trip back to the city was going much faster that the trip to Albany. The pilot advised Jack that they had a strong tail wind and it actually cut the flying time. Jack could see the lights strung out on the bridges around New York City. They were a shade of blue that made them stand out from all the other lights in and around the city. Jack noticed that the pilot and co-pilot were both looking at him and talking. They didn't seem to be watching where they were going.

Jack didn't want it to look like he was worried but he did notice that they seemed to be traveling directly into the string of lights that illuminated the Brooklyn bridge. Jack didn't want the morning headlines to read "Police Goombas tangled up in Brooklyn Bridge." Jack stated as nonchalantly as possible as the helicopter crew made eye contact with him, "Hey, those lights seem to be getting awful close." The pilot responded, "Yeah, sometime we go under the bridge, sometime over and sometime between the bridge and the lights." Jack closed his eyes as they approached. He didn't care how they handled the bridge. He just knew that he didn't want to see it. They landed quickly and Jack was picked up by a detective and returned to One Police Plaza.

Jack entered the office at a little after nine in the evening. It was quite evident that everyone had been busy. Jack could see all the paperwork set out on the desks. Jack for the first time thought to himself that he was glad he went to Albany. Granted he had to do a report but it would be a short one. He knew that the guys in the office would all no doubt be producing volumes of official police reports. Jack formulated his report in his mind. "On such and such a day at such and such time I accompanied, Oh, shit, I didn't get the names of the pilots, no big deal. I accompanied two Italian guys to Albany. We landed I picked up a picture from some guy and we came back to New York. End of report. Jack thought to himself he would make sure Bob reviewed it and made any necessary changes. This report writing wasn't so bad after all. A piece of cake.

The clock was approaching eleven p.m. It had been decided that Martin, Trombetta and Nerney would travel to Lower Township in the morning to show the photo array to the witnesses. Tom would pick the guys up at seven am at the Nasprettos and they would be on their way.

Ernie intended to work his day tour and then meet up with the guys in the late afternoon. It had been decided that if anything happened they would call Ernie and he would find a way to get himself assigned to Major Case.

Detective Henry Waite had been assigned to assist Rybicki and Taylor as they updated the Search Warrant affidavit. They knew information would be coming in all day, from various investigators and agencies. They wanted to make sure nothing was left out. Jim Rybicki was constantly reviewing all the facts and utilizing those that he felt would provide a judge with the best case scenario possible. Piraino and Martin would receive the information. Martin would provide it to Rybicki and he would make an intelligible, chronological account of the case. When Jim completed a page on the computer screen he and Martin would then review it, make changes and Jim would go on with the next page.

Joe Piraino continually coordinated all activities in New York and handled all work assignments. He and Martin were constantly having three or four minute conversations and then they would move on to another step in the investigation.

Trombetta and Martin seemed to have a working relationship that didn't require a lot of conversation. These guys had been together as a team for so long that they seemed to read each other's minds. Everyone kidded Jack about not doing reports but it was evident that he always was aware of what was going on and Martin would confer with him regularly. They would just make eye contact and it seemed that information was transferred. Certainly they could make it without each other, but they knew that as a team the investigative process seemed to flow, no matter what the obstacle. Some cases just took longer than others.

A positive feeling was in the air. Something told the

investigators that the case was getting down to the wire.
They only needed a positive identification to make them all
feel at ease with the suspect. Sure they had gut feelings
but judges wouldn't sign warrants based on gut feelings.
Captain Duke and Lt. Pollini constantly reviewed the work
of all the investigators. They were happy to see that not
only their own investigators but the guys from Jersey were
all "top notch." It wasn't often that they found a problem
with the investigative procedures that were being utilized.
They seemed to be on top of everything and everyone.

It was decided that everyone should get some rest and
return in the morning for what they hoped would be the last
step leading to the arrest of Dave Douglass' killer. The
majority of the guys went to the Metropolitan for a late
sandwich and a couple beers. They talked about the case
and were putting all their hopes into the photo array.
They knew someone would ID Hop Chung.

Lt. Pollini went along with the guys and figured he would
lighten up the conversation by picking on Trombetta with
regard to his helicopter flight.

They kidded Jack about his helicopter ride and pending
report. Ernie asked if Jack would be able to spell his
name or did Bob do that for him. Jack took a lot of heat
while the guys were sitting around the table washing down
the sandwiches with the well deserved cold beers.

Bob laughed when everyone busted on Jack. Ernie
caustically said, "It's obvious they sent you to Albany
cause' you're so dispensable and basically worthless."
Some of the New York guys had to be reminded that Jack and
Ernie were actually friends.

Bob knew, however, that without Jack aiding in the
investigation things would not have moved along as they
did. Martin was glad that he and Trombetta worked best
when they worked together. Each of them always talked
about being partners in some type of business upon
retirement. They had been a successful investigative team.
They would no doubt be a successful business team, after
all, they were the "HONEYMOONERS."

Ernie continually mentioned the fact that his ability to
coordinate case investigations was the stepping stone to
the culmination of the case. Gene Taylor just kept his
stoic face even when everyone else was spitting out their
beer from laughter. Ernie thought about breaking Gene's
balls but thought better of it. Maybe this guy was the
strong silent type who hated all living things. Ernie
didn't want to find out. Ernie thought about Simon Kok and
the fact that he referred to Gene as Sergeant Slaughter.

Ernie decided he wanted to be on Gene's side when he kicked Kok's ass for mocking him. Gene just had a way with looking miserable even when he was having fun. No one was able to tell the difference. This guy didn't seem to have emotional highs and lows. He just seemed to look right through everyone and everything.

Jim Rybicki took a lot of heat about paying for the bill and he attempted to make a last ditch effort to get Trombetta to pull some money from his pocket. Needless to say Jim failed. Everyone threw in a few bucks for the bill and tip, everyone except Jack. Not only did he not reach into his pocket. He talked Jim Rybicki into buying him a pack of cigarettes. Jack loved it when a plan came together.

It was a little after midnight when it was decided that they should call it a night and get some sleep.

Everyone quickly departed. Taylor and Rybicki were staying at a motel nearby. Martin and Trombetta were once again staying at the Naspretto home. The rest of the guys went home.

Martin, Trombetta and Ernie traveled to Glendale to Ernie's home. They conversed about all that had taken place and the conversation was generally upbeat. Ernie asked if there would be problems if the witnesses couldn't identify the suspect from the photo array. Jack indicated to Ernie that there would be other alternatives to identifying the suspect if the witnesses didn't come through. They had to be able to show that Chung was linked to the restaurant, the burglaries, and to Dave's murder. A positive ID would just make things easier for the investigators. Bob was silent as Jack talked. Bob didn't think he would get the positive ID.

The next morning found everyone awake bright and early in the Naspretto home. Grace was given an update by Ernie and Angelina watched Barney the dinosaur.

Bob and Jack had packed all their things and figured that no matter what happened during the day that they would return home that evening. Jack made a remark about the fact that it was April 1st. April Fools Day. The guys all hoped that they were not fooled by anyone on this day. It also happened to be Good Friday and Jack's twentieth anniversary on the job.

Tom Nerney left his vehicle at Ernie's and drove the Jersey unmarked vehicle while Jack sat in the front passenger side and smoked cigarettes and changed the radio channels. Bob sat in the back reviewing a bunch of reports. He was

attempting to extract information providing the phone
numbers and addresses of the witnesses. It was their
intent to contact the people and then schedule a meeting so
they didn't miss anyone.
They conversed about the case during the entire trip to
Jersey and at about noon pulled into the Lower Township
Police Department parking lot. They entered the building
and immediately met with Chief Douglass and Captain Maher.
The introductions were completed and they updated the
Administrators with regard to the case.

The Lower Township Administrators treated Tom like royalty.
Tom continually tried to minimize what he and NYPD had
done. Tom advised the Chief and Captain that Martin and
Trombetta were the reason the case was coming to closure.
Tom indicated that the two man team was relentless,
experienced investigators that didn't allow anyone or
anything to distract or deter them from finding a cop
killer and bringing him to justice. Bob and Jack were
embarrassed by Tom's statement but they were also
flattered. They knew that this NYPD investigator had been
around and for him to bestow these accolades upon them was
an honor.

Lunch was provided and as they ate Martin contacted the
various witnesses and set up appointments to meet with
them.
The three investigators had some time to kill before they
could meet with the witnesses. Tom was given a quick tour
of Lower Township and Cape May. Tom Nerney indicated that
he would like to visit the area under different
circumstances. Bob and Jack felt the same way about New
York City.

It was three in the afternoon when they went to meet with
the owner and two of the English speaking workers at the
resturant. During the short trip to the restaurant Tom
Nerney indicated to Trombetta and Martin that he didn't
think the restaurant personnel would be helpful. Tom felt
that even if they could make the identification they would
probably be reluctant to do it. If anyone, the bus driver
would be able to provide the best results with regard to
the identification of the photo line-up.

Tom explained that he didn't want Martin and Trombetta to
feel as though he was trying to take over the case with
regard to the photo line-up procedure. Tom indicated that
he wanted to hear first hand the description of Dave's
killer directly from the person who actually saw the
perpetrator. Tom knew from many years of experience that
he wanted to see the perpetrator through the eyes and
recollection of the best eye witness.

Tom knew that once he heard the bus driver's explanation of his account and heard him provide a description he would be able to pick Dave's killer out of a large crowd. Nerney knew what worked best for him so Martin and Trombetta complied.

The Jersey guys had never felt that anyone from NYPD ever tried to take over the case. It had been an investigative partnership from the beginning. Bob and Jack certainly were not worried about any such thing. They just wanted to catch Dave's killer. What Tom Nerney said made sense to them. They each had a picture of Dave's killer in their mind. They formed that picture from all the information they had received. Tom Nerney only wanted the same investigative information. He would in turn utilize that information to etch a picture of the killer into his mind's eye.

Tom knew that when he entered Chung's residence he would know upon seeing Chung's face if this was the killer of Officer Dave Douglass.

Martin and Trombetta also knew that the witnesses would be a bit more intimidated and possibly more cooperative due to the fact that Tom was from NYPD. It was decided to introduce Tom to the witnesses and he in turn would conduct the photo line-up. Martin and Trombetta intended to watch closely the reaction of the witnesses as they observed the six photographs of Chinese subjects.

A waiter was the first to review the photographs. Tom explained the procedure to the subject and opened the folder of pictures. The witness's eyes were scanning the photographs. His eyes locked on the photograph of Hop Chung and hesitated for what seemed an eternity. It was evident that he recognized the subject as a past employee. The witness then reviewed the rest of the pictures, looked at Tom Nerney and stated, "I recognize no one." Nerney said, "Thank you for your cooperation." Trombetta immediately stated, "You don't recognize anyone in those pictures." The subject shook his head in the negative. Tom immediately stated, "Would you please go get the cook." The waiter did so. Jack looked at Tom and stated, "He friggin' knows who Chung is. Who does he think he's kidding? I wanted to grab him by the throat. Bob, did you see his eyes when he noticed the picture of Chung?" "Yeah, that sucker knows who he's looking at," stated Martin.

Without saying it, Bob and Jack were both wondering what would happen if Keith Ng was conducting this line up. They smiled at the thought.

Tom stated, "Don't worry about his failure to identify. We

know he recognized Chung. Let's watch the cook real
closely."

Moments later the cook was given the photo line-up. It was
quite evident to the investigators that the cook had
already been prepared by the waiter. The cook looked at
the eight photographs in record breaking time and stated,
"I not know anyone heerr." He then turned and walked away.

"I'm gonna kill one of these suckers," said Trombetta.

"It was evident he didn't even see what was in front of
him," said Martin. Both witnesses were standing in the
front of the restaurant as the investigators began to exit.
Nerney looked at them and stated, "Thank you for your more
than negative input and your ability to remain
uncooperative." The investigators walked to their vehicles
as the door slammed behind them. Martin started the car
and Jack stated, "One day that place will pay for all their
shit."

Martin and Trombetta went into a tirade about the
restaurant workers and owner. Why did it always seem these
people were not being cooperative? Even when they were
being helpful it took forever to get them to provide useful
information.

Nerney was listening and said, "Listen, we are wasting our
time with these people. Let's not even do the owner. He
has been reluctant to help from the beginning. Let's go
meet the bus driver."

The guys quickly entered the Garden State Parkway and were
headed to the Atlantic City bus terminal. They had
arranged to meet the driver at the station around two p.m.
They were on their way to the meeting hoping for more
positive results.

When the investigators arrived at the bus terminal it was
ascertained that the bus driver was on his way. They were
directed to an office and moments later the bus driver
arrived. Tom Nerney spoke to him with regard to what he
had observed and witnessed when he had provided
transportation to the Chinese suspect. The driver provided
a very good description of the suspect from physical
attributes to clothing. He advised how the haircut of the
individual reminded him of Moe of the "Three Stooges."

Tom took in everything the driver said and after some small
talk he provided the photo line-up. Tom knew that the bus
driver would not pick out Chung. Jack and Bob figured he
would pick him out immediately. Tom felt that the guy was

going to base his decision on the hair of the subjects in
the photographs. Tom knew that the picture of Chung was
not a good representation of Chung's present features or
hairstyle. The best likeness of Chung was the picture they
were utilizing and it was twenty years old. Tom Nerney was
not disappointed. The driver had done exactly what Tom had
figured. The three investigators had watched as the bus
driver looked at the photographs. He had spent a lot of
time looking at Chung's picture but he was not going to say
for sure that Chung was the guy. It just wasn't exact
enough.

The three investigators left the terminal at five p.m and
started the two and a half hour trip back to the Big Apple.
They called the detectives in New York and advised them of
the failure to make positive ID. Jim Rybicki started
revamping the affidavit.

While the three investigators had been in Jersey the New
York Team continued to obtain information and track down
investigative leads with regard to Chung. Joe Piraino felt
that they had more than enough to obtain a search warrant
for Chung's residence. Piraino also believed that once
inside the house they would come up with enough
incriminating evidence to arrest Chung for the murder of
Dave Douglass.

It was seven fifteen p.m when the three investigators
walked into the Major Case office.

CHAPTER FIFTY SEVEN

"We've been working our asses off. Where ya been, terd?"
Ernie asked Jack.

"You don't work. You stamp overtime cards and try to look
busy, Captain Naspretto. Can I help you? Don't ask me
about police work. I get a little confused," mocked
Trombetta.

Joe Piraino immediately grabbed Bob. Jim Rybicki and Henry
Waite sat down with them and it was evident things were
happening. Before long Bob was reviewing the affidavit and
commenting about the fact that Rybicki had done an
outstanding job. Trombetta said to Ernie and Gene Taylor,
"I taught those guys everything they know. I'm Bob's
mentor. He's gonna turn out to be a good cop." Ernie
laughed and couldn't believe that there was someone on this
earth who actually bull shitted more than him, Jack
Trombetta. Gene just maintained his normal I'm looking
through you glare.

Lt. Pollini entered the room and said, "Bob, Jack come in
my office I want you to see something." The guys followed
and Joe placed a cartridge into the VCR in his office. He
explained that it was a tape of the people entering and
exiting the apartment complex that housed the Chung family.

The TARU surveillance van had taken the tape during their
monitoring of all who exited and entered the apartment.
Jack and Bob watched closely as the tape began to play.
They observed a Chinese man in a green army style jacket
wearing a blue knit watch cap on his head. Almost
immediately they stated simultaneously, "That's our guy."
Pollini stated, "We think so, too," and smiled. "We also
know that when he returned he entered the Chung apartment,"
added Joe Pollini. Bob and Jack couldn't believe how much
Chung resembled the composite provided by the bus driver.
It was almost a perfect likeness.

The guys could see that everyone's face indicated that they
all knew they had the right guy. The arrest of Dave's
killer was about to take place. They tried to make
themselves aware that a let down could occur but they
didn't want to believe it. They had been through a lot of
let downs in this case. It was about time that they turned
things around.

Martin returned to the computer where Rybicki was placing

the finishing touches. Rybicki made a few minor revisions
to the affidavit and then Waite, Rybicki, Taylor and Martin
left to meet with two assistant district attorneys to
review the document. They reviewed the paperwork and gave
their okay. Martin, knowing that the case was getting
close to making an arrest, used the telephone and put a
call into Chin and Ng at Queens Robbery. He wanted to
advise them that it was going down. He knew that if they
weren't busy and could make it that they would like to take
part in the arrest. The guys weren't there. Martin left a
message for them and asked that they be paged and advised.

Within the hour the guys were all sitting in night court in
the City of New York. They sat for approximately one hour.
Henry Waite was use to the court activities. The Jersey
guys, however, were quite interested with the Judge and the
way he handled cases.

A derelict drug user was standing before the judge in what
appeared to be clothing that had never been removed from
his body. The guy was wearing a mask like those worn by
medical personnel. He was very thin and scruffy looking.
He was explaining why he had been in possession of crack
cocaine. His appearance was for sentencing but for some
reason he seemed to be attempting to conduct a retrial of
his case. The Judge continually reminded him that the case
was completed and that he had been found guilty. The
derelict stated, "Ya don't understann', ya Honna. I am a
vicum' of circunnstance. Since I was here I got real bad
sick. Ya see, I have ta wear dis mask so I don't breathe
bad shit. If I get anymore bad shit in my lungs I could
die."

The derelict continued to talk as the Judge was handed
paperwork by a court officer. The Judge's eyes were
looking at the papers but his ears were listening to the
last ditch efforts of this guy who didn't want to go to
jail.

"Ya, Honna, I am placin myself on the mercy of dis herre
court. Ya gots ta understann I need medical attencion all
da time. I can't be breathin anymore shit or I might
die."

The Judge was looking at the papers before him. They were
investigative reports that were provided by the
investigators whose job it was to conduct pre-sentencing
investigations. The Judge stated, "Sir, is it not true that
only three days ago you were once again arrested for use of
crack cocaine."

"Ya, Honna , Sir, I was framed on dat one. I swear."

431

"The report before me indicates that you were smoking a pipe that was believed to contain crack cocaine. Preliminary test indicate that to be the case."

"Ya, Honna, haven't ya been listenin' to me. The Doctor says I can't breathe dat shit no moe. It could kill me. Dats what I been tryin' ta tell ya. I won't breathe dat shit no moe if ya don't put me in jail. I need constant medical care. I'm a sick man, ya Honna."

The Judge looked stoically upon the convicted drug user and stated, "Sir, I am quite concerned about your health. For that reason and your eloquent plea for help I am sending you to County Jail where you will be for three hundred and sixty four days. During that time I will make sure that you won't have to breathe as you put it,'any moe shit'. Best of health to you. Officer, take him away."

The Jersey guys liked this Judge. The Judge subsequently reviewed the affidavit and after asking a few questions of Waite and Martin he signed it. The guys quicky returned to the Major Case office and formulated their plans. It was decided that they would set up a three way phone conversation between Quey, who was in North Jersey at a County Prosecutors office, Rybicki, who would be monitoring at the office of the DEA in New York, and Chung who would be at his home. Quey was going to get Chung on the phone and keep him there as long as possible. Quey would call and advise that he may have a job for Chung at a Chinese restaurant. When they had exchanged telephone numbers they had talked about getting each other jobs, if possible.

Quey felt that he could pull off the conversation. Quey was also advised to engage in some small talk to place Chung at ease during the conversation. They wanted to make sure that Chung was present in his home before they entered. They also figured that if he was on the phone that indirectly they would have some control over him as they entered his apartment.

Martin noticed that Jim Rybicki had been called to the phone. Jim was talking to someone and had a perplexed look on his face. He saw Martin watching him and motioned for Martin to approach. Bob did so and Jim while holding the phone mouthed that he was talking to the prosecutor. It was evident that Jim was not happy with what he was hearing and he continually engaged in verbal responses that indicated he was not happy with what he was hearing. Martin realized that Jim was in a four way conversation. He was on the telephone with the Prosecutor, Assistant Prosecutor and the Chief. Jim may have been out numbered but he was holding his own. Martin heard Jim indicate that he felt the Feds were not needed. At that point Martin started yelling, "No way man, No Feds, from up here are going to be involved with this arrest."

Jim then advised the people on the other end of the phone that Martin had made the statement. Jim then added Martin wanted to talk to them. Jim put his hand over the phone and advised Martin that they wanted the Feds to make the arrest, interview, charge and process Hop Chung. Jim advised he didn't agree but that they wouldn't listen to him. Gene Taylor along with Jack and Ernie were now paying close attention to what was being said.

The entire room was listening. Bob grabbed the telephone.

Jack was ready to grab it but Bob beat him to it. Jack could tell by the look on Martin's face that the shit was about to hit the fan. Ernie stated to Jack, "Do you believe this shit? You don't even look pissed."

"My man Bob Bo is going to take care of the problem right now."

Martin grabbed the phone and stated, "Yeah. This is Martin. What's up?" Martin listened for a few minutes while each of the people on the other end of the phone attempted to explain why the Feds should be involved and further why they should affect the formal charging, arrest and subsequent interview of the perpetrator. Martin continually made faces and gestures as he was listening. The guys were all getting a kick out of his animated activity.

After a few minutes Martin declared, "The only Feds that can get near this case are Jack Reemer and Gary Chan and even then there is no way I would stand by while they did the charges and made the arrest. Not to mention the fact that there is no way they will be doing the interview. No it's not gonna' happen. Your wastin' your breathe." The AP started to get a little mouthy and stated, "You don't quite understand, I...." Martin cut him off and stated, "No, you don't understand. We've been eating, sleeping and living this case why you people have been sitting around thinking about how you could screw it up." The Prosecutor stated, "Bob, you know that's not the case. We want this case to be perfect."

Martin took offense and stated, "It has been perfect and it will be more perfect when we finish it without the help of the Feds up here. They have been worthless from the beginning and we sure as hell aren't going to let them screw this up. These Feds up here couldn't even do the simple things we requested. When they finally did they screwed it up. No. No Way. It's not gonna' happen."

Jack said to Ernie, "No way, I'll kick the Pros' ass. I'll kick all their asses."

Captain Duke had exited his office and heard what was going on. He asked Martin for the phone and as he did so he placed it to his ear and stated, "This is Captain George Duke of Major Case, NYPD. Let me just say that if the Feds are in, NYPD is out." Duke handed the phone back to Martin.

Martin heard a silence at the other end of the phone and stated, "My man wasn't kiddin'. I should also advise you that if a Fed even walks in this office someone will be lockin' me up because I'm gonna kick his ass." Jack broke into a big wide grin as Martin said, "So, Mr. Prosecutor, what's your pleasure?"

The Prosecutor stated, "Bob, would you please give the phone back to Jim?" Martin did so. In seconds Jim hung up the phone and with a smile stated, "The Feds are out and Martin and Trombetta just made three enemies for life."

Martin laughed and said, "I got broad shoulders." Jack looked at Ernie and stated, "I told ya my man, Bob Bo, would take care of the problem. If he had big problems he couldn't handle I would jump in and take care of it. That's the way we work." Ernie laughed and thought to himself that both Bob and Jack may be sickos, but they were fun to be around. Never a dull moment.

Things quickly calmed down and the guys got back into the problem at hand. The men were provided their assignments with regard to the entry and subsequent search. By nine fifteen p.m. they were on their way to the Chung apartment.

When all the teams arrived near the Housing Complex Rybicki was notified to make the call. The call was quickly connected and Rybicki advised the Search Team Leaders that Chung was in the apartment and on the phone.

Duke, Pollini, Nerney and Martin would be the initial entry team. It would be Martin's job to insert the key and unlock the door to the apartment to gain entry. If the door didn't open completely or easily Trombetta, Taylor and Naspretto would utilize a battering ram to force the door open.

Jack would from that point on tell the story about how he carried a two hundred pound battering ram up two flights of stairs in record breaking time. When Jack was asked why he didn't have Ernie help out he answered, "That terd is a weakling." Ernie replied, "I hope ya get a hernia." Jack decided he would handle the battering ram by himself.

Joe Piraino, Detective Christine Leung and Sergeant Mike
Lau would follow. Lau was called in to assist from a
patrol command. Prior to his promotion to sergeant he had
worked in Major Case. It was their job to make sure that
the other subjects in the apartment were contained. Lau
would serve as interpreter during the entry, search and
subsequent transport of any prisoners that didn't speak
English. He would also carefully listen for any
spontaneous statements uttered by Chung. Piraino was to
take total control of all search efforts once the apartment
was secured.

Martin was wearing a jacket that had the Lower Township
Police insignia printed on the chest and POLICE in white
letters across the back. The printing and insignia where
hidden and could be exhibited when required. Martin
prepared the jacket as everyone began to display their
shields either around their necks, on their chests or
belts.

Martin slowly placed the key into the door lock. Chung
could be heard talking on the telephone and three other
distinct voices could be heard. Captain Duke held up four
fingers indicating that he believed four subjects were in
the apartment.

Pollini and Duke drew their weapons as Martin turned the
key. The occupants didn't notice that the door was slowly
opening. Trombetta quietly placed the ram on the floor of
the hallway. Everyone had their weapons drawn. They all
actually hoped Chung would give them a reason to shoot him.

In an instance Martin, Pollini, Duke and Nerney had
entered. They were all yelling "POLICE, POLICE." Pollini
yelled, "Put the fuckin' phone down." Lau was yelling in
Chinese at the occupants of the apartment. Chung was
standing across the room from the door talking on the
telephone. His face registered shock. Mrs. Chung along
with her two year old son, teenage son and daughter were
sitting on a couch to the left of the door and across the
room. The occupants were frozen in their positions. Chung
looked at Martin's jacket and his attention was drawn to
the Lower Township Police insignia. Chung's eyes seemed to
open as wide as possible. His chin fell, leaving his mouth
opened wide. A loud gasp exited his mouth as he dropped
the telephone receiver and shrugged his shoulders while
looking down at the floor.

Both Martin and Nerney could see that Chung had just
admitted he had killed Dave Douglass. They each had been
involved in enough interrogations to know the physical
signs of guilt. Chung was the scumbag that shot and killed

435

Patrolman Dave Douglass. They each approached him quickly.
Mrs Chung was speaking and neither Nerney nor Martin could
hear her. Detective Christine Leung indicated that Mrs
Chung was advising that her husband had an injured hand and
that she didn't want anyone to hurt him.
Nerney knew that the investigators figured Dave Douglass
probably shot and wounded Chung and immediately looked at
Chung's hands. Nerney observed that the left index finger
was recently scarred. Nerney showed the hand and finger to
Martin. Nerney stated to Martin in a whisper,"It looks
like it could be a defensive wound." Martin knew that
Nerney was referring to the fact that perhaps Chung had
raised his left hand in a defensive movement when Dave
fired his weapon, probably at close range. Martin
immediately thought that such a movement would provide the
reasoning for the fact that Dave's weapon had "stove piped"
and jammed. Tom had his handcuffs in his hand and he with
the help of Martin placed the cuffs around the wrists of
the cop killer.

Chung began to speak in Chinese. Tom Nerney looked right
into his eyes from a distance of about three inches. Tom
placed himself into the mind of the bus driver. There was
no doubt he was looking at the killer. Nerney then stated,
"What do you speak? Cantonese, Mandarin or how about
English, you fuckin' cop killer." Martin thought to
himself that it was the first time he had heard Nerney
curse.

Gene Taylor was walking toward Chung as Captain Duke and
Lt. Pollini and Sergeant Piraino began to walk down the
hallway of the apartment to check for other individuals.
Trombetta saw them start down the hall and his SWAT
training came into play. Trombetta immediately observed
that the bosses were placing themselves in a dangerous
position by the way that they were beginning to enter the
rooms. Jack immediately approached them and took the lead
position. He then directed their approach and movement
throughout the rest of the search. The two bosses followed
Jack. They could tell he had been down this road before.

Ernie was following Jack with his weapon drawn. They
completed securing the interior of the apartment and
returned to the livingroom. The family members were the
only occupants in the apartment. Lau and Leung had them
under control and they were all seated on the couch.

Chung had no shoes on. He was told to put some on. Gene
Taylor just watched patiently as the shoes were put on
Chung's feet. He then said, "Wait a minute. Let me see
those shoes." He bent Chung's leg backward and looked at
the sneaker's sole design. Immediately Gene turned and
with a look that betrayed his normal stoic glance he

stated, "These sneakers are mine. The guy that wore them killed Dave Douglass." Ernie thought to himself that he remembered Jack saying that Gene had indicated he would never forget the imprint left by the sneakers of the killer of Dave Douglass. Ernie thought that he saw a smile on Gene's face. Every cop in that room knew Gene's faint smile meant this case was solved.

Lau had taken control of Chung and was advised by Nerney to give him his rights. Lau began talking in Chinese with Chung. Martin and Nerney started to walk around the residence.

Nerney grabbed a Buddha that was on a shelf and as he lifted it he observed that a Lottery ticket had been placed underneath it for good luck. Tom read the numbers out loud. "One, three, seven, eight, eighteen, thirty eight. The second series is two, five, fourteen, sixteen, seventeen and thirty two. This 'fucko' is still playing the same numbers." Nerney looked at Martin and added, "We just found ourselves a cop killer." Martin and Nerney had grins on their faces.
Everyone recognized them as the same numbers found on the Lottery ticket at the scene of the murder. Simultaneously, Ernie was pointing out a bicycle in the hallway. It was the one stolen from the Chinese residence in Lower Township.

Almost immediately Martin, Trombetta and Naspretto were in the hallway outside the door to the Chung apartment. They were all hugging, crying and trying to speak at the same time. Here they were three hardened cops all exhibiting emotions that they would rather hide. Bob kept saying, "We got him, man, we got him." Ernie said, "This fuckin' mutt has had it. He's history." Jack said, "It's him, it's him." They were hugging and kissing each other as they all embraced in a circle. It was almost like they would not allow anyone to break the chain. Bob said, "Thank you God for making this happen."

Jack stated, "Dear God, Thank you for allowing us to get Dave's killer in spite of ourselves. Thank you, Lord." They continued to sob and cry. Gene Taylor and Tom Nerney exited and joined in the hugs and kisses.

Ernie noticed that not only did Gene have a big smile he was also crying. Ernie thought that Gene was human after all. Tom Nerney looked at Jack and Bob and while embracing them stated, "Well, you did it. You got him."

Jack said, "Not with out the help of the best damn police department in the world." Bob stated as they all embraced, "We love you guys." Tom and Gene returned to the

apartment. Bob, Ernie and Jack were too overcome with
emotions to be helpful with anything. Everyone eventually
exited the apartment and expressed their feelings to the
Jersey guys.
Captain Duke, after hugging the guys stated, "All right,
Bob, he is your prisoner now go get a confession." Ernie
noticed that Martin turned from an emotional wreck into a
man on a mission. Ernie could tell by the look on Martin's
face that once again he was all business. Martin went over
to Joe Piraino to discuss transportation and assistance.
Ernie looked at Jack and said, "Man, did you see the look
on Bob's face." Jack said, "That's the way he gets when
it's time to do his thing." "Are you going with him?"
asked Ernie. "Right now, I feel like I'm gonna puke,"
answered Trombetta.

Martin once again exited the apartment and saw Jack bent
over holding his stomach. "Hey, you all right?" asked
Martin. "Yeah, I just feel a little sick," answered
Trombetta.

"Jack, you have to stay here," said Bob. "One of us should
be here at the scene."

Jack stated, "I don't mind staying here. I'm not ready to
talk to that bastard yet," added Jack referring to Chung.
"I'm not ready either, but you can bet I'll put on a good
act," Martin said.

"Where did Ernie go?" asked Bob. "He went down the hall,"
stated Jack. At that time Ernie came around the corner and
said, "I gotta get to a phone. I gotta call Grace. She'll
never forgive me if I don't call her with the news."

Bob and Jack laughed as Ernie knocked on a door, pulled out
his badge and as a lady answered the door stated, "Mam,
official Police business. I have to use your phone."
Ernie walked right passed the woman before she had a chance
to answer him.

He picked up the phone, dialed and said, "Hello, Grace, we
got him! I gotta go." Grace was in bed when the call
came. She handled the news the best way she knew how. She
jumped out of bed and cleaned the entire house that was
already clean. She had never been so proud to be a cop's
wife and Ernie was so happy that he could make Grace happy
with the news. Grace deserved it. She had been a rock to
lean on for her husband and the Jersey boys during this
ordeal.

Moments later Ernie exited and they all began hugging once
again. Ernie with a smile stated, "Grace is really happy."
Everyone laughed at Ernie's statement. Joe Piraino then

came out into the hallway and the crying started again. Jack finished kissing and hugging Joe and then started to gag as though he might throw up. Joe made him sit down and take deep breathes.
Ernie started to feel a little queasy and he too was taking deep breathes. Bob in the mean time had met with Lau and Leung who had exited the apartment with Chung. Martin advised that he would go down stairs and get the vehicle and bring it to the entrance to the complex. Lau and Leung would wait until he arrived before they exited with Chung.
 They figured newspaper reporters who may have been listening on police scanners would have set up shop at the entrance to the Housing Complex.

Martin quickly ran down the steps and as he exited the building he couldn't believe his eyes. Standing in a row shoulder to shoulder were uniformed and plainclothes personnel of NYPD. Martin recognized Henry Waite and Greg White at the beginning of the line. The uniformed guys numbered about fifteen. He had never seen the faces before. Counting Henry and Greg there were about eight other plainclothes guys that Martin had seen around One Police Plaza in the past.

Henry and Gregg approached Martin as Martin said, "We got him." Gregg hugged and picked Martin up off the ground as Henry hollered for all to hear, "We got'em, we got'em." Everyone began to cheer and applaud. Martin was overcome by the display and started crying all over again. Greg and Henry had tears in their eyes as the guys shook hands and hugged.

Each uniformed policeman in the line stood out in a display of blue. Martin thought that it was quite a sight. Everyone referred to cops as the "Thin Blue Line." Martin thought about the fact that it was a "Thick Blue Line" that appeared before him. It had been this "Thick Blue line" that had teamed together and caught a cop killer. Martin would never forget the display of brotherhood before him.

Each man, uniformed and plainclothes, extended his hand in brotherhood and in congratulations on a job well done. Bob was overwhelmed by the display and even though each man had something to say to him he could not remember what it was.

Eventually, Bob returned with the vehicle as Chung was led from the building. He was taken past the same "Thick Blue Line." Chung only received stares. The officers saw only a dead Police Officer when they looked at Chung.

Leung entered the driver's seat. Martin rode shotgun and Chung and Lau were in the back seat. Martin noticed that all the cops were clearing out from the front of the

439

building. Martin asked Leung, "Where did they all come from?" Leung stated, "They're from a lot of different precincts. They heard we were going to get this guy tonight and they wanted to be here.
Some of them decided to sneak over here and some were probably getting off duty." Christine Leung could tell that Martin was overwhelmed by what he had experienced. She reached over hugged and congratulated him. Chung sat in the rear of the car starring at the two. He probably had no idea why everyone seemed to be hugging, kissing and shaking hands.

During the ride Chung was talking to Lau. Every now and then Lau would advise as to what was said. Lau stated that Chung didn't want his family to worry and that he was sorry for anything he had done. Lau advised that Chung was sounding like a guilty man.

Jack and Ernie were standing in the hallway talking to Joe Piraino when it became quite evident that Jack had passed the gagging stage and was about to lose his lunch. Captain Duke, saw what was happening and said, "Joe, get him out of here before he pukes on my scene." The guys all laughed and Joe quickly approached Ernie. "Listen, the absolute best thing you can do for us now is get him out of here." Joe knew that a substantial amount of work remained to be done at the apartment and Jack was not in shape to help out. Ernie grabbed Jack and walked him downstairs. As they were leaving Jack and Ernie heard Joe Piraino say, "I'm declaring this a crime scene." The words signaled every cop there that it was time to get meticulous. Tom Nerney and Gene Taylor were born to be meticulous.

Just as Ernie and Jack reached the unmarked car on 14th Street Jack began to vomit. He was throwing up, gagging, crying and smiling all at the same time. Ernie assured Jack that he would not tell anyone what he had just witnessed. However, within one hour Ernie told everyone associated with the case that Jack had thrown up.

Joe Piraino knew he had to start coordinating the search of the apartment and had to contact Police Photographers to record the scene. Joe had already made up his mind, Gene Taylor would control the search for evidence along with the confiscation and recording of every item that was found. Joe knew that the Search Warrant listed every item that had been taken from the Chinese workers in Lower Township. He knew that it also listed other items that they hoped to find, most specifically a gun, the gun used to kill Dave Douglass.

Tom Nerney would stay at the scene and he and Joe Piraino along with the photographers would assist Gene. Duke and

Pollini would also stand by until they felt comfortable leaving the scene and returning to One Police Plaza.

Meanwhile Ernie and Jack were sipping coffee that Ernie bought in a corner deli. He also bought himself a Robert Burns "Black Watch" cigar. In Red Auerbach Celtic victory tradition, Ernie lit up and puffed away. It was the first cigar he had smoked in a while and he loved it. Every now and then Jack would throw up what he was drinking. At least if he had something in his stomach he wouldn't have the "dry heaves."

Ernie looked at Jack and stated, "You're a pathetic sight. Do you realize that everyone is busy except you and me? But, at least I'm off-duty. What's your excuse?" Jack stated, "Do you realize that from where we sit we won't have to do a report? We will provide moral and technical support. Do I have to teach you everything about being a good detective?"

"You really do have method to your madness, don't you?" said Ernie. Ernie thought for a moment and stated, "Man, did you see Bob's face? He was like a robot on automatic pilot. Once he was told to get the confession he changed completely. One second he's cryin' his eyes out the next his eyes looked like they were sharpening a knife to cut Chung's throat. You can tell when he starts work. It's as if there is nothing else on his mind. He's like a crazy man on a mission."

Jack said, "Well, if we get back to the office, watch Bob at work. Maybe you'll learn something. If you are lucky enough to watch both of us interview somebody together you'll really learn something. Stick with me Ernie I'll make you a hero yet."

"You're so full of shit your stinkin' up Joe's car. What are they doing up their now?" asked Ernie. Jack proceeded to explain to Ernie everything that was taking place. Jack provided a perfect synopsis of all that would occur. Ernie was impressed with Jack's knowledge. Ernie thought to himself that perhaps Jack really did know his stuff. Bob had told Ernie that there was no one better to have around than Jack. Bob was probably right. Ernie, however, was not going to make Jack's head big by saying so.

Ernie looked at Jack and asked, "Hey, Jack, did your pee-pee get hard when they got this ass hole? It was almost like the time I had these three strippers in the back of my patrol car. Did I ever tell you about that?"

Jack threw up again and after wiping his chin said, "Do you see what you do to me, you stinkin' pervert? There won't be a place in heaven for you if you don't clean up your act."

Ernie said, "If you don't try to sell me on being born again, I won't tell you any sex lies."

"Hey, Ernie, it would be easier for you to get into heaven than it would be for you to make me believe you had three strippers in the back seat of a patrol car."

CHAPTER FIFTY EIGHT

Chung had been taken to the Major Case office where he was cuffed to a chair next to a desk. Martin immediately asked Leung and Lau to make sure that Chung was aware that he had been read his rights. Martin had recorded the time they had left the apartment and now recorded the time they arrived at Major Case. It was 10:15 p.m. Martin intended to keep a log of every occurrence with regard to Hop Chung. Martin knew that sooner or later a defense attorney would try to show that his poor client was not afforded the normal creature habits. Trombetta was usually the one who thought of and handled this aspect of the interview and interrogation but Martin knew he would be on his own until Jack returned from the scene of the search. Martin was wishing Jack was present. It seemed that things went better when they were able to work together. It was easier for each man because they knew that if one was about to make a mistake the other would realize it and get things back on track.

Martin and Trombetta fed off of each other and what one man missed the other would find and then pick up the slack. Martin would generalize and Jack would be more specific. Jack thought more like an attorney and would think, about what he was going to say. Bob would get on a roll and ad lib as the situation required. Most often, people that knew both Bob and Jack would think that Jack was the one who generalized and Bob was the fact and figure guy.

Bob decided that he would not formally interview Chung until the search was complete. He figured that he would then be better prepared to ask questions with regards to the findings of the search team. In the meantime Martin was aware that Chung had been given his rights and Martin had made it a point to make sure that Chung was given something to drink and made sure that he was afforded the opportunity to use the bathroom. Mike Lau was in charge of making sure all went well with Hop Chung.

Martin then went to the telephone and called Chief Douglass at his home. He advised the Chief that they had the killer under arrest and that he was talking. The Chief had a million questions but knew Martin would be busy. The Chief stated, "Make sure you and Trombetta interview this guy." Martin advised the Chief that Trombetta was at the scene. The Chief then stated, "Well, don't let anybody drag you away from interviewing that shithead." The Chief knew he didn't have to tell Martin to be there during the interview. "Listen, Chief, would you call the Captain and fill him in. Then if you would I would appreciate it if you would call Debbie Douglass and tell her you wanted to come over and talk to her. When you get there tell her you want her to make a phone call. Here is the number to give her." Martin gave him the direct line to Major Case and then ended the call. Martin had promised Debbie that when the arrest was made he would be the one to notify her.

It wasn't long before the phone rang and the Chief was on the other end. He stated he was putting Debbie on the line. "Hello." "Hello, Deb, this is Bob. Remember I told you that when there was good news you would here it from me?"

Debbie listened as Bob said, "It's over, Deb. Jack and I got him a few minutes ago. It's over, he is finished." Debbie started to cry with tears of joy and pain. "Oh, I'm so glad you got him, I'm so glad. Thank you, thank you. I hope the bastard gets the chair," added Debbie. "Well, Deb, we had a lot of help up here but now the cop part is over. It's up to the prosecutor to do the rest." Some more was said and they hung up. Martin felt good.

Martin then advised Lau to make small talk with Chung and hoped Lau would extract worthwhile information in the process. Lau would provide Christine Leung with his findings and she in turn would advise Martin. Martin jotted down notes as he received the information.

Chung was advising Lau that he was a hard working man who had been humiliated by Chinese Resturant owner. Chung, after being fired, actually made believe he was going to work so his family would not be embarrassed with the fact that their father was not working. Chung stated that he borrowed money from friends to bring home and give to his wife to make it appear that he had been paid. He advised that he would spend most of his time in employment agencies in an attempt to secure a job. He stated that it had gotten to the point that he could no longer borrow money from friends.

Back at the arrest scene Joe Piraino had looked at his watch and noticed that the time was eleven p.m. He went downstairs and sat in the car with Jack and Ernie. It appeared Jack had gotten over the case of the nerves and he and Ernie were reflecting on everything that had occurred. Joe wanted to provide the guys with some news of the search.

Joe in his usual quiet subdued manner and voice stated, "Jack, I have some good news. We found about ten of the stolen items from the house that was burglarized in your town. We have items that link him to every one of the burglaries." Jack and Ernie couldn't believe what they were hearing. Jack stated, "You mean to say this guy saved the stuff from the burglaries."

"Yes, Jack, that's the case," replied Joe Piraino softly.

Ernie realized what was said and said, "This fuckin' mutt kept the stuff that he took even after killin a cop?"

"That's correct, Ernie," said Joe as he smiled.

"This guy is a total fuckin' idiot. Thank God," added Ernie.

"Jack, are you alright now?" asked Joe, in his most caring voice. "Yeah, I'm doing better," answered Jack. Joe returned to the search and left Jack and Ernie to each other.

They remained at the car, Ernie being animated in all their conversations and Jack being somewhat subdued because he still felt that he might puke at any moment. Joe Piraino came down to check on the guys on a couple of occasions. Each time he had another bit of information with regard to something that had been found. Joe visited the guys at about 12:15 am and said, "This guy had a piece of some kind of weed or blade of grass on his bureau. It was wrapped up like a memento. Gene Taylor says it is a weed that he recognizes from the crime scene search where Dave and the perp were struggling."

Ernie looked at Jack and stated, "Man, you and Bob were right. Sergeant Slaughter knows his shit. Can you believe this mutt would keep this stuff around? Not to mention Gene recognizing a certain kind of weed to be indigenous to the crime scene." Ernie thought his statement sounded real professional.

Jack looked at Ernie and then to Joe and said, "We are going to find out this guy didn't know he killed Dave. He'll probably try to say he didn't know he shot him. Even a fool wouldn't keep all those items around if he knew he killed somebody, especially if that somebody was a cop." Joe went back into the Housing Complex.

Martin and Leung were listening to Lau talking to Chung. Christine Leung asked if Chung wanted a drink or needed to go to the bathroom. Martin motioned to Lau to help Chung. Lau uncuffed Chung and as he did Leung looked at the injury to Chung's finger and made a comment. Martin then told Lau to ask Chung if he wanted a shot and a beer rather than a soda. Lau looked at Martin as if he was crazy but asked the question. Chung answered and Lau stated to Martin, "I told him that if I could I would give him a beer or some whiskey. He told me that he isn't a drinker, he would rather have a soda." Martin was trying to obtain as much, back ground information, from Chung as possible. Martin just didn't want Chung to know he was providing it. Martin did not want Chung to say during the formal interview that he was drunk when he killed Dave. Martin then told Lau to ask if getting shot in the finger was very painful. Chung replied in Chinese, "It hurt bad." Leung looked at Martin with a smile and stated, "When they come out of the bathroom we have to find out where the gun is located." Martin stated, "Christine, you are reading my mind."

Martin had just got Chung to admit his injury was due to a gun being discharged. Now that he brought up the fact that a weapon was involved they should ask him if he owns one. Lau returned from the mens room with Chung and as he handcuffed Chung to the chair said, "He told me the gun he took to the place in Jersey is in a coat pocket in the closet of his bedroom. He also said that maybe he shot himself during a fight with the policeman." Martin and Leung were out of their chairs and Leung was making a call to the guys at the search scene. Martin knew that Chung was now getting talkative and was starting to come up with his reasoning for doing what he did. Martin knew that Chung would now come up with as many fabrications as possible to justify his actions. Chung was starting to feel comfortable in his surroundings. Martin knew it would be that comfortableness that would lead Chung down the primrose path to prison for the rest of his worthless life.

Jack and Ernie were talking about how stupid Chung had been when Joe approached the vehicle they were seated in. Jack had now been feeling pretty good and had a cigarette in his hand. No doubt Ernie had gone to the corner store and purchased them for his sick buddy.

Joe slowly and methodically approached the guys and stated, "I have some really good news." Jack thought to himself that Joe Piraino was the most controlled and subdued individual he had ever met. When he was excited you couldn't tell unless he told you. He and Jim Rybicki had a lot in common when it came to appearing very calm.

Joe spoke slowly and softly and stated, "You won't believe this but Bob called and says that Chung will go for the works and he even found out where the gun is located." Ernie and Jack had looks of relief on their faces. Joe then added the coup de grace, "It gets better. We got the gun." Jack and Ernie weren't sure what Joe had said. Joe smiled and repeated himself slowly, "We got the gun."

Jack and Ernie began to expose large smiles as Ernie jumped from the open door of the car out of his seat and onto the sidewalk. In, his most animated fashion Ernie was jumping and running around the police vehicle screaming, "YA' GOT THE GUN! YA' GOT THE FUCKIN' GUN! I DON'T BELIEVE WE GOT

THE GUN! JACK, WE GOT THE FUCKIN GUN!"

Jack, Joe and Ernie were once again hugging each other as
Ernie kept screaming. Even in the early morning hours the
foot traffic on 14th Street in New York is busy with
vehicles and pedestrians. Jack thought that the people
traveling by must think these guys are idiots.

Jack and Joe became apprehensive about their show of
excitement while on the streets of New York. Ernie on the
other hand was running up to pedestrians screaming "WE GOT
THE GUN! WE GOT THE FUCKIN' GUN!!!" The pedestrians just
looked at him and figured he must be high on drugs or
something. One old guy carrying what appeared to be a bag
of groceries from the all night market down the street
stated to no one in particular, "Where's a cop when you
need one?" If he only knew.

Jack and Joe tried to calm Ernie down. It wasn't easy.
Jim Rybicki returned to the Major Case office. When he
entered he and Bob shook hands and hugged. Rybicki had
been in charge of the County aspect of the case since Lt.
Jim McGowan had gone to Florida. Jim often thought that
perhaps the case would never be solved. He also thought
about the fact that dealing with Martin and Trombetta would
be an experience he would rather forego. Jim knew that Bob
and Jack did their own thing no matter what anyone said. He
also knew that you could appeal to them but you didn't want
to come across like you were their boss. Jim knew they
could get the job done. He just hated having to put up
with their explosive personalities. Martin and Trombetta
had considered Jim just another Prosecutor's Office crony.
They, however, changed their minds during their time
together in New York. On many occasions they watched and
listened while Rybicki constantly argued with the County
Prosecutors with regard to the case. Both Bob and Jack
listened while Rybicki would be talking on the telephone
with a prosecutor and telling him he basically didn't know
what he was talking about.

Bob and Jack liked the way Jim worked. He rarely got upset
or raised his voice. He would just raise his eye brows and
smile each time he made a point. Yeah, Bob and Jack
witnessed Jim coming around. They knew that they would now
be on this guy's side for life. That's how they were. Be
normal they loved ya. Be an ass that wouldn't listen and
learn and you had two enemies for life. Bob and Jack
always said that if you had something good to say about
either one of them they would be glad to listen. Just
don't talk negative about one of them to the other. They
weren't interested in listening to you. Not to mention the
fact they may get a little goofy and you would wish you
kept your mouth shut. Perhaps that was another reason why

their partnership was so productive.

Rybicki advised Martin that the Assistant District Attorney, ADA, would be arriving along with a video and audio technician and a court appointed translator. Jim advised that they would be sitting in on the interview. Martin immediately went ballistic. What the hell was he going to do with all those people sitting in a room while he was trying to get a guy to admit to burglary, theft, arson and the murder of a police officer. Jim knew Bob wouldn't be happy with the scenario. Jim began to explain that the procedure in New York mandated the interview process. Jim explained to Bob that he also would be sitting in on the interview as a representative of the Prosecutor's office. Only because he was ordered to do so. Jim continued to try to calm Bob down. Eventually Jim stated, "Listen, I will make sure that you, the translator and Chung are the only ones talking. I'll make the ADA agree to that stipulation. I'll give him some line of bull crap. I tell him if he has anything to say or ask that he has to write it down and hand it to you. I'll do the same thing. That way if perhaps you overlook something we could bring it to your attention."

Martin knew that Jim was right he just didn't like the idea of all those people in the room. Chung would think he was at an inquisition. Martin wanted Chung to be comfortable as possible with the surroundings. Martin also wanted to be sure that if he had to turn up the heat of the interview that no one would interrupt.

Jim Rybicki knew he had to talk Martin into accepting the fact that everyone would be in the room during the interview. Jim utilized his cool calculated demeanor and brought Martin around. Martin knew Jim was right but he didn't want to admit it.

Martin made sure Chung was receiving all the creature comforts and then sat down with Christine Leung. Bob asked Christine about the rest of the Chung family members. Bob wanted to know if Christine thought she could gain their confidence and speak to them about the actions of Hop Chung over the last three months. Christine assured Bob she knew what he wanted and that she could do it. It was then Christine's job to soften up the family members for Bob to interview. He wanted to know what they knew before he actually had to speak with them. Christine knew that Martin was mentally reviewing in his mind all the excuses that Chung may devise. Christine also knew that Martin wanted to be able to combat these excuses not only with the statements of the family members but also with the statements Chung had already made prior to and after his arrest. Detective Christine Leung then began to coordinate

the transportation to the office and the subsequent
informal meetings with the members of the Chung family.

Mike Lau was still taking care of Chung and making sure
that he was afforded every comfort that could be provided.
The log that Martin had kept would show that Mr. Chung was
treated very fairly while at NYPD.

Martin went into Captain Duke's office to formulate
questions with regard to the interview of Chung and his
family. Martin reached over and turned on a radio that was
sitting on the cabinet. Bob turned it on and was met with
Led Zeppelin and their song SINCE I BEEN LOVING YOU.
Martin listened as he wrote. He always liked the song
because it sounded like old time blues.

In a while Christine Leung entered the office.   Martin
turned off the radio. "Bob, I'm sure the family will be
helpful.   They are all very talkative and I made some
notes." She handed them to Martin. Bob looked at them and
stated, "Yeah, this is perfect. Good job.   I take back
almost everything bad I said about female cops." Christine
laughed and stated, "You just never worked with one as good
as me."

"You're right," said Martin.   "Listen, should we get Chung
something to eat?"

"Yeah, let's get Chinese," replied Christine.

"The rest of the guys are back. I'll tell ya what, I'm
buying", she added.

"No, you can't do that. Lower Township is buying,"
insisted Martin.

"Listen, Bob, I'm not gonna argue with ya. I'm buying and
you can go with me. You need a break. I'll take you to
the best Chinese place in New York City." Martin thought
to himself how he and Jack hadn't eaten Chinese food since
Dave had been killed. What the hell it was time to
celebrate. Everyone that had returned from the search
scene was standing around back slapping and shaking hands.
Christine went around the room taking orders. Before long
she went over to Chung and also took his order. He sat
solemnly with his head down looking at the floor. He did,
however, place his order which was, pork and vegetables.

Christine had recorded eight different dinners and some
appetizers. She made a phone call, placed the order and
then she and Martin took the elevator to the parking area
where they entered her vehicle and were on their way. She
exited the building and pulled over at a convenience store

449

that was open all night. She ran in before Martin could ask
her why they stopped. She exited quickly, hopped into the
car and laid a pack of cigarettes on the seat. "Don't tell
me. Jack needed smokes," stated Martin.

"Yep, but he did give me the money, even after I offered to
buy them," said Christine. Jack really is celebrating,
thought Martin.

They stopped in front of a small Chinese restaurant and
they both ran in. Christine spoke to the owner who she
knew and followed him to the kitchen. In seconds she was
exiting with bags in her hands. She was followed by the
owner who was also carrying bags of food. They approached
the counter and Martin reached for his money. Christine
stated, "You take out money and I'm gonna pour this won ton
soup all over ya." She looked like she meant it so Martin
put the money back in his pocket. Bob thought to himself
that Jack would be so happy.

They returned and everyone ate. The food was excellent.
Bob and Jack had their first taste of authentic New York
Chinatown cuisine. They vowed to bring their wives to the
Big Apple and do it again. As they ate they conversed about
the fact that Bob was waiting for the ADA, a translator and
a technician before he could start the interview. Bob and
Jack ate and reviewed all of Bob's notes and talked about
how Bob would conduct the interview. Martin advised Jack
that after he completed the interview and formal statement
of Chung he and Jack would take statements from the other
family members.

"Hey, if we can I want to let Ernie sit in and see what
goes on," Jack suggested.

"Sounds good," responded Bob.

They finished eating as the ADA showed up with his people
and things started to get underway. Bob, Jim, the ADA,
translator and technician entered the room. Chung was
brought in by Mike Lau. Martin asked the translator if he
could be as demonstrative as Martin may become. The
translator assured Martin that he would be as animated and
vocal as Martin indicated while asking questions. The
translator advised he had done this type of interview in
the past and that he would act out all of Martin's actions
and statements as if Martin was doing the talking in
Chinese. Martin was happy with the arrangement.

The translator did all the introductions. Martin then read
the rights in English and gave Chung the prepared Chinese
language version to read and sign. The entire procedure
was being recorded. Chung was seated at Captain Duke's

desk, next to him was the translator. Martin was facing
Chung from the opposite side of the desk. The ADA and
Rybicki were to Martin's right and far enough behind him
that they couldn't be seen in the video. The technician
had the camera set up on a tripod behind Martin. The
interview was underway as Martin stated, "This will be a
formal taped interview and statement of Mr. Hop Chung. The
date is 4-2-94 and the time is 2:30 am."

Martin went on to name all the people in the room and then
stated, "Mr. Chung, would you now tell me everything you
know in regard to burglaries, thefts, arson and subsequent
shooting that occurred in Lower Township, New Jersey during
the months of January and February of this year?" Martin
was impressed with how fast the translator was providing
the information to Chung.

Chung went on to indicate that he had worked for at the
restaurant for a few weeks in December and into January of
1994. He stated that he never got along with the owner
because he expected too much from him. Chung had an
arthritic problem in both hands and elbows and was always
too slow for the owner. He continually berated and
embarrassed him in front of the other employees. Chung
indicated that he stayed in the group home owned by the
resturant and would go home on his days off to his family
apartment. He advised that he was sending his daughter
through college and that his son would be starting soon.
He also advised that he had a young son and a wife to take
care of.

Chung provided that he couldn't speak English and taking
the bus back and forth was facilitated by a business card
he possessed that had directions printed on it. It had
been given to him by a guy named Liu. Liu had used it
initially and when he quit Chung used it. Chung was fired
in early January after a verbal argument with the
restaurant owner.

Once again the restaurant owner had verbally berated and
embarrassed him in front of all the employees. Chung got
his belongings and left. He didn't want to return home so
he stayed with a friend in New York and thought about how
the Chinese Resturant owner was ruining his life. He had
no job and no place else to obtain one. Many restaurant
owners knew he was too slow in the kitchen. His friend got
him a job that lasted two days before he was fired. He had
to do something to feed and provide for his family. He
returned home, as it was his normal two days off. He
decided he would not tell his family he had been fired. He
would even continue to travel back and forth to New Jersey
and make the family think that all was well. It was on his
first bus trip back to Jersey after being fired that he

decided to start robbing the house where he had stayed with the other workers.
Chung decided that he would steal from those who had given him a hard time. He would not steal from those employees who had helped and been nice to him.

He robbed the people of their belongings when no one was at home. He was aware of the work schedule and knew when the occupants would be working or in New York City during their days off. He advised that whenever he entered the house he would try to damage the property. He wanted the owner to pay for what he had done. He took items of clothing that were new and that he could give to his family members as gifts and also toiletries to be used by his family. He also took items such as electronic equipment, bicycles, luggage, money and other personal items that he could sell or give to his family as gifts. He was providing a belated Christmas for his family.

Chung explained how he traveled by bus and transported even the bicycles on the bus trips with the help of the drivers. He advised that often he would have the same two drivers and that they were only doing their job by helping him. He would always be left off and picked up at the corner just past the residence that housed all the workers.

Chung continually damaged the doors, windows and on one occasion left the hot water running because he thought that possibly the water heater would be damaged. It was his intention to make him pay for what he had done.

During Chung's rendition of what had taken place Martin would ask pointed and direct questions with regard to anything he wanted to clarify. Martin led Chung through the initial burglaries and thefts and then everyone in the room listened intently to what had taken place the evening of February 18th, 1994, the night Patrolman David C. Douglass of the Lower Township Police Department was shot and killed while responding to a call of a suspicious person.

CHAPTER FIFTY NINE

Hop Chung arrived by bus and was left out almost in front of the residence where he had lived with other Chinese restaurant workers. He carried a suitcase with him that he had stolen from the house on a previous visit. In the suitcase was a jacket he had also stolen previously and had been wearing since he had stolen it. He looked around and knowing that no one would be in the residence he walked to the back yard. He broke a window in the rear door and opened it and walked in. In seconds he heard a loud beeping noise and he saw a light blinking on a little panel on the wall. He immediately ripped it off the wall and threw it out the back door into the rear of the yard.

He wasn't sure what it was. The owner of the property had it installed since Chung's last visit. The owner was tired of the place being robbed. As soon as he had a chance he was suppose to register the alarm with the Police Department and they would be advised when an unauthorized entry took place. He hadn't had time to get to the Police Department. Hence the alarm would only produce a beeping sound that might scare off an intruder.

The Chinese intruder now feeling secure after stopping the noise started to slowly walk through the residence. Once again he noticed that the people living in the house had put padlocks on their doors. He knew that he would force them off as he had done in the past. He knew that one of the rooms he would not enter. The room belonged to two workers who had been very good to him. He would not steal their items.

Chung slowly and methodically went from room to room going through the drawers and closets. He found one suitcase that was packed with women's clothing. He placed it near the rear door where he had entered. He continued to take things from throughout the house and placed them near the back door. He found a upright suitcase with wheels and filled it with items. He placed a small television on top and pushed it out the back door into the yard. He then slowly and methodically started pushing it down the main street, Townbank Road, along the sidewalk. He pushed it about a block and crossed the street. He left it near a fence back from the roadway. He wanted it to be right where he would catch the bus to return to New York City. He had done the same thing in the past. It always made it easier to load the bus with his stolen items if they were close to the location where the bus would stop. The bus drivers were always helpful and if he needed help they would assist him.

As he walked slowly back to the house he thought about how he had gotten on the bus in New York and took it to Atlantic City. It actually was like a free trip if you got the roll of quarters from the casino. Sometimes you even got a meal. You were almost reimbursed for the full fare. It was a cheap mode of transportation for the Chinese workers in the area who had family in New York City. The majority of them did.

He grabbed the gun that was in his right front pants pocket. It was heavy and cumbersome but he brought it along this time because he had decided to kill the owner if he saw him. It was the owner who had ruined his life and the life of his family. This man had humiliated and embarrassed him. If the owner showed up he would not live to ruin the life of anyone else. He almost hoped that hewould pull up in his fancy Mercedes Benz. He would not drive away.

Many thoughts were going through his mind. He had to find another job. How long could he live on the proceeds of the robberies? He knew this would be the last time he came to New Jersey. He had been lucky he had not been caught.

Why couldn't he win the New York Lottery? He played it regularly, always playing the same numbers. He thought about the ticket he had in his coat pocket which was in the stolen suitcase he had brought with him.

He was wearing a plaid flannel type shirt and dark pants. He had a dark color knit cap that was also in the suitcase. He wanted to put it on as he was getting cold. He returned to the house and grabbed two suitcases he had loaded with radios, tape players and toiletries for his family. He then remembered he wanted to put on his cap. He put it on and left the suitcase he had brought with him opened on the floor. He didn't want to put on the jacket just yet as it was too bulky. It was a ski type jacket and if he wore it he would have trouble carrying all the items.

Once again Chung walked down the street on the sidewalk as traffic rolled by him. He noticed some people looking at him as they drove by, but he figured they were use to seeing the Chinese workers moving into and out of the residence. The bus drivers were sure use to it. He crossed the street looking down at the ground as he always did. He once again placed the items near the place where the bus would stop. He figured that with the next trip he would move them closer to the roadway in anticipation of the bus arriving. It was a little after 7:30 p.m. and the bus would be coming anytime. It usually arrived at about

7:45 p.m.

He began to hurry across the street and hadn't been looking
when a car screeched to a stop as it attempted to turn the
corner. He was staring at a young girl who had almost run
him over. He could tell by the look on her face that she
was as scared as he was. He lowered his head and walked
away toward the house. He would make one more trip and
then return to the house and get even with the owner for
the last time.

Chung went in the door and immediately put on his jacket.
It was now too cold to go without it. He loaded up the
suitcase he had brought with him and made the last trip.
He didn't notice but there was a car following him. He had
not been aware but a nearby resident had been watching him
and at first thought, perhaps, he was just one of those
Chinese guys. The resident, however, just thought the guy
was being too sneaky. The guy slowly followed and kept an
eye on him as he walked and then dropped the suitcase off
at the location directly in front of the guy's home. He
returned to the house.

The resident quickly pulled into his driveway and hollered
to his wife, "Call the police, this guy is really acting
suspicious." Dispatch received the call and at exactly
7:37 p.m., the responding officer was dispatched to a call
of a suspicious person.

The complainant didn't know that the guy after returning to
the house was crouching down on the floor placing a match
on the gasoline he had put on a mattress and the floor. He
had found a can of gas next to a lawnmower that had been in
a side entryway to the house. He knew the owner would be
very surprised when he found his house burnt to the ground.
He deserved to be mad. He deserved to be dead. If only he
would drive up.

Patrolman Dave Douglass was parked only a short distance
away looking at a 'Street Survival' magazine. He would
often review them and pass on important information to his
fellow Swat Team members. Dave was into weapons training
and survival techniques. The article mentioned the
importance of wearing the bullet proof vest. It basically
indicated that if you were shot while not wearing a vest
you didn't have much of a chance of surviving. If you
couldn't function you didn't have to worry about disarming
someone or saving your own life. Dave put the book on the
seat and adjusted his bullet proof vest as he reached for
the radio.

Douglass advised he was at the scene. He was closer than
the Rookie and figured he would help out his fellow officer

even though it wasn't his call. Dave's job was to function
as a back up responder but he knew he was closer to the
call.

Dave saw a small man cross the street and enter the yard as
Dave pulled onto Sunnyside Drive off of Townbank. Dave
hears the complainant say to the man, "Hey, buddy, did you
lose something?" Dave turns on his alley light and
illuminates the subject as he runs behind some hedges on
the side of the property. Dave was familiar with the area
and knew that the guy had to come out at the rear of the
property on Fieldview Drive.

Dave hoped that the guy would get caught up in the strand
of barb wire that was about knee high at the rear of the
yard. Dave could see the complainant and his wife watching
the action from their doorway. Dave sped up and rounded the
corner on to Fieldview at the rear of the yard just as the
guy trips over the wire and seems to be tangled up. Dave
throws his car in park and hollers over the radio that
he'll be out on Fieldview. The Rookie is just pulling onto
Sunnyside drive, the location where Dave had illuminated
his alley lights. The Rookie is on the side of the
complainant's yard.

Dave is out of his car just as the guy gets free of the
barbed wire and is back on his feet. Dave can see that the
guy's jacket was stuck to the barbed wire. It was
apparently ripped off of him as he tried to get free off
the barbed wire after falling.

Dave was surprised at how fast the little guy could run.
He didn't seem real coordinated and seemed to be older but
he was moving pretty fast. Dave increased his speed and as
he approached he yelled, "Freeze, you mother fucker." The
guy hesitates slightly but continues to run. Just as Dave
grabs his shoulder the guy is reaching into his pocket with
his right hand. Dave pulls his gun as the guy turns and
thrusts a 38 caliber revolver directly at Dave's throat.
The guy fires. They are so close that the shot leaves
powder burns on Dave's neck and shirt. The shot enters
Dave's throat just above his bullet proof vest. Dave
instinctively reacts and fires his weapon just as the guys
left hand comes up to defend himself against the shot. He
grabs the end of Dave's gun as it discharges. The weapon
is unable to complete its cycle to discharge the bullet
casing. Dave pulls the trigger of his Smith and Wesson 9mm
but nothing happens. Dave realizes it jammed. The guy
screams in pain and turns holding his hand and is running
across the vacant lot toward the rear of the house where
all the Chinese workers live.

The Rookie who had exited his car was in the yard of the

complainant and upon hearing the two shots he immediately crouched down behind a tree and looked around to see where the shots had came from.

Dave, clutching his throat, realizes that the face he saw was the face of an older Chinese guy. He must live at the house. He probably works at the Chinese Resturant. Dave with his hand to his throat can feel the blood. He reaches for his portable but can't find it. It had been dislodged from his belt when he had chased or scuffled with the guy. Dave knew he didn't have time to look for it. He ran to his car and could feel the blood pumping through his fingers. Dave got back to his vehicle as quickly as he could.

He reached in for the radio and at 7:45 p.m. Dave said his last words, "Get me Rescue, I've been shot." He dropped the radio handset and as he turned he observed the guy running into the woods. Dave looked at the gun he still held in his hand. He could now see why it hadn't fired. It was jammed. He dropped it to the ground as he collapsed and took his last breath. The time was 7:46 p.m.

The Chinese guy was running for his life. He saw the marked police car approach him and he was scared. The policeman grabbed him and he automatically drew and fired his gun at the officer. He couldn't believe what he had done. He had just fired his gun at a policeman. Why did he do it? He was just scared. He had to get home to his family. His finger was hanging off and bleeding. He stopped for a minute, crouched down in the woods and ripped his shirt and tied it around his hand. He could hear the sounds of emergency sirens and see flashing lights through the woods. He wanted to get to the next location where the bus would stop to pick him up. He ran through the woods making sure that he would be a safe distance from all of the activity. He could see smoke going into the sky. The Chinese Resturant owner's house would burn to the ground. That made him happy.

He eventually got out to the roadway just as a bus was approaching. He tried to contain himself and slowly entered the bus and took a seat in the rear. Later not one bus driver could ever remember picking him up. Either Chung was lying or the drivers didn't want to admit they had given a ride to a cop killer.

Towards the end of the interview Martin could sense that Chung was beginning to change his demeanor. He continually would say that he was confused or maybe going crazy. He stated that maybe it was all the alcohol he had been drinking. Ever since he had been fired he was drinking an awful lot. Chung also stated that he would never burn the owner's house on purpose. Maybe he dropped a cigarette or

457

something.

Martin could tell that Chung had given it up and was now having second thoughts. Chung continued to say, "I crazy, I crazy man. I not remember too good. I real crazy. Booze make me nuts." The translator was providing a word for word translation as all in the room listened.

Martin could see that Chung was now going to try and negate everything he had admitted thus far. Martin decided to finish up the interview and by asking if Chung had been afforded the chance to drink, eat and use a bathroom. Martin even had Chung indicate what he had to eat and drink. Chung even indicated that everyone had treated him fairly and that they had not hurt him in anyway.

Martin asked some personal questions with regard to smoking, alcohol and drug use and how he treated his family members. Chung kept saying that he was so crazy that he verbally and physically abused his own family members. Mr. Chung didn't know that any defense his attorneys with regard to his demeanor and well being would initiate would be going down the tubes.

Rybicki and the ADA had handed Martin a few questions to ask and Martin had done so prior to asking the personal questions.
Martin had also ascertained that after getting on the bus Chung went to Atlantic City and subsequently to a New York City Hospital. He advised the Doctor that he had cut his finger on a slicing machine at work. Chung was in the hospital for a couple days and his family visited him there.

Chung advised that he always told his family that he had purchased the items from people that were returning to China and wanted to sell their belongings. He also advised that he told them he injured himself on a meat slicer and that he had lost his job for that reason.

The statement was concluded and Chung was taken to lock-up and processed. He would be incarcerated from that point on. It was then decided that Martin and Trombetta would interview the wife and daughter of Chung and that Rybicki would interview the oldest son.

Mrs. Chung required a translator but the daughter and son spoke perfect English. The ADA and his people had left immediately after Chung's interview so Martin and Trombetta utilized Sgt. Mike Lau to translate.

Jack grabbed Ernie and instructed, "Listen, Bob and I are going to interview the two females. If you want to see how

it is done, slip in and sit behind the subject and be quiet."
Ernie sat in on the interviews and placed himself behind the person being interviewed. He listened and paid close attention to their faces, their gestures, their movements and their verbalizations. He noticed that Bob and Jack seemed to converse with their eyes. It was almost uncanny. They seemed to know what the other was going to say. They also seemed to have a way of passing information back and forth without talking to one another. They never interrupted each other and when one stopped talking the other immediately took up the slack. If one of them seemed to have a better rapport with the person that one would do the most talking.

They continually changed roles and were always more than a step ahead of the person they were interviewing. Upon completion of the interviews Ernie had a lot to say.

"You guys are unbelievable. You talk to each other without saying anything. How do you know what each other is thinking? I could tell one of you would have a look that indicated you had a question and then you would blink your eyes or move or something and then the other guy would get the message and ask the question you were thinking of. It's fuckin' unbelievable. How do you do it? It's like you are working with one mind that started out as two but ended up on the same wave length. Why did you ask all those questions about Chung smoking, drinking, and using drugs?" Before he got an answer Ernie continued. "You asked them if he gets angry around the house and how he disciplines the kids." Ernie was rambling on making statements and asking questions but not allowing anyone to answer.

Jack and Bob let him go on until he seemed to tire from hearing himself talk. Jack stated, "Everything we say or ask is done for a reason, Ernie." Bob added, "You see, Ernie, we are sure, by the way that Chung acted towards the end of his statement that he is going to claim he is nuts, uses alcohol and drugs or is an all around prime candidate for the funny farm. We wanted to have an answer for everything he could possibly come up with."

Jack stated, "You see, Ernie, Bob knows that Chung is going to say he must have dropped a cigarette on the mattress and hence a fire. So he already knew that Chung didn't smoke but he wanted to get independent family members to provide the answer. You heard them say that Chung hasn't smoked in ten years. So you can rest assured he didn't start the fire with a cigarette. The best part about what we did is the fact that the family members think they are advising us about all the positive virtues of their husband and father.

That's fine. That's what we want. Chung's wife and daughter gave us enough info to hang the guy. They figured they were helping him and they were glad to do so."

Ernie looked at them both and said, "You even had me believin' you cared about his health and well being and I know you'd like to kill the fuck."

Bob said, "Ernie, somewhere along the line they are going to say that he is a psycho. We will be able to show that he is as sane as Jack."

"That ain't saying much," said Ernie.

Bob was then directed to the office where Rybicki was talking to the son. Rybicki asked Bob if he wanted to ask the kid any questions. Bob quickly ran down some of the personal information about the kid's father and then Rybicki finished up the interview.

It was close to five in the morning before the office of the Major Case Squad was looking empty. The guys that had stayed around were finishing up as much as they could. Everyone had been working for many hours. Martin and Trombetta had been awake for twenty four hours and were at that stage where they were just going through the motions.

It was seven in the morning when the remaining investigators Martin, Trombetta, Naspretto, Rybicki, Taylor, Piraino and Nerney decided to go out for breakfast. They conversed about the problems that would no doubt start to surface now that the case would be in the hands of the lawyers. They all knew that the prosecutors and defense counsel would now begin to evaluate and re-evaluate everything that had taken place with regard to the investigation. They would theorize and hypothesize until they had reached their own conclusions as to what really took place. Once they had taken almost unlimited time to reach their conclusions and seemed content with them, they would change their minds. They would then chastise a cop, who had most likely made a split second decision with regard to an action or inaction he took, as to why he did what he did.

The guys had seen it before and would no doubt see it again. It didn't matter whether the case was high profile or not. Lawyers, over the years, had been able to place themselves in the most bureaucratic and money making profession known to man. It was interesting. They lobbied for the laws, wrote the laws and after the cops enforced the laws the lawyers made money on the laws they and their cohorts had initiated. Maybe it was a good profession to get into. The government of the United States,

interestingly enough comprised of a lot of lawyers, seemed
to go along with the entire bureaucratic, self serving
mumbo jumbo mess.

Perhaps lawyers are like women. You can't live with them.
You can't live without them. Then again, God made women.
Who the hell made lawyers?

The guys finished breakfast and returned to Major Case.
Ernie Naspretto bid farewell and went home to get some
deserved rest. He no sooner went home and the reporter for
the local Chinese newspaper showed up to take pictures of
the investigators. Ernie couldn't be a hero, no matter how
hard he tried.

Chief Douglass telephoned Martin and Trombetta and advised
them that he wanted them to attend a news conference at one
in the afternoon. Neither Jack nor Bob were interested in
attending. They had a three hour ride home and had been
thinking about seeing their families and getting some rest.
The Chief explained that he wasn't making a request. Chief
Don Douglass had a way with giving orders when orders were
called for.

By this time everyone except for Tom Nerney had left. Bob,
Jack and Tom spoke for a few minutes and Tom told them to
hit the road. The guys embraced, shed some more tears and
promised that they would all stay in touch. Tom Nerney
said it best when he stated, "We are partners and friends
for life. If one of us needs the other we will be there."

Bob and Jack left the office of NYPD's Major Case Squad.
Bob turned to Tom as he walked away and said, "See ya,
Harvey."
Tom replied in kind........

461

CHAPTER SIXTY

Martin and Trombetta exited One Police Plaza and made it out of the Big Apple in record time. They were traveling southbound on the Garden State Parkway. They were conversing about the fact that they didn't want to attend a news conference. They knew they had to hurry. They both needed to clean themselves up and put on some fresh clothing. The Chief stated that he wanted them in suits and an order was an order.

They were traveling at a high rate of speed and would make the trip home, in just short of two and one half hours. During the ride home they vented. They talked about Dave Douglass, his family, their own families, the members of the Lower Township Police Department and about all of the many people who had taken part in the investigation.

At one point Jack began to smoke a Marlboro Light. Bob looked at him as he turned down the window and said, "You said you were going to stop smoking after we caught Dave's killer." Jack looked at Bob and said, "I'm gonna stop as soon as the case is finished in court." They each laughed and talked about the fact that the hand of God had been touching their investigation from beginning to end. They were very grateful. They got quiet. Jack reached over and turned on the radio. As usual, he searched the stations. Bob heard a familiar song and told him to stop. Jack listened for a second and said, "I know this one. It's STAIRWAY TO HEAVEN." Martin shook his head in the affirmative and said, "Yep, it's another LED ZEPPELIN song." The guys listened and the tears flowed down their faces. Patrolman David C. Douglass was still on their minds.

Martin and Trombetta stopped at home, got hugged and kissed by their wives, then got showered, shaved and dressed. They arrived at the Prosecutors office fifteen minutes before the news conference.

Bob and Jack met all their "kids" along with Jack Reemer and Jim McGowan and were shaking hands, hugging and exchanging congratulations. Reemer and McGowan both apologized for not being able to be in on the arrest of the shooter. They both had to either appear in court or handle family business that they couldn't postpone. Bob and Jack thanked them for all that they had done.

A few minutes later Martin and Trombetta met with Reemer's boss and verbalized their feelings about the worthlessness of the Feds in New York. Jack stated, "I wish those worthless pieces of shit were here." Martin led Jack from the office.

Martin and Trombetta found themselves standing in a hallway. They were listening to a conversation the baldheaded Assistant Prosecutor was conducting. He was indicating that a death penalty in the case would probably not be appropriate.

Martin and Trombetta both expressed their feelings that it would be appropriate but they didn't think it would happen. They knew that good old New Jersey was as liberal as any state in the union.

Jack whispered to Martin that Debbie Douglass was in a nearby room. They knew that this conversation was the last thing she had to hear. Jack could tell that Martin was waiting for the AP to make another remark. Almost on cue the AP then stated he could prove from the available evidence that the perpetrator probably shot him self in the hand by mistake.

Jack knew Martin was going off. Martin stepped into the personal space of the AP. He kept his voice low so that Debbie would not hear what was going on. Martin pointed his finger and stated, "You are welcome to all your theories and ideas. Debbie Douglass is in that room. If she hears what you are saying she will lose it. She has been through more than enough. If you say one more shitbird statement you are gonna wish you never met me. I hope you understand me."

Jack thought to himself, "Way to go, Bob Bo." Jack looked at the AP and stated, "ditto".

Trombetta grabbed Martin's shoulder and the hallway cleared, except for the AP who was now standing alone.

The news conference went quickly. During the conference Jack whispered to Martin that he still didn't feel like speaking. Martin eventually spoke for himself and Trombetta.

"We wish to thank everyone who assisted with this case. The public along with local, county, state, federal and international law enforcement officers helped us do what had to be done. We want to thank our brother officers in the City of New York who not only helped with the investigation but allowed us to live in their homes. Most of all we want to thank the Lord, our God, for being with us and bringing this case to a close."

EPILOGUE

Hop Chung attempted to fight extradition from the State of
New York and at one point attempted to prove that he was
insane and therefore incompetent to stand trial even for
the extradition proceedings. The Cape May County Assistant
Prosecutor was reminded of the statements Trombetta and
Martin had obtained from the Chung family members. It
would be difficult proving insanity when your family was on
record indicating what a normal person you had been prior
to and at the time of your arrest. Chung was extradited
without a defense.

On March 2nd, 1995 more than a year from the murder of
Officer Dave Douglass his killer was brought to justice. A
plea agreement was entered that had been agreed to by
Debbie Douglass and members of the Lower Township Police
Department.

Hop Chung pled guilty to the murder of Officer Dave
Douglass and received a life sentence, with a, thirty year
parole ineligibility. Chung will be eighty three before
parole would even be considered.

Lower Township Detective Sergeants Bob Martin and Jack
Trombetta along with their "kids" and administrators
listened to the proceedings. New York City Police
Department Captain Ernie Naspretto, Detective Sergeant Joe
Piraino and Detective Tom Nerney were also present. When
the hearing was completed they found themselves at the
Villas Fishing Club having a drink to the memory of Lower
Township Patrolman David C. Douglass.

Jack was smoking a Marlboro light. He said he would quit
smoking after Chung was denied his first parole. Jack said
to Bob, "Ya know, this whole case would make a good book."
Martin thought for a moment and said, "Yeah, it would,
except that you know me and book writing. I just never get
around to it. Jack said, "Well, what you do is get Ernie
involved. He does that newspaper article. That way with
two guys writing you would pressure each other into
producing. Listen, if you guys write a book I'll use all my
influence to make sure someone buys it."

Bob knew Jack wouldn't write any chapters but he also knew
that Trombetta could talk anyone into buying him food,
beverages and just about whatever else he desired at that
moment. Martin replied, "I'll talk to Ernie and see what
happens." Jack was already thinking about who he could
sell the book to. He knew he might have a problem selling
it to the Feds in New York. Jack took a drag on the
cigarette and thought to himself that maybe he could sell

them the book. If they wouldn't buy he would just kick some ass.

They started talking about the way things had gone at the court proceeding and Jack then asked Bob what he had said to the reporter as they left the court room.

Bob Martin said, "It was no great statement Jack. I just said, I am happy with the outcome. It's been sitting here confronting everyone for the past year and having it finished feels good."

All the guys congratulated each other repeatedly while enjoying the cocktails that the patrons of the club graciously provided. Eventually all the guys left the Villas Fishing Club.

Life and police work goes on. Joe, Tom, and Ernie said so long and were on their way back to the Big Apple. Jack and Bob got in their car and headed home. It was a quiet trip. There was no conversation but Bob and Jack were thinking the same thing:

Nobody knows why the Lord took Dave, but the Lord sure had his hand in this investigation from the beginning to

THE END......

This book was written by Bob Martin and Ernie Naspretto. Jack Trombetta never liked writing reports. Why would he want to write a book? However, without him it certainly would not have been as interesting nor as complete and factual. When Bob and Ernie had trouble recalling certain facts Jack always had the answer.

Jack, Bob and Ernie were relentless in their quest to bring to justice a cop killer. They did so….However, they did not do it alone. A family of cops put their hearts, hard work and souls together and justice prevailed.

Bob and Jack retired from the Lower Township Police Department. Ernie retired from New York City Police Department.

This book is dedicated to Officer Dave Douglass and all the fallen officers whose names appear on the Law Enforcement Memorial in Washington, D.C. along with every cop from every jurisdiction that took part in this investigation. Know that because of your efforts this case was closed by arrest and conviction. What more can we really expect?

Our Fallen Brothers might well state the following:

We can only do our best to make this world a better place, in which to live. We, do so through the guidance of our Lord and God. Some of us are asked to give more, and do so, leaving behind many whom may not understand. To those we can only say, "We swore to serve and protect. Rest assured we did so and because of that we are in a better place."